SMOKESCREEN

ALSO BY IRIS JOHANSEN
(IN ORDER OF PUBLICATION)

EVE DUNCAN SERIES

The Face of Deception
The Killing Game★
The Search
Body of Lies
Blind Alley★
Countdown★
Stalemate
Quicksand
Blood Game★
Eight Days to Live★
Chasing the Night
Eve
Quinn
Bonnie
Sleep No More
Taking Eve+
Hunting Eve+
Silencing Eve★+
Shadow Play+
Hide Away+
Night and Day
Mind Game★
Shattered Mirror
Dark Tribute

★Starring Jane MacGuire
+Featuring Margaret Douglas

KENDRA MICHAELS SERIES

(written with Roy Johansen)
"With Open Eyes" (short story)
Close Your Eyes

Sight Unseen
The Naked Eye
Night Watch
Look Behind You
Double Blind

CATHERINE LING SERIES

Chasing the Night
What Doesn't Kill You
Live to See Tomorrow
Your Next Breath

STANDALONES

The Ugly Duckling
Long After Midnight
And Then You Die
Final Target
No One to Trust
Dead Aim
Fatal Tide
Firestorm
On the Run
Killer Dreams
Pandora's Daughter
Silent Thunder (Iris & Roy Johansen)
Dark Summer
Deadlock
Storm Cycle (Iris & Roy Johansen)
Shadow Zone (Iris & Roy Johansen)
The Perfect Witness
No Easy Target (featuring Margaret Douglas)
Vendetta

SMOKESCREEN

IRIS JOHANSEN

GRAND CENTRAL
PUBLISHING

NEW YORK   BOSTON

Grand Central Publishing
Hachette Book Group
1290 Avenue of the Americas, New York, NY 10104
grandcentralpublishing.com
twitter.com/grandcentralpub

First Edition: July 2019

Grand Central Publishing is a division of Hachette Book Group, Inc. The Grand Central Publishing name and logo is a trademark of Hachette Book Group, Inc.

The publisher is not responsible for websites (or their content) that are not owned by the publisher.

The Hachette Speakers Bureau provides a wide range of authors for speaking events. To find out more, go to www.hachettespeakersbureau.com or call (866) 376-6591.

Library of Congress Cataloging-in-Publication Data

Names: Johansen, Iris, author.
Title: Smokescreen / Iris Johansen.
Description: First Edition. | New York : Grand Central Publishing, 2019.
Identifiers: LCCN 2018048366| ISBN 9781538713082 (hardcover) | ISBN 9781538715543 (large print) | ISBN 9781549141409 (audio book) | ISBN 9781549141416 (audio download) | ISBN 9781538762974 (ebook)
Subjects: | GSAFD: Mystery fiction.
Classification: LCC PS3560.O275 S66 2019 | DDC 813/.54--dc23
LC record available at https://lccn.loc.gov/2018048366

ISBNs: 978-1-5387-1308-2 (hardcover), 978-1-5387-1554-3 (large print), 978-1-5387-5101-5 (Canadian trade), 978-1-5387-6297-4 (ebook)

Printed in the United States of America

LSC-H

10 9 8 7 6 5 4 3 2

SMOKESCREEN

PROLOGUE

Headlights!

Jill Cassidy's fingers stabbed into the mud as she saw the light spearing the darkness on the road ahead. The vehicle was going slowly, but they'd never see her on this side path. She had to get to the main road. But she had no shoes, and every muscle was aching, throbbing. She'd tried to get to her feet and walk as soon as she'd heard those bastards leave, but she was too weak. She had only managed to crawl slowly, painfully, through the jungle.

She could *do* this, she told herself desperately as she forced herself to propel her body through the mud on the path. The pain wasn't as bad as it had been when they'd first left her. Ignore it, think about the story. Always think about the story. It wasn't the pain, it was the shock that was causing her to shake and feel so weak.

The shock and this gentle, warm tropical rain that had started to fall just as she'd finally managed to pull herself together and force herself to move. Strange that warm rain could make her feel this cold. So gentle, she thought dazedly. Why on earth had that word occurred to her when there seemed to be no gentleness left in her world?

The headlights drew closer.

She had to get to the road before the car passed her.

She tried to move faster.

It was a jeep, she realized. The motor was so loud... Would they hear her if she called out? She *had* to catch their attention. She made a last effort and rolled out onto the road.

"Jill!" The jeep screeched to a halt. "Dammit to hell!"

Novak, Jill realized. It was Jed Novak, and he was angry... That was okay, let him be angry. All that mattered was that he had come, and nothing else could happen to her as long as he was here.

He jumped out of the jeep. "Jill." He was striding toward her. "I almost ran over you."

"You... wouldn't do... that. Spoil your... image. CIA to the... rescue."

"Shut up." Then he was kneeling beside her, the rain beading off the brim of his hat as he looked down at her. "Just look at you, Jill," he said hoarsely as he wrapped his jacket around her. "I told you to be careful. What happened? Why wasn't someone with you?" In spite of the roughness of his tone, his hands were gentle as he picked her up and set her inside the jeep. "How badly are you hurt?"

"I don't know. It... feels bad. But I made it through that jungle... so I guess it's not—" Jill struggled to keep her voice steady. It was over. Those bastards were gone. Don't let them *do* this to her. "I thought they—were going to—kill me. But it turned out they—only wanted to teach me a lesson and get me sent home."

"You have some nasty bruises." He stiffened as the dashboard lights fell on her torn blouse and upper body. "Blood. Shit. I shouldn't have moved you."

"Not—my blood. Hadfeld. They—wanted to show me—his head. They threw it at me... He's dead, Novak."

"You're not in good shape yourself. Those bruises are really bad, and they're all over you." He was carefully feeling her arms and body. "Here, too. Your head? Concussion?"

"I don't think so. I never totally blacked out." She'd wanted to black out, but she'd been afraid that if she stopped fighting, she'd never wake up. She started to shake again. Don't think about it. She'd made it this far, and she'd be fine. Just don't think about it.

But she couldn't stop *shaking*.

"Hey, it's okay. You're safe." Novak had pulled her into his arms and was holding her tight. "Breathe deep. Just take it easy. We'll talk about it later."

Safe. She lay there against him, letting his heat warm her, shut out the chill. He was so strong, and she felt as if his strength were pouring into her and shutting out that horrible weakness. Yet more than five minutes passed before she could stop shaking.

She finally sat up and pushed him away. "I'm sorry," she said unsteadily. "I fell apart. You asked me why—there wasn't someone—with me. I got the phone call from Hadfeld. But it was a trap. They were waiting for me."

"How many were there?"

"Four."

"Can you describe them?"

Describe the pain? Describe the smell of them? Describe the helplessness she'd felt? But she had to focus and try. She shook her head. "Scarves over the lower...half of their faces. One black man, three white. Two of the white men had dark hair, one was fair-haired. It felt like...straw. Most of the conversation was in a Maldara dialect."

She had to stop a minute before she could go on. "They...wanted to hurt me and...they did. The one who was fair-haired kept driving the others to hurt me more and more. He beat me himself, then he told the others what they had to do and how to do it. He said they'd been sent here to do a job, so do it." Say it. She had to tell him. She swallowed. "I have a little blood—down there, and I'll need a rape kit."

Silence. "They raped you?"

"Three of them did. The one with fair hair only seemed to want to beat me. He seemed...angry."

"Son of a *bitch*." Then Novak began to swear softly and viciously. "We'll get you to the local hospital in Jokan," he said. "Another fifteen minutes."

"No hospital. Not here," Jill said jerkily. "You're CIA, and I've seen you pull strings. You can get me anything—I need—without throwing me into the system. Do it, Novak."

"The system isn't all that bad when you've been savaged the way you've been, Jill. You're one of the best journalists I've ever come across, but not even a Pulitzer is worth this." He added harshly, "You should have done what I told you and stayed out of it. Would it have been too much to leave it up to me? You knew I'd follow up."

"Yes, I knew you would," Jill said wearily. "Because you're as obsessed as I am. But it was my story—you might have been—too late." She was getting weaker, she realized. That temporary adrenaline rush when she'd felt so safe with Novak was fading. And there was something she had to do, she remembered vaguely. "Do you have a first-aid kit in this jeep?"

"You don't have to do it yourself. I'll get you help right away, Jill."

"It's not for me. I need some medical gloves. I couldn't describe those men, but I—fought them. When they surprised me, they took away my gun, but they'll have scratches." She looked numbly down at her hands. "And I might have some DNA beneath my nails if it survived my trip—through—all that mud."

He muttered another curse, reached into the backseat for the first-aid kit, and handed it to her. The gloves were on top of the bandages, and she quickly pulled them on to protect her nails. She set the first-aid kit on the floor at her feet. Better. One more thing done to rid herself of that terrible feeling of helplessness. "You were driving slow. You were looking for me, weren't you? How did you know I was here?"

"My informant at the embassy intercepted an anonymous call to the secretary shouting about how U.S. journalists were to blame for the ruin of his country and claiming that he'd taken care of one tonight. Their directions were pretty damn accurate. They *wanted* you to be found. I was lucky to reach you before the soldiers from the embassy."

"No, I'm the lucky one." Though luck was a bittersweet concept tonight. But she could imagine how she would have felt if anyone but Novak had found her. "Now take me somewhere you can get those gloves off to a lab so I can get clean again. Then I'll try to figure out how to find out how they knew it was me Hadfeld had contacted."

He was silent. "It might be my fault."

Her gaze flew to his face. "You've got a lead?"

"Better. I think I might be able to get my hands on the skull. So go home and let me work on it," he said roughly. "You've gone through too much as it is."

"Yes, I have." Her hands clenched into fists. "And I'm not the only one. Do you actually believe I'd ever let those bastards get what they wanted? Can't you see? They knew the first thing that the embassy would do if they found out about this would be to notify my publisher. And then they'd send me back to the U.S. to some discreet hospital to go through debriefing and therapy. That's why that bastard told those other men that they had a job to do. That's why they kept beating me. That's why it was rape." Her eyes were suddenly blazing at him. "After all that's gone down here in Maldara, the last thing those diplomats would want would be to have a journalist injured and raped at this stage of the game. Six hundred thousand people were murdered here. Genocide. Now they think they've put Humpty Dumpty back together again. So they'd need to hush any disturbance and wrap me in tender loving care. Why else do you think this happened?" Her voice was shaking. "I told you, those men *knew* what they were doing. They *wanted* to hurt me. They had their orders. Well, I won't let them get away with it."

"Easy," Novak said quietly. "I'll take care of it. No one's going to let that happen."

And if he took care of it, it would mean anyone in Novak's way would be destroyed. She had seen it before. But she didn't want it to go down that way. "You bet they're not. Do you know how weak they made me feel? The pain kept coming and wouldn't stop, and I couldn't do anything about it. I'm never going to be that weak ever again." She wanted to close her eyes and just stop arguing with him. She needed to shut out the world, and maybe, for a little while, those four monsters would vanish with it. But she had to get Novak's promise first. "So this night never happened. Because you're going to let me see to it myself, aren't you? It will take a little while for me to get over this, but you're not going to let anyone sideline me. You're going to let me go after them. I *deserve* it, Novak."

"Do you think I don't know that?" he asked hoarsely. He looked away from her. "Okay, you don't go back to the U.S. I use you and let you help me take them down. And, if you get hurt again doing it, I just consider you collateral damage. Is that the plan?"

"That's the plan." She could close her eyes now. She could relax her body and attempt to block out the pain...and the memory. "Just get me fixed, and then you can tell me how you're going to get the skull."

"And just how am I supposed to fix you, Jill?"

She was getting so blurry she wasn't sure she understood. "You're right, I spoke without thinking. My responsibility...Just take me somewhere, and when I'm better, I'll take care of it."

He was cursing beneath his breath. "Never mind. You're not thinking straight enough to recognize monumental frustration when you hear it." He said slowly, clearly, "Listen. Stop trying to be strong. I know you're strong. You don't have to prove it to me. And I'm not leaving you until I know you're okay. We're in this together." He reached out, grasped her hand, and pressed it tightly. "Do you understand? I'll not let you go."

And, in spite of Novak's being one of the toughest men she'd ever met, he was having trouble with her being hurt and not being able to put her back together again. Strange...

But she couldn't help him now. Maybe later...

Right now, she could only cling desperately to his hand and take whatever comfort he could give her. Because she was starting to shake again, and he had said she didn't have to be strong. "That's very...kind. Do you mind if I—don't talk anymore, Novak?"

"Hell, no." His grip tightened. "Look, this is what we're going to do. I'm taking you to Baldar, the private airport we use near the border, and flying you to Nairobi. There's a hospital there where I send my men when I need absolute secrecy. No reports. No leaks. No one in Maldara will know where you are." He muttered a curse. "Even though I don't want to do it because it will take about an hour and a half to get you there."

"That doesn't matter." Yet she could see he was upset again, and she had to make one last effort. "None of this was your fault. Your decision. My—choice. Stop blaming yourself."

"That's right," he said bitterly. "Collateral damage."

She didn't reply. She was at the end of her strength, and she just wanted to crawl away somewhere until she could heal.

Collateral damage.

It wasn't an accurate description of her role in this nightmare. She had gone after the story with her usual drive and determination. Novak might have thought that the decision he had made caused this to happen to her, but she did not. She'd not been smart enough to read the signs of betrayal when Hadfeld had phoned her. She'd been too eager to get to him and obtain the proof she needed. Even if Novak had found a way to get the skull, things might still be on the verge of exploding.

And there might be true innocents on the horizon who could be hurt by what had happened here at Maldara.

Collateral damage...

CHAPTER

1

LAKE COTTAGE
ATLANTA, GEORGIA
TWO WEEKS LATER

I thought you'd be finished with her by now." Michael was tilting his head and gazing in disappointment at the reconstruction of the skull on Eve's worktable. "I wanted to see Nora before I left today. Did you have trouble with her?"

"No." Eve made a face at her son as she wiped the clay off her hands with her work towel. "I had trouble with you. I was busy packing your bags and making arrangements for that summer camp your sister, Jane, is so set on taking you to. Nora had to wait."

"She won't mind." Michael wasn't taking his gaze off the skull of the six-year-old child who was Eve's current forensic sculpture. "She'll know you're trying to do what's best for her, that you're trying to bring her home, Mom."

His voice was gentle. Even as a toddler, he had never had a horror of these skulls of the victims that had appeared in her studio through the years. Now, though he was only ten years old, that understanding and gentleness seemed to have deepened. Eve had never had to explain to him about the monsters who had killed these children, then tried to burn them, bury them, toss them away as if they had never existed. Michael just accepted that Eve was trying to fix something that was broken, that those children were lost and had to go home. Lord, she was lucky.

She gave him a quick hug. "Well, Nora may understand, but the Chicago Police Department isn't that patient. I have to finish this reconstruction and get it back to them so that they can start sending out photos to the newspapers and TV shows. We have to see if anyone can identify her." She turned him around and pushed him toward the hall. "And you have to gather all the treasures you can't bear to leave behind for the next month and pack them in your duffel. Last chance. We have to be at the airport in four hours."

"Right." He smiled at her over his shoulder, his amber eyes shining with mischief. "You're first on the list. Can I take you, Mom?"

She wished he could. She didn't know what she was going to do without him and Joe for a month. "I wouldn't fit in your duffel. But we can Skype." She made a shooing gesture. "Get going."

He laughed and ran down the hall.

She turned back to the reconstruction with a sigh. Noise. Laughter. Family. She was going to miss all of it. She reached out and gently touched the reconstruction's cheekbone. "Sorry, Nora. You're important, too. I'm just having a few issues at the moment."

"Then come with us." Joe was standing in the doorway, looking at her. "A month is a long time." He crossed the room and took her in his arms. "Or let me come back to you." He kissed her. "Screw that seminar. I'll go next time."

"Scotland Yard doesn't offer them that often. And everything is cutting-edge when they do." Joe was a detective with ATLPD and was always interested in all the bells and whistles connected with crime fighting. "And the timing is just too good to miss. Jane is taking Michael to that dig in Wales, and you'll at least be close enough to keep an eye on them."

"Come on, Jane adores Michael. And she's introducing him to digging for ancient Roman treasure at that Welsh castle. Treasure and playing in the dirt. A ten-year-old's dream. He wouldn't miss me."

"He'd miss you." She kissed him again. "Just as I will. But I'm not ten, and I'd feel better if one of us is near him. So would you." Michael had become the center of their lives since the night he'd been born, but neither of them could deny that he was...unusual and always a challenge. "And you can never tell which way he's going to jump."

"Tell me about it," Joe said dryly. "You could come and work in London."

"And then you'd feel guilty about spending all those hours at the Yard." She gave him a quick kiss. "I'll tell you what I told Michael. Skype. Go finish packing. I need to clean up before I take you to the airport." She grimaced. "And I gave in and agreed to give an interview at one this afternoon. Annoying, but it was the only time the reporter could fit me into her schedule. I'll take her out on the porch and try to get rid of her as quickly as possible. But you guys are on your own until we leave here at two."

"We'll manage." He kissed the tip of her nose. "Reluctantly. Why the interview? Does it have anything to do with Nora? She's not even finished." He frowned, puzzled. "And you don't usually give interviews anyway. You say it's a waste of your time."

"It is a waste. They tend to focus on me and not the victim."

"Imagine that," he said mildly. "The foremost forensic sculptor in the world who is both charming and beautiful. How could you possibly compare to a hideous skull that's been buried for decades?"

"Not beautiful, interesting-looking. And I'm not charming, that would require effort. I always opt for kind and intelligent. You must already be missing me if you're resorting to flattery."

"You've got that right."

She cleared her throat. "Me too."

"So why the interview?"

"It's Jill Cassidy. I liked the story she did on that DFACS scandal. She never gave up and fought those politicians who were ignoring the child abuse and fraud claims all the way."

Joe nodded slowly. "I remember. She won a Pulitzer for it." He gently touched her hair. "I should have known it would have something to do with kids. She wants to do some kind of profile on you?"

She shrugged. "I guess she does. We didn't discuss it. I said I could give her an hour if she insisted on its being today. It seemed worthwhile. I don't think she'd waste my time on trivial junk."

"You mean like telling the public how brilliant and famous you are? Heaven forbid." He was heading down the hall. "Not only trivial, but totally boring..."

Eve shook her head as she watched him disappear into the bedroom. Wry, mocking, yet as full of mischief as their son. Nothing boring about Joe. She was already missing him. Their relationship had taken them through valleys and mountains, and they had come out of both with a closeness and love that no longer faltered no matter what strain was put upon it. She frowned as she had a sudden thought. Good Lord, what if that interview involved Joe and Michael? The last thing she needed was a journalist looking for a tell-all piece that violated her privacy. She could not permit it.

Don't jump to conclusions.

If she saw that was the way the interview was heading, she'd just end it immediately. She wasn't shy about protecting her family's privacy.

And she'd taken the interview because Jill Cassidy had shown herself to be a responsible journalist. Joe had been joking about Eve's being boring, but it was true that she was not someone whom social media would find particularly fascinating. She was not only a workaholic, she was too complicated... and very private.

She just had to hope she wasn't getting mixed signals from Jill Cassidy...

———◆———

"Hello. I'm Jill Cassidy." The young woman at the door was smiling warmly at Eve as she shook her hand. "Please call me Jill. I can't tell you how eager I've been to meet you, Eve Duncan. Thank you for agreeing to see me."

"Come in. I'm sorry I can't give you very long. I have to take my husband and son to catch a flight." Eve was studying the reporter and feeling distinctly relieved. Jill Cassidy must be late twenties or early thirties, a little on the thin side, with medium-length brown hair and wide-set blue eyes. Full lips that had a touch of sensitivity and humor and clear, glowing skin. But those eyes were steady and honest, and Eve felt the honesty was also very real. She was dressed in dark slacks and a simple white blouse that made her appear businesslike yet perfectly natural and unassuming. "I expected you to be older. You won that Pulitzer two years ago."

"I got lucky. Right story. Right timing." She was looking around the open living room and kitchen. "This is wonderful."

"It's home," Eve said simply.

"That's why it's wonderful. You can feel it. I'm traveling most of the time, so my home is usually the nearest hotel." She gestured to the smiling portrait of Eve dressed in her old blue work shirt on the wall beside the window. "That's terrific. Relaxed, but there's still a sense of purpose. Your daughter, Jane MacGuire, painted it?"

Eve's eyes widened. "Yes. You're right, Jane is terrific. Her career as an artist is zooming these days. How did you know about her?"

"I do my homework." Her gaze was wandering around the room. "You have a longtime relationship with Joe Quinn, a police detective whom you married eight years ago. You have a ten-year-old son, Michael; and besides Jane MacGuire, whom you adopted when she was about Michael's age, you and Joe Quinn took in another young girl, Cara Delaney, and made her your ward. She's not with you now either, since she's a promising violinist and she's on tour." Her gaze returned to Eve's face. "Now, I found her background to be very interesting indeed."

Eve stiffened, instantly on guard. That remark had been too full of meaning to miss. "Really? But you asked to interview *me*, didn't you? I don't consider my husband or children to be fodder for the press. I believe you'd better leave."

She shook her head. "Do you think I'd have mentioned Cara Delaney if I'd meant to cause you problems? I just had to make certain you knew that I could hurt you if I chose and had no intention of doing so. Otherwise, you'd be worried all the time I was talking to you that I was going to cause some kind of scandal by revealing that your ward is the granddaughter of Sergai Kaskov, a known figure in the Russian Mafia." She gestured impatiently. "I don't care about that. All I care about is that you're brilliant and have devoted most of your career to helping children who have been murdered and abused. Evidently, somewhere along the way, you've also been able to build a life for yourself and your family that I envy with all my heart. Good for you."

"You couldn't have hurt Cara." Jill Cassidy seemed to be sincere, but Eve was still wary. "She wouldn't give a damn about scandal. All she cares about is the music. Though you'd find the rest of the family very protective and might find yourself in an extremely uncomfortable situation." Eve stared at her. "You could have just not mentioned my family at all. This was all very deliberate."

She nodded. "Because as I said, I do my homework. You're sharp and very protective. You'd start questioning what I was asking of you the minute you realized I wasn't being totally honest with you."

Eve frowned. "That's not quite clear."

"And you like everything crystal clear," Jill said brusquely. "And you said we don't have much time. Can we sit down somewhere and talk?" She smiled crookedly. "Unless I've completely misread you, and you're going to throw me out?"

"I came close a few minutes ago," Eve said slowly. "I'm still not sure about you. I believe I might have to do a little homework on you, too."

"It's a good idea," Jill said soberly. "Don't trust me. I promise I'm not trying to hurt you or your family. But you don't know me." She smiled. "And all that honesty might be intended to disarm you. But can we still sit down and talk? That won't hurt you."

Eve hesitated. And that honesty *was* disarming her, she realized. Her first wariness was fading, and she was beginning to like Jill Cassidy. "We can talk." She gestured toward the porch. "I'll give you a cup of coffee on the porch. It's our only guarantee of privacy. Joe and Michael might be all over the place while they're packing."

"Great." Jill started to turn away; and then her attention was caught by the skull reconstruction on the worktable across the room. "You work here?" She moved across the room. "I thought you'd have a separate studio." She was reaching out and touching the skull. "May I?"

"It appears that you may," Eve said dryly. "And will."

Jill looked at her. "I just wanted to see your work. She's not finished?"

Eve shook her head. "Close. But Nora will take a few more days." She gazed at her curiously. "How did you know she was female?"

"The lips. The nose. Both very feminine. The rest is blurred and incomplete, but she's there, waiting to be born."

"No, she's not. Nora was born six years before a monster decided to snatch that life away from her. Now all I can do is help her to try to find someone who loved her as much as that monster hated her and send her home." She added grimly, "And hope I can find the monster and send him to the electric chair."

"Amen," Jill murmured. "I understand you've managed to do that a number of times."

"Not enough. Never enough." She gestured to the porch door. "There are too many monsters out there."

"Yes, there are." Jill was still staring at the reconstruction. "You called her Nora. You have some idea who she was?"

"No, I always name my reconstructions. It helps me to connect with them." She started for the door. "Now I have a question for you. You appear familiar with skulls and reconstructions. You not only have a good eye, you know what to look for. Have you been taught?"

Jill shook her head. "Heavens no. Self-taught on the Internet because it's both your profession and your passion. But the key word is familiarity. I only wanted to know what I was seeing."

"Are you planning a series of articles instead of just interviewing me?"

"No." She grinned. "And that's two questions." She opened the porch door. "I'll wait on the porch while you get me that cup of coffee. But I'll give you a teaser to make you want to hurry it along." She looked back at Eve. "I don't want to interview you at all. I want to offer you a job that I hope I can convince you to take. Gross misrepresentation. If you're too pissed off to even let me try, you can toss me in that beautiful lake. Okay?"

Jill didn't wait for an answer. She closed the door behind her.

———◆———

"I don't have time for this," Eve said as she handed Jill her coffee five minutes later. "You picked the wrong day, Ms. Cassidy."

"We've gone back to formality?" Jill asked. "At least you didn't choose the lake option."

"I considered it."

Jill tilted her head. "But you were curious. You have a certain amount of respect for me and were willing to risk being disappointed. But you also have an innate curiosity, which is natural considering your profession."

"That curiosity will be fading away if you don't satisfy it soon. You don't wish to interview me." She asked bluntly, "What the hell do you want with me?"

"Basically the same thing you've done during your entire career," she said quietly. "I want you to identify a number of skulls and bring resolution and peace to their families and loved ones." She paused. "I want you to bring them home."

"I already have a waiting list of cases," Eve said impatiently. "I don't need any more. There are other forensic sculptors you can hire."

"But they're not you." Jill leaned forward. "And they won't give those children the skill and dedication you would. They were murdered, and now they're already being forgotten."

"Children? Plural? How many children?"

"Twenty-seven."

Eve felt a ripple of shock. "A mass murderer?"

"Oh, yes. Though not what you might think."

Twenty-seven children. It made Eve sick to her stomach. "Then tell me what I should think."

"Maldara."

Eve went still. "My God."

Jill slowly nodded. "Though I haven't seen any sign of God in Maldara since the moment I stepped off the plane two years ago. What do you know about Maldara?"

"What everyone knows. Two warring groups in the depths of the Congo struggling for supremacy. Civil war. Blood. Gore." She swallowed. "Another Rwanda. So many deaths. The ruling party managed to triumph about eighteen months ago." She searched for a name. "The Kiyanis I think. Their president was able to persuade the U.N. to support her."

"Yes, Zahra Kiyani is very persuasive," Jill said. "Over six hundred thousand people died in Maldara during that conflict, and only fifty thousand were laid at her door. She was Teflon."

Only fifty thousand. Eve could only vaguely remember the details of that horror she had seen on TV and the Internet two years ago. "Men, women, and children. Butchered. I didn't want Michael to watch it." She lifted her head as a sudden thought occurred to her. "Children. You want me to do reconstructions on the children of that massacre?"

"Not all of them. You'd be there for decades." Jill's lips twisted.

"There are far too many. But there's a school in the village of Robaku, near Jokan on the northern border, where I've been doing volunteer work. Twenty-seven students were killed by a machete brigade led by Nils Varak, a mercenary who was hired by the Botzan faction because it was practically on the Kiyani doorstep. The children were chopped to pieces. Then the school was burned to the ground."

"Terrible," Eve said, sick. It wasn't difficult to envision the terror and pain that must have enveloped the children that day.

"Yes, every minute of it was terrible," Jill said jerkily. "Some of the children weren't dead when the fires were lit. Varak was too impatient to wait. He wanted to lure the people from the village to the school with the screams." She drew a shaky breath. "But you're in a hurry. I have to tell you why I need you. Almost half the villagers were killed that day, most of them parents. But some are left, and there are other relatives, grandparents, uncles, aunts, who also loved those children. But after the massacre, those relatives were devastated. They don't even know which of the children are their own. The damage was too great. The government of Kiyani offered a common grave, but they've refused the offer. They want to bury their own children in the village where they were born." She added softly, "It seems the feeling is universal. They want to bring their children home, Eve."

Eve nodded. The story had touched her unbearably. "Have they tried DNA?"

"It was a bloodbath. With the fires and scattered remains, only a few had enough quality DNA left to be matched. And even those parents wouldn't be satisfied. These are simple village people, Eve. They don't want to be given a piece of paper with a DNA result. They're willing to wait for the years it will take to DNA the bodies, but not the skulls. They want to see, to touch, to recognize." Her eyes were glittering with moisture. "They need *you*, Eve."

"Not necessarily me, Jill. I'm good, but I'm not the only one who could do this. Besides, it would be a massive undertaking to gather those remains and send them to me. The U.N. should hire several forensic sculptors and set up studios on-site at Robaku. That would be the quickest way to get it done."

"The quickest, not the best. Having you do it would be the best." Jill shrugged. "And U.N. funding isn't an option. They've already refused to approve anything but the least expensive methods of disposing of those children. Maldara has turned into one huge cemetery they don't want to face. If a mass grave wouldn't be such bad press, they'd probably even approve that over working with DNA."

Eve felt a ripple of shock. "That's pretty harsh."

"It's the way of the world," Jill said wearily. "The U.N. has too many fires to put out for sentimentality. They regard Maldara's fate as settled, so they want to put a period to it and move on in the most economical way possible. That's only good business. Zahra Kiyani would even like everyone to forget about that massacre and has been pushing to move the villagers to another location. I've been writing story after story about Robaku to keep the interest and sympathy high and not let the wishes of those relatives be forgotten."

"There are many charitable organizations not connected to the U.N.," Eve said. "I've worked with a few over the years. Ask for money and volunteers."

"I am," Jill said simply. "I'm asking you to volunteer. I can gather enough money together to pay you to come to Maldara and do the reconstructions on those children. You're the best one for this job, and they deserve the best."

"I'm sure they do, but there are other fine forensic sculptors." Eve had seen where this was going and had tried to offer alternatives to avoid having to refuse her. She could see that Jill Cassidy was passionately committed to helping those children. The story had touched and horrified Eve, and she could almost feel the agony of the parents who had lost their children to those butchers. "Not me, Jill," she said gently. "I have a career with commitments. I have a family who needs me. I can't go flying across the ocean to work in a country in the middle of Africa."

"I know I'm asking a lot." Jill's face was tense. "But they need help. If you could see..." She reached in her briefcase and pulled out a manila folder. "Here. You *can* see them." She thrust the folder at Eve. "You could put off your other commitments for a little while, couldn't you? These people have lost so much already. Someone should care enough to give them something to make—" She broke off, then said, "I can talk about your work, but there's nothing I can say that would make leaving your family any better. I don't even have a family any longer, but I know it would suck." She drew a deep breath. "But if you could give those kids just a few weeks, it would give me time to try to work something else out for them."

Eve shook her head. "I have a life, Jill. You're asking me for a major disruption. And I don't even know if it's the best thing for those village families. You're asking me to trust your judgment."

"Yes, I am. Or your own judgment after you look at the biographies and photos in that envelope." She reached out and grasped Eve's hand. "Look, I know it's a sacrifice. Who wants to go to a wild, underdeveloped country and set up shop in a jungle for those weeks? But if you agree to do it, I know you'll come back feeling good about it. And maybe it's not so underdeveloped any longer. It has a U.S. embassy, there's a temporary U.N. headquarters, and reps come in and out of Jokan, the capital city, on a regular basis." She grimaced. "It's practically civilized compared to when I first visited."

"You said that was two years ago." She frowned. "The fighting was still going on then. I'm surprised they let you in the country."

"They didn't. But I had a few friends in high places and even more in low places who managed to smuggle me under the radar. I had an idea it might be the story of the decade, and I wanted to be there." Her lips tightened. "I knew it was a second Rwanda, but I thought I was tough enough to take it. And I did take it, I just didn't realize I'd be caught up in the nightmare and start bleeding myself. You don't go through an experience like that without its changing your life."

"Changing?"

"I was first on the scene, and I told the stories." Her face was haunted. "But you can't do that in a place like Maldara without becoming part of the story."

"Yet you want me to go and tell stories of my own when I do those reconstructions," Eve said quietly. "And you know that it will probably hurt me to do them. Every single one I've ever done has hurt me, Jill. It goes with the territory. And this time, I wouldn't even have the comfort of doing it to try to find the butchers who murdered them. They had to have been killed or imprisoned by now."

"I know." She nodded jerkily. "So do it for their parents or grandparents. Nothing is perfect. Particularly in Maldara." Her hand tightened on Eve's. "Just *do* it. I promise I'll make it safe for you and as comfortable as I can."

"I know you would." Eve gently pulled away her hand. "And I admire you and what you're trying to do for these people. But I have my own commitments I have to think about. Maldara is half a world away from them. But I promise I'll try to find an organization that will be able to give you the help you need."

"Thank you." Jill's voice was unsteady. "I guess I couldn't expect anything else from you." There was desperation in her eyes as she held Eve's gaze. "But you're the help I need. *Please.* Will you promise to think about it?" She reached in her pocket and handed Eve her card. "Just call me, and I'll arrange everything."

"I'll think about it," Eve said. "But I'm afraid I'll disappoint you, Jill. I can't do—"

"Mom, we're ready to go!" Michael was standing in the doorway, his eyes shining with eagerness. "Dad's grabbing the suitcases and that present I made for Jane." His gaze was on Jill. "But if you're still busy, I'll help Dad take the suitcases down to the car and we'll wait for you there."

"No, I believe we're finished here." Eve got to her feet. "It took a little longer than I thought." She held out her hand to him. "This is my son, Michael, Jill. This is Jill Cassidy, Michael, come and shake hands with her. She's a very famous journalist, and you'll probably be seeing her stories in newspapers and on the Net."

"Really?" He was across the porch and smiling at Jill. "That will be neat. I'm very glad to meet you, Ms. Cassidy." He shook her hand and looked her straight in the eye. "I'll be watching for them. I think you must be very smart if you're this famous so young."

"Not so young." Jill smiled. "Compared to you, I'm ancient. I'm happy to meet you, Michael. I can see why your mother is so proud of her family."

"We're proud of her, too." He turned away and went back to Eve. "I think I'll go back inside and help Dad. He might need me." He leaned forward, and whispered to Eve as he passed her, "She's so *sad*, Mom. Be nice to her." Then he was through the door and talking to his father.

"Sweet kid." Jill was looking after him. "You're lucky."

"Yes, I am." She shouldn't have been surprised at Michael's instant insight, but she was. Jill had been hiding that vulnerability very well, even from Eve, until those last moments. But then Eve and Joe had known since the moment he was born that Michael saw deeper than other people. "But like all kids, he has a few issues." One of which was to make her feel guilty when she agreed with what he saw, she thought crossly. Gazing at Jill Cassidy right now, Eve was acutely aware of the scars that had been born of the emotional battles the woman had fought over the years. "He can be very demanding on occasion."

"I see absolutely nothing wrong with that," Jill said with a smile. "I can be demanding myself. I believe we'd get along fine." Her smile faded as she turned toward the porch steps. "But I'm in your way. You said you had to take your husband and son to the airport. Thank you for seeing me."

"You're welcome. I'm sorry I can't help you." She followed Jill to the steps. "I meant what I said, I'll get on the phone tomorrow and try to talk to several charities."

"I'm sure you will." Jill looked back at her, and Eve was once more aware of that hint of desperation in her expression. "Just look at the family photos and read my biographies of the children. That's all I ask. After meeting your son, I know that's a lot. But I have to ask it."

Eve gazed at the manila envelope on the cushions of the porch swing. "I'll look at them." She shook her hand. "But I can't let them change my mind. It was nice meeting you, Jill."

Jill nodded and made an effort to smile. "Yeah, I hope Nora turns out the way you want her."

"That depends on her," Eve said. "I never know until the last sculpting."

"Why doesn't that surprise me?" Jill waved and ran down the steps.

Eve stood there and watched her as she got into her dark blue Volvo and backed out of the driveway. Jill smiled again as she waved and drove down the lake road.

Smiles?

She's so sad, Michael had said.

"Hi." Michael was suddenly standing beside her, his gaze on the car. "Did we stay inside long enough? Did you have time to fix it?"

"No," Eve said. "Sometimes people have to fix their own problems. Though I'll make a few calls for her tomorrow." She gave him a little push to stop the protest she could see was coming. "But right now I want to spend time just being with you and your dad and not thinking of anyone else until you get on that jet. Go get your luggage."

———◆———

Jill pulled onto a side road a few miles from the lake cottage and turned off the engine of the Volvo. She realized she was shaking. Stupid. Everything had gone well, and there was no reason for her to be this upset. Yet she had felt like she had to take a few moments before she got on the freeway. She had wanted to catch a final glimpse of Eve Duncan and her family before she took the next step that would send Eve spiraling into the coming nightmare.

Maybe it would not happen. She had tried to take precautions that might keep Eve safe.

Or might not.

Either way, Jill was committed, and all the regrets in the world wouldn't alter what she'd done. So stop this nonsense and make certain that the rest of the plan was set as well. She quickly dialed Jed Novak before she could change her mind. "It's okay," she said when he picked up. "They're on their way to the airport, and Eve Duncan isn't getting on that flight with them. The only worry I had was that she might change her mind. She's very close to her family, and that could have happened."

"But you said it wasn't likely," Novak said dryly. "And I built the entire scenario around your judgment. I'm glad you didn't disappoint me."

"You would have just made me come up with something else. You don't allow failure, Novak."

Silence. "No, I don't. Not once you were committed. The stakes are too high." He paused. "Is she going to do it?"

"I think she will. She turned me down, but she'll look at the photos and the children's stories. They'll be very effective. Then she won't be able to resist going back and finding out more about Maldara. She'll allow a little time to pass, then she'll find a way to do what I asked."

"You seem certain."

"I'm as certain as I can be considering how intelligent she is. As I told her, I did my homework." Jill added curtly, "She doesn't want to do it. She wants to keep her commitments with all those law-enforcement bodies she had on her agenda. And she has family responsibilities and knows that there's always a possibility of harm when you go to a country like Maldara. That's why you have to reassure her that the risk is minimal when she starts checking. Have you set it up?"

"Of course," he said dryly. "This isn't my first rodeo, Jill."

"No, you were probably there when they built the Colosseum. I'm the one who doesn't have the experience. But I have to do this right, Novak." Her hands tightened on the steering wheel. "And the risk has to be as minimal as we're letting her think. You have to keep her safe, Novak."

"It will go right if you've read Eve Duncan right. You've told me all the things that are con, what are the pros?"

"Only two things. I'm good at what I do. I made very sure the photos of the massacre and the families will shock and touch her. And I guarantee my stories in that envelope will do the rest. They're going to haunt her, she won't be able to forget them."

"And the other thing?"

"She likes me," she said simply. "And I know it's hard for her not to trust someone she likes." She drew a shaky breath. "Because I like her, too. So make sure we don't get her butchered, Novak."

"I'll work on it."

She braced herself. "And while you're doing that, I should tell you that on that last day before I left Maldara, I thought I was being followed."

"You were. Don't worry. I'm on it. I'll get back to you."

"That's comforting," she said dryly. "Kind of you to let me know." She cut the connection.

She didn't feel as if she could talk to Novak any more right now. He was a master at the games that all those covert organizations played, and she was a rank amateur. That was fine with her; she had never wanted to be anything but a journalist and tell the story.

But not this story.

She stiffened as she glimpsed Eve Duncan's Toyota driving down the lake road. She was at the wheel, and her son and husband were smiling and talking to her. She was also smiling and looked happy as if life was good and there was no Maldara in the world.

And Jill could make certain there would be no Maldara for Eve Duncan. She could step away and take the story in another direction.

But she knew she wasn't going to do it.

She was going to let it happen.

CHAPTER

2

I'll call you from London as soon as we get in," Joe said. "Jane said that we'll be going out to breakfast after she picks us up, then drop by her apartment to rest until she and Michael leave for Wales tomorrow evening."

"And you'll be using her apartment while you're at the seminar," Eve said. "I told you it was meant to be. The timing was almost too good to be true."

"Not if you're not with us." His hand reached up to cup her cheek. "Change your mind?"

"I'm tempted." More than tempted. The idea of going back home while they flew off into the wild blue yonder was already causing her an aching sense of loss. "Maybe after I finish Nora. I'll see in a few days."

"Good." He kissed her. "I'll keep after you."

"If you have time," she said ruefully. "During that last seminar at the Yard, you were busy from dusk to dawn. And afterward, you and the guys were cementing international relations at every pub near Scotland Yard."

"Only the one on Whitehall. The others closed too early. But I might just have time for you." He grinned. "Try me." He slipped his arm around her waist, and they walked toward the jetway, where Michael was waiting, playing a game on his computer. "Though I'll have to think about it. I was a little insulted when you sent Michael in to tell me we had to sit down and wait until you finished that interview with Jill Cassidy."

"It wasn't exactly an interview. It turned out to be something different." That was an understatement. "And that wasn't me, that was Michael. He liked her. He was feeling sorry for her and thought I should help her."

"Why?"

"You know Michael. He just said she was sad." She shrugged. "And maybe she is. Journalists don't have tremendously happy lives. They see too much. Big-time stress. But I told him sometimes people have to fix their own problems." She turned and kissed him again, hard. "And the only problems I want to fix right now are yours and Michael's," she said fiercely. "You take care of yourself, and I'll expect at least one Skype a day. Even if it has to be from a pub on Whitehall Street."

"You'll get it." His hand gently caressed her cheek. "Don't work too hard. I don't want to come back to a haggard wife who will send me running back to that pub to drown my sorrows." He grinned. "Now go say good-bye to Michael. I'm sure he wants to lecture you about your mistreatment of Jill Cassidy."

"No, he won't. Not this close to the time he's going to have to leave me. I'll get a break." She was moving toward Michael. "But he might do it on our first Skype call!"

◆

Dammit.

Eve could feel her eyes sting with tears as she drove up the driveway to the lake cottage. The place seemed just as empty as she'd been afraid it would without Joe and Michael. It had been bad when she'd watched the plane take off, but this was worse. This was where there were a million memories, and she'd have to fight them every single day.

She wanted to run back to the airport and jump on the next plane.

Yeah, that would be mature and responsible. It would be good for Michael to spend time with his sister. He and Jane didn't get a chance to bond that often. And she'd be in Joe's way while he was networking. Just get busy and this month would fly by and they'd all be together again.

She ran up the porch steps and threw open the door. It was getting dark, and she flicked on the light. That was more cheerful. She threw down her purse and moved to her worktable in the studio across the room. "Hi, Nora." She looked down at the reconstruction. "It's just me and you, kid. But we'll get along just fine, won't we?" She touched the clay of her cheekbone with her index finger. "And after that, we'll find someone else to help."

Nora gazed up at her from blind eyes. Eve hadn't put the glass eyes in the eye orbits yet. That was always the last touch. Usually she didn't even notice that emptiness, but she did today. Probably because she was feeling so empty herself. "Maybe we won't work right away." She turned away. "No offense. I'll just have a cup of coffee, then call Jane and tell her they're on their way. We'll get together later tonight."

But the call to Jane went straight to voice mail. Jane was always busy, and she might even have a gallery showing. Later. Everything seemed to be later today.

She took her coffee to the porch and looked out at the lake. Beautiful as usual. But it wasn't as lit by sunlight as it had been earlier when she'd been out here with Jill Cassidy. The sun had gone down, and it was a little somber.

Jill Cassidy.

Promise you'll look at them.

Her gaze went to the manila envelope she'd left on the porch swing. She didn't want to look at those photos. She'd seen more than enough horror photos in her career in forensics. She was depressed enough today.

Promise me.

She could almost see Jill standing on those steps, pleading desperately.

She's so sad.

And Michael had ganged up on Eve.

Oh, well, just do it. She crossed to the swing, plopped down, and reached for the envelope. It might be better that her mood was as somber as that lake out there. She pulled out the photos and switched on the light. It couldn't be any worse than what she'd seen before . . .

———◆———

Wrong.

Two hours later, the tears were still running down Eve's cheeks. So much worse than anything she'd ever encountered in her career thus far. Not only the butchery and the burning of innocents, but Jill had researched and interviewed parents, relatives, friends, and siblings of each child in the village. Then she had written their stories from birth to the day of their horrible death. Each word simple but poignant until Eve had felt that every one of those children belonged to her.

She leaned her head back and closed her eyes, but the tears still flowed. She could still see that day, feel the darkness of terror as the militia had come and hacked and hacked with their machetes. Would she ever not see it? Jill Cassidy had made every moment come alive for her and anyone else who read those damnably beautiful, agonizingly human, stories.

Close it out.

Impossible.

Jill had known it would be impossible. That's why she had made Eve promise to look at them. Brilliant, wise, Jill Cassidy, who had done her homework and had no trouble reading her. She would have been resentful except for the fact that Jill could not have written those words if she hadn't been caught up in the same agony as Eve was feeling now. They were bound together by the pain of those helpless children butchered in that village.

But don't let Jill Cassidy manipulate her. Push it away. Don't give in to it. Six hundred thousand people had died in Maldara. These were only twenty-seven children.

But now, she knew every single one of them.

She opened her eyes. She would *not* cry again. Tears did no good. Find a solution or accept the pain. She reached for her computer and flipped open the lid.

Maldara . . .

———◆———

It wasn't Joe but Jane who called her four hours later. "I'm calling from the apartment. Michael and Joe are here and safe," she said. "But there's something missing. You. I thought I was going to be reasonable and not harass you, but then when you didn't show up at customs, I decided that was bullshit. Get on the next plane. I don't care if you smuggle that skull through customs and just work here at the apartment. Or if you decide to go with us to the dig. At least you'd be here. That's where you belong. Now do what I say, dammit."

Eve could almost see her toss her red hair as she said those last words. Jane was always passionate when it came to family, and this wasn't totally unexpected. "I'm thinking about it. Though we both know that you're all going to be so busy that you probably wouldn't know I was around."

"We'd know." She sighed. "I just thought that I'd add my two cents' worth to the guilt trip Joe has no doubt been bombarding you with. I guess I'll just have to leave it to him."

"You'll have enough on your plate with supervising Michael on that dig. He's so excited about it. I know it's going to be wonderful."

"I think it will. Most of the time, they only permit older students on these digs. I went on my first one when I was a teenager, remember? So when I ran across the information on this one in Wales that was allowing younger kids, I jumped on it." She chuckled. "And I'm not sure who's going to supervise whom. Michael is already making plans and reading all my literature on it. I'm expecting sunrise to sunset to be the time-frame agenda."

"See? You'd have to squeeze me in."

"I'm not handling this well. I'd better hand you over to Joe. He has more experience at bulldozing you. I love you."

The next moment, Joe came on the line. "As Jane said, we're here and already missing you. She insisted on trying her powers of persuasion one more time. We stopped for breakfast on the way from the airport. Did I wake you?"

"No, it's only a little after midnight here, and I've been busy," Eve said. "Good flight?"

"Passable. Michael and I played cards. He's decided that counting cards shouldn't really be considered illegal in the casinos, and he's perfecting his technique."

"Heaven help us. Don't you dare take him to a casino."

"I think he'll be content with Jane once they start working at the dig in Wales. Why weren't you sleeping? Nora?"

"No." She paused. "Just doing some research about some skulls found in Maldara. I didn't know much about it."

"Maldara? From what I remember from the news stories, you'd do better researching almost anything else. Nightmare stuff. I remember you were very careful to keep it away from Michael's eyes."

"Which meant I had to ignore a lot of it myself. I only knew it was a civil war between the Kiyanis and the Botzan factions in central Africa that tore the country and most of its people apart. It went on for almost two years before the U.N. sent in forces to stop it." Her hand tightened on the phone as she remembered the photos of what those troops had found when they'd crossed the border. "The Botzan had hired a mercenary, a guerilla leader, Nils Varak, to run rampant over the country and attack the Kiyanis. Most of the butchery and burning was done by him and his men. He used the Botzan militia machete troops on occasion, but mostly he liked the personal touch." She added harshly, "The news stories said he had more blood on his hands than Hitler before the U.N. forces managed to kill him."

"Not soon enough," Joe said grimly. "When he first started that bloodbath, every police department in the world was canvassed for information about him. When I read his rap sheet, I was tempted to volunteer to go after the son of a bitch myself. Varak was into everything from child trafficking to terrorism. Pay him enough, and he'd do anything."

Even kill twenty-seven small children who had done nothing to deserve it. "I agree, he wasn't killed soon enough. I don't remember your telling me about that query."

"It was hardly dinner conversation. Since I decided not to do anything about it, I didn't see why I should discuss it. I was just as glad you were in Michael-protecting mode. You didn't need any more darkness hanging over you." He paused. When he next spoke, his voice was curt. "And why were you researching skulls in Maldara? Whose skulls?"

She didn't want to get into this now, but she wouldn't lie to him. "Children. I don't really know. When do I ever know, Joe? I just heard about this massacre at a school in Robaku village from Jill Cassidy and felt I had to know more about it. But I couldn't find out much. In spite of the U.N. presence, that country seems to still be in chaos."

"I can believe it," Joe said grimly. "Which is why I don't like you even thinking about it."

"Maybe if someone had thought about Maldara before that chaos started, I wouldn't have had to hear about those children's skulls today." She drew a deep breath. "Go to bed, Joe. All I did was do a little research. No big deal. I'll talk to you tomorrow. Right now, I'm going to put in an hour or so on Nora. I've been neglecting her today."

Silence. "Yes, you have. And you were so anxious to get her finished. Now I'm anxious for you to do it, too, because I want you here, Eve." He paused. "I love you. Being without you sucks. I'll talk to you when I get back here to the apartment tomorrow night."

"I love you, too. Tell Michael I'll call him before it's time for him to leave for Wales this evening. Good night, Joe." She cut the connection.

She had worried Joe, and it might be for nothing. She should have just kept her mouth shut about Maldara. No, she shouldn't. She rejected the thought immediately. Their relationship was based on total honesty, and silence could also be dishonest. Besides, they were so close, he would probably have sensed her disturbance.

Just work on Nora for a few hours and go to bed and get to sleep. Maybe by the time she woke tomorrow, that aching unrest would have lessened.

She picked up her ruler to check Nora's mid-philtrum measurements one last time. That space between nose and lips was so small, so delicate, on a child. Six years old . . .

There had been six-year-olds in that classroom in Maldara, too. One girl and two little boys. Robaku had been a village school, and one teacher had taught various ages and grades. Jill Cassidy had spent a good deal of time and effort detailing the short lives of those six-year-olds.

Eve had to stop working and close her eyes for an instant as the wave of horror and heartbreaking sadness overcame her once more. Then she got control again and put the ruler down and started to fill in the clay around the mid-philtrum.

It might be a long night.

Damn you, Jill Cassidy.

———◆———

NEXT DAY
2:35 P.M.

Do it!

Eve stabbed in the phone number on the card that Jill had given her. She wasn't surprised when Jill answered the phone in two rings. "Get over here. I want to talk to you."

"I thought you might," Jill said quietly. "Actually, I thought it could be—"

"Get over here," Eve interrupted. "I'm angry, and on edge, and I want to see your face while I'm listening to what you say to me. You went to a hell of a lot of trouble to tear me apart, and I have an idea why. How quick can you be here?"

"Ten minutes. I'm in a motel just off the freeway."

"I thought you'd stay close," Eve said curtly. "I'm surprised you didn't camp out in your car."

"I thought about it."

"I'm sure you did. I'll expect you in ten minutes, and don't expect either coffee or politeness. We've gone past that now." She hung up.

She got to her feet and moved toward the door to the porch. She needed air and to calm down a little before she confronted Jill. She hadn't realized until she'd actually made contact with her how the anger had been building in the last few hours. Or perhaps it had started building earlier, during all the hours she'd been working on Nora last night.

She took a deep breath and gazed out at the lake, trying to steady herself.

Sunlight. Beauty. Peace.

Everything that she wanted to surround her while she was working on Nora and others like her who had been robbed of all three.

And this was Eve's life, her *home*.

The anger was growing again.

But now she had a target.

Jill was driving down the lake road and pulling into the driveway.

Eve met her at the top of the stairs. "You're early. You must be eager to see me."

"I broke a few speed laws. I figured that you needed to vent before you exploded," she said. "You don't get angry often, but when you do, it's supposed to be impressive."

"Of course you'd know that about me, too. Research."

"Yes." Jill's gaze was studying her face. "Circles. You didn't sleep last night. I'm sorry."

"Are you? I don't believe you. I think it was all part of your plan to manipulate me. You knew exactly how to do it. You knew which buttons to push and took time to coordinate them in the right order." Her lips tightened. "Those photos and biographies were a masterstroke. They brought me down as if I'd been run over by a fifty-ton truck. You knew they would, didn't you?"

"Yes. It was your principal weakness." She added, "And your greatest strength. I had to use it."

"You're not even denying it."

"Why should I? You'd know I was lying, and I wouldn't insult you." She paused. "Besides, I've won, haven't I?"

Eve stared at her in frustration. It was difficult to hold on to her anger as she gazed at the reporter. Jill wasn't boasting; there was only vulnerability and that sadness Michael had noticed. "Not yet. I *hate* being manipulated. Last night, I started thinking about every way you'd done that since you walked in here yesterday afternoon. It took me a little while to get it together because you were so clever and so good at what you do. Even those photos weren't close-ups of the children. Just loving family shots. Because you knew I never looked at facial photos of my reconstructions." Her lips tightened. "And then you hit me with the photos after the massacre."

"I didn't want to do it. But I had to convince you." She moistened her lips. "We need you, Eve. You don't realize how much. But I promise if you come, that you'll see how worthwhile it is."

"I can tell that you think it is. But you're asking me to put my life and career on hold while I do those reconstructions."

"Only for a few weeks. I told you, I wouldn't expect more from you."

"How generous of you," she said dryly. "It's what I expect of myself that matters. You've been playing me to get what you want, but that's over." She was silent. "I'm the only one in charge of what I do, but there are things I have to know before I commit." She stared her straight in the eyes. "Is everything you told me the truth?"

Jill's gaze didn't waver. "Absolutely. Every word."

"Even those stories you wrote about the children at the school, *their* stories?"

Jill nodded. "I swear it. You can ask their parents and grandparents. You believe me?"

Eve couldn't help but believe her. "You're so good at what you do. I had to be sure."

"I *am* good. I'm a fantastic storyteller. It's my primary talent. I have others, and I've always had to use whatever skills I have to survive. But I try to be honest, Eve."

"I had to be sure about that, too. You told me not to take you at face value. I didn't. I spent a little time this morning finding out about you."

"I thought you might. Did you discover anything interesting?"

"You spent your entire life until you were eleven years old trailing around the world with your father, who was a photographer. When he was killed in Tibet, it took the U.S. consulate over a year to get you back to the States. But you had no relatives, so you were fostered out for the next five years. Then you worked your way through a community college and started freelancing. Your gift for languages helped you to get ahead, but the first couple years must have been hard."

"Not that bad. I liked traveling around on my own again. I was a little gypsy until my father was killed." She added, "But you didn't find anything incriminating, did you? Other than being a loner, I'm pretty much what I appear on the surface."

"I *wanted* to find something."

"I know you did. It would have been an excuse to close your eyes again." She paused. "Are you going to come with me?"

"I'm close," Eve said jerkily. "Not because you want me to do it. Whether it was for a good cause or not, you tried every weapon in your arsenal to make me do what you wanted. And I could see how you'd pried and researched into who I was to make that happen. That's probably what I resent most. Talk about violation of privacy? And you did such a damn good job." She gestured impatiently. "No, it's because last night I realized those stories were like a poison inside me. I couldn't forget them. And I knew the only way I might be able to was to do something to help, to heal, those children. But you probably knew that would be my reaction?"

"I thought it was likely. You're very caring."

"And I *can't* heal them, but I might be able to heal those closest to them."

Jill nodded silently.

"So when I decided that those stories might have trapped me into doing this, I decided I had to look the situation over and explore how bad it might be. First. My family. I have a husband and a son who need me. And I need them. From what I've been able to find out, Maldara is still too unstable to be considered safe on any level. Yet you said that I'd be safe while I did those reconstructions. How?"

"I have friends at the embassy. And the U.N. staff on-site think reporters have to be given special protection. No bad press. I'll just convince them to extend that protection to you."

"From what you said, they don't even want the work done at Robaku."

Jill grimaced. "But I've been a thorn in their diplomatic asses over the last year. They'll be glad to shut me up and get rid of my nagging as long as it doesn't affect their budget." She added, "But, you know, it might be a good idea for you to call one of those charities you mentioned and tell them you're volunteering to do the job. You have tremendous name recognition, so there's no question they'll jump at sponsoring you. Just ask them if they'll contact the U.N. and advise them you're operating at their request. That way you'd get the official protection and not raise any U.N. hackles by mentioning me." She shrugged. "And the charity would get credit in the international community that might translate to donations later. Everyone wins."

"And more manipulation," Eve said.

"Would you rather I do it? I'll do anything that will make you feel more comfortable." Jill was obviously being perfectly sincere.

"No, I'll take care of it." Eve ran her hand through her hair. "If it's even possible. I just remembered I don't have a visa, no documents. That could take—"

"Twenty-four hours," Jill said. "Give me your passport, and I'll have it processed. We can stop and have the necessary shots on the way to the airport."

"Twenty-four hours?"

She smiled. "I told you that I have friends in high and low places. This is a piece of cake." She turned and strode toward the door. "And while you're getting me your passport, I'll make *you* a cup of coffee." She glanced over her shoulder. "If I'm forgiven enough to be let back into your good graces?"

"Marginally." She followed her into the house. "I'll let you know when we get to Maldara."

"Then you might never forgive me. It's hot, humid, and the poverty will break your heart." She started pouring the water into the automatic coffeemaker. "How will your husband take your decision?"

Eve was not about to deal with that now. Later. "That's not your concern."

"It is if it's going to make you unhappy." Jill was frowning. "He's a detective. Let's see... He'll be worried about your safety. I'll give you a couple of names of law-enforcement officials in the Kiyani government for him to contact. And I know a few agents with the CIA and MI6 who operate in Maldara who might reassure him."

"I wouldn't bet on it." Eve's brows rose. "Is there anyone you don't know in Maldara?"

"Not if they're useful." Jill handed her the cup of coffee. "Survival. You'll only have to be there for a few weeks. But I've been there for two years."

"Two years..." Her gaze narrowed on Jill's face. "Okay, I need to know what I'll be facing there that I couldn't find on Google. According to what I read, for decades Maldara has been torn by conflict between the Kiyanis to the north and Botzan to the south. The Kiyanis possessed most of the wealth in the country, which was based on rich farmlands and diamond mines. They even managed to develop a fairly stable republic in the last thirty years. The Botzans were poor by comparison, mostly mountain people, except for a decent fishing industry, and they changed rulers every couple years. The mountain population were principally made up of roving bands who made the majority of their living stealing from the Kiyanis, whom they hated. They'd been raiding the Kiyanis' properties for years before the Kiyanis suddenly decided to go on the attack. Civil war. The Botzan faction was finally defeated by the Kiyanis after the death of that mercenary, Nils Varak, and with the help of the U.N." She paused. "Is all of that correct? Is there anything else I should know? Is Botzan still a danger?"

Jill shook her head. "It's pretty well broken up now. The U.N. was getting too much static because of the Varak massacres, and they saw to it that the Kiyanis took over most of Maldara." She grimaced. "And Zahra Kiyani, their president, is taking full advantage. She's even charmed the U.N. into giving her the right to speak at the next General Assembly meeting."

"I think I read something about her. She's a modern-day Madame Chiang Kai-shek?"

"Yes, that's who they're comparing her to. But you'll hear a lot more about her now that she's been able to draw a breath and start taking stock. Her father, President Akil Kiyani, was assassinated six months after the conflict started, and she tearfully accepted the presidency to honor him."

"Sarcasm?"

"I'm not a fan. When I interviewed her, she reminded me of Eva Peron. She's quite beautiful and much more flamboyant, of course. But her grateful people had just erected a statue of her in the main square of the capital city of Jokan. I found that odd after a war that had almost destroyed the country." She shrugged. "But that's politicians. She seems to have everything under control. She's built a hospital and gives to charity. The army and police seem to do their jobs. Everyone is fairly safe as long as they stay in the capital and don't go running around the countryside. She might even invite you to tea. That village where the massacre occurred is just outside Jokan. She's visited it twice and had a splendid and tearful photo op. Unfortunately, I wasn't able to attend."

"I don't believe I would either." Eve could see how that political circus would have hurt Jill. "And I'd think you'd be ready to leave Maldara. Isn't your story almost finished?"

"It's finished when it's finished. I'll know when it's done. Like your reconstructions." She'd turned away and was gazing at the reconstruction of Nora on the worktable across the room. "You've made a lot of progress on her since yesterday. She looks close to completion."

"I had a lot of time to work on her. Thanks to you, I couldn't sleep last night." She took a sip of her coffee. "And looks can be deceiving. The final will probably take me another twenty-four hours or even longer. I'm going to need this caffeine."

"But I might be able to get you out before that."

"Wrong," Eve said flatly. "I don't leave until Nora's finished and sent off to Chicago. It's bad enough I'm having to put off other commitments, I won't push *her* aside."

Jill nodded. "Sorry. I knew that, I just didn't think. If you'll give me your passport, I'll get out of your way so you can get back to her."

"Fine." Eve went to the kitchen cabinet where she and Joe kept their documents in a lockbox. "You're being amazingly cooperative." She handed her the passport. "I'll call you when I'm available to leave."

"Cooperative?" Jill's brows rose as she slipped the passport in her pocket. "I know how lucky I am that I talked you into going. I'm not about to rock the boat. Anything you need, just let me know."

"I'll do that." Eve gave her a cool glance. "And neither of us should pretend that luck had anything to do with your persuading me to commit to several weeks doing the reconstructions on those children. You were clever. You made sure you knew what would push every button. And you played me."

"Yes, I did," Jill said quietly. "But I still consider myself lucky that you allowed me to do it. If I work hard enough to make this trip easy for you, I hope you'll forgive me." She smiled with an effort. "I'll be in touch soon if you don't mind. Just to see if there's anything you need." She turned and walked quickly toward the door. "In the meantime, I'll e-mail you those names and contacts I mentioned might be useful to you." She looked back over her shoulder. "I'm sure your Nora will turn out wonderfully. Good-bye, Eve." Then she was gone.

Eve stared after her for a moment. There was no reason to feel as if she had somehow hurt Jill and should try to heal the hurt. Eve was the one who had been maneuvered into throwing her life into chaos for the next few weeks. And Jill Cassidy had not even denied it was done deliberately. Yet the emotion she felt for those children had to be genuine, and where was the line drawn in the sand where brutality toward children was concerned? Eve had never found it.

Forget Jill Cassidy. Eve had made the decision. Now she had to cope with making the best of it.

She was still drinking her coffee as she crossed the room toward the skull on her worktable. As she'd told Jill, she'd need the caffeine.

"Okay, Nora." She stopped in front of the reconstruction. "We're almost there, but now you have to help me. You're going to have to tell me who you are, show me what to do..."

———◆———

Jill dialed Jed Novak as she walked toward her car. "It's done," she said jerkily. "She'll be ready to leave in twenty-four hours if she finishes the current reconstruction by then. I think she will. She's driven right now."

"Putty in your hands, Jill?" Novak asked mockingly.

"Don't *say* that," Jill said fiercely. "It's stupid. She's not putty in anyone's hands. I made a situation impossible for her, and she's just trying to survive it. She's a completely private person, and she knows I probed deep to get what I wanted from her."

"Easy," Novak said. "Bad joke?"

"Very bad joke." She stopped as she reached her car and drew a deep breath. "And a very bad meeting with a woman I admire, Novak. She's smart, and nothing really gets past her. So you need to prepare very carefully. I've given her your name and a few others to pave the way. She might call you. Make her feel comfortable." She paused. "Have you heard anything from Jokan?"

"Not yet. Only a few rumbles. We still have time."

She wasn't as sure about that as Novak. "Let me know if it changes. I'm not going to let Eve go near the place if it does."

"But you'd go yourself," Novak said softly. "Who's going to stop you, Jill?" He added wearily, "It probably wouldn't be me. Never mind. I'll let you know." He cut the connection.

No, it wouldn't be Novak, Jill thought. She had never known anyone as tough or more ruthlessly motivated than Novak. He would get the job done no matter who fell by the wayside.

Yet he hadn't been ruthless after he'd taken her to that hospital in Nairobi, she suddenly remembered. He'd swept her into the ER, giving orders and making everyone snap to attention. Then he'd stayed with her, guarding her, watching that she was given the best possible attention.

And he'd been there, moving shadowlike in the background, for the entire four days she'd been forced to spend at the damn place.

But there had been nothing shadowlike about those nights he'd sat beside her bed and fought off the dragons that attacked from the darkness. There had been moments when she had hated how strong and dominant he had been during that period when she had been so weak. But there had been other times that he had seemed her only path to survival...

NAIROBI HOSPITAL

She screamed.

Darkness.

Pain.

She couldn't move!

She was smothering!

She sat bolt upright in the hospital bed, her hands tearing off the sheet.

"No." Novak was suddenly sitting on the bed beside her. "You're fine. Only another dream, Jill." He was holding her, rocking her back and forth. "I'm here with you. Nothing can hurt you."

She was clutching at him. Her heart was pounding so hard that she could hardly breathe. "I hate this." But she couldn't let him go yet. Another minute... Then she would be strong again.

No, she couldn't allow herself that time. It was another sign of weakness. She drew a deep breath and pushed him away from her. "Thank you. I'm okay now. I don't need you any longer." *Need. How she detested that word.* "In fact, I don't know why you're here anyway. As you said, it was only a nightmare. I'm not a child who can't deal with bogeymen." *She leaned back against the pillows and said impatiently,* "For that matter, I shouldn't even be in this hospital. It's been three days, Novak. I thought I'd be in and out of here in a matter of hours. Why won't they release me?"

"You know that besides severe bruising you had a cracked rib and a few other less obvious problems. I told them not to let you go until they could promise me that they'd done all they could for you." *He got off her bed and settled back in his chair.* "I guarantee they didn't want to break that promise. I tend to get a little testy. Now go back to sleep." *He paused.* "Same nightmare?"

"I don't want to talk about it." *She was glad of the darkness. His stare was always laser sharp, and she didn't want to face it right now. When he came to her at night, he was always only a deep, soothing voice, a strong hand that wove a barrier to keep out the weakness and the terror.* "Tell them to let me leave here, Novak. I would never have come if I'd known you'd make me a prisoner. You even have a shrink coming in to talk to me every day. I don't need all this. I'm not one of your agents. Give me a week or two on my own, and I'll work it out for myself."

"No harm in getting a little therapy. The doctor says what you're going through is PTSD. I think talking to the psychiatrist is doing you good. I've noticed that you're not as tense as you were that first day." *He added,* "And only one nightmare so far tonight."

"I can work it out for myself," *she repeated.* "That's the way it has to be. It's my story, and I have to tell it."

"What?"

She hadn't meant to say that, it had just tumbled out. What did it matter? He had learned more intimate things about her during these last days. "When I was a kid, I had trouble understanding everything that was happening to me. But I loved books and reading, and the stories always made sense to me. There seemed to be a reason for everything, and I thought the writers had a kind of magic that could always make it that way if they tried hard enough." She added, "And it still makes sense to me to think of myself as writing my own story, incomplete, a work in progress, but totally in control of who I am." She shrugged. "Weird, huh?"

"Interesting. And totally logical for a premier storyteller."

"And you're probably being polite and think that I'm nuts. That's okay, it works for me."

"And that's all that's important."

"See? You're being polite. Look, you're a busy man, you don't need to be wasting your time on me. I'm going to leave here tomorrow and go back to Maldara."

"We'll see." He leaned forward and took her hand. "Maybe if you don't have another nightmare tonight. So concentrate on keeping them all at bay."

"I'm going to leave tomorrow." But she found her hand instinctively tightening in his grasp. He had been her anchor in the storm, and she didn't want to let him go quite yet. She could go to sleep holding his hand as she'd done for the past three nights. She was nearly healed, but she could be with him for these next hours. She would be strong tomorrow. "No more nightmares, Novak..."

And the next day Novak had taken her back to Maldara, and she had started to make the plans and do the research that had brought her here to Eve Duncan.

She looked back at the lake cottage as she got in her car. Eve was probably already working on that reconstruction. In a way, Eve reminded her of Novak as far as motivation and steely determination were concerned. But Eve lacked the kill gene that made Novak lethal. She didn't doubt that Eve would kill to protect family or friend, but that was different.

But she knew others who possessed that kill gene, too.

And she and Novak were sending Eve right into their target zone.

CHAPTER

3

Her hair was just right, Zahra Kiyani thought with satisfaction as she watched her maid, Dalai, straighten the strands at her temple. Her chignon was dark and sleek and shining, with just the right touch of sophistication. It accented her high cheekbones and slightly slanted eyes and made the deep gold of her skin glow. She'd wear it like this when she went to New York next week, she decided. Then everyone would realize that she was truly a woman of style and power.

"Send her away," Edward Wyatt said roughly from her bed across the room. "You've kept me waiting long enough."

"You'll spoil my hair." She met his eyes in the mirror. The Honorable Edward Wyatt might be considered important to his cronies at the U.N., but she knew exactly how to control him. "And then I'll have to have Dalai do it again. Such a waste." He was naked and fully aroused, she noticed. She'd kept him watching her and anticipating for the last thirty minutes, and he was ready and eager for the game to begin. But she was not, and she was annoyed that he should speak to her with so little respect. Make him wait. She turned to Dalai. "I think the ruby comb tonight. Did I tell you how much I enjoy wearing it? It has such meaning for me."

"Yes, madam, you told me." She met Zahra's eyes in the mirror as she hurriedly placed the ruby comb in the chignon. Her maid was probably remembering the details of the deadly story of the comb, Zahra thought with amusement. Dalai was so easy to frighten. "It will be beautiful."

"Yes, it will." Zahra glanced back at Wyatt. "Do you think I'll look beautiful when I give my speech at the U.N. General Assembly? Will you be proud of me?"

"Stop teasing and come over here."

"But you like me to tease you. You like everything I do to you." And she had found out early in their relationship that the thing he liked most was for her to dominate him. The twisted bastard went wild when he was forced into submission. She'd seen the signs on that first night she'd seduced him and had her agent, Lon Markel, check him out. Wyatt spent a good deal of money at several specialty houses when he was in London. That information was all Zahra needed. His particular addiction suited her very well. Domination could be used in many ways other than sex. She got to her feet and came toward him. "Do you think that your wife will think I'm beautiful? Perhaps we can have a threesome when I'm in New York. Shall I call her in London and tell her to join us?" She slipped off her robe and dropped it on the floor. "But perhaps she thinks a woman's duty is only to provide pleasure to a man . . . and whoever else he chooses. Haven't you taught her?" She slipped naked into bed. "I'll teach her for you."

He started to reach for her, and she pushed him away. "No, my rules. Always my rules."

"Bitch," he said through his teeth. "I'm going crazy. Let me *in* you."

"I told you, you'll mess my hair." She ran her fingers down his belly. "But I might allow you to persuade me. But you'll have to give me something that will please me to make up for it."

"What a whore you are."

"No, I'm a queen. I've told you that before."

"You keep saying that. Being president isn't enough for you?"

"No, presidents rely on elections. A queen has power because she is what she is. That's why it hurts my feelings that you don't believe me. You should feel honored that I let you have my body."

"Stop playing this game, Zahra. Just let me—" He gasped as her hand closed on him. "What...do you want?"

"I want you to tell me that you know I'm a queen, and you'll do everything you can to make sure that's how I'm treated in New York."

"You—know—I—will."

"How do I know it?" Her hand tightened around him. "Prove it to me. I haven't noticed you doing anything to make my position here in Maldara stronger lately."

"I do everything you ask." He gasped again as her nails dug into him. *"Shit."*

"I don't appreciate how unfriendly the newspapers have been to me. You have influence. Do something about it."

"I told you, interfering with the free press would be a mistake. It would shine too bright a light on me and my office here in Jokan. I can't do it."

"All I wish is for you to get rid of just one journalist. Jill Cassidy. That's not too much to ask."

"She's very well regarded, and it might cause a stir. You said you'd take care of it yourself."

And she would have, if only those fools had been a little rougher with the bitch that night in the jungle. She'd given explicit instructions, and it should have worked beautifully. But Jill had disappeared for only a few days after the attack; and then she was back in Jokan and still very much in the way. "It didn't work out. I want you to do it."

Wyatt was silent. "I'll do it. You know I'll do anything you wish. But you should know they will probably recall me. Is that what you want?"

No, it wasn't what she wanted. Wyatt was still useful, and it would take her time to develop a relationship with a replacement. "You know it's not," she said curtly. "Very well, I'll find another way. But you will be sure and block anything she tries to do here?"

"Of course." He looked relieved. "Whatever you want. That's a much better—"

He gasped. She was suddenly above him and he was deep inside her. *"Yes."*

She reached up and took the ruby comb from her hair and held it in front of his eyes. "Isn't it beautiful? Full of glitter and power. But there's always danger with power. What if I'd coated these prongs with a deadly poison?" She brought the prongs closer to his throat. "Then you'd really know how powerful I am, wouldn't you?"

He was staring in fear and fascination at the comb. "Yes."

"But it excites you, doesn't it?" She brought the comb still closer to his throat. "I can see it does." Then she was taking the comb away and putting it back in her hair. "Whatever I want?" She was moving fast, controlling him, not letting him touch her, totally dominating. "Stay still. Don't move. You have to be punished for not giving me everything I need tonight. I'll permit you to have this, but then I'll tell Dalai to use the quirt on you. You'll like that, won't you?"

His cheeks were flushed, his mouth open to take air. "Yes. But I— want you—to do it."

"Why should I care what you want? You're only my slave, and so is Dalai. I'll lie here as a queen should and watch the two of you perform for me." She leaned over him, her dark eyes glittering. Her sharp white teeth sank deep into his shoulder. "Say it."

"Whatever pleases you." He shuddered as the blood ran from the wound. "Yes...watch us...as a queen should..."

———◆———

LAKE COTTAGE

"It's crazy," Joe said curtly when Eve finished telling him why she was going to Maldara. "I knew that there was something going on last night. I just didn't know I wasn't going to get a chance to talk you out of it."

"You have a chance now," Eve said. "I called you as soon as I was positive I was going. I won't be leaving until tomorrow afternoon at three." She added sarcastically, "It seems Jill has arranged with one of her friends in high places to lend her his jet and pilot to give us a lift to Maldara. For all I know, she might have even set it up before she came to see me. But at least that will eliminate a lot of red tape and give me more time to send Nora off and postpone my other commitments." She paused. "Please don't give me a hard time, Joe. It won't do you any good. I've decided I have to go."

"You *don't* have to go, dammit. You told me yourself that Jill Cassidy played you. Why should you let her have her way?"

"Because she made sure that I'd know her way was my way this time. I can't do anything else." She added wearily, "I'll e-mail those photos and biographies Jill gave me to you. Then I think you'll understand."

"Oh, I'll understand," Joe said. "But it won't make me want to keep from boiling her in oil at the earliest opportunity. I did a little more research after I hung up with you last night. I could see this coming. Granted, Maldara isn't the powder keg it was two years ago. But between Zahra Kiyani's power grab and all the other ex-mercenaries and crooks who are trying to line their pockets with what's left of that country, it could still be lethal. I don't want you there."

"Three weeks. A month tops. It's all I promised Jill." Then she realized what she'd just said. "No, to hell with Jill. It's what I promised myself. And I may not be able to do reconstructions on more than a portion of those children. I'll have to examine the skulls and make a decision. I may be done sooner. But if I'm successful with only a few, it will show what can be done and might encourage the U.N. to hire someone else to complete the job." She paused. "Remember when I said the timing was just right for you to go to Scotland Yard and Michael to take his trip with Jane? Well, maybe this timing is right, too. Maybe if I can help the relatives of those children, then it was meant to be."

"I'm not in the mood for you to bring up fate at this particular time." Joe was silent another moment. "I'm going with you."

Just what she'd expected. "No, you are not," she said firmly. "I wouldn't get anything done with you floating around like a drone ready to strike. You're going to stay at Scotland Yard, keep an eye on Michael, and call me on Skype as you'd planned to do. If I get nervous about anything, I'll let you know."

He didn't reply.

"Look, Joe, I gave you the names of those officials at the embassy and the U.N. that Jill sent me. She even supplied you with a CIA operative and someone from MI6 to call. Check them out. They should be able to tell you anything you need to know."

"Maybe. I recognized one of the names. I ran into Jed Novak two years ago when I was over here picking up a counterfeiter in Paris." He was silent again, thinking. "They'd given Novak a team and sent him to go after a terrorist ring in southern France. He has a reputation that's...impressive. I wonder what he's doing in Maldara..."

"Discuss it with him and find out." Jill had been right, Eve thought. A detective like Joe would feel more secure about her if he knew she was going to be surrounded by law enforcement he knew and understood. "I'll call you when I get there. I'm sure by that time, you'll have all the information you need."

"Are you trying to get rid of me, Eve?"

"Lord, no." The sound of his voice, the knowledge that he cared, was a comfort even when she had to argue with him. "I just have to get back to Nora if I'm going to finish her tonight. So just do all the things that will make you feel better about my going because it's going to happen."

He didn't speak for a moment. "I think it is, dammit. So by all means I'll do everything I can to prepare for it. Count on it. Good night, Eve."

Eve put down the phone after he'd disconnected. There had been a tinge of grimness in that last sentence. He was already planning what he could do, whom he could use to protect her. She wished she was like Joe and could prepare and make plans for the weeks ahead. There was no way she could do that this time. She just had to go with what she felt.

Because she couldn't see anything but the pitiful photos of those slain children and the siren call of the tales Jill had woven about each one of them.

———————

JOKAN, MALDARA
THIRTY-SIX HOURS LATER

"We'll be landing at Jokan in forty-five minutes." Jill had come out of the cockpit and dropped into the passenger seat next to Eve. "I wanted to let you rest as long as possible, but now there are things I have to talk to you about." She grimaced. "You'll notice I've tried to stay out of your way during the flight."

"I could hardly miss it," Eve said dryly. From the moment the Gulf Stream had taken off, Jill had either been in her own luxurious leather seat across the aisle or in the cockpit with their pilot, Sam Gideon. She had been polite, seen that Eve had drinks and food, given her updates on their progress, but other than that, she had worked on her computer and allowed Eve total privacy. "I appreciate the effort, but you didn't have to treat me as if I had Ebola."

Jill smiled. "I didn't want to push my luck. I know you resent me.

No one has a better right. You'll meet a lot of people here who have problems with me, so you won't feel alone."

"You mentioned that the U.N. officials here weren't your fans. The Children for Peace charity had no problem dealing with them. They found the undersecretary, the Honorable Edward Wyatt, both charming and cooperative when they called him and told him they were sending me."

"Because I wasn't involved." Jill shrugged. "If they'd known I'd convinced you to come, they would have stonewalled you. Lately, it's been a solid wall whenever I need something from them." She made an impatient gesture. "And that's okay, I can work around them. I just have to warn you that I'm going to have to do that. It will be easier and safer for you if no one knows that I had anything to do with bringing you here."

She raised her brows. "You're abandoning me?"

"No, I'd never do that." She made a face. "Though you'd probably prefer if I did. But this is a country that's not like Main Street U.S.A. I know people, you might need me."

"If they don't hate you?"

She nodded wryly. "There is that to consider." She leaned forward, and said urgently, "You won't be alone. I'll surround you with people you can trust. And I'll be able to be on hand for you in a few days. I've had Sam Gideon set up an interview with the press on Thursday, to which I'll be invited. We'll have a nice meeting and find we have everything in common. Everyone knows I've been trying to convince the government to give the villagers what they want for their children. They just can't know that I brought you here."

"Why not?"

Jill hesitated. "Zahra Kiyani didn't like me any more than I did her. I told you, Robaku is a village practically on her doorstep. She was born and raised as Kiyani royalty, and now she's the president of the country. Her father gave up the throne to become president, which I don't believe pleased her. She also has more control than I'd like and is the prime mover in the effort to get the village moved to another location. I don't want her to influence anyone against what you're doing."

"You didn't mention that the deck was already stacked against me," Eve said dryly.

"It's not. I just have to deal around a possible bad hand," Jill said. "And I'm doing it. And I'm telling you about it."

"And letting me know the possibility that this Zahra Kiyani might get me ousted from the country before I can start doing one reconstruction. After a very long trip and a good deal of inconvenience." She shook her head. "And now you tell me?"

"You won't be ousted. We're working around it." She smiled. "And I thought this was the best time to tell you. You won't be likely to give up easily after traveling all this distance. And it's not as if I'll force you to stay. Gideon will take you directly to Robaku after you get off the plane, and you'll meet Hajif, the head of the village. He'll take you to the school and show you where you'll work if you choose to help them. President Zahra ordered the place be made into a sort of memorial, and you'll have to do the reconstructions on-site." She paused. "If you don't want to do it, just tell Gideon. He'll bring you back here, and you'll be on your way to your lake cottage within the hour."

"But you're confident that's not going to happen." Her eyes were narrowed on Jill's face. "You think you know me so well. I might surprise you."

Jill shook her head. "I'm not confident. I know you can surprise me. You're very complicated, and bad things can happen to any plan. I'm just hoping I'm not wrong about you in this instance." She got to her feet. "I'll go back to the cockpit. I'll stay on the plane until I'm sure I won't be seen getting off. After Gideon lands, he'll take care of you from then until we stage our meeting at the press interview."

"Gideon," Eve repeated. "You've dropped that name through the entire conversation. You're talking about Sam Gideon, our pilot, whom you introduced me to at the beginning of the trip?" She vaguely remembered a good-looking, dark-haired young man with a flashing smile. "I'm to put myself in his hands? I take it he's another friend of yours who is a bit more than a pilot?"

Jill nodded. "Well, he does own this Gulf Stream. And flying would be his career of choice if it were up to him." She made a face. "But he owns mega stocks and diamond mines and other boring stuff here in Maldara that tend to get in his way."

"Poor guy."

"Don't be sarcastic," she said quietly. "He's my friend, and he did me this favor. He's helped me before, and I trust him. The fact that he inherited a good portion of the entire wealth of this country made that a hell of a lot easier. I've known Sam Gideon ever since I first came to Maldara. He was born here and lived on a family plantation near Jokan before he graduated from Oxford and moved to London. He knows everybody who's anybody in the country. He won't let you get in trouble. And if he does, he has the man who can get you out of it on speed dial." She stopped at the door of the cockpit to look soberly back at her. "You might find him a little unusual, but you can trust him, too, Eve. I'd never turn you over to someone you couldn't trust." Then she was opening the cockpit door. "I'll see you Thursday if you're still here."

Eve watched the door shut behind Jill. That last sentence had probably been said to convince her that she wasn't being taken for granted. Yet every word Jill spoke sounded sincere. But the fact that she'd let her get here to Maldara before she'd told her that she happened to be having trouble with the ruling head of the damn country was both frustrating and suspicious. Trust her? Trust this Sam Gideon?

Eve shouldn't even get off the damn plane.

But she was already here in this place where savages had thought nothing of killing children as they studied in their classroom.

And she knew she was going to go to Robaku.

———◆———

"Jill says you're very important to her and I'm to be polite and respectful." Sam Gideon's dark eyes were twinkling with mischief as he came out of the cockpit after he'd landed the Gulf Stream. He had just a hint of an English accent that made the mockery in his tone take on an additional slyness. In his thirties, he was very good-looking, with olive skin, dark hair cut close to tame a tendency to curl, and that smile that was definitely reckless. "I told her that I'd been so polite to you when we were introduced that I'd never be able to do a repeat. So what you see is what you get." He shook her hand. "But I did promise her not to try to seduce you. Though it was a sacrifice since I do have a thing for intense, stormy women."

"Stormy?" Eve studied him. Jill had warned her that he was unusual, but it was clear there was much more to Gideon than what he seemed on the surface. He had chosen that remark deliberately because sex was blatantly inappropriate in this situation and definitely would have been forbidden by Jill. That opening could have been meant to either put her at ease or shock her. "Then it's lucky you're wrong about me. I have a very calm nature and avoid turbulence at all costs. Besides being married to a man who makes every effort to keep me from having to deal with the storms of life."

He chuckled. "And you've firmly put me in my place and given just a hint of a threat in case I step out of it. But I notice you don't deny the intensity, which means the storms probably come to you. Jill didn't really need to try to protect you from me, did she? But she tends to go the extra mile." He took her elbow and nudged her toward the door. "Now we've taken each other's measure and can get down to what's important to you." He threw open the door. "Welcome to Maldara, Eve."

A wild study of contrasts...

She stood on the steps, her gaze taking in the sleek commercial jets and military planes that occupied the hangars and runways of the small airport. Everything was new and modern and shining. In the distance, she could see a few skyscrapers on the horizon that contrasted sharply with the dense jungles surrounding the city. On either side of the road leading to Jokan, she could see ragged men, women, and children who had put up their booths of fruits and vegetables and brought their animals to sell at market.

"It's very... different," she murmured as she went down the steps. She was suddenly assaulted by heat, humidity, and the smell of gasoline from the planes on the tarmac. "Though I guess I expected more damage from the fighting."

"Jokan had less destruction than Botzan," Gideon said. "Amazing, since Varak's ghouls were hired by Botzan to decimate it. Our magnificent President Zahra claims her advisors and loyal people managed to hold them at bay by the grace of God." He was leading Eve toward the wire enclosure that she assumed was the parking lot. "The presidential palace wasn't touched. She was able to welcome all the diplomats with her usual grace and style when they liberated Maldara."

"Do I sense a little antagonism?" Eve glanced sideways at him as he opened the passenger door of a tan Land Rover for her. "Yet I don't believe Jill would refer to her as being magnificent in any sense of the word."

"Well, that's where we differ. I've had a closer relationship with Zahra than Jill has. I had an opportunity to assess her qualities." He tilted his head, considering. "I think she has a magnificent opinion of her own worth. I think she's not brilliant but has a magnificent talent for self-preservation." He paused, thinking. "Physically, she has magnificent breasts and possibly interesting, but not magnificent, sexual abilities. So Jill is not being entirely fair."

Her gaze narrowed on his face. "Yet you don't have any use for her."

"Not any more than I would have a use for a spitting mamba I ran across in the jungle." He smiled gently. "Except to sell the venom—

and then the snake would have to be alive to milk it. Much too much trouble." He was driving out of the airport onto the road. "But fair is fair. One has to be accurate. How else can you be allowed to make your own judgments?"

"I hope I won't even have to meet her," Eve said. "I intend to keep a low profile while I'm here."

"It will be difficult for you to do that. You're very famous, and you're in Zahra's kingdom. If she doesn't know that now, she will soon. And she's possessive of Robaku. Didn't Jill tell you?"

"Zahra's *kingdom*? But she's the president of Maldara."

"Zahra has a few bizarre ideas of her own regarding that." He shrugged. "Which are entirely in keeping with her opinion of her own magnificence. But I won't go into that since you're going to make the attempt to avoid her."

"You do know her very well, don't you?" Eve asked curiously.

"You mean, were we lovers? Oh yes. When I came back to spend the summer with my parents after graduating from Oxford, I was ready for a great passion. Zahra was the president's daughter, but she considered me deserving of her attention. I'm very rich, and she automatically associates wealth with royal entitlement. She thought she might be able to mold me into the prince she felt was her due. We had an interesting summer."

"A great passion?"

"No, but erotic and fascinating, until I saw the mamba raising its head. Then I left her and went back to London." His lips twisted. "She wasn't pleased. She'd thought she'd found someone who could survive her bite; and then she had to start over." He gestured to the curve of the road ahead. "Robaku is just ahead. I called from the cockpit and asked the headman, Hajif, to come to meet you at the school. Jill said you had a decision to make and to give you the information you needed to make it."

"And then you'll take me back to Atlanta immediately if I decide I don't want to stay?"

"Of course. Jill always keeps her word. Even if it means I have to bear the brunt of it." He gave her a keen glance. "But I think I'll probably get a good night's sleep tonight here in Maldara. I'd wager that intensity usually wins out when it comes to children. Why else are you here?"

"Your friend, Jill, conned me," she said flatly.

"Then she had her reasons," Gideon said. "And it probably hurt her more than it did you. Jill is one of those rare people who take honor seriously. She'd agonize over it." He paused. "And I bet she made it as painless for you as possible."

"The hell she did," Eve said curtly. "She wrote me a biography on each of those children that would tear your heart out."

Gideon gave a low whistle. "Ah, that pen of hers can be a lethal weapon. She's a great wordsmith. But she is usually responsible about how she wields it. Maybe you'll find that she was this time, too." He'd negotiated the turn in the road, and they'd suddenly left all semblance of the modern world and were in the jungle. He drove on a bumpy dirt road for another few minutes, then pulled to a stop and gestured to a large, square structure several yards away. "Robaku."

Eve stared in shock. Destruction. Chaos.

It was a burnt-out shell of a building. No roof. Only blackened, jagged openings that had once been windows. There was a wide, gaping opening that must have been a door, which vines and shrubs were trying to devour.

Eve could almost smell the acrid scent of the smoke from the flames that had destroyed the school. It had been a long time, but she could swear the smell lingered. She had thought it would at least have been cleaned up, perhaps flowers planted. Some attempt made to have the painfulness of the scene erased.

"Nothing...has been done." She got out of the Land Rover and stood looking at that gaping mouth of a door. "Jill said Zahra...some kind of memorial."

"This is Zahra's concept of a memorial. She ordered the villagers not to touch the school." Gideon got out of the car. "She said that everyone should see the horrible destruction that the war brought to her country so that they would never be tempted to repeat it. Unusual, but it sounded vaguely patriotic when she was quoted in the newspapers." He was striding toward the door. "Step into Robaku's pride and joy, Eve."

No hint of either pride or joy here, she thought, sick. She followed him slowly until she reached the doorway and stood staring into the half darkness. It was worse inside than it was outside.

The desks...

Most of them were blackened and destroyed, but a few of them had escaped the fires and sat there on the burnt-out floors as if they were waiting for the child who came to occupy them every day.

Eve could feel her eyes sting. "Oh, shit."

She moved into the huge room. The blackboard...broken and melted.

Something dark streaking the floor that was neither ash, nor dirt, nor burnt-out boards.

"Jill was told that's not blood on the floor," Gideon said. "That Zahra had given permission for the blood to be cleansed when the body parts were taken from here." His lips curled. "But since Zahra's own people extracted the bodies, I wouldn't give odds that they were careful about cleaning up the blood."

She couldn't take her eyes from those dark streaks.

He was looking at her face. "You don't look well. Maybe I'd better get you out of here."

She paid no attention to him. She was being bombarded by visions of what must have happened here that morning. The children at their desks...The teacher at the blackboard...probably chatter and smiles filling the room. Everything normal and right, as it should be for children in a classroom. As it was in her son Michael's classroom.

"Did...they have any warning? Why didn't they run away?"

"No warning. The school is located on this hill at the far end of the village. It's about a ten-minute walk to the village itself. Varak's militia struck the school first, then went on to burn the village. Hajif said they heard the screams from the children and ran toward the school to save them. But it had already been torched by the time they got there. A few of the bodies found inside were parents who ran into the flames to try to save their children. But most of the villagers were hacked to pieces by the militia, who were waiting for them. The children were only bait." He took her arm and was moving her toward the door. "And now I'm getting you out of here. Jill won't be pleased that I let you get this upset. You're done. You've seen it, you won't forget it."

No, she'd never forget it, Eve thought. It wasn't just the terrible ruins, it was as if the spirits of those children were still here...still waiting.

She pulled her arm away. "It's not as if I'm going to break down or anything, Gideon." She concentrated on keeping her voice steady. "I've seen terrible things before in my career. It's just that this is...overwhelming. I feel if I look over my shoulder, I might see them there." She did not look over her shoulder, but at him. "I thought this Hajif was going to meet us here."

"He always asks if he can meet us at the museum a little down the road. It's only a few yards away, and he finds this place pretty hard to take." He was leading her farther into the jungle. They were passing a beautiful brook surrounded by tall boulders. It seemed odd that anything beautiful could exist this close to that atrocity, Eve thought dully. And Gideon was saying quietly, "Hajif's grandson was killed in the massacre at the school."

Hajif. Eve thought for a moment, then made the connection with the biography Jill had written. "Hajif, grandfather of Amari, nine years old. Amari liked building model airplanes with his father. He wanted to be a pilot when he grew up..."

"You have a good memory. His father was also killed in the massacre. Now there's just Hajif and his wife, Leta, left."

"It doesn't take a good memory to remember what Jill wrote about Robaku." She changed the subject. "Museum? Jill never mentioned a museum."

"It's part of Zahra's memorial. Not that there are many museum artifacts there. Just a few trinkets and photos. She just wanted a place to entertain dignitaries and news media that would show her off to advantage and keep her designer outfits from being contaminated by the soot of the schoolhouse." He lifted his head as a small black man with grizzled hair and lined face, dressed in flowing trousers and a loose white shirt, appeared, coming toward them. "Hajif." He moved quickly toward the man and bowed. Then he rattled off something in an African dialect and turned to Eve. "Eve Duncan, Hajif. She came to see Amari and his friends and hopes she can be of service."

"Jill Cassidy told me of her." The old man's English was broken but his expression was desperately eager as he turned to Eve. "It's we who should strive to serve you. Ask us, and it will be given."

"I don't know if I can help you," Eve said gently. "I'll have to examine the skulls and see if the damage will prevent me from being able to measure and do the sculpting. I understand there was considerable..." She hesitated. She didn't want to say that during fires, the brain often exploded and shattered the skull. "The fire might be a problem..."

"But Jill said you are wonderful and can work with such problems. Is that not true?"

"If there are no other elements that cannot be overcome."

Hajif was silent. "Please." His dark eyes were glittering with moisture. "We need to see him at least one more time as he was. My wife, Leta, keeps hoping that Amari escaped into the jungle and is afraid to come home to the village. She will not listen to me. She said that head in the box is not her Amari."

Eve frowned. "Head in the box?"

Gideon said quickly: "The remains of the children were sent to the American embassy to be kept at the medical lab there until they could be ID'd. But the villagers made such a fuss about the skulls being taken that they were allowed to keep them on-site until it was decided how to dispose of them."

"*She* kept them," Hajif said. "It should not be. They belong to us."

"Zahra stepped in and took over the preservation of the skulls until the decision could be made," Gideon said. "She put the skulls in her museum."

Eve stiffened. "What?"

"With all due respect, of course," he said ironically. "Blessed by the church. Properly preserved in specially crafted boxes." He gestured to a sleek, modern, one-story, gray-stucco building. "Would you like to see them?"

"Yes, I would." She was already striding toward the museum. "Now!"

The first thing she saw as she approached the building was the huge glass-enclosed gold-framed portrait of Zahra Kiyani beside the front door. Dressed in a white designer suit, she looked beautiful, sad, and dignified. Her arms were outstretched as if in welcome.

Eve ignored it, threw open the glass door, and went inside. Clean, bright, beautifully tiled green-and-beige floors. Several glass cases with very few artifacts, as Gideon had said. "Where are those boxes?"

Gideon nodded at a row of rust-colored leather boxes with elaborate gold lettering on the front. No names, just numerals. Not simple, dignified numerals, they were scrolled, then encircled with a fanciful design.

Hajif came to stand beside Eve. "Her soldiers told us that Amari is probably in the fourth box. And if we would consent to have the DNA test, Madam President's experts would be able to tell for certain."

And, until he consented, his grandson's skull would remain in that beautifully crafted box like a forgotten library book on a shelf only yards from their village. Or even worse, a macabre reminder of his death at the hands of Varak and his butchers. Jill had told Eve that the U.N. officials wanted those children to be buried and forgotten, and it was clear Zahra Kiyani was also systematically working to make that happen. Why? It could only be that as the surviving ruler of the conflict, she wanted everyone to forget the details of that brutal struggle to secure her new image. Children were so often used as pawns.

Eve could feel the anger begin to rise within her. It was all *wrong*. No one should forget those children. It was even worse than what had happened to Nora. At least the police were trying to find out what had happened to her. It didn't matter that those butchers who had killed the children of Robaku were known and probably ended up butchered themselves. Their victims needed to come home to the people who had loved them.

"Four?" Eve went behind the counter and looked at the glossy Roman numerals. "They said your grandson was numeral four?" She found the box and pulled it out. "And he was nine years old?" She laid the box on the counter and carefully opened it. The skull was blackened by fire but as carefully preserved as Gideon had said. "Let's take a look..."

"May I ask what you're doing, Eve?" Gideon was gazing over her shoulder with interest.

"Just checking to see how competent Zahra's experts are. It's not all that difficult to establish approximate age if you have the experience." She took the skull out of the box and set it on the glass counter. She carefully went over the skull, paying particular attention to the teeth. "It's a male, but the age is wrong. And the long bones of the face indicate he's at least twelve. One of the older boys in the class." She was trying to remember Jill's notes. "There were two older boys...one was...Maha?"

"Or Shaka," Hajif said eagerly. "Shaka was thirteen, Maha twelve."

"I'd have to examine him more closely to determine which one he is." Eve carefully replaced the skull in the box. "But he's *not* your grandson, and that 'expert' who said he was is no expert." She took the box to the back shelf and slipped it back in its place. "Your wife was right, Hajif. Your grandson might be in one of these boxes, but it's not that one."

"But you will find him?" Hajif asked. "You will bring him back to us?"

She stared helplessly at him. He wanted promises, and there were so many pitfalls that could get in the way of her giving him what he wanted. She wasn't even sure if these were the skulls from Robaku. That had been a stupidly careless mistake about Amari's age.

"My wife needs to know," Hajif said. "She...hurts."

And so was he hurting.

And, dammit, there should be some way to ease that pain. They had lost enough, they had a right to *know*.

She reached out and touched his shoulder. "Then we'd better do something to help her," she said gently. "But I'll need your help first, Hajif."

A brilliant smile lit his face. "You will do it? Anything. I will do anything."

"Will you get some men from the village to come here and take out all these display cases and shove them outside the building? Then I'll need a level table put in the center of the room. I'll show you how high it will have to be. And I'll need a stool of some sort."

"Right away." Hajif turned and moved quickly out of the museum.

"Any orders for me?" Gideon was smiling faintly. "Am I to assume that you're going to be delving into those boxes in the near future?"

"Yes," she said curtly. "Jill is going to feel very satisfied, isn't she? I don't give a damn. Those neat little boxes crafted of the finest leather with all those pretty gold letters made me go ballistic. They look like fashion accessories. I use boxes myself for transport. But this is pure showmanship, no dignity, no feeling. Zahra Kiyani made them part of her personal scenario. I want those kids out of those boxes."

"Obviously. You didn't answer me. What can I do?"

"Get me a cot to set up in here. I'll probably be spending most of my nights in this blasted museum."

"That's not necessary. And unless you're into communal bathing, the hygiene arrangements will be awkward for you in the village. I've made reservations for you at the one decent hotel in Jokan. I can run you back and forth."

"Keep the reservations. I'll need to use the room to shower occasionally. Otherwise, I can wash up in the bathroom here."

"How do you know there is one?"

"Of course there's a bathroom. You said that Zahra used this place to receive the media." She was looking around the room. "And I bet it has a lovely mirror for touching up her makeup." She saw a door across the room and strode toward it. She opened the door and glanced inside. "Yes, a great mirror with her traditional gold frame. I think I'm beginning to know Zahra Kiyani."

"Then heaven help you," Gideon said softly.

"I won't need divine intervention. I'll just stay out of her way and rely on Hajif and his people. I'll work hard and fast and get through this job as quickly as possible."

"Twenty-seven children, Eve," Gideon reminded her.

"I'll do as many as I can in the next month. I'll arrange for the others to be done by someone competent after I have to leave." She gave a last appraising glance at the bathroom and started to close the door. "Make certain I have towels, shampoo, and soap. That's all I need for the time being. Bring in my duffel from the car, will you? How many people in the village speak English?"

"Probably only a handful. But you have Hajif if you need a translator. He said he'd do anything as I recall." He paused. "And I'll stay within ten minutes' distance from you in case of emergencies."

"I'm not expecting any emergencies," Eve said. "This is what I do. I'm in control here. I can handle anything that comes along."

"I can see that." Gideon's gaze was on her flushed cheeks and glittering eyes. "And you can't wait, can you? Well, just know that I'm available." He turned toward the door. "I'll go get your duffel and find you a cot somewhere. You're really staying here tonight? Why don't you let me take you out to dinner and start tomorrow?"

"Because tonight I'll be going through all those skulls until I find one that fits Amari's age and description. Then I'll have to examine it and see if I can do what Hajif wants me to do."

"So Amari is going to be first?"

"He *has* to be first. His grandparents want it so much that I couldn't do anything else. After that, I'll be able to try to be more selective."

"Then I'll tell Jill that you have the initial process going at full speed." He looked back over his shoulder. "Anything else?"

"Bring in my computer and make sure I'll have no problem with Internet while I'm here. That's essential."

"You'll need it for your work?"

"Possibly for the final. But it's principally because I planned on using it to Skype. I prefer it to my smartphone to contact family, and I won't be stranded out here in the jungle and lose contact with my husband and son. That's *not* acceptable."

"Ah, yes, the protective husband in the background? Dedication and total devotion on both sides of the coin. You're an interesting woman, Eve Duncan. I believe I'm going to enjoy you."

"Interesting? You haven't seen anything, Gideon. And I couldn't care less if you enjoy me. Just get me what I tell you I need."

He chuckled. "I'll definitely get you what you need. It will be my goal in life while we're together." He mockingly flipped his hand to his head in a half salute. "I'll be back in a flash with the first install-ment."

He was gone.

Eve gazed after him with impatience and frustration. She still didn't know what to think of him after these hours in his company. He had smoothed her way seamlessly with Hajif and furnished her with both information and a subtle challenge. She hadn't the faintest doubt he would continue to do so until she could wrap up her work here. But he had almost casually admitted to having an affair with a woman about whom she was beginning to be very wary. And he was clearly loyal to Jill Cassidy and her agenda. And that agenda was aimed at using her to do whatever Jill wished here at Robaku.

Forget it. None of this is important right now, Eve thought impatiently. Jill Cassidy wanted to use her? Good luck to her. Since she had told Gideon that she was committed to doing these reconstructions, it meant that she automatically took charge of everything to do with those children. It was how she worked, and she would have it no other way. If Jill interfered, Eve would have to roll right over her if necessary. Jill had started this, but that didn't mean that Eve couldn't finish it...

CHAPTER

4

She's a powerhouse," Gideon said when Jill picked up his call. "Eve listened. She questioned. She let me see the horror she felt. Then she took over. She's setting up shop even as we speak. She's even ordering *me* around. Doesn't she realize what a blow to my ego that is? You might have trouble with her."

Jill had known that from the beginning. The moment she had chosen Eve Duncan, she'd been aware that manipulation could only go so far and felt fortunate that she'd at least gotten Eve here. "Your ego will survive. I believe the only trouble we'll have right away is that she's a workaholic, and we'll have to keep her supplied with materials. Hajif is cooperating with helping her?"

"She's going to do the reconstruction of his grandson first. He thinks she's an angel from heaven." He paused. "She wanted to make certain that her computer and phone would operate at top efficiency. What do I do?"

The phone. Jill could see problems looming on the horizon. "Stall. It might be fine. I'll check with Novak. He's supposed to be here in five or ten minutes to smuggle me off this plane. I'll get back to you." She cut the connection.

She sat there staring out the window of the plane. It was starting.

The first step. Eve had now committed, and she'd be working on the skulls. Jill just hoped that they could move to the next step with more speed, and—

She tensed and whirled to the door as she heard the steps come down outside. She dived to press back against the wall as she saw a strong, brown hand open the door.

"Easy, Jill," Novak said dryly as he came into the cabin. He was hauling a broom and a large, stainless-steel waste-disposal container behind him. "I'd appreciate it if you'd neither shoot me nor hit me in the head with your object of choice." His skin was stained chocolate brown, his contact lenses were the same color, and he was dressed in red coveralls and hat with a cleaning-company logo on the brim. "It would spoil any chance of getting you out of here without being noticed. I'm supposed to tuck you in this waste-disposal container, and who would tote you out of here if you dispose of me instead?"

She let her breath out in relief. "I don't know why you're here anyway. I'm hardly important, and you could have sent one of your men to get me."

"Yes, I could have done that." He paused. "Just as you could have come back into the country alone without going near Eve Duncan and causing me this trouble."

"I had to make sure she'd get here safely. She's my responsibility." She held up her hand as he started to speak. "I know that Gideon could have taken care of her, but she's mine now. It was my plan, and I have to own it."

"That's right," he said mockingly. "She's an important figure in what you call 'your' story. It has to be as you dictate it."

Nairobi. She'd revealed too much to him that last night. "I'm surprised you remember I said that," she said lightly. "It must have been the sedatives."

"I could hardly forget it. I believe it defined your philosophy of life. I'm always on the lookout for clues to understand you."

"You're always on the lookout for clues, period. You take everything apart, then put it back together again." She dropped down in her chair again. "What about Eve's computer? She'll be Skyping her family and telling them everything that's going on. That means anyone who is hacking her will get a complete report via Joe Quinn."

He nodded. "I can't see that would be a problem right away. There's no reason why anyone would believe Eve's here for anything but the obvious. Besides, interfering would send up a red flag to Quinn. I'd rather not do that until the last minute. I've met him, and he'd be a son of a bitch to get rid of if he decided he had to step into the picture." He frowned thoughtfully. "And I've monitored her telephone conversations to him, and I think we'll let her take care of it. She's as protective of him as he is of her. She doesn't want him here either."

She gazed at him in surprise. She had never seen Novak this wary of anyone. He was always cool, always totally in control, and the smartest man she'd ever met. Even sitting here in those ridiculous red overalls and tennis shoes, he didn't appear anything but assured and able to conquer his particular world. She tried to smother the tingle of tension as she gazed at him. After their time together in Nairobi, she should have gotten over that edginess. But he'd always had that effect on her, a combination of wariness and fascination. The lean face, the intelligent, deep-set eyes that always seemed to see too much, the firm lips. There might be handsomer men than Jed Novak, but Jill had always found his super intelligence and quiet strength to be mesmerizing from the moment she had met him over a year ago. "I never actually got to meet Quinn. Have I missed something?" She smiled. "You're being very cautious."

"And so should you. Quinn respects her. He'll stay out of her business as long as he believes she's safe. The minute that changes, he'll go into overdrive."

"I would, too. That's why she has to stay safe." She tensed. "And when is that going to change, Novak? When do we get the skull?"

"Soon. I'm hoping not too soon. When I get word it's a go, we'll have to move fast." He met her eyes. "Whether or not you think Eve is ready for it. You'll have to go in and convince her."

"I know that," she said jerkily. "I'll do what I have to do. It might even be a relief." She got to her feet. "And now you should get me out of here. You've taken long enough to clean this plane. I need to get to the embassy, check in, and annoy the ambassador's secretary to give me any story that he has available on a dull news day."

Novak lifted a brow. "And make sure that no one makes the connection between Eve's arrival and you?"

"No one should if you've done your job. You said you'd arrange it so no one would realize I'd left Maldara."

"No one will. Your tail only caught glimpses of a look-alike as she moved through the streets or visited a friend or restaurant."

She smiled with an effort. "And now Eve appears here courtesy of a notable charity while I've been here all the time and obviously had nothing to do with it." She moistened her lips. "Did you, by any chance, manage to identify the man who's been following me?"

"Not 'by chance.' You insult me." His lips tightened. "We knew the day you showed up in Jokan a week after the attack. I had my own men on you, and he was spotted immediately. His name is Ken Bogani, and he's one of Zahra Kiyani's agents." He paused. "But I don't think he's one of the men who attacked you. We checked DNA, and there was no match for the specimen under your fingernails or the trace evidence on your clothes."

Not under her nails.

Think of the words, don't let the ugly pictures bombard you.

Novak's voice was cool and without expression, and she must be equally calm and composed. She'd already revealed too much to him when he had stayed with her while she was recovering in that hospital in Nairobi. She knew it was dangerous that she had become so dependent on him. But the situation was different now. She was a professional, and she mustn't show him any more weakness.

"But that doesn't mean he's not on the backup team, does it? It's odd you haven't been able to locate any of those men when you're so good at what you do. It's as if they dropped off the face of the earth."

"I'll find them, Jill."

"I know you will. But that shouldn't be a high priority anyway right now." Then she wearily shook her head. "And there's probably no connection between this Bogani and Hadfeld's death, or what happened to me. It wouldn't make sense. Zahra wouldn't have anything to do with Varak, a man who nearly destroyed her country. It has to be something as simple as the fact that I got in Zahra's way at the Robaku school, and I'm suddenly on her watch list."

"Not necessarily. I don't believe in simple answers when it comes to Zahra Kiyani."

Her gaze flew to his face. "You do think she's involved?"

"I didn't say that. You're right, it's not logical, considering who she is. It would be at odds with both Zahra's past and everything she stands for. I just don't discard the possibility because it might be complex."

"And she *is* complex." Jill was thinking quickly. "If you'd heard the bizarre stories Gideon told me about her...But if you think there's even a possibility, we need to pursue it. It's not that I'm afraid. It's not about me. We just have to look at everything, and—"

"It *is* about you." Novak's hands were suddenly hard on her shoulders. His eyes glittered down at her. He muttered a low oath. "I can see you thinking, trying to find a way to go after them. Are you crazy? It's *all* about you. They hurt you. Do you want it to happen again?"

"I believe you know the answer to that," she said unsteadily. "I didn't behave with a great amount of courage that night, did I? And I wasn't any better after you flew me to Nairobi. You had to...help me and I—" She broke off. "And now you're feeling guilty because you think it happened because you wouldn't give me what I asked you. I could see it coming that night you picked me up on that road. *I* made the decision. It was a big story, and I went after it. You had nothing to do with it."

"The hell I didn't."

"Okay, you want to feel guilty, go ahead." She pulled away from his grasp. "Though you don't have that reputation, and I don't know why on earth you're focused on me."

"Neither do I." He gave her a push toward the stainless-steel disposal cart. His voice was rough, but his hands were gentle as he lifted her into the cart and closed the lid. "Now shut up until I get you out of here and into the work van."

The waste container was hot, small, stuffy, and she had to curl pretzel-like inside. She could hear him open the door, and the sunlight pouring on the stainless steel made it even hotter. She knew she should be silent now. But he had been angry with her, and she had to make sure it wouldn't make a difference. She whispered, "You made me a promise. I won't let you break it, Novak."

"Don't you ever give up?" His voice was no longer angry but weary. "I can't break it. We're too close, and you have Eve Duncan, the only wild card in the deck." He started to maneuver the cart down the steps. "Let's hope I can keep her alive for you."

———※———

"It's about time," Joe said as he answered Eve's Skype. "I know you asked me to wait until you called me, but you didn't say it would be at three in the morning."

"Sorry." She leaned back on her stool and took a swallow of coffee. Bless caffeine, she just might make it through the night. "It took me longer than I thought to set up my lab; and then I had to go through the skulls to see if I could find Amari."

"Amari?"

"Hajif's grandson. He has to be the first reconstruction." She started to go into the reasons for the selection, but he cut her off.

"Later," he said grimly. "All I want to know right now is that you've definitely decided to do the reconstructions. You said it wouldn't be a done deal until you got there and looked the situation over. If you've set up your lab, it means that you're committed. Right?"

"I have to do it, Joe," she said quietly. "I'll get them finished as quickly as I can."

"I know you will. I'll admit I was hoping it would go the other way." He paused. "You look tired. Don't work yourself into a nervous breakdown because you think I'm pressuring you. I'm behind you whatever you do."

"You're not the only one who's pressuring me," she said ruefully.

"Jill Cassidy? Tell her to go to hell."

"She's being very subtle. It's hard to have a confrontation when she dumped me on this Sam Gideon the minute the plane's wheels hit the tarmac here. I think she's designated him to do the pressuring for the time being."

"Sam Gideon?"

"Our pilot. I imagine he's several other interesting things as well. He mentioned casually that he'd been Zahra Kiyani's lover at one time. But Jill said I could trust him."

"Providing you can trust her."

"Neither really matters. I'm back at work. I'm the only one I have to trust now."

"Wrong. You have to trust me. You might have gone into your cocoon, but I have to make certain that no one messes around and tries to break into it."

"From long-distance," she said pointedly.

"For the time being."

She tried to change the subject. "Tell me what you're doing. Do you like the guest instructors at the Yard?"

"They're superb. I'll tell you all about them after you finish telling me about Robaku." He paused. "I want every detail, Eve. Every impression."

She laughed. "Joe, are you debriefing me?"

"In a way. Partly. But I've already been away from you too long.

I *need* you. It will help if you just let everything flow out and share
with me."

"It's been quite a day. I don't even know if I'll remember everything. It's sad here. Some things will hurt talking about..." But she
suddenly knew she needed to share them anyway. She always needed
to share with Joe. It kept the bond firm, doubts at a minimum, and
the love shiny and new. Do as he asked and let it flow. "I guess it
started on the plane when Jill came to tell me that everything wasn't
quite as I thought it was going to be..."

———◆———

An hour later, Eve turned off the computer, sat there, and gazed
around the room. For that short hour she'd been with Joe, it had
faded away, and she wanted to keep it at a distance. She didn't want
to face that schoolroom only yards away, nor the memory of those
children who had died so terribly. She wanted Joe and Michael and
the life she'd had only days before. She wanted to close her eyes and
forget about anything else.

But there was always a price to pay if you allowed yourself to forget the madness and the horror.

It could come again.

She took a deep breath and pushed her computer aside. Then she
took the skull she'd mounted on the dais and started to examine it.
First, she'd have to repair the damage. Next, she'd start to measure.
She was very tired, and she'd probably have to catch a nap on that
cot before she actually started. Her hands tended to shake if she was
too exhausted.

But she needed a little time with this young boy now that they
had come together.

She looked down at the hideous, blackened skull and gently
touched the cheekbone. "Hi. You've been through a nightmare, but
you're not the nightmare," she whispered. "I think you probably

know that by now, but we have to make certain everyone else does, too. We're going to make you as handsome as you were before that day, and that will make your grandmother very happy. Okay? And I usually give my sculptures names, but I believe I know yours, Amari. So we'll go from there. Are you ready?" She began to check for breaks in the orbital socket. "Let's clean you up a bit, then we'll get you started on your road home..."

"You're a fool, Wyatt," Zahra said savagely. "I don't *want* Eve Duncan at Robaku. Why would you permit her to come to my city and work on those children? I've worked hard to try to filter all publicity about them through me, and now you let some charity send a world-class forensic sculptor here? She's bound to attract attention."

"They went through the London office. I was told to accommodate them. What could I do?"

"What I want you to do." She drew a deep breath and tried to smother her anger. This was not the time to alienate Wyatt when everything must go smoothly over the next few weeks. "You said Duncan has already arrived? Did Jill Cassidy have anything to do with bringing her here?"

"The home office didn't mention her. But you know that her stories about the massacre did stir up a good deal of sympathy. It might have influenced the charity to act."

"Tell me about it. That's why you should have gotten rid of her. But she had no direct connection with Duncan?"

"No, I believe Duncan called the charity and volunteered her services. Though I was told she arrived on Sam Gideon's plane. Perhaps he had something to do with it."

Gideon. Zahra's hand tightened on the phone. Son of a *bitch*. Yes, he could have done it, just to annoy her. She'd made no secret of her views about Robaku. He was constantly getting in her way, and it was dangerous for her to do anything to put a stop to it. His plantation might have been burned to the ground during the conflict, but he still had enormous economic influence in Maldara. She wished he'd been burned up with the damn place, she thought savagely. "That doesn't mean she isn't involved." But her temporary chief agent, Bogani, had told her that Jill Cassidy had been in Jokan for the weeks since the attack. If she was involved, it had not been directly, and Gideon was quite capable of raising enough hell on his own. "I'm going to meet this Eve Duncan. I'll be able to tell if she's just a do-gooder or if she'll get in my way."

"Let it go, Zahra," Wyatt said. "What harm can she do? I'll keep an eye on her, and in a few weeks she'll be gone. She's probably doing it for the publicity and working on a few of those burnt-out skulls will be enough to discourage her."

"I want her gone now. Robaku is mine, and it's time all these arguments about the DNA ended." She was done talking to him. "Let me know if you find out anything else." She cut the connection.

She sat there for a moment. She didn't like this. She needed to talk to Lon Markel, her primary agent, and discuss how far she could go to discourage it happening. She started to dial her cell again, then stopped. Markel had been involved in the attack on the Cassidy woman, and she'd been told not to call on him again unless it was an emergency.

Screw it. No one could tell her what to do. Markel was *her* agent, her employee, and she trusted him more than she did the others in her service. He'd been with her for years before he'd been yanked away from her these past months. She'd only tolerated Bogani since she'd been told she couldn't have Lon Markel for the time being. But she would *not* have him hijacked and permanently taken away from her. She paid his salary, and she would do what she liked with him. She began to dial again.

She stopped and put the phone down.

It wasn't fear, she told herself. She was never afraid. It was just that perhaps it wasn't wise to use Markel again so soon. There was a slight chance he might have been recognized by Jill Cassidy that night. Of course, it was entirely her own decision. It would be better to handle this herself.

It was entirely her own decision...

———◆———

"How is it going?"

Eve looked up from her reconstruction to see Sam Gideon standing in the doorway. "Well enough." She arched her back to ease the stiffness. "Amari isn't easy. Just reconstructing the damaged bones of the right temple took me almost a day. It must have been a machete blow to be that shattered. But the measuring isn't causing me too much trouble. I'm almost done with it." She tilted her head. "I haven't seen you for two days. Weren't you supposed to stay around and be at my beck and call?"

"I was around. I peeked in a couple times, but you were so absorbed that I decided to let Hajif handle everything. He seemed to be doing a good job, and I'm always tempted to ask questions." He was looking at the reconstruction. "What are those red flags all over his face?"

"Depth-measurement markers."

"Not flattering. But the rest of him is looking a hell of a lot better than that first night, when you pulled him out of his box."

"Thank you for your critique. Now go away, Gideon. I'm busy."

"Presently. I just thought I'd drop by and give you fair warning. I just got word that Zahra Kiyani is on her way to pay you a visit. I thought you'd want to be prepared."

Eve frowned with annoyance. "I don't need this. Can't you get rid of her?"

"No, you'll have to do it. Zahra doesn't listen to me. She'd prefer that I didn't exist. I actually thought she'd be here before this. She obviously took a long time to make up her mind whether you were worthy of her personal attention." He paused. "It would be best if you didn't mention Jill. Zahra can't hurt me, but she'll try her best to hurt Jill. And Zahra has enough power in Jokan to make it...uncomfortable for her."

"You want me to lie?"

"That's up to you." He smiled. "No one is going to stop you from saying anything you wish to say. If you think what you're doing here isn't worth doing and that Jill should be punished for being involved, by all means have a chat with Zahra about it." He turned and headed for the door. "I'll just hang around outside until her entourage shows up and greet her." His smile was a combination of both mischief and malice. "That should make her day..."

She gazed after him with exasperation. She didn't want to deal with Zahra Kiyani, and she didn't want to have Gideon telling her how to handle the woman. She just wanted to go back to work and finish Amari.

But it was too late. She heard the roar of several automobiles exiting the road, then the slam of car doors as they reached the museum. Eve got to her feet and wiped her hands on her work towel. Then the door was being opened ceremoniously by a uniformed soldier, and Zahra Kiyani was sweeping into the museum. She did not look pleased, Eve thought. Evidently, seeing Gideon had definitely *not* made her day.

She was dressed in a designer gold-paisley suit and was just as beautiful as she appeared in her photos. Her frown disappeared, and she gave Eve a flashing smile. "How happy I am that you're here in my country." Her English was faultless, with just a hint of an accent. "And doing such good work. I thought I'd drop by and personally welcome you." She looked Eve up and down. "But I should have let you know. You're obviously working so hard that I might be in the way..." She trailed off and shrugged. "You do look so tired. I hope you'll forgive me."

The needle was faint but definitely there. Eve was annoyed enough about the interruption not to let it get a pass. "I'm not at all tired. When I become this involved in my work, I forget everything else. I'm looking forward to many engrossing hours spent here at Robaku," she said. "Thank you for coming to welcome me. But I know how busy you must be, so I won't keep you." She gestured to the skull. "And I'm busy as well. He's one of your own people, so I know you'll want me to finish as soon as possible."

"Yes, of course." She gazed at the skull. "One of the children..." Her glance shifted back to Eve. "I understand you have a child. Aren't you worried about leaving him to take care of my problems here? Children can be so very fragile."

Eve went still as she looked at her. Zahra's voice had been soft, and her expression was serene, but Eve had felt a chill. Could that have been a threat? "My son is always safe even when I'm not with him. And my work is too important to leave it undone when a charity says I'm needed."

Zahra nodded. "You appear to be very talented." She forced a smile. "Though I do prefer the certainty of DNA over a pretty sculpture. I suppose Jill Cassidy told you that we disagreed on that score?"

"Jill Cassidy? Isn't she a reporter or something? I believe I've heard of her. But it was Sam Gideon who told me about you."

She stiffened. "Really?" she said warily. "What did he say?"

"He used the word 'magnificent' quite a bit. I can see why he thought it applied to you." She inclined her head. "Now if you'll excuse me?"

But Zahra Kiyani was still looking around the room. "I can't say I like what you've done to my beautiful museum. It's in shambles. I'll tolerate it for now because I don't wish to be unfair. However, if I find that your work isn't what it should be, I'll have to ask you to leave. I'll be back next week to see if that charity that sent you has made a mistake." She moved toward the door. "I'll see you then, Ms. Duncan."

Then she was gone. A few minutes later, Eve heard the low roar of the cars as they departed Robaku.

Gideon came back into the museum a moment later. "That was very short. She didn't waste much time on you."

"No, *I* didn't waste much time on *her*," she corrected. "She only came to threaten and find out who had sent me here. I said enough to satisfy her so that she'd get out and let me work."

"Satisfy?" he repeated. "She looked almost triumphant when she glanced at me when she left."

"That's because I told her you thought she was magnificent. She probably thinks that if she made the effort, she could have you worshipping at her feet again."

He flinched. "That was wicked of you, Eve. When she has time to think it over, she'll realize I must have been lying to you." He tilted his head. "But you must have been doing a little prevaricating yourself if you let her believe it."

"I didn't lie. She asked what you'd told me about her, and I told her the truth. I just didn't elaborate."

"And were you equally truthful when she asked you about Jill?"

"I might have been a little less open. She had a perfectly good target in you, and bringing in Jill would have confused things and wasted more time."

"And you wouldn't have wanted that to happen," he said softly. "It was all for the benefit of Amari and friends."

She was silent. "I didn't like her." She was remembering that instant when Zahra had mentioned her son. She was still feeling that chill. "I've met women before who are antagonistic toward other women. I've never understood it. She was trying to be subtle, but underneath, she was practically bristling."

"She believes she has no need for them, and they might prove competitive. Not that she'd admit the latter." He smiled. "After all, she is magnificent."

Eve smiled back at him. "You left out one descriptive noun.

Magnificently arrogant." She waved her hand. "Now get out of here and let me work. If I'm lucky, I'll get Amari finished tonight or early morning and reward myself by letting you take me to that hotel so I can shower."

"And sleep in a real bed?"

"That's too much luxury. The cot is fine. I'm usually so tired I have no trouble sleeping. Out, Gideon."

"I'm going." He hesitated at the door. "But I should tell you that Zahra wanted to leave one of her soldiers on guard here. I'm sure she'd say it was for your protection, but I still sent him on his way."

"Does she think that I'm going to steal one of these skulls?"

"No, I'm sure she's checked you out thoroughly. She just likes to be in control, and you didn't fall into line. It probably wouldn't have done any harm to let the guard stay as long as I knew he was around. I just didn't want you to stumble over him if you went to get a breath of air." He grimaced. "As if you would bother." He lifted his hand in a wave. "I'll be back around midnight to see Amari in all his glory."

"No glory." Eve was already sitting back down on her stool. "Just a little boy spruced up and ready to go home to see his grandparents..."

Then she closed everything out as she settled down to spend the next hours working on completing and checking the measuring. It was undeniably the most important if least satisfying part of the sculpting process. It was the precise building block of features and contours that made Amari who he was. But it was only the final stage of sculpting that revealed the details that gave him the personality and presence that brought him to life for Eve.

So do the hard, gritty work and make sure that she made no mistakes. Then she'd do the initial smoothing and make ready for that final step. She felt her fingers tingling at the thought.

Stop it. Not yet. This boy deserved care and certainty.

The measuring...

It had not gone as well as she'd hoped with Eve Duncan, Zahra thought impatiently as she gazed out the window of her limo. She'd hoped to impress her enough so that she would be able to oust her during the next visit. But Eve Duncan was one of those women who thought so much of themselves that they didn't realize how far above them she was. Station and beauty meant nothing to them because they had some idiotic skill and thought they could compete. It was not only laughable, it was an annoyance. Now she would have to spend more time than she'd planned on getting rid of her. It would probably mean trying to influence that charity to—"

Her phone was buzzing.

She stiffened as she saw there was no ID.

Dammit! She had been afraid of this.

She punched in the access code and typed rapidly.

IT DIDN'T GO WELL. DUNCAN IS STUPID AND I CAN SEE SHE WON'T COOPERATE. IT WILL TAKE ME A LITTLE LONGER THAN I PLANNED.

A pause, then the answer.

WE BOTH KNOW THAT'S NOT ACCEPTABLE. I TOLD YOU I NEED HER GONE. MAKE IT HAPPEN.

Orders? She tried to smother the bolt of sheer rage that shot through her.

I'LL DO IT AS QUICKLY AS I CAN. HOW DARE YOU TELL ME WHAT TO DO. YOU HAVE NO IDEA HOW COMPLICATED IT IS TO KEEP ALL THE BALLS IN THE AIR.

Another pause.

HOW DO I DARE? YOU KNOW HOW I DARE, ZAHRA. NOW STOP STALLING AND GIVE ME WHAT I WANT.

She should have been more cautious. She might have made a mistake. She typed in quickly. AS SOON AS POSSIBLE.

The answer came back instantly.

MAKE IT HAPPEN!

———◆———

Eve finished the initial smoothing of the clay just after midnight.

She leaned back and gazed at the reconstruction as she wiped her hands. Everything was there, and smooth, and presumably correct. But he was like a baby asleep in the cradle, waiting to be roused. It was time to wake him up and bring him back to those who loved him.

Her hands were tingling again. But that was okay now. The blood flow usually helped the process and kept her from becoming exhausted.

"It's time for you to get to work, Amari," she said softly. "We're almost at the end, and I need a little help here. I'll be with you all the way, but there are so many tiny things I could miss that would make them sad if I didn't catch them. We don't want that to happen, so let's make sure it doesn't. Okay?"

She reached out and delicately touched the place on his skull that she'd repaired. "Let's do this, first. Let's make it go away forever..."

Smooth.

Careful.

Delicacy.

Don't hurry. It has to be perfect.

Don't let anyone know the pain that caused that wound.

See? It's gone now, Amari.

Perfect.

Smooth.

Mold.

Go on to the cheekbone.

It's going faster now.

Smooth.

Mold.

Hollow the left cheekbone a little more.

The clay was cool beneath her fingers.

Ears. Make them generic. Hajif could tell her if she'd gotten it right.

Smooth.

Mold.

Fill in.

The clay felt warmer now as her fingers moved faster.

Eyes.

No, not yet. There was something troubling about the eyes...

Go on to the nose.

Pay attention to the measurements of the space between the nose and upper lip.

Smooth.

Fill in.

Mouth.

So difficult.

Just go with what seemed right.

Eyes?

No, not yet. What was wrong with the eyes?

Go back to the cheekbones.

Not full enough, he'd not reached puberty and was still a child.

Smooth.

Mold.

Fill in.

Her fingers were flying now.

What's wrong with the eyes?

Check the measurements.

Measurements correct.

But something was wrong.

Not with the right eye, she realized.

Left eye. Outer corner of the left eye.

Too smooth.

Indent.

No, build up.

It didn't matter if she didn't know the reason.

Just do it.

Now it was right.

Go on to the curve of the lips.

Something was missing.

Mold.

A deeper crease.

Her fingers were hot, fast, mindless.

Let it all come together.

Smooth.

Fill in.

Mold...

CHAPTER

5

"F inished?" Gideon said behind her from the doorway. "It's almost three. I gave you an extra—"

"Almost," she interrupted. "I just need to put in his eyes. Go get Hajif and his wife."

"It's three in the morning. You want me to wake them up?"

"Yes, by the time they throw on some clothes, I'll be finished. And they're not going to care if it's three in the morning. They deserve to be the first to see him. Go!"

"You're continuing to order me about," he complained. "I can't say I'm accustomed to such treatment..."

He was gone.

And she was reaching for her eye case. There was no question about the color, they would be the same rich brown as Hajif's. She carefully inserted the glass eyes in the orbital sockets and sat back to look at him.

Yes.

Only Hajif and his wife, Leta, could tell her if this was Amari, but the skull had come alive as she'd wanted it to. She'd put the hint of a smile at the corners of his lips, and the shining brown of his eyes appeared oddly eager as he stared up at her. She'd engraved gentle curves that mimicked short curls or waves framing that face. It had just seemed right.

"Are you ready for them?" she whispered. "They're ready for you, Amari."

She stood up as she heard them coming. She stood to one side as she saw Gideon open the door and Hajif and his wife appear in the doorway. "I thought you wouldn't mind getting up a bit early, Hajif." She gestured to the reconstruction. "Is this what you wanted from me?"

Hajif stood stock-still in shock.

He was silent, staring dazedly at the sculpture. "I . . . did not expect this. It . . . is magic." He drew his wife, Leta, toward the worktable. His eyes were shimmering with moisture as he slipped his arm around her waist. "You see, Leta, he has returned to us." He reached out, and his index finger gingerly touched the raised scar at the corner of his left eye. "Remember how upset you were when the propeller flew off his toy plane? You kept saying one more inch, and he would have been blind. But he was fine, wasn't he?" He looked at Eve. "How did you know?"

"I didn't. Some things just seem right. Is it Amari, Hajif?"

He nodded. "It is my grandson." He turned to his wife, whose eyes had never left the face of the reconstruction. "Is it Amari, Leta?" he asked gently. "Has she brought our Amari back to us?"

"Yes." The tears were suddenly running down her cheeks. "He is not alive. He's not hiding in the jungle waiting to come home to us because he's afraid. They killed him, Hajif." She was sobbing. "They *killed* him."

"You knew that." He pulled her into his arms. "But does he look sad and afraid now? He is our Amari, and there is no fear."

"No fear," his wife said brokenly. "I have nightmares about how afraid he was when those butchers came."

"I know. I know." He held her close. He looked over her head at Eve. "Words cannot—I thank you. May we come and visit him here in the museum?"

She shook her head. "I don't believe he'd like staying here. Why don't you take him home?"

His eyes widened. "But he belongs to—"

"He belongs to you now." She grimaced. "As long as you promise not to ever put him in that box again." She took a step closer to Leta. "Leave him here for the time being," she told her gently. "Go home and make a place for him. No fancy shelves. Just a place where he'll be safe, and you can see him every day. Use his favorite colors, put things he loved around him. If you see something you think he'd like, give that to him, too. See him as he is now and let him become part of your life." She paused. "And maybe that will make the night-mares go away."

"I hope that is true." Leta suddenly launched herself into Eve's arms and was embracing her. "But if it's not, when I wake, I will have him with me." She awkwardly backed away, embarrassed. "Come along, Hajif. We must go home and find this place for him. It will not be as easy as she makes it out to be."

"But I'm sure you will be back in just a few hours with the perfect place." Hajif smiled again at Eve as his wife pushed him toward the door. "There is nothing I will not do for you," he said quietly, "You have only to ask."

"Oh, I'll ask," Eve said. "I have twenty-six other skulls to deal with after this. I'll need help."

"Skulls," he murmured, his wondering gaze on Amari. "It does not seem possible. He is . . . alive." He smiled brilliantly. "Magic."

"No, skill and experience," she called after him, as Leta pulled him from the room. She made a face, and said to Gideon, who was still leaning against the wall beside the door, "I don't think Hajif believes in witch doctors, but this is Africa. You can never tell."

"He may not be far wrong." Gideon straightened and strolled across the room toward the reconstruction. "This is pretty incredible."

"It's hard work and making sure every measurement is correct." She moved toward her duffel beside her cot. "And now you can take me to that hotel and let me spend the next hour under a hot shower." She slipped the strap of the duffel over her shoulder. "I need it."

"Give me a minute." Gideon was closely examining the reconstruction. "You're selling yourself short. Probably intentionally. I've never seen anything like this. It's superb."

"Yes, I'm very good. I want to go, Gideon."

"Hmm." His index finger was tracing the scar at the corner of Amari's left eye. "I just wanted to get a closer look at this. Hajif was impressed. I agree." Then he gave her a slanting glance that held pure mischief. "Magic..."

She ignored him, already on her way toward the door. "Bullshit. Haven't you ever heard of inspiration? Get me to that hotel."

She heard him laugh as he followed her from the museum.

◆

The Soran Hotel was one of the few skyscrapers in Jokan, and it looked like a luxurious Ritz-Carlton, Eve thought. It even had a uniformed doorman who rushed to open her door. "You said it was a decent hotel," she said to Gideon. "This is several steps up from that. Zahra's intervention?"

"No, my father had it built when he still thought Zahra's father could make a difference here in Maldara. Once Zahra took power, she couldn't bear to give up a quality hotel when she could use it to her advantage. Though it irritates her that I prevented her from nationalizing it and still have major control. She tries to exert her influence whenever she gets the chance." He walked with Eve into the lobby and handed her a key. "Suite 735. It's the room I keep on reserve for myself. You'll find it comfortable. Enjoy your shower. I'll give you an hour, then have them bring you your meal. I'd guess you haven't eaten for hours."

She couldn't remember when she'd grabbed that bowl of soup yesterday. "No, but I think I'm getting hungry."

"Then I'll call Pierre Gaillon, the chef, and get him out of bed. I hired him from the George V in Paris, and he does miracles with coq au vin. You won't be disappointed."

"I'm sure I won't. But I'm not accustomed to gourmet cuisine, Gideon. I'd be satisfied with a sandwich."

"I wouldn't. I told you that I'd take care of you." He walked her to the elevator. "I'm tempted to join you for dinner, but this is the time for you to relax, and I'm much too stimulating."

"I didn't notice," she murmured.

"Of course you did." He punched the elevator button. "You're just dedicated to keeping me humble. So I'll stay here in the lobby and talk to the manager and wait for you to call me and tell me how much you enjoyed that coq au vin. Try to get a nap if you can afterward. Call me if you need me."

"No nap." The doors of the elevator opened, and she stepped inside. "And I'll be ready to go back to Robaku as soon as I've eaten. I need to start the next reconstruction. I think I'm going to do one of the six-year-olds. But I'll call you as soon as I've finished that gourmet meal you're ordering for me." She said quietly, "Thanks, Gideon. I appreciate your making everything easier for me."

"My pleasure." He smiled. "It's been an interesting few days. If you don't mind, while I'm waiting around, I'll give Jill a call and tell her about Amari. She'll want to know."

"I don't mind." Being able to help Hajif had caused her resentment toward Jill to lessen, she found. There was no doubt that so far her work here had been worthwhile and caused a major difference in Hajif's and Leta's lives. "Tell her if she wants to see it, she should visit Hajif's home."

"And not get in your way?"

She found herself smiling as the elevator door started to close. "And not get in my way."

"I won't get in her way," Jill said. "In fact, I'll wait until the press meeting day after tomorrow to even show up at Robaku. Do I detect a little softening?"

"A little." He paused. "She's got a different mind-set. Doing that reconstruction meant something to her. She's pretty fantastic, you know, Jill. You chose the right person."

"I'm well aware of that, Gideon. There wasn't a choice when I realized how amazing she was."

"But I like her," Gideon said. "And I'm not cut out for all this secretive bullshit." He returned to Eve. "And she covered for you with Zahra. But that isn't because she was fond of you but because she didn't like Zahra or the way she'd used the kids as a display for her museum."

"I thought that would push her buttons," Jill said. "It did mine. I deliberately left it as a surprise." She'd be glad when all this manipulation ended, she thought wearily. "But if she's so involved with the kids, it might make it more difficult when I try to move her away from them."

"No word about the skull?"

"Anytime now," Jill said. She was as impatient as Gideon. "Novak said he'd let me know as soon as he does. It has to happen, Gideon." She changed the subject to Eve. "Take care of her. I don't like that Zahra wanted a guard stationed at Robaku."

"She didn't get it. I'll be there for Eve," he said quietly. "The worst thing that will happen is that she'll drop from exhaustion. I don't seem to be able to control that possibility. Now let me go and order her dinner. The other possibility is that she might forget to eat and starve to death." He cut the connection.

Gideon seemed almost big brotherly, Jill thought as she hung up, and that was never Gideon's style. He was cool, sometimes amusing, sometimes sensual, and always wary these days. He tended to keep everyone at a distance. But he had said he liked Eve, and that might have made the difference.

They had both developed feelings for Eve since they had brought her to Maldara. It was becoming more and more difficult to face drawing her even deeper into the quagmire.

Novak, get that damn skull!

———◆———

"I'm clean at last." Eve stopped drying her hair and tossed aside the towel as she grinned at Joe on the Skype. "Sorry you have to put up with my soggy hair, but I wanted to catch you before you went to the Yard. I didn't get a chance to call you yesterday. Did you get my message that I was finishing Amari?"

"I got it," he said dryly. "Or I would have been on the next plane to Jokan. I take it that it went well? You're practically floating."

"I am floating. It was so *different*, Joe. You know I usually have to just send the reconstructions back to a police department and they do the follow-up to find who the child is and the killer. This time I was able to see that boy go home to the people who loved him five minutes after I finished. I got to see their *faces*, Joe."

"And it meant the world to you," he said gently. "That's wonderful, Eve."

"Everything's wonderful tonight." She chuckled. "I sent Amari home, Gideon brought me to this five-star hotel so that I could dine in style and shower, and I got to share it all with you. It can't get any better."

"Until next time." He smiled. "I'm not going to be able to get you away from that place, am I?"

"I'm needed here, Joe. But I'll leave when you and Michael are finished there. I promised you. Besides, I couldn't stand being away from you any longer than that." She heard a knock on the door. "That must be my room service. Gideon said that the chef was preparing me coq au vin, and it was guaranteed to be delicious."

"Evidently, I'll have to trust your opinion of this Gideon," Joe said.

"Though I'm not certain how I feel about his being able to whisk you to five-star hotels and ply you with gourmet meals. I'll have to tell you when I meet him. But as long as you're not sharing that meal with him, soggy hair and all, I guess I'll be able to tolerate it."

"You're joking," she said as she got to her feet. "I have to answer the door. I'll tell you tonight if it's as good as Gideon said. I love you. Have a good day."

"Only half joking. My humor is suffering drastically since I've been limited to Skype to see you. You'll remember I don't like sharing you. But I'm glad you've already had a wonderful day. I love you, too. Be safe."

Eve headed for the door as she disconnected the call. Those last remarks had had an edge, she thought. Joe had been very patient, but she knew he was worried. She had to be careful to reassure him that though everything was strange, and there were annoying elements like Zahra Kiyani, there had not been anything obviously threatening during these days.

A smiling waiter wheeling a white-draped cart with several silver-domed serving dishes bowed as she opened the door. "The chef sends his regards and hopes his offering will please you."

"I'm sure it will." She was suddenly ravenously hungry. She stood aside as he rolled the cart into the room. She would have to tell Joe about the elegant presentation when she talked to him tonight. It would amuse him. Or maybe it wouldn't. She'd have to think about it. But it would certainly emphasize that everything surrounding her at the moment was ultracivilized and completely without threat...

———◆———

Eve pushed back her chair and sighed with contentment.

The meal had been as fantastic as the presentation, and this coffee she was drinking was excellent as well. She was tempted to call Gideon to tell him how well he'd done, but she decided against it.

She'd call him after she got dressed and was ready to leave. That would be time enough. She was eager to get back to Robaku and start the new reconstruction.

She quickly dressed in slacks and a work shirt and brushed her hair. She did feel fresher and able to cope now. She'd been right to take this little break between reconstructions. She'd be able to attack the new work with a clear head, and that would make it go faster than—

Pain!

She bent double as agony knifed through her stomach.

She felt so sick.

Then her stomach was suddenly heaving.

She had to hold on to the vanity to make it to the toilet.

Then she was throwing up . . .

Time after time, trying to hold herself upright, fighting the violence of the vomiting.

Her head was throbbing, pounding . . .

And then the cramping attacked her stomach.

Hideous cramping.

Her legs gave way, and she fell to the floor.

Her head was on fire.

Her phone . . . She had to get to her phone. She reached blindly toward the vanity where she'd laid it.

No strength . . .

Only the pain and the terrible nausea.

She felt as if she must be dying.

Because everything was going dark . . .

<hr />

"I don't have much time, Jill," Gideon said curtly when Jill picked up his call. "I'm in an ambulance heading to the embassy hospital. I found Eve unconscious in her suite, and I couldn't bring her around. I have to get her to the ER right away."

Jill stiffened. "Gideon, what happened? You said she was fine when I talked to you before."

"I don't know what happened, dammit. No obvious wounds. She'd obviously been throwing up, but I don't know if it was drug-induced. All I know is she's damn sick."

Panic seared through her. "I'll meet you at the hospital."

"No, I'll call you when I know more. You can't do anything I can't do. Novak doesn't want you near her."

"That's too bad. I don't *care*. I figure all bets are off now. She could *die*, Gideon. She wasn't supposed to get hurt. There's no reason. Not for what she's doing at Robaku."

"Evidently, someone disagreed. And she might not be that sick. Let me find out." As she started to protest, he cut in harshly: "I told you I'd be responsible for her, and I screwed up. Do you know how that makes me feel? Now let me take care of her. I won't let you blow everything we've worked for because you're panicking. There's too much at stake. Now call Novak and tell him to check her suite and see if he can find out who or what brought her down. I ordered dinner for her, and she'd finished it. But you stay away from the hospital unless I call you, Jill." He cut the connection.

Jill *was* panicking. She was terrified. And there was no way she wasn't going to go to the hospital to see Eve. Gideon said he was responsible, but he was wrong. She was the one who was responsible for everything that had happened to Eve. She had chosen her, then done everything possible to make her come here.

Yet if she did show up at the hospital, it would make Eve more of a target than ever. Any association with Jill might draw attention to Eve. But this couldn't go on. She had to *do* something.

One step at a time.

First, do as Gideon suggested and phone Novak.

She quickly dialed Novak's number. "I suppose you already know what happened," she said unevenly. "Gideon asked me to call you. But you always know what's going on before anyone else does."

"I know an ambulance just took Eve to the embassy hospital," Novak said. "Stay away from there, Jill."

"I've already heard that song, and I'm trying to do it. Because if Eve manages to live through this, I don't want to make it any more dangerous for her than it is already."

"I know you're upset, Jill. But we don't know what her condition is right now. We'll do everything we can to—"

"Upset?" Her voice was shaking. "You bet I'm upset. I can't take this any longer. You go find out exactly what happened to her. And you make certain that Gideon lets me know as soon as possible whether I've killed her or not."

"It isn't your fault that—"

"Don't tell me that," she said fiercely. "I am to blame. I'm going to pray that I didn't hurt her too badly, but I won't try to escape the fact that if I did, the fault was mine." She drew a deep, shaky breath. "But it's not going to happen again. We thought she was safe, but she wasn't. And we let her walk right into it. It's got to change."

"I don't like the sound of that."

"And I didn't like it when Gideon said he couldn't wake Eve up." Those words were still chilling her. "It's got to change, Novak."

She hung up the phone.

———◆———

EMBASSY HOSPITAL
12:40 P.M.

"Eve? Open your eyes. I have to talk to you."

Gideon, Eve realized dazedly. It was good he was here...She'd been trying to phone him when she'd been so sick.

"Eve. Open your eyes, dammit. This might be my only chance to talk to you."

He sounded so urgent that she forced herself to open her lids. His face above her was as strained and urgent as his voice had been. He was frowning, and Gideon seldom frowned. Then he was smiling at her. "That's right. Now stay awake. These hospitals suck, and I have to try to get you out of here."

Hospitals? Green walls. The smell of antiseptics and cleanliness. Definitely a hospital. Eve had been around enough of them to recognize one when she saw it.

And Gideon's face above her was sober again. A hospital face...

"I was sick..." she whispered. Her throat was sore, and she could barely speak. She was sore all over, she realized vaguely. "Fast... it happened so fast. What happened to me, Gideon?"

"I don't know. They're calling it food poisoning." He was putting a straw between her lips, and she was sipping ice water. "But it was a damn violent strain if that was what it was. Besides the nausea, it caused unconsciousness. When you didn't answer your phone, I went up to your suite and found you crumpled on the floor. I couldn't wake you." He took her hand. "It scared me. So I called the American hospital that the embassy uses and had them send an ambulance. You still weren't awake when you got to their ER. They diagnosed it as food poisoning and pumped your stomach."

That was why the muscles of her stomach felt this sore... "Food poisoning... not such good coq au vin after all."

"Maybe. But I'll swear that chef would never give you anything contaminated. I know him."

"I might argue with you about that." She swallowed to ease the soreness of her throat. "I felt so sick. But I'm going to be okay?"

He nodded. "Very nasty case, and it's going to leave you weak for a few days. They say you'll have to rest. But you'll be fine eventually."

"That's good." She closed her eyes again. Then they flew open. "No, it's not. I can't stay here in the hospital. I have too much to do. I have to get back to Robaku."

"I thought that would be your reaction. That's why I wanted to get to you before anyone else had a chance to try to brainwash you." He smiled. "I prefer to do it myself."

"Go to hell, Gideon." She lifted her hand to her aching head. "Just tell me what you want, and I'll see if I want the same thing."

"I want you out of this hospital. I want you back at Robaku. I'll pull all the strings I have to in order to get you there. But you'll have to put up a fight to do it. All those nice kind people who want only what's best for you are going to go on the attack in about fifteen minutes. And then, if you don't cave, they'll bring in the big guns."

"Don't be ridiculous. No one can keep me here if I want to walk out of this place. I'm already feeling better. I'll just take a couple more hours to rest, then I'll leave." Not totally the truth. She was still feeling terribly weak, and her head was throbbing again. "I can't just lie around. It would drive me crazy. I always feel better if I'm working."

"I'm not arguing with you. I'm on your side. But I can't be the one to force the issue this time. I'll just tell you that when I get you to Robaku, I'll take care of you, and you'll be better off." He got to his feet. "Now the first one to see you will be Dr. Jeremy Santiago. He'll be comforting and reassuring but will tell you that you should rest here for a few days and let the ambassador send you home to the U.S. for a longer rest. When you refuse, you may even get a visit from Ambassador Sandow himself. The message will be the same. And that may only be the beginning. Your phone is on that nightstand. When you get through running the gauntlet they set for you, give me a call, and I'll whisk you out of here." He touched her hand gently. "I'm sorry, Eve. I wish I could do more for you, but that's not possible right now."

"It's okay." She only wanted to close her eyes and rest. "You didn't cook that damn coq au vin. But you should really hire a different chef for that fancy hotel."

"I'll try to do that." He was on his way toward the door. "As soon as I locate him. He seems to have disappeared..."

Disappeared. That sounded all wrong, she thought wearily. But she was too tired to work out why right now. She'd get a little rest, then she'd think about it.

"Ms. Duncan, how glad I am that we were able to help you. I'm Dr. Santiago." A tall, plump man in a white coat was entering the room. "You were a very sick woman." He was beaming at her. "But you're going to be fine, and we're going to make you comfortable for the rest of the time you're in Maldara. But we do have to talk about plans for your recovery..."

"Get me *out* of here, Gideon," Eve said in exasperation when he answered the phone two hours later. "I can't take much more of this. I've talked to two doctors, the head nurse, and I just had a telephone call from the ambassador. They want to keep me in this hospital for another week, then send me back to Atlanta."

"Told you so," Gideon said. "I'm just surprised the ambassador didn't visit you in person. Did you feel slighted?"

"Stop it. No one is listening to me. I tried to explain that I'm fine and need to get back to work, but they said they don't want to take the responsibility for my recovery since the attack was so severe."

"It was very bad, Eve," he said soberly. "You have to know that was true."

"*Get me out of here.*" She pronounced every word with emphasis. "Everyone agrees I'm not on the critical list. There's no reason why I can't go back to work."

"You're certain that's what you want to do? I don't mind persuading you, but I won't coerce you."

"You listen to me, Gideon. The last thing the ambassador said when I turned him down was that he thought it might be a good idea if I talk to President Kiyani, who had expressed concern I'd become this ill in her country. My head is already aching. I won't sit here and get a migraine from having to deal with her."

"I'll be there in thirty minutes." He cut the connection.

Eve put down her phone, leaned back on her pillows, and closed her eyes. She felt totally exhausted. She should probably have told him to bring her something to wear, she thought wearily. The clothes she had worn when the ambulance had brought her here must have been a total disaster. Oh, well, let Gideon worry about it. She had found him quite capable of producing anything she wanted while she was here in Maldara. Except maybe that coq au vin, she thought wryly. He hadn't done such a great job at that particular—

There was some sort of bustle in the hall . . .

Oh, shit.

Her door was being ceremoniously opened by the same uniformed guard she had seen at Robaku yesterday.

Zahra Kiyani entered the next moment. "What a terrible thing to have happened to you," she said sweetly. She motioned to the leather chair beside Eve's bed. "Dalai, do something with that chair. You know how careful I have to be to avoid germs in places like this." A young, pretty maid in an ankle-length tan sarong scurried forward and put a gold-silk shawl on the chair before fading into the background. "This hospital is truly deplorable," Zahra said. "You should have been brought to my hospital when you were taken ill. I had it built this year." She gracefully sat down on the silk-draped chair. She wore an exquisitely draped scarlet dress that contrasted boldly with the gold shawl. "It's like a wonderful palace but with all the modern facilities."

"This hospital seems entirely adequate," Eve said. "And I'm not certain patients who are as ill as I was would appreciate being treated in a palace. It's a little over the top."

"It's all what you become accustomed to." Zahra studied Eve. "And you still appear to be quite pale. Would you like me to have Dalai do a makeover to give you a bit of color? She's quite clever about all sorts of different things."

And one of them was evidently how to please Zahra at any cost,

Eve thought. The girl had seemed almost frightened as she'd scurried around at her command. "No, thank you. All I need now is a nap. I'm planning on checking out of this hospital soon."

"So I've been told. I've come to try to dissuade you. We don't want someone of your stature to take any chances with your health. What if you had a terrible relapse? It would look very bad for my government when I'm trying so hard to show the world that we are not savages after that terrible war." She smiled. "Why don't you transfer to my hospital, and we'll take great care of you? Then when you're well, I'll either send you home or you can return to Robaku."

"I intend to return to Robaku today," Eve said. "And I don't need to remain in your hospital or any other. My work is going very well."

Zahra's flashing smile remained, but it was now fixed. "As I said, I'll have to visit you again and make that judgment. It would be unfortunate for you to go through so much when we might have to send you home anyway."

"I'll take my chances," Eve said. "You'd have to have cause, and, as I said, I have proof that my work is going very well. And I'll have more proof when I finish the new reconstruction."

Zahra's smile was now a mere baring of teeth. "I hate the idea of your being so stubborn. Look what's already happened to you. That horrible bout of food poisoning. Did they tell you there was a possibility you might die? Wouldn't that have been terrible? It's really too bad they don't have food tasters in this day and age."

Eve's eyes widened in shock. There had been a thread of intimidation in those words, and that last remark had been totally bizarre. "Food taster? I'm sure that my food poisoning was accidental, and I'm glad we have no use for food tasters."

"Yes, of course. But I admit that I've often thought that they did have their uses. When one is of a certain importance, naturally there are people who wish to take that stature away from them in any way possible." She met Eve's gaze with defiance. "I'm sure my own ancestors must have felt bound to protect themselves by such means.

After all, the food tasters at court were only slaves and considered of no importance. The royal line had to be preserved."

"Why? The idea is totally barbaric." Then something Zahra had said caught her attention. "Court? I don't know anything about your family background except that your father was the president of Maldara before you, and it was a republic." She added dryly, "But I doubt if he appointed any food tasters to his cabinet."

"No, of course not." She was smiling again. "But we're a very old family, and our traditions go back over two thousand years. Did you think that we'd emerged from the same jungle as those crude Botzans?" Her lips curled. "When he was president, it suited my father to pretend that we were one with all these people, but I would never be so stupid as to give up my heritage. We did not make the Great Journey from the north and struggle all through the years to keep our lineage pure just to sacrifice it to those uncivilized barbarians. I told my father that he couldn't do it." She drew a deep breath. "And I was right, the Botzans killed him. So you can see why I believe that one must protect oneself in any way possible. When death comes near, you should take it as a sign to stop and consider all the consequences."

There was that hint of a threat again. "I don't believe in signs and portents," Eve said. "And I do believe in doing what I think is right in spite of consequences."

"Too bad." Zahra shrugged as she rose to her feet. "I do hope you'll change your mind. Let me know, and I'll send someone to make accommodations for you." She snapped her fingers at the servant girl. "Dalai!"

The young woman jumped forward and snatched up the gold shawl on the chair. Her subservience annoyed Eve. In that moment, she could imagine Zahra indulging herself in any cruel arrogance she chose with those she considered beneath her. She found she wanted to strike out. "Thank you for coming." She paused. "Oh dear, I just had a thought. How do you know that all those stories about your so-called pure lineage weren't a fairy tale? You said yourself that it was a long time ago that your family came to Maldara." She smiled gently. "Who knows? Maybe the Botzans were really your first cousins."

Zahra stopped and whirled to face her. "You insult me," she hissed. "It was no fairy tale. *Look* at me." Her eyes were blazing. "I am everything she was and more." Her voice was shaking with anger. "She made mistakes I will never make. And someday, I will have the world she lost to her own stupidity."

She turned on her heel and left the room.

What was that all about? Eve wondered. She had clearly opened up a nasty can of worms when she had taken that potshot at Zahra's august family tree. And who the hell was *she*?

Later. Gideon should be arriving at any moment, and she needed these few moments to pull herself together. At least she had gotten rid of Zahra before she had to confront Gideon. She was in no mood to referee the explosiveness she sensed between them. She glanced at the clock on the night table. It was almost five in the evening. It seemed like days had passed since she'd talked to Joe early this morning. She'd promised him she'd call him back tonight and what was she going to say to him? He'd be worried and immediately on the attack.

Think about it on the way back to Robaku.

Too many questions. Too many decisions.

And where the hell is Gideon?

"That bitch!" Zahra's lips were tight with rage as the chauffeur opened the door of her limousine outside the hospital. "How dare she? Did you hear her, Dalai?"

Dalai knew that Zahra didn't want an answer, only an audience, but she nodded as she slipped into the backseat beside her. One could never tell what would offend Zahra and cause her to take that rage out on the nearest target. Her anger with Eve Duncan was so intense that Dalai had to be extremely careful.

"She *insulted* me." Zahra leaned back in the seat, fuming. "And she doesn't even realize how lucky she is to be alive. Stupid. Incredibly stupid."

Agree. Then try to distract her. "Yes, madam," Dalai said. "And very rude. She doesn't have any idea how wrong she is. She's just a peasant, and you're a queen. You should pay no attention to her."

"Are you telling me what to do?" Zahra asked sharply. "You were stupid, too, today. You weren't quick enough when I told you to fetch that shawl."

The distraction hadn't worked. It had only served to transfer the anger from Eve Duncan to Dalai. She had been expecting it. Eve Duncan could not be touched right now. But Dalai was always available as an outlet. Be humble. Show Zahra fear. She liked the fear. "I know, madam. Forgive me."

"Why should I?" Zahra's smile was malicious. "You should be punished. You're obviously getting lazy. I'll think about it on the way back to the palace."

So that Dalai would have time to anticipate what was to come, she thought wearily. It was all part of the fear Zahra liked to make her feel. Dalai would almost certainly be beaten if she didn't think of some other way to distract Zahra once she got back to the palace. But it would be easier to distract her there, where Zahra had decisions to make and Dalai could make herself useful in helping her. If she was beaten, it would probably not be severely.

"What are you thinking about?" Zahra asked suspiciously. "You're very quiet."

"Nothing, madam." Dalai's eyes widened with fear. "Nothing at all."

It was a lie. She was thinking that it was worth a beating to have seen Eve Duncan cause that look of outrage and indignation on Zahra Kiyani's face.

And that someone should warn the woman what a dangerous thing it was to do.

CHAPTER

6

Gideon arrived ten minutes later, and he was a whirlwind of activity for the next hour. Somehow he managed to persuade one of the nurses to help Eve dress in the slacks and shirt he'd brought with him. Then he ignored all the protests of the doctors and nurses, negotiated a miraculously fast exit, and whisked her to his Land Rover, parked in front of the hospital.

"Now lean back and relax. I'll have you at Robaku in forty-five minutes." He buckled her seat belt. "You did good, Eve."

"So did you." She closed her eyes and took a deep breath. "I wasn't sure that they wouldn't call security. They were very determined, weren't they?"

"Very." He started the Land Rover. "I could see it on the horizon once they got you settled in that room. It seemed to be a concerted effort."

"It was annoying, but it's hard to be angry. After all, it's the job of a hospital staff to do whatever they think best to get their patients well. The only one I had problems with was Madam President. But then, that was a given."

"Sorry I didn't get there in time to spare you."

"So am I. You might have been able to keep me from insulting her." She shook her head. "No, I doubt it. I rather enjoyed it. She was so ugly to that young maid, and all that arrogant bullshit about royal tasters and such..."

Gideon went still. "Tasters?"

"It was almost a threat." She looked at him. "Some nonsense about her family having had poison tasters in the past and that it wasn't a bad idea. I found it peculiar she'd mention it in the same breath as telling me how sad she was that I'd become so ill. Is there any reason why I should consider it a threat?"

"There's always a reason to suspect Zahra of any effort at intimidation. She doesn't want you here, and she'd take advantage of any opportunity to make you feel afraid and uncertain."

"But there's no reason to think that my food poisoning was anything but an accident?"

Gideon was silent. "Not as far as I know. The food was examined, and it contained mushrooms that could have made you very ill. And we haven't been able to talk to the chef yet. We're still trying to locate him."

"And it would have been crazy for Zahra to slip me anything that would make me that ill just because I wouldn't get on the next plane and take off for home," Eve said. "She's the president of the damn country. She must have more important things to worry about." She made a face. "Though tonight I wasn't sure if she wasn't a little off base when she started talking about her Kiyani ancestors. That's when I lost it and told her that her ancient history could all be bullshit."

"What?" Gideon burst out laughing. "You do like to live dangerously. You couldn't have said anything to make her more angry."

"It didn't seem to matter at the time. She was talking something about the Great Journey and how much better she was than *her*. Whoever that was." She rubbed her temple. "It got pretty confusing."

"Not for Zahra," he said quietly. "It means everything to her. And I guarantee she doesn't think it's bullshit."

She nodded as she looked at him. "That's right, you'd know, wouldn't you? You were ... intimate."

"Not exactly. But we had sex, and that was entirely different from intimacy." His lips twisted. "But she enjoyed me enough to consider me a candidate. It was amusing to watch her. If I'd stuck around, I might have gone from candidate to consort. Pity I didn't find her that exciting."

"Consort?"

"Yes, Zahra always considered herself a queen, and naturally, she needed a consort. Her ancestress had taken many important men as consorts, and she eagerly followed in her footsteps. I had enough power in Maldara to be fairly impressive, and she thought I'd be a good enough match."

Eve frowned. "Ancestress?"

"Oh, you didn't get that much in depth? Zahra only acknowledges two of her ancestresses, and only one earns her reluctant respect. One is Kiya, the founder of the Kiyani family. The other is Kiya's mother." He smiled. "But to get to the answers, you have to travel on the Great Journey. I can't tell you how often Zahra bored me with looking at her map of that journey." He took out his phone and pulled up a Google map of Maldara and the rest of northern Africa. "We sit right here above the Congo and directly northeast is Ethiopia, then South Sudan, Sudan, and Egypt." His index finger touched a destination on the Mediterranean coast of Egypt. "And here is the city of splendor that is no more. At least in its original state. Don't you think it's a fine birthplace for our Queen Zahra's ancestors?" He smiled. "Now reverse it, and we have the Great Journey that's now Kiyani history, whether or not it's true."

Eve looked at the city. "Alexandria? Zahra is claiming Egyptian heritage?"

"She will be soon. It serves her purpose right now to please the nationalists here in Maldara, but there's a certain glamour to the stories connected to the Great Journey, and Zahra will want to take advantage of them. Maldara is a small fish compared to Egypt. I'd bet Zahra will start climbing as soon as she makes her position unassailable here."

"The Great Journey." Eve was frowning. "I don't understand any of this, and you're making my headache worse. Tell me what you're talking about."

"I'm getting there. I told you that you'd have to go back to Zahra's favorite ancestress for clarity. Work it out for yourself. Who would Zahra accept as an acceptable predecessor?"

"I'm not ready to play games. You're enjoying this too much." But she was intrigued and thinking in spite of herself. "An ancestress who started her journey in Alexandria and traveled south to the jungle country of Maldara."

"Go on."

"Why would she do that? Alexandria was a queen city for thousands of years. It had the greatest library in the civilized world and the Pharos lighthouse, which was one of the seven wonders of the world. It had famous scholars and scientists."

"Which Zahra would not appreciate as you do, Eve. What would make that city acceptable as a place of origin for her? You said it in that first sentence."

Her eyes widened. "Queen city. The Pharaohs had their palaces on the bank of the Mediterranean." She took the next giant step. "And the most famous queen was Cleopatra. Zahra actually thinks she's related to Cleopatra?"

"By George, I believe you've got it. Not thinks, knows. She couldn't be more certain."

"She's got to be nuts," Eve said flatly.

"Perhaps. But you have to accept that she believes it, so you'll understand who she is. All her life, she's identified with the royalty of Egypt and particularly with Cleopatra VII. You can either call it bullshit or you can use it to manipulate her."

"Which did you do?"

He smiled. "I did what I had to do at any given moment. But I'm afraid you're too honest to follow my lead. Jill had problems doing it. Though she did become interested in the literary aspects of Zahra's fantasy. But then, Jill's a storyteller."

"So I've discovered," Eve said dryly. But she couldn't deny that her curiosity had been aroused. "What literary aspects?"

"The Great Journey wasn't only a map, it was a journal. It was passed down from generation to generation in the Kiyani family."

Her gaze flew to his face. "Whose journal?"

He chuckled. "Not Cleopatra. Gotcha."

"No, you didn't. I'm not that gullible. Everyone knows how Cleopatra died. And it wasn't on a Great Journey to this steaming jungle in the middle of Africa. Whose journal?"

"Does everyone know how she died? Zahra would disagree."

"Gideon."

"Just a little food for thought." He grinned. "And a warning not to take anything for granted in this world. You're right, it isn't Cleopatra's journal. But it was written by an ancestor of Zahra's whom she viewed with a certain respect and tolerance. Her name was Kiya."

"Kiya? That's right, you mentioned Zahra respected her. You're saying a woman made her way from Alexandria to Maldara and founded the Kiyani dynasty?"

"I didn't say she was alone. She had slaves and at least one consort. That was in a day when a woman had to be able to use a man to get what she wanted. That was why Zahra had respect for her in spite of her many flaws. But Kiya was powerful enough to pull things together and set up her household and family to suit herself." He paused. "And it was her name that remained on all the record books from the time she crossed the Maldara border." He smiled. "Kiya, beloved daughter of Cleopatra VII."

"What? It was actually true?"

"Perhaps. If it wasn't, Kiya told a good story."

"You said record books. Not just her journal?"

"Come on, what do you think? It was over two thousand years ago. The records were only vague references other than Kiya's accounts. And the Kiyanis became almost as savage as the natives who attacked them when they invaded their territory. But they were smarter, and they had more civilized methods of torture and murder than the tribes had seen before. So they beat them back and started to build their empire."

"Which evidently was no Alexandria. It's pretty much as undeveloped now as when they came here."

"They had several obstacles to overcome. A few Zahras and similar male counterparts appeared over the centuries. They were low on family values and high on world domination." He was driving off the highway and onto the bumpy dirt road that led to Robaku. "Like most families, good and bad. But with the Kiyanis, it just seems to be exaggerated. They go up and down like a roller coaster." He pulled up to the museum and shut off the car. "Here you are." He got out and ran around to open the door for her. "See? What else could you want? Chauffeur service, and I even provided you with entertainment to keep you amused." He was unlocking the door to the museum. "Now I'll get you settled and make sure that it's okay to leave you."

"Of course it's okay." She got out of the car and joined him as he opened the door. "I only have a little headache now." And her knees were still damnably weak. But she ignored both because she was still fascinated by the story with which Gideon had been regaling her. "Did Zahra ever show you this journal?"

"Of course." He nodded. "Not the original. But it had been copied multiple times over the centuries." He smiled mockingly. "It was at a time when she was still enthralled with the idea of me as a consort and wanted to impress me."

"And were you impressed?"

"It was ... interesting. But her take on it was even more interesting."

He stepped aside for her to enter. "Now story time is over. Sit down. You're not as steady on your feet as I'd like."

"I'll get a cup of coffee and an aspirin and I'll be fine."

"I'm sure you will." He turned on the lights. "Go sit down," he said again. "I'll make the coffee. I could use one myself. I seem to have been telling you tales like some male Scheherazade all the way from Jokan. Do you suppose Scheherazade got hoarse from talking all night?"

"She had motivation. She was under a death sentence if she didn't keep the sultan entertained." She dropped down on her stool. "And you're no Scheherazade, Gideon." She suddenly chuckled. "Sorry, I just had a vision of you dressed up in a veil and harem outfit. I may never be able to look at you again without seeing it."

He flinched. "You really know how to hurt a guy." He was pouring water into the coffeemaker. "Oh, well, I have enough confidence in my manly vigor to be able to suffer through it." His gaze went to the reconstruction of Amari, which was still on the dais on her worktable. "He's still here. It seems a long time since I brought Hajif and Leta here last night."

"It was a long time." Her gaze shifted to Amari. "A lot happened..." She suddenly straightened on the stool. "And Hajif must have wanted to get in here to get Amari. They were so eager to take him home. But the door was locked, and we weren't here. I thought I'd be back before they were ready for him."

"And then you were so rude as to develop food poisoning and kept them out. I believe they'll forgive you."

"But I'm back now, and there's no reason why they have to wait any longer." She got to her feet and steadied herself on the worktable for a minute as that blasted weakness swept over her. "I'll go down and tell them that they can—"

"No," Gideon said firmly. "I'll go down and get them if you don't think they can make it through the night." He pushed her back down on the stool. "Rest."

He was out the door before she could protest.

Gideon was being a little too protective, she thought with exasperation. It wasn't as if she were tottering on the edge of death. She might as well have had Joe here. No, Joe would not have been that obvious. He would have been subtle and warm and...Joe.

Damn she missed him.

She looked at the clock. Eight-ten. No, it wasn't time to call him yet. She usually waited until she was sure he wasn't at an evening session at the Yard. That was about ten or eleven Maldara time.

And she needed that coffee if she was going to keep alert until it was time for her to make that call. She got to her feet and went to the cabinet where the coffee was brewing.

She'd just poured herself a coffee when Gideon came back into the museum.

"Caught you," he said. "What didn't you understand about the word *rest*?"

She was frowning. "Where are Hajif and Leta?"

"They weren't quite ready for him. They said they'd see you in the morning." He came to the coffeemaker and poured himself a cup of coffee. "So sit down. You don't have to be hostess to me. We're way beyond that, aren't we?"

"Yes." She was still staring at Amari. "I don't understand. They were so eager and Leta said only a few hours..." She shifted her gaze back to Gideon. "Unless you gave them the impression they wouldn't be welcome?"

He grimaced. "I wouldn't do that when I know you'd have my head. I was charming and caring, I just explained that the reason we didn't show up earlier was that you'd been very ill and had to go to the hospital." He held up his hands. "All very truthful."

"And you knew Hajif and his family probably wouldn't go to a hospital unless they were dying."

"It did occur to me that might be the effect."

"But you knew I wanted them to come."

He nodded. "People make their own decisions, Eve. I just gave them the facts."

And he was so clever that he knew just how to shade them. "I could go down to the village and bring them back with me," she said coolly. "I don't appreciate manipulation, Gideon."

"I know. Even if I didn't realize it, Jill told me. She was afraid that it might be the one thing that would keep you from coming here." He said quietly, "But I told you that if you left the hospital and came back to Robaku, I'd take care of you and you wouldn't suffer for it. I was acting instinctively with Hajif to keep that promise."

"Because you want me to rest?"

"Partly." He smiled. "I imagine it's difficult for the people around you to take care of you without a little manipulation and sleight of hand. Admit it. Doesn't your family have to resort to it on occasion? What about your husband?"

"Joe and I are honest with each other. Besides, that's different."

"Which means that you *try* to be honest with each other."

"Which means that you don't have the same rights and privileges."

"Unfortunately." He chuckled as her eyes widened. "I told you I liked intense women." He shook his head. "I'll back down now. You left yourself open, and I couldn't resist. I know you're as faithful as Penelope was to Odysseus."

He was impossible. "Now you're delving into *The Odyssey*? First, it was that wild tale about Kiyani, and now you're into mythology?"

"Well, I did minor in English Lit when I was at Oxford. And there was a two-headed female monster in *The Odyssey*. When you think about it, there might be some connection with Zahra Kiyani." His smile faded and he added soberly, "But I'm really still trying to distract you as I've been attempting to do since we left the hospital. That's not being fair. You've had a rough day, and some of it was my fault. You like honesty, and I should give it to you."

Eve frowned. "Distract me?" She didn't understand any of this, and it was beginning to frustrate her. "Distract me from what?"

"Any number of things." His lips twisted. "That's been my main duty since Jill called me into this with you. Protect and distract. I'm very good at both though you'd never know it by today. But Jill says she can't take any more, so evidently there's a change coming. I might as well begin again now. Yes, I did want you to rest, but only because you're going to have enough with which to contend when Jill gets here. That should be in about ten minutes. You're going to get all the honesty and absence of manipulation you can stand." He grimaced. "Which is completely wrong for the situation. I'm surprised Novak is letting her do it. I guess he thinks she deserves it. She paid the price."

"Who is Novak?" Then she remembered. "CIA. Jill gave me his name to pass on to Joe. What has he got to do with this?"

"You can ask Jill. I don't know how honest she's going to be. If she tells you about Novak, then you'll probably have the entire picture." He moved toward the door. "Now it's time I went into protection mode again. This time for Jill. She wants to make sure that Robaku isn't being watched. She doesn't want anyone to know that she's coming to see you tonight. I'll see you later, Eve."

He left the museum.

What the hell?

Eve put her coffee cup down and leaned back against the cabinet. Her knees were still shaky, and she hadn't needed those enigmatic words from Gideon to make her any dizzier. She hadn't understood what he was talking about, but she didn't like the sound of it.

Well, she would soon find out and handle it. She just wished that Jill Cassidy hadn't picked a night when she was feeling this weak and vulnerable to spring something of which even Gideon seemed to disapprove.

Forget it. Stop dwelling on something she couldn't change until she was confronted with it. She went back to her stool and began to prepare Amari for his final trip to Hajif and Leta tomorrow.

Then she stopped as she realized what she was doing. Not

questioning, just accepting what was happening to her no matter how strange she thought it. Meekly going back to this work she had chosen to do.

Or that had been chosen for her to do.

And Jill would be coming in that door soon, and, in spite of what Gideon had said, the reporter might try to manipulate her once again.

No way.

Clear your head and get ready for her, dammit.

◆

"It's wonderful," Jill said quietly from the doorway behind Eve, her gaze on the Amari reconstruction. "Or should I say *he's* wonderful. Your Amari seems almost alive again."

Eve looked over her shoulder. "That's what you wanted, isn't it? You wanted him to come alive so that Hajif and Leta would have something besides a DNA report to file away? That's what I wanted, too." She turned on the stool to face her. "And I did it. But that isn't all you wanted, is it, Jill? That isn't why Gideon is outside cruising around in his 'protective mode' to be sure no one will know you're here. By the way, you're twenty minutes late. He must have been worried. Or maybe he isn't as efficient as he told me he was." She added coolly, "But what can you expect when you choose an errand boy who was born with a silver spoon in his mouth?"

Jill went still as she studied Eve's expression. "Gideon did his job. It was my fault. I had to make sure I wasn't followed." She crossed the room toward her. "I didn't want to ruin everything because I was having an attack of conscience. There was still a possibility that I could salvage bits and pieces even if you socked me, then threw up your hands and took the next flight out."

"You seem to think that a possibility. I probably will, too. Particularly since Gideon was talking about honesty, which was clearly lacking, and manipulation, which was obviously present. Though I'm not surprised he brought them up. I've known since the day I met you that you were very good at luring people into doing what you wish." Her lips tightened. "And yet I didn't realize that you were lying to me. I consider myself a good judge of character, and when you answered my questions, I would have sworn that you were telling me the truth."

"I was telling you the truth. I just couldn't tell you everything." Jill shook her head. "Otherwise, you wouldn't have come, and we had to have you here." She continued in a desperate rush: "And I thought it would be okay. I was sure we could keep you safe. I didn't expect this to happen. There was no reason."

"You mean that the food poisoning was no accident? I tried to tell myself that it didn't make sense that anyone would want to hurt me. But I've been sitting here waiting for you and trying to put everything together from what Gideon said, and that stuck out in living color. He was very tentative, but he didn't really deny it. I might have been too woozy to figure out the whys and wherefores, but the fact that it was intentional became crystal clear as I thought about it. Evidently someone believed they had reason not to want me here. Zahra?"

"I'm not...sure. I knew Zahra wouldn't want you here, but I didn't believe she'd feel strongly enough to actually strike out at you. She just wants control of Robaku. She's very careful of her image, and there's no way she'd want even a suspicion touching her."

"Yet Zahra Kiyani was in my hospital room this afternoon expressing her sympathy and her opinion that I should get the hell out of Dodge. Diplomatically, of course. Well, as diplomatically as she was capable of. But I was having trouble appreciating anything but the fact that she'd come running when there was a chance to get rid of me." Now Eve was having trouble suppressing her anger. "I was so sick, and I was told I could have died. When I woke up, the entire world seemed only to want to get rid of me. It pissed me off, and I didn't even know then that it had been a deliberate attempt. Then I got Gideon's 'distractions' laid on me and his irritation that you weren't behaving as everyone wanted you to." She glared at Jill. "That about topped off my day. If you hadn't come tonight, I was going to go after you. I'm mad as hell. I want answers, Jill."

"That's why I'm here." She looked for a place to sit down, saw only the cot across the room. She shrugged, dropped to the floor, and crossed her legs tailor-fashion. "That's what I've been trying to tell you. There are still things I don't know, but you'll know what I know."

"How refreshing. You're not denying that someone tried to kill me?"

"I'm not denying it could have happened. But Novak said that the poisoning was done by an expert, and you weren't meant to die. The mushrooms were blended with an additive from Egypt that altered the toxicity. They just meant to discourage you, just like they did me. It was meant to make you a little ill to encourage you to leave. That's the only reason why I think there was even a possibility that Zahra might have anything to do with it. This was more of a threat than an attempt on your life. She'd use every threat before she'd endanger her position."

"That threat was very painful. I thought I was dying. I couldn't tell the difference at the time." Eve went on to the next item on her agenda. "Novak. Jed Novak is the name of the CIA operative you gave me to reassure Joe. Gideon said he didn't think Novak would let you talk to me. Do you work for the CIA?"

"No." She grimaced. "Though Novak did do his best to keep me from coming here tonight. I told him I couldn't do anything else, and we'd have to make other plans if you blew up. I've only known Novak since I came here to Maldara, but I'd heard enough about him to reach out when I needed him."

"One of your friends in high places?"

"Novak operates on both levels. That's why he's so valuable." She added wearily, "He's gone to a lot of trouble and expense to set up the switch. He's got a right to be angry with me. But I'm not like him, and I can't go by his rules. Please believe me. I knew there might be some danger to you, but I thought we could get you out of here before it—"

"Became fatal?" Eve interrupted. "You're not making your position any more sympathetic. And you're certainly not making this situation less muddled. Now, I'm going to ask you questions, and you're going to answer me clearly and concisely."

"Whatever you say," Jill said quietly.

"You said that doing these reconstructions was important to you, but that's not the real reason why you put all your time and effort into luring me here. What was that reason?"

"I needed the best forensic sculptor in the world to come here to Maldara. I had a job that had to be done by the very best."

"What job? Not the children?"

She shook her head. "But I knew that would bring you. I hoped that once you were here, I could persuade you to do the other reconstruction."

"The honorable thing to do when offering a job is to give terms and let me decide."

"I couldn't take a chance. It was too important. We didn't even have the skull, and to get it might have made you—" She stopped.

"Made me what?" Eve said impatiently.

"An accomplice." Jill didn't let her absorb that but went on quickly: "We wanted to switch a skull that's being held in the vault at the U.N. headquarters in Jokan for a counterfeit so that you could do a reconstruction to verify the identity."

Eve stared at her, openmouthed. "What?"

"I know. It's not the kind of... You would never have done it."

"That's quite correct."

"That's why I wanted you to be here. I wanted you to see that schoolroom." Her voice was shaking. "I wanted you to see what he'd done to this village. I wanted you to see what he'd done to this *country*."

She stiffened. "He? Who are you talking about?"

"Nils Varak. You know it was his men who butchered those children."

"Of course I do. He was a monster. What does that have to do with anything? Varak was killed right after the U.N. forces invaded Maldara. Some kind of helicopter explosion."

Jill was shaking her head. "That's what I thought." Her voice was unsteady. "And, after what I'd seen while I traveled around the country writing my stories, I wanted to send up fireworks when I heard it had happened. I'd interviewed people who told *hideous* stories about him that I couldn't write about, that I didn't even want to remember." Her voice was jerky. "Robaku wasn't the first school he'd destroyed. He *liked* to kill the children. He told his men that it made their parents more likely to cave when they saw the remains of their children. Besides, it brought him a particular pleasure to take their lives before they'd barely started to live. And he didn't want to make it quick...he liked the machetes..."

"Stop," Eve said. Jill's face was tense, pale, her words hoarse and feverish. Eve could see that she was reliving those stories, and she suddenly couldn't stand for it to go on. "Okay, so he was a monster. Monsters should be destroyed, and that's what they did. The French forces said there was absolute proof that they'd cut the head off the snake."

Jill nodded. "Absolute. That's what they said."

Eve's eyes narrowed on her face. "You're saying it's not true?"

"I'm saying that I hope it's true. But I'm afraid it's not." She moistened her lips. "And what if it's not true, Eve? What if he's out there somewhere, waiting until all the smoke clears so that he can come out and start all over again? If not here, then somewhere else. Six hundred thousand people dead, and he killed a hell of a lot of them. And he'd do it again, he wouldn't stop. He liked it too much."

"I can't believe this. Why do you think Varak might still be alive?" She was trying to remember all the details of the account she'd read on Google. "He was killed in a helicopter explosion in the mountains in the south Botzan area. The French blew him out of the sky as he was trying to escape. But they immediately retrieved his skull from the wreckage, and he'd been positively identified by DNA." She went still, her eyes widening. "The skull? I can't believe you'd want me to do a reconstruction on Varak. Are you crazy? Absolute DNA ID. Everyone knows it."

"That doesn't mean it's true."

"It means that it will be accepted in any court in the world. And any reconstruction I do would not have a chance over DNA results. Even if I showed the skull didn't resemble Varak, it wouldn't make a difference. DNA rules."

"But it would insert an element of doubt with people who would go after Varak full throttle if they thought he was still alive." She paused. "One of them is Novak. The director of the CIA accepted the proof that Varak was dead. Novak would have to have some credible reason for them to reopen the investigation. But regardless, he'd never stop if he was sure that Varak was still alive. He almost caught him twice while he was on the hunt for him in the mountains. He was the one who notified the French he'd be on that helicopter."

"And he thinks that Varak slipped away?"

"He doesn't know, but he wouldn't put it past Varak. But he has to be sure. When I came to him, he promised me he wouldn't stop until he was certain Varak hadn't played him and everyone else for fools."

"*You* came to him? And he believed you with no proof?"

"No. Novak is a cynical bastard who doesn't believe in much of anything but himself. But I had a shred of information that caught his attention . . . as it caught mine."

"What information?"

"I had an informant with the Botzan faction, Ralph Hadfeld, a mercenary. After the war ended, he wanted to get out of Maldara with enough money to start again in another country before he ended up being caught and tried. He called me and tried to sell me the story of the century. He said that he had been in the hills with Varak that last day, and Varak didn't get on that helicopter. The last Hadfeld had seen of him he was in a jeep heading north."

"How reliable was this informant?"

"He'd never steered me wrong." She paused. "He said he'd taken a photo of Varak in the jeep when the helicopter was taking off. And the price he asked for the story and the photo was over a million dollars. I think he knew I'd put that info under a microscope. He said he'd give me two weeks but no longer. He wasn't sure if any of Varak's men had seen him take that photo, and he wanted out of the country."

"And you went to Novak for the money?"

She nodded. "I knew the CIA would authorize any amount to Novak. He's their golden boy." She drew a deep breath. "But he wouldn't give it to me. He listened, then he said that Hadfeld could be playing me. He said he'd go after him himself, and he even had an idea how the info could be verified. He said that I should keep out of it."

"And you didn't do it."

"It was *my* story, my informant, and I had to know if it was the truth. But if Novak wouldn't give me the money, I had to go somewhere else. So I called Sam Gideon. I knew I had a chance with him. There was no way he'd want Varak to slip away after what he'd done here. Gideon agreed to make the buy, and I called Hadfeld."

"You got the story and the photo?"

"No, he said he'd call me later with arrangements. And he did call me one night a few weeks ago and set up a place in the jungle to meet him." She looked away. "Emphasis on *set up*. It was a trap. When I got there, Hadfeld was dead, a very bloody death. He'd been tortured. Evidently, Varak's men had been tracking him and forced him to make the call. They wanted to make sure that I saw what they'd done to him."

"But you got away?"

There was the faintest hesitation. "Yes, I got away." She looked back at Eve. "But if they did that to Hadfeld, I didn't need much more to convince me that what he was going to sell me was the real McCoy and that Varak was still out there. Wouldn't you feel the same?"

Varak *alive*? Eve felt a ripple of shock. She had been so involved with listening to the horrific details of Jill's story that the idea that Varak had not been killed in that helicopter crash had not actually gotten through to her. But as she stared at Jill, a chill went through her. How could she not consider it? Because Jill Cassidy thought it was true and had gone to this extreme to prove it. "I might feel there was a chance except for the DNA."

"Novak says that DNA can be faked if you know the right experts. Particularly in an explosion, when only minute amounts can be extracted."

"I've never heard of its being done with complete success. Particularly not in a circumstance where the scrutiny is so intense."

"Novak says it can be done. I believe him. But he wants to be sure that skull isn't Varak's before he goes to the people who matter. It's a scenario that will have everyone from politicians, to noted scientists, to Novak's own CIA director, ready to tear it apart. And in the furor, Varak could disappear."

"And you want me to be caught in the middle."

"No. But you might be anyway," Jill said. "I don't know what's happening. No one should have targeted you just for doing these children's reconstructions. I could see it if they thought you were working on trying to prove Varak is still alive."

"Which you want me to do at the earliest possible opportunity." Eve shook her head. "I can almost see why you decided to set up this elaborate charade. You needed to hold all the cards possible to even think I might do it."

"And even then I knew you might tell me to go to hell," she said soberly. "I only hoped that you'd remember that Varak had created all this carnage. He should pay for it, Eve. And he shouldn't get a chance to do it again." She looked at the reconstruction of Amari. "Those villages were helpless before his militia. They were savage. Varak even hung some of the body parts in the trees . . ."

Eve flinched. "Shock value, Jill?"

"Anything I can do." She got to her feet. "I'm sorry I wasn't completely honest with you. You know everything now. I'm praying that you won't let my duplicity affect your decision. Let me know what you're going to do, and I'll make it easy for you." She grimaced. "Unless a miracle happens, and you decide to help us. Then I can't promise it will be easy, only that we'll try to keep you safe." She headed for the door, then stopped before she opened it. "No, I still wasn't totally honest. I'd better tell you all of it. Even though it's going to make you even angrier. After I decided it had to be you who did Varak's reconstruction, I told Novak what he had to do. We had to get rid of Joe Quinn, so Novak pulled strings with some bigwigs in London and got the Scotland Yard seminar pushed up so that it would fit in with our plans."

"What?" Eve's eyes widened. "You went to those lengths?"

"You love Quinn," she said soberly. "You were right when you said I'd probed every facet of your life. That was a very big part. The chances were very slim that you'd leave him unless the circumstances were right."

"You're damn right."

"Your Michael was easier. Novak just had to find a conveniently located dig in the U.K. and send Jane MacGuire folders that described it with glowing references to how healthy and fun it was for children. Jane doesn't see your son that often. She grabbed at the chance to give him a treat like that."

"And you did your research and knew that Jane had gone on digs before."

She nodded jerkily. "I had to make sure that if I took you away, it would be worthwhile for them. You had to be certain they were safe and happy."

"How very kind," Eve said sarcastically.

"No, completely selfish. I interfered in your life. I had to do it in the most painless way possible. You have a right to be furious about that, too." She paused. "I'm sorry," she whispered. "I wouldn't have done it if I hadn't thought that it was necessary. We can't let a Robaku happen ever again."

Then she was gone.

Leaving Eve alone with her confusion and anger... and terror. She didn't know how long she sat there just trying to comprehend all that she had been told. At least ten, fifteen minutes passed while she struggled to understand both the horror of the possibility Jill had shown her and this feeling of betrayal and being used.

She closed her eyes and let the emotions flow over her, not trying to sort them out yet. She could still see Jill's face before her. She'd looked like a little girl sitting on the floor at Eve's feet, her blue eyes big and so full of fear yet terribly earnest as she tried to do what she'd thought was honorable and right.

She would *not* feel sorry for her, Eve thought fiercely. Jill had been totally manipulative and moved them all around like chess pieces to get what she wanted. It didn't matter that she'd thought she was doing it to keep that monster from getting away to strike again.

But how could it not matter? It was what Eve did every day of her life. Bring the children home so that monsters would be punished and not be free to kill again.

But she did not lie or cheat or use anyone else to do what had to be done. There was no question what she should do now that she knew why Jill had brought her here.

"Are you okay?"

Her eyes flew open, and she saw a tall man wearing a black-leather jacket standing in the doorway. She had never seen him before. "Who are you?"

"Jed Novak." He held up his hand. "Sorry to startle you. I'm no threat."

That was a lie. Novak might not be a threat to her at this moment, but she had been around dangerous men for most of her life. She was married to one. She knew she was facing one now. "You're CIA. Jill told me about you. Did she send you to try to convince me that everything she did was fine and for the greater good? Go away, Novak."

"No, she didn't send me. She told me not to come." He smiled faintly. "She was afraid I might attempt to intimidate you. She wanted to be sure to be fair to you. She's having a major guilt trip. She was scared to death when she thought you might die this morning."

"She should feel guilty. I can see you're not similarly prone to it. What a surprise."

"I have my moments. But I've learned that guilt has no place once I've made a decision. I'd end up in a psych ward with all the blame that can be laid at my door. Jill, on the other hand, has a conscience that constantly gets in her way."

"Not so I'd notice."

"You should have noticed. Jill fought me and Gideon and herself to come to you tonight. She knew it was the wrong thing to do."

"Then why are you here, too?"

"Because I need to try to save the mission." His lips tightened. "If you won't help us, Jill will go off in another direction and might get herself killed. She's vulnerable, they know her name, they know her face." He paused. "And they know she'll never stop. So that's why I'm here to repair the damage and ask you to forget everything but why she did it. I know that it was a shock, but you're tough. I can see you're okay."

"No, I'm not okay." Her voice was cold. "I'm angry, and I feel as if I've been treated like a marionette in a puppet show. How did you think I'd feel?"

"Just like that." He walked toward her. "That's why Gideon and I both tried to talk her out of it. She knew it was a risk, too. She told you everything?"

"Yes," she said tersely. "Even down to how she pulled the strings with Joe and Michael."

"I was hoping she'd leave that out." He made a face. "That must have struck a little too close to home."

"It was an invasion," she said harshly. "And I can't believe that she'd be able to talk Gideon into helping her do this. He's not even CIA. It's crazy."

He nodded. "And it was crazy that his home was burned to the ground and his parents butchered by Varak. Did he mention that?"

"No," she said, shocked. "And neither did Jill."

"He doesn't like to talk about it." His lips tightened. "I was with him in the mountains when he heard about it. He knew those mountains like the back of his hand, and he was trying to help the farmers who had fled their villages to find safe havens. The killing of his parents was particularly brutal even for Varak. It was clear that Gideon had been targeted to discourage him from throwing in more help and money to fight that son of a bitch." He added softly, "And then to find out that we might not have killed him after all? He has to know, Eve."

"Well, I don't. Not if it means risking my freedom and my life with my family because I became involved with this madness. Stealing a skull, doing a reconstruction, when it could mean absolutely nothing?"

"You wouldn't have to steal the skull. The skull is being held in the main vault at the U.N. headquarters in Jokan. I've arranged a bribe to one of the guards to switch the skulls. It would be brought to you, and you'd do the work in total privacy here at the museum. Then, when we have an answer, you document it, and your work is over. If the skull is really Varak's, then we return the skull to the U.N. headquarters and make another switch. And that would be the end of it."

"No, it wouldn't. I'd have to undo the reconstruction and bring it back to the way I started. And what if it's not Varak?"

"Yes," Novak said softly. "What if it's not, Eve?"

Eve couldn't answer. It was a question that frightened her more than anything else. What if her work uncovered a horrible truth about the man who had killed those children here at Robaku and all those other children slain in this bloody land?

"It's something to think about," Novak said. "I promised Jill that I wouldn't reveal you as a source, but there would probably be suspicions."

"Of course there would be," she said impatiently. "She brought me here because I have a reputation. I'd be the first one anyone would suspect. There would be so much uproar, I could lose that reputation, and the entire world would think I'm some kind of radical crackpot."

"Or a brave woman out to save that world," he said quietly. "It could go either way, but in the end it would depend on how much it means to you. No matter how we try to protect you, you'll probably go through a firestorm. I'll try to move fast enough to get my hands on Varak right away, but no guarantees."

"There are too many ifs and mights in this scenario. And I seem to be the one who's bearing the brunt of all this violence and ugliness that's going on. I was *poisoned* today," she said through set teeth. "It's easy for Jill to wring her hands and talk about how Varak has to be stopped when she's not taking the punishment."

"None of it's easy for Jill," he said roughly. His coolness had suddenly become ice. "You don't know what you're talking about. I gave her every chance to get out of this, and she still went after them. And if you bail on us, she'll still do it. No matter what they do to her. And there are worse things than a bout of food poisoning, Eve."

His violence had caught Eve off guard. All the smoothness and persuasiveness had disappeared in a heartbeat when she'd attacked Jill. And it had been triggered by that one comment Eve had made. Why? Then she was suddenly remembering two sentences that Jill had spoken that had been lost in the bombardment of information she had been throwing at Eve.

They meant to hurt you and discourage you as they did me.

And that tiny hesitation, *Yes, I got away.*

She met his eyes across the room. "She said she got away after she found Hadfeld. It wasn't true?"

"Oh, they let her get away afterward. They wanted to teach her a lesson first. There were four of them. They beat her and they raped her and left her to crawl out of that jungle to find her way back to the road. So don't tell me about her not paying her dues. The only thing she asked me when I found her on that road was to let her be the one to go after them."

"And you agreed?"

His lips twisted. "At that point I would have given her anything she asked. She believed that Hadfeld was telling the truth, and she'd paid the price. I could have negotiated that payment and handled the transaction. I didn't do it. I wanted to go after him my way. So she did it on her own."

And Jed Novak was not as cynical as Jill had said, Eve thought as she gazed at him. She didn't know what he felt for Jill, but she could tell that what had happened to her that night had struck a deep chord. And it had struck a deep chord in Eve as well. The mere fact that Jill had not tried to arouse Eve's sympathy by letting her know about the attack made the feeling even more poignant.

But that didn't change the situation. It merely made it more painful. "Do you believe that skull is Varak's, Novak?"

"Maybe. I was convinced he was dead at the time, and I tend toward doubting everything that comes my way. The attack on Jill made it seem less likely. I do believe that skull could be a phony.

I've been sending agents into the mountains asking questions of the people who were there the day of the explosion. There are a few who have doubts that Varak was on that helicopter. The others are afraid to admit to anything that would disturb the status quo." He shrugged. "And I've already started to trace a few scientists who could possibly fake that DNA. But I can't make a move on them until I'm sure I know what I'm doing. Varak would be quick to get rid of any witness."

"If he hasn't done it already," Eve said. "You're not being at all reassuring."

"Jill made me promise not to lie to you. The decision is yours. I'd appreciate it if you'd make it quickly. The switch is supposed to be made tomorrow night. It would be foolish for me to spend a fortune in bribe money if I have no forensic sculptor of your caliber to do the work. By the way, I'll have to ask you not to talk to Quinn on your Skype about any of this. It was safe to let you contact him before, but not now. There's the possibility that you might be hacked." He met her eyes. "This would take only a few days, and you might be able to keep a monster from coming back out of the shadows. Jill thinks that it's worth it. Let me know if you agree."

He turned on his heel and left the museum.

CHAPTER

7

There was no decision to be made, Eve thought. Particularly after that last remark about her not talking to Joe about it.

She shouldn't even think of doing that reconstruction. There were so many reasons why it was a bad idea.

And there was only one reason why she should do it.

To stop a monster from coming out of the shadows and striking again.

Someone had killed Hadfeld to keep Jill from getting evidence that the monster was still out there, waiting.

And that violence and horror done to Jill. Eve's own pain and sickness. Maybe Varak was no longer hiding but was on the move.

Her gaze went to Amari on the dais in front of her.

"I don't know what to do," she murmured. "But that was a terrible thing he did to you. We have to be sure that he paid for it, don't we?"

He gazed back at her with those big brown eyes and the eager expectancy that she had unknowingly sculpted in his expression. Eagerness to go home, to end the sadness of that final parting.

But could that sadness be ended if those shadows remained?

"In my court?" Eve nodded slowly. "Yeah, I know. You've had enough to deal with." She got to her feet. "Okay. I'll think about it and get back to you." But not here, where she was surrounded by those lavishly trimmed boxes, and Amari, who was both her triumph and despair. She headed for the door. She needed *air*.

She stood outside and breathed deep, her gaze on the night sky. There was moonlight, the bright orb barely visible over the canopy of trees. Just stand here and look and listen to the night sounds and don't think about anything that Jill had told her earlier.

She had come here for a specific purpose, to help Amari and all the other children who had been so terribly mutilated and destroyed. It wasn't right to put that aside and go on a wild-goose chase that could be a senseless waste of time.

It wasn't right.

Then why was she walking through the overgrown brush down the path toward that schoolroom she'd never wanted to see again?

Go back.

There's no one there.

No way she could help what had happened in that room.

Those lonely desks, the dark streaks on the floor...

She stood in the gaping opening and gazed at that broken blackboard. Had the teacher been standing there when the school had been overrun? Had the children had time to scream before the machetes began to tear into them? They must have been so afraid...

"Eve." It was Gideon standing beside her. He asked gently, "What are you doing here?"

"I don't know." That desk couldn't have been Amari's. It was too small. Maybe one of the six-year-olds... "I'm just... They were used to kindness... They wouldn't have known why..."

"No, they wouldn't." He touched her wet cheek. "We have to hope it was very quick. Come on, I'll take you back to the museum." He was propelling her away from the schoolroom and down the path. "It's been a bad day for you. You need to get some rest. We all ganged up on you, didn't we? We should have waited until you'd had time to heal at least."

"Yes, you should." Now that she was no longer looking at the schoolhouse, she was beginning to function again. Though she was unutterably sad and weary. "And you'll hear from me about it later. Right now, I have to take it all in and start thinking instead of feeling." They had reached the museum, and she turned to face him. "How did you know I was down there?"

"Jill told me to keep an eye on you." He smiled. "Though I would have done it anyway. I care about you, Eve. You may think that we all just wanted to use you, but it's not true. Yes, we had to do what we had to do, but that didn't change how we feel, who we are."

"And what you had to do dominated your life," she said soberly. "You didn't tell me about your parents, Gideon."

His smile vanished. "They were good people. I loved them. What else was there to say? Except that I have to be certain Varak died in that helicopter." He held the door open for her. "So many people died here in Maldara. After I went back to our plantation, which Varak had burned to the ground, I thought it was only one more graveyard out of thousands."

She shook her head. "I'm so sorry that you lost them, Gideon."

His brows rose. "But not sorry enough to forgive me?"

"No. I have to understand it first, and I'm not nearly there yet." She grimaced. "Particularly since I'm feeling so alone right now. Your friend, Novak, asked me not to call and talk to Joe about this. Do you know how difficult that is for me?"

He nodded. "But you're not as angry as you were, or you'd want to do it anyway and to hell with whether or not your phone was being tapped."

"No, that isn't an option, whatever I decide." She moistened her lips. "Because I can't be sure you're not right. I told you before that I felt that if I looked over my shoulder, I'd see one of those children? What if I looked over my shoulder and saw Varak in that classroom? What if he's out there somewhere?"

"Welcome to our nightmare," he said quietly.

"I have enough of my own." She turned and went into the museum. "Good night, Gideon. I'll see you in the morning."

"Night. Try to sleep."

She might actually manage to sleep, she thought as she locked the door. She had thought she might start to work, but she was too exhausted. Tomorrow would have to do.

She went to the bathroom, washed, then brushed her teeth. Then she went to her cot and sat down with her computer.

How she wanted to Skype Joe, to see his face, to release all the tension and share everything with him. But Novak had said there might be someone listening, spying, and even the idea of that intrusion made her angry. It was as if she were being robbed. Hell, she *was* being robbed.

Don't think about it now.

Just make sure that Joe wouldn't worry without totally lying to him.

And she hated the idea of that half-truth, too.

She texted.

WILL CALL YOU TOMORROW EVENING. HAD A BIT OF FOOD POISONING AND I'M HITTING THE SACK EARLY. I'M FINE, BUT YOU KNOW HOW THAT KIND OF THING TAKES IT OUT OF YOU. A GOOD NIGHT'S SLEEP WILL FIX ME RIGHT UP. I LOVE YOU.

EVE

LONDON

Son of a bitch!

Joe clicked off Eve's text message and leaned back in his chair. He didn't like this at all. Knowing Eve was ill was bad enough. But the fact that she'd played down the severity of her illness and hadn't Skyped tonight made it worse. She either didn't want to answer questions, or she didn't want him to see the toll that food poisoning had taken. Or it could be both.

She had been so happy when she'd called him from that hotel early this morning. He'd even felt a little of the uneasiness he'd had about her being in Maldara fade.

Now it was back in full force.

He wasn't going to be able to take much more of this.

Eve did not like him hovering, but then she shouldn't have taken off for a country like Maldara. Even food poisoning could be danger-ous if not properly treated, and he wasn't sure what kind of medical facilities were available. And how had she gotten food poisoning anyway? She knew all the rules about not eating fresh products in foreign countries.

It wouldn't be a bad idea if he took a flight to Jokan and checked out what—

His phone was ringing.

Michael.

"Shouldn't you be in bed by this time?" Joe asked when he an-swered Michael's call. "Jane was telling me that you were up before daylight, and they were working you like slaves at that old castle."

"Yeah, but it's fun. Every time I find something, I go look in Jane's archaeology book and see if it's anything that could be interesting." He paused. "But I was wondering if maybe it would be more fun if we went over to that Maldara place where Mom is right now. You said that it was in the middle of the jungle, where there are all kinds of wild animals and stuff. What do you think?"

Joe stiffened. This coming out of the blue from Michael was weird as hell. Particularly since he'd been raving enthusiastically about his work on the dig since he'd arrived there. "I think that your mom would tell you that she's not there to have fun and that she wouldn't have time for either one of us. She's doing the same kind of work she does at home, and it has nothing to do with jungles or wild an-imals." He paused. "But I believe you knew that, Michael. I don't remember discussing the wild animals when I was telling you about Maldara."

"No, you just said it had jungles. I looked the rest up on the Internet."

And what else had he found on the Internet about that war-torn country that would have sent up red flares? "Well, you don't have to worry about your mom hiking around the jungle and getting eaten by tigers. She's working in a museum doing her work, and you know how boring museums can be."

"Not all museums are boring," Michael said. "Remember that movie *Night at the Museum*? That was cool, wasn't it?"

"In a crazy kind of way." Michael was being entirely too persistent, Joe thought. Which meant he was genuinely worried. Time to cut to the chase and get to the bottom of this. "So why are you calling me now when you should be sleeping? Did your mom say something the last time she phoned you?"

"No, she's only called me a couple times, and she was asking about what Jane and I were doing. She seemed okay." He was frowning. "But I was just thinking today that maybe we should go be with her. I don't like her there alone."

"She's not alone. She was very careful to give me an entire list of people she could call on if she ran into trouble."

"But they're not us."

"No, they're not us." And Joe felt exactly the same as his son about that. He wanted to be the one who was there for her. But something Michael had just said was making him uneasy. Michael had always had an almost psychic bond with Eve, even before he was born. She might not have said anything to him, but that didn't mean he hadn't sensed something. "Today? Why would you suddenly feel like that today, Michael?"

Silence. Then Michael said simply, "Something was wrong. I got scared."

"Why?"

"I don't know. It was really bad, then it was gone. She's okay now. I just don't want her to be alone anymore."

"Neither do I," he said gruffly. "I'm working on it." He had to try to reassure Michael even though his son's words had done the opposite to him. "It might be nothing. Your mom had a touch of food poisoning today. But, as you said, she's fine now."

He shook his head. "It was...really bad, Dad. Can we go, please?"

"Not right now. You know your mom, she wouldn't like it if we showed up on her doorstep without an invitation. I'll work it out." He added brusquely. "In the meantime, stop worrying. Enjoy the dig and take care of Jane. She went to a lot of trouble to give you a good time."

"I know she did." He paused. "You probably won't take me with you if you go, and that's okay. I know you'll take care of her. She'll be safe." He paused. "She's *got* to be safe."

"I believe I know how to do that," Joe said dryly. "I've been taking care of your mom for a long time, since long before you were born. Now get to bed. Let me keep an eye on her for both of us."

Michael was silent. "Sometimes it seems to be easier for me to keep an eye on her. But, okay, whatever you say. Good night, Dad." He cut the connection.

She's got to be safe.

And Michael had been very worried that Eve *wasn't* safe.

So was Joe supposed to rush out and take the next plane to Jokan because his son was getting some kind of psychic vibes that all was not well with Eve's world?

Why not? It was what Joe wanted to do anyway, and Michael's instincts had been almost a hundred percent correct in the past.

But that meant trusting Michael's instincts over Eve's explanation. Which would definitely not please her.

Okay, he didn't like it, but he'd give Eve the twenty-four hours she'd requested and talk to her tomorrow night. She'd be honest with him. If something was wrong, she'd tell him then.

Or he'd be able to know just by looking at her face. As he would have tonight if she hadn't sent him that damn text instead of Skyping.

It was really bad, Dad.

———◆———

ROBAKU

3:40 A.M.

Machete!

Varak liked killing children, Jill had said.

And he was there in the schoolroom waiting for Eve to come so that he could show her that bloody machete.

She didn't have to look over her shoulder, she could see him now, smiling, waiting...

But she couldn't see him clearly because she didn't know his face. She could see the evil, but how could she stop him if she didn't know his face?

And he was raising that machete...

———◆———

Eve jerked wide-awake, her heart pounding. She was panting, unable to get her breath. She sat upright on her cot.

Only a nightmare. Only? She felt as if she'd been there that day and been helpless to stop that carnage. She got sluggishly out of bed and went to the bathroom. She drank a glass of water and stood there looking in the mirror. She was pale, and the hand holding the glass was shaking. She looked as helpless as she'd felt when she'd faced Varak in that nightmare.

She *wasn't* helpless. She couldn't be helpless. She steadied her hand as she put the glass down on the vanity. And she wouldn't let herself spend her life looking over her shoulder, wondering if he was still there, waiting with that bloody machete.

Eve grabbed her phone and punched in Jill's number the minute she left the bathroom. "I want you over here. I want Novak, too. Right now. If I can't sleep, I'm not going to let either one of you sleep, either."

"Twenty minutes," Jill said. "And I'll find a way to get Novak there."

"I know you will. I'll make the coffee."

Silence. "That sounds promising."

"Not necessarily. I desperately need the caffeine, and I want both of you to be awake enough to give me answers." She cut the connection.

Jill arrived fifteen minutes later. "Novak is right behind me." She went over to the cot and pulled it into the center of the room. "If you don't mind, I'll try to avoid sitting on the floor at your feet this time. I don't mind being humbled, but I have an idea I might need all the dignity I can gather together for this session. You really should have Hajif find you a few more chairs."

"You do it." She gave Jill her coffee. "I like the idea of your being humble, considering what you've put me through." Her lips twisted. "Though I can't see Novak being humbled in any situation."

"He pretends well." Jill sat down on the cot. "But you're right, he knows what he wants and goes after it." She glanced at Novak as he walked into the room. "I've saved you from groveling, Novak. Come and share my cot."

"How can I resist? I've never had that invitation from you, Jill." He strolled toward Eve. "But I think we should get down to business before pleasure. Since you summoned both of us, I assume you do mean business?"

"*My* business," Eve said. "I had one hell of a night. I have to be sure that Varak won't ever come back. And the only way I can do that is to do a reconstruction and see for myself that I don't have to worry about it." She added, "Which could get me into all kinds of trouble. You're going to go after that skull tonight?"

"That's the plan," Novak said. "We'll try to keep you from being hurt by this. All you'll have to do is perform the reconstruction and the computer measurements and photos. We'll keep your identity confidential."

"Which will be fine if this skull is Varak's. It will be bullshit if it's not," Eve said. "We all know that my identity will be secret only if we return that skull to the U.N. vault before the switch is discovered. You won't do that if you think that I've proved Varak is alive. You'll want to take the next step and find the person who falsified the DNA." She looked him in the eye. "And then you'll try to hunt down Varak and trap or kill him. Isn't that right?"

He nodded slowly. "I've told you that I would."

"And that's why it's a miracle she's even considering doing it," Jill said.

"More than considering," Novak said softly, his gaze studying Eve's face. "She's going for it. She only wants us to tell her the best way to do it."

"Wrong. I want to tell you how *I'm* going to do it," Eve said. "When you leave here, I'm going to start on the reconstruction of the six-year-old girl who's next on my list. I'll get as much done as possible today and tonight before you give me the Varak skull. I hope to get past the measuring to the initial sculpting. At that stage, a layman can't tell how much is being accomplished. Then I'll start work on Varak. That will be slower; depending on condition, it may take me up to three days. If I'm interrupted or have to leave the museum for any reason, I'll hide Varak away and put the six-year-old on the dais in his place."

"Only three days?" Jill leaned forward, tense. "Are you certain?"

"No, not if the damage from the explosion is more extensive than I think. But they would have had to have found some kind of basic bone structure to even begin to identify Varak and start to search for DNA. You said there were five passengers on that helicopter?"

"Including the pilot," Novak said. "But according to my inter-rogation of Varak's men we captured after the explosion, Varak was wearing a leather jacket that day. There was melted leather in the rubble near the remains of the body." He grimaced. "Which was ba-sically the skull."

"And the jacket led you to the right victim," Eve said. "How con-venient that they didn't have to waste time beginning their search for the DNA. Particularly since the whole world was so very eager to know that Varak was dead."

"Do you think that didn't occur to me?" Novak asked. "But the French forces had made the kill and were in charge of the investiga-tion. The U.N. told us to back off. Why do you think I even listened to Jill when she came to me with that story about Hadfeld?"

"Because you're not an idiot," Jill said. "Though you should have—" She broke off and turned back to Eve. "If the skull isn't too degraded, it will only be three days. That would be enough time. Novak said that the safe is only opened for a visual check every five days."

"Only? You appear to like that word. I'm glad you think it's going to be so easy," Eve said dryly. "It doesn't seem like that much time to me to do the reconstruction, determine if it's Varak, then erase all signs I'd even done the work so that you can slip it back into the safe as if it had never been touched." She added grimly, "And, if it's *not* Varak, then everything will probably blow up in my face."

"Our faces," Jill said quietly. "You're not alone in this. Anything that happens to you happens to me from now on." She smiled faintly. "If you get tossed into jail, they'll have to give me the next cell."

"I'd prefer to avoid that possibility," Eve said. "I have a son to raise, and I don't want to leave it up to Joe." She glanced at Novak. "Which brings me to what I have to do to keep Joe from going bal-listic about this. Joe told me that you'd met him. Did you actually think you could keep him out of it?"

"I was hopeful. But I was considering options. Unfortunately, developments are escalating."

"You mean because I was poisoned yesterday? You mean because no one told me what had happened to Jill before she drew me into this nightmare? Yes, I think either one of those events might have caused Joe to believe the situation here had escalated out of control." She added, "And I haven't told Joe any of the details about either one, but I'm going to have to do it. Jill gave me your name to reassure Joe, but he's not going to be reassured by the fact that I almost died and you can't find the chef who was responsible for the poison. Has that changed?"

"No, Gaillon hasn't shown up back at the hotel. I suspect he might have taken a bribe and skipped the country, or he might have proved embarrassing to whoever hired him and was taken out. I'm exploring both possibilities. I'll let you know as soon as I know."

Eve was shaken for a moment by Novak's coolness and complete lack of expression. But then she should have expected it. Jill had told her he was ruthless, but she found she wanted to disturb that coolness. "How nice of you. But you can see how Joe wouldn't believe you're particularly efficient." She glanced at Jill. "Look what you let happen to her."

His lips tightened, but there was only a flicker of expression in his eyes. "That's true. So what's your remedy for the situation? How do we keep him out of this?"

"We can't. It's too late. If there were any way that I thought I could keep him in London, I'd do it. But the minute I ended up in that hospital yesterday morning, I knew it was the end. Even if I left this place, he'd be back here checking out that hotel and why it happened to me. Joe never lets go, it's not his nature."

"I repeat, do you have a remedy?"

"I can't keep him out, so I tell him the truth." She paused. "And we invite him to help clean up this mess. He'll be here anyway the minute he hears what's been happening." She shrugged. "And he can be a great help, he's a superb detective. Give him all the facts and turn him loose. You'll be surprised how good he is."

"I don't doubt it. He has that reputation. I would have ordinarily welcomed his help. But I remembered that when I met him, I thought he'd probably be a difficult man to control, that he'd always go his own path." He was searching her face. "And you don't want him here, do you?"

"You're damn right I don't. But I can't go away until I know about Varak. And Joe will come regardless when he knows I was targeted." She added curtly, "And I might still be targeted. You can't deny that, can you?"

"Not as long as you're working on the skull. After that, you might be safe."

"Might?" She shook her head. "Then your job is to keep Joe so busy that he's nowhere near me while I'm working on that reconstruction. Otherwise, you can forget about my doing it. I won't risk him. Do you understand?"

"I understand. Anything else?"

"Evidently you don't trust me to Skype him. Get me a satellite smartphone that's virtually impossible to hack. And make sure my security is good enough that Joe will feel comfortable about leaving me alone here."

"I would have done that regardless."

"I had to be certain. Joe would notice."

"I imagine he would," he said. "But you should know that Gideon is fully capable. After his parents were killed, he came to me and asked to be sent to a training camp the CIA runs in Afghanistan. He did very well."

"You mean he's fairly lethal." She nodded. "I can see he'd be motivated. But he just doesn't give off those vibes."

"He's complicated," Jill said. "He adapts to the situation. I think you've found that out."

"Yes, I have." She added, "But then so do you, Jill. But I don't think you persuaded Novak to send you to a training camp to increase your kill quotient."

"I was tempted to blackmail her into it at one time," Novak said grimly. "I still might decide to do it. She's damn vulnerable."

"Back off, Novak," Jill said. "I'm not that vulnerable. I made one mistake. You keep coming back to it."

"Because I can't forget it," he said grimly. "Though you appear to have managed."

"Do I?" Jill asked. "No, I haven't forgotten. Though I try very hard."

Novak muttered a curse as he turned back to Eve. "I'm supposed to take possession of the skull at eleven tonight. Can you put off talking to Joe Quinn until I'm certain the switch has gone through? You might not have to bring him here. That guard, Swanson, is very edgy, and even the prospect of retiring with a fortune may not overcome his nerves. I might have to start all over if he panics."

"I can't believe you'd let that happen," she said caustically. "Joe said you were the CIA's go-to man."

"Which only means in situations like this I can't delegate, I'll have to be there tonight when the switch is made."

"Then you won't let this Swanson change his mind." She shrugged. "I'll wait, but the result will probably be the same. Once I let Joe know how sick I was, it will be all over. If I don't tell him I'm on my way to him, he'll be coming here." She stared him in the eye. "So handle it, Novak. Having Joe hovering over me while I complete that reconstruction would be suspicious to say the least. Joe's reputation is remarkable, and no one would believe he'd fly here from Scotland Yard just for a conjugal visit."

"I'll handle it," Novak said. "Just stall him. Okay?"

"No, it's not okay. And it won't work for long. Get me that phone so I can talk freely to him, or it won't work at all." She made an impatient gesture with her hand. "Now both of you get out of here. I have to start to work." She got to her feet and strode over to the row of leather boxes on the shelf. "Did I tell you how much I hate these boxes? But no more than I hate everything else that happened here." She took down the box with the skull of the six-year-old girl that she'd set aside in preparation. "Her name is Mila. She has a right to expect my full attention, but instead I'm making her part of this charade."

"You'll make it up to her," Jill said quietly as she got to her feet. "And I believe she wouldn't mind that she has a role in catching the man who did this to her and her friends. Do you, Eve?"

"No." Eve opened the box and gazed down at the small, blackened skull. "Very clever, Jill. Just the right thing to say."

"Not clever. It's what I feel. From now on, that's what you'll get from me." She headed for the door. "Now I have to get back to my apartment and change. I'm supposed to be back here for that press interview Gideon has set up for this morning." She smiled as she stopped at the door. "It's good that you'll be in the midst of working on a new reconstruction. I'll be able to be admiring and ask dozens of questions."

"Not dozens." Eve was frowning with exasperation. "And I completely forgot about that damn press interview." Too much had been going on that was more important. "I have to *work*. Tell Gideon to get everyone in and out within an hour."

"Don't worry. It will be just long enough to make me appear to be only another journalist out to get a feature story. Along with trying to convince Zahra that it was Gideon and not me who was behind bringing you here."

"Zahra's going to be at the interview?"

"It would surprise me if she wasn't," Novak said as he joined Jill at the door. "She seems to be ever present. She'll want to take some of the media attention away from you and focus it on herself." He glanced at Jill. "And her agent, Bogani, is still following Jill everywhere she goes."

"She's being followed?" Eve frowned. "Why? Just because she's trying to keep Zahra from swallowing up this village?"

"Interesting question," Novak said. "I'm looking into it. I'll see you this evening, Eve."

Eve turned to Jill as he left the museum. "Why?" she repeated. "Novak may be 'looking' into Zahra Kiyani, but I think she's weird as hell, and I want more than a look. I wouldn't put anything past her and her 'food tasters.'"

"Gideon told me about that conversation." Jill shrugged. "Novak's 'looks' are very thorough. But I agree she's a piece of work. It seems to run in the family. Remind me to tell you about Kiya and her journal. It's enlightening." She lifted her hand in farewell. "I'll see you at the press interview. You won't have to suffer through it for too long. Gideon is a master at this kind of bullshit. He was trained from childhood to be head of the Gideon financial empire. This is nothing."

"No wonder Zahra wanted him as prince consort," Eve murmured. "Well, all I want is for him to get those reporters and Zahra out of here and let me keep on working."

"He'll do it." Jill turned to leave. "One hour. No more."

One hour.

Jill had kept her word, Eve realized, as she watched Gideon whisk the six reporters he'd invited out the door. He'd managed to get them all individual interviews with her that were at least five minutes long, and he hadn't allowed them to take control or ask her any awkward questions. More important, he'd made Jill just one of the crowd with no special privileges, and Jill had played her part to perfection. She'd been eager, intelligent, and no one would have been able to guess she'd ever met Eve before today.

Then he'd turned the spotlight on Zahra Kiyani and switched the reporters' focus to her. Thirty minutes of Zahra's exuding charm, and he'd started herding the reporters toward the exit.

"He's very good, isn't he?" Zahra was suddenly at Eve's elbow. Then she frowned. "Though I could have used a few more minutes with the media before he decided to get rid of them. But it's difficult to control Gideon."

"I thought the timing was just right," Eve said. "I have to get back to work. It was kind of you to take the time to come."

"I couldn't do anything else." Zahra's flashing smile illuminated her beautiful face. "I had to make sure that you were all right after that horrible food poisoning yesterday. You're a little pale, but better than I thought. But, of course, you'll have to worry about a relapse. These things do happen." She didn't wait for a reply but gestured at Jill, who was now being ushered out the door by Gideon. "What did you think of Jill Cassidy? She and Gideon know each other, but I notice he didn't give her any more time for her interview than the other reporters. I was expecting . . . more."

"That wouldn't have been fair, would it? What did I think of her? She seems very competent and appears to know quite a bit about the village. She said I could ask her anything I needed to know, but I don't believe it will be necessary. I'm only interested in working."

"And besides, you can ask me," Zahra said softly. "I'm the only one you should consult. Robaku is really my property. My father allowed these villagers to live here, but now it's time for them to settle somewhere else. Keeping this village alive only keeps the memories of the war fresh to everyone. I've been trying to make that clear to you. It's just as well you stay away from busybodies like Jill Cassidy, who can only cause trouble."

"I'll keep it in mind." But she found she was too annoyed to leave it at that and be diplomatic with Zahra at the moment. The woman always managed to push her buttons. That comment about evicting the villagers from their homes had been a jab too deep to ignore. "But I did enjoy reading her stories. Now that I think of it, I might want to discuss them with her. It's always wise to get a few viewpoints." She turned and moved toward her worktable. "Thank you for coming, but you really didn't have to check on me. I'm doing very well. Not a hint of a relapse."

"It's early days," Zahra said. "Dalai!" Before she swept toward the door, Zahra gestured imperiously to the young servant girl who had been hovering in the background. "You might keep that in mind as well." She brushed past Gideon as if he weren't there. "And you might have given those reporters their story for the day, but you saw how eagerly they turned to me. You mustn't feel bad about that. In the end, they'll always come back to me. I have a certain glamour that you'll never possess." She lifted her chin. "I'm a Kiyani."

Then she was gone.

Gideon gave a low whistle as he gazed after her. "Her ego is flying high today." He turned to Eve. "Did she do you any damage?"

"Only a not-so-subtle hint that I could have a relapse if I wasn't careful." Now that Zahra was gone, Eve found she felt chilled. "I don't like it. There's something very savage about Zahra Kiyani. And I'm tired of threats, subtle or not. She might have had something to do with my getting ill, right?"

"It's possible."

"Then I want to know if it's more than possible. I want to know why. I want to know everything about her."

"Then we'll have to accommodate you. But I assume that's not first on your list? You appear to have a full agenda."

"Yes." And her agenda tonight included looking at a skull that might be that of Nils Varak.

Another chill.

"You might say that." She quickly looked down at the measurements she'd started on Mila. "Not first, but Zahra is definitely on the list."

———◆———

Zahra braced herself as soon as she got in her limousine. She'd like to wait until she got back to the palace, but she'd found that wasn't an option. Now she seldom had a choice, and nothing she did was private any longer.

Not from him.

She typed the text.

DUNCAN'S WORKING ON ANOTHER DAMN SKULL. SHE'S NOT PAYING ANY ATTENTION TO ME. IT'S NOT MY FAULT.

The return text came immediately.

OF COURSE IT'S YOUR FAULT. I TOLD YOU TO GET RID OF HER. YOU DIDN'T DO IT. YOU WERE TOO FRIGHTENED. NOW I MIGHT HAVE TO HANDLE IT.

She'd known she'd get the blame. It made her furious.

YOU DON'T UNDERSTAND. I WON'T GIVE UP WHAT I'VE WORKED FOR ALL MY LIFE BECAUSE YOU'RE IMPATIENT. IT COULD HAVE WORKED. FEAR AND PAIN ARE WEAPONS TOO. THEY JUST DIDN'T WORK ON DUNCAN. I'LL TRY SOMETHING ELSE.

The reply came explosively:

YOU'RE RIGHT, I AM IMPATIENT. YOU MADE ME PROMISES. YOU'RE NOT KEEPING THEM.

She couldn't let him get away with that bullshit.

YOU MADE ME A PROMISE TOO. YOU SAID YOU'D GET IT BACK FOR ME AND YOU DIDN'T DO IT. IT'S MINE. I WANT IT BACK.

He didn't answer, and Zahra began to get nervous. It was all very well to defend herself, but the result could be unpredictable.

STOP WHINING. IT'S ALREADY IN THE WORKS. BUT THAT HAS NOTHING TO DO WITH YOUR NOT GETTING RID OF DUNCAN. I'LL GIVE YOU A FEW DAYS BUT AFTER THAT I'LL TAKE OVER. DO YOU WANT THAT TO HAPPEN, ZAHRA?

The threat terrified her.

I'LL MAKE IT WORK. I'LL GET HER OUT OF THERE. JUST A LITTLE MORE TIME.

She had to wait for a full moment.

FOUR DAYS. SHOW ME YOU'RE NOT A COWARD AND WE'LL COME TO TERMS. OTHERWISE IT WILL BE MY TERMS.

The text conversation was clearly ended.

She drew a deep breath and tried to keep control. She had expected anger, not an ultimatum. But she could work with it. She would try to fix Duncan her way, but if necessary, she'd do whatever she had to do. The alternative was too dangerous to accept.

Four days...

CHAPTER

8

I've brought you dinner," Jill announced from the doorway of the museum. Her arms were full of take-out sacks. "I'd bet you haven't eaten today."

"You'd lose," Eve said. "I had a sandwich before that ghastly interview. I know I have to take care of myself when I'm working."

"Well, this Chinese takeout is much better. It's the only restaurant in Jokan that I'd trust to have genuine ingredients that have nothing to do with monkeys or reptiles." She was taking cartons out of the bag and putting them on the worktable. "Sweet and sour soup and a bland beef lo mein. I figured your stomach might still be tender."

"Good guess." Eve was looking at the cartons. "But this isn't necessary. I shouldn't take the time."

"Yes, you should. There's no telling when you'll allow yourself to eat after Novak dumps that skull in your lap. You know that's true." She smiled. "Besides, I hate to eat alone." She set her own cartons on the desk. "So eat, and if you want an excuse while you're doing it, so you won't feel you're wasting your time, ask me any questions you wish about Zahra Kiyani. Gideon told me that you were becoming very wary about Madam President. Since he let me read the Kiya journal, he thought that I'd be less likely to be biased."

Eve gazed at her for a moment and reached for a carton and utensils. "You're sure about the reptiles and monkeys?"

"I have a friend in their kitchen. He wouldn't steer me wrong.
Trust me." Then she made a face. "You really can trust me, Eve.
About everything."

"Really?" Eve said noncommittally. Then she changed the subject. "Why didn't you bring another meal for Gideon? Isn't he still
drifting around the village?"

"I didn't see him. I think Novak sent him off to do something
or other after he finished staging that interview." She handed her a
handful of paper napkins. "But don't worry, Novak would have sent
a man here to replace him."

"I'm not worried. Though I'm sure Gideon would say that no
one could replace him." She tried the soup. "Excellent. Now tell me
about Zahra. Gideon said that there was a possibility that she was to
blame for my very painful morning yesterday. Do you agree?"

"I agree it's a possibility. Zahra is capable of anything. How far
would she go? I'd judge to the limit if she thought it safe. But she's
cautious, and she'd make certain that the end result would be worth
any action she takes." She was gazing thoughtfully down into her
soup. "She's into power, and she believes it's her due. It's all part
of that royal bullshit she's embraced since childhood." She looked
up at Eve. "Gideon told you she believes that she's descended from
Cleopatra?"

"Are we back to this Kiya again?" Eve asked impatiently. "I ask
about Zahra, and I get a tall tale about Cleopatra's daughter."

"Because when I first came to Maldara and was trying to get a
handle on how to keep Zahra from kicking all those villagers out of
their homes, I had to understand her. I didn't even come close until Gideon told me about Kiya. Then it started to come together. In
many ways, Zahra *is* Kiya. With a generous sprinkling of Cleopatra
thrown in."

"How?"

"You take a psychotic personality and throw in the idea that nothing is forbidden and everything is your right to take. The final result you come up with is a very dangerous woman. Zahra really admires Cleopatra, you know. If you look deeper into who Cleopatra really was, you can see the similarities. She wasn't the gorgeous, tragic queen that the movies portrayed. Intelligent, yes. And she possessed a kind of glamour that had its own attraction. But she killed her brother and sister. There were even rumors that she might have killed her own father. No one counts how many of her slaves bit the dust. Food tasters were a way of life, and any cruel indulgence was allowed with slaves. According to Kiya's journal, Cleopatra even threatened her with death and torture innumerable times when she was angry with her. It didn't matter that Kiya was her daughter."

"Gideon said that you appreciated the literary aspects of her journal," Eve said. "Do you think it was fact or fiction?"

"It . . . was persuasive."

"But Cleopatra only had one daughter, Selene, who later became Queen of Mauretania."

"Only one acknowledged daughter," Jill said. "According to Kiya, she was the result of a sexual liaison between Cleopatra and a soldier in her army while Caesar was away. She gave Kiya to her slaves to raise, and later, Kiya herself served as a slave to Cleopatra. Evidently, she wasn't treated too badly. Cleopatra ordered her named Kiya after Queen Kiya, who was a queen to Akhenaten during the Eighteenth Dynasty. She was one of Cleopatra's favorite ancestors because she was known as the Beloved Wife. Other of his queens were called royal and powerful, and Nefertiti was famous for her beauty, but Cleopatra thought Akhenaten probably loved Kiya more. Wherever her name was inscribed, it was followed by Beloved Wife. Anyway, maybe Cleopatra wanted to tell her daughter she loved her even though she'd made her a slave. At times, Cleopatra actually did show her affection." She added ironically, "Providing Kiya kept in mind her lowly place in the scheme of things."

"Which would have been very painful considering that she knew she was Cleopatra's daughter."

"True. But she seemed to have inherited Cleopatra's toughness because she adapted and played her mother's game while she waited for her chance."

"Chance?"

"To be a queen herself." Jill finished her lo mein and pushed the carton away. "I wonder if she actually managed to outthink Cleopatra, or if she took advantage of circumstances."

"What are you talking about?"

"The Great Journey." Jill leaned back. "What do you know about how Cleopatra died?"

"What everyone knows. When she knew Octavian was on his way to capture her, she locked herself in her mausoleum and committed suicide by letting an asp bite her."

Jill nodded. "Partially right, according to what Kiya related in her journal. Not complete enough. No one gives more than a mention to the slaves she took with her into the mausoleum to die with her. They were the maids Eiras and Charmion. But there was one more slave who went with her."

Eve stiffened. "Kiya?"

"According to Kiya's journal, she went there with her mother by her own choice. She makes a point of saying she felt it her duty to do whatever her mother wished her to do. Or whatever seemed wisest." She paused. "Do you know what else is seldom mentioned? Cleopatra's burial treasure that was in the mausoleum. One of the greatest treasures ever compiled. That was why Octavian was rushing to reach her—he needed that treasure."

Eve stared at Jill, guessing where this was going. "And did he get it?"

"Oh, yes, it was a vast treasure, and he was very pleased with it." She smiled. "And, according to Kiya's journal, there was so much that Octavian never even missed the wagonload of treasure that was taken out of the mausoleum during the time before Cleopatra actually got around to committing suicide."

"My, my," Eve murmured. "Kiya, again?"

Jill nodded. "Remember her line about whatever was wisest to do? It seems that what was wisest for Kiya to do was not to kill herself with Cleopatra. Her mother had sent Caesarion, her son and heir, away to hide from Octavian. Kiya convinced Cleopatra that she should spare a little of her treasure to make certain her heir was safe and had enough funds to fight Rome. Then Kiya magnanimously volunteered to risk her own life to take the treasure to Caesarion." She sighed. "But unfortunately, Octavian found Caesarion and murdered him before she was able to get to him. What a pity. The only good thing was that Cleopatra had already killed herself and didn't have to hear the sad news." She shook her head. "But what could Kiya do with this huge fortune in the back of her wagon? What a conundrum."

"The Great Journey," Eve said.

"Well, she obviously had to leave Alexandria or Octavian would kill her. The only solution was to go somewhere far away, a wild, mysterious place that she had been hearing about in the market." She nodded. "The Great Journey."

Eve chuckled. "You're a much better Scheherazade than Gideon. How much do we believe?"

"As much as you like. It's a great story, so I prefer to believe it all. Particularly since Kiya was such a scheming bitch that she reminds me of Zahra. If she was that clever, couldn't she have found a way out for Cleopatra? Was this her master plan from the beginning, or was she making it up as she went along?"

"Probably a little of both."

"I believe you're right." Jill got to her feet and went over to the coffeemaker. "She had been waiting for a long time, but when the opportunity came, she was ready. She even knew where she was going." She made the coffee and leaned back against the cabinet. "But after that first journal about the Great Journey, the treasure isn't mentioned. I found that interesting."

"Dispersed by her heirs through the centuries?"

"Not much to buy in primitive Maldara. It seemed to disappear when they reached the border." She shrugged. "A mystery to solve. But, then, the entire story is something of a mystery all bound up in True or False." She suddenly smiled. "And, speaking of True or False, that story about the way Cleopatra died wasn't entirely true, according to Kiya. She didn't die of the poisonous bite of an asp though she wanted everyone to think she did. The snake was a symbol for royalty, and Cleopatra liked the idea for that reason. But she wanted her death to be as perfect as her life, so she wasn't going to take any chances. Kiya said that she did extensive research by having several slaves bitten by asps so that she could study the effects before she made her decision."

"Charming."

"Entirely practical from Cleopatra's viewpoint. When a goddess dies, it must be with glory and dignity. But she found when an asp bites, it causes swelling and ugly discharge and intense pain that lasts up to six hours or longer. It's a horrible death. There was no way she was going to put up with that agony and loss of dignity. So she opted to have the snake brought to the mausoleum for effect, but she arranged to have her jeweled hair comb coated with a fast-acting poison. She pressed the prongs of the comb into her arm when the time was right."

Eve's brows rose skeptically. "Definitely another True or False."

"But think about it. Consider what we know about the era and Cleopatra herself. It's possible." Jill shrugged. "And, if you believe in Kiya, then it's more than possible." She smiled quizzically. "Anyway, did I manage to help you to get a glimpse of Zahra's character by studying Kiya?"

"With a few major differences. Kiya was a survivor. Everything she did was because she had to fight or die. Zahra doesn't have that excuse. It's pure ambition."

"How very perceptive." Jill poured coffee into a cup and took it back to Eve. She mockingly inclined her head. "Your after-dinner coffee, madam." She looked at the scant remains of the food. "And you managed to get most of your dinner down. That's good." She took the sacks, plastic plates and utensils and tossed them into the trash can in the corner. "That should hold you until I get back. I have to go now. I'll see you about midnight."

Eve stiffened, her eyes widening. "You're going with Novak? Neither of you mentioned it."

"It's my story," she said simply. "In more ways than one. Novak would have just argued with me. It's better if I just present him with a fait accompli." She headed for the door. "Get back to work on Mila. With any luck, we'll have a replacement for her within a few hours."

If they weren't caught and killed by those guards at the U.N., Eve thought. The soldiers guarding that vault might shoot first and ask questions later. This would be considered robbery on an international scale. She was sure Varak's skull must be the principal prize being held there. Villains on the mega scale of Varak were rare, and proof of his demise was even more rare. Trying to steal Varak's skull would have been like trying to steal Bin Laden's corpse. Eve had not been worried about Novak. He was a professional, and Joe said a good one. But Jill was different. Novak had said she was vulnerable, and she'd already been terribly hurt. She said impulsively, "Jill."

Jill looked back over her shoulder and grinned. "What's the matter? Going soft on me? I'm the bad guy, remember? I'm the one who got you into this mess."

"I remember." But she still had to say it. "But it won't hurt you to be careful, Jill. You're...valuable." She turned back to Mila's reconstruction, and said lightly, "Who else knows where to get Chinese food with no serpents or monkeys?"

U.N. HEADQUARTERS
JOKAN

No Novak.

And it was only fifteen minutes until he had to meet with Swanson, Jill thought tensely. She'd gotten here twenty minutes ago and expected to see some sign of him before this.

Her gaze narrowed on the huge mansion on Wabona Street that had formerly belonged to the owner of a diamond mine before it was taken over by the U.N. The house and grounds were enclosed by a twelve-foot stone fence that the U.N. said was necessary for their employees' security. Though she knew most of the employees had been given quarters in the city after Edward Wyatt had taken residence in the mansion. The house itself was dark now, and there was only one uniformed guard at the gate.

And there was a camera mounted on that gate.

Jill's hands tensed on the steering wheel of her Volvo. She was parked some distance down the street from that front gate, but she'd be in view of that camera the minute she walked within several yards of it.

But Novak would have taken care of that camera, wouldn't he?

And how had he been planning to get rid of the guard?

No way to be sure without checking. She would have had to call him anyway, but now the need was imperative. It was getting very close to that eleven o'clock deadline.

She dialed his number. "Where are you, Novak?" she asked when he picked up. "I need to know if you've taken out this damned camera."

He muttered a curse. "I knew it. I was hoping that you wouldn't do this. Why couldn't you leave it up to me?"

"Where are you?" she repeated.

"In the garden behind the building. Swanson is going to meet me here with the skull."

"How do I get back there?"

"You don't. Stay where you are, and I'll call you after I've left the garden."

"That won't work for me. I started this, I need to take my share of the risk. Tell me a safe way I can get to you."

Silence. "There's an unlocked gate on the north side of the block. No guard. Camera is disabled. Get here quick. I only have five minutes to make the switch and get out after Swanson shows." He cut the connection.

Yes!

Jill was out of the Volvo and running down the street.

North side of the block...

Where was the gate?

There!

She was inside.

She paused for a minute, breathing hard, leaning against the gate, her gaze searching the darkness.

A large fountain. A courtyard...Paths leading toward the main house. The windows were dark here, too.

Where the hell was Novak?

"Keep quiet and follow me." She hadn't heard him approach and could barely make him out in his dark garb. He was carrying one of the gaudy paper totes sold in the marketplace. He added curtly, "The courtyard."

She had to almost run to keep up with him as he moved toward the courtyard. She skidded to a stop as he put out his arm when they reached it. No one was there. "Shouldn't he be here by now?" she whispered.

"If he hasn't gotten nervous." He glanced at his watch. "And turned me over to his captain. Be quiet, Jill. I need to—" He stopped, his gaze on the doors at the far end of the courtyard. "Okay..."

A young soldier in a British private's uniform was hurrying toward them. He was pale, obviously nervous, and carrying a medium-size brown-leather suitcase. It had to be Swanson, Jill thought with relief.

He stopped short as he reached Novak, his gaze fixed warily on Jill. "Who is she? You were supposed to be alone."

"Yes, I was," Novak said dryly. "Plans changed. You're not compromised. She's just an expert to make sure that you're not trying to pass off bogus merchandise."

"I couldn't do that. The imprint of the ID on the skull can't be counterfeited."

"She'll verify it." He handed Swanson an envelope, then the shopping bag. "The replacement. And if anything is wrong, I'll be back for you."

"Nothing will be wrong." Swanson stuffed the envelope in his jacket pocket. "But you have to have it back by Monday. When the inspectors come, I can't cover for you."

"I know that. Get out of here and get that replacement skull in the vault."

Swanson turned away. "I'm going. You have only three minutes before that guard will be back at the gate after his smoke. You'd better hope he doesn't come back early."

He was gone.

And Novak was grasping Jill's arm and running with her toward the gate. He pushed her through it and was locking the gate behind them. "Run! South to the end of the block and around the corner."

Jill ran.

She didn't look back.

Three minutes.

But it must be less than that now...

Then Novak was passing her, and the next moment pulling her around the corner.

She pressed back against the high stone wall, breathing hard.

"Don't stop. Keep moving." Novak jerked her back into motion. He was still running, holding tight to the suitcase. "My jeep's a half block down."

She saw it, the black jeep he usually drove. She dived into the passenger seat as soon as he pressed the lock release.

Novak shoved the suitcase onto her lap and slammed the driver's door. The next instant he was starting the car and pulling away from the curb.

Jill's heartbeat didn't slow until they were three blocks away from the U.N. headquarters. "So I'm an expert?" she asked after she got her breath.

"What else was I supposed to say? It was as good a lie as any. I would have been ready with a better one if I'd known you'd do this to me."

He was angry, she realized. It wasn't unexpected. He liked to be in control. He probably thought he had a right to be angry with her for interfering with his plans. Too bad. She hadn't been about to let him do this without her.

"I think you did know. You even said it when I called you. So stop growling about it. You know I had to be here."

"The hell I did. If I hadn't thought that you might do something to blow the switch if I didn't monitor you, I'd have hung up when you called."

"I would have been careful. I wouldn't have done anything to put you in danger. That's what this was about." Why couldn't he understand that? "We've been together since the beginning. I wasn't going to let you be alone. You might be CIA's golden boy, but stealing this skull could cause you big trouble if anything went wrong."

"I can take care of myself." He was gazing at her incredulously. "What could you have done to save my ass anyway?"

She shrugged. "I'd just say that I was the one who was going after the skull because of the story potential. Everyone would believe me. Reporters have the reputation of doing anything for a story." She added quietly, "And I'd tell them that you were trying to stop me. But I had to be there at the switch tonight or it wouldn't have worked. Swanson had to see me."

Silence. "Oh, he saw you all right." He looked straight ahead. "And he'll remember you. You're crazy, you know."

"Maybe. And it might have all been for nothing. Everything seems to have gone smoothly. But I had to do it."

"Why, dammit?"

"I owed you," she said jerkily. "The night I was . . . hurt, you came after me. You didn't have to do it. You'd already told me to stay out of it. But you found me, and you took care of me." She moistened her lips. "It was a bad time for me. I've been alone most of my life. I wasn't alone that night."

"Your thinking is wonky as hell," he said hoarsely. "That's not how I remember it."

She shook her head. "And then you did everything you could to let me help, to let me find them. I *need* to do that." Her hand touched the suitcase he had thrown on her lap. "And it's brought us to this. One step closer." She had a strange, tingling feeling in her palm. The skull was here, separated from her only by the sleek hardcover leather of the case. Was it the head of the monster? "How could I not be here, Novak?"

His glance shifted back to her face. "*You* couldn't," he said. "Because you don't see things like other people. But do me a favor and don't try to save me again. Okay?"

"You didn't listen to me." She changed the subject. "Swanson was nervous tonight. Do you think he'll be able to hold himself together until we can get the skull back to him on Monday? What's to keep him from going on the run before that? That would trigger instant suspicion."

"I only gave him half of his money. He'll be motivated to keep cool and do everything right until he gets the other half Monday. After that, I don't care what he does. One way or the other, we'll have our answer by then." He paused. "Provided Eve comes through for us."

"Yes." Her hand tightened on the case. "After tonight it will all be up to Eve."

"Everything went well?" Eve carefully moved her reconstruction of Mila to the cabinet she'd cleared in readiness. "No problem?"

"It depends on how you look at it," Novak said as he placed the case on her worktable and opened the snaps. "And also how you look at this skull. I don't think Swanson had the guts to double-cross me, but you'll have to tell me." He opened the lid of the suitcase. "Check the ID number on the skull interior below the left-ear cavity before you go any further. It should be 1066." He gave her a small vial. "One drop should bring it out."

She carefully took out the skull and put it on the dais. "This is like something from a James Bond movie," she grumbled. "Ridiculous, Novak."

"The CIA is much more advanced than 007 these days," he said dryly. "But the Brits did work out a way to guarantee the authenticity of this skull. It's foolproof." He watched as Eve put a minute drop of liquid on the back of the ear bone. It fizzed, and four tiny numbers appeared—1066.

"Though it's a bit showy," Novak said. "I could have done without the sound effects."

"But you're always understated." Jill took a step closer. "This is the skull they took from the helicopter? We're certain?"

"The Brits would be insulted. The skull had almost a guard of honor before the French forces turned it over to the scientists the Brits flew in to tag it," Novak said. "And I was there in the lab watching as they did it. I'm naturally suspicious, and I wanted to be sure. I stayed with it through the entire ID process until they put the skull in the vault." He turned to Eve. "This is the skull taken out of that helicopter. Now can you find out if it's Varak's?"

"I can find out what this man looks like. If it's a strong resemblance to Varak, then it should be fairly simple," Eve said. "If it's not, you'll have to prove whether or not he's Varak to your satisfaction.

But I told you, the DNA specimen taken from that back molar was judged absolute proof." She frowned as she examined the skull. It was badly burned, and it was no wonder that other DNA was not available. It was going to be very difficult to do the reconstruction. "I can't promise anything else."

"We can't expect you to do anything but your best," Jill said. "I'm grateful you're going to do it at all." She grimaced. "Particularly since you have a perfect right to tell me to go to hell."

"Yes, I do." Eve was securing the skull to the dais. "But then I'd never know if Varak is down there ready to greet you." She shrugged. "So I guess I'll have to forgive and forget until I find out for sure. After that, we'll go into it again."

"Works for me," Jill said. "I suppose you're going to start on him tonight? A little rest would do you good."

"I'll get some sleep tonight. I'm going to need it. But I'll work on repairs for a few hours before I go to bed." She turned to Novak. "But now I talk to Joe. Did you get my phone?"

"Yes." He took a sleek, small gray phone out of his jacket pocket and handed it to her. "Very safe."

"I'm glad something is safe around here," Eve said. "I guarantee Joe isn't going to be impressed by it. Alarms are going to go off the minute the call doesn't come in on my computer Skype." Her gaze shifted back to the blackened skull. It seemed to be staring malevolently back at her. Foolishness. Those stories that Jill had told her about Varak were causing her imagination to run riot. "Why don't you both get out of here? You've done your part. Don't worry. Nothing Joe says will change my mind. I've agreed to do this. Now I'm committed."

"I'm not quite finished here." Jill put up her hand as Eve started to speak. "I'm not hanging out to eavesdrop on your conversation. It's time we trusted each other." She glanced at Novak. "I speak for myself. Novak has been playing in the shadows for so long it comes natural to him. Most of the time, he can't help himself. But he won't do anything to hurt you."

Novak's eyes narrowed on her. "What are you up to?"

"I'm just trying to tell her that she has to put up with having me bunk here at the museum from now on until the reconstruction is finished."

"What!" Eve said. "No way."

"My thought exactly," Novak said to Jill. "After all you've gone through to make sure that no one was aware of the connection between you?"

"The press interview already established that, and you'll just have to make certain there's no one snooping around here. You'll do that anyway."

"Why?" Eve's lips twisted. "Because we trust each other so much?"

"I want you to have someone here to protect you. I think that has to be me."

"I have her guarded, Jill," Novak said. "You know that."

Jill shook her head. "How quickly could they get to her? It might not be soon enough." She turned back to Eve. "I won't bother you. You won't know I'm here. Unless you need me."

"I don't want you here."

"I'm sorry," Jill said sincerely. "It has to be this way. I got you into this, and I have to be responsible for you."

"The hell you do."

Jill smiled slightly. "Then we'll have to be responsible for each other. Earlier today, I told Hajif to have a cot ready for me. I'll go down and tell him to bring it up now." She headed for the door. "It will be fine, Eve."

"It's not *necessary*, Jill," Novak said.

"Yes, it is." Jill looked at him over her shoulder. "I don't want her to be alone."

"That seems to be her mantra these days," Novak said to Eve between set teeth, as they watched her walk out of the museum.

Eve repeated, "I don't want her here, Novak. I can take care of myself."

"I'm sure you can. Quinn would make sure that you would never be helpless. It doesn't seem to make any difference to Jill." He looked back at Eve. "Oh, she can take care of herself, too. She survived here in Maldara for two years. And she might not have gone to one of our training camps like Gideon, but she knows karate and is an excellent shot."

"You said she was vulnerable."

"Because she does things like this," he said harshly, his eyes glittering in his taut face. "Because she knows that no matter how good anyone is, there's always a situation where being good isn't enough. She was hurt in one of those damned situations recently. She doesn't want anyone else to be hurt." He gestured impatiently. "You might as well give in to her. You're not going to win. She'll make it work for you. But she won't let you go through this alone." He turned and headed for the door. "I'll go help her. First I have to send someone to pick up her car at the U.N. building, then talk to the guards so that we can get her settled. Go ahead and call Quinn."

Eve shook her head ruefully. So much for privacy and being in total control of the reconstruction process. She supposed it didn't really matter if Jill stayed. If Jill annoyed her, then she would just toss her out.

She doesn't want anyone else to be hurt.

Those poignant words had touched Eve in spite of her resistance to this invasion of her privacy. That memory of Jill's attack must be a constant battle to overcome. But she was dealing with it and not trying to hide away.

Courage . . .

And, dammit, Eve's own admiration for the blasted woman that had flowed in and out like a tide was back again.

Until Jill did something else to infuriate her.

She looked back at the skull.

She shivered again.

It might not be entirely unwelcome to have someone else in this place while she worked on the skull.

Think about it later.

Joe.

She reached for the phone Novak had given her.

"What the hell is happening?" Joe said the instant he picked up the call. "Why aren't you using your computer? I want to *see* you."

"Well, I don't want to see you right now. Later we'll arrange face time on this smartphone," she said wearily. "But now you're going to be pissed off, and it's enough that I'll have to hear you. But I would have bitten the bullet and continued on the Skype if Novak hadn't said this phone he gave me was guaranteed not to be hacked. That was important."

Silence. "Why? No, don't answer that. First I want to know exactly how ill you were yesterday. That's what's important and was driving me crazy. What the hell happened to you?"

"And that will go back to why the new phone is necessary. I'll tell you everything. Just don't say anything until I've finished. Okay?"

"I'm listening," he said grimly. "But I don't think there's going to be anything okay about it."

And it wouldn't get any better, she thought. *Just go for it.* She dived in, and started, "It was right after I hung up from talking to you when I was at the hotel..."

He was ominously quiet as she related the entire story of the last twenty-four hours. When she stopped, he only asked, "That's all? Nothing else?"

"That's not enough? Say something."

"Give me a minute. Right now, anything I'd say would be obscene."

"I went down that road, too. But here I am, sitting here staring at this ugly skull that I hope is Nils Varak's." She added quietly, "Because I don't think I could bear it if I find out that it's not, and he's still out there. Yes, I was drawn into this by deceit and subterfuge, but in the end, that's the bottom line. I can't let a monster who almost butchered an entire nation walk away."

"You told me that you could have died," he said harshly. "I can't think of anything else right now."

"But I didn't." She had to batter through that protective side of him, which was always present and paramount and make him start looking at the entire picture. "But the fact that I came close makes me wonder if Hadfeld wasn't telling the truth as Jill thought. Even Jill can't figure out why anyone would try to hurt me just for doing those children's reconstructions here at Robaku. It was the perfect red herring."

"It certainly lured you," he said curtly. He didn't speak for a moment. Eve could almost hear the volatile storminess in that silence. "I want you out of there. But I'm not going to be able to persuade you to come, am I?"

"Not now. I have to be certain."

"Eve."

"I know. But I can't leave until I know the man who killed those children is dead, Joe." She said with sudden passion, "You told me yourself what a monster he was. Since I've been here, I've seen it with my own eyes. If you could have seen that schoolroom, you'd understand."

"Yes, he was a monster, and that monster is making you go through hell even now that he's dead."

"*If* he's dead."

"You wouldn't question those DNA results if Jill Cassidy hadn't conned you."

"She conned me to get me here. She's not conning me about her belief that Varak is still alive. Neither is Gideon or Novak. They're all very smart and taking big risks because they think Varak might not have been on that helicopter."

"They *should* be the ones to take the risks and not drag you into it."

"All I'm doing is the reconstruction, Joe."

"And you won't give that up," he said. "Okay. Then do the damn reconstruction. But I'm not going to trust anyone else to keep the heat off you while you're working on it. I'll take the next plane out."

"I didn't expect anything else," she said. "But it's not what I want, Joe. I believe that Novak will see that I'm safe. I don't want you involved in this."

"And I don't want you working on that reconstruction that could either get you thrown into jail or murdered. It's a standoff." He paused. "I'm involved in everything you do. It will always be that way. And prepare to see me involved up to my neck in this fiasco. I'll make a few preparations, call Jane and Michael, then I'll be leaving."

"Michael," Eve repeated. "Don't say anything to him that would worry—"

"He's already ahead of you. He called me yesterday and wanted us to take a trip to Maldara. I stalled him, but he won't be surprised that I'm leaving. It was almost a direct order that I go and take care of you."

"Shit."

"Exactly. That's why I have to call Jane and make sure she'll see that he won't try to find a way to join me."

"Heaven forbid."

"And why I have to wrap this up as quickly as possible. No doubts, no strings. Finished. I'll call you when I know when I'll arrive in Jokan. Bye, Eve." He cut the connection.

Michael.

Eve had realized that he might be a problem since they'd always had that special sensitivity to each other. But recently he had also been reaching out to Joe in a similar manner. She should have been just as worried about that as Joe's reaction. The mere idea of Michael's being here in Maldara frightened her. Her gaze flew back to the skull on the dais in front of her.

He liked to kill children.

She didn't want Michael anywhere *near* this place where so many children had died. Even if there proved to be no physical danger, he might sense that overpowering aura of death.

"How did it go with Quinn?" Novak had come in and was standing behind her. "As expected?"

She nodded. "He'll be on his way soon. He's not happy with any of us. He says this has to be wrapped up quickly. No doubts. No strings. Finished. That's the way Joe always works his cases." She stared into the skull's gaping, empty eyes. Evil. Death. Terror. Had those eyes looked out with pleasure at the bloody savagery he had created? That's what Jill had said, that's what Eve had felt, when she had stared into the darkness of that schoolroom. "Joe's right, Novak," she whispered. "No matter what I find, I can't stop until it's finished."

CHAPTER

9

Two hours later, Joe left Jane's apartment and headed for the taxi
stand on the corner of the block.

"Could I give you a lift, Quinn?"

Joe tensed, then he whirled to see a dark-haired man standing beside the door of the apartment building. Joe's gaze raked his features
with one quick glance. "You're Sam Gideon. What the hell are you
doing here?"

"Easy." Gideon put up his hands. "Just offering you a lift as I said.
I expected you to be a bit edgy but not on the attack. And how did
you know who I was, anyway?"

"Did you think I wouldn't find out every detail about everyone
Eve was connected with at Robaku?" he asked coldly. "I could tell
that she was beginning to trust you. That made you dangerous. And
now she tells me that you were responsible for getting her poisoned.
That might make you dead."

"I don't blame you," Gideon said. "I screwed up. I was supposed
to take care of her, and I didn't do it. I thought she was safe." He
made a face. "I really don't want you to attack and make me defend
myself. I'm pretty good these days, but you were a SEAL and can
probably cause me intense bodily pain or death. Besides, I think Eve

has forgiven me and might get pissed off if I end up seriously damaged. Wouldn't it be better to just put up with me and let me help you to get to her as soon as possible?"

"I'd have to think about it," Joe said. "The other option is much more tempting."

"I was afraid of that." Gideon sighed. "Novak warned me that you'd probably be major pissed off. But he also said you were smart and that might make a difference. How long is it going to take for you to think about it before I prepare for personal Armageddon?"

"I repeat, what are you doing here? The last thing I heard from Eve was that you were in Maldara." He was quickly processing the information he'd acquired about Sam Gideon. "You're the rich guy who was banging Zahra Kiyani. Not a good recommendation. I don't like what I hear about her." He added, "But you also pilot a Gulf Stream, and I assume the lift you offered wasn't just to the airport. How quickly can you get me to Maldara?"

"Shall I go down the list? One, yes, I am rich, and I did have an interlude with Zahra that might prove beneficial to us. Two, the reason I'm here is that Novak knew that when Eve agreed to do the reconstruction, it wasn't going to work unless we brought you into the mix ASAP. So he immediately sent me here to put myself at your disposal. Three, it took me seven hours and thirty minutes to get here from Maldara today, and I believe I can guarantee to get you back in the same time. Anything else?"

"Novak sent you? Then he owns you?"

"Was that meant to insult me?" Gideon smiled. "I have many talents, but I'm new to this game Novak knows so well. Yes, I let Novak own me because he's an expert at what he does. I'd let you own me if you show me you're better than Novak." His smile faded. "I'd let the devil himself own me if it meant that he could deliver Varak to me. Is that clear?"

Joe studied him. "It seems to be. I'll have to give it time to verify whether you're being honest or just telling me what I'd consider acceptable." He turned on his heel. "In the meantime, get me to Maldara. And seven hours and thirty minutes is not what I wanted to hear. So be prepared to spend that time filling me in on every phase of what you and Novak have been doing regarding that damn skull. Eve might be a major part of this, but I know Novak isn't waiting for verification or permission from his director. He's already on the move, isn't he?"

"You'd have to ask him."

"No, I'm asking you." Joe's smile was tiger bright. "And by the time we reach Maldara, I'll have answers. I believe we'll start with the DNA..."

ROBAKU

"Hey, you said you were going to nap for a while. Isn't it time you stopped working?"

Eve looked up from the reconstruction to see Jill standing beside her. She realized she hadn't heard her leave her cot on the other side of the room. But then she had been so absorbed that she hadn't been aware of anything but the reconstruction in front of her. "Soon." She stretched her stiff neck around in a circle. "I got carried away with doing Varak's repairs. It took awhile. But I have a clean slate now. I can start with the measuring."

"He doesn't look clean to me." Jill was gazing at the blackened skull. "He still looks like something from a horror film." Her glance shifted to Eve. "And you're calling him Varak. I know you told me that you always have to name your reconstructions so that you can connect, but this is different, isn't it? You're assuming he *is* Varak?"

"No." Eve shrugged. "I didn't know what to name him, so I decided to give him the benefit of the doubt. If he is Varak, then I'll have it right; if he's not, then I still might be close." Her lips tightened. "Because it would be almost certain that he's a Varak victim, maybe even one of his butchers who was on that helicopter. Either way, this is a Varak entity."

"Complicated. Sort of a reconstruction with a split personality. But what else could we expect from Varak?" She asked curiously, "How does that affect you in making a connection with him?"

Eve felt herself stiffening. She quickly looked back at the skull. "I won't have to worry about that yet. There's a lot to do first. The measuring, the initial sculpting."

"And you'd prefer not to dwell on it," Jill said softly, reading her expression. "Have you ever done a reconstruction before on someone...like Varak?"

"You mean an evil son of a bitch who scared the hell out of me?" She moistened her lips. "Once. Several years ago. I hoped I'd never have to do it again. Call me crazy. But when a soul is that evil...it seems to linger...And I imagine Varak would be a million times worse." She straightened her shoulders. "I'll face that when it comes. Now I have work to do."

"After you sleep a few hours," Jill said. "You said soon."

"This isn't soon," Eve said flatly. "I let you stay with me, but I won't have you ordering me around."

"I'll back off. I just didn't want you to get too tired." Jill paused. "I was wondering after Joe Quinn called back and told you that he was on his way whether you might be waiting up for him. It will be a few hours yet before he gets here."

"I know that, Jill." She found her lips curving with amusement. "It's not as if I'm pining away and burning a candle to light his way."

"I wasn't certain," Jill said quietly. "You love him. I wasn't sure how that worked. I've heard it's different for different people."

Eve's brows lifted. "You've heard?"

She shrugged. "I had a major crush on a guy in college, but that went away fairly soon. And, though I'm usually too busy, I do love sex. But I've been around long enough to realize that it's more than that to some people. It would be for you."

"Yes, it is," Eve said. "But Joe and I have been together long enough that we don't need burning beacons to find each other in the darkness. We know who we are and where we are, and there's no question that we would ever lose each other. Burning beacons are fine, but they tend to be a little wistful." She chuckled. "We just go straight for the heart of the flames."

"Which is very difficult to research," Jill said. "Sorry that I misunderstood. But you have to admit I've been very good about keeping out of your way. You didn't even know I was here all night."

Eve couldn't deny it. Once Jill had set up her cot on the far side of the room and settled down, she had been totally silent. "The reality might have been better."

"Maybe. But you wouldn't have had anyone to keep you company in warding off the monster." She smiled. "I know about monsters, too, Eve. Company can be a help." She turned away. "Could I get you a cup of coffee?"

Yes, Jill knew about monsters, Eve thought. They were unlike in so many ways, but in that one way, they were sisters. Sisters... That thought had come out of nowhere. They had both grown up fending for themselves and fighting for survival. It would have been nice to have someone like Jill there to share that struggle. She felt a sudden rush of warmth. "Coffee? No thanks. I've had too much caffeine tonight as it is." She leaned back on her stool. "For that matter, I've had more coffee since I met you than I've had in the last six months. I seem to need it to survive. Does that tell you anything?"

"Sorry. But you can't blame me entirely. You're a workaholic, and you do like your coffee. Can I get you a water?" She was going over to the ice chest. "If you're going back to work, I'll stay with you in case you need a reminder that you promised you'd nap. Is it okay if I drag up one of those chairs I got Hajif to bring up and sit and watch you? I promise I'll be quiet and won't ask questions." She took out two bottles of water from the chest and brought them back to the worktable. "Though it will be torture." She wrinkled her nose. "You know how curious I am."

Eve shrugged as she took the bottle of water. "I don't mind questions while I'm doing the basic measuring. It's almost automatic since I've done it so many times. And it's so important that I recheck it several times anyway. It's when I get into the layers that I have to concentrate."

"Good." Jill was dragging a chair over to the worktable. "I only had time for an overview of your work process while I was researching you, and I've been frustrated ever since. When I'm interested, I have to know everything." She plopped down on the chair. "Now tell me where we're going with this."

Eve laughed. "We? I wish it could be a joint operation. I could use a little help on this one." She paused. "Okay, I'll answer your questions, but then at some point you have to answer mine. You're not the only one who is curious. All I got was a thumbnail sketch about Jill Cassidy." She added mockingly, "And I have to know *everything*."

Jill was silent, wary. "That's not... easy."

"Take it or leave it."

"I'll take it. You have a right. But maybe not tonight." She smiled with an effort. "Now tell me why you have to concentrate on 'layers.'"

"Because it tells me what I need to know." She started to measure. "There are more than twenty points of the skull for which there are known tissue depths. Facial-tissue depth has been found to be fairly consistent in people the same age, race, sex, and weight. There are anthropological charts that give specific measurements for each point. For instance, in a Caucasian male like Varak, the tissue-depth thickness between the mid-philtrum point, which is the space between the nose and the top lip, is ten millimeters. The architecture of the bone beneath the tissue determines whether he has bulging eyes or jutting chin or whatever."

"What happens next?"

"I insert the depth markers and take strips of plasticine and apply them between the markers, then build up all of the tissue-depth points. Kind of like a connect the dots game in three dimensions."

"Only that's an enormous simplification," Jill said quietly.

Eve glanced at her. "Enormous," she agreed. "But that's the basic step. Then you worry about being absolutely true to your measurements and keeping track of the placement of facial muscles and how they influence the facial contour. And so on and so forth. Are you bored yet?"

"No way. I want to know about noses and mouths." Her gaze was narrowed on Eve's face. "But you're getting tired. You're fading. I can see it. I don't want to be an extra stress on you. I'll just sit here and watch quietly until you give up and go to bed."

She was right, Eve realized. She was suddenly feeling drained. She had thought she'd be fine for another hour or so, but if she wanted to finish these basic measurements, she needed to gather her strength and concentration. "Whatever." She shrugged. "Later."

She closed Jill out and focused entirely on the hideous skull before her. Strange, she never considered skulls hideous. It must be the thought of Varak...

Whatever it was, she wanted to be done with him for a while.

But the last measurements, which should have taken her another thirty minutes, stretched out to an hour. She was totally exhausted when she pushed back her chair. "Enough," she told Jill as she headed for her cot. "Now I need a nap."

"At last," Jill murmured as she flicked off the overhead light and followed Eve. "Can I get you anything? Another glass of water?"

"No...too tired." She crawled onto the cot. She was yawning as she pulled up the sheet. "You wanted to know about mouths and noses? They can be difficult. I'll tell you about it some other time..."

"You do that. Don't worry about it. That's another story. I can wait."

"Another story...Sounds like you. But sometimes the story turns out to be a mystery and has to be guesswork that you have..."

Eve was asleep.

Jill shook her head as she gazed down at her before she gently tucked the sheet higher around Eve's shoulders. She was glad that Eve had finally given in, but she wished it had been before she was this exhausted. Yet she'd known it had to be Eve who made the call. She turned and glided away from Eve's cot.

She should probably go back to her own cot across the room and try to get a few hours sleep herself, but she knew she was too wired to relax. Too much had been going on in the last twenty-four hours, and she hadn't had Eve's nonstop work to burn off adrenaline and energy.

And these nights, she had to be as exhausted as Eve had been before she could sleep without the nightmares coming.

Don't think about them. It was only a matter of time before she'd overcome that damn weakness.

Fresh air.

Clear her head and listen to the soothing night sounds.

She quickly moved past the worktable, avoiding looking at the Varak reconstruction as she headed for the door. Not now. She'd face that battle again later. He was part of this village's nightmare as well as her own personal nightmare. She needed to get away from him for a little while.

She drew a deep breath as the cool night air hit her face.

Bright moonlight.

Night sounds. Jungle sounds. Birds. Animals... Was that a monkey?

That was better. She could feel some of the tension leaving her. She sank down and leaned back against the stucco wall of the museum. Twenty minutes, and she'd be ready to go back inside and try to sleep...

"Is everything okay?"

She jumped.

Novak was a dark silhouette a few yards away.

"It would be if you didn't move like a damn panther," she said wryly. "I didn't hear you. What are you doing here?"

"Making phone calls. Checking on the sentries I set up. Waiting for Quinn to show up and raise hell. According to Gideon, he's as pissed off as we thought he'd be." He dropped down beside her. "I didn't think that you should be the only one to take the flak."

"I was prepared for it." She leaned her head back against the wall and gazed up at the night sky. "After all, it was my plan. When will Quinn be here?"

"Three or four hours. He would have gotten here sooner, but he's having Gideon drop him off at our private airfield at Baldar and will make his way here on his own."

She frowned. "Why?"

He shrugged. "He was a SEAL. His instincts are to go in and make that first strike before anyone knows he's hit the ground running. He'll want to slip in and look the situation over. Particularly where Eve is concerned, and he trusts no one in Jokan." He grimaced. "And that includes us."

She studied his expression. "And you'd do the same?"

"Certainly. I have a few problems with trust myself." He was suddenly bending toward her, his eyes narrowed on her face. "You didn't answer me. Is everything okay? I saw the lights go out in the museum, and I thought you'd both be going to sleep."

"Eve's asleep. I thought I'd get some air before I tried to settle down."

His gaze was still searching her face. "Why?"

She was suddenly aware of something different about him tonight, a tension, a recklessness, and that tough ruthlessness that was such a part of him seemed more obvious than usual. It was making her uneasy. "For goodness sake, because I wanted some air. Stop interrogating me, Novak."

"But I do it so well," he said mockingly. "Check my credentials. Though I'm better with Al-Qaeda and Isis. You're really not worth my expertise." He changed the subject. "You didn't think Quinn would go easy on you?"

"Why should he? I think Eve is beginning to forgive me, but I knew her family might never do that. I can take any flak Quinn hands out."

"Yeah, you're just collateral damage," Novak said bitterly. "How could I forget?"

"I don't know. I guess because it seems to bother you." She was trying to keep her tone light. "We've discussed this before. In your job, you usually accept it as a fact of life. Yet you seem to be making some kind of exception for me." Her gaze shifted to his face. "You were even kind to me those days in Nairobi. Extraordinarily kind."

"Imagine that," he said dryly. "Since I'm sure you didn't deserve it. You've caused me nothing but trouble since the day you came to me with that wild tale about Hadfeld. And when you showed up at the U.N., I was ready to break your neck."

"I know." She moistened her lips. "But I had to do it."

"You made that clear. No debt left unpaid." He added harshly, "What did you say? You'd been alone all your life, but I hadn't left you alone when you needed someone that night. So I had to have my payoff, too."

"I was grateful. I don't understand why it upset you."

"Then you should have thought about it," he said curtly. "I *know* you, Jill. You forget that I was there with you after those therapy sessions that shrink put you through in Nairobi before he'd release you. I know what kind of life you've led." His words were suddenly spitting like bullets. "Talk about collateral damage. You trailed all over the world behind your father from the time you were four, and he paid more attention to his camera than he did to you. It's no wonder that you were so confused you had to develop your own concept of who you are and how to survive. You had to fend for yourself."

"I never said that," she said quickly.

"No, but you made a few slips, and after I left Nairobi, I did a check to fill in the blanks. Your father never even made provisions for you if anything happened to him. When he was killed in Tibet, you ended up in an orphanage in Hong Kong for over a year until you managed to convince the local U.S. ambassador that you were a U.S. citizen. You were only eleven years old, and you had to do it yourself."

"My father never intentionally hurt me," she said quietly. "I just wasn't high on his list of priorities. Some men aren't meant to be parents. I'm not a victim, Novak."

"No, you didn't let yourself be a victim even when you were bouncing through five foster homes, who accepted you only for the paycheck and treated you less decently than that orphanage in Hong Kong."

Novak was really on the attack, she realized in bewilderment. His intensity was overpowering, and she could almost feel the electricity he was generating. What was happening with him? Suddenly, she didn't care. He had no right to bring back the memories she kept firmly tucked away. She sat up straight. "You're damned right I didn't let myself be a victim," she said fiercely. "You're only a victim if you don't learn from a bad experience. It was one of the first things I found out when I was a kid. Do you know how I won that Pulitzer?"

"You wrote a series on the corruptions in the DFAC system," Novak said. "I made the connection. But it wasn't enough. Not unless it ended with your own foster parents ending up in jail."

"Maybe they did. I don't know. I wrote the series years later. I was past any desire to punish individuals. I just wanted to punish the system, so it couldn't happen again to someone else."

"I wouldn't be so forgiving." His smile was suddenly savage. "As a matter of fact, I have to admit to taking down their names for future reference."

"What?" she said, shocked. "You're joking?"

"If you want jokes, call on Gideon. As you've said, I don't tend to be soft and easy. I grew up on the streets of Detroit, and I guarantee that everyone who ever caused me problems ended up regretting it."

"I can believe it. But these are *my* problems, Novak."

He shrugged. "I've decided you're entirely too philosophical and I should take over the handling of this type of difficulty myself."

She gazed at him in disbelief. "Are you crazy? Not if it's my business."

"It's all how you view it. That doesn't seem to make any difference to me." He added through set teeth, "Which really is beginning to piss me off."

"I'm the one who should be pissed off. You're not making sense. Why are you being like this?"

"It was bound to come out sooner or later. I've been holding it in too long." His lips twisted. "I don't *want* this. I want it to be like it was when I first met you over a year ago." His light eyes were glittering. "You were smart and gutsy, and I wanted to go to bed with you three minutes after I met you. That was all I wanted, very simple and clean, with no complications. That's what should have happened."

"What?" She inhaled sharply. "You never said anything. You never made a move."

"We were both busy and at opposite ends of the country most of the time." He smiled sardonically. "But tell me you didn't know it was there waiting to happen."

She was silent. The words had shocked her, but she couldn't deny that what he'd said was true. Yes, she had known, but she had refused to acknowledge it. She had instinctively blocked even thinking about him sexually. She was still doing it. Because along with that instant explosive sexual attraction had come the realization that he would demand too much of her. She had a career she was passionate about, and he wasn't like anyone else she had ever met. He . . . disturbed her. Novak was too difficult, and she had not wanted to have to deal with him. She swallowed. "Well, then it was a good thing that it never got past that first three minutes."

"The hell it is," he said roughly. "If we'd just gone to bed together, then it might have been over by this time. It wouldn't be like this. I don't like feeling what I'm feeling now. It's too damn complicated. And I don't have any way to control it."

"I don't know what you're talking about. All I'm getting out of it is that you're angry and it's somehow my fault that we didn't jump into the sack together. That's not complicated, it's plain nuts. And it's bullshit that you're not in control. You're always in control of yourself and everyone around you."

"If I were in control, we wouldn't even be having this conversation. After Nairobi, I swore to myself that it wasn't going to happen, that you were off-limits, that you were walking wounded, and that's how I had to treat you."

She stiffened. "Walking wounded?"

"What do you think? It *killed* me to see you like that. I didn't expect to feel that way."

"Walking wounded," she repeated. "You son of a bitch. How do you have the nerve to say that?"

"With extreme trepidation. You don't want anyone to know you're not invulnerable. It doesn't go along with the story you've created to always keep your personal world in order. But I was there with you when you woke from those nightmares. You're still having them, aren't you? I think I might have held on if you hadn't lied to me tonight." His eyes were blazing. "That's why you came out here, not because you wanted a breath of air."

She didn't answer him. "I'm *not* walking wounded. So you can stuff your pity, Novak."

"You're not listening. Don't worry. There wasn't pity even when I was there with you in that hospital. I don't know what it was. I was just . . . aching and wanting to kill someone, anyone." He added fiercely: "And there's sure as hell no pity now, or I wouldn't have decided to toss out all that crap about going through this by myself. I don't know what I was thinking. So I'm going to be my usual selfish self and take what I want any way I can get it."

"Going through what by yourself?"

"I *feel* something for you, dammit." He added fiercely, "It's that same sexual attraction multiplied about a thousand times, all mixed up with what I felt in that hospital and what I've learned to feel about you since then. You don't want pity? Great. Because sex was my first choice anyway. Though I doubt if we can go back to square one. It probably wouldn't be enough for me." He was suddenly on his feet, looking down at her. "I just had to give you warning that if you really are walking wounded, you should get away from me. Run, not walk. Because these days, whenever I look at you, I want to take you to bed. If I can talk you into it, that's where we'll end up. And I don't know where we'll go from there because I'm not sure I'll be able to let you go after that." He reached out his hand and pulled her to her feet. "And now you'd better go in and get to bed. You shouldn't have to worry about having nightmares unless they're about me. I've given you enough to think about to distract you." His voice was suddenly low and intense. "But remember that I'd never hurt you, and it would always be your choice."

Electricity. Intimacy. His hand grasping hers was warm, vital, and she could feel her pulse pounding in her wrist. He must feel it, too, because his thumb was rubbing back and forth on the pulse point. She was shaking, her breasts firming, tightening. He was too close... No, he wasn't close enough.

She needed to pull away from him. Why didn't she do it? Because her emotions were in such a shambles that her responses were purely physical. She couldn't think, she could only feel. Don't let him see it. She had sworn she'd never be weak again, and no one was more dominant than Novak. She nodded jerkily. "Of course it's my choice. And you won't hurt me because if you did, I'd pull out the Beretta in my jacket pocket and shoot your nuts off."

He blinked. "Point taken." Then he threw back his head and laughed. "And that side of you is another reason why I'm finding handling you so complicated."

"Then don't try to handle me." She turned toward the door. She had to get away from him. Because she wanted his hands on her again, dammit. He had only touched her hand and wrist, yet her pulse was still pounding crazily. "I was right, the first time. It was good that it never really started. It would never have worked out."

"Maybe." Then he was smiling recklessly. "But this is a new game with new rules. And we can change those rules as we go along. Anything you want to do." He reached out and gently touched her cheek with his index finger. "Go to sleep. I had to be honest with you, but I'm not going to let it get in the way of what we have to do. Good night, Jill. If I can deter Quinn, I'll try to do it."

Her skin was warming, throbbing beneath that gossamer-light touch. She moved her head to avoid it. She had an idea that "honesty" couldn't help but get in the way. It was as if he had ripped down a safe, sheltering barrier between them and left only heat, electricity, and vibrant awareness. "I told you I didn't need your help." She opened the door. "Good night, Novak."

"Jill."

She looked over her shoulder.

He was standing there, lean, muscular, infinitely male. "I just wanted to tell you that you've convinced me." His smile was both intimate and knowing. "After careful observation, I can see you're no victim and definitely not walking wounded. What a relief." He turned away. "Let the games begin..."

Games? Jill's pulse was pounding, and her breath was uneven as she closed the door behind her. This wasn't any game she wanted to play. No, that was a lie. It was obviously one that she wanted passionately to play in every single physical way possible. She just couldn't permit it to happen.

If she could stop it. Because Novak had decided that wasn't the way he wanted it. Screw it. It was only sex, dammit. Why didn't she just go back outside to him and find somewhere to make it happen?

Because it was never only sex to her, and she couldn't risk its being anything more to her with Novak.

I wanted to go to bed with you three minutes after I met you.

That had been an exaggeration. He'd been too angry with her during those first three minutes on that mountain in Botzan. And she'd only been concerned with persuading him to get out of her way so that she could get to that bandit, Abdi Zolak, and keep him from getting killed...

BOTZAN MOUNTAINS
ELEVEN MONTHS AGO

"What the hell are you doing here?" Jed Novak was skidding down the hill toward Jill. His blue eyes were glittering with fury in his taut face as he pulled her down behind a banyan tree. "Do you want to get killed? There's a band of roving bandits camped up on that hill. I gave orders that this area was to be cleared."

"I know you did, Novak," Jill said impatiently. "You didn't make any secret about it in any of the villages I had to go through to get here." She jerked her arm away from him. "You wanted to send a message to Zolak that the big, bad CIA were on their way and that he'd better not throw in his lot with those Botzan mercenaries. He was just to meekly give up his weapons and let you take him down." Her eyes went back to the top of the hill. No movement. But there probably wasn't much time before Zolak would get edgy that she hadn't shown up yet. "Only he won't do that, and you're stupid if you think he will. He's too scared of not dying a brave death that will make his sons proud of him." But Jill knew that Novak's reputation was that he was far from stupid. She had only seen him from a distance since he'd arrived in Maldara, but she'd made it her business to research him. He was superintelligent, and the word was that he'd been sent here to Maldara by Langley to try to find a way to stop this hideous war. So reason with him. Persuade

him. It was her only hope to get Abdi Zolak home to his village. Her gaze shifted back to Novak's face. "He'll fight you. He has fifty-two men in this band he's gathered. There would be deaths on both sides." She leaned forward, her voice urgent. "But I can keep that from happening, Novak. The only reason he's here at all is that he agreed to come down from his hideout and meet with me. Wouldn't it be better to let me go up there and talk to him?" She wasn't getting a response. Okay, try harder. "Look, I'm Jill Cassidy, and I'm a reporter, not some missionary out to save Zolak's soul. I know he's been a thief and a bandit most of his adult life. But he's always taken care of his family and his village. And he's not a murderer... yet. But if he joins those mercenaries, he'll become what they want him to be. Here in Maldara, that means butchery. And the only people who can stop him are his wife and family. He cares about them. I might be able to talk him into going back to them so they'll have a chance to do it."

"I know exactly who you are, Jill Cassidy." Novak's eyes were fixed on her face. "I had reports on you from my men watching that village down the road. I'm used to handling reporters getting in my way, but I didn't think I'd have to deal with one who seems ready to get herself killed for the damn story." He looked up at the hill, then turned back to her. "I have credible info that Zolak is up there, and I'm going to go get him. I have orders to find any way I can to keep those mercenaries from recruiting any more local people to add fuel to the fire that's burning up this country. Zolak's an experienced fighter, he's exactly what they're looking for." His voice hardened. "And I don't give a damn about Zolak's soul or the story you're hoping to get from him. I'd prefer you stay alive, but that's up to you."

"I'm not going to get myself killed. Not if you stay out of my way." She had to get through to him. In spite of his coldness, she could tell that Novak was listening, his face was very intent. She had an idea he always listened, was always thinking, trying to put everything together. "Zolak only became involved in this war because he thought that it would be just like the raids he'd been doing most of his life here in the mountains. From the time he was a young boy, that was what he was taught. But he didn't count on all the deaths, and the slaughter of children all around him when this country

exploded. He told his wife it made him sick. There's no way he wants to join those cutthroat mercenaries Botzan hired. He wants out if we can find a way to bring him home honorably." She reached out, and her hand closed on his arm. "Help me to do that, Novak. I've heard you're smart and have enough influence to pull it off. Or just let me do it on my own."

He was silent, gazing down at her hand on his arm. Then he looked up at the top of the hill. "You said he agreed to meet with you?"

She drew a relieved breath. "Yes, but he said I'd have to come alone. I've been writing my stories from his home village for the last month. I've grown to know his wife and children. They're the ones who told me how he felt about the war. I talked to him on the phone myself last week. He wants to go home to protect his own village from all the Varaks of the world. I believe him." She added: "But he's very proud, he could be forced to go the other way if we don't let him keep his dignity."

Novak's eyes were narrowed on her face. "You think you know him that well?"

"Some stories are easier than others to read. Will you stay here and let me go up there?"

His lips indented in the faintest smile. "What would you do if I didn't?"

"Find a way to go around you. But I don't think I'll have to do that. You have a job to do, and you'll do it. What do you care if some egotistical reporter thinks she can do it better?" She paused. "As long as you think I'll get Zolak to go home, you're going to let me go up that hill." She took her gun from her pocket and handed it to him. "Will you keep this until I get back? Zolak said I can't be armed."

Novak looked down at the gun for an instant. "Then of course you have to obey his rules." He put the Beretta in his jacket pocket. "Go on. You don't want Zolak to get nervous. You can tell him that I'll work out something for him once he's back at his village if you think it will help."

"It will help."

"Good." Then he reached for his automatic rifle and settled down on his stomach, sighting down the scope before lifting his head to look at her. "But you'll have to put up with me covering you for the entire time you're up there with Zolak. I'd find explaining away the death of a reporter much too awkward."

"Don't interfere, Novak."

"Did I say I'd interfere? I'll give you your chance. But we've just met, and how do I know whether or not I'd regret it if Zolak decided to kill you? I do hate regrets." He smiled. "But you'll learn what I hate most is to lose an opportunity."

She inhaled sharply. She wasn't sure what he meant. Yet she found she couldn't look away from him. The intensity, the force, the intelligence that was far more interesting than just good looks. She wanted to stay and see what else was there . . .

He nodded at the hill. "Get going. It will be fine. I've got your back."

She hesitated for only a second, then she was turning and swiftly climbing the hill. She could see the bushes move as Zolak's sentries spotted her. She felt she was safe from Zolak, but she didn't know how nervous those sentries would be.

Forget it. Think of what she had to say to Zolak. How to persuade him to save his life and that of his family. How to keep him from joining those butchers. She couldn't worry about anything else right now.

Not even that strange, intimate moment before she had left Novak.

Besides, she found that anxiety was ebbing away. She could almost feel Novak down there, watching her, aiming that rifle, protecting her. With every step she took, she was beginning to have a feeling that everything was going to be okay. She was going to pull this off. She was going to be able to convince Zolak to change his story or start a new one.

And somehow it all had something to do with the fact that this time she wasn't alone and that Novak had been there for her. Strange. When she was almost always alone.

You'll learn what I hate most is to lose an opportunity, Novak had said.

Well, so do I.

But at this moment, my opportunity is with Zolak waiting for me on that hill. I don't have time for you.

But I do admit it does feel good that right now you have my back, Novak.

———◆———

And that day Jill had talked Abdi Zolak out of going to join the mercenaries and gone with him back to his village to get him settled with his family. But the next week she'd been sent to Jokan to cover an attack. Novak was right, they'd been at opposite ends of the country for almost a year, only seeing each other casually.

But there had been nothing casual about him tonight, nor the way she was feeling. Which was an indication she should regard it as even more dangerous. Damn right, they couldn't let it affect the work they had to do.

So forget everything but getting rid of the monster who might already be knocking on their door.

———◆———

DAWN

The first pearl shading of dawn was lighting the sky as Joe punched in Jed Novak's number. He'd just done an initial reconnoitering of Robaku. "Your security sucks, Novak," he said curtly. "Two sentries? And they were deaf and blind. I could have taken them down in my sleep. Is this how you're supposedly keeping Eve safe?"

"No," Novak said. "There's another sentry nearer to the museum that you didn't see who informed me that you were near the village. Plus there's another guard down the road furnishing surveillance on anyone approaching from Jokan. I'm also using a drone that's equipped with an infrared monitor to make a pass over the village every ten minutes. It just identified you as an unknown object and will notify those three sentries immediately."

"Two of whom would already be dead," Joe said. "But the drone is a decent idea if you increase the number of flyovers."

"I'll consider it." He paused. "And those sentries are good men, you're just better. If you're through critiquing my arrangements, would you like to come and have a civilized discussion? Where are you?"

"In the palmettos behind you." Joe moved out of the trees. "And I'm not feeling particularly civilized at the moment." He swiftly covered the yards that separated him from Novak. "But we might as well get this over with before I go to see Eve." His gaze went to the stucco building behind Novak. "That's the museum?"

"Yes, but you probably already know that. I imagine you had Gideon draw you a map of the village or you wouldn't have been so familiar with it. And you have plenty of time. Eve's asleep, and Jill said she's been pushing too hard and really needs it."

"That should make you both very happy," Joe said bitterly.

"It doesn't. We don't want to drive her to exhaustion," Novak said. "But the sooner we get this over with and have an answer, the better for all of us. We can't do that without Eve." He met Joe's eyes. "I realize you want her out of here, but you don't have a chance until she finds out if that skull she's working on is Varak's. I believe you know that."

"Oh, I do. Because you have her caught in your net. So by all means let's move fast. Tell me what else you're doing other than depending on my wife. You wouldn't be able to stand in the background any more than I would. You'd go straight to find the scientist who could have created the DNA evidence. Gideon said he knew you'd been investigating, but no details." His lips twisted. "He said you were a very secretive man. Imagine that."

"Wouldn't it only be practical to wait for Eve to give us some evidence of proof?"

"But that's not your style. I'm surprised you didn't ask for the money to pay off Hadfeld in the beginning. Politics in the director's office?"

Novak nodded. "The U.N. was being difficult. And I'd already been accused of being something of a fanatic about Varak." His lips tightened. "But Jill wouldn't wait. She went for it herself. Which ended with her going after Eve."

"Big mistake," Joe said. "I still haven't decided what I'm going to do about that. But I do know that if that reconstruction is not Varak, I'm not going to stand around and wait for politicians to decide what to do. I've got to be ready. So go back to the DNA evidence. Who do you believe to be responsible?"

Novak gazed speculatively at him. "No questions about the possibility of even being able to defeat the mighty DNA? What do you know about falsifying DNA evidence?"

"Enough," Joe said curtly. "I had a murder case two years ago in which I was positive I knew who the murderer was but couldn't prove it. I *knew* that Richard Sander had killed his wife. But the DNA blood evidence seemed infallible. So I assumed that it was a big lie and went out to prove it."

"And you did it? Interesting. How?"

"Followed the money. I traced a bank draft from Sander to Tel Aviv to a dummy company. Then, when I started digging, I found out that one of the scientists, Sol Goldfarb, who had set up the company, had previously worked for an Israeli think tank that created a way of proving whether or not DNA evidence had been falsified." He shrugged. "And if you know how to prove that, then it's the next step to be able to create a better way to do it yourself."

"And did you get your killer convicted?"

"No, I had an extradition problem getting Goldfarb out of Israel. But I'm still watching him. I'll do it someday." His expression became more serious. "And then I'll hang them both out to dry."

"I'm sure you will," Novak said. "And Israel did do some groundbreaking work in that direction. You must have learned a lot while you were trying to gather in Goldfarb. But I don't think that the person who falsified the DNA on Varak is in Israel. I'm betting on Egypt."

"Why?"

"Because Yusef Dobran is the most talented scientist I've ever run across in that line of work. His execution is nearly foolproof. He's also the most expensive, and it would take big money to hire him. He's got money to burn these days, and he can afford to be picky. Besides, anyone undertaking a replication of Varak's DNA would think twice about doing it. Not only would it be dangerous because of the consequences of being caught, but the first thing Varak would do is eliminate the witnesses."

"Then why would Dobran do it?"

"I have no idea. Fear? Blackmail? A staggering amount of money that he just couldn't refuse? We'll have to find out."

"If he's still alive."

Novak nodded. "He's alive. He's rich enough to be able to afford excellent protection and lives in an exclusive area just outside Cairo, with a bevy of bodyguards." He paused. "But everyone has an Achilles heel. He has an assistant, Hassan Sebak, who's willing to co-operate for the right price."

"And he's already told you Dobran did the job?"

"No, he's very cautious. But he did tell us that Dobran had recently done a very big job. For a price, he's willing to find a way to bypass Dobran's guards and get me in to see him. After that, it's up to me to find out if he did the job and who hired him." He paused. "Or up to you, Quinn."

"You'd rather risk my neck than your own?"

"Any day of the week." He smiled faintly. "But I realize it's your decision. We'll play it your way. My highest priority is keeping Eve working, and I'll do that any way I can. I don't want you to persuade her to do anything else."

"You must realize that's bullshit," Joe said impatiently. "Jill Cassidy researched her, and you know exactly what Eve will do. I've done all the persuading I can, and now I have to jump in and help her try to stay afloat."

"She thought that would be your plan, so I'm offering you the opportunity. I'll send Gideon with you to Cairo along with any backup you need. Find out what you can about Dobran and everything he knows. It's not many men I'd trust to go after him, but you'll be able to do it. I'll stay with Eve and protect her while she's finishing the reconstruction." He paused. "Or you can stay here and hold her hand, and I'll go to Cairo."

"And that remark is obviously aimed at sending me down the road. I'll think about it." He started toward the museum. "But right now, I want to see Eve."

"Not yet." Novak was suddenly moving past him. "Give me ten minutes. Jill insisted on staying with Eve to protect her, and I don't want her shooting you. I'll go and get her out of there." He disappeared into the museum.

Joe muttered a curse. Patience. But he was not feeling patient. Ten minutes? He didn't want to stand here twiddling his thumbs. He wanted to see Eve *now*. He wanted to talk to her, see her face, and he wanted to know why she was willing to risk everything for this madness.

If you could have seen that schoolroom, you'd understand.

The schoolroom. The place that had horrified and captured Eve in a way that Novak and Jill Cassidy would never have been able to do.

The schoolroom...

He turned on his heel and started down the path.

———◆———

"Joe..."

He was near her. The familiar scent of him surrounded her. Eve could feel his warmth, sense the strength...

"Shh," he said softly. "It's not time to wake up yet. Just let me hold you..."

He was here, gently sliding onto the cot and turning her into his arms. Safety... Love... Home...

Her arms slid around him, and she nestled closer. "Not much room on this ... cot, Joe."

"We'll manage." His lips brushed her temple. "We always manage. Though I agree it's not conducive to doing what I've been wanting to do since I left you in Atlanta. So just rest a little longer and let me hold you. That will be good, too."

Yes, they always managed to be together. And it was wonderful just having him here beside her.

She relaxed against him and lay still, listening to his heartbeat. "Jill was ... here. Where is she?"

"I have no idea. Nor do I care." He kissed her ear. "I believe Novak removed her from the premises to avoid conflict."

"She meant well."

"And she's won you over," he said grimly. "She won't find me that easy."

"I wasn't easy. She just proved to me that I wouldn't be able to live with myself if I didn't do the reconstruction." She rubbed her cheek against his shoulder. "I have to do it, Joe."

"I know." He was silent a moment. "I saw the schoolhouse. I could see the effect it would have on you." Then he burst out, "Hell, it tore *me* apart."

"It's the children," she whispered. "I keep thinking about Michael. Outside of the home, a schoolroom is where a child feels safest. What if Michael had been in that classroom facing Varak with those other children? You wouldn't be able to keep from trying to stand between them either, Joe."

"No, I wouldn't." Joe was silent again. "Then let's get moving and make sure no one else will ever have to face him." He brushed a strand of hair away from her forehead and gave her a kiss on the tip of her nose. "So much for you getting a little extra rest." He carefully released her and moved off the cot. "That wasn't going to happen, was it? Lights?"

"Wall switch beside the door." She was already missing the *feel* of him. She saw him silhouetted against the faint light pouring into the glass of the windows as he lithely crossed the room. It must be almost dawn. "I slept longer than I intended anyway." She sat up and swung her legs to the floor. "I've got to get back to work."

The lights flashed on, and Joe's gaze immediately zeroed in on the skull on her dais. "This is him?" He went to the workbench and examined the reconstruction. "You've only done the basic measuring..." he murmured. "You have a long way to go."

"Not so long," she said defensively. "I had repairs. It will go faster now."

"I'm not on the attack," he said. "I'm just trying to gauge the time frame I have to work with." He paused. "Novak wants me to go and check out a scientist who might have been capable of doing the DNA substitution. Did you know anything about that?"

"Not about the DNA." She had to be honest with him. "But I told him I didn't want you hovering over me while I did the reconstruction. I would have trouble concentrating. Is what he wants you to do something that would be helpful?"

He nodded slowly. "It would have been my first move anyway. I just don't like leaving you again." He was still looking down at the skull, thinking. "But Novak seems to have your security well in hand." His lips twisted. "And your friend, Jill, is apparently ready to stand guard over you. Which is only right considering that she got you into this."

"I don't think I could call her a friend, but she will protect me as much as she's able." She met his gaze. "I'll be okay here, Joe. Don't worry about me."

"Of course I'll worry about you," he said roughly. "You're barely recovered from being poisoned. You look exhausted and pale, and you'll drive yourself until you get this finished." He tapped the skull. "But I can't help you do it, so I'll have to go and find another way to reach the same goal. I suppose I'll head for Cairo."

"Cairo?" Eve repeated. "Egypt? That's where you're going to find this scientist?"

He nodded. "Yusef Dobran. Why the surprise?"

"Not surprise really. But Egypt has been turning up in the conversation ever since I got here. Zahra Kiyani has a passion for it. But it had nothing to do with Cairo."

"One can never tell where a passion will take you." He turned away from the reconstruction. "I'll go tell Novak I'll head to Cairo to talk to his scientist. I'll be back before I leave."

"You'd better. Otherwise, I'll track you down."

"Promises. Promises." He smiled at her over his shoulder. "It's going to be okay, Eve. And that's another promise."

She watched him walk out the door. She wanted to go running after him, to touch him again…Instead, she got to her feet and headed for the bathroom to wash up and change her clothes. They both had their jobs to do, and the sooner they were done, the sooner they could be together.

It was best that Joe was leaving, she told herself. Best that he wasn't going to stay here in the center of the hurricane, where she had to be with the reconstruction. After all, it was what she had wanted.

But Joe never stayed out of the eye of the hurricane for long. How did she know there wasn't a worse storm waiting for him in Cairo?

CHAPTER

10

J oe saw Novak standing by the path the moment he left the museum. "I'm going to Cairo."

"I thought you might. I'll call Gideon unless you prefer someone else to accompany you. He's been involved with investigating Dobran from the beginning. He's very good, and he has advantages that my other men don't have."

"Money and contacts?"

Novak nodded. "Those, too. But I was thinking that he learns from every situation and adapts to find a way to win the next one. Didn't you find that to be true?"

Joe nodded. "Gideon will do." He looked him in the eye. "As long as you make it clear that he obeys my orders instead of yours. And as long as I find him valuable. The minute I find he fails me in either category, I'll send him back to you and work on my own." He paused. "He wouldn't tell me anything on the way here. He lies very well, but he's obviously clever, and I realized he'd know more about you than what he told me."

"I'm glad you didn't force the issue with him. I like Gideon, I might have had to address it with you." He added, "Yes, he knew. As you say, he's clever, and I needed him. But he's his own man, and I'll let him know that he can trust you. You'll have to forge your own relationship with him."

Joe nodded. "Whatever. And I'll need to know everything there is to know about Yusef Dobran and his assistant, Hassan Sebak. Right away."

"What Gideon doesn't know, he'll find out for you. When do you leave?"

"In the next hour or so."

"I'll assign someone to take you back to the airport and let Gideon know you're coming. Backup?"

"Get someone local to Cairo that Gideon can call if needed. I'll let him know when I think—"

"Hello. You're Joe Quinn?" It was a woman's voice from the path behind him. "I'm Jill Cassidy. We've never officially met." She was coming out of the brush from the direction of the village. She slanted a cool look at Novak. "You lied to me, Novak. Hajif didn't need to see me. I told you I wasn't going to hide from Quinn." She turned back to Joe. "You deserve to meet the person who hurt Eve and manipulated your family." She lifted her chin. "Is there anything you'd like to say to me? Whatever it is, I'll listen and agree with every word. There's no apology I can make that will make what I did any better." She held his gaze, and said quietly, "But I owe you, and I promise I'll find a way to make it right."

"Believe me, she will, Quinn," Novak said dryly. "Which isn't always a good thing."

"You're right." Joe was gazing straight in her eyes. "Your apology sucks. What you did to Eve is unforgiveable. Eve may have come up with some way to find excuses for you, but I won't. If you need to kill a snake, then cut its head off. Don't make Eve do it for you. You could have gotten her killed."

"I know that," Jill said steadily. "It's all my fault. And even if I wanted to stop her now, I couldn't do it. It's too late. All I can promise is that I'll take care of her."

"Yes, you will," Joe said fiercely. His hands clenched into fists as the rage tore through him. His gaze went from her to Novak and back again. "Because you're right, it is too late. So Eve is going to do what you asked her, and I'm going to find where the snake is hiding. And you will both make certain that nothing happens to Eve. Not a scratch, do you hear? If anything does, then I'll come after you, and I'll never stop until I kill you." He whirled back toward the museum. "Call Gideon, Novak. I need to get out of here."

Eve was coming out of the bathroom when Joe walked into the museum. "That was quick," she said warily as she studied his expression. "What's wrong?"

"Nothing. It's just time that I left." He took her into his arms. "No, that's a lie. I just ran into Jill Cassidy and blew my cool." He held her close. "And uttered dire threats if she and Novak didn't take care of you." His arms tightened. "And meant every one of them."

"I'm sure you did." She looked up at him. "They both want to keep me safe, Joe. Just take care of yourself."

"Always." He kissed her. "I'll call you when I can. Try not to work too hard." He cupped her face in his two hands. "Yeah, that's not likely. I'll see you soon, love."

She nodded and blinked to keep back the tears. "I'm sorry that I pulled you into this, Joe."

"I'm not. I just wish it had happened sooner." He pulled her close again for a long moment, then he was turning away. "I'll call Michael on the way to Cairo and reassure him that you're doing well."

"I'll have to call him again myself soon. It was just difficult . . ." She made a face. "He'd see right through me and worry."

He nodded. "He does that anyway even long-distance." He suddenly whirled back and was across the room again. He kissed her, long, hot, passionately, then he let her go. "Change your mind. Let me take you out of here. I'll find another way to do this."

Her arms tightened around him. "What if you can't? I have that skull here, now. Give me the time, and I can do this. You know I can."

He muttered a curse and pushed her away from him. "Yes, you can do it. I thought I'd try one more time." He turned away again. "Hell, I would have tried sex if it wasn't for that damn cot and a whole roomful of skulls glaring down at us."

Eve shook her head with a smile. "The cot was a problem, but the kids wouldn't have been glaring; children usually think sex is funny." Her smile faded as her gaze fell on the Varak reconstruction on the dais. She suddenly shivered. "But I think he might have been a challenge."

"No, he wouldn't. We wouldn't let him," Joe said. "But I prefer you not have the distraction. He bothers you. So get rid of him, and when I come back, we'll discuss the other hurdles to overcome." He paused at the door and looked back at the reconstruction. He smiled, then deliberately gave the Varak skull the finger. "Get rid of him," he repeated. "He's no threat to you. Alive or dead, we won't let him touch you."

Then he was gone.

Jill opened the door of the museum ten minutes later. "Quinn is on his way," she said. "Novak got him out of the village as soon as he could. I think he was afraid he'd have to protect me from him and that would have caused all kinds of trouble with you." She hadn't moved from the doorway. "Am I allowed to come in? I have to do it anyway because I have to be near you. But I hope that you'll still permit me to do it. I know that Quinn was terribly angry with me."

"For heaven's sake, come in." Eve shook her head with exasperation. "And you should have expected him to be angry. Your research should have told you that Joe can be very cool most of the time, but he has his limits."

"And you're definitely one of those limits." Jill shook her head. "No, you're the supreme limit. I did realize it, I just hadn't experienced it." She came into the room. "It's going to take me a long time to find a way to get him to forgive me."

"No question." She sat down at her worktable. "Does it matter?"

"Yes. Making amends is always important. I'll just have to do something very good that will make up for the bad. It's all a question of balance. The monks taught me that when I was a kid."

"Monks?"

"In Tibet. They were cool dudes." She looked at Eve with a frown. "You haven't had breakfast yet, have you?"

"I'll eat later."

She shook her head. "You'll get involved and put it off. I'll go down and get some fruit from Hajif, then send someone to Jokan for something more substantial." She frowned. "Tea or coffee? I can make you decaf."

"Tea will be fine. And now isn't the time for decaf."

"No, it isn't." She started to turn away. "Thank you for not letting him turn you against me. I know that I'm nothing to you, and he's everything. But you won't be sorry. I'll keep you safe."

"Just don't let anyone disturb me until Varak is finished. That's all I need from you." She grimaced. "And that's all Joe will want also. To have this over."

Jill shook her head. "But he wants something else more. He told Novak and me he'd kill both of us if you got even a scratch while we were taking care of you." She smiled. "So I have to make certain to pay attention to his priorities even if they conflict with yours." She headed for the door. "I'll be right back. Please don't acquire any scratches while I'm gone."

Eve shook her head ruefully as Jill disappeared. She had known Joe was in a fury when he'd come back to the museum, but she'd hoped he'd been exaggerating when he'd said he'd been threatening dire things. She should have known better. Well, Novak and Jill would have to learn to accept Joe as he was and be damn glad to have him on their side.

She forced herself to turn back to the Varak reconstruction. Blank gaping holes for eyes stared at her from that scorched, blackened face. Joe had realized that she had been nervous about doing this reconstruction. And though he hadn't wanted her to do it, he had offered her his support in typical Joe fashion. She smiled as she remembered that scornful, insulting finger Joe had given Varak before he left.

Lord, she loved him.

"He's right, I can do this," she murmured as she gazed into those gaping eyes. "Screw you, Varak."

She leaned closer, her gaze intent, as she started to measure again.

———————◆———————

Gideon was standing beside the steps of the plane when Joe was dropped off at the airfield. "I hear we're going to Cairo," he said as he turned and went up the steps. "I thought that's where we'd end up after you talked to Novak."

"But you still didn't tell me anything about Yusef Dobran on the way here," Joe said as he followed him into the plane. "That could have been dangerous. I was frustrated as hell."

He shrugged. "It was the chance I took. You were an unknown quantity." He grinned. "And what I did know was explosive. I had orders to bring you here. I wasn't certain that you wouldn't make a detour to Cairo on your way if you thought you had a chance to bring this to a close a bit faster." He headed for the cockpit. "And after all the effort I put in setting up Hassan Sebak, I wasn't going to let it all go down the tubes because you were in a hurry."

"You set up the deal with Sebak?"

"Novak can't do everything." He dropped down in the pilot's seat. "Though he'd prefer to try. But I convinced him that I could handle this better than he could. It was quite an accomplishment, since Novak thinks very highly of himself." He was doing the checklist.

"Rightly, of course. But I'm a bit impatient. He has too much on his plate, and I *want* Varak." He looked at Joe. "So sit down, buckle up, and we'll get out of here. I'll tell you everything I know about Cairo on the way."

Joe slowly sat down in the copilot's seat. "You think Dobran did the DNA. You believe Varak is alive? Why?"

"Because Jill does, and I trust her. Nothing has changed that since the day she came to me and asked for the money to give to Hadfeld." His lips twisted. "Besides, I can't do anything else. It's a puzzle I have to solve. I'll use you or anyone else to help me do that." He started the Gulf Stream checkdown. "But I'll let you use me as well, Quinn. When I get this baby in the air, I'll be at your disposal."

"Yes, you will," Joe said grimly as he buckled his seat belt. "And I'm pretty good at puzzles, Gideon, but I don't intend to spend much time on this one. I want an answer before Eve gets finished with that damn reconstruction." He leaned back in his seat as Gideon started to taxi. "And you don't know what impatient means yet."

"Five minutes," Gideon said, as the plane left the ground. "Just five minutes..."

It was only four minutes before he gained the altitude he needed and turned to face Joe. "What do you want to know?"

"Dobran. Everything."

"He was born in Cairo to an upper-middle-class family, his parents were both prestigious professors of arts and antiquities at the Cairo University. But Yusef chose to go for a medical degree at the Sorbonne in Paris and went on to get both a medical and chemistry degree there. He was totally brilliant, but when he was at the Sorbonne, he developed a drug habit that required he make more money than he could earn in medicine. That led him to explore other alternatives that took him into the DNA netherworld, and he found his niche. He spent six years in Paris, and by the time he returned to open his own lab in Cairo, he had developed a stellar reputation among the criminal underworld. For the last fifteen years, he's built on that reputation, and I'm sure Novak told you that Dobran is probably our man."

"And what do you think?"

"That Dobran is an arrogant asshole who will do anything to prove how clever he is. He likes money, but he also considers himself one of the elite intelligentsia like his parents. Unfortunately, both his parents and his social set don't agree and have ostracized him."

"What a pity. Does he have a wife? A mistress?"

"He changes mistresses every few months, but he always visits them in town and never permits them to come to his Asarti estate." He glanced at Joe. "He's very careful. Only his guards and his drug dealer and Hassan Sebak are permitted on the property. That's all."

"And what does Sebak do for him? What kind of assistant? Does he help in the lab?"

"Sometimes. But he's more of a gofer. He runs interference and errands for Dobran." He smiled faintly. "And he makes sure that all is secure and well in his gallery. That may be his most important task as far as Dobran is concerned."

"Gallery?"

"Dobran is a collector. Paintings, sculptures, antiquities. He has a fabulous collection that he's acquired since he came back to Cairo. It's what he spends those fat fees that he gets for his work on." He shrugged. "It's almost as much an addiction as his drug habit. Though it could be that he just wants to stick it to his father and all those other people who don't recognize how superior he is."

Joe's gaze narrowed on his face. "But you don't believe that."

"No, but I'm giving you both sides of the coin. Though it could be a little of both. He was exposed to fine art and antiquities from childhood, so the appreciation has to be bred into him. But he's shown himself to be vengeful and selfish all of his adult life. I'm certain that adds to the pleasure enormously. Hence, the addiction."

Sharp. Very sharp, Joe thought. Gideon was impressive. "Two addictions. Drugs and his art collection. Which can we use?"

"That's up to you," Gideon said solemnly. "Novak said that I'm to let you lead the way. I gave you possible weapons, so now I'll meekly let you take charge."

"Meekly?" Joe's brows rose. "Is that supposed to be amusing? You're like a chameleon adapting to your surroundings to get what you want. That's a dangerous talent."

"Only if you don't want the same thing." He handed his phone to Joe. "Check out the photos of Dobran and Sebak. You'll want to know them on sight."

"That goes without saying." Joe glanced at the two photos. Dobran was in his early forties, hollow-cheeked, thick, dark eyebrows. Sebak, older, receding hairline, a little plump. "What else do you have?"

"Shots of his estate, Asarti, outside Cairo. It's a château he bought from a French businessman five years ago and had renovated. You'll notice the placement of his exterior sentries are clearly indicated." He gave Joe a glance. "Just in case you don't want to rely on Hassan Sebak to get us in to see Dobran. I dangled the money, and he snapped at it, but he's a little too comfortable with Dobran. He tends to be nervous. He's still tempted, but it's possible he could change his mind before the deal is struck. He might decide that trapping us is a safer option for him."

Joe flipped through the photos. "No interior shots?"

"No, but you'll find a copy of the original renovation plans filed by his architect when he bought the château. That should do it."

Joe examined the plans. "Yes, that should do it."

"So do we ignore Sebak and go for his boss?"

Joe thought about it. "Not immediately. There are things Sebak can tell us that might help us. And you've already proved that he can be tapped." He held up his hand as Gideon opened his lips to protest. "You haven't set the deal in place, so he won't have a decision to make that will impact us. Where are Sebak's quarters? Is he in the house?"

Gideon nodded. "Dobran assigned him quarters near the gallery. I told you that was his main duty to Dobran. Care and security for his treasures."

"Yes, you did." His gaze was raking the house plans. "And yet there's something missing..."

"What?"

Joe didn't answer, his gaze still on the plans. "You can get us to the house, but after that, we're on our own?"

"I can do better than that. I hijacked the Internet info of the company who installed his security system and got one of Novak's experts to figure out the codes to both the exterior and interior. I can disable the alarms, video cameras, and the motion sensors to everything but the gallery. That's on a separate circuit and code. The security there is foolproof against fire, theft, earthquake, and acts of God or Satan. Dobran doesn't want anyone touching his treasures."

"But we can get to Sebak's quarters?"

"If we can get past the guard stationed near the French doors in the library." Gideon's eyes were narrowed with interest on Joe's face. "Look, we can have Herb Nassem, the operator Novak set up as backup, drop us off and pick us up at the château. And I can manage to get us into the place. But all this would be difficult. If you still want Sebak, why not let me set up a meeting with him in the city instead?"

"I don't want to waste the time," Joe said curtly. "I want it all. I want Sebak. I want Dobran. I want answers. And I want it all to go down tonight." His lips tightened. "And since you've done such good prep work, we might be able to pull it off."

Gideon blinked. "If we don't get killed. You were right, I don't understand the word impatience as you define it." Then he smiled slowly. "Go for the entire jackpot? It's very appealing. Providing you have a plan?" When Joe just looked at him, he said, "You don't have a plan."

"Not yet." Joe went back to flipping through the photos on

Gideon's phone. He added absently, "I'll get there. We have all day. But the first order of business is that we've both got to memorize this floor plan. Now tell me about Dobran and his drug addiction. He obviously has to keep it under control, or he wouldn't be this successful. What does he use?"

"Opium pipe. He started off on pills, but after he came back to Cairo, he found himself an antique pipe that I'm sure made him feel like a caliph. But you're right, he keeps control. He likes money too much to do anything else. Sebak said he locks himself in his suite at night and goes into never-never land. But during business hours, he's not a user."

"That could be bad or good. Do you know his typical schedule? We need him coherent but not troublesome . . . "

ROBAKU
2:45 P.M.

"You've got your red voodoo markers in place," Jill said as she handed Eve a bottle of water. "Don't argue. Drink it and take a deep breath. You've been racing nonstop all day." She tilted her head critically as she gazed back at the reconstruction. "Now he looks more like a ghoul than ever. Does it bother you?"

"No." Eve took a drink of water and leaned back. "That's a necessary process that leads to a successful conclusion. Why should it bother me?"

"You said you weren't looking forward to working on a man like Varak. Just checking." She made a face. "And I suppose I shouldn't have even mentioned it. It's my damned curiosity again. I'm glad that he's not putting his mojo on you."

"If he were, it would be because I let him. If evil lingers, it could be because we invite it into our minds." She took another drink of water and looked directly into the skull's gaping eyes. She hadn't realized until this moment that she had not done that since she had started working. Well, why should she? she thought defensively. She'd been doing depth measurements. It wasn't because she'd been afraid. "The trick is to concentrate on the work and not give in to imagination." She was speaking as much to herself as to Jill. "I've probably blown Varak's mystique out of all proportion because of what I've learned from reading and hearing about him." And the horrible nightmares. The machete glittering in the darkness of the schoolroom. She forced herself to keep her gaze on the skull. "Do you realize I don't even know what he looks like? That's not a bad thing since I avoid it anyway. But I only saw a couple photos of him on Google, and none of them were close-ups. I wasn't interested in him, only the children. I just got a vague impression that he was very big and had dark hair. Then when I came here and saw what he'd done in that schoolroom, I didn't want to look at him. He's not even a human being to me any longer. He's a Hitler or Bin Laden."

"Close," Jill said. "But you have to add a little Jeffrey Dahmer to be exact."

"You should know." She tore her gaze from the skull. "I'm sure you've researched him ad nauseam, just as you did me."

"As much as I could. He was a big part of the story of what happened here in Maldara, and I had to try to understand him." Her lips twisted. "I never succeeded. I felt like one of those FBI profilers trying to see into the mind of a serial killer. There has to come a time when there is no answer but the fact that Varak was a monster." She paused. "But I think you should know about Varak. Because he didn't look like a monster. He was quite good-looking in a Slavic kind of way, and he's over six-five and very powerfully built. Strong. Exceptionally strong, and he liked to break things...and people." She moistened her lips. "And everyone around him sensed that he did, and it gave him power over them. He loved power from the day he was born. He searched for it in violence, sex, money, or anything else that gave him the same thrill."

"You seem to know him better than you thought you did," Eve said slowly.

"Maybe I wanted to be like you and close my eyes to the monster. But I'm not allowed to do that because I have to tell the story. And now you don't get to do it either because I brought you into this. You have to get to know him. I'll try to make it as brief as possible." She paused. "Varak grew up in the slums of Johannesburg and was the first of three children born to Marta Varak, a worker in a local clothing factory. His father was a soldier who deserted Marta after eight years, and she became a whore to support her children. She treated them all well enough, but she was besotted with Nils. She spoiled him rotten, and he might have been the reason her husband deserted her. Nils didn't like the competition, and there's no telling what he did to push his father out the door. There was no doubt he was the perfect sociopath and was as smart as he had to be in every category. He had temper tantrums until he learned it didn't get him what he wanted, then he became devious. But he had all the signs of a psychopath from the time he was a toddler. There were rumors that were never proved that he killed small neighborhood animals. Then, when he was nine years old, his eleven-month-old baby sister suffocated in her crib when he was supposed to be taking care of her. It was said to be accidental. His mother said the poor boy was devastated even though he always complained about her crying. The only family member Nils got along with was his younger brother, Oscar, because he let Nils totally dominate him. When he was fifteen, he took Oscar with him to Venezuela when he joined a rebel group as a mercenary. But when Nils formed his own army two years later, Oscar took off and went back to Johannesburg. He was evidently tired of being his brother's punching bag." Jill paused a moment. "You know the rest. Varak has been building his reputation country by country and one massacre at a time. Only the massacres and the butchery kept getting worse and worse. Maldara was just the last in the line of his bloodbaths."

Eve looked back at the skull. "I hope this *is* Varak. Somehow we have to put an end to him, Jill."

Jill nodded, her gaze on the reconstruction. "You're working very quickly, aren't you? As I said, you're on fire. But you said three days..."

"I said *maybe* three days, he's going very fast." She took another drink of water. "But it may slow down as I do the fill-in. I have to be very careful."

Jill was studying her expression. "But you don't believe it will slow down, do you?"

Eve didn't answer for a moment. "No, sometimes a work just takes off and leaves me far behind. I can't seem to do anything wrong. This could be one of them."

"So how long?"

Eve shook her head. "I have no idea. Right now it's a fever. But sometimes a fever breaks." She finished her water. "And I won't know if I don't get back to work."

"I'm dismissed?" Jill asked. "When am I allowed to disturb you again?"

Eve started to put on another depth marker.

"When?" Jill persisted. "Next on my list is a cup of beef soup. I have to keep you strong. Give in, and the interruption will go faster. Tell me when it will be convenient."

Jill obviously wasn't going to surrender, Eve thought resignedly. "Before I begin the final sculpting."

Jill's eyes widened. "Shit. You're going to finish tonight."

"I didn't say that."

"But you are, aren't you?"

"Perhaps. More likely tomorrow."

"I think...tonight." Jill's gaze went to the reconstruction. "What did you say about sometimes a work's just taking off?" She murmured, "Maybe we're not the only ones who are impatient..."

———◆———

ASARTI
1:40 A.M.

"You're sure the kitchen entrance is the safest?" Joe asked as he went down the path after Gideon. "I've always found less obvious—"

"Have I been wrong yet?" Gideon interrupted. "Face it, I've been bloody perfect. After Nassem dropped us off down the road, I led us right past those sentries, didn't I? You shouldn't mess with perfection, Quinn." He'd reached the kitchen alcove, and his fingers were racing over the security panel. "Particularly since I'm not at all sure that I'm not the only perfect thing about this venture."

"Perfection is overrated," Joe said. "It doesn't leave room for innovation." Yet he couldn't argue that Gideon had fulfilled every need. He had been a constant surprise to Joe. And this door was opening silently with no alarm. "Okay, you're awe-inspiring. Meet me at Sebak's quarters. I'll go take out the guard in the library."

"I'll do it," Gideon said as he moved down the hall. "The guard will be easy. I'll let you handle Sebak. You want him alive, and my impression is that he's very edgy. I bet he has a gun in his bedside table."

He probably knew Sebak did, Joe thought as he turned in the opposite direction and made his way through the darkness toward Sebak's suite.

Sebak's door was locked. Definitely edgy.

It took Joe two minutes to silently pick the lock. Then he was inside.

More darkness.

But Joe's eyes were accustomed to it now, and he could make out a bed across the large room.

Joe moved silently toward it.

Movement!

The bedcovers were suddenly thrown aside, and the man who had done it was lunging toward the bedside table.

Joe was across the room in seconds, and his hand came down in a karate chop on Sebak's wrist as he fumbled to get the drawer open.

Sebak cursed in pain as he turned and launched himself upward at Joe. "Son of a bitch. What are you doing? One scream, and I'll have guards all over the place." He struck out blindly and hit Joe in the chin. "They'll *kill* you."

Enough.

Joe's hand cut down on Sebak's neck in a karate chop and put him out.

He went limp.

Three or four minutes maximum before he'd regain consciousness, Joe thought. Get ready.

He flicked on the bedside light, checked to make sure the man was indeed Sebak, and removed the .38 revolver from the drawer of the bedside table. Then he took out his handcuffs and snapped them on Sebak's wrists.

"No trouble at all?" Gideon was at the doorway, his gaze on Sebak. "I admit I'm disappointed. I wasn't aiming for serious, but a few minor problems would have made me feel better about having to be so wary around you. I don't like not feeling totally in control of the situation."

"Then you shouldn't have told me that he'd go for that gun." Joe took a small roll of duct tape out of his jacket pocket. "Did you take down the guard?"

Gideon nodded as he watched him tape Sebak's mouth. "Complete with the duct tape. I did a neater job than you." He closed the door and walked toward him. "I think he's coming around. Maybe you'd better be the first one he sees. You're more threatening. I concentrated on being intelligent and charming when I was trying to lure him to our side. That's not the impression we need right now." He stepped out of Sebak's field of vision. "So be intimidating, Quinn."

"I will," Joe said grimly as he moved forward and jerked Sebak's head back. Sebak's eyes flew open, and he gazed up at Joe in alarm. He tried desperately to open his lips and speak.

"I'll let you talk soon," Joe said harshly, "when I'm sure you understand what will happen to you if you scream or cause me any trouble. Nod if you understand."

Sebak nodded but then tried to lift his arms and strike out. When he saw the handcuffs, he began to struggle frantically.

"Helpless," Joe said. "I can do anything I wish to you, and you won't be able to stop me. And you might be able to get out of this alive if you don't make me angry." His voice lowered. "But it's going to be very easy to make me angry. I need information, and you've been playing games with my friend. Do you know there's a pressure point I can press here on your neck that can make you very sorry that you did that?" He reached down, and his thumb and forefinger found the exact place. "Ah, there it is."

Sebak opened his lips, trying to scream as pain jagged through him.

"But I never play games, Sebak. I just make certain the pain keeps coming and coming until I get what I want. I want this information very much because without it, someone I care about is going to suffer." He pressed the cord again and watched Sebak's face as it twisted in agony. "I won't permit that to happen. I'll do anything I have to do to keep it from happening. But I don't care if you suffer at all. I believe you understand that now, don't you?"

Sebak nodded frantically.

"Good. Then you won't try to escape, and you'll cooperate with everything I ask of you. Is that true?"

Sebak nodded again.

Joe leaned forward. "Then I'm going to take off the tape, and we'll begin." He stared deep into his eyes. "But you'll have to remember that if I see any sign of trickery, I won't hesitate. You're expendable, Sebak. And, if I don't get what I want, then I'll have no hesitation about showing you that." His fingers moved gently on Sebak's neck, and he could feel the muscles tense. "You're in my way. It's up to you to prove that I should keep you alive." He suddenly reached up and ripped off the tape with one motion. "Are you going to scream, Sebak?"

"No!" His gaze was holding Joe's. "I promise. I won't—" He stopped. "I want to live. Tell me how I can do that."

"I fully intend to do that." He said over his shoulder to Gideon, "It's over. Come out, come out, wherever you are. Sebak isn't going to have any trouble believing that I'll do anything I have to do now."

"I can see that." Gideon moved forward. "Intimidating, indeed. Is that how you treat the prisoners at your precinct when you're interrogating them?"

"No, that's my job, and there are rules. This is Eve, and there are no rules." He looked back at Sebak and gestured to Gideon. "You'll remember him, he was going to give you a great deal of money. But now you've decided that's not necessary, haven't you?"

"I remember him." Sebak's tone was surly. "We can still deal. I'll get you in to see Dobran. You didn't have to hurt me."

"Yes, I did," Joe said. "I don't have time to do anything else tonight. But I could learn to enjoy it if you don't cooperate." He took a step closer to Sebak. "And we will pay a visit to your boss, but I think you know a good deal, and that will save me time. Gideon tells me that he indulges in his favorite opium pipe in the evening and might be a bit bleary when I wake him."

Sebak hesitated. "Gideon said that he wanted info about some DNA project Dobran was doing. I don't know anything about his business." He looked suddenly alarmed as he met Joe's eyes. "Well, maybe a little. But you'd do better to talk to him."

"I think you'd know about this," Joe said softly. "It was a very big job, perhaps the biggest Dobran has ever done. It would have been very difficult for him not to call in all the help he could get to keep himself safe and the work secret. You're his errand boy, and he trusts you. You might not know anything about the lab work, but you'd be drawn into the job itself."

"He doesn't trust anyone that much."

"I thought we had an understanding," Joe said. "Now I'm going to ask questions, and you're going to answer quickly and fully. Or we go back to the moment before I ripped off that tape. Do you want that, Sebak?"

"No! I just—" He was breathing hard. "He knows bad people. He could have them kill me."

"That's your problem, but you have a bigger one with me." Joe smiled. "Don't you?"

"Yes."

"Then we go forward. What do you know about that DNA job Dobran took on several months ago?"

He was silent, then said reluctantly, "He didn't want to do it. From what I overheard when he was talking on the phone, the money was more than he'd ever been offered before, but he said it was too dangerous. He said that he had plenty of money and didn't need to run that kind of risk to get more."

"And who was on the phone?"

Sebak shrugged. "I don't know. Somebody important. Dobran said something about not caring how big they were, it was nothing to him. He had enough business, and he wasn't going to run the risk."

"But evidently he did run it."

Sebak's lips twisted as he nodded. "Dobran was offered a price he couldn't refuse. A box was delivered here a few days later, and he sent me to take it to Caladon that same day."

"Caladon?"

"Kalid Caladon. He's Dobran's favorite art expert. He's expert *and* discreet. Dobran has all his artifacts appraised by him."

"And this was an artifact that Dobran sent to him for appraisal? What kind?"

"A gold statue. Dobran was excited about it. He was even more excited when I brought the report back from Caladon. He had me set up a special glass case in the gallery for the statue and arranged maximum security for it." He added, "And he started work on the new DNA project the next day."

"How? Did he meet with someone? Did he go to the lab?"

"He didn't go to the lab. But he must have met with the client because he flew out that morning." He added quickly, "And that's all I know. I did what Dobran told me to do, then I was out of it. Dobran spent the next three weeks at the lab before the job was finished."

"You know nothing else?" Joe asked.

"Only that Dobran is crazy about that statue and spends time with it every day." He thought of something else. "Oh, and he told me to put two more guards on the property." He added sourly, "But they didn't keep you out, did they?"

"Names," Joe said. "I need client names."

"I don't have any names. I've told you all I know." Sebak's voice was shaking. "You'll have to get it from Dobran."

Joe was afraid that was true. Sebak was still too frightened not to tell him if there was anything left to confess. "Then that's what we'll do." He pulled Sebak to his feet. "Let's go."

"And am I to be allowed to interrogate Dobran?" Gideon asked. "I'm getting very bored, Quinn."

"Maybe." He pushed Sebak across the room and out the door. "But we're going to make a stop before we go to see him. I want to take a look at that statue."

"I told you that I don't have the code for the gallery. You'll have to rely on Sebak."

"I'm certain he'll cooperate," Joe said as he nudged Sebak toward the gallery. "Isn't that right?"

"I don't know why you want to see it," Sebak said. "It's just a statue."

"Maybe I'm an art lover. Besides, I want to see what Dobran sees in it and why he wanted it so badly." He stopped before the ornate carved doors of the gallery and gestured to the panel. "Do your thing. If you set off an alarm, I don't have to tell you that you'll regret it."

"No." Sebak was quickly putting in the code. "I wouldn't do that. Haven't I done everything you've told me to do?" The carved door opened to reveal steel panels that slid silently to each side. "You see?"

"Yes," Joe said. "You've made a good start. But it's all in the follow-up. Where's the statue?"

"At the end of the second row." He hurried on ahead. "I'll show you."

Gideon gave a low whistle as he fell into step with Joe. "I've seen rooms at the Louvre that don't have this many treasures." His gaze was on the rows of glass cases on either side of them containing Egyptian artifacts of every description. "No mummies? I half expect to see King Tut in one of those cases. I bet there are artifacts in here that the government would never permit to be owned in a private collection."

"No bet." The gallery was very heavy on Egyptian artifacts, but there were also priceless originals on the walls by Cezanne, Rembrandt, Titian . . . "It's clear he sometimes took his fee in fine art. That Titian is worth far more than this château."

"You have a good eye," Gideon said. "And whoever sent Dobran that artifact must have known that it would be irresistible to him."

"Here it is." Sebak had stopped before a softly lit case at the end of the row. He gestured impatiently. "I told you, it's just a statue."

Joe inhaled sharply as he gazed at the superb artistry of the work. It was no more than eighteen inches but was made of pure gold, and every complicated detail of the slim Egyptian woman it represented was done to perfection, from her crown headpiece to her sandals. "Yes, you did. Only a statue." He bent closer. "Take it out of the case. I want to examine it."

"I'm not allowed to do—" He met Joe's eyes and reached out to press the coded release on the top of the case. "Be careful. He'll kill me if it's damaged."

"It's gold. I'm sure it's already very old, and gold isn't that fragile." He took the statue and looked at it. It was just as magnificent as he'd first thought. "But I can see why he was impressed by her."

"I can't," Sebak said sourly. "I don't know why he wanted it. He has others, you know." Sebak nodded at the row of cases across the room. "Probably older than this one. Age is everything to value according to Caladon. This one is only 44 B.C. But Dobran couldn't wait to get his hands on it."

"Why?" Joe murmured. "It's exquisite, but why would it mean that much to him?"

Sebak shrugged. "He told me to make sure Caladon cleaned the base carefully so that every engraved hieroglyph was clear. I think he hoped it would be a name, but it wasn't. Yet he didn't seem disappointed. When he got the statue back from Caladon, he even had a gold plaque made for the case itself with the same words inscribed." He gestured to the small rectangular gold plaque inside the case. "And that wasn't even done in hieroglyphics."

"No." Gideon was suddenly pushing forward to shine the beam of his flashlight down on the gold plaque. "It's ordinary, modern Egyptian script, and it only shows that Dobran is a true collector. He wanted to see the proof, know what he had, every time he came to see her. It was his way of claiming her as his property, bringing her into his world where she didn't belong." His gaze was narrowed, focused on the delicate script. Then he abruptly went still. "Shit." He muttered an oath beneath his breath. "Let's get to Dobran fast, Quinn. No wonder he put on extra guards. I'm surprised that he's still alive. We have to get the hell out of here. I think we've found out all we need to know."

"In a minute. I don't want Sebak around when I'm talking to Dobran." He pushed Sebak down on the floor and fastened his manacles to the leg of the case. When Sebak started to protest, Joe taped his lips shut again. "And you might have found out all you want, Gideon. But evidently I haven't," he said. "I don't speak Egyptian, much less read it. What does it say? Is it a name?"

"No, Sebak is right, no name." Gideon turned toward the door. "Just a kind of title."

"What title?"

"Three words." He threw open the door. *"Great Beloved Wife."*

CHAPTER

11

"Take it away." Eve pushed the bowl of beef soup to one side. "I can't eat any more, Jill. And if you argue with me, I'll throw this bowl at you."

"I'm not arguing." Jill took the bowl and turned away. "I'm lucky I got that much down you. But you had to eat something, you've been on fire all day." She glanced over her shoulder at the skull. "I can tell he's waiting for you. Or that you're waiting for him. Or something..." She shook her head. "He's blurred. I look at him, and I can't tell anything about him. Can you?"

Eve nodded. "Like you, I can tell he's ready and waiting."

"Are you nervous?" Jill asked.

"No. Yes. I'm a little sick to my stomach, but I need this. I have to know." She drew a deep breath. "Now be still and let me get back to work. I don't want to hear from you until I've finished."

"You won't." Jill sat down in a chair across the room. "Promise. I won't even watch what you're doing. But I do have to be here to watch your back. Okay?"

"Okay," Eve said absently, as her fingers reached out to tentatively touch the brow bone on the reconstruction. "You have that photo of Varak?"

"In my briefcase under my cot. It's waiting for you, Eve."

Waiting.

She sat there gazing at the smooth clay before her. Everything had been waiting for this moment. The measurements had been taken and checked. The initial sculpting done, the part that told her basically nothing but laid the groundwork. Now it was time to make him come alive.

She shuddered. No, she couldn't think of it like she did other reconstructions. She didn't want him to come alive. Ever since she'd put that skull on the dais, she had been fighting not to think of the person he could be, so that she could block out all the evil and think only of the work itself.

But now she could no longer do that, she had to accept who and what he was so that she could sculpt that face. Was it her imagination, or did she feel something dark and angry stirring?

She moved her shoulders to release the tension, her gaze never leaving the skull. "Okay, are you ready?" she whispered. "I'm not afraid of you. Be as angry and ugly as you like. I'll still get what I want from you. You took so much from so many. Now you have to give at least some of it back."

Her fingers moved down to his right cheek.

Come to me.

Smooth.

Mold.

Fill in.

Darkness.

Anger.

Pay no attention to it. Keep working.

Go to the ears. That should be easier. They had to be generic. She had no idea whether they stuck out or had longer lobes. Just let it flow and do what seemed right.

Anger.

I don't *care*. I'm doing this.

She could no longer even attempt to block him out, but she could keep to the flow and work through that anger and do what she had to do.

Smooth.

Mold.

Fill in.

Hatred.

Work faster. Go to the mouth.

Generic again. She knew the width but not the shape. Better to make the lips closed and without expression. Because the only expression she'd be able to put would be anger and hatred.

Concentrate.

Her fingers were flying now, hot and facile on the clay.

She could do this.

Lips done.

She was moving too fast.

Check the measurements. They were still important.

Nose width, 31 mm. Correct

Nose projection, 18 mm. Okay.

Now concentrate and do the job.

Anger.

Go away!

More shaping to the nostrils.

Mold.

Smooth.

Creasing on either side of the nose.

Good.

Smooth.

Mold.

Fill in.

It was better now. She could still feel the darkness dragging at her like a huge lodestone, but it was only exhausting, not frightening.

She was working feverishly.

Start the creases beneath the orbital cavities.

Fill in.

Mold.

Smooth...

———◆———

ASARTI

"Great Beloved Wife?" Joe repeated as he followed Gideon down the hall toward Dobran's suite. "What the hell is that supposed to mean?"

"Trouble." He glanced over his shoulder at the statue Joe was still carrying. "And very revealing. Plus as dangerous as a flesh-eating parasite for Dobran to possess. That's why we've got to get out of here ASAP. There's no way that Zahra would let that statue out of her hands if she hadn't intended to get it back. She probably has her own version of a SWAT team watching the house, ready to take Dobran out."

"Zahra Kiyani?" Joe said. "You're saying she hired Dobran. Why would she want to fake Varak's death? He worked for the Botzans, her enemy. She had every reason to want him dead. He almost destroyed her country."

"You'll have to ask Dobran. All I know for sure is that she almost certainly did the hiring."

"Because of the statue." Joe looked down at the statue. "It belonged to her? You've seen it before?"

"No, but it's a statue of Kiya, one of Akhenaten's queens during his reign in the Eighteenth Dynasty. On every artifact bearing her name, it was followed or preceded by *The Great Beloved Wife*. That's what's engraved on that statue you're holding. Zahra has always had an obsession about her. Kiya, Zahra's ancestor who founded the Kiyanis, was named for Akhenaten's wife by her mother, Cleopatra. Even in Kiya's journal, she mentioned that the reason that Cleopatra gave her the same name was because of the stories, passed down through the centuries, of how Queen Kiya was so loved by Akhenaten. Didn't Eve mention any of this to you?"

"Probably. It's vaguely familiar. But I guarantee I wasn't paying much attention to any tall tales about Cleopatra. I had other things to think about. As I do right now." He added grimly, "And there could have been other people who had access to a statue of Akhenaten's queen."

"But maybe not one sculpted between 50 and 30 B.C., when Cleopatra and her daughter were alive. That's unusual in itself when Akhenaten and his wives died back in the Eighteenth Dynasty." He slowed and gestured ahead. "Dobran's suite is the second door on the left. Let's see if he can give us a few answers, provided he can focus through his usual haze. Though it might not be possible. Either way, we have to get out of here. Agreed?"

"Agreed." Joe moved quickly down the hall and unlocked the door.

The heavy scent of opium.

A man dressed in loose trousers and an open white shirt was lying sprawled on the couch with an opium pipe in his lips. He appeared to be asleep.

Shit.

"Not much chance of getting answers," Gideon said. "Still want to try?"

"Hell, yes," Joe said. "I don't like the alternative of having to take him with us and get answers later."

"You didn't mention that alternative," Gideon said. "I don't like it either."

"Hold this." Joe thrust the statue at Gideon. Then he was across the room and yanking the pipe out of Dobran's mouth.

No response.

He shook him. "Wake up, Dobran."

Dobran opened his eyes. "Go away." His voice was slurred. "You have no...right to be here. Son of a bitch...I'll have you...castrated."

"Oh, now that does make me mad. Wake up." Joe slapped him. No response. Once again. "Keep your eyes open, dammit."

"Tired..."

"Give me the statue, Gideon." He dug his hand in Dobran's hair and jerked his head back. He held the statue squarely in front of his face. "If you don't keep your eyes open, I'm going to hammer this statue into a pile of rubble."

"No!" Dobran's lids flew open. "Mine. I'll kill you..."

"Is it yours? Who gave it to you?"

"Bitch. Arrogant bitch...Only a down payment. She promised she'd give me more. She said she had lots more..."

"Who?"

"But she never gave me anything else...and she even wanted that statue back. Bitch." He reached out and tried to grasp the statue. "So beautiful...Mine."

"Who?" Joe repeated.

"Did I tell you I was going to castrate you?"

"Who?"

"Maldara...Kiyani..."

"Why?"

"How do I know? She wanted it done..." His eyes closed. "They pay me, I do it. But he was too dangerous. She shouldn't have cheated me."

"Who was he?"

"You know who he is. Everyone knows him..." He was dozing off to sleep again. "But she shouldn't have tried to take the statue back..."

And no matter how Joe shook him, he only got mumbles and complaints. Joe was cursing low and vehemently beneath his breath as he released Dobran's hair and let his head fall back on the pillow of the couch. "Dammit, it's not *enough*."

"What do you mean? You know it was Zahra. He said as much."

"Yes, but I'm going to have to squeeze more out of him. I can't risk his going on the run or ending up a corpse if Zahra decides he has to be taken out." He put the statue in his backpack. "And Eve may need him to testify if all this shit comes tumbling down around her." He slipped on the backpack. "Come on. Help me. We've got to take him with us."

"That was the scenario I wasn't looking forward to facing." Gideon helped him get Dobran onto his feet, and they half carried, half pulled him toward the door. "How do you intend we do it? Go right through all those sentries, lugging him along behind us?"

"No, we go back to the gallery, pick up Sebak again, and let him show us the other way out."

"What other way out? We have the house-renovation plans. Every exit leads out front or to the side gardens protected by sentries."

"But there was something missing." They'd reached the grand staircase and were having to balance Dobran's weight to keep him from falling down the stairs. "I told you that it wasn't right."

"But you didn't tell me why."

"The gallery. You said everything was built around keeping the gallery safe. But there was only one door, and it led to the hall and the front doors. Dobran would have wanted another way to get his treasures out of the château in an emergency. Only he wouldn't have wanted it put in the house plans for everyone to see."

"You're guessing."

"Of course." They were on the staircase landing. "But it's a good guess, and I'm banking on it. It's better than trying to yank Dobran through that garden and having to deal with—"

An explosion rocked the house.

Fire!

Flames were suddenly ripping through the foyer below them.

Then another explosion.

"The gallery." Joe and Gideon were dragging Dobran down the rest of the steps. "Get him to the gallery."

Smoke.

Another explosion. This time from the kitchen.

It was hard to see now.

It took them twice as long as it should have to reach the gallery.

A minute more to punch in the code he'd watched Sebak enter.

Then they were inside.

The heavy steel door slid closed behind them.

Joe released his hold on Dobran and pressed the lock on the door. "Bring him. I've got to get to Sebak." He was running down the aisle. "We've got to get out of here before the local fire department shows up with the police and an antiterrorist unit. And those grounds out front will be teeming with Dobran's sentries by now." He'd reached Sebak and knelt to free him from the handcuffs and rip off his tape.

"What did you do?" Sebak screeched. Tears were streaming down his chalk-white face. "I heard the explosions. Are you trying to kill me? I did everything you told me to do." Then he saw Gideon and Dobran. "I thought you were only going to question him. He's the one who will kill me."

"Not if you get us out of here," Joe said as he jerked him to his feet. "You'll never see Dobran again if you help me get him away from here before anyone breaks in and tosses another bomb. I didn't set off those explosions."

"You're lying," he said uncertainly.

"Have it your way. I don't have time to argue. I have to find a way out." He pushed him down to his knees again. "I'll put the manacles back on you and you can wait for someone to come . . . or not."

"No." He struggled back to his feet. "I'll show you. But then you'll let me go?"

"We'll talk about it. I'm still not sure you don't know more. But we're not going to let Dobran go, I need him. So he won't be around to go looking for you. Move!" He was gazing around the gallery. "No doors. But there's another way out, right? Show me. Hurry!"

"I will. I'm hurrying." Sebak was running toward the back of the gallery. "The mummy..."

"Mummy?" Joe was helping Gideon move faster with Dobran. "What are you talking about?"

Sebak was standing before an upright ornate mummy sarcophagus whose top was a huge, carved hawk. "It's a passageway that leads out of the back of the house and down a tunnel toward the road." He was opening the lid, then swinging the five-foot shelf containing the wrapped mummy to one side. "Dobran liked the idea of using the mummy to hide the door." He ducked inside. "Follow me."

"Wait a minute." Joe had a thought. "Gideon said that everything in the gallery was on a separate control. Does that include video cameras?"

"Of course," Sebak said. "Everything."

"Then where can I pull the tapes?"

"They have a special code to release each section of the display areas. There are six kiosks."

"Six!"

"Sirens, Quinn," Gideon said quietly.

Joe heard them, too.

"Shit." *No time to stay and grab the videos. Worry about it later.* "Get going, Sebak."

Sebak disappeared into the darkness.

"Macabre," Gideon said dryly as he dragged Dobran farther into the sarcophagus. "This decision must have been made during one of his more bizarre narcotic episodes."

"Whatever." Joe was negotiating the entrance to the tunnel while still trying to help Gideon with Dobran. "Pull that lid shut behind you, then call Nassem and tell him to meet us at the road in back of the château."

"I'm sure it's bad luck to close the lid of a coffin on oneself." Gideon slammed the lid behind him. "Oh, well, I look to you to protect me."

"Don't count on it."

"But I most certainly do, Quinn. Otherwise, I'll drop Dobran and let you lug him out yourself." Gideon reached for his phone. "And I think those sirens are closer..."

———◆———

ROBAKU

It was done.

Eve was breathing heavily, as if she'd been running.

She was shaking from exhaustion.

But you didn't beat me, you son of a bitch.

No, he wasn't quite done. But only the eyes were left to insert. The eyes were always the last step in completing a reconstruction.

Her hands were trembling as she reached for her eye case.

"Eve?" Jill was beside her. "Can I help you now? You don't look so good."

"Tired..." Eye case. "I have to get the eye case. We can't look at him until I put in the eyes."

"I won't look at him. I know this choice is as important to you as the sculpting itself." She gave Eve the eye case and opened the lid. "Which ones?"

"Brown. We'll try brown first. Brown eyes always predominate." She took out the right eye and carefully put it into the socket. She didn't look at the face, her gaze fixed only on that dark, shiny eye. "I think it's time you got that photo, Jill."

"I do, too." Jill squeezed Eve's shoulder. "I'll be right back. Put in the other eye."

Eve was already doing it. She carefully inserted the left eye.

Anger.

Screw you. I've *done* it.

"Here it is." Jill handed her the blown-up photo. "May I look now? I don't need the photo. I know what the son of a bitch looks like."

"Go ahead." She forced herself to look down at the features of the man in the photo. She felt a ripple of shock as she gazed into those dark eyes so much like the ones she'd just inserted. The shape of the orbital cavities were identical to the ones she had just created. Varak? It must be Varak. What other features were the same? She identified the curve of the cheekbone immediately. She remembered those bold, Slavic cheekbones. She couldn't take her eyes from the photo, caught by the sheer power of that face. Dominance. Power. Intensity. And darkness, so much darkness.

"Eve," Jill said gently.

Eve glanced up from the photo. "You should be relieved. It has to be him. It was lucky that I was able to repair those orbital—"

"Eve. Look at him."

Eve's gaze followed Jill's to the reconstruction.

She stiffened. Her hand was shaking as she reached for her phone. "I've got to call Joe."

———◆———

ASARTI

Joe's phone was vibrating in his pocket.

Not now. Later.

He couldn't answer it. He was almost at the end of the tunnel. He could see Sebak ahead, rolling aside a large boulder.

"No!" Joe called. "Don't go out there yet. We don't know what's happening. This might be too easy. It doesn't take a mental giant to figure out that there might be a back way out of that gallery. Explosives. Fire. Then someone waits to see who goes running. Let me take a look." He pushed Dobran at Gideon and strode to the opening. Shrubs. A thin stand of trees. A stretch of lawn that led to the road several yards away. As he watched, he saw their driver, Nassem, pull to a stop at the curb of that road.

No sentries. No police. No fire trucks. They all seemed to be at the front of the house, where he could hear sirens, shouts, breaking windows.

"Safe?" Gideon was beside him.

"How the hell do I know? Probably not." Joe's gaze was scanning the trees. "But it's safer than any other option."

"What are you doing to me?" Dobran had raised his head and was staring blearily at Joe. His voice was slurred. "You won't get away with this." He saw Sebak a few feet away. "Call the guards. Why are you just standing there?"

"You said you'd keep him away from me," Sebak said to Joe. "He saw me with you. Knock him out or something."

"Sorry," Gideon said. "With the drugs, he's handicapped enough. Yes or no, Quinn?"

"Yes. But you head for the car and let me follow. Zigzag. Don't give anyone a good shot. I'll cover you." He unlocked Sebak's manacles, then pulled out his gun and pointed it at him. "Help him get Dobran to the road. If you cause us any trouble, I'll put a bullet in you, Sebak." His gaze was scanning the trees. "Go!"

Gideon moved. Joe stood in the shadows for an instant, letting his vision become accustomed to the dark as Gideon and Sebak streaked toward the car. No one on the grounds or behind the trees. What about those upper branches? If he were a sniper, that's where he would be.

But a sniper would now have to change positions because he had a prey constantly moving in a zigzag pattern.

Watch.

Look for any motion.

Which tree?

A rustle in the leaves of the oak tree.

Joe swung his gun to cover it.

An owl flew out of the branches.

But something nearby might have startled it.

The pine next to the oak.

A rifle barrel aiming, then leveling.

Shit!

Joe was aiming even as he ran toward the tree.

His shot was only a second behind that of the sniper.

That second was enough, dammit. He heard Sebak scream with terror as he watched the sniper plummet from the tree to the ground.

Joe barely glanced at the man's bloody skull as he tore across the grass toward Gideon, who was kneeling beside Dobran.

Gideon looked up at him and shook his head. "Head shot. Dead. Either the shooter was good, or I wasn't zigzagging at my top potential."

Joe muttered a curse. "He was good, and there's no doubt Dobran was the target. It was no random shot. He was being slow and careful, or I would have seen him before I did. And I went for the head. So I can't even question him."

"Then may I suggest we get out of here?" Gideon asked. "With all that noise going on in the front, I doubt if anyone heard the shots, but it's best not to risk it." He glanced at Sebak, who was curled up, frozen, a few yards away. "What do we do with him?"

"Take him with us," Joe said curtly as he turned and ran toward the car. "You're right, we have to get back to Robaku. We came up almost empty with Dobran. I'll let Novak question Sebak and see what else he can drag out of him. And as soon as we get back to the plane, I want you to call Novak and tell him to find a way to get those security videos out of the gallery museum before the police yank them and get around to scanning them. The last thing we need is for anyone to know we were here if they didn't know already. There has to be a reason why there was only one sniper waiting here for the rats to run out of the trap. We've got to have time to put everything together."

"You're calling me a rat?" Gideon jerked Sebak to his feet and pushed him toward the car. "Most unkind and inaccurate, Quinn. I've been more a beast of burden tonight..."

———————◆———————

Joe glanced at his phone the moment they were a few miles away from Asarti.

Eve.

He muttered a curse as he punched in the return. "What's wrong?"

"That's what I was about to ask you. Why didn't you answer me?"

"I was involved. Things didn't go as expected. Are you all right?"

"No." She went on quickly: "I'm okay. It just doesn't seem as if anything is all right at the moment. I just finished the reconstruction. I thought it was going to be fine, that we'd gotten lucky." She paused, then said shakily, "I was wrong. It isn't Varak."

"No, it isn't," Joe said. "Look, I have to get off the line, you stay where you are until I get back there. We'll be boarding Gideon's plane in another fifteen minutes. Let me talk to Jill."

"Why?"

"Because I don't want to relay a message through you. I have a few orders to give, and you might phrase them as requests. They are *not* requests."

Silence.

"You weren't surprised about Varak, were you? Why not?"

"Not now. You'll know everything I do as soon as I get back there. Until then, all I want is to make certain you're safe. Let me talk to Jill."

Silence.

Then Jill's voice on the line. "What's happening? Eve is upset enough without having you worry her."

"Does Novak know about the reconstruction yet?"

"No, Eve wanted you to know first. I'll call him when she hangs up from you."

"No, you will not. Novak doesn't know until I'm there to control him."

"Control? Novak? And he deserves to know. He's been in this from the beginning."

"The only one who deserves to know is Eve. But I'll probably need the two of you to get her out of this nightmare, so you'll both know as much as I do once I'm certain that I can trust Novak. He's entirely too accustomed to running the entire show, and I won't risk Eve because he has some plan I don't know about."

"He wouldn't risk her."

"And I don't trust either of you, so how would I know? We'll discuss it when I get back. Until then, no one finds out that the reconstruction is done. Eve is still working on it. As long as no one knows there's a weapon to be wielded, then no choices will be made that might put a bull's-eye on her chest."

"I won't lie to him."

"That's up to you, but if you ever want me to trust you as Eve appears to do, you'll handle it so that only you will have the responsibility. You *will* do this, Jill."

Silence. "I'll consider it."

"No, you'll keep her *safe,* and when I get there, we'll let Novak join the party. I'll see you in a couple hours, Jill." He cut the connection.

He glanced at Gideon. "Any comment?"

He shrugged. "Not unless you expect a vote of approval. I'm playing this straight down the middle. From your point of view, you might even be right about Novak. He does have an obsession about Varak that might lead him to be a little impetuous." Gideon looked him in the eye. "But then so do I. That doesn't mean I'd do anything that would hurt Eve. I don't believe he would either. But you'll have to make up your own mind. I won't get in your way as long as you don't put obstacles in my path." He smiled faintly. "It was an interesting evening. You do keep things moving, Quinn..."

—◆—

"He knew that it wasn't Varak," Eve said, as Jill handed her phone back to her. "Something happened there tonight."

"Well, we obviously won't know what it was until he gets here," Jill said sharply. "He could have spent the time he used trying to intimidate me on telling us. But evidently he didn't want to do that. And something pretty important happened tonight with us, too." She shook her head. "Sorry. I'm a little annoyed with him."

"He told you that you couldn't tell Novak," Eve said.

"Novak has a right to know. He's not going to run out and start some kind of bizarre offensive just because we're certain."

"We might be certain, but proving it is a different matter. We always knew that would be true, Jill." She looked at the reconstruction. Why could she still not shake this feeling of darkness and hate as she gazed at the skull? "And I can see why Joe might not want to jeopardize either my life or freedom."

"Do you think I can't?" Jill grimaced. "But he's put me on the spot by not letting me tell Novak. We've been on the same team, and now I'm not supposed to trust him? At least he said that it would only be until he got back here."

"You're going to do it?" Eve gazed at her in disbelief. Then she smiled faintly. "I don't believe it. You're angry with him. Why are you doing it?"

"He offered me a price I couldn't refuse. The bastard said it would help him to trust me." She got to her feet. "But I don't intend to lie to Novak. It will only take Gideon a couple hours to get Quinn here, and you're not going to be finished with this reconstruction until he walks in that door." She took out Eve's computer and opened it. "You said there were all kinds of computer details and comparisons to complete a reconstruction job. Sit down and start doing them."

Eve slowly dropped back down on her stool. To her amazement, she couldn't smother her smile. Only moments before, she had been swirling downward through confusion and terror, yet now she was feeling an instant of welcome humor. "And what if I finish before Joe shows up?"

"I've got it covered. I'll be nagging you and asking questions to make certain that computer reconstruction will have so many minute details that it will take you twice as long as it usually does." She opened her own computer. "Though I might annoy you a little."

Eve brought up her forensic programming. "And all to keep from lying to Novak?"

"And to stop your idiotically stubborn husband from saying I didn't obey his damn orders. He said to keep you safe and not tell Novak." She was focusing on the photo. "It's up to me if I do it in a way that may please both of them..." She suddenly looked up at Eve. "Do you think I'm being manipulative again?"

"Perhaps. But I can see it's sheer self-defense." And it would keep Eve busier until Joe did walk in that door. She had been frightened when he hadn't called her back, and she didn't want to think about what he'd been doing during those minutes. "I'll permit myself to be manipulated as long as I'm aware it's happening."

"It just seemed easier."

"You sound like my son, Michael. He's always certain everything would be easier if he did it."

"I'll take that. You love the kid." Jill looked down at the photo again. "Now I'll get back to doing a facial analysis, while you get busy with the victim."

Victim.

Eve felt a ripple of shock at the word.

All the time she had been working on this reconstruction, she had never consciously thought of this skull as that of a victim. The possibility had always been there, of course. But she had only felt the darkness, the antagonism, the hate. Even now, it was difficult to feel sympathy for this man who had died in Varak's place. Split personality, Jill had called it, when Eve had given the name Varak to the reconstruction. Was it the reason that lingering darkness remained?

Or was it the ferocious anger that his identity had been stolen as well as his life taken from him in this horrible way?

Either way, she had to change how she thought about him.

Not a monster but a victim.

CHAPTER

12

J oe and Gideon walked into the museum two hours and fifteen minutes later, followed closely by a very grim Novak.

"Surprise. Surprise," Novak said sarcastically as he glanced at the completed reconstruction, then at Jill. "At least a surprise for me until Quinn showed up here fifteen minutes ago and told me. But I appear to be the only one who wasn't on the need-to-know list."

"I really just finished his computer input ten minutes ago," Eve found herself saying quickly. "Stop glaring at Jill, Novak."

"But you knew two hours ago it wasn't Varak." He made an impatient gesture. "I'll deal with that later."

"No, you won't," Eve said. "My job. My decision." She turned to Joe. "How are you? I was worried. What happened in Cairo?"

"Not much that was good," Joe said. "Except that we might have acquired some valuable information to coordinate with what you found out about the ID of the reconstruction."

"But you got Dobran killed," Novak said bitterly. "He's the only witness we knew about, and he's dead. And we needed his information. I'll interrogate Sebak, but from what Gideon told me, I doubt if I'll get anything. By all means, tell them what happened at Asarti. It will be interesting to have all the cards on the table for a change."

"I'm sure it would be a great change for you," Joe said coolly. "That's why I didn't want you to know anything before I could be here to keep an eye on what you were doing." He turned to Eve. "I did get Dobran killed. As I said, there was as much bad as good that happened at Asarti." He spent the next minutes filling her in on the events of the last twenty-four hours, and ended with, "And I don't give a damn about Dobran's death, we can work around it. What I'm worried about is that whoever staged those explosions and the sniper attack will probably know in a matter of hours who was taking Dobran out of that château tonight."

"What?"

"Dobran had to be the target. We were careful, and no one knew we were in the château. It had to be a random accident that we were there at the same time as the attack. But I killed that sniper, and once they find him, they'll look for more answers."

"And who are 'they'?" Jill asked.

Joe's gaze returned to the reconstruction. "You tell me. Someone who wanted to eliminate Dobran as a witness but also wanted something Dobran had in his possession that could be plucked from his gallery in the confusion of the fire."

"But why will they know you were there?" Eve asked.

"Sebak said there was video surveillance in the gallery. Gideon was able to eliminate the cameras everywhere else but not in the gallery. And we were in too much of a hurry to get out of there with Dobran to stop and disable them."

"Amateurs," Novak said sourly.

"Walk in our shoes," Joe said curtly. "I needed Dobran. You'd do the same."

Novak was silent. "Maybe."

Joe turned back to Eve. "And once I'm identified, it will only be a short time before they'll make the connection to you. The first thing we've got to do is get you out of here."

"Do we?" Eve had known this was coming. It was Joe's protective instinct at work again. "I don't think so. Not the first thing, Joe. The first thing we have to do is figure out what happened and why. I'm not going to run away and hide from being arrested by the U.N., or whoever killed Dobran, until I know what I'm facing."

"I can take care of that once I know you're safe."

"No, Joe," she said quietly.

"Dammit, Eve." His eyes were blazing. "Dobran was a witness, and he's dead. Tonight, you proved with that reconstruction that Varak's death was a big lie. Do you think they'll let you live?"

"I haven't proved anything as long as the courts believe in the DNA. Dobran is dead, and I'd bet any lab evidence has been destroyed by now." She held up her hand as he opened his lips. "I'm just saying that we might have time to figure this out because they'll have to figure out what we know, too. I have no intention of getting myself killed." She smiled at him. "So back off and stop pushing. Now show me that statue. That could be very interesting." She looked at Gideon. "You really think it had to belong to Zahra Kiyani?"

He nodded. "Everything Dobran said indicated that it had to be her." His lips twisted. "Particularly the part where he called her a bitch. That definitely struck home." He watched as Joe dug into his backpack and pulled out the gold statue. "And it's the statue of the first Kiya. Who else would have it?"

"Who, indeed?" Jill came closer as Eve took the statue from Joe. Her gaze was lit with eagerness and curiosity as she stared down at it. "And why would she have it?" she murmured. "It's beautiful, isn't it? It must have nearly killed Zahra to have to give it up." She reached down and traced the script. "Great Beloved Wife..." She glanced at Gideon. "She never mentioned this statue to you?"

"There were things that she didn't confide. I imagine a multimillion-dollar artifact might be included in that range since she wasn't sure I was totally besotted with her." He glanced at the statue. "She should have told me about it. The fact that she had it would have definitely sparked my interest."

"She told Dobran that she had a lot of other artifacts. That it wasn't going to be the only payment," Joe said.

"I remember you said that." Eve was still looking down at the statue. Exquisite. And the idea that it might have been created in the court of Cleopatra VII added to the mystique. "Which leads us to the distinct possibility that the treasure that Kiya mentioned in her journal did exist, might still exist, and Zahra has it in her possession." She frowned. "And she still gave him this one artifact, which must have meant a good deal to her, to get him to falsify that Varak DNA."

"And in the end, that's the only thing of real importance," Novak said curtly. "All this talk of artifacts and Zahra Kiyani's obsession with them is bullshit. If Zahra is guilty of being an accomplice to Varak, then it doesn't matter whether she did a payoff at a bank in the Grand Caymans or with these artifacts. It means she's as guilty as that son of a bitch, and we have to go after her."

"No one is denying that," Jill said. "I just find it interesting as a storyteller that the story appears to be growing in scope." She met his eyes. "And I don't agree that it's not important. The fact that Zahra has a secret treasure cache worth millions, possibly billions, that she can tap at any time, automatically furnishes her with weapons. For one thing, it could have lured Varak into her camp. And since everything to do with Kiya is important to Zahra, it has also somehow become woven into this terrible connection to Varak. That makes it very important, Novak. You're just still pissed off that I didn't let you know the reconstruction was finished."

Silence. "Yes, I am." He turned to Joe. "When Gideon called me from the plane, I arranged for a couple agents to go to Asarti and blend in and see what was going on out there." He paused. "And how we can manage to cover your tracks. I should get a report soon."

"It better be very soon. Or everything may come crashing down on us." He looked at the reconstruction. "Do we agree that Zahra Kiyani has to be working hand in glove with Varak to maintain the lie that he's dead? The question is why, and how far it goes." He paused. "And how far it went while the war was still going on. If Varak was allowing her to use him as a double agent to defeat Botzan, it would make sense why her casualties were so slim."

Gideon gave a low whistle. "Oh, I can see that happening."

"But where is Varak right now?" Jill asked quietly. "Would he run the risk of staying in Maldara?"

"Questions," Eve said wearily. "So many questions." She looked at Joe. "But we still have time to get the *answers*. Let's just take a deep breath, then go after them."

"We'll see," Joe said. "As long as I don't see any sign of your becoming a target while you're doing deep-breathing exercises." He glanced at Novak. "And as long as I get that report from your people at Asarti right away."

"You'll get it," Novak said. "And now I'm going to go interrogate Sebak. I'll let you know if I find out anything more from him. It's not professional to hide information from people with the same goals." He turned and headed for the door. "You might keep that in mind, Quinn."

"I will," Joe said. "As long as you set the example." He turned to Gideon as Novak left the room. "One more thing. I want to know everything Zahra Kiyani does from now on. I need to know it all. You're familiar with the palace and know her routine better than anyone else, so you're the best one to do it."

"Lucky me. You do realize that my face is also on those videotapes? It's only a matter of time before Zahra realizes I'm not only an inconvenience but a threat." He shrugged. "So I guess I'd better get busy doing the advance prep work we need before she decides to target me." He strolled toward the door. "But you're right, I still have a few contacts in her personal entourage, and I'm very familiar with the gardens and every room in that overdone monstrosity of a presidential palace."

"Not only the bedroom?" Jill asked dryly.

"You underestimate me. I never limit myself when it comes to keeping a relationship fresh." He paused at the door, and said soberly, "Zahra's very complicated, but you can count on her striking fast and hard when she decides she's being threatened." His gaze went to the statue in Eve's hands. "And that's a threat, Eve."

The next moment, he was gone.

Eve drew a shaky breath as she shook her head. "Well, that appears clear enough." Her hands tightened on the statue for an instant before she handed it back to Joe. Why was her hand shaking? The statue wasn't that heavy. But it seemed heavy. "But I can't let myself worry about Zahra Kiyani. I created that reconstruction for only one reason, and that was to find out if Varak was still out there." She wearily rubbed her temple. "And he's alive, Joe. I haven't been able to really comprehend that yet. He's out there...waiting."

"Because you're so exhausted that you can scarcely sit on that stool," Joe said roughly, his gaze raking her face. "You've pushed yourself until you're ready to collapse." He turned to Jill. "Get out of here. Leave us alone."

"Joe, she didn't do anything," Eve said quickly.

"I know that. Not this time," Joe said. "And no one would have been able to stop you. I've been there. But now all the adrenaline is gone, and you're crashing." He glanced at Jill. "You did as good as you could under the circumstances. I just want you out so that she can draw a breath without looking or thinking about Varak for the next few hours." He stepped toward Eve and pulled her to her feet. "Come on. I promise you that we're on our way to getting the son of a bitch." He slipped his arm around her waist. "We'll just take a little time together now, okay?"

"Do I have a choice?" His arm felt strong and warm around her, and she felt secure for the first time since he'd left her so many hours ago. "I guess I do, and I choose you, Joe." He was leading her toward her cot. "I'll always choose you."

"Because you're very smart." His lips brushed her temple. "Smarter than Varak or Zahra and sometimes even me. That's why you're going to rest now." He glanced over his shoulder at Jill, who was on her way out the door. "See to it. You understand?"

Jill nodded, gazing thoughtfully at Joe, then Eve. "I believe I'm beginning to understand quite a bit." She turned back and opened the door. "Don't worry. She won't be disturbed. I'll take care of it."

———◆———

KIYANI PRESIDENTIAL PALACE

He wasn't answering her!

Zahra gazed furiously down at her blank screen. She'd texted him twice, and he was ignoring her. Arrogant bastard.

She texted again.

DID YOU GET IT? WHEN CAN I PICK IT UP?

No answer.

YOU SAID I COULD HAVE IT BACK TONIGHT. WHERE IS IT?

At last an answer.

THERE'S A PROBLEM. I'LL TEXT YOU LATER.

She stiffened. No, this couldn't be happening. He had promised her!

I WON'T TOLERATE THIS. I'VE BEEN WAITING TOO LONG. I WANT IT NOW.

The answer came with swift brutality.

YOU'LL GET WHAT I CHOOSE TO GIVE YOU WHEN I CHOOSE TO DO IT.

The screen went blank.

Rage.

She closed her eyes, trying to subdue the anger. This was her fault, she had allowed him to intimidate her until he thought she was just another one of his cowed whores. And it had come down to this indignity.

It was over. She would not let it go on!

"Dalai!" She got to her feet as the maid came running out of the anteroom. "Come with me. We're going out."

Over an hour later, Dalai was driving Zahra off the main road and through the thick foliage of the jungle that surrounded and hid the armed compound and large house.

Zahra phoned as she got closer. "I'll be there in a few minutes. Call off your men, Varak."

"I've known exactly where you were since you got off the road. What a fool you are. I'm tempted to sit here and watch them blow you to bits."

"You won't do that. I'm too valuable to you. I'm not afraid of you." That was a lie. There were moments when she was afraid, but not of physical abuse. She was afraid of his reckless egotism and his power to send all her plans toppling. "So threaten all those idiots around you who can't see through you. I'm done with bowing down at your altar to feed that ego." She hung up.

Five minutes later, Dalai drove her up to the gates of the stockade, where Lon Markel was standing guard. Zahra leaned forward and nodded curtly at him. "Open those gates. I have to see him, Markel."

"Did he give you permission?" Markel asked with the hint of a sneer. "You know that he—"

"Open those gates!" Markel was *her* agent, only on loan to Varak, and he was daring to question her! It just showed how much respect had been stolen from her by that son of a bitch. "Now!"

He shrugged, opened the gates, and stood aside.

Two minutes later, Dalai screeched to a stop before the long porch of the house.

"Do you wish me to come in, madam?" Dalai asked. She was tense with nervousness as she watched the door open and Varak come out on the porch.

She was actually trembling, Zahra noticed impatiently. You'd think she'd have learned to control herself by now. But just one glimpse of Varak, and she was falling apart. "I haven't decided." She got out of the car. "Stay here, I'll let you know." She strode up the steps, her gaze on Varak. He was staring straight at her, and she could see why a weakling like Dalai might be afraid of him. The expensive plastic surgery for which Zahra had paid an enormous fee might disguise his features, but those dark eyes were piercing, and the power and ferocity were unmistakable. His black hair had been dyed to a pale sandy shade and allowed to grow longer than his usual cropped cut because she had thought it might soften his appearance. Perhaps it did at first glance, but that was also a failure in Zahra's opinion. All these temporary measures were only safe as long as everyone was certain Varak was dead.

"What do you think you're doing?" Varak said harshly. "I told you not to come here again. You could have led them right to me. People are always watching you."

"And I'm supposed to pay any attention to what you tell me to do?" She stopped before him, glaring. "And I'm no fool. I went out the secret panel, and I leave a car parked in a garage down the street. No one saw me."

"I know they didn't, or I wouldn't have let you come near here. Do you think I didn't know you'd do something like this?" He turned and walked back into the house. "Come in. I don't want my men seeing your tantrum." His lips twisted. "Or I'd have to either beat you or cut your throat. I don't allow myself to show weakness to them as I've demonstrated to you on many occasions." He poured himself a drink from the bar just inside the door. "You like that about me, don't you, Zahra?"

"I like to see power at work. It amused me to watch them grovel." She added through set teeth, "But I'm not amused now, Varak, and I won't grovel to you. What are you trying to do? Give me my statue."

"I'm trying to give it to you, bitch," he said. "I told you that there was a problem. I'm not playing mind games with you." He drank down his whiskey. "And I have more to worry about than your fancy statue. Something weird happened at Asarti last night that might be more important to both of us."

"Nothing is more important. Give me my statue."

"I'd have to find it first. Because it wasn't at Asarti."

She went still. "What?"

"Interested now?" Varak asked. "You weren't interested in anything about the way I was going to get the statue back. You just snapped your fingers and said you wanted it."

"You said you'd get it back from Dobran a few days after the skull was identified as you. You *promised* me. But he still has it."

"He has nothing. Dobran is dead. I had a sniper set up to take him out last night."

"Good. Then why don't I have my statue?"

"You were going to have it," he said harshly. "I was tired of hearing you nag me. I thought I'd get you off my back about the statue in case I had to go to Robaku and take out that Duncan woman in the next couple days. I knew I couldn't trust you to do it."

"My statue," she reminded him.

"I was going to eliminate Dobran as a witness and take the statue at the same time. I sent in a team to bomb the place and start fires that would block all the entrances and force them to use the one through the gallery. Dobran liked that statue, too, and I knew he and Sebak would go after it and out the gallery exit if they were forced to run. Then all I had to do was put several of my men with the fire and police departments who answered the alarm. They'd only have to break into the gallery and find a way to grab the statue and smuggle it out of the château. Not a difficult job in all the confusion that would be going on." He poured himself another drink. "It should have worked. I should have rid myself of Dobran, and you would have had your statue."

"Should?"

"I got Dobran." He lifted his glass to his lips. "Unfortunately, Nolan, my sniper, was also taken out by someone equally efficient." He sipped his whiskey. "And I just heard from the team who went into the gallery to get your damn statue that it had already been stolen. No sign of other thefts, just that one artifact. Unless Dobran decided to sell it."

"Not *my* statue." Her eyes were blazing. "Stolen? What really happened to it? Dobran loved it, he wouldn't have let it be stolen, and certainly not purchased."

"Maybe not. I'm leaning toward agreeing with you. We have the murder of my very talented sniper to consider. As I said, something weird happened up there last night. We might not have been the only ones who were after Dobran, and that's much more threatening than anyone's taking your statue."

"Then you should have gotten all this taken care of before anyone else had a chance to go after Dobran or my statue. I told you enough times that I wanted it done."

"Forget the statue!" He suddenly hurled his glass across the room to crash against the wall. Then his hands were around her throat. "You listen to me," he hissed. "You're not stupid. I wouldn't have gotten on your merry-go-round if I'd thought you were. Now stop acting as if you're an imbecile. I might have saved us both by taking out Dobran last night, but it might be too late if someone is onto us and got to him first. We've got to think about saving our asses."

His grip was bruising her throat. For an instant, she was feeling panic mixed with her fury. He always liked to hurt her. She knew how brutal he could be. "Let me go, Varak. How dare you speak to me this way. Stupid? I'm the one who had you brought to me when you were only one of Botzan's dirty mercenaries. I gave you the chance to come out of this war alive and richer than you ever dreamed." She stared him in the eye. "I've protected you, hidden you. I've done everything for you, and I've only asked you to do a few small things to keep our heads above water during a difficult time."

"A few 'small' things?" His thumbs pressed harder into her neck. "Play a double game and attack when and where you told me? Help you to set up your fancy image with the U.N., so they'd choose you to run this son of a bitch of a country?" He bent his head and his tongue touched the hollow of her throat. He whispered, "And make certain that papa dearest was killed in a timely manner so that you could take over the presidency?"

She inhaled sharply. "I did what was necessary. He wouldn't listen to me. He wanted to negotiate peace with them. You made no objection at the time." She went on the attack. "And as long as you continue to cooperate, I'll protect you . . . provided you protect me. But I won't let you destroy what I'm building. I'll get you out of Maldara as soon as it's safe. Then all you'll have to do is arrange to move my treasure safely out of Maldara for me, and I'll give you the share I promised."

"If it even exists; you've never let me see it." His fingers pressed harder. "I'm beginning to doubt you, Zahra. You don't want that to happen."

"Don't be foolish. It would be dangerous to take you there. I showed you the Great Beloved Wife, didn't I? Dobran jumped at getting it. You could see how valuable it is." She met his eyes. "I promise that as soon as I have the treasure secure, I'll buy you an island somewhere, and you can set up your own little kingdom."

"You have it all planned." He dropped his hands from around her throat. "But it's my decision, and an island sounds boring. I liked the life I was living before you dropped into my world. When we split that treasure, I'll look at my options."

That was what she was beginning to fear. She reached up and massaged the bruised flesh of her throat. The prick had hurt her this time. "I just want to keep you safe."

"I'm touched, Zahra." His lips twisted. "But you'd do better to think about keeping us both safe by helping me find out what happened at Asarti."

"You said you'd take care of that." She paused. "You really think that it might be more than just a theft? That someone knew that Dobran did the DNA?" She was getting more nervous as she thought about it. "It might not be so bad. No one could trace the statue to me. I took it from the treasure."

"You're back to covering your ass."

She made an impatient gesture. "What are you going to do?"

"My team at Asarti who slipped in with the firemen haven't been able to get the security videotapes of the gallery yet. They'll go back later and try again. That might tell us something. But that's not all. Hassan Sebak has disappeared. We need to track him down."

"Sebak didn't know about you. I made it a condition that the DNA remain absolutely confidential." She shrugged. "But, by all means, go after him. He might have stolen my statue, and all this worry might be for nothing. Besides, we have to remain safe."

"I notice which one you put first," he said sarcastically. "How nice of you to give me permission. But I've already set it in motion." He turned away and stripped off his shirt. "Now take off your clothes and lie down on that couch."

She had half expected it. Her resistance always aroused a sexual response in Varak. On occasion, she had actually used it to stir the passion hotter. But that was when she had attempted to use sex to bind them tighter together, when she'd had hopes that Varak might be someone she could control as she hadn't been able to control Gideon. But lately she had realized that Varak would not be controlled either, and the sex was only to subdue her.

He snapped his fingers and repeated mockingly, "Take off your clothes, Zahra."

Arrogant bastard. She shook her head. "I have to get back to the palace."

"But our agreement is that I'm never to be without amusement out here in the wilds. Have you forgotten?"

"I send you women to amuse you all the time."

"But I'm bored with them. They're whores, and nothing is new or exciting. No matter what I do to them, they just accept it." He smiled. "While you accept nothing without a battle. I want you to scream for me."

For a minute, she was tempted to pit her skill against his. But it was a struggle she was never sure she could win with him. She couldn't afford to lose when so much was at stake. "Not now." She turned to go. "But you enjoyed Dalai the last few times you had her. Fear is also exciting for you. I brought her with me in case I needed to negotiate." She looked at him over her shoulder. "I imagine you have no trouble making *her* scream?"

He smiled. "No trouble at all. She's like a startled doe most of the time. But you've trained her well, she never says no. Though I always prefer your services."

"She'll have to do. Don't damage her too badly. She's valuable to me. And I'll need her back by tomorrow."

She opened the door and motioned for Dalai to come into the house.

The girl was already tensing as she got out of the car, Zahra noticed. She had gone pale and was looking beyond Zahra at the open door.

Panic.

No, Varak would have no problem making her scream.

———◆———

ROBAKU

Jill called Novak the moment she walked out of the museum.

He didn't answer.

She called again.

No answer.

And then again.

He answered curtly, "What do you want, Jill?"

"I need to talk to you. Quinn just kicked me out of the museum, and I can't just sit and do nothing. Where are you?"

"In the village. Hajif set me up with a vacant hut to use as an office, and I'm trying to coordinate the men I sent to Asarti to gather information."

"Can I help?"

"No."

Time to eat crow. "I realize you're pissed off at me, and you have a right to be."

"Damn straight."

"Quinn doesn't trust you. Not me either, but I'm working on it." She paused. "And I knew it would only be a couple hours delay. It didn't seem too bad. What can I do to make it right with you?"

He didn't answer.

"What can I do?" she repeated.

"The eternal question with you." He was suddenly walking toward her out of the brush and turning off his phone. "You should have stuck with Quinn. As you said, I'm more pissed off with you than he is right now."

"It wasn't really Quinn, it was Eve. I had to balance what she—" He had put his fingers over her lips, and she looked up at him, startled.

"Hush," he said. "I'm trying very hard not to confuse this anger with anything more emotional or sexual. But since it's always there, it's a factor. Along with the fact that I find myself oddly hurt that you didn't trust me to handle this situation. That's very weird in itself. But it will help if you don't make excuses or tell me you owe me anything." He took his fingers away. "Now why did Quinn kick you out?"

Her lips still felt warm and tingling even though his touch was gone. "He wanted her to rest." She moistened her lips. "I was just another disturbance."

"Yes, you are." His lips twisted. "So he tossed you to me?"

"No, he wouldn't care where I went. She's the only thing important to him. It's kind of nice. Warm..." She met his gaze. "It was my choice to come to you, Novak. Because I do trust you." She added simply, "How could I do anything else after what you've done for me? No matter how much you want your own way, you'd never do anything to hurt me. I'll always come to you if you'll let me."

He was silent. "Oh, shit." He took a step toward her. Then he stopped abruptly. "You leave yourself wide open, dammit. You haven't been paying any attention to what I've been saying to you, have you?"

"Sure I have." She smiled with an effort. "Some of it sort of scared me. I'm really not the kind of person anyone would obsess about. I don't know what I'd do with you if I didn't believe you'd probably change your mind before all this is over."

"I can offer suggestions," he said thickly. "And you must be wrong because the obsession is definitely there." He paused. "But there's nothing I'd do to you that should scare you."

"You're back to walking wounded again?" She shook her head in exasperation. "For Pete's sake, it's not about sex." Though that was patently untrue. She couldn't get near him without this feeling of heat and electricity. She drew a deep breath. "Is it okay if we don't talk about this? I just wanted you to know that I do trust you. And it's important that you not shut me out of anything when everything seems to be exploding around us."

"Heaven forbid that you miss one single minute of any combustion coming our way," he said dryly.

She nodded. "Heaven forbid," she echoed quietly. "It's my story, my responsibility, and if I don't tell it, then it might not get told. And I brought Eve into this, and now Quinn is involved." She made a face. "You might say I even brought you into this, Novak."

"The hell you did."

"I came to you. Just as I'm coming to you now. You turned me down then. Don't turn me down this time."

He swore under his breath. "Low blow, Jill."

She nodded. "Yes. But I speak fluent Egyptian and Arabic. Can't you use me to find out what's happening in Cairo?"

"Possibly."

"Novak."

"Hell, yes, I'll use you," he said roughly. "Haven't I done that from the beginning? Quinn's right, we've got to either eliminate or delay anyone's finding out who killed that sniper and was in the château tonight. And we need time to get a plan together. Which means we have to get our hands on those gallery videotapes. I'll see if I can patch you into the local Cairo police from the Museum of Egyptian Antiquities, and you can express concern that some of the antiquities on loan to Dobran might have also been stolen. In short, lie through your teeth and work your magic."

She nodded, frowning thoughtfully. "I can do that. But it might be better if I contact a friend of mine, Matt Kimbro, who's a reporter for the *Cairo Messenger* and also does freelance. He knows most of the players in the government and police department. I worked with him during the nine months when I was covering riots in Cairo. He's been there for years, and he knows where all the bodies are buried." She grimaced. "And believe me, in Cairo, that's a hell of a lot of bodies. He owes me a favor, and I could ask him to call a few people and maybe follow up with the police and security company." She shrugged. "Or I could do both."

"Yes, you could." His lips were quirking. "And probably will." His smile faded. "And I'm glad there's someone who owes you a favor instead of your being obsessed with payback."

"I'm not obsessed, there just has to be a code, or nothing makes sense." She was taking out her phone and checking the directory. "And in my profession, I've found it's always more valuable to have someone owe me. It just didn't turn out that way with you."

"And why does this Kimbro owe you?"

"I'll never tell." She grinned as she started to punch in Kimbro's number. "Because that would be breaking the code."

"I'll find out, you know," he said softly. "I can always find out whatever I need to find out. And there's nothing I'm not going to know about you, Jill."

"The CIA showing all its black hat–white hat power. You have a tendency to surround and conquer." She met his eyes. "Did it occur to you that might be why you scare me? Who wants anyone to know everything about them? I'd feel smothered. Stay out of my private life, Novak."

He was silent. "I don't know if I can." He paused. "I'll have to see how it works out." He turned and headed back toward the village. "When you finish setting up Kimbro, come and let me know, and I'll give you something else to do. I wouldn't want to waste your talents."

The long facial bones...

Not right. But so close.

Eve could see them before her even though her eyes were still shut. She moved restlessly on the cot as she realized how close...Just like the shape of those orbital cavities...

Too close.

It seemed impossible that all those details could be that identical and not actually be Varak. It didn't make sense, Eve thought frantically. Had she done something wrong? They all thought she was perfect. But she wasn't perfect, she could make mistakes. And what if Varak was the biggest mistake of her life? She had told them the reconstruction wasn't Varak, but the resemblance was too close. It didn't make sense. But what had she done wrong? Why had she made that mistake? Why were those orbital cavities—

"The brother!" Eve's lids flew open, and she sat bolt upright on the cot. "He has to be the brother."

"Shh, go back to sleep," Joe said. "Nightmare?"

"Only the same one that I've been living with while I've been doing this reconstruction. And I can't go back to sleep. The minute I woke up, I started to worry about the shape of his damn eyes." She threw aside the sheet and swung her feet to the floor. "When I was first looking at the photo of Varak, I thought that the reconstruction I had made had to be him. There were so many similarities. It was only when I actually compared them that I realized that I hadn't been working on Varak's skull." She was moving across the museum to her worktable. "But I got caught up in the computer verification; and then Jill was upset with what you were forcing her to do about Novak. Things kept getting in my way." She was dropping down on her stool and looking at the reconstruction. "And I didn't make the connection. I should have made the connection, Joe. It was stupid of me not to realize who he was."

"And it only took five hours of sleep to send the stupidity packing." Joe was on his feet and strolling toward her. "Before you start working again, don't you think you should put on some clothes?"

"I'm not going to work," she said absently. "I just wanted to take one more look at him. I was so scared, I'd made a mistake. There was all that darkness and anger... And the bone-structure similarities. If you compare it with the photo, you can see it."

"I'll accept your word for it." He put his hands on her shoulders as he stood behind her, gazing down at the reconstruction. "The brother? You think this was Varak's brother? He's never been mentioned. I don't remember his even having a brother."

"I didn't know either until Jill told me about him. He had no part in Varak's life after he was a teenager. He was Varak's younger brother, Oscar, and, as far as I know, they hadn't seen each other for years. He was afraid of him because he'd been bullied all his life." She shivered as she gazed at the reconstruction. "He had good reason to be afraid. There's nothing more cold-blooded than choosing your own brother to die in your place." She reached out and touched the orbital bone of the left eye with her finger. "But it was a clever choice. Not only was the bone structure similar, but even the DNA would have been similar if the minutest trace was found outside of Dobran's work. Insurance, Joe."

"You're fairly certain?"

"It's a very good bet." She looked up at him. "And that's going to help us, isn't it? We needed to find out who he was before we could claim he wasn't Varak. He was a murder victim, Joe. There's a chance that there might have been a witness to it. Or at least someone might have seen Varak with Oscar during the period right before his supposed death." She was trying to think of everything Jill had told her. "Johannesburg. His brother was supposed to have gone back home to Johannesburg after he split with Nils Varak. Can we trace him that way?"

"I'll trace him, you'll stay out of it." Joe held up his hand. "Look, you've done what you set out to do. No one is more dangerous than you to Varak now. You've shot holes in the fancy scenario he rigged up with Zahra Kiyani." He shook his head as she started to speak. "And don't tell me it doesn't mean anything if the courts accept the DNA over your work. It does mean something because you're so well respected. Why do you think Novak wanted you on his team? Jill might have wanted your expertise, but Novak knew that you could influence people and change minds. You'll stir up a hornet's nest, and Varak will come out and try to squash you before you do damage."

"But that's a good thing," she said quietly. "We want to bring him out, don't we? It will be easier for us."

"To use you as bait?" Joe shook his head. "Forget it. I want you out of Maldara. I'm going to send you to London and pull strings to surround you with every man from the Yard that I can beg or steal."

"I notice you say you're going to send me, not take me. Because you told me this had to be finished, didn't you? There's no way you're going to let Varak get away now that you know he's alive. You'll stay here and do what I should be doing while I'm palling around with all your buddies from Scotland Yard."

"It's the reasonable thing to do. You don't have to be here, Eve."

"No? I don't see it that way. I brought you here, Joe." She looked back at the reconstruction. "And *he* brought me. Jill thinks she's responsible for involving everyone in this nightmare, but it was Varak. Because he's alive, we're all swirling around him, drowning in what he is and what he's done. I won't go away and take a chance on letting him pull anyone else into that whirlpool." She smiled with an effort. "But you've convinced me how important I am, so I'll stay here at Robaku, where Novak and you can protect me." She paused. "Unless we can think of a way to use me with more efficiency."

"Eve."

"No, it's not done. *I'm* not done. I can't stir up any hornet's nest right now because if Varak doesn't go after me, he'll go on the run. We can't afford to have him do that, Joe. So I'll stay here and work on Mila, be a thorn in both Varak's and Zahra's asses, and we'll try to think of a better way to build a rat trap to catch them." She drew a deep breath and had to stop. This had been too painful. She always hated conflict with Joe when she knew it was pain and worry driving him. She had to get away from him and recover. She got to her feet. "And now I'll go get dressed. You're right, nudity lacks a certain dignity when I'll probably have to argue about this with Jill and Novak, too."

A muscle jerked in Joe's cheek. "Not Novak."

"We'll see." She headed for the bathroom. "I've been getting a different viewpoint about him lately. Jill trusts him."

"Eve," Joe said. "Don't do this."

She stopped at the door of the bathroom. "I know you're unhappy about it. But I can't do anything else." She opened the door, and added simply, "Because whenever I close my eyes, I see that schoolroom, Joe."

CHAPTER

13

Jill was waiting when Eve came out of the bathroom forty-five minutes later. She was staring at the reconstruction and looked up as Eve crossed the room toward her. "You really think it's the brother?"

"I do. I'm surprised you didn't think of it before I did. You're the storyteller. It's definitely a macabre twist on the story of Varak."

"It probably would have come to me eventually. I was just upset and a bit scattered at the time. But it does make sense."

"Now we have to find proof that Varak murdered his brother or try to discover when and where he disappeared. Hopefully, it will be about the time that helicopter exploded in the mountains."

"Quinn and Novak are already working on it. Dobran took a flight somewhere the day after he accepted that statue. It would be logical if it was to Johannesburg to examine and accept the body of Oscar Varak and prepare it for the DNA implant," Jill said. "Why do you think I'm here? Quinn came storming down to the village and told Novak that he had to put a trace on Varak's brother and determine if this is really him." She nodded at the reconstruction. "He wants all the puzzle pieces we have to be in place before anyone discovers that the skull is gone from that U.N. headquarters." She grimaced. "I got the impression he was trying desperately to stave off having you tossed in jail. I told him I wouldn't allow that to happen."

"If I remember correctly, you didn't give me the same promise," Eve said dryly. "You just said you'd be in the cell next to mine."

"Well, I didn't think that would go over well with him. He's still very tentative with me. Instead, I decided I'd come here and let Novak deal with him and see if you need any help."

"Only with information. What's been happening? It seems as if I slept for a long time."

"Not for a normal person." She shrugged. "I managed to get a reporter friend, Matt Kimbro, to go and squeeze information out of the local Cairo police. The police did collect all the security videos in the château, but they hadn't gotten around to viewing them yet. They're still in the evidence room."

Eve stiffened. "But they will view them. It's only a matter of time. And they'll find out it was Joe in that gallery."

"Maybe." She paused. "I told Kimbro it was important to me that I get hold of those gallery tapes. The evidence room might not be a problem for him if his contact is on duty. It's like the rest of the police department in Cairo. Bad and good. It's not that unusual for things to go missing...if the price is right. He said he'd let me know."

"A very good friend," Eve said. "To risk getting arrested."

"Yes. But he's smart, and I told him if it gets down to taking any serious chances, he's to call me, and I'll get him help. I'll go myself if necessary. Together, we'll be able to do it."

"And get yourself arrested, too?"

"We have to get those security tapes. It could hurt Quinn *and* you."

"Then let Novak go help your friend Kimbro."

"I will if it's more efficient. But Kimbro trusts me, and he was more likely to be accommodating if I was in the background. He's *my* friend, and he owes *me,* not Novak." She smiled. "And Kimbro might not need help. I told you, he's smart." She changed the subject. "Now, what other information do you need? Oh, Gideon has already gone to the presidential palace in Jokan to see what information he can gather about Zahra Kiyani. That's all I know right now. Sorry, more later."

"Nothing to be sorry about. It's fairly substantial." She was rifling through her cabinet and pulling out the reconstruction she'd begun on Mila. She carefully put the Varak reconstruction in the cabinet in its place. "And certainly more productive than what I'll be doing."

"I can't believe that."

"Believe it," Eve said curtly. "Sitting here and working is the only way I'll be able to keep Joe from going ballistic. He wanted me to fly back to London to cozy up with Scotland Yard."

"He told us." She hesitated. "Not a bad idea, Eve."

"You should have thought of that when you brought me here," she said curtly. "There's no way I can go back and forget everything I've seen and learned in Robaku." She glanced at her. "And you knew that would happen, so don't let me hear that again from you."

"Just a comment," Jill said. "Maybe because I wish I could take it all back."

"I know you do." She began to put in the depth markers. "Too late." She added, "So make amends and work with me to find that son of a bitch who killed these kids."

"You know I will." She turned away. "I'll go down to the village and get you something to eat. You've lit a fire under Quinn, and I doubt if he'll be here anytime soon. Maybe by the time I come back, I'll be able to give you another report. Anything else I can do?"

"Not unless you've taken up forensic sculpting." Eve waved her hand. "Out with you. Let me get into Mila."

"On my way." Jill headed for the door. "I guess I'm used to staying close and watching out for you. No need of that now. Quinn and Novak have arranged a virtual army to guard you."

I don't doubt that, Eve thought. The knowledge tended to smother her. But she shouldn't complain, it was all part of the surveillance which she'd told Joe she'd accept.

And she wasn't complaining; it was just difficult.

Mila. This little girl deserved her attention. Think of Mila.

———◆———

"Fruit. And a salad creation that Leta made for you from Hajif's garden. The dressing is spicy but good," Jill said as she came back into the museum two hours later. She set the tray down on Eve's worktable. "No protein. But I'll work on that for your supper." She glanced at Mila as she went to the cooler to get Eve a water. "How's it coming?"

"Fine." She pushed back and started to eat the salad. "You're right, this dressing is good. What's Joe doing? I take it not making salad. Did he find out anything from Scotland Yard?"

"Only the brother's background. After Oscar went back to Johannesburg, he was into everything from petty thievery to gunrunning. No connection with his big brother during that time. It's pretty clear he wanted the break to be permanent. For the last seven years, he was involved with piracy in the Indian Ocean. He was first mate on a schooner that raided corporate ships and held executives for ransom. At least two of the prisoners were executed during those years. Oscar definitely was not a pleasant man. He learned a lot from big brother."

"But he was an amateur compared to Varak," Eve said. "And the last lesson he learned evidently was a horror story. Was he definitely back in Johannesburg at the time Dobran flew down for a visit?"

"Novak is checking that out." She shook her head. "It seems Quinn and Novak are working in tandem. Pretty scary, huh?"

"Intimidating. But it probably won't—"

Jill's phone was ringing. "Hold that thought." She glanced at the ID. "Cairo. It's Kimbro." She answered. "What's the word, Kimbro? Can you get the tapes?"

He sighed. "I'm afraid not. It's impossible." Then he chuckled.

"Because I've already got them. You persist in underestimating me, Jill. They're tucked in my camera bag right now. Piece of cake."

Jill breathed a sigh of relief. "No trouble?"

"Just a return of favors. I slipped in and slipped out of that evidence room with my customary grace and style, leaving a hefty bribe behind. Which you will return to me with interest."

"Why should I? You owed me." She added teasingly, "And it was a piece of cake."

"So that I won't consider you in my debt now. I know you, Jill." He paused. "But to make sure, I'll accept another bribe. I want to know why you were ready to let me run that risk to get these tapes. You're usually boringly protective." He added, "And I want in on the story."

Jill's smile faded. "No, you don't. Not this story. Not now, Kimbro."

"It must be one hell of a scoop," he said softly. "If not now, when?"

"Soon. Don't push me, Kimbro. I won't shut you out. I promised you that you'd get the story of a lifetime. Just don't go probing into anything concerning Asarti. Okay?"

He sighed. "Okay. I guess you want these tapes right away? Where can I drop them off?"

"Where are you now?"

"Having breakfast at a sidewalk café about six blocks from the police station."

"Cocky."

"Why not? I told you it was a piece of cake. No problem at all. Really simple. You'd have been proud of me."

"Yeah." But she was beginning to be distinctly uneasy. "But sometimes things can be too simple. We've both gotten in hot water when we least expected it. Look around you, is there anyone there in the restaurant who looks familiar?"

"Not really. You're too suspicious." Silence. "Maybe that guy in the gray suit with no tie who's reading the newspaper. But I can't be sure."

"Then pretend you *are* sure and do me a favor. Get up and walk out of that restaurant. Don't look as if you're in a hurry. Stroll, don't run. Take a taxi and go back to your apartment and lock the door. I'll send someone to meet you and pick up those tapes."

Silence. "What is this, Jill?"

"Just do it, okay? I'm not sure if it's necessary. But it will make me feel better. Don't play games. Be careful. Call me when you get to your apartment." She hesitated. "And I think perhaps it might be a good idea if you go with the person who comes to get the tapes. I'll let you know when you call me."

Silence. "You're nervous about me. This must be nasty."

"Very nasty. I told you that in the beginning."

"You're going to feel very foolish about this if you're wrong. I'll rub it in, you know."

"I can take it. Are you leaving the restaurant?"

"I just threw some cash down on the table. I'm strolling, not running. There's a taxi down the street. You'll owe me for cab fare, too."

"Fine. Has the man in the gray suit moved?"

"No, he's still reading his newspaper. Looks like you're wrong."

"Good. Thanks, Kimbro. Call me as soon as you get to your apartment."

"You can bet I will. I didn't finish my breakfast. I'll use it as a guilt trip to make you tell me why you wanted these tapes. See you, Jill." He cut the connection.

"What's happening?" Eve asked.

"Maybe nothing." Jill was dialing Novak. "But Kimbro managed to get hold of those tapes, and I'd really like Novak to have them picked up right away."

"And your friend, Kimbro, too?"

"It might be a good idea to have Novak's men look over the situation and see if it's a good idea." She was biting her lower lip. "I don't have a good reason. I guess I'm allergic to having everything go just as it should. It's not been happening much since I came to Maldara. It makes me nervous." Novak picked up, and she said quickly, "We've got the security tapes. Kimbro is on his way to his apartment now." She rattled off the address. "Send someone to pick them up right away." She paused. "And make certain whoever you send knows what he's doing. Okay?"

"Why?"

"Because Kimbro is my friend, and I'm not taking chances. Don't argue with me, Novak. I've got what we needed. Now you do your part."

He was silent. "Orders? I'll send Nassem." He hung up the phone.

"Mission accomplished?" Eve asked as she watched Jill slip her phone in her pocket. "You were pretty sharp. You don't usually speak to Novak like that."

"He'll survive. I wanted him to get off the phone and do what I needed." She shrugged. "I know it was overkill, and he'll make me pay for it later. It seemed the thing to do at the time." She looked at the food on the tray in front of Eve. "You've scarcely touched your salad. Can I get you anything else?"

"No, I'll finish this. I've been a little busy listening to you." She made a face. "Stop hovering over me. I know you want to go back down to the village and make sure Novak is doing what you want him to do. Go!"

Jill smiled. "As you command." She headed for the door. "It's ridiculous, you know. I'm overreacting."

"Or it might be instinct," Eve said soberly as she gazed back at her Mila reconstruction. "I believe in instinct. I hope that you *are* overreacting. Let me know when Novak's agent actually has those security tapes in his hands."

"You'll be the first to know."

"I'd better be," she said wryly. "It appears that I'm the only one who is out of the loop."

Five minutes later, Jill had reached the hut where Joe and Novak had set up shop. Joe was no longer there, but Novak appeared to be just as busy as when she'd left. She hesitated at the door.

"Stop dithering," Novak said without looking up from his computer. "Yes, I did contact Nassem, and he'll be at Kimbro's apartment in thirty minutes. Satisfied?"

"Yes, you did the best you could." She came into the hut. Hajif had only managed to produce the one small bench where Novak was sitting for the makeshift office, but there were colorful blankets placed around the hut against the walls. Jill dropped down on one of the blankets and leaned back against the wall. "And it might not even be necessary. He was pretty sure he wasn't followed."

"But he's your friend." Novak's voice was without expression. "And with you, that means commitment and, therefore, possible inconvenience for me. I'm beginning to become accustomed to it."

"Poor you." She grinned. "Where's Quinn?"

"He received a call from his son. He wanted privacy."

"And probably to ensure that he not reveal a softer side to you," she said. "That's reserved for Eve and company." She took out her phone. "What other calls do you want me to make now that we've nailed down the security tapes?"

"You can call Gideon and see if he's made any contacts in Zahra Kiyani's august household yet."

"Busywork?"

"Maybe. You seem to be a little edgy. But useful busywork. Gideon sometimes gets carried away and goes in depth with any project. He needs structure."

"He's brilliant. You're lucky to have him."

"But I don't have him, that's my point. No one has him. He might go off in any direction if it pleases him. But he might be less likely to stray from the path if you're around."

"I'm not his guardian." She added slyly, "If that's what you want, then I should have gone with him."

"That's not what I want," he said flatly. "And you know it. Stay away from Zahra. Just check on Gideon. If nothing else, it will keep your mind off Kimbro."

"Busywork," she repeated. But she still dialed Gideon's number. No answer. She tried it again. In the middle of the ring, she got another call.

Kimbro.

She quickly pressed accept. "Are you in your apartment?"

"Locking the door now. Happy?"

"Moderately. Herb Nassem, a CIA operative, will be picking up the security tapes in about twenty minutes. Don't give them to anyone else."

"Can I ply him with liquor and see if I can talk him into telling me why those tapes are so important?"

"No, he has no idea. You weren't followed?"

"No. Not even that guy in the restaurant. He never stirred from that table when I got in the cab." He paused. "All kidding aside, you're not getting into anything over your head? I'm here for you if you are. Iron Man is my middle name. You don't need to get involved with these CIA guys. They can be trouble."

"Tell me about it," she said dryly. He might still want the story, but she was touched anyway. "I'll call you if I need to ditch them. But I hear Nassem is reliable. If he wants to pull you out of there, go with him."

"If you insist . . . and promise to keep in touch."

"Absolutely. When Nassem gets there, let me know. Thanks, Kimbro." She cut the connection and looked up to see Novak gazing at her. "He says he wasn't followed and that CIA can be trouble. I agree. But I'll give them the benefit of the doubt if this Nassem comes through." She grinned. "Probably not you. You're too far gone."

"Definitely." He tilted his head. "You're relieved."

"So far. I'll feel better once Kimbro gives the tapes to your guy. He should be there in another twenty minutes. I want this over."

Novak nodded and turned back to his calls. "It sounds as if you've got it covered."

"I hope I do." She started to dial Gideon again. "I couldn't reach Gideon before. While I'm waiting for Kimbro's call, I'll try him again..."

———————◆———————

But it wasn't over in twenty minutes.

No call from Kimbro.

It didn't mean anything, Jill told herself. Nassem could have been stuck in traffic or something. Cairo was always a traffic nightmare...

Another fifteen minutes.

No call.

She started to dial Kimbro.

It went to voice mail.

Shit.

Her hand was shaking as she started to punch in the number again.

"I've already tried him twice," Novak said quietly.

She went still. "What?"

"Nassem always has orders to call his superior, Karim Absar, when he makes contact with the subject. He was on his way up in the elevator after he reached the apartment building when he checked in twenty minutes ago. But he didn't call back after contacting Kimbro." He paused. "And he didn't answer when Absar called."

"So you called Kimbro," she said shakily.

"Twice."

"You said that." She moistened her lips. "Something must have happened. We should call the police or an emergency number." She rubbed her temple. "No, not the police. Stupid. We just robbed the damn police. The medical-emergency number. I think it's 123 in Cairo."

"My people will be faster. When they couldn't contact Nassem, I told them to get over to Kimbro's apartment right away. They should be arriving any minute."

"Efficient. You're always so efficient, Novak." She was having trouble concentrating on what she was saying. All she could think about was Kimbro. "You called him. Why didn't you tell me?"

"You were already worried. There was no use making it worse until I was sure that it was necessary. It could have been anything. It didn't have to be—" He stopped. "We're still not sure what problem they might have run into. We won't know until Absar's team gets there."

"But you have an idea, don't you?" She drew a deep breath. "Of course, we both do. But he didn't think he was followed, Novak."

"And he might not have been. If they had an ID on him after he took the tapes, they might have just gotten his address and been there waiting for him to show. Or his tail might have been very, very good."

"He might not have had to be that good. Kimbro was cocky. Piece of cake." She could feel her eyes stinging. "He said it was a piece of cake."

He muttered a curse. "We don't *know*, Jill."

She nodded. "We have to wait. You're right, we should find out soon." *Keep control.* Novak was being his usual professional self, and she had to follow his lead. But it was so hard. She linked her arms around her drawn-up knees and held them tight. "I told him to hold off, and I'd get him help, but he thought he could do it without any help. Cocky. He's always so cocky. And he had the deal made before I even knew it. I should have known he'd do something like that. I should have expected it."

"Shut up," he said roughly. "I can see where this is going, and I'm not letting you take either one of us there. It could be okay, Jill. I'll get a report from Nassem or Absar any minute, and we'll—"

His phone rang. "It's Absar."

She stiffened, her eyes flying to Novak's face as he answered the call. Whoever Absar was, he was spitting out words as soon as Novak answered, not giving him a chance to reply. Her gaze was focused desperately on Novak's face as he listened, but his expression told her nothing. "The tapes?" he asked once.

Still no expression.

Then, evidently, he was asked a question because he did answer. "No, don't wait. Take care of it. It has to be clean." He cut the connection.

She sat up straight, her gaze on his face. "Not good," she said jerkily. "Though I don't know how I can tell. I never know what you're thinking. Kimbro?"

"Dead."

She couldn't breathe. She felt as if she'd been kicked in the stomach.

"Dammit!" Suddenly Novak was on his knees beside her. His face contorted, his hands grasping her shoulders. "I had to say it fast and hard and get it over with. I *know* you. I couldn't play around with it when you knew it was coming."

"Yes, I knew it was coming," she said stiltedly. "I was just hoping I was wrong."

"Well, you weren't wrong." She was suddenly pulled into his arms, his hand on the back of her head, her face buried in his chest. "Kimbro's dead. Nassem's dead. Both found in Kimbro's apartment. Stop shaking. I can't take it."

Jill couldn't take it either. She was clutching desperately at him. He seemed to be the only warmth in her world right now. "How?"

"Will you let me tell you later?"

"No. Now."

"The attack was probably made when Kimbro opened the door for Nassem. It appeared to be an assault from the rear. Absar thinks they might have been waiting in a vacant apartment down the hall for their chance to go after Kimbro. Nassem was almost decapitated by a knife blow to the back of his neck." He paused. "Or possibly a machete."

Machete...

"Kimbro?"

"Same weapon. Two blows to the chest and abdomen, one kill blow to the throat. It had to be fast, he would have bled out very quickly."

She closed her eyes tightly. "Is that supposed to be comforting?"

"The only comfort I can give you."

"It sucks, Novak." But she was still holding tightly to him. "The tapes?"

"Gone."

"And machetes are a strange weapon of choice for a thug in Cairo." She added unsteadily, "But it was Varak's favorite weapon."

"Varak wouldn't have been the one who did this, Jill."

"But he had an entire troop of machete killers in his personal army. Who knows what kind of force he has now? He could have sent one of them to take care of this small job. Nothing much, just killing a reporter who got in his way. A reporter who *I* put in his way." She couldn't stop talking, couldn't stop the tears from flowing down her cheeks as she lifted her head to look up at him. "That's why I was afraid. All those deaths...I thought: What if Varak is still alive and comes back to do it again? And he *is* back, Novak. I brought him back. I set out bait for the tiger."

"The hell you did." His hands were cupping her face as he glared down at her. He said fiercely, "You know that's not true. Stop feeling sorry for yourself. I won't *have* it."

"I don't feel sorry for myself. I feel sorry for Kimbro, dammit. And I have to accept responsibility for the—"

"I gave you the assignment. You didn't even realize that anyone but you knew what Kimbro was up to. And you told me yourself he not only wanted to repay a debt, he wanted the story. If he hadn't moved too quickly, we could have had someone to protect him from the moment he left that police station. He was careless and overconfident, and it got him killed."

"It's not that easy. I drew him into the web because I was worried about what those tapes would do to Eve and Quinn. You can't absolve me of blame, Novak."

"Then let me share it. Because I sure as hell can't take watching you like this."

He meant it. All the fierceness and the almost brutal intensity that electrified him were naked in his face. It shocked her. She instinctively pushed him away. "You can't do that, Novak. You have your own problems." She shook her head to clear it. "And you shouldn't have to deal with all this angst I'm going through either. You had a man killed today also. Did you know Nassem?"

For an instant, his face still retained that shockingly fierce intensity. Then it was gone, and he said without expression, "I'd met Nassem a couple times. He was a good operator and supposed to be a good guy."

"Very vague. Is your life usually that vague?"

"It's safer to keep it that way in my job."

But there had been nothing safe or vague about him only a moment ago. Forget it. She shouldn't have even asked the question. Keep away from anything personal with Novak. "I can't do that." She got to her feet. "I used to try, but it doesn't work for me. People pop up, and suddenly there's a Kimbro or a Hajif or a Gideon." She was wiping her cheeks with the sleeve of her shirt. "Or even a Novak."

"And you get hurt."

"It depends on how the story goes. Sometimes I can make it come out right. I'm not sure about this one. I'm beginning to doubt it." She said unsteadily, "I suppose I should take care of arrangements for Kimbro. He doesn't have a wife or kid, but he used to talk about his mother in Toronto."

"Later perhaps. Not now."

Her gaze flew to his face. "Why not?"

"It's better if the bodies just disappear for a while. We don't want

the police or Egyptian government involved in this yet. I told Absar
to do a cleanup."

"What about the evidence? I don't want it cleaned up. I want the
people who killed Kimbro to be caught."

"We'll send in a forensic team. Absar's already on the job. We'll
find the murderers and take care of it. I promise you."

"He was my *friend*."

"Then be a friend to him. Don't go after the errand boy, go after
Varak. They have those tapes now, and all hell may break loose." He
met her eyes. "It's starting, Jill."

She stared at him for a long moment.

It was starting.

It had already started when Eve completed that reconstruction.
But Kimbro's death had marked the beginning of the battle to come.
There was no turning their backs on the struggle now. Those secu-
rity tapes would light a fire that could cause a gigantic bonfire.

Accept it. Stop this clinging and weeping and wailing that wasn't
going to help.

But Kimbro...

"All right. Then let's find Varak." She turned and headed for the
door. She added fiercely, "But you keep your promise, Novak. I'm
holding you to it." She paused at the door. "How quickly can we
expect those tapes to explode in our faces?"

"Not long. I wouldn't say that either Zahra or Varak have a great
degree of patience, and their underlings will know it. It's possible
they could be seeing them in the next few hours."

"And then we wait for the explosion."

"Or attempt to cause one of our own." His gaze was scanning her
face. "Are you okay now?"

Her lips indented in a ghost of a smile. "No, but I'll be better
when we figure out how to cause that explosion. I don't like to feel
this defeated. It's got to change."

"Michael just called, Eve," Joe said grimly when he came into the museum. "He was phoning from the dig site in the middle of the day. I believe that constitutes big-time worry on his part." He shook his head. "Though I managed to stave off any action, Jane might have to face problems later."

"Dammit." Eve frowned as she turned to face him. "How did he sound?"

"Calm. Reasonable. Just trying to talk me into bringing him here to see you. He's worried, not panicking. Being Michael."

"And even when he panics, we wouldn't know it," Eve murmured. "He'd just do what he thinks he should do. Which scares me to death." Her lips twisted. "And he has perfect timing, doesn't he? You want me to go to London. He's putting pressure from his end. I'm caught in the middle."

"No conspiracy, Eve."

"I know." She sighed. "I'll call him back and try to reassure him. But he can read me like a book. Honesty is great except when you have to deal with someone like Michael."

"It will help if he just hears your voice," Joe said. "The vibes are always there between you, but just talk to him." He moved over to stand beside her. "It always helps me." His hand reached out to caress her cheek. "Even if you say the wrong thing."

"And even the times when you turn a deaf ear." She held his hand to her cheek for a moment. "But you must be more concerned about him than you're letting on if you ran here right after you talked to him." She looked up at him. "Or did you consider it an opportunity?"

He shook his head. "I wouldn't use Michael as a pawn, no matter how much I want my own way."

"I didn't think you would, but you really wanted me to get out of Dodge." Her gaze was searching his face. "What else, Joe? How bad?"

"Not good. Right after I hung up from Michael, I got a call from

Jill. It seems that her friend Kimbro is dead, and the gallery tapes were taken."

"She must feel terrible," Eve said, sick. "I know she was worried."

"She should be worried," he said. "We should all be worried about those tapes."

"Are you blaming Jill?"

"Why should I blame her?" he said impatiently. "She was only trying to help. I'm the one who left those tapes in the gallery. I should have found a way to get them out of there myself."

"Sure, you had so much time, and nothing at all was happening around you," Eve said. Joe's first instinct was always to shoulder the burdens. "Forget it. How can we make it right?"

"It might be too late. As soon as they view those tapes, they'll go after me, and that will lead to you. The only thing we can do is brace ourselves for the impact. We're already doing all that's possible to go after Varak at top speed."

Brace for the impact. Eve shuddered at the words. Brace for Varak's striking out at them like a vicious rattler. Brace for Zahra's moving forward, sleek and dangerous and totally without conscience. "At the moment, it doesn't seem like top speed to me."

Varak wielding his glittering machete in that schoolroom.

Varak striking out at those helpless children.

He likes to kill the children.

She inhaled sharply as she remembered Jill's words.

"No!" Her hands closed into fists. "I don't have to wonder what else the son of a bitch might do. He uses children, Joe. That's why he staged the massacre at the schoolroom. He wanted to lure their parents to the school from the village, so he attacked the children. He knew it would be the one sure way to trap them." She met his eyes. "Because there's nothing a parent wouldn't do for their child." She paused. "There's nothing we wouldn't do for Michael. We have to be prepared that one of Varak's moves might be to go after our child." Even as she said the words, she could feel the fear and panic rising. "You were so worried about me, Joe. But forget about me. We should be worried about Michael. We should concentrate on keeping him safe."

"Slow down. You or Michael? That's no choice at all."

"But it's always been the right choice for us." She drew a shaky breath. "First, we have to keep Michael away from Maldara and away from me. We don't want to draw Varak's attention to him. Particularly not in connection to me. But we can't be sure he's safe at the dig either. Varak probably has all Zahra's power behind him, and judging by the appearance of that sniper at Asarti and Kimbro's death in Cairo, he must still have his own scumbags at his command. He could send someone to find him."

"I'll tell Jane to disappear with him until this is over."

"You know that would only make Michael more determined to go his own way. It's better to keep him busy. Besides, Jane should be protected, too. And while we're at it, even Cara's probably not safe. You'll have to make sure he can't touch anyone in the family. But I'm most worried about Michael and Jane. I'll call Jane and tell her what we're facing." She got to her feet and went into his arms. "I believe it's time for you to call those buddies of yours at Scotland Yard and persuade them to assign him that army of detectives you were going to surround me with." She laid her head on his shoulder, and said softly, "It was a good idea, just not the right person."

"Exactly the right person." His arms tightened around her. "I don't suppose I can talk you into going to be with Michael?"

She shook her head. "I have to stay away from him. Haven't you been paying attention?"

"I wish I could tell you that you're all wrong about this." He paused. "I might, if I hadn't gone down and looked at that schoolroom for myself." Joe's lips twisted. "Okay, then I suppose I'd better get on the phone again with the Yard. I just spent half the morning harassing them about Oscar Varak." He gave her a quick kiss before he turned away. "We'd better get ready to defend the gates."

"And brace for the impact," she repeated somberly as she reached for her phone to call Jane.

———◆———

"Why didn't you tell me all this before?" Jane asked quietly. "All Joe has been saying is that I should keep an eye on Michael because he might decide to take off and go to see you. That was worry enough, but now you're telling me that he might actually be in danger on this dig? Not fair, Eve."

"I know it wasn't. I was so grateful to you for giving Michael such a great time, and I guess I was hoping that what was happening here wouldn't get in the way. I just wanted to keep you out of it as long as I could. That time just ran out."

"I'd say it did," she said dryly. "And you had no business keeping me out of it. I'm supposed to be merrily playing in the dirt with Michael while you're being hunted down by this Varak. I should be with you."

"No, you shouldn't," Eve said firmly. "You should be exactly where you are right now. Joe has arranged to give you and Michael all kinds of protection, but those Scotland Yard people don't know Michael as you do." She paused. "And Michael would never be anything but honest with you even if he thought you were getting in his way. We both know he wouldn't be quite as honest with anyone else. This might be a bad time for him. He's going to need you."

"Now you're scaring me."

"I just mean he's going to be worried about me, and there aren't many people who can handle a kid like Michael when he's determined to do something." She made a face. "I wish I had ten of you at that dig."

"Do you?" Jane shook her head. "I can see why you're concerned, but I still want to come there and—" She stopped. "Okay, I'll do what you want. But no more trying to keep me out of this. Be honest with me. And be honest with Michael. Though he probably knows what's going on anyway. But it might be making him uneasy for you not to be perfectly open with him."

"You could be right," Eve said. "Sometimes it's hard to know what to do. First instinct is always to protect. Very well, honesty all the way. Thanks, Jane."

"And that's not all. If I'm responsible for taking care of Michael, then I'll do it my way." She added, "You're right, Joe's friends at the Yard might not cut it as far as Michael's concerned. And I can't furnish ten of me who could handle him. But I'll make a call, and I'll have at least one person who's capable of doing it here at the dig tomorrow."

"Who?"

"Seth Caleb's at his estate in Scotland." Her lips twisted. "I don't think you'd argue that Michael would be no problem for him. Michael adores him, and they're soul mates. Half the time, I don't even understand what's going on between them."

Jane was talking about Michael's relationship with Caleb, but she wasn't mentioning the off and on, tumultuous and passionate relationship she'd had with Caleb in the past. Eve hesitated. "The last thing I heard from you was that you weren't seeing Seth Caleb any longer. Has that changed?"

"No, I'm not seeing him, but Caleb has no qualms about dropping in on me whenever he pleases. And it will please him that I need him to come and guard Michael."

"I don't want to make things difficult for you, Jane."

"Things are always difficult when Caleb is around. We might as well make use of him. You and Joe will feel safer that Caleb is with Michael, won't you?"

Eve couldn't deny it. "He's totally remarkable."

"And that's all that's important." Jane smiled. "If I can't be with you, then you'll know that you've nothing to worry about as far as Michael is concerned." Her smile faded. "But you'll have me to worry about if you don't call me every day to tell me what's happening. This can't happen again, Eve."

"It won't. Never again. Good-bye, Jane." She ended the call. She knew Jane too well not to realize that having Caleb at that dig might be a strain considering the volatility of her relationship with him, but she also knew she wouldn't be able to talk her out of it. Jane would make any sacrifice, do everything she could to safeguard Michael and the entire family. It was her nature.

"Everything all right?" Joe was studying her expression.

"Great." She smiled with an effort. "Jane is in fine form. Michael couldn't be in safer hands. And that dig will definitely be braced for impact."

———◆———

"Get over here!" Varak's voice was crackling with fury as Zahra picked up the phone. "Right now, Zahra. Or I'll come to that fancy palace of yours." His disconnect was a crash in her ear.

He was clearly in a rage, Zahra thought, but he had no right to speak to her like this. She had already been out there to see him earlier today, and she wouldn't be at his beck and call. Then she stifled her own anger. She couldn't take a chance with Varak's volatile temperament right now.

And he must not come here. How many times had she told him that they must not take any chances? She would have to go, but he would hear from her about this when she got to his damn compound.

She tore out of the palace and, a little over an hour later, screeched to a stop in front of his house. She jumped out of the car and was climbing the steps when the door flew open and Varak came out on the porch.

"I won't take your rudeness, Varak," she said. "Next time, I'll tell you to go to hell."

"You'll take whatever I give you." He grabbed her wrist and was pulling her inside the house. "You've put me at risk for the last time. You promised me that you'd make certain I'd be safe if I played your game. Now everything is falling apart, and it's your fault."

"Nothing is falling apart except that I don't have my statue."

"The hell it's not." Varak's face was livid, twisted with anger. "I told you that you had to get rid of Duncan. But you were so frightened that all those diplomats who suck up to you would turn their backs and walk away. Now look what you've done."

"I *tried* to get rid of her. I even had Bogani drown that chef to protect us. I haven't done anything else but put up with your arrogance and insults." She glared at him. "And I've reached the end of my patience with you. What's supposed to be my fault, Varak?"

"It *is* your fault." He strode across the room toward the desk. "Do you want to see why you don't have your precious statue? I just got the security tapes from the gallery at Asarti." He pressed the button on his computer. "And guess who was dragging Dobran through that gallery."

She was looking over his shoulder at the computer screen. "How should I know who—" She stopped. "Gideon? It was Gideon at Asarti?"

"You told me he was once your lover. He seems to have forgotten old loyalties and formed others. He wasn't alone." He fast-forwarded the tape. "Do you recognize this man, Zahra?"

"No, I've never seen him before."

"Neither have I. So I ran a check through a database I use. Actually, he's very well known in some circles. He's Joe Quinn, a detective with the Atlanta Police Department." He took a step closer to her, his eyes glittering. "And he's married to Eve Duncan. Now what would he be doing at Asarti, Zahra?"

She inhaled sharply. "How should I know? None of this is my fault."

"And it's not your fault that he was obviously trying to extract

Dobran from that château when my sniper shot him? Not your fault that the one man who could tell the world that I'm still alive was being snatched away by the husband of the woman who is the premier forensic sculptor in the world? You don't see the connection?"

Zahra was afraid that she did, but she'd have to be wary about admitting it to Varak while he was in this foul mood. "Perhaps. But I don't know how the connection would be made. Duncan was working on reconstructions of those children. I saw them when I went to the museum for the press conference. Nothing to do with you. There was no threat."

"And was there no threat from bringing an expert forensic sculptor within a stone's throw of the U.N. headquarters where the skull was placed? Why do you think Quinn wanted Dobran? He already knew that Eve Duncan had been working on that skull and was certain it wasn't me. She fooled you. Can't you see it? Gideon brought her to Maldara, and everyone knows he and Jill Cassidy are friends. They all fooled you."

"I asked Wyatt, and he told me that Cassidy had no connection with the Children for Peace charity that contacted the London office."

"Just as she had nothing to do with trying to skewer me by paying Hadfeld for that story about my still being alive? I wanted to kill her then, but you persuaded me that I should only hurt and scare her. You should have realized that she wouldn't give up. She just went in another direction. So don't tell me that she had nothing to do with Eve Duncan's coming here." His voice was low and thick with rage. "Or that Duncan wasn't pretty damn sure of what Quinn would find at Asarti. Joe Quinn wouldn't have risked his reputation if Duncan hadn't thought she had proof that the skull in the U.N. vault wasn't mine."

"How could she know that?"

"That's what we're going to find out." He whirled to face her. "And I know you're ready and willing to help, aren't you?"

"Of course, I gave you my word." *Keep him calm. And this might affect both of us.* "Tell me what I can do."

He reached in her handbag and took out her phone. "You're going to call Edward Wyatt and tell him that you're in the mood for something different and are coming to see him at the U.N. residence tonight for your fun and games. You'll tell him to send everyone away so that no one will recognize you. You'll make it sound erotic enough that he'll be panting to do anything you want him to do."

He grinned. "But then he does that anyway. Right?"

She ignored the question. "What are you planning, Varak?"

"You'll get me and my men into that vault room, where I can check out that skull. Wyatt's already given you the code ID imprinted on it. If that code's not on that skull at the U.N. vault, then we'll know what Eve Duncan has been working on at that museum at Robaku."

"And what good will that do?"

"Then we start covering our bases and nullifying any gains Duncan and those others might believe they've made. The minute I know for sure that she has the skull, the game changes." His eyes were flickering, blazing with intensity. "I have a plan ready. Do you think I spent all these months cooped up in this compound without thinking of ways to protect myself and end up back on top, where I belong?" He nodded at the phone. "Make that call."

She was still glancing down at the video. "They do have my statue."

"I don't want to hear about that statue again," Varak said between clenched teeth. "*Listen* to me. You're going to do as I wish, or I'll blow all your plans to hell and take what I want in my own way. I'm sick of your stalling about giving me my share of that gold. Do you understand? I'm done with taking orders from you. From now on, you'll do what I tell you to do. Make the call."

"You will hear about it again," she said fiercely. "Because I will get it back. Don't give me orders, Varak." She was thinking, trying to figure out which way to go. She couldn't let him see that he'd intimidated her, but she could tell he was ready to do exactly what he threatened. The blowup she'd feared all these months was very close. Play along. Give him what he wanted now and see how she could turn it around. "I'll do this because it seems the best way to be certain that we're in as bad a situation as you're telling me. You do have your uses, and you might even be able to point a way out of it." She had a sudden thought. "But Wyatt is accustomed to having Dalai join us. I'll need her to come with us tonight, and I gave her to you earlier today. I have to have her back. Where is she?"

"Bedroom." He shrugged. "If she'll be any good to you."

She didn't like the sound of that. "I told you not to damage her." She was heading for the bedroom. "Now what have you done?"

"I enjoyed myself." He followed her into the bedroom. "You promised me more time than just these few hours, but I made them count. But you can have her now. If you think that it won't turn him off."

Zahra was gazing critically at the young girl. Dalai's wrists and ankles were tied to the four posts of the bed. Her naked body was bruised, her nipples bloody. Tears were running down her cheeks, her eyes were desperate, pleading, as she looked at Zahra. "Please..."

"She's not too bad," Zahra decided. "I'll tell Wyatt I did it, and it might even excite him." She went over to the bed and untied the ropes. "Though if I'd left her with you until tomorrow, it would have taken me weeks to repair her." She tossed a sheet to Dalai. "Wrap up and go get in the car. And stop crying, it's not as if it hasn't happened to you before. You should be accustomed to it by now. You're making me angry."

"I'm...sorry." The girl was frantically trying to get to her feet. "Don't leave me, madam. I'll do anything you want me to do."

"Yes, don't leave her, madam," Varak said mockingly. "She was a complete bore."

Zahra ignored him. "Just get out of here, Dalai. You'll have to make yourself presentable when I get you back to the palace." Zahra heard Varak laugh behind her as she began punching in Wyatt's number.

She drew a deep breath when Wyatt picked up the call. "I've been thinking about you. I've been amusing myself with Dalai today, but she's not enough for me right now. I'm coming to you tonight, and I want you to send everyone away and be prepared to entertain me..."

CHAPTER

14

Now what had Zahra been up to? Gideon wondered.

He drew farther back in the shadows of the old coach house as he watched Zahra drag Dalai out of the maze bordering the street and into the far end of the coach house.

He knew exactly where they were going. He had used the secret passage hidden in that last stall many times to get into Zahra's quarters during the summer when their affair had been red-hot.

Whatever it was that was causing Zahra to have reason to creep around in the dark and use those passages at a time like this was probably worth exploring...

What the hell? More than probably. He hadn't had much luck so far today.

He had spent most of the day moving around the exterior of the palace and refreshing himself on any changes that might have occurred in the years since he'd broken with Zahra. Most of the new guards were unknown to him, but there was one he remembered who might be willing to deal if the money was high enough. He'd been holding off going inside the palace to explore and had only just verified that the secret passage leading to Zahra's wing was still available and intact. Then, when he'd seen Zahra and Dalai moving from the maze into the coach house, his curiosity had flared.

Dalai... The girl was draped only in a sheet, and she looked very much the worse for wear. Not good for her, but it might be an opportunity...

What a bastard I am, he thought bitterly. The girl was like a frightened rabbit around Zahra, and he was thinking about using her? Rabbit... He vaguely remembered Zahra scornfully calling her that in those days when she'd first come to the palace all those years ago. He scarcely remembered Dalai Sadar from the old days. She had been a new servant in Zahra's entourage then and not even into her teens, still a child. She had been brought from one of the Kiyani farms in the north when Zahra had said she needed a new maidservant. He only recalled Zahra's being impatient with her and telling him that she scurried around like a frightened rabbit and that it was going to be boring having to train her.

He recalled feeling sorry for the girl at the time and had often tried to ease the sting of Zahra's scathing words. But he had already been trying to edge away from Zahra, and a few months later, he'd made the break and was on his way to London.

And Dalai had grown up under Zahra's less than tender care and become the pretty, well-trained rabbit that Zahra had intended.

Had there been blood on that sheet?

His phone was vibrating in his pocket.

Jill. He took the call.

"I've been trying to call you for the last few hours, Gideon," Jill said in exasperation. "Why didn't you pick up?"

"I was busy. Granted, I'm very familiar with this palace, but when your aim is to spy on the enemy, you don't want to draw attention to yourself by chatting on the phone as you stroll around the property. It defeats the purpose. You caught me this time in the old coach house, where I could talk."

"Coach house? Zahra has a coach—Never mind. I've reached you now. Have you talked to Novak?"

"Would I answer his calls when I refused to answer yours? That would be rude."

"Stop it, Gideon. I have to tell you something." She paused. "We weren't able to get the security tapes back. Novak's agent, Nassem, was killed, and so was my friend, Kimbro. Kimbro actually had the tapes in his possession, but we have to assume that when he was killed, the tapes were taken by one of Varak's men."

"Shit. Nassem?" Gideon repeated. "He was a good guy, Jill."

"That's what Novak said." She cleared her throat. "So was Kimbro. But the reason I was trying desperately to get in touch with you is those tapes. If Zahra and Varak don't know that you were involved in that break-in already, they will soon. You shouldn't be there, Gideon. We don't know what they'll do if they think we might be getting close."

"I'm careful." He added grimly, "And all the more reason why we should find out what's going on with Zahra. I remember she has an office that adjoins her suite. I thought that I might rifle through her desk and see what I can find out. There are too many blanks that need to be filled in."

"It sounds too risky to do it alone. Come back here, and we'll find a way to work on it together. Haven't you been there long enough?"

"Maybe. I spent most of the time finding out that I knew practically none of Zahra's personal guards any longer. There's one I might approach if necessary." He paused. "But I did have what you might call an encounter with Dalai Sadar this evening. Do you remember her?"

"The young girl that runs around at Zahra's beck and call? There's not much to remember. She obviously tries to fade into the background. I feel sorry for her, and Eve was really irritated at the way Zahra treated her. Was she around when you were playing your sex games with Zahra?"

"Barely. She was just a kid, not even in her teens yet. I remember trying to get Zahra to be easier on her. But I wasn't around that long. Our ship had sailed."

"But you met Dalai this evening?"

"As I said, more of an encounter." He changed the subject. "I'm going to stick around for a little while. Quinn would say that would be a waste of time coming back to Robaku for help when I'm already here at the palace. He's all for conquering by combining tasks." He paused. "I'll see how I feel about that office when I get within striking distance. If I decide against going for it, I still have one other path I can try before I come back to Robaku."

"What?"

"Never mind. It's a long shot, but you can never tell what will work. I'll call you when I leave here. Don't phone me again. I won't be able to answer you." He ended the call.

A long shot. He stood for a moment in the darkness, staring at the wall passage into which Zahra and Dalai had disappeared. He had to admit he was curious... So go for the long shot?

And perhaps... reparation?

Gideon had no trouble remembering the layout of the rooms once he reached Zahra's wing. The maid's room was two doors down from Zahra's suite. She always wanted privacy but also to have instant service when she required it.

He moved silently down the hall, listening for activity from Zahra's suite or the guards on the floor below. He had waited almost an hour before he'd entered the passage. If it had been blood on that sheet, Zahra would probably have needed time to take care of Dalai's wounds.

He hesitated. Time to make the decision. Go to Zahra's office? Or go to Dalai?

Either would be a risk.

He stopped outside the maid's room.

No decision. That blood... He'd known this would be the choice.

He listened.

No sound of activity.

He silently opened the door and slipped into the bedroom. The room was so plain and without color, it appeared almost sterile. A bed. A pine washstand. A chair against the far wall.

He could see Dalai sitting on the edge of the bed, still wrapped in the sheet, her eyes fixed dully on the floor.

"Dalai," he said gently.

She stiffened, her gaze wide with alarm as she saw him.

Oh, shit. She was going to scream.

This was turning out to be a stupid idea, he thought. "Shh. Please don't scream. I'm Sam Gideon. Do you remember me? I'm not going to hurt you."

She didn't scream. She just sat on the bed, panting, looking at him with those wide, dark eyes. "Of course . . . I know you. What do you want with me? Did Madam Zahra send you? I wouldn't think she'd choose to permit you to have me."

"All I want is to talk to you. Zahra didn't send me." He grimaced. "In fact, she would be very angry with me if she knew I was here. I'm surprised you remember me. You'd just come to the palace when I first met you, and I didn't stay around for long. Your Madam Zahra and I were once what you might term an item, but that was long ago. She can't stand me now."

"I remember everything about you." She was still stiff and unrelaxed. "But you're right, now Madam feels differently. You have to leave here. I didn't think she'd send you to me. But she'll still punish me if she finds you here." Her voice was trembling. "She does hate you. I can tell every time she sees you or talks about you. You make her angry. She *must* not get angry."

"Because she'll punish you?" He came toward her, his gaze on the sheet. "You're bleeding. Did she do that to you? And those bruises on your shoulders?"

"Go away."

"I thought I knew what a bitch she was, but I might have been way off." His lips tightened. "You don't have to take this, Dalai."

"Go *away*."

"Did she do it?"

"No. Yes. Go away. You'll make things worse if she comes in and sees you."

"Then we'll keep our voices down, and she won't come in. Unless she decides to come in and clean you up. I was thinking I'd given her time to have done that already."

"Take care of me?" She gazed at him in bewilderment. "Why would she do that? She told me to take care of it myself because she had to take me out again later tonight." Her hands clenched on the sheet. "You have to leave. She'll be angry with me. She'll think it's my fault. She'll give me to him again."

"Him?"

She was shaking her head. "You have to go. She'll hurt you, too." She was beginning to tremble. "And I can't take any more right now."

"I'll leave soon." He was having trouble keeping his temper. She might be a rabbit, but she had clearly been mistreated, and she was displaying a courage that touched him. "Maybe you shouldn't have to put up with any more of this. That's what I want to talk about. But first things first; it annoys me that Zahra didn't take care of you." He went to the washstand and poured water in the basin. "So I believe I'll do it myself." He grabbed a towel and washcloth and came back to the bed. "You looked like you could use a little help when I came into the room. You were just sitting, frozen."

"I'm just...tired. I was...resting." Her hand clutched at the sheet. "Go away. I'll do it."

"But I'm not in the mood for Zahra to get her own way right now. I'm very irritated with her. So sit very still." He was pulling the sheet down as he spoke. "And I'll take care of—" He went still, staring at her breasts. "You look as if you've been savaged by a wild animal."

She had gone still. "It doesn't hurt much anymore. I don't believe she'd like you to see it."

"No?" The anger and pity were growing more by the second. "Who did this?"

She didn't answer.

"Maybe later?" He dipped the washcloth in the water. "Sit still. I'll try not to hurt you." His lips tightened. "Though I don't know how I'm going to do that. You look...raw." He was dabbing carefully at her breasts. "You should probably go to a doctor. I'm tempted to take you with me when I go."

"No!" She was frantically shaking her head. "I'm fine. She'd be angry. It won't matter. She said it wouldn't. Some men aren't like you. Some men like to see—" She broke off. "Why don't you just go away?"

"Easy." He lifted his eyes to her face. "I went away a long time ago and that's why I don't want to do it now. I was thinking about that when I saw you downstairs. I was such a selfish bastard, just out of college, and I didn't care about anyone but myself. I thought you'd be okay, but what did I know? I broke with her and went my merry way. Hell, I've hardly thought of you all these years."

"Why should you?" She was looking at him with bewilderment again.

"That's right, you don't expect anyone to think about you or watch out for you." He held up his hand as she opened her lips. "But I'm not going to make it difficult for you. I can see this isn't the time. Do you have any salves you can use on these wounds?"

She nodded jerkily.

"Why doesn't that surprise me?" His lips twisted. "Then I'll let you do it so that Zahra won't be angry with you. Just let me finish this bit to make sure you won't get rabies from the son of a bitch."

She nodded slowly, her gaze fixed on his face. She sat very still while he finished washing and drying her upper body. Then, when he sat back on his heels, she asked quietly, "Is that all? I can see you're angry. Have you changed your mind? Do you wish anything else of me?"

It was clear what she meant, and he felt another ripple of rage mixed with pity. He shook his head. "Just get your damn salve."

He watched as she dropped the sheet, got to her feet, and walked naked across the room to a drawer beneath the washstand. Her body was exquisitely fragile, and he realized that there were more bruises than he had thought. That delicate gold skin had to have been brutally beaten. She took a small round tube of salve from a drawer and rubbed it over her wounds. Then she turned to face him. "It's done. But it might be a waste if she wishes me to bathe later to prepare myself again."

"Prepare for what?"

She didn't answer.

"Or should I say whom?"

She didn't answer. "What do you want with me? Why did you come?" She moistened her lips. "I'm very confused, and I'm so tired. I'm forbidden to complain. But, if it pleases you, I would like you to go so that I can rest."

"What would please me is if I knew what else you were going to have to face tonight from Zahra." He took a cotton throw from her bed and wrapped it around her. "Sit down. Rest. I'll be out of here soon. I didn't mean to stay this long. You threw me a curveball I didn't expect. I just have a few things to say, and I'll be gone."

Where to start? She was looking at him with those doe eyes that were making him feel as if he were aiming a rifle at her. *Start at the beginning. Start with honesty.*

"I didn't come here to cause you any trouble. But I'm going to ask you to help me. There's no reason why you should because it's clear no one has helped you all these years. Certainly not me." He shook his head. "And it might even be dangerous for you. If Zahra can treat you like this, there's no telling what else she'll do to you."

He paused. "But I have to ask it because it's very important, and you may be our only hope."

"Help you?" She was frowning. "I don't understand. I can do *nothing*. She hates you and wouldn't permit me to help you. She would punish me."

"Permit? Punish?" He paused. "You're not a slave, Dalai. Even in Maldara, slavery is forbidden. I won't tell you that there wouldn't be danger, but I will tell you that I'll protect you if you help me." He added, "And I promise Zahra will never be able to punish you again."

"You lie to me." She shook her head. "I belong to her. My father sent me to her and told me I must always do as she commands."

"You belong to no one but yourself. He was mistaken." He wasn't getting through to her. How could he expect to overcome the brainwashing Zahra had been giving her all these years? But every word she spoke was tearing him apart, and he had to keep trying. "You've lived here in the palace and heard all the speeches the diplomats made about freedom. You know that Zahra wasn't telling you the truth. You're free to do as you wish."

She shook her head. "I've heard all that, but I'm different. She said that I belong to her, like the slaves that Kiya brought from Egypt on the Great Journey belonged to Kiya. That I have to do everything she wants me to do." She added wearily, "And she *can* punish me. So that's another lie, too. Will you go now?"

"Not yet. I have to tell you what I need. Then I'll let you kick me out."

"Kick you out?" she asked in horror. "I could not do that."

He smiled. "Yes, you could. You just need the practice, and it would come naturally to you. But you might need my friend, Jill, to help you get over the first hesitation."

"Jill," she repeated tentatively. Then she said slowly after a moment's thought, "Jill Cassidy. I've heard Madam speak of her. She does not like her either."

"No, Jill has gotten in her way, and she doesn't like it." His eyes narrowed on Dalai's face. "But you probably knew that, didn't you? That's why I need your help, Dalai. You know everything that goes on with Zahra. You've been with her for years, and she obviously treats you like wallpaper when she's not mistreating you. You see and hear everything. She'd never think that you'd betray her."

"Because I would not. You do not know what she would do to me."

His lips tightened. "I can imagine, judging by what I've seen tonight. But I'm asking you anyway. Terrible things have happened here in Maldara, and Zahra is part of a plan to start it all again. There were so many deaths. My friends and I are trying to keep it from happening, but we're working in the dark. We need names and faces." He paused. "Particularly the name and face of one man who Zahra might be protecting. I believe you probably have information that might shine a light on that darkness. Information that can save lives. I *need* it, Dalai." He paused. "And in return, I'll promise to take care of you, and protect you, and give you a life that will give you all the choices you could wish. Is it a deal? Will you trust me?"

"You want *me*?" She was gazing at him in horror. "She would kill me. She would let him hurt me."

"If you helped us, we'd keep you safe. Just furnish us with what we need to stop Zahra...and anyone else with whom she's dealing. We'd protect you and even send you far away if you wish."

"I cannot answer questions." Her voice was shaking. "She said she would treat me as Kiya would someone who betrayed her. She even showed me the place with no air."

"What place?"

"Go away!"

"I'm going." He moved quickly to the door. "I understand why you're upset. But I had to do it. If you help us, it could save lives. I know you think of me as an enemy, I've never done anything for you. But getting rid of Zahra might even save your life someday."

"You don't understand *anything*." Her eyes were glittering, blazing. "I don't want to die like a Kiya slave. I don't want to die at all." Her voice was no longer shaking but very strong and hard with determination. "I won't let you or her or anyone do that to me."

That sudden change of demeanor from meekness to ferocity had startled him. "I'm trying to understand, Dalai." Gideon looked over his shoulder as he reached the door. Ferocity? He must have just frightened her. Except for those huge, blazing eyes, she looked infinitely fragile, and he couldn't leave her like that. "Don't let anyone else hurt you the way you were hurt tonight. Do you have a phone?"

"Of course, Madam might need me. I must always be available to her."

"Of course," he repeated. He strode back across the room and threw his card on the bed. "I'll leave. But if you change your mind or get in trouble, call me, and I'll come and get you. And you won't have to tell me anything if you're afraid to do it."

Her eyes widened. "Why would you do that?"

"I told you. Because I didn't do it when I should have done it all those years ago. When I got bored with her, I just took off. I didn't give a thought to you."

Her eyes were still bewildered. "Of course, you didn't. Why should you?"

"I can't explain it if you don't know. Anyway, deal or no deal, call me if you need help."

"I cannot do that," Dalai said jerkily. She was silent another moment. "I think you are trying to be kind to me. But if I'm not very good, she said he will punish me again, and I can't risk it." Her voice was shaking again. "I could not *stand* it."

His eyes narrowed. "Zahra's not always truthful. She might not keep her word. If she changes her mind, you might remember that I'm offering you your own choices." He added with sudden urgency, "No strings, dammit. Just use the card and call me."

"I'm going to tear it up and throw it away. She might find it," she said unsteadily. "But I'll remember your number. I have a very good memory. But don't expect me to use it."

It was a small victory, but he'd take it. "I never expect anything. I hope for everything." But she was still so damn defenseless. He impulsively reached into his pocket and pulled out his pearl-handled switchblade knife and threw it on the bed beside the card. "Take this in case you need it. My father gave it to me when I came home from Oxford. I think he'd want you to have it." He smiled. "Now you can't tear that to pieces. It's a keepsake."

"No, but I can never use it." She reached down and gingerly touched the pearl handle. "I'll have to hide it away so that no one will ever see it." She shook her head. "Why don't you understand? I can't resist, or it makes it a thousand times worse for me."

"No, I don't understand. Because if you'd let me help, we could beat this." He turned and moved back toward the door. "Just trust me." He carefully opened the door and cautiously looked up and down the hall. "Take care of yourself, Dalai," he said. "Since you won't let me do it. And no one else seems—"

"I've never thought of you as my enemy."

He stiffened at the words and looked over his shoulder. "What?"

"I never blamed you for leaving me," she burst out suddenly. "Why should I? Everybody leaves. And I never thought I was important enough for you to worry about." She stared him in the eye. "And I liked it when you were with her. You smiled at me and joked. It was different than it was later. You were nice to me."

He was silent. "You have a very limited experience in that area. And that makes me feel like even more of a bastard than I did before. But *call* me. Let me help you."

She shook her head. "Go away."

He had to go, he thought in frustration. But she was sitting there, fragile, helpless, and he wanted to scoop her up and take her somewhere safe. Another casualty in this damn war that had taken so much from so many. But a casualty that he thought he might have prevented.

"Call me!" He closed the door and moved swiftly down the hall.

———◆———

ROBAKU

"It's about time you got here." Jill came down the path toward Gideon when he arrived at Robaku an hour later. "Would it have hurt to have phoned me as soon as you could? Did you find out anything when you were going through Zahra's personal quarters?"

"I didn't get that far," Gideon said. "I was checking out something else, and I got involved." He held up his hand. "Don't ask. I came up with zeros all around."

"And you're upset." Jill was reading his expression. "You didn't by any chance run into Zahra while you were 'involved.'"

"If I had, I would have probably broken her neck," he said grimly. "I was ready to do it tonight."

"Why?"

"A poisonous combination of personal guilt and a few revelations that were particularly infuriating." He stopped, then said, "Okay, I was thinking about using her maid, Dalai, to help us. I thought she could be a fount of information. But I blew it. And besides, she's been used enough." He made a face. "At one point, I believe I even offered your services, Jill. Be prepared if I drop her on your lap if I change my mind. Why should I be any different? Do you know Zahra even used the Kiya card on Dalai to convince her that she was only a slave and didn't have any right to argue about how she was treated?"

"Kiya," Jill repeated. "It doesn't surprise me. After all, a queen must have her slaves. It was clear she seemed to consider Dalai her special property."

"Exactly."

"That sounded bitter." She was thinking. "I did feel sorry for her. And I remember that Eve was angry about the way she was treated." She nodded suddenly, and said recklessly, "Go ahead. By all means, hand her over to us. We're so frustrated that we'll be glad to find a way to get some of our own back."

"Easier said than done. I'd have to fight Dalai as well as Zahra." He changed the subject. "No word about whether the security tapes were delivered to Zahra or Varak yet?"

"Not as far as we've heard. I was hoping you'd know something when you got back from the palace."

"Well, Zahra was definitely on the move this evening, and she had plans for later tonight." His lips twisted. "I was tempted to follow them, but it sounded as if it might concern Dalai more than any connection to Asarti."

"Novak is monitoring the chatter, but nothing yet," Jill said. "Other than that, we're just trying to think of a way to make certain Eve's safe and find proof that it's Oscar's skull that we have in that museum. We'll probably hear about what Varak plans to do about those tapes soon enough." She shrugged. "But I don't think anyone is going to sleep well tonight."

"Then I might as well go have a drink with Novak and confess that I had an utterly worthless day. I don't dare go to Quinn. He won't accept any report that won't contribute to keeping Eve safe and out of jail."

"By all means go get a drink. You look like you need it. I might join both of you later before I go to Hajif's to turn in. He offered me a mat in his hut, and I'm trying to give Eve and Quinn their privacy." She turned and strolled toward the museum. "But first I'll go tell Eve that you're back and that we might have to adopt Dalai before this is over..."

U.N. HEADQUARTERS
10:32 P.M.

"You look beautiful tonight." Edward Wyatt stood at the top of the
grand staircase and watched Zahra walk up the curving stairs toward him. Her dark hair shone as she passed beneath the huge crystal
chandelier. His eyes lingered on her breasts, spilling out of the low
neckline of her nude-colored silk gown. "Fantastic. Do you know
how many times I've imagined you walking up to my bedroom toward me here in my own place? This is my domain, everyone has to
kowtow and fawn to me. But all I could do was wonder what you
would do to me if I could ever get you here."

"But I'm the one who arranged this. I'm always the one in
charge," Zahra said coldly. "And if you didn't do as I told you to do,
I will not stay. You've sent everyone away? I mustn't be seen here or
I'll be known as your whore when I go to New York for my speech,
and all those diplomats will not give me the respect I deserve. I'll
be angry if you've made this visit difficult for me, Wyatt. I've been
looking forward to it since I called you."

"Do you think I haven't?" he asked hoarsely. "I couldn't think of
anything else. Of course I sent them away. I told my private secretary that I was having a confidential meeting with a member of the
Botzan secret service who wanted to speak to me about a possible
terrorist threat he might need our help to solve. That's what you
wanted, right?"

"That's exactly what I wanted. We'll see if you can please me in
other ways tonight." She had to get Wyatt out of the hall and into his
bedroom right away. Varak had said he wanted the way clear to bring
his men down to the vault ten minutes after she and Dalai arrived.
She turned and said to Dalai behind her, "Come along. I want to see
him perform. He's sure to be better than you were today. Where's
your bedroom, Wyatt?"

"Third door." He gestured as she swept by him but paused to

watch Dalai hurry after Zahra. "Hello, Dalai." He smiled maliciously. "How are you? You appear to be moving a bit stiffly. I hear she gave you a hard time today. I hope you're not going to spoil things for me tonight."

She quickly shook her head. "I'm fine, sir."

"You wouldn't lie to me?"

"Of course she wouldn't lie," Zahra said impatiently. "I'll allow you to strip her down so that you can see the bruises. I thought you might enjoy it. Providing you don't waste my time with this chatter."

"I'm sorry." Wyatt moved down the hall and flung open the door for her. "I promise I won't waste your time."

"We'll see. Dalai, come and help him undress. I find I'm eager to see just how much he's been anticipating this." She gave him a cat-like glance over her shoulder. "And judge what kind of torment it will take to make it worth my while to have come here tonight."

———

Varak carefully drew the heavy bronze box out of the vault and laid it on the desk. "Get me the liquid, Markel."

Markel had it ready. "You're sure this will work?"

"Don't question me." Varak flipped open the lid and stared down at the blackened skull. "Hello, Oscar. How nice to see you again," he murmured. "It seems okay, Markel. He's as ugly a son of a bitch as the day I burned him to a crisp." He took the skull out of the container and turned it over. "Did I tell you that I'd been wanting to do that since the prick took off and ran back to Johannesburg, Markel? Well, actually since he annoyed me when he was a kid. I just hadn't gotten around to it yet."

"You told me," Markel said nervously. "Why don't you check the number so that we can get out of here?"

"There's no hurry now. Zahra will keep Wyatt busy." He was opening the vial. "And who knows, this might actually be Oscar. It could be that Duncan didn't go this route. If she did, then I'll act accordingly. I've got my plan in place." He put a drop of liquid on the bone near the ear. "And I'm actually looking forward to showing that bitch, Duncan, there's no way she can beat me." He added with sudden harshness, "I'm tired of hiding away when all I want to do is break out and let them all see what I can do."

"You said that the gold would be worth it." Markel's gaze was focused on the skull. "Did you make a mistake?"

Varak's head swung around like a striking cobra. "I don't make mistakes."

Markel backed away. "I only thought maybe circumstances had changed," he said quickly. "Is there anything I can do to help you with that skull?"

Varak didn't speak for a moment, and Markel tensed. Then Varak said, "No, I've got it." He looked back down at the skull. "Just be still and let me see how this is going to play out. Whatever goes down, I'll get what I want." He added, "Because I don't make mistakes, Markel."

He waited as the liquid did its work.

"Anything?" Markel asked.

Varak didn't answer. His eyes were on the skull.

Son of a bitch!

No numbers appeared. Nothing.

It was *not* Oscar.

And the rage was beginning to sear through Varak.

It was an insult that Eve Duncan had thought she could do this to him. Of course, she was only a woman, and Joe Quinn might have manipulated her. But she had to have been the one to do the actual reconstruction to prove that skull wasn't Varak's. He was suddenly furious with everyone connected to this defeat. Gideon, Joe Quinn, Eve Duncan, Jill Cassidy. He wanted them all *dead*.

No, he wouldn't accept that they had defeated him.

"Varak?" Markel said tentatively.

"Shut up," Varak hissed. He took the skull and hurled it across the room to smash against the wall. "The bitch thinks she fooled me." His hands clenched into fists as the white-hot rage tore through him. "Let's show them how wrong they are. Set the C-4."

"Where?"

"Everywhere, you fool. Everywhere."

Markel hurried out of the vault room.

Varak strode across the room and jammed an explosive in the empty eye socket of the skull lying on the floor.

Markel was back in the room and setting the charges.

"When you finish, get the other charges set throughout the house," Varak said. "Then tell the men to do the other blocks. Be ready to detonate when I call you." Then Varak was running out of the vault, down the hall, and up the staircase. Where the hell was she? Then he heard voices behind a door down the hall. A second later, he was throwing open the door of Wyatt's suite.

Wyatt was naked and kneeling before an equally naked Zahra. His head swiveled, and he stared in shock at Varak. "No one is supposed to be here. What are you—doing—"

"Blowing your brains out." Varak shot him directly between the eyes.

Then he glared at Zahra as Wyatt fell to the floor. "It's the wrong damn skull. It had to have been switched by that bitch, Duncan. You should have gotten rid of her. You should have gotten rid of all of them." His eyes were blazing. "That's why she sent Quinn to Asarti. You're to blame for this. Now I have to protect myself."

"And you call killing a U.N. diplomat protecting yourself?" She was staring in horror at Wyatt's shattered head. "How am I supposed to handle this?"

"I don't give a damn. I've already made plans to get rid of all the evidence. You just find a way to keep them from coming after me. Fix it. Put your clothes on and get out of here. This place is going to blow in another seven minutes. I won't wait for you."

"You're blowing it up?" She shook her head dazedly. "You are insane. Do you know what kind of nightmare you're going to—" She was gasping, choking as his hands closed on her throat.

"Listen to me," he hissed. "And keep listening. From now on, you're going to do exactly as I say. I'm done playing with you. Do you know how much I want to squeeze just a little harder and break your damn neck? I won't tolerate your ordering me about. I'm in charge now. Do you understand?"

She couldn't speak, so she nodded.

He released her, and she backed away, holding her throat. His smile was savage. "Yes, you do understand. Now get out of here and do what I told you. You're always telling me how clever you are. Now prove it. It's my game now, my orders, Zahra." He whirled and strode toward the door. "Fix it!"

Zahra gazed after Varak for an instant as anger and shock struggled within her. Fix it? How was she supposed to fix this catastrophe? She looked down at the blood spattered over her naked body. It was like him to barge in and make things as difficult and horrible as possible for her, she thought bitterly. And this time it had been far worse. She was trying to swallow. She reached up and touched her bruised throat. This time she'd thought he was going to kill her. She knew he'd been very close.

"What do we do?" Dalai whispered from the bed across the room as she scrambled to sit up. "Do we have to do what he says?"

Zahra had forgotten she was there. She whirled on her as she grabbed her gown. "You do what you always do. You obey my orders." She slipped the gown over her head. "And my orders are that you do whatever he says until I tell you differently. I don't want you causing me any trouble while I work this out. I might have to do some delicate negotiations with him before I get what I want." She headed for the door. "Now get dressed and go down and get in the car."

"Negotiations," Dalai repeated numbly as she threw on her top and sarong skirt. "Then I'll have to do what he wants. That's what you mean?"

"That's what I said, isn't it? Hurry. We have to get out of here. He's a little crazy right now. He *hurt* me. The bastard almost killed me. I have no idea what he's going to do next."

"Yes." Dalai's voice was trembling as she hurriedly stumbled after Zahra down the grand staircase. "He's very angry. I can see there's no telling what he'll decide to do now..."

———◆———

ROBAKU

"Wake up, Jill!"

Novak, she realized sleepily. He was shaking her, and he sounded really—

Then she was wide-awake. Her eyes flew open.

Darkness, but Novak was kneeling above her with a flashlight. "What's wrong? What are you doing here?" She sat bolt upright on her mat. "Is Eve—"

"Eve is fine as far as I know," he said roughly. "You can check yourself as soon as we get to the museum. I've called Quinn, and they're waiting for us. Put on your shoes, and we'll get over there." He pulled her to her feet. "Because there's a hell of a lot wrong. I just got a call from my agent, Palmon, in Jokan to tell me to check my computer."

"Jokan?" She was slipping on her tennis shoes. "What happened in Jokan?"

"What didn't happen in Jokan?" He was pulling her toward the door of the hut. "I don't believe there's any doubt now that Zahra and Varak believe they know why Eve sent Quinn to Asarti to get corroborating evidence from Dobran."

"Stop talking in riddles. Just tell me." She tried to stop at the door of the hut. "And give me just a second to tell Hajif and his wife I'm leaving. I don't want to frighten them."

"I'll send someone." He was pulling her down the path toward the museum. "As for telling you, it's not really necessary. That should give you a hint." He gestured to the night sky to the north. "What do you think, Jill?"

She halted, frozen, her gaze on the baleful red glow that lit the entire horizon.

"Screw your hints," she whispered. "What happened, Novak?"

"The entire block that the U.N. occupied was blown to kingdom come. Along with two of the side streets on either side. Pretty clear that whoever set those charges didn't give a damn if they blew up the entire city to make certain of that U.N. building."

"Casualties?"

He shook his head. "It only happened forty-five minutes ago. But my agent says that no one could have lived through the primary explosions at the U.N. site. Initial information from Wyatt's staff is that he was the only one there tonight. But it's a total inferno, and the soldiers and police can't even get near it to try to recover bodies. The neighboring streets are even worse. There were definitely multiple deaths in those shops and houses. I'll be given updates as soon as they're available."

"Why?" she asked dazedly. She swallowed to ease the tightness of her throat. "Why would they do it? An attack on a U.N. facility would cause an uproar. Zahra wouldn't want to be associated with anything like that."

"Unless it wasn't her call," Novak said grimly. "Unless she's lost control of the agenda. We'll probably know soon enough. This is her city, she'll have to be involved in explaining and mopping up this disaster."

"And soon," Jill murmured. She couldn't take her eyes off that glowing red horror in the distance. "I don't see how she could possibly talk her way out of this holocaust."

They had reached the museum, and Jill saw that it was ablaze with lights. Joe was throwing open the door. "What the hell?" His eyes were glittering, his lips tight. "What's happening there, Novak? You've got to know something."

"You know as much as I do right now," Novak said curtly. "I'll find out all I can when I get to Jokan. I sent Gideon on ahead when I got word, and I'm on my way. I only wanted to bring Jill to you before I left." He turned away. "Take care of her. There's no telling what's going to happen next."

"You're leaving?" Jill asked, startled. Then she recovered. "Of course you are. This is a disaster, and you're CIA. I should be going also. I have contacts, I might be able to—"

"No," Novak said. "You'd get in my way. I don't want you seen there. Eve may be the prime target, but you've got to be high on their list by now. It's not as if I won't let you know right away. For once, just do as I say for—" His phone rang. "Gideon." He answered and listened for another minute. "When?" he asked. "Find out and get back to me. I'll be there as soon as I can."

"What is it?" Eve asked as she joined them at the door.

"President Zahra Kiyani has just requested TV time to address the nation in response to this national disaster. Gideon believes that she'll be speaking in the next hour or so. He'll give me a definite time in the next fifteen minutes." His lips twisted. "It probably won't be immediately. She'll want to give every news agency on the planet time to chime in and give her maximum exposure. I imagine the palace newsroom is already packed."

"Of course, it is," Jill said. "It's a great story. I should be there." She stared him in the eye. "I *will* be there, Novak."

"You'll have to pass," he said coolly. "You have another story to cover. Anything Zahra has to say will almost certainly have a direct influence on Eve. You're the one who chose Eve to be the one to put her neck on the line. Hell, you've been in agony about your responsibility for getting her poisoned." His voice became crisp and cold. "So suck it up and forget about that story luring you to the palace. You haven't finished this one yet. Stay here and make sure she lives to read it." He turned and strode down the path.

Jill stared after him, stricken.

"Pretty rough," Eve said quietly. "He probably didn't mean it all."

"Yes, he did." She shivered. "He always means what he says. You can always count on that." She drew a deep breath. "And the bastard is so damn smart that he's usually right. He sees right through you and cuts out all the bullshit like he has a scalpel." She turned to Joe. "You can see that, can't you? You know he's right about my being to blame for Eve's being in this position."

He nodded. "He's right. You had plenty of help, but you're the one who worked and made it happen."

"And yet I was ready to run back to Jokan as soon as I saw another story beckoning, another way to go after Zahra and Varak. It was fresh and new, and all I could think about was that maybe this was the direction I should go."

He was silent. Then he said, "Do you think that wasn't my first thought?" He made a face. "I've been frustrated as hell, and I don't respond well to it. But it's second thoughts that matter, and I knew it was impossible."

"But I had to have that second thought drummed into me." She turned to Eve. "Forgive me. It won't happen again."

"Stop talking as if this is all about me," Eve said, disgusted. "Joe is bad enough. But I have to put up with him." She turned and went over to the computer on her worktable. "I'll stand only so much from you, Jill." She turned on the computer. "Now let's see if we can find out what's happening in Jokan."

CHAPTER

15

The local Jokan television station switched from the shots of the U.N. disaster to the newsroom at the presidential palace two hours later.

Zahra Kiyani walked slowly up to the stage from a carved door opened by two uniformed soldiers. She was wearing an elegant white suit, and every glossy hair in her chignon was in place. She looked absolutely stunning as she turned to face the audience.

But her expression was tense and sober, and she paused a moment before she started to speak. "I grieve with you, both my own people and the loved ones of those friends from foreign lands who died tonight in that terrible massacre." Her voice was shaking, and her eyes were suddenly shining with tears. "You will notice I wear white instead of black for mourning. For those who are not familiar with Kiyanis, this is the custom of my family to honor our dead." Her voice broke. "And everyone who died tonight I regard as a member of my own family." She stopped a moment, struggling. "This is a monstrous thing that happened, and there are no words I can say that will explain or give comfort to you. All I can do is give what answers I can and grieve with you. First, I have to express my heartfelt condolences to the family of the Honorable Edward Wyatt, whom I've been told almost certainly perished in that explosion tonight. We had become friends during these last months. His Herculean efforts to help me bring health and happiness back to my countrymen after the devastation they had suffered will live in my heart and memory forever." Another emotional pause. "Unfortunately, that bravery and dedication very likely caused him to be targeted. The police are still investigating, but we suspect Botzan terrorism. They have informed me after questioning the wife of Edward's private secretary, Peter Greville, that Edward had scheduled a confidential meeting tonight with a Botzan secret agent who was attempting to capture a radical, terrorist group who were trying to revive the terrible war that killed so many of us." She swallowed. "Including my own father. I had received reports and threats to my life from this group for the last few months, but my own secret service had not succeeded in apprehending them. I can only believe that Edward thought the force of the U.N. might bring them to justice and risked his own life in order that the peace would not be broken." She cleared her throat. "Because that was the kind of noble, giving man the Honorable Edward Wyatt has been since the moment I first met him. May God bless his family and my eternal thanks to Great Britain for sending him to my country so that I could learn from him." She lowered her head and was silent a long moment, struggling. "Forgive me. This is as difficult for me as it is for you all. I know I promised you information, and I will give it. Naturally, because this hideous disaster has just occurred, that information may be sketchy, and I beg you to understand. I can only tell you what I've been told. The consensus of those around me is that the terrorist group got wind of the meeting with Edward and wished to set an example. It was easy for them because he had sent all of his guards and employees away for the night in order to satisfy the demands of the Botzan secret agent. That was like the Edward I have come to know, risking everything..." She went on: "But in the last hour we've found out that he was not the only target. The terrorists weren't satisfied with only killing him. His private secretary, Peter Greville, and several of the guards were attacked and shot in their residences in the early hours of the morning. The police told me that there's reason to believe that they wanted to make certain everyone connected with the death of Nils Varak paid the same price. You might remember that Varak's skull was being held at the U.N. headquarters." She shuddered. "It shouldn't surprise us that the monster who almost destroyed my country should be worshipped by those murdering terrorists." The tears that had been brimming were suddenly running down her cheeks. "But it does surprise me. I can't understand anything about people like this. Shouldn't the deaths stop sometime?" She looked directly in the camera. "But we all have to understand it because we have to stop it. It can't go on any longer. Together we *can* stop it. Help me, and I will help you. I will let you know whatever I find out about this atrocity so that we can share knowledge as well as our sorrow. I will set my own agencies and soldiers to seek out those answers. I'm going to cancel my trip to New York to speak at the U.N. in order to devote myself to keeping those beasts from devouring my country." Her voice was suddenly ringing with resolve. "That is my duty, and I will give every minute of every day to it. I ask for your prayers and your support." She stepped back. "Good night and God bless."

She turned and walked away.

Jill gave a low whistle as she looked up from the computer screen. "She aced it. I bet every reporter in that room is giving her a standing ovation. Hell, I'd probably do it, too, if I didn't know she was lying through her teeth."

"But you do know," Eve said. "Gideon told me once that she was magnificent in a number of ways. This is apparently one of them." She leaned back, and added thoughtfully, "Do you know what I was thinking about when she speaking? She was totally beautiful, totally persuasive, and able to move everyone with whom she came in contact. Mesmerizing. She reminded me of her favorite ancestress."

"Kiya?" Joe asked.

"No, she tolerated Kiya, but she identified with Cleopatra. Cleopatra had the power, and Zahra adores power. Pity. Because Kiya was probably more intelligent." She shook her head. "But Zahra definitely covered all the bases with that speech. She produced a logical villain based on recent history. She glorified Wyatt and Great Britain and the entire civilized world. She even gave a reason why those guards were killed when they weren't even at the U.N. headquarters tonight and why the place was chosen to be targeted. You can bet that Swanson and anyone connected to that skull was on the hit list. All very logical and acceptable." She grimaced. "And then she sealed the deal by setting herself up as a combination Joan of Arc and Mother Teresa with all the glamour of Cleopatra. That YouTube video is going to get millions of hits, and the Zahra Kiyani legend is going to grow and grow."

Jill nodded. "Hell, she might decide to bypass using Egypt as a stepping-stone and go straight to Washington. After that speech, it's going to be nearly impossible to make her out to be anything but a heroine. It's like Jackie Kennedy in that bloody pink suit."

"That's what she intended," Joe said harshly. "What they both intended. What the world believes to be Varak's skull is now totally destroyed, and if we brought up the skull on which Eve just did the reconstruction, it would be an uphill battle to prove it wasn't a complete forgery. It throws everything into confusion. Very smart. Zahra and Varak make a formidable team."

"Murderers," Eve said with a shiver. "Another massacre, and she managed to sugarcoat it."

"Yes." Joe met her eyes. "It just goes to show how determined they are to protect themselves. They assassinated Dobran and killed your friend Kimbro, Jill. That explosion tonight was just another safety measure. They're going down the list and checking off the hazards to eliminate." He paused. "And you're probably next on the list, Eve. You have a spotless reputation, and that's dangerous to them." His tone was suddenly urgent. "The game's changed. *Now* will you let me take you out of here?"

"Do it, Eve," Jill said. "As he said, it's going to be an uphill battle from now on. If you stay, you'll be vulnerable to anything they decide to do to you."

"What am I supposed to do? Let Joe bury me in the mountains somewhere and hope Varak won't dig me up?" Eve shook her head. "I won't live like that. I won't let Varak believe he can roam the earth and get away with all this slaughter. There has to be a better way to handle this. We just have to find it." She was thinking, trying to see some way out. "We have to take advantage of any weakness they might have. Zahra has to have a different agenda than Varak. Jill says she's always been cautious, and she must feel as if she has a tiger by the tail."

"This is all guesswork," Joe said impatiently. "And all it means is that I'm not getting what I want and that Eve is still in danger as long as she's here." He drew a deep breath. "Because who's to know if Zahra won't think of some clever reason to blow up this village as well? I wouldn't put it past her." He strode toward the door. "I need some air. Then I'm going to call Novak. I'm having problems with your 'logic,' and I want solutions."

OUTSIDE U.N. HEADQUARTERS
JOKAN

Gideon's eyes were stinging from smoke as he closed his computer after watching Zahra's speech. "Interesting. She's either amazingly improved from the time when we were an item or she was inspired. What do you think?"

"I have no idea." Novak added, "But Jill would say she told the

story with incredible conviction and that she came across as a combination of Angelina Jolie and Mother Teresa."

"I believe she was inspired...maybe by Varak," Gideon said absently as he gazed at the ambulances still racing from the homes and
shops on the streets surrounding the U.N. toward the hospital. He
was realizing that some of the smoke he was breathing was carrying
the scent of the burnt flesh of those victims caught in the flames. It
was too damn familiar. "But I don't think even Mother Teresa could
inspire any mercy for the people who did this. What's the count?"

"More than fifty. If the staff of the U.N. hadn't been sent home, it
would have almost doubled."

"She mentioned that some of the guards who took care of the
vault had also been assassinated. Swanson?"

Novak nodded. "They wanted to get anyone connected to the
skull. It was a well-planned raid."

"Varak can be brilliant." Gideon's lips twisted. "The smell of this
smoke reminds me of the day I came back home to bury my parents. He was very thorough. Everything stank for weeks of smoke
and flesh. He burned every living soul on the property."

"You never told me that."

"It was over," he said. "Until it wasn't." He looked away from
the ambulances. "Do you need me any more tonight? I think I
should—" His phone rang, and he glanced down at the ID. Presidential palace. No designated name.

He quickly turned away from Novak. "Excuse me. I've got to take
this."

Novak's brows rose. "Confidential?"

Gideon didn't answer as he moved a few more steps away. He
punched the access key. "Gideon."

"I've got to see you right away." Dalai's voice was shaking. "You
said you'd help me. Will you still do it?"

He stiffened. "Yes. But I'm a little busy right now. I'm sure you
can hear the sirens."

"I've been hearing them ever since I got back to the palace. I think I'll hear them forever."

"Then I imagine you heard more than the sirens. How close were you to the explosion?"

She didn't answer. "I need to see you. I'll be at the coach house in thirty minutes. Please come."

"How can you get away? I'm standing here watching the U.N. headquarters burn to ashes. And I just heard Zahra give a speech to rock the ages."

"She's surrounded by all those reporters. She doesn't want me around to get in her way. She told me to stay in my quarters."

"She never did like to share the spotlight."

"Will you come?"

"I'll come." He cut the connection. He turned back to Novak. "I'll see you later. I have something to do."

"Curious. Or someone to see?"

He smiled. "Perhaps."

Novak's narrowed eyes were studying his face. "It's that young maid of Zahra Kiyani."

Gideon's smile never wavered. "Perhaps."

"Be careful. It could be a trap. It's odd that you'd hear from her after Zahra probably blew up a good bit of the city. She could be dangerous. Are you sure it's worth it?"

"No. But it's promising." He lifted his hand. "I'll call you later and let you know."

———◆———

Dalai wasn't in the coach house when Gideon slipped inside the back entrance twenty minutes later. But the entire palace seemed to be teeming with activity, he noticed. He'd been lucky not to be seen coming here.

It could be a trap.

Yes, it could. He was taking a chance that Dalai had not gone to Zahra and told her that he had been to see her. Or more likely, she might have lost her nerve and was still cowering in her bedroom.

Then, suddenly, the door of the passage opened, and she was there, running toward him. "I was afraid you'd leave. Madam called me down to the press office to redo her hair. She said it wouldn't photograph well if she—" She broke off and drew a deep breath. "But you didn't leave. So it's all right."

"Yes, it's all right," he said gently. "Why did you call me? Did someone hurt you again?"

"No, not like that. Usually it's only him. It was the blood...he shot Mr. Wyatt in the head. There was so much blood." She was biting her lower lip. "But he *will* hurt me again. I know it. She's too afraid of him. She'll do anything to keep him from hurting her. But I don't matter to her. She'll use me again and again to please him." She was gazing desperately up at him. "But I can't *bear* it. I can stand most things, but not that. I'll tell you whatever you want to know. It's a kind of bargain, isn't it? But you don't have to promise to keep me safe, or send me away somewhere. Just keep me away from him."

"Hush." He reached out to stroke her hair. "I will promise to keep you safe. But I can't do that unless you help yourself. You're still not telling me names. Give me his name, Dalai."

She was silent. "It's very...hard. She said no one is supposed to know it. She said she would send me to—" She swallowed. "Varak. His name is Nils Varak." She was looking searchingly at his face. "But I think you knew it, didn't you?"

"But I had to be absolutely certain. Now I am." He added grimly, "I believe you're aware that Varak's presence here in Maldara is a huge secret. There aren't many people who would be brave enough to say his name."

"Yes, I knew it was a secret. That's why Madam spent all that money for that plastic surgeon to change his face. And I'm *not* brave. I had to do it. After I came back tonight, I was lying in bed and shaking. Because I knew I was going to have to do it. I knew I had to ask you to help." She braced herself, and, suddenly, she was no longer trembling. "Because I'm not strong enough. I don't know any of the ways that you would. I'll have to learn them. You were always so strong when you were with her. You were never afraid. You even laughed at her when she tried to order you about. If I do what you wish, you'll keep her from giving me to him again." She paused, then said quietly, "Or because I believe you hate him, you will kill him. That would be much better."

Gideon felt a ripple of shock. He had not expected those last words. Dalai had spoken with no passion, only simplicity and determination. But who could blame her after all she had been through? "I'll never let you go back to him." He smiled grimly. "And, if you can tell me where to find the bastard, I have friends who will be glad to go with me and see that Varak will never live to see another day."

She closed her eyes for a moment. "I'm sorry to make you do this. I know it should be me." She opened her eyes. "But I will repay you."

"Just tell me where I can find him."

She nodded. "He has a compound deep in the rain forest over an hour from here. It's off Nagali Highway, and the roads going to and from the property are patrolled by Madam's soldiers. And he has his own soldiers at the compound. Many soldiers. I don't know how many." She paused, thinking. "He likes explosives. I've seen them in the warehouse there."

"Yes, I'm aware that he likes explosives," Gideon said harshly. "Anything else?"

She shook her head. "I'm sorry. I was always in the bedroom."

He felt another bolt of rage and pity. "Nothing to be sorry about. You've told me a great deal. We don't have to talk about him anymore. Let's talk about Zahra. She's very important, too."

"She can't help you get to the compound," Dalai said quickly. "Varak doesn't like her to come there. He's afraid she'll be followed."

"No, forget about the compound for a moment. I need to know

everything about her relationship with Varak. We might be able to use it. Are they lovers?"

She shook her head. "She used to sleep with him. But she doesn't anymore. She sends him whores . . . or me."

"That doesn't surprise me. Well, why does she put up with him? What binds them together?"

"I don't know what you mean." She was backing away from him. "I have to go now. I've been here too long."

She was suddenly on edge, he realized. She had started to shake again. The minute he had started to question her about Zahra . . . He was thinking back to the conversation in her room. "You're frightened. You said something about Zahra's sending you to the place where there was no air. What did you mean?"

"It's not important to you. I've told you about Varak. He's the only one you have to worry about." She started to back toward the stable.

"Wait. I could try to take you out of here now."

"No, you couldn't. Not while Varak is still alive. You might not be able to do it if you did." She glanced back over her shoulder. "And then she would know. It would be worse for me."

"I'll make sure that we're very careful when we go after him, so that won't happen. But I can't just leave you here." He reached in his pocket and scrawled numbers on a card. "This is my friend Jill's phone number." He came toward her and put the card in her hand. "If you don't hear from me, if something happens, call her, and she'll take care of you."

"No," she said fiercely. "Nothing is going to happen to you. You're strong. No one can hurt you. Do you think I'd send you to him if I thought—" She broke off and whirled away from him. "I will call you if I hear of something that might hurt you."

Then she was gone.

Gideon gazed helplessly after her for a moment before he turned toward the maze that led to the street. After this night of fire and death, he hadn't dreamed that Dalai would furnish them with the weapon that might bring Varak down. He should be happy and full of hope. But that vulnerable young girl who had been a victim all her life was still here, and he had no real grasp of what she was facing.

Stop thinking about her. He could only help Dalai by eliminating the threat that was terrifying her the most. So they'd have to go over what she had said about the compound and start planning.

He reached for his phone to call Novak.

———◆———

ROBAKU

"Varak," Jill murmured. "It seems too good to be true. I thought everything was going down the tubes when Zahra came out with that save earlier tonight." She was gazing at the night sky over Jokan, which was still glowing malevolently. "I was afraid to hope."

"And it might be too good to be true," Novak said. "We won't know until we check out that compound where Dalai said we could find Varak." He looked at Gideon. "I told you it could be a trap. You said the girl seemed almost as terrified of Zahra Kiyani as she was of Varak. Zahra has been brainwashing her since childhood."

"It wasn't the same," Gideon said. "She's scared of Zahra. But she thinks she'll only be safe from Varak if he's dead. There's a distinction."

"One of which I approve," Joe Quinn said, turning to Eve, Jill, Novak, and Gideon, who were standing in front of the museum. "It's the first break we've had. Let's go for it. You can check out the terrain and make sure it's as safe as it can be for us, Novak."

"I appreciate your faith in me," Novak said dryly. "I definitely want to check out everything connected with the girl. Gideon is being a little too trusting."

"Only because he's feeling guilty about not having helped Dalai when he had the chance," Eve said. "He was trying to persuade us to adopt her."

"Maybe," Gideon said. "But now we might owe her." He turned back to Novak. "How do we verify the information?"

"I'll send a team to the property to take a good look as soon as it gets light. In the meantime, I'll order a couple infrared drones to scan the area." He cocked a brow as he glanced at Joe. "Providing that meets with your approval?"

"It does." He added, "As long as I'm heading the team that goes in at daybreak."

"No!" Gideon was adamantly shaking his head. "You head the team, Novak. Keep Quinn out of it."

"That's not going to happen," Joe said curtly. "What the hell is wrong with you, Gideon?"

"I've seen how you operate," Gideon said. "It's half instinct and half intellect and all exactly how you want it to go. It might be effective, but I don't want to rely on your decisions when I promised Dalai that we'd be careful not to tip our hand and get her in trouble with Zahra. I wouldn't want Zahra to cut her throat if she thinks she's been betrayed."

"You shouldn't have made her promises," Novak said slowly.

"Well, I did." He met Novak's eyes. "I knew there was a possibility you'd want to move fast. But we've known each other a long time, and I didn't believe that you'd let her get killed if there was any way to keep it from happening. I don't care if you send me or someone else to pull her out of that palace if you make a decision to go for it. I just don't want any action taken without warning." He paused. "And I trust you not to do it."

Novak stared at him for a moment. Then he shrugged and turned away. "I'll do whatever is possible. No promises." He glanced at Joe. "It appears that I'll be heading that team. No offense. I'd trust you implicitly. You're just a little too volatile for Gideon at present." His gaze shifted to Eve. "I wonder why?"

"Joe wouldn't let anything happen to Dalai," Eve said quietly.

"Unless he thought there was reason to think your safety was on the line," Novak said. "Then no one else would have a chance. But hopefully that won't happen today." He looked back at Joe. "Right, Quinn?"

"Hopefully." Joe added impatiently, "It doesn't matter. I'd rather be checking the area for land mines anyway. The girl mentioned explosives."

"Whew." Gideon smiled. "That was close. Defusing land mines seems an ideal job for you. Sorry, Quinn."

"You might be very sorry if you pull that shit again." He turned to Novak. "What time do we leave?"

"Six."

"Then we'd better get some sleep." Joe took Eve's arm. "If you don't mind sharing a bed with a callous bastard like me."

"Ouch," Gideon murmured as he watched them leave. "I knew that was a mistake. But I wasn't able to do anything else for that poor kid."

"I knew it was a mistake, too," Novak said. "You're lucky you didn't piss him off." He turned and headed down the path. "And now I'll go back to the village and do a check to see if Dalai is telling us the truth about the location of Varak's compound and find out everything I can about it. I'll encode and send out two of the X-4 drones. Gideon, I want you to go to the airport and see that there's no slip-up. Got it?"

"Got it."

"Make sure they're functioning properly with the codes I enter. I want accurate information before we start out. In the past, Varak's hideouts have always been almost impregnable. I have to know what to expect, or I'll have to make adjustments." He added, "And try to get a couple hours sleep."

"All those goals might not coincide," Gideon said dryly as he disappeared down the path.

Jill stood hesitantly, gazing after him. She felt totally useless, when she should have had a hand in helping to make this plan work.

"What are you waiting for?" Novak was looking over his shoulder. "An invitation?"

She went still. Then she was running after him. "I'm glad you remembered your manners," she said lightly as she fell into step with him. "I was wondering if I was going to have to barge in on you."

"I knew that would be your next step. You wouldn't have been able to go back to Hajif's hut and try to go back to sleep. That would have been far too sensible and normal."

Yes, Novak had developed an almost paranormal ability to read her, Jill thought. It should have made her uneasy, but she was finding it oddly comforting to have him there, understanding who and what she was. Not always approving, often frustrated, volatile, and disturbing, but an undeniable part of the fabric of her life.

"I wouldn't have been able to sleep," she said. "I'm excited. Can I do something to help you get those drones programmed?"

"Perhaps." He saw her frown and grinned. "Okay, I'll put you to work. Why not?"

"Right." She nodded. "You can never tell when I'll run across a time when I'll need information like that. Drones seem to be an essential part of my life these days." She ducked through the opening of the hut. "How long will it take?"

"Not that long if all goes well. We have Gideon on the other end double-checking." He lit the lantern. "He'll be very careful about not making any mistakes. He knows I'm not pleased with him."

"He was doing what he thought was right," she said quietly. "And you must have thought he was right, too, or you wouldn't have let him talk you into doing what he wanted."

"I hadn't decided one way or the other when Quinn stepped in. It would have been more diplomatic to let him take the reins." He shrugged. "But Gideon didn't allow me the choice. I don't like to be put in that position."

"Joe Quinn is almost a stranger to Gideon, he had to go with the man he trusted. It was important to him." She stared him in the eyes. "I'd be the same. I trust you. If it was important, I'd go to you, Novak."

He went still. "Don't trust me too much, Jill. That's what I told

Gideon. I only do what I can." His lips twisted. "And since I'm such a selfish bastard, what I can do sometimes alters from minute to minute."

She shook her head. "I don't believe you."

"No?" He gazed at her for a long moment. Heat. It came lightning fast out of nowhere. Taking her breath away. She couldn't look away from him. "Well, I did warn you," he said as he took out his computer. "Let's get to work. I'll show you how to look up the address and directions and coordinate it into the drone's memory."

She was relieved that electric moment had passed. Or was she? She was feeling a strange sense of loss. Of course she was. "It sounds complicated." She came closer to look down at the screen. Then she was beginning to get excited again at the challenge before her. "You're sure it won't take more than an hour or so?"

———————

It took an hour and five minutes to program the two drones.

It was not nearly as complicated as she had thought to learn the codes and keep them straight. She had followed Novak's lead, and it was like learning a new game that was as absorbing as it was exciting. She found she was disappointed when she had put in the last equation. "Is that all?"

Novak was grinning. "Unless you want to teach it something else. We're supposed to be gathering information, but I suppose we could rig up a bomb or two to drop on that compound."

"No, that would be breaking your word to Gideon." She was still looking at the computer screen. "It's very sophisticated, isn't it?"

"State of the art." He held up his hand. "But I can see you already creating a story about it. Don't do it. Drones are constantly being upgraded, but this one is very special."

"Okay." She sighed. "But it was great fun. Thank you for letting me play with it."

"My pleasure. It was fun watching you. Your cheeks are still flushed, and your eyes are shining like those of a kid opening a Christmas present." He chuckled. "Next time I'll show you how to set the bomb capability."

"It was fascinating." Her smile suddenly faded. "And dangerous. Bombs and all those technical spy devices...I shouldn't be this excited. I just got caught up in the moment. It's not a game."

"It's whatever you make it." He signed out of the program. "And for you it was a game and a story unfolding and excitement."

"But not for you."

"No. Much darker," he said. "But it was good stepping into your world for a little while." He turned to look at her. "Maybe I'll remember it when it gets a little too dark in mine." He reached down and pulled her to her feet. "Now go to Hajif's and get to sleep. You should still have a few hours."

Heat, again. Out of nowhere. Tingling through her body, causing her breasts to swell. She quickly pulled her hand away. "Hardly seems worth it."

"I don't suppose I could talk you into not getting up when we take off? There's no reason why you should."

Other than the fact that she should be going with him. The darkness of which he'd spoken was suddenly overwhelming her. This was her fight as well as his, and now he was going to face the monster while she was supposed to stay here and snooze. "There's a reason," she said tightly. "You know there's a reason." She turned on her heel. "I'll see you at six."

A few minutes later, she had reached Hajif's hut. She stood outside the door, breathing hard. She couldn't go in right now, she was too upset. She sank down on the ground and leaned back against the wall. Her hands clenched into fists.

She *hated* it. She felt helpless, and it shouldn't be like this. She was the one who had gone to Novak in the beginning and asked him to help her go after Varak. Now he was going to leave her behind when she was responsible for everything that had happened since that night? Reason told her that she would not be an asset if she insisted on going with Novak. She had no military experience and might even be a danger to the team. He had a right to expect her to stay out of it.

But she wanted to go. She *needed* to go with him. Varak was a devil from the depths of hell. He had reached out and killed thousands of people. Who knew what kind of force he still had at his command? It might be intended to be an exploratory foray into that jungle, but that didn't mean it would stay that way. The panic was rising as the thought stabbed through her. How many stories had she written about good plans gone wrong?

They could all die.

Novak could die.

No!

She jumped to her feet. She tore across the short distance that separated her from Novak's hut in seconds. The next instant she was inside. "This is all wrong!" she said fiercely. "I can't have it like this."

He whirled to face her. "What's wrong?" He was instantly on the attack. "What happened?"

"I won't be cheated." She hurled herself at him. She was in his arms. She was kissing him. "I won't have *you* cheated. Varak has already taken too much. Take off your clothes."

"What?" He pushed her away from him to look down at her. "What the hell are you doing, Jill?"

"Nothing that's in the least thought-out, or probably even sane. And you have a perfect right to say you've changed your mind and don't want me. But I think it's still there, or I wouldn't be feeling—"

"Shut up," he said hoarsely. "You're damn right it's not sane. And every word is making me rock-hard. Get out of here."

She shook her head. "You want it. You want me. You've told me you do." She broke free of him and pulled her tee shirt over her head and threw it aside. "And I wish you'd take your clothes off so that

I won't feel as if I'm some kind of sex maniac. I'm not very good at this seduction bullshit. I've always thought that kind of thing was phony." She was trying to undo her bra. "But if that's what you want, then I'll try to—"

"Stop it." He grabbed her wrists and held her still. "You're killing me." He drew a deep breath. "Talk to me. Tell me what brought this on before I throw you out."

"That's just like you. You tell me what you want, then all of a sudden you're worrying and pushing me away because you think that I'm so damn vulnerable." She glared up at him. "I'm not weak. Sometimes bad things happen to me, but I can handle them. I'll always be able to handle them without you taking care of me. So back off, Novak."

"You're not answering me."

"Because when you come into the room I tense up because I know your just being here will change everything. It shouldn't be that way. I write my own story, dammit. But not when you're around. Why do you think I've been fighting you? But now Gideon pulls this thing with Varak out of his hat, and suddenly it doesn't matter." She repeated through set teeth, "It doesn't *matter*. So take off your clothes, Novak."

"Not quite yet." His gaze was narrowed on her face. "Why did it make a difference?"

"Don't be stupid. I can't go with you, dammit. I'd be a liability. What if something happens to you? What if you die? Then Varak would win because we'd both be cheated by him. We wouldn't be able to have this." She was trying to steady her voice. "I won't have that, Novak. I want you to have everything you want. And I want to have everything I want. And we both know what we've wanted since the day we met." She swallowed. "So will you please let go of my wrists and take me down on those blankets over there and do something about it?"

"So I'm to thank that bastard, Varak, for you?" His hands tightened on her wrists. "I don't think so, Jill. I don't find that prospect appealing." His lips twisted. "What am I saying? I'm going crazy at the thought of dragging you down on those blankets. I just can't stomach the idea that he'd have anything to do with it." He suddenly smiled recklessly. "So I'll have to make sure that it's only between you and me. Because I'm not going to be fool enough to walk away from you no matter what brought you here." He dropped her wrists and started to unbutton his shirt. "Though I admit I had a crazy idea that I should be noble and all that crap. But I'm way past that. I've been wanting you too long."

"I never asked you to be noble. You're the one who called me walking wounded." She watched him drop his shirt on the floor. His body was so lean and sleek and muscular, like a panther's. She couldn't take her eyes off the corded muscles of his stomach. "And I just didn't want you to think I wasn't strong. I've never shown any-one as much weakness as I've shown you."

"That's supposed to be weakness?" Two movements, and he pulled her into his arms. He was rocking her gently back and forth. "Just be quiet, will you? You're making me crazy. I don't want to feel like this about you right now. All I want to think about is how much I *need* you." Then she realized her bra was gone and he was rub-bing her breasts back and forth against his chest. She gasped as she felt the warmth of his flesh against her, the faint abrasiveness of his chest hair against her nipples, which was causing her to tighten and swell. "That's right," he murmured. "This is what I want...But it's not enough. I want my mouth on you."

And the next moment, his mouth closed on her nipple.

Suction.

His tongue...

His teeth...

Her back arched as she felt the pressure.

"Wait," she gasped. She was wildly shedding her clothes as his mouth never left her. "I can't take—"

"Yes, you can. You can take everything. This is how strong you are." He pulled her down on the blankets. "So don't tell me you're not strong." He was shedding his clothes as he spoke. "I'll show you what you can take." He stopped suddenly as he looked down at her. "I'm going wild. I'll try to let you set the pace, but I can't promise. The last thing I want to do is hurt you. Don't let me do that. Just tell me."

She was panting, moving against him. The feel of his hips against her... "Will you stop worrying? I *know* you, Novak. Just *touch* me." Then she suddenly lunged upward and took him instead. "Yes!"

He froze. His face contorting. "Well. That ends that, doesn't it?" he said hoarsely. "It's up to you from now on. I'm gone..." He started to move.

Fast.

Hard.

Heat.

Hot. So hot.

She heard herself gasping, crying, as she met him, tried to take more of him.

Crazy.

It went on and on. He was moving her, positioning her, so many positions... until she thought she couldn't take any more; and then she found there were no limits.

His face over her, tense, almost in pain.

Then it was going faster, harder.

"Novak..."

Darkness.

Light.

Pressure.

Impossible that it could go on.

But it had to go on, she couldn't let him leave her...

Then he was gathering her close, lifting her. "Jill?"

But he wasn't leaving her she realized out of the haze of madness. He was taking her with him.

Her fingers dug into his shoulders.

She thought she screamed. But there was no sound, she realized. Because she had no breath and was clinging helplessly to him as wave after wave was overwhelming her.

"Okay?" His chest was moving in and out with the force of his breathing. "I didn't do—"

"Don't you dare," she gasped. "I'm quite sure you wouldn't ask that of any other woman at a time like this. I'm fine, better than fine."

"You're not any other woman." His voice was low against her throat. "I'm not sure I'll ever be able to compare you to other women." He lifted his head to look down at her. "So don't expect it."

She met his gaze. She wanted to pull him down and return to the hot, erotic intimacy that had gone before. She couldn't read his expression and it was making her uneasy. Sensuality. Intensity. Something else . . .

"That's fine with me." She smiled with an effort. "I don't mind being unique. As long as you understand who I am and realize you can't change me."

"Ah, yes, I mustn't try to influence your story." His lips twisted. "I'll try to keep that in mind." He kissed the hollow of her throat. "But you evidently don't mind me taking action on this level. You came to me."

"Yes."

He licked her lower lip. "And you didn't once think of Varak, did you?"

He knew she hadn't. She still wasn't sure what he was thinking. "Novak, what are you doing?" She paused. "Are you angry?"

"I wouldn't be so ungrateful. I don't really know what I am at this moment. I'm having problems sorting out what I'm feeling about this particular chapter in your story." His lips moved down to her breast, and his tongue flicked lazily at her nipple. "But I do know that we're both in complete agreement that this was entirely success-ful." He moved over her. "And we want more. You're ready for me. Am I wrong?"

She was more than ready. It had been such a short time, but she was burning. Dangerous. It was so dangerous to feel that sexual intensity for him. She wasn't even certain that it was only sex. She had always been confused about her emotions regarding him. Admiration, respect, gratitude were all mixed with that wariness. It would be even more dangerous if it was more than sex.

Worry about it later. She bit her lower lip as the waves of heat moved through her. She couldn't think now that his hands were moving, teasing, entering. Just take what he was offering. "No, you're not wrong." She pulled him down to her, and whispered, "There's nothing I want more than this now, Novak."

———◆———

Voices.

Novak was on the phone, Jill realized drowsily.

Then she was wide-awake. Her eyes flew open, and she saw Novak sitting at the bench across the hut. He was fully dressed and gazing at his computer.

"What is it?" Then she shook her head as she realized what it must be. "What time is it? Did you get the drone results?"

He nodded. "About ten minutes ago. They came in a little after five. I've been going over the results with Gideon."

"What were they?" She was quickly throwing on her clothes. "Why didn't you wake me?"

"No need. You didn't get much sleep," he said absently, his gaze on the computer. "It's not as if you could do anything about it."

That was true enough, Jill thought. She had probably drifted off to sleep only minutes before he'd received those results. And it only heightened her frustration that he was perfectly right about her not being able to help him in any way. That was what had started the sexual marathon that had caused her to still be here when those results had come in. "You're probably right," she said curtly. "Call it curiosity. I'd like to know."

He turned to face her. "I'm sorry. I didn't think." He tapped the screen. "Very heavy foliage and tree cover. Glimpses of what could be a residence and four bunkhouses. Several possible vehicles. Farther back on the property, a concrete pad that could be used for a helicopter." He looked up at her. "And the infrared showed at least forty or fifty figures under that heavy canopy of foliage."

"Then it could be true." She inhaled sharply as excitement gripped her. "Dalai must have told Gideon the truth. It could be Varak."

"It could be Varak," he agreed. "Particularly since the drone also detected the presence of explosives throughout the area. Varak has always been fond of his land mines. But that foliage is like a thick blanket, we won't know until we get there. And several of those figures were probably sentries moving around the property. One false step, and we could get ourselves killed, or tip Varak off that we're on the property. We've got to be careful."

"Then you won't be able to go in and get him right away." She tried not to sound as relieved as she felt. "You'll have to mount surveillance until you're certain?"

"Probably. I want to know everything about the place, and I want a visual on Varak."

"Dalai told Gideon that Zahra had paid for plastic surgery."

"I've been on the hunt for Varak ever since he showed up in Maldara. I studied him for years after he started his killing sprees here. He might change his face, but he's a big bastard, and he won't have been able to change the way he moves. I'll know him." His lips tightened. "And then I'll find a way to go in and get him."

"Unless you find an opportunity to get your hands on him today," she said bitterly.

He nodded. "Maybe."

"That's what I thought." She turned and headed for the door. "Do let me know when you make a decision."

"Jill."

"Look, I know you have to do this," she said jerkily. "But next time, I want to be there when it happens, so you find a way to not get yourself killed today."

"I'm not going to get myself killed," he said quietly. "What happened between us blew my mind. I have no intention of cutting what we have short. Will you come back here tonight, and we'll do it all over again? Plus more erotic embellishments?" He added mockingly, "Provided that Varak doesn't kill me."

He was actually joking? "You bastard."

"I admit I'm a little raw about your having to use such a sleazy excuse as Varak to come to me. Particularly since I've discovered that you've become an obsession." He added softly, "I'll come to you with no excuse at all. From now on, I won't be able to leave you alone. Expect me."

"The hell I will." She left the hut and strode toward Hajif's place. She'd wanted to *hit* Novak. The news that the possible strike on Varak might be temporarily averted had thrown her from despair to relief, then to anger. He was annoyed that it was Varak that had been the impetus to bring her to him? Screw him. She had been in a turmoil of emotion all night. Scared to death that he might get killed, then having probably the most erotic sexual encounter she'd ever experienced.

She had reached Hajif's hut, and she stopped to get a breath and calm down. It wasn't sunrise yet, but she knew that it was almost time for Novak to go to the museum to meet with Joe Quinn. She couldn't hide away here. She would wash, change her clothes, and be on her way there, too. Eve would expect her, and it wasn't professional to do anything else. Though she knew Novak would have made certain Eve was guarded, if Joe was going with Novak, Jill should be there to protect and support Eve.

Screw Novak.

But please keep him safe today, dammit, she added quickly

CHAPTER

16

I'll call you as soon as we know anything," Joe said. He kissed Eve and headed for the door, where Novak was waiting. "Don't worry. I checked Novak's security arrangements, and you'll be fine."

"Yes, I'm really worried about that," Eve said dryly. "I'm not the one who's going to be checking out land mines."

"I know what I'm doing, Eve," he said quietly as he glanced over his shoulder. "You know that's true."

"I know, but that doesn't help much." She gestured impatiently. "Get out of here. The sooner you leave, the sooner you'll get back. Keep safe."

He nodded, and his glance shifted to Jill. "Make yourself useful. Watch over her."

"I will," Jill said. "Why do you think I'm here? I realize she's my responsibility." She was trying not to look at Novak. The anger she had felt was dissipating, lost in the panic, and she tried to hold on to it. "Good luck." Her gaze shifted to Novak. "You, too, Novak. Don't do anything stupid. You promised Gideon."

He smiled mockingly. "I'll keep that in mind. I'll definitely see you later, Jill."

Then they were both gone.

And Jill found herself going to the door to watch them go down the path. Her hands clenched into fists. "Look at them. They can't wait to get out there and play their war games. They could get themselves blown up."

"Yes, they could." Eve came over to stand beside her. "And it's really getting to you." Her eyes were on Jill's face. "Maybe more than I would have thought."

"And it's not bothering you?" Jill shook her head. "I know better than that. I've never seen anyone as crazy about a man as you are about Joe Quinn. I didn't expect you to be this controlled."

"I have to be controlled," Eve said quietly. "Joe is a detective, and he's in danger every day. I face this too often to let myself fall apart every time he walks out the door in the morning. It's his job, and it wouldn't be fair to him. And he's fantastically efficient at that job, and that helps."

"Is he really that good with land mines?"

"Yes, trained by the SEALs, and he kept up with advances. He's done work on cases where he had to defuse them. And once when we were in Scotland, he got rid of a number of them planted on the road bordering a lake we were exploring. He knows what he's doing. So I trust him with those damn bombs as well as everything else." Her lips twisted. "Even though at times like this it nearly kills me. Particularly since this time I'm to blame for his being here."

"No, you aren't. I am," Jill said in frustration. "Joe knows that, everyone knows that. Which is why I should be going with them today." She raised her hand. "Mistake. You don't have to tell me it would be a mistake. I know it would be a mistake. I'd be a liability. I don't have the training." She added gloomily, "I think I should get Novak to send me to that same CIA training camp in Afghanistan where he sent Gideon."

"What? I don't believe you'd stand a chance in persuading him," Eve said. "And he'd probably be right. That's not where you make a real difference in life. You don't shoot people. You use your brain and figure out how to change the way they think so that they'll do what you want. It's part of your ability as a storyteller. That's where you make the difference. That's your talent, and who should know better than I how good you are at it?" She grimaced. "Though considering the kind of situations in which you become embroiled, it might not be a bad idea to keep that training camp on the back burner as an alternate plan. But I'd find another way to reach the same goal."

"Easy to say. Right now I feel like one of those medieval women who were left home to tend the castle while the men rode off to save the world. It's driving me crazy." Her gaze suddenly narrowed on Eve's face. "And I bet it's driving you crazy, too. You'd hate it as much as I do. How do you cope?"

"Like you, I try to be reasonable about the greater good. I have a son to think about, and that has a tremendous influence." She suddenly smiled recklessly. "And when I can't stand it any longer, I go for it, get on my trusty steed, and ride hell for leather and leave that safe, boring castle behind."

Jill smiled back at her. "I thought as much." Her smile faded. "But what are you going to do today?"

"I'm going to work on Mila." Eve went over to her worktable. "Because that's where *my* expertise lies. And I'll try to get lost in my work and forget that Varak might have a more sophisticated land mine than we've seen yet. I'm going to trust Joe and Gideon and Novak. I'm going to wait for Joe's call. If I have to stay in the castle, I'll be as productive and inventive as I possibly can. So that next time, I might be the one to save the world." She glanced over her shoulder. "Sound like a plan?"

"It sounds like you," Jill said. She turned away. "I'll have to think about it. I'm having trouble adjusting at the moment. Thanks for letting me vent. I needed it."

"I could see that. No problem." She smiled. "It was good talking just to remind myself of all the things I knew were important. Sometimes emotions get in the way." She paused. "I'm scared, too, Jill.

Varak seems like the ultimate bogeyman. He's escaped so many times during these last years. No one has been able to touch him. And now he's got Zahra Kiyani in his corner. When Gideon told us about the compound, I thought that it was going to be okay. But what if it isn't? Novak's drones uncovered some nasty surprises."

"They'll find a way to get around them. It might just take a little while."

"Yeah, I know." Eve forced her gaze to shift back to her reconstruction. "Definitely time for me to get to work."

Jill watched Eve's hands flying over the clay. Eve was focusing, her determination unquestionable as usual. It was a quality Jill envied at this moment.

Then do something about it, she thought impatiently. She turned and went out the door. The morning sunlight was getting stronger, and it was warm on her arms as she sat down beside the door. She had promised to watch over Eve, but she needed a little distance now.

Because Eve's words had struck a strong, resounding chord. She had to think about them, examine them, let them begin to come alive. She knew about words. They were a part of her mind, part of who she was. And these words might be some of the most important of her life.

You don't shoot people. You use your brain to figure out how to change the way they think so that they'll do what you want. It's part of your ability as a storyteller.

That's where you make the difference.

That was true. All her life that was what had made the difference. Yet from the time she had brought Eve to Maldara, she had stepped back because of guilt and uncertainty. She had relied on Novak, Gideon, Joe Quinn, and Eve herself to make most of the moves forward. She'd been content to merely sit on the sidelines and watch over Eve.

And Kimbro had died. Eve had been poisoned. There was no

telling how much blame Jill had to shoulder about the bombing of that U.N. building because she hadn't been more aggressive.

She had to close her eyes for an instant. She couldn't be sure that everything would have been different if she'd been more true to herself. But what if it had been? When you wrote a story, every chapter, every paragraph, every plot point made a difference.

She opened her eyes and drew a long breath. Okay, don't look back. Look forward. Do what Eve said she could do, use her primary talent. Figure out a way to change the way the story would go. Pray that trip to Varak's encampment would yield dividends but don't count on it. Rely only on yourself.

Look at the principal characters and how they would behave. Explore weakness, strength.

Varak was a sociopath, almost impossible to judge.

But Zahra...

What had Eve said about Zahra?

And now he's got Zahra Kiyani in his corner.

But did he really have her in his corner? Could her character be moved, shifted?

Think about that...

And who else had moved into the spotlight?

Dalai.

Strange to think of that slender, vulnerable girl in anything as bold as a spotlight. She had fluttered in and out around Gideon, then had run away. But there had been no doubt that she had been honest and helpful about Varak. Jill hadn't realized until now that something about her encounter with Gideon had made her uneasy...

Put the thought aside. Let it simmer.

Go back to the beginning, when she'd first gotten that offer from Hadfeld.

That was really the start of the story...

NAGALI RAIN FOREST
2:35 P.M.

"Quinn's not back yet?" Gideon murmured to Novak as he crawled
back from checking on the other men on the team. "It's been almost
an hour. I don't like it. He stopped us four times before we got half
a mile into the property to disarm land mines. I have an idea this
whole jungle is one big time bomb."

"So does Quinn," Novak said grimly. "That's why he wanted to
explore ahead to make sure that it would be minimally safe for us to
go forward without blowing ourselves up. The sentries are the least
of our worries."

"Well, they may not be the least of Quinn's worries. I didn't
hear any explosions, but one of the sentries might have gotten
him." Then he shook his head. "No, Quinn's too sharp. Forget I
said that. I just want to get moving. So do the rest of your team,
Novak."

"Do you think I don't?" He paused, struggling with his own impatience. "Quinn knows what he's doing." He added, "I hope."

"That didn't appear to be a sincere vote of confidence." Joe Quinn
was suddenly moving out of the palmetto bushes next to them. "But
I can see why. I thought I'd be back before this."

"Why weren't you?"

"I knew after a half hour that I wasn't going to be able to bring
any of the team much farther than this point. I've never seen an area
so heavily seeded with land mines. Varak must be truly paranoid. I
watched one of his sentries, who obviously had a defined path, and
he was very careful about not going off that path. He probably didn't
know where all those land mines were either."

"And that surprises you?" Novak asked. "Varak would have been
amused if one of his men was careless enough to get himself blown
up." He asked, "Where were you for the rest of that hour?"

"Taking photos. Trying to determine sentry placement. I found the helicopter pad." He looked at Novak. "And I located the main house and bunkhouses."

Novak tensed. "Varak?"

"I didn't see him. And that area is so heavily fortified, there's no way we'd be able to get into his house or get a shot at Varak without being blown away ourselves." His lips twisted. "I thought I'd better get back instead of staking him out. After all, you are heading this team."

"Not so that anyone would notice," he said. "You said that the team wouldn't be able to go any farther, but you managed to flit all around the damn encampment."

"I knew what I was doing. One man with experience. An entire team tramping through there would end up in pieces. The odds are someone would make a mistake." He looked at Gideon. "And that young girl you were so concerned about would pay for it when Varak got spooked. Do you want that?"

"No. But I *do* want Varak." He turned to Novak. "What do we do?"

Novak thought about it. Dammit, he couldn't see any options at the moment. He muttered a curse, then said to Gideon, "Go back to the men and get them out of here and back to Robaku." He whirled back to Quinn. "You said one man could do it. How about two? Can you take me back to that house so that I can verify that bastard is Nils Varak?"

Quinn gazed thoughtfully at him. "Maybe. You want to stake him out?"

"I want to see him *move*. And maybe there's some way we can get in that house for DNA. If we can't, I want to get a video to send to our lab for facial analysis and verification. They'd be able to determine if his basic facial structure would support that plastic surgery Zahra paid for. It's not much, but I don't want this all to be for nothing. Can you do it?"

Quinn was thinking about it. "You do know that it gets dark very early in rain forests like these. Those tree canopies block out all light. You'd have only a limited amount of time to stake him out. We'd have maybe three or four hours." He added grimly, "And it's hard as hell to avoid those land mines when I can see. Even at dusk, it would be a risk. I can't use a flashlight because of the sentries."

"Stop telling me about the problems. Will you do it?"

"Shit," Gideon said. "Novak!"

"Answer me, Quinn." Novak held his eyes. "Can you get me there?"

Quinn suddenly smiled. "Sure, no problem. I know the way now. Providing you can follow in my steps without a single deviation. Not even an inch." He added dryly, "That would be nearly impossible for you considering that you don't like to go any way but your own."

"But not quite impossible," he said curtly. "I'd have the comfort of knowing you'd be blown up before I would." He turned away. "Let's go, Quinn."

Quinn nodded. "By all means. I was pissed off about having to stop and come back to you anyway." He moved back into the palmetto bushes. "Stay close, Novak. I'm going to be moving very fast."

ROBAKU
5:50 P.M.

"What do you mean they went back into that jungle?" Jill stared at Gideon in horror. "Gideon. Why did you just leave them there?"

"I had orders, dammit," Gideon said. "I couldn't go with them, but I could get the team safely back. That's what I did."

"Since when did you ever obey orders," Jill's voice was shaking. "You do what you like."

"Not when it comes down to sacrificing thirty-two men by not obeying two men who have a hell of a lot more experience than I do."

"No, you'd rather sacrifice—"

"Easy, Jill," Eve said. "It's not his fault. Would you like to go up against Novak or Joe?"

"Yes, I'd like to knock their heads together." But she realized Eve was right. It was just the shock that had caused her to attack Gideon. Shock and sickening fear. But she had to control it. Eve was just as frightened as she was, and she mustn't make it worse for her. She forced herself to nod at Gideon. "You did what you could. I'm just scared."

"Me too." He made a face. "I nearly flipped when Novak wanted to go back with Quinn to stake out Varak. I would have done anything I could to stop them. I was worried about Quinn's being a wild card, but Novak was just as bad today."

"Or just as good," Eve said quietly. "They're both professionals, and they wanted to get the job done. What can we do to help them, Gideon?"

He shook his head. "Not much of anything. Just wait. I left two men on the road that borders the property to send me word if anything...unusual occurred."

"You mean if one of those land mines blew up," Jill said.

Gideon nodded. "That was what Quinn was worried about. I told you that he told Novak he wanted to get out of that jungle before it got dark."

"Yes, you did." Eve was looking out the window at the fading light. "It should be dark soon."

Gideon didn't say anything.

Jill's gaze flew to his face. "Gideon?"

"Not in that rain forest," he said. "It's probably been pitch-dark for the last thirty minutes."

She inhaled sharply. She felt as if she'd been kicked in the stomach.

Gideon said quickly, "You know they'll call as soon as they get to a safe area."

"Whenever that is," Eve said numbly. She straightened her shoulders. "Yes, Joe will call me as soon as he can. I know that."

"Of course you do. Let's go outside and get some air." Jill strode toward the door and opened it for Eve. "Like you said, they're both professionals."

She watched Eve go out the door before she turned to Gideon. "How bad was it out there?"

"Deadly. What you'd expect from Varak," he said soberly. "It's set up to be a killing field, between the land mines and the multiple snipers. If the team had gone in, the chances are we'd have never come out. Novak knew that, but he was desperate."

"So he took the chance himself." Her lips twisted. "And he'll do it again." She started out the door toward Eve. "If Varak didn't kill them both this time." Her hands clenched into fists at her sides. "We'll have to see if Eve gets that call."

———————◆———————

The call didn't come until almost an hour later.

Jill's heart jumped, and she whirled to face Eve.

Eve nodded and quickly checked the ID. "Joe."

Relief so great it made Jill dizzy. "Thank God."

Eve answered the phone. "You're an idiot, Joe," she said huskily. "Are you both all right?" She nodded at Jill at his answer. "You don't deserve it. When will you be here so that I can tell you in person?" A moment later she hung up the phone. "Another forty-five minutes. They didn't leave the stakeout until it was almost fully dark, and it took them longer to get back through the jungle."

"I would think it would. Was the risk worth it? Did they get what they needed?"

Eve made a face. "Joe said partially successful. But partially is never enough for Joe."

"Nor for Novak." Jill tried to keep her voice steady. "I'll go inside and tell Gideon that they evidently didn't get blown up. Coming?"

Eve shook her head. "I'll wait out here. I'm too edgy to be cooped up right now."

"And you want to see Joe the minute he walks down that path."

"You might say that," she said lightly. She leaned back against the wall. "Though I do intend to be very stern with him."

"Yeah, sure." Jill opened the door and went into the museum.

Gideon immediately looked up. "Eve heard?"

Jill nodded. "Both okay. They'll be here in about forty-five minutes. You'll probably hear from Novak soon."

Gideon gave a low whistle. "I'll call the airport and let the team know."

"Do that." She was silent a moment. "They didn't get everything they needed. They'll probably go back, won't they?"

He hesitated. "It depends on how successful they were."

"The only results they'd consider successful enough to stop them from going after Varak would be if they'd managed to kill him or had gotten some scrap of DNA material that would prove his identity. Neither of those things was likely to happen according to Joe. Right?"

"That's what he said," Gideon said warily.

"Then no way should they run the risk of going after him again," she said flatly. "We need to leave him alone and try another direction."

"It's Varak, Jill," he said gently. "He's out there waiting for us to scoop him up."

"It's the wrong thing to do. I sat here all day, going over everything that has happened since I got that first message from Hadfeld, until the moment you showed up with the location of that compound from Dalai. It's like a story with huge gaps missing, but nothing I thought of or tried to put together made going after Varak in that jungle the right thing to do." She held up her hand as he started to protest. "And I'm not going to argue with you. I know where you're coming from. I'll talk to you later." She turned and headed for the door. "Will you stay here with Eve until Joe and Novak get here? I'm tired, and I think I'll go down to Hajif's hut and rest for a while."

His eyes widened in surprise. "You don't want to wait until they get here?"

She shook her head. "So I can hear about how they avoided the killing fields? Maybe later. Right now, it doesn't appeal to me. It makes me feel sick to my stomach." She headed down the hill toward the village.

She needed to be alone. She didn't know what her attitude would be when she saw Novak again. The day had been fraught with tension and worry and attempts to forget that he might not be coming back. That first moment when she had realized he was safe had been dizzy and shocking and put her on an emotional roller coaster. What they had between them was only sex and passion and the strange bond of fascination that had formed these past months, she told herself. Last night, she had been swept away, and today had been so emotional that she couldn't regain her equilibrium. It was better if she took a step back until she was more cool and able to analyze her responses.

And there was no way that would have been true if she'd been there when he'd walked into the museum tonight. No, she needed to go to see Hajif and Leta, have a light meal, then go to bed.

She would deal with Novak tomorrow.

———

Her phone rang three hours later.

She tensed, then rolled over on her sleeping mat and reached for it.

Novak.

Bite the bullet. He wouldn't stop calling until she answered. "Hello, Novak."

"Get out of there and come to me. I need to see you."

"I'm already in bed."

"I don't care. Come to me, or I'll come and get you. You don't want Hajif and Leta to be upset." He cut the connection.

No, she didn't want Hajif to be drawn into this. She rolled off the mat and threw on her clothes. A moment later, she'd stalked out of Hajif's hut. She saw Novak in the doorway of his hut, framed against the lantern light behind him, and strode toward him. "What do you want, Novak? That was completely rude, and I don't appreciate you—"

"Shut up." He pulled her into the hut and jerked her into his arms. "I'm having a very bad day." He kissed her. "And I didn't need to have you hiding out and avoiding me at the end of it. Particularly after Gideon was telling me how weird and stiff you were being." He kissed her again. "That's not going to happen. If you don't want to screw me, that's your decision, but you're going to be with me. I need you." He pushed her down on the blankets. "Do you want a drink? I could use one right now. A glass of wine?"

"How polite." She sat up, trying to get her breath. What had started out as anger was transforming into that same electricity she had felt last night. Her breasts were swelling, her lower body tingling, readying. "And you can't force me to be here. What's wrong with you, dammit?"

"Wine," he answered himself. "You like wine." He poured a merlot from a bottle into a glass. He poured himself a whiskey and sat down cross-legged in front of her. He handed her the goblet. "No force. I merely made a suggestion."

"Bullshit."

He grinned. "Okay, I wanted to catch your attention."

"I almost decked you."

"And I wanted a little sympathy after a hard day."

"Not the way to get it. And since when have you ever come to anyone after something goes wrong? I've never seen anyone so self-sufficient."

"It's a new era." He took a sip of his whiskey. "Maybe I've never found anyone with whom I wanted to share my very rare failures. Or maybe I just wanted to see you sitting here and know that there was someone I cared about whom Varak hadn't been able to touch. Anyway, I was frustrated as hell when you weren't there when I got back to that museum. I needed you."

He had said that before, and suddenly Jill's impatience was dwindling before it disappeared entirely. It would take a lot for a self-assured man like Novak to admit to needing anyone. "Gideon said that it was bad out there." She took a sip of her wine. "A setup for a killing field." She added with sudden fierceness, "So why did you go back with Quinn and try to get yourself slaughtered? Varak's killed close to six hundred thousand people in that war, and he clearly built that compound as a trap. You knew it, and you still talked Joe Quinn into staking out that house."

"I didn't have to talk very hard. Quinn wanted him as much as I did. I only had to let him control how he got me through that land-mine tangle. Quinn likes control."

"And you don't?" She shook her head in frustration. "The two of you together are a complete disaster."

"Actually, I found we worked very well together today."

"And that could be an even bigger disaster." She drew a deep breath. "Would you like to tell me why you waited until after dark to start trying to get back out of that jungle when Quinn told you how dangerous it would be?"

He shrugged. "It wasn't that bad. Quinn had the route pretty well memorized, including land-mine placement. And we had no choice. We didn't get even a glimpse of Varak until almost twilight. I was afraid we might have to give it up for the day." His lips twisted. "But then Varak's true nature came to the rescue. He evidently hadn't had his quota of blood recently. He had one of his soldiers dragged to that dirt yard before the front porch to be punished for some infraction at the attack on the U.N. headquarters. At least that was the excuse. I think he probably just wanted his men to witness how all-powerful he was." He paused. "He used a machete. He took a long time. I had no problem getting the videos."

Jill felt sick. "You said that you'd know him just by the way he moved. Was it really Varak?"

He nodded. "I'd swear to it. But that wouldn't be enough, of course. Not now that Zahra has convinced everyone that Varak's skull was destroyed at the U.N. headquarters. Probably the videos won't be enough either, but we can send them through our photo techno unit at Langley to establish what he could have looked like before surgery. But we'll have to go back and break into that house in the compound and get a DNA specimen so that I can get the director to let me stage a raid powerful enough to bring Varak down."

"That means you're determined to go back there," Jill said tightly.

"It's our only option if we want to grab the bastard before he decides to leave the country. We're lucky to get the chance."

"I don't believe there's any luck connected to Varak unless it's bad luck. He definitely couldn't be recognized?"

He shook his head. "His face has been changed, his hair is sandy-blond, not black. The only thing that's the same is that muscular, powerful body and the way he walks. The arrogant bastard strides around as if he owns the world..."

Muscular and powerful . . . As arrogant as if he owned the world.

Jill went still. "His hair is dyed blond now? I only remember Dalai telling Gideon that he'd had plastic surgery."

"Very good plastic surgery. But his hair is kind of dirty blond now."

Fair hair. Suddenly, her chest was tight, and she was having trouble breathing. It couldn't be the same man, could it? Varak wouldn't take the risk of exposing himself just to inflict that act of terror on her. And she hadn't been able to see what shade her attacker's hair was in the darkness, only that it was light, fair. But she had felt the straw-like texture beneath her fingers when she'd been fighting him.

But it had done her no good to fight him, she remembered in a panic. She'd felt so weak, and he'd been brutally strong...

As if he'd owned the world.

"Jill?" Novak's gaze was narrowed on her face.

"You said you took a video." She moistened her lips as she put her glass of wine carefully on the floor beside her. "I want to see it."

"No, you don't," he said flatly. "You don't want to ever see that bloodbath."

"You took it. I want to see it."

"Why?" he asked roughly. "So that you can add it to your collection of nightmares? There's no need for you to see it."

"That's up to me, isn't it?" She had to keep her voice steady. "You thought it important enough to risk getting yourself killed. Show it to me."

"I tell you, it's the stuff of nightmares. You don't want to—" He suddenly broke off. "Nightmares..." His gaze was searching her face. "Don't make me show you this, Jill."

"I want to see it."

He muttered a curse. "And it seems I'm going to let you see it." He got to his feet, went to the phone lying on the bench, and brought it to her. "Do me a favor and don't watch more than the first five minutes. He does a lot of strutting during that period and doesn't get into the carnage until you see him take his machete."

She was bracing herself to press the PLAY button. "He loves that machete." She swallowed. "That's how he killed those children."

"Press the button," he said roughly. "Just watch it and get it over with."

She pressed the button.

Fair hair. Eyes glittering as Varak strode out on the porch and looked down at the man kneeling in the yard.

Ferocity.

His lips pulled away from his teeth like that of a feral animal.

Malicious pleasure.

Anticipating the pain to come.

He was speaking, hurling threats at the man on his knees.

Then he was walking down the steps.

Power. Arrogance. As if he owned the world...

She couldn't take her eyes off him. She was staring in helpless fascination.

Even when one of Varak's men handed him his machete.

"No, dammit!" Novak was there beside Jill, jerking his phone away from her. "No more."

"No more," she repeated dully. She didn't need any more. She'd seen enough. "Thank you. I... couldn't seem to stop. He was like a snake that was weaving back and forth and hypnotizing me. Not letting me move." She hadn't been able to move that night in the jungle either. "I couldn't move at all. Only snakes aren't that strong..."

"Shh." She was suddenly in his arms. "No, they're not that strong. And I'll be chopping the head off this particular snake very soon. He's just jumped even higher on my kill list." His hand cupped the back of her head, his lips at her temple. "It was him?" he asked softly. "He was one of those sons of bitches who raped you that night?"

She shook her head. "No, he was the one who was telling the rest of them how to do it." Her voice was shaking. "He kept saying they weren't hurting me enough. That it wouldn't do any good unless they broke me. He seemed angry about it. He was the one who kept beating me and beating me..." She had to take a deep breath. "It was him. I recognized the eyes." She added, "And the voice. I didn't realize I'd remember so much. It was such a hideous blur. Or maybe I just tried to block him out." She recalled something else. "And that laugh. I'll always remember him laughing when he leaned over me and asked how I liked it—" Her fingers bit into his shoulders. "But he never actually raped me, and I didn't get a chance to scratch him. He must have been very careful about DNA. He'd know how dangerous it was to him... Maybe that was why he was so angry. He'd hate it that he couldn't make me suffer as much as he wanted." She buried her face in his chest. "But you were right—arrogant. As if he owned the world."

"He won't own more than six feet of it when I get my hands on him," Novak said harshly. "I knew you thought he was one of them when you kept insisting on seeing the video. I couldn't stop you when you had a right to know." His lips tightened. "And I had a right to know, too. I've been wanting to kill those bastards from the night it happened."

"It never occurred to me it could be him," Jill said. "I just thought it was a few thugs hired by the people who killed Hadfeld to make certain I left Maldara. Why would Varak become involved in . . . that . . . when it would automatically put him in danger?"

"Why would he use a machete on that man today? The idea probably amused him. I'll have to ask him before I gut him."

His voice was colder than she'd ever heard it, and Jill was beginning to be afraid she'd made a terrible mistake. Novak had already been determined enough to go after Varak in that hellish jungle, and she might have tipped the scales even more. She rushed to repair the damage. "Don't use me as an excuse. I've told you time after time that none of that was your fault. I wasn't your responsibility. Do you hear me?"

He didn't answer.

"And what if you're wrong about making another run at Varak?" she said harshly. "I've been thinking about it today, and it seems too dangerous. He's sitting there with his land mines and his damn machete ready to strike. I know you believe it's the logical way to go, but it could get you—"

"Hush." He pulled her down and fitted her spoon fashion against him. "Just lie here and let me hold you. We'll talk later. You're upset, and I didn't handle any of this right."

"No, you didn't. You should believe me when I tell you something. I know it's partly my fault. I got upset when I realized Varak—" She stopped and started again: "How can I persuade you not to go back into that jungle after Varak?"

"You can't." His lips were brushing her ear. "I can make this work, Jill. All I have to do is figure out the best way to do it."

"You mean to keep him from using that machete on you. It's the *wrong* thing to do," she said passionately. "We can go at it another way."

He didn't answer.

And he wouldn't answer, she thought. "Stubborn jackass."

"Only when I know I'm right. Relax. We'll talk later."

But he wouldn't listen then either. "No, we won't. You're already making plans, and they don't include me. You're scared that I'll break apart. It's been like that from the beginning." She added, "So you shouldn't be upset if I make plans that don't include you."

He stiffened against her. "What's that supposed to mean?"

"It means that this is *my* story, and I'll do anything I can to make it come out right. You're about to mess it up."

"I don't like the sound of that."

"Ditto. Do you want it more clear? It seems I'm going to have to take events into my own hands." She tried to relax her muscles and took a deep breath. "So I'm going to do as you suggest and lie here and take a little while to pull myself together. Because you were right, that video shook me up. But it probably shook you more than it did me because I promised myself that I'd never let any of those men hurt me again. They're no more than a passing memory to me now, and soon, they won't even be that. And it doesn't change anything that one of them was Varak. It will just take a little longer to forget him." She closed her eyes. "I'm going to try to sleep. When I wake up, I hope you'll make love to me because I found it wonderful, and I'm not at all sure that we'll ever do it again."

"Are you finished?" Novak kissed her ear again. "I don't know what's happening with you, but I'm very good at working through problems. That all sounded very final. But I assure you it is not." He held her closer. "By all means rest. Because once we start, we'll be doing it again and again and again..."

CHAPTER
17

J ill moved silently across the dimness of the hut.

"Come back," Novak murmured, as she reached the door. "There's still plenty of time."

She glanced over her shoulder. Novak was only a glimmer of strength and sensuality in the half darkness, but she still felt a hot tingle of sensation run through her. Ignore it. The hours with him that had gone before had made her body too accustomed to the sheer sexual eroticism of what they were together. Her breasts still felt heavy. Her skin felt satin-smooth and pliant. "You're wrong. We're out of time. Maybe I'll see you later, Novak."

The next moment, she was out of the hut. She drew a deep breath of the moist, humid air and started up the path toward the museum. It was only a little after six, and she'd been tempted to go to Hajif's, but she'd be too close and available to Novak there. Last night, he had shown her that he would have no qualms about bursting into Hajif's home if he wished.

And she did not wish to see Novak anytime soon. The sex had been too hot, and there had been that element of domination of which she was always aware with Novak. He hadn't liked it that she'd refused to communicate with him in any other way than the one that had driven both of them to the edge and beyond. If she'd stayed any longer, she would not have been able to fend off either arguments or conversation.

Conversation? They were so far apart, it was a totally foreign concept. He just wanted her to say that he was right, and he wasn't listening to her. And she was so frightened that Varak would kill him that she was desperate to try anything that would leave Varak out of the equation.

And that meant leaving Novak out of the equation as far as she was concerned.

Okay, then, start as she intended to continue.

Check in with Eve, then explore the path that had been beckoning to her since yesterday afternoon...

———◆———

"You've been very restless this morning." Eve looked up from her Mila reconstruction as Jill put coffee in front of her. "Everything okay?"

"As okay as it can be." Then Jill was silent. But she couldn't leave it at that. "Did Joe mention when they'd be going back to Varak's compound?"

Eve shook her head. "Just that they want it to be right. They were frustrated as hell yesterday." She added soberly, "I don't like it either, Jill. But I can't convince him that we have any other option. Joe doesn't like it that they found that helicopter pad. It would be too easy for Varak to get a helicopter pickup and fly out of there if he took the notion."

"And that means they probably won't wait longer than tomorrow or the next day." Jill forced a smile. "And that's not long to come up with another solution. But miracles happen, don't they?" She tilted her head. "Now I should let you get back to work. Is there anything else I can get for you?"

"No. How many times do I have to tell you that you don't have to wait on me, Jill?"

"It's no trouble. I don't have anything else to do now that Joe is here. He's eliminated my primary job of making sure that you're safe. He's so good at it that I feel useless. You don't really need me any longer." She lifted her hand as she headed for the door. "If you think of anything you want, give me a call. Till then, I'll stay out of your way."

"You've made sure never to be in my way," Eve said quietly. "And no one could ever call you useless."

"That's good to hear." She smiled as she opened the door. "See you later."

Jill moved quickly down the path and into the jungle several yards from the museum. She wanted complete privacy, and this area had seemed the best way to ensure it.

She sat down beneath a kapok tree and took out her phone. She paused, looking down at it. She could still change her mind. She might be wrong. But she had to go with her instincts. She drew a deep breath, took out the slip of paper with the phone number Gideon had given her when he'd come back from the palace the night before last.

This is how you make a difference.

She hesitated, then dialed the telephone number.

It rang once.

No answer.

It rang again.

Nothing.

On the third ring, it was quickly picked up.

"This is Jill Cassidy, Dalai," she said quickly. "Is it safe for you to talk? If it isn't, hang up on me."

Silence. "Is he dead?" Dalai's voice was a mere agonized breath of sound. "Gideon said you would only come to help me if he couldn't. Did I kill him?"

"No," Jill said quickly. "He's still alive. Can you talk? Where is Zahra?"

"The British prime minister is here. She took them to the hospital to visit the victims." She brushed the question aside. "Tell me. Is Gideon *hurt*?"

"No." Jill added deliberately, "But he could have been. It was very close."

Dalai struggled to get control. "Thank God. How I prayed that he would be safe."

"That's very kind." The girl was obviously sincere, but Jill had to harden her heart against the impulse to soften. Difficult to do since all she could think about was how much Dalai must have gone through over the years. "But you still sent him out to that compound."

"He *wanted* to go. You all wanted to go. You all knew how evil Varak is. I told you everything I could to help you."

"We realize that. It wasn't enough. Though Gideon was still grateful. And he did what he could to protect you before he went into that jungle to go after Varak." She added, "But that compound was one huge trap. It was a miracle they got out alive." She paused. "And they're going to go back if you don't stop them. Help me to stop them, Dalai."

Dalai was silent. "You know *nothing*. How can I do that?" She paused, her voice edged with panic. "Varak has to die, and I cannot do it. Do you think I haven't thought about it? But when I'm with him, it's as if he devours me."

"It's the fear that devours you," Jill said. "Do you think I don't know how that feels?" But she couldn't be too sympathetic or Dalai wouldn't take that final step they needed her to take. The girl had come so far against tremendous odds. Just from listening to Gideon about their encounters, Jill could read between the lines. Dalai was clearly a fighter but not a trusting one. She had even been afraid to trust Gideon. So give her something to fight against, someone to fight beside. "But don't expect me to let you cover your head and send people I care about to do what you should be doing. This is your battle, too. What you gave us didn't work. As I said, every step at that compound is a trap. We need more from you." She paused. "Gideon told me about the way you handed him Varak on a platter but dodged talking about Zahra. He accepted it because he felt sorry for you." Her voice became flat and uncompromising. "I don't feel sorry for you. I can't afford to do that. It's too dangerous for all of us. I won't pity you, but I'll respect you and work with you. Because I believe you can do anything you have to do to help us, Dalai. I thought a long time about how you fit into the picture, everything that you'd discussed with Gideon, your background, what you must have felt, what you wanted out of life. What your story really was . . . And then I realized that Gideon was letting his guilty feelings blind him to the fact that you aren't quite the victim he thinks you to be. Yes, you've been mistreated and threatened and terrorized. Who could deny that's true?" She paused. "But I believe you've managed to survive it because you're very, very strong. You had to be strong to live with Zahra Kiyani since you were a child. She's a powerhouse and as evil as they come. Gideon believes you've been brainwashed, but I think you've just done and said the things you had to in order to survive. I did the same thing when I was living in all those foster homes when I was a kid. But you had it even rougher than me. It took someone very smart and patient to fight that silent battle with Zahra all these years. I imagine most of the time she doesn't realize you're doing it. You're still fighting, but I'd bet somewhere down deep you've been waiting for your chance to get away from her. You might even have a plan? I think that first night that Gideon came to you, the reason you were so upset was that you were afraid he'd get in the way of any plan you might have to free yourself from Zahra. Is that true?"

Dalai didn't reply.

It was pure guesswork and instinct, but Jill had to go with it once she'd started. "But then Varak showed up on the scene, and it was a horrible scenario that you couldn't tolerate. You had to do something, anything, to get rid of him. You're frightened of Zahra, but in the end you didn't see her as the prime immediate threat. You thought you'd have time later to find a way to escape from her. So you distracted Gideon from discussing anything about her so that he'd concentrate on Nils Varak. Varak had hurt you terribly and would hurt you again if given the opportunity. It was to your advantage to have us go after him with full force right away and prevent him from doing that." She smiled sadly. "So you called Gideon and delivered the message you wanted to send. When you left him, Gideon had a mission."

Dalai was silent. Then she finally said, "You're...very clever. Madam said you were." Another silence. "That's the reason she hated you. She tried to get that Wyatt man from the U.N. to stop you. But he couldn't do it, so she had to go to Varak."

It wasn't that frank admission that surprised Jill but the fact that Dalai's voice and manner had altered in the space of that silence. Both were no longer trembling or fearful, only troubled.

"Gideon is clever, too," Jill said quietly. "He would have realized what you were doing if he hadn't been so conscience-stricken about how he treated you when you first came to the palace. He has a great heart, and it tends to get in his way."

"There's no reason for him to feel badly," she said jerkily. "He treated me very well. Everyone else was afraid of her." Then the words tumbled out. "I didn't *want* to do this. But he was always so smart and strong. It's what I most remembered about him. I thought he'd be all right. I didn't mean not to tell him the whole truth." Then she stopped. "No, I guess I did. But I gave him Varak, someone I knew he wanted very much. And, yes, I knew it would also keep me from being hurt again. There's nothing wrong with that. I thought I could tell him all the rest about Madam later, when it would be safer for me."

"No, there's nothing wrong with that," Jill said. "I can understand how you might feel you had to protect yourself any way you could." She paused. "As long as it didn't hurt anyone. Because I realize what you went through. We're alike in many ways. We've both been victims." She added, "I believe you know that, don't you? You said Zahra had to go to Varak to help her. You heard exactly what Zahra asked Varak to do to me when she couldn't get what she wanted from Wyatt."

Silence. "She was very angry with you. He told her it would be better to kill you, but she said that would be...awkward, and that they should just hurt you." Another silence. "I knew what that meant. I was very sad. You should have done what she wanted."

"No, that would have been the wrong thing to do." Jill hesitated, then said deliberately, "Because that would have made me the slave she's tried to make you, Dalai. You know that if you don't fight, that's what happens. I was hurt, but I healed, got to my feet, and started to fight again. I'm fighting now. And that's what you've got to do."

"Do I? Even though she said she's like Kiya, and I was meant to be her slave?" Jill realized there was actually a trace of sarcasm in Dalai's words, and it only showed how far they had come toward honesty in these last minutes.

"Bullshit. How do you know that you're not the one who's like Kiya? You can be whatever you want to be. Look at you. You've already started to fight." She added dryly, "Though definitely in a manipulative manner. I'm afraid we're also alike in that quality, and lately, I've become very aware how destructive it can be. I've sworn off it myself unless it's an emergency." She changed the subject. "But it's time to admit that the only way you're going to get rid of Varak is through using everything you know about Zahra. Zahra's the key. It's too deadly going after Varak. There are too many traps. So you'll have to give me a way to use Zahra to bring Varak to us."

"There's no way to do that," she said quickly.

"I believe we'll think of a way. We'll talk, and something will come to us. It probably won't be as slick and efficient as what you were planning to have Gideon do. But we'll get there."

"You don't *know* her." Her voice was suddenly harsh. "Stay out of this. Let me handle her. I know how she thinks, how she reacts. You could spoil everything. You don't know what she'd do."

"No, but you do. You know everything about her." It was time to stop pushing. She had to step back and let the decision come from Dalai. "If you're ready to help us, then find a way to call me. I don't want to put you at risk again. Let me know, and I'll somehow find a way to get you out of there so that we can talk more freely." Her voice took on an urgency that could not have been more genuine. "But we don't have much time. People will die." Now add the single plea that might change the story. "Gideon will die."

She cut the connection.

Jill drew a deep breath. It was done.

Now all she could do was sit here and wait for a call that might not come.

———◆———

The call came three hours later, when the sun had just started to go down.

Her heart jumped as she saw the presidential palace ID on her phone. *Yes.*

"I will help you." Dalai's voice was intense and angry when she came on the phone. "I have no choice. Though you'll probably be like all the rest of them who care only about themselves. But you mustn't be stupid or careless. Do you hear me? I won't be put in that . . . place again."

"Hopefully, I won't be either of those things," Jill said. "How can I help you? Should I send someone to the palace to get you?"

"You're already being stupid. You'd spoil everything if you did that." Dalai drew a deep breath. "Besides, I'm already here."

Jill stiffened in shock. "What? Where?"

"Robaku. I knew that's where you were. Madam was angry enough about it. I decided there was no sense my trying to tell you anything on the phone. I'd have to come there anyway."

Jill was stunned. "Just like that? You walked out of the palace and just decided to come here to see me. How?"

"Madam leaves a car in a garage two blocks from the palace that we use when she goes to see Varak. Most of the time, she likes me to drive, so I have the keys."

Jill shook her head in bewilderment. "Then you could have escaped whenever you chose."

"No, I couldn't. She would have chased me down and caught me. It wasn't the right time. Neither is this, and you keep on asking questions," she said, exasperated. "I only have a few hours before she'll be back from that meeting with the British prime minister. I've parked down by this brook with the boulders. I've come this far. Now you come to me."

"I'll be right there." Jill was jarred out of the shock as she realized what the consequences were of Dalai's decision. "How long have you been here? No, you had to have just gotten here, or they would have been all over you. Look, you might have visitors before I get there. Don't run away. Just wait for me."

"Visitors?" Dalai repeated, alarmed. "Not Gideon. I don't want to see Gideon. I came to see you."

"Fine. Just wait for me." She hung up and called Novak. "Did you get the drone intruder report?"

"It just came in. How the hell did you know?"

"She's no threat. Don't do anything. Don't tell anyone you got it." Dalai had mentioned Gideon, she remembered. "Don't tell Gideon. She particularly doesn't want Gideon."

"Who is no threat?" he said sharply. "What are you doing, Jill?"

"Dalai. And I'm trying to get off this phone so that she won't run away." She was already striding down the path toward the brook.

"But I can see that's not going to happen unless I let you come. Okay, meet me at the brook. And don't you let anyone hurt her." She cut the connection as she rounded the bend and saw Dalai standing beside the brook. She was wearing a black cloak over her top and sarong skirt, and she looked as if she were going to fly away any minute. Jill drew a breath of relief. "I was afraid you'd be gone. It would have been wise of you to give me a little warning." Jill skidded to a stop before her. "I'm sure you must have picked up information from Zahra and Varak that this place is a virtual armed camp."

"No, they've never mentioned it." She was frowning. "Varak doesn't like having Eve Duncan here, but Madam told him to stay away from Robaku. She didn't want to cause an incident if—" Dalai broke off, then said impatiently, "And I wasn't sure I was coming here, so how could I give you warning? I didn't know if I'd change my mind. But no one saw me."

"Except the spy in the sky. Which means Novak saw you." She looked down the path. "Don't get spooked. Here he comes. It was easier to bring him here than argue."

Dalai froze, her gaze on Novak. "I have to go."

"No, you don't. This is Jed Novak. I trust him. Gideon trusts him." She turned to Novak. "Don't you do anything intimidating. She's here to help us. She's already literally gone the extra mile. So let me handle it."

Novak stopped, staring at Dalai. "She doesn't appear to be a threat. Though her coming here automatically makes her suspect." He took a step closer. "And she doesn't seem to be intimidated, only wary." He smiled at Dalai. "Maybe we should have a truce to see if either one of us has cause for concern." His smile faded. "Though I didn't like it that she didn't want Gideon here."

"I was...ashamed," Dalai said. "He was kind, and I knew he pitied me." She looked him straight in the eye. "I used it."

"Not good." He glanced at Jill. "Why is she here?"

"Because I don't want to see anyone get blown up by that homicidal maniac. She might be able to tell us how to work around it. She knows Zahra, inside and out."

Dalai was still holding Novak's eyes. "And she says Zahra is the key. Do you believe that, too?"

"Jill and I are at odds on that score. But I'm always willing to listen to differing opinions." He was gazing at her searchingly. "Do you think she's right?"

"She might be. That's why I'm here." She shivered. "Though I don't want to be. I *hate* this place."

"Because of the children," Jill said. "I understand."

"Yes. No." She shook her head. "It always frightens me. I want to leave here." She said impatiently, "But I'm here, so what do you want to know?"

"Everything," Jill said. "But you told me when you first got here that you couldn't tell me anything on the phone. You said you would have had to come here anyway. Why?"

"Because you think you understand, but you can't. I knew I'd have to show you." She whirled on her heel and strode along the bank toward the tall boulders that bordered the north side of the brook. "Let's get it over with."

Jill was running after her. "Where are you going?"

"The boulders." Dalai was hurrying down the path. "Now don't talk to me. I'm nervous about this, and I'm afraid I'm doing the wrong thing. I've never trusted anyone but myself before. I still don't." A moment later, they'd reached the edge of the creek, and she was skirting around it until she reached a group of tall boulders that bordered it to the south. "The third one..."

Then she fell to her knees and was digging at the dirt at the base of the boulder. *"Yes."* She had revealed a nine-inch-square keypad. Then she froze, gazing down at it. "Give me a minute. I'll be all right in just a minute."

"What the hell is this?" Jill fell to her knees beside her. The girl was clearly terrified. She reached out to take her hand. "What's wrong? Let me help you, Dalai."

"No one can help me." Dalai was staring down at the keypad. "That's what she said. No one can help you, Dalai."

"Zahra?" Jill was frowning in confusion. "She was the one who said that to you?" Then she stiffened. "Zahra was *here?*"

Dalai drew a deep breath. "Of course she was here. She's always been here. She regards Robaku as her special place. She brought me here several times a year from the time my father sent me to her. Usually at night, when she considered it safe." She pulled her hand away from Jill's. "And she hated it when you got in her way."

"You mean when she built the museum?"

"No, she thought that was a triumph. It was all your stories and keeping those villagers from being moved." She was looking down at the panel, bracing herself. "There's a code." She was punching in a four-letter code. "She gave it to me when she first started training me to help her take care of this place. She waited almost a year before she trusted me with it." Her lips twisted. "When she thought that I'd been taught to obey every rule she'd set out for me as a slave should." She paused. "And the consequences if I failed in any way."

"Dalai, what are you talking about?" Jill asked quietly.

"You wanted to know about Zahra Kiyani. I'm telling you about her." She met Jill's eyes as she punched in the final letter. "This is who she is. Shall I tell you what the four letters of the code are?"

Jill was beginning to make a wild guess.

Then she heard a click, and the rocky ground around the boulder appeared to shift. The next instant, it slid open to reveal a trapdoor with a metal ladder.

She heard Novak mutter a soft oath behind her.

"The ladder is very sturdy and safe," Dalai said. "So is the cavern below. It was built by Zahra Kiyani's great-grandfather, but the Kiyani family kept it updated and repaired through the years. You can understand why she didn't want the village disturbed in any way."

Jill was gazing down into that darkness. "You've known about this for years?"

"She needed someone to come with her to check and make certain all was in order. She trusted me. She made certain I could be trusted." She reached in her cloak and pulled out a flashlight and thrust it at Jill. She made an impatient gesture toward the ladder. "Go and see for yourself. I can't go down there yet."

"Stay here, Jill," Novak said. "It could be a trap."

"She's still shaking. Just look at her," Jill said. "For heaven's sake, it's no trap. I'm going down, Novak." She turned on the flashlight. "You can keep an eye on her if you want—" Novak was already climbing down the ladder. "It's okay, Dalai. You can wait for us here." Jill headed for the trapdoor and started down the ladder.

There were over twenty steps, and she saw Novak standing on the ground beside the ladder. She jumped from the fourth rung and caught hold of him to steady herself. The earth was soft and mushy beneath her feet, and the smell was a blend of earth scents and rotten vegetation. And something else that was causing Jill's stomach to tense. She moved the beam of the flashlight to pierce the darkness. Stone walls, a path leading south, away from the creek.

"I think we know what that code is." Novak had pulled out his pen flashlight and was looking around at the stone walls. "She gave us enough clues."

And he'd already figured it out, she thought. He'd probably done it before she had. That intelligence and the amazing ability to put puzzles together... "I need to be sure." Jill started down the narrow, rocky path.

"I don't suppose you'll let me go ahead, Jill," Novak said.

"No. My story." She gave him a smile over her shoulder as she moved faster. "I brought you here. Are you trying to cheat me?"

"Perish the thought. I just wanted to be sure there weren't any snakes down here."

"Keep an eye out. But I don't think Zahra would permit that. I'm sure she always sent Dalai down to check it out."

Then she made the turn in the stone path.

She stopped and inhaled sharply.

"It's true..." She had to gather her composure before she glanced over her shoulder at Novak again. "Now you can tell me what four-letter code Dalai punched in at that boulder."

"Kiya," he said softly. His gaze was traveling around the sizeable room and all the treasures it held.

"Too easy." She was dazzled as the beam of her flashlight fell on wonderful vases, trunks overflowing with gold and precious jewelry. And several truly superb gold statues. "If Zahra hadn't been so arrogant, any security expert would have told her that was the least safe password she could have chosen." She crossed the room and touched one of the statues. "Well, we found where Zahra grabbed that wonderful statue she gave to Dobran. But none of those statues are as fantastic as the Great Beloved Wife."

"Amazing." Novak was examining one of the engraved gold coffers. "There's so much here. I know that it was supposed to be a wagonload of treasure. But that was a long time ago. You would have thought the family would have gradually let some of it go."

"Family tradition," Jill said. "Gideon said that Zahra was an absolute fanatic about family history and tradition. Evidently, it was a trait passed down through the ages." She drew a deep breath, then wished she hadn't. That sickeningly familiar scent...

"Jill?" Novak's gaze was on her face.

"I'm fine. I just want to get out of here. We should get back to Dalai."

"I'm here." Dalai was standing behind them. Her face was chalk pale. "I told you I'd only be a minute." She pulled the cloak closer about her as if to ward off a chill. "Have you seen enough?" She was gazing searchingly at Jill's face. "Maybe more than enough. You're very clever, Jill. I believe you see things that others wouldn't see."

"I see that you look ill." Jill moistened her lips. "And frightened.

Why are you so frightened to be down here?" She was thinking back, trying to put together everything she knew about Dalai. "Gideon said that you were terribly afraid of Zahra." She was trying to remember. "He said you said something about the place with no air." Her gaze flew to Dalai's face. "Is that this place, Dalai?"

Dalai nodded. "I can't breathe down here." She swallowed. "I know it's my imagination, but it doesn't make any difference. My heart starts to pound, and I want to scream."

"Just being underground?"

"What?" Dalai looked at her as if she were crazy. "No, it's the cage." She moved jerkily across the room to a row of large, gold, bejeweled chests against the far wall. "That's what Madam called it, the night she made me get into it." She paused beside an elaborate gold chest whose top was thickly patterned with a beautiful, closely woven, openwork design. She threw open the chest, and Jill saw that it was empty. "It was that first year she brought me here, and she had to make sure I was broken enough that I'd never betray her." Her voice was trembling. "So one night she made me climb into this chest, and she locked it. It wasn't quite airtight, but I thought it was. It was dark and I couldn't breathe and I thought my heart was going to jump out of my chest. I screamed, and I couldn't stop screaming. I heard her laughing. She said she was sure Kiya had punished her slaves this way, and I had to learn that every time I failed her, she would put me in this cage. If I was lucky, she'd remember to take me out." She was looking down at the coffin-like interior. "She remembered in thirty-two hours."

Dalai couldn't have been much more than a child, Jill thought in horror. An experience like that would have scarred anyone, much less a vulnerable girl totally dependent on that monster. It was a wonder that she had not been totally crushed. "I don't know what to say," she said gently. "You'll never be able to keep from remembering that time, and I can't help what happened to you." She added with sudden harshness, "But I'll be there to lend a hand when you're ready to throw that bitch into her own cage."

Dalai looked at her in surprise. "I didn't tell you that to make you feel sorry for me. I just had to make you understand." She turned away from the chest. "She only put me in that chest one more time, and I knew what to expect, so it wasn't as bad. But I couldn't stop remembering that first night whenever she made me come down here."

"I can understand why," Novak said grimly. "But I don't understand why you even came down today. We saw what you wanted us to see. You were right, we had to experience it for ourselves."

Dalai shook her head and turned to Jill. "No, I had to make sure that you knew everything that happened here." Her gaze was searching Jill's face. "I think you do. You figured it all out. When I first saw your expression after I came down, I could tell." She met her eyes. "Do you want me to put it into words?"

Jill couldn't look away from her. That scent was surrounding her... The panic was rising. "No." She whirled away from her. She couldn't go yet, she knew there was one more thing to check. "I'll be right back, Novak. Take care of her."

Then she was out of the treasure room and stumbling down another short path. The pungent scent was stronger now, and she could see broken boards on the ceiling up ahead. She had to stop as she saw the dim light piercing the cracks in that wood.

Sickness.

Horror.

"Jill." Novak was holding her. "Come on. Let's go back."

"I had to be sure," she said numbly. "I couldn't believe what Dalai was trying to tell me." She was clinging to him. "That's the schoolroom, Novak. It's only a few yards away from Kiya's treasure. The Kiyanis allowed that schoolroom to be built practically on top of their precious treasury. Dalai said Zahra's great-grandfather moved the treasury here, and that was very smart, wasn't it? I'm surprised it wasn't Zahra. Because no one would disturb a village school or suspect what was below it." She swallowed. "But I could smell the scent of that schoolroom the minute I came down here. The chalk, the burnt walls and floorboards...All that death...I know it so well."

"I know you do." He'd turned her and was leading her back toward the treasure room. "And it's going to hit you harder any minute, so I want to get you out of here. That's why I left your Dalai and ran after you."

"She's not my Dalai, she doesn't belong to anyone. But someone should help—" She stopped and closed her eyes. "There's more...She was trying to tell me, but I didn't want to listen. I didn't want to hear the end of the story." Her eyes opened. "But I have to hear it now." She pulled away from him and strode back into the treasure room. Dalai was still standing where she'd left her beside the golden cage. Jill crossed the room toward her. "The schoolroom." Her hands clenched into fists at her sides. "It was all coming together before, but I need the words now. It wasn't just a random attack, was it? Tell me."

Dalai shook her head and said unevenly, "Zahra didn't have enough cash to keep paying Varak, and she was afraid the Botzan army might take Robaku."

"Go on," Jill said.

Dalai was shivering. "So she told Varak about the treasure and promised him a share if he stayed, kept working for her, and found a way to keep her treasure safe until the war ended."

"And he took the deal," Jill said hoarsely.

"Yes, he wants that gold. It's still all he talks about."

"The gold," Jill repeated jerkily. She had to get the words out. "And his solution to get it was to stage a massacre that killed all those children and half their parents and made that schoolroom a memorial site that no one would want to desecrate."

Dalai nodded.

"One more question. Did Zahra approve of his 'solution'?"

"Not right away. She said that it appeared to be a practical plan, but he would have to lower his fee since she was going to have to do a good deal of the publicity and diplomatic work herself."

"Yes, that would enter into any negotiations," Jill said unsteadily. "Couldn't you tell someone?"

"I wanted to live," Dalai said simply. "I was afraid. I'd only heard bits and pieces of the plan, and I didn't know about the schoolroom. But I know that I will go to hell forever for being such a coward." Her voice broke. "When I heard about the children..."

"Yes, the children..." Jill said dully. The children who had died only yards from where she was standing. She couldn't stand here, thinking about it. She had to get out of here. She turned and headed for the ladder.

A few minutes later, they had all surfaced by the boulders. It was only twilight, Jill realized. It had seemed a very long time ago that she had descended that ladder. She looked at Dalai as she got to her feet. "Yes, you're sorry," she said jerkily. "I can see it. But now you have a chance to change your story. To not let a massacre like that ever happen again. Can we count on you?"

Dalai looked away from her. "I'm here, aren't I? I've told you things that would get me killed...or worse." She lifted her chin as she turned to face her. "I'll do whatever I can. But I'm still a coward. Don't expect me to be something I'm not."

"All I want now is for you to listen and call us if there's anything we should know." She added, "And I'll do the same. We'll do the rest together, Dalai."

Dalai gazed at her for a moment before she turned and went toward her car. Then she suddenly looked back at them. "You're going to do it, aren't you? You're actually going to take them both down?"

Jill nodded. "I promise you. And you're going to be there when we do it. No one deserves it more."

"I...believe you." Her dark eyes were filled with wonder. "And I think I might be able to...trust you."

"Good." Then Jill had a sudden thought. "Have you been here too long? What if Zahra's missed you?"

"Then I'll lie to her. I've learned how to do that very well. I'll make her believe me." She shrugged. "Then Madam will beat me, and I'll weep and be very contrite and afraid. She's too busy right now to do anything else to me."

"I wish you wouldn't call her Madam," Jill said bitterly. "It sounds so subservient. It reminds me of the way she's treated you all these years."

"It's what she wants me to call her. If I stopped, she would think it odd and punish me. But someday I will not care what she thinks." She got into the car. "Because she won't be able to use her fine, golden cage if Robaku is no longer available to her. Isn't that sad?" She didn't wait for an answer but drove away from the brook area and headed for the road.

"She's certainly not the rabbit Gideon said Zahra called her." Novak's thoughtful gaze was following her. "And she might say she's a coward, but I don't see that either. It's as if she was opening, changing, revealing new facets, every moment she was here."

"She's a survivor," Jill said. She turned and headed for the museum. "And what she's done today may make us survivors, too." She glanced at Novak, and said fiercely, "Because we know how to fight Zahra and Varak now. We know what holds them together. You know damn well we have a weapon if we use it right. And it's got nothing to do with Varak's compound. So don't tell me that you're going back there."

"I wouldn't dare," he said dryly. "You're so savage, you might throw me in that golden cage."

She shuddered. "Don't even talk about it. I don't understand how Dalai was able to go through what she did." She looked back at the tall boulders, which suddenly appeared threatening in the gathering darkness. "I made her a promise, Novak. Now you have to call everyone up to the museum and get a plan together to make sure that I didn't lie to her."

CHAPTER

18

Kiya?" Gideon shook his head. "It seems impossible that treasure has been here in Robaku all this time. You'd think Hajif
or someone else would have stumbled over it at some time or other."

"Dalai said Zahra was careful," Jill said. "And who would believe
that it was right under their feet for all those decades." She smiled
bitterly. "And after the massacre, no one wanted to go near that
schoolroom. Just what Varak thought would happen." She turned to
Eve, who had been very quiet since Jill and Novak had returned to
the museum over an hour ago. "I couldn't believe it when I saw it.
Don't go down there, Eve. It . . . hurts."

"I have no intention of looking at that treasure," Eve said. "It
would make me ill." She leaned back against the cabinet. "All I want
to do is find a way to use it to get our hands on Varak." She crossed
her arms tightly across her chest. "Soon."

Joe nodded. "That's the aim," he told her quietly. "If Varak has
been sitting there in that compound waiting to get his hands on that
gold, all he'll need is a push. He set up his compound as a trap, and
we can do the same thing with Robaku. Dalai said that they had no
idea how we were fortified. We can just make sure that it appears to
be a simple, sleepy village with only a minimum number of guards

to give Varak trouble. And we'll have to find a way to get the villagers out of the line of fire. We just have to make sure it's all handled
right."

"So that no one gets a machete in their throat," Eve said wryly.

Jill had heard enough. "But first we have to get him here." She
was on edge. Yes, both Joe and Novak had plans that would probably
work once Varak was lured to Robaku. They were already thinking
of strategy, and that was fine. But that wasn't her priority. "Zahra."
She got to her feet. "We have to make her be the one to spur him
to leave that compound. That's what I told Dalai, and that hasn't
changed. And I should be the one who does it." She smiled faintly.
"I'll weave her a fine story and make her believe it's her own. As
Eve said, it's what I do well. The rest of you can think and scheme
and spend your time making Robaku the most splendid trap on the
planet. Just let me get him within your range."

Novak was shaking his head. "And let yourself be within the range
of a woman who would have no compunction about tossing you
into the deepest dungeon if she can get away with it. Even Dalai said
she hates your guts."

"Then as Joe said, it's my job to handle it right. I'm going to call
my publisher when I get back to Hajif's hut and ask him to set up an
interview for me tomorrow with Zahra Kiyani. That's the first foot
in the door." She met his eyes. "I'm going to do it, Novak. Don't
get in my way."

"No promises," he said curtly.

"If you do, I'll just work around you. I'm going to do what I do
best." She headed for the door. "Now you all do what you do best,
so mine won't be for nothing."

Then she was out the door and moving down the path toward the
village. She carefully didn't look at the path that led to the sparkling
brook and those tall boulders. The horror and sadness were still too
close to her. She just wanted to get away from them for these next
few moments.

"Jill."

She stopped and looked behind her.

Eve was coming down the path after her.

"It's going to be okay, Eve," Jill said quickly. "Don't try to talk me out of it. It's the only way that makes—"

"Hush," Eve said, still coming toward her. "Stop talking and start listening. I have something I have to say to you."

———◆———

THE NEXT DAY
10:40 A.M.
KIYANI PRESIDENTIAL PALACE

"What a pleasure to see you, Ms. Cassidy." Zahra's tone was almost a purr as Jill walked into the small, elegant office where she'd been escorted by both a uniformed soldier and a bespectacled young clerk. Zahra was sitting in an elaborately carved chair behind an equally graceful desk. She was dressed in a deep teal-colored maxidress and looked stunning as usual. "But then it's always a delight to have you visit the palace. We have such a long-standing relationship. Of course, it's not always been harmonious, but I believe we'll be able to iron that out now. I'm sorry you weren't among the journalists here the other evening to hear my speech. I was truly spectacular."

"I was a little busy, but that's what I understand." Jill paused. "It was superbly done. But then, you're always ingenious." She glanced around the office. "I assume this office is totally secure? You wouldn't have had me brought here if it wasn't. And your clerk gave me the equivalent of a strip search before they let me in to see you." She smiled. "As you said, you can't count on my being either reasonable or harmonious. You've always considered me a troublemaker."

"And so you are." The purr had suddenly vanished. "I thought I could discourage you, but you were too stupid. You kept insisting and getting in my way. Robaku is *mine*. You had no business writing all those stories objecting to my moving those peasant families out of the village."

"Actually, I *was* stupid," Jill said. "I agree with you on that score. Because I thought our battle was entirely about Robaku and those children. I had no idea you had another agenda entirely on the back burner." She paused. "Or that you'd gotten yourself involved in something that was more ugly than I could ever dream. Not until Joe Quinn went to Asarti that night and came back with this." She pulled a photograph out of her bag and pushed it across the desk at Zahra. "She's very beautiful, but you should have known that Gideon would recognize it as the first Kiya."

Zahra stiffened, her hand clenching the photo. "I don't know what you mean." But her gaze was almost hungry as she stared at the statue. "I've never seen it before."

Bingo. Jill realized she had hit a nerve. Move the needle a little farther. "What a pity. It's extraordinary. Joe Quinn gave it to his wife as soon as he got back from that fishing expedition. Because she's an artist, too, he thought Eve would appreciate it."

"He gave it to *her*?" Zahra couldn't seem to take her gaze from the photo, and her lips were tightening viciously. Then she forced herself to look away. "It doesn't make any difference. It's just a statue. It has nothing to do with me."

"But the fact that that crook, Dobran, had it in his possession, and did the DNA falsification on Nils Varak, might be very awkward for you if it came to light."

"No proof," Zahra said. "I know nothing about Nils Varak other than he's a monster who almost destroyed my country. We've taken whatever weapon you thought you had away from you." Her eyes narrowed on Jill's face. "See what response you'll get if you take that nonsense to the media or anyone else. You should have seen how that British prime minister was bowing and scraping to me yesterday. I'm a heroine, haven't you heard?"

"Yes, and you won't be easy to topple," Jill said. "But you've made me very angry, Madam President. I'm going to try exceptionally hard to see that happen. I've found political figures aren't that difficult to bring down once you find their Achilles heel. I won a Pulitzer doing that a few years ago."

Zahra's lips curled. "Threats?"

"Not yet. First, I'll tell you what I'd do to win another Pulitzer. I won that first one totally on my own. This time I'd have help. I'll bring Eve Duncan in to give interviews and tell her story. It won't have quite as much weight after you and Varak destroyed the skull at the U.N., but she has an amazing amount of respect and credibility. It would stir up a good deal of talk and cause people to start asking questions." She smiled. "And I'd be there to answer those questions. You thought my stories were troublesome before? I'd never stop. Eve has already been speaking to the U.S. embassy and asking them to intercede with the U.N. to grant extended permission to continue her work at Robaku. She can be very persuasive."

She leaned forward across the desk, her eyes shining, her words firing like bullets. "We're planning to set up permanently at Robaku, and you'll never get rid of us. Before we're through, you'll never say that Robaku is yours again. It will be *mine* and Eve Duncan's. We've already drafted plans for tearing down that hideous schoolroom and building a fine chapel where families can come and pray for their slain children. I'll be taking pictures of the schoolroom and showing what it could be with public support. I'll spend a lot of time describing the children who died there. You'll remember how much sympathy my stories have aroused in the past year? Well, before we're through, anyone who reads those stories about Robaku will want to get in there with a jackhammer and tear that schoolroom down themselves." Jill could see the shock in Zahra's face at the picture she'd drawn. Okay, hit her with another one from a different direction. "And you might be interested to know that in another fifteen minutes, Eve Duncan will make an announcement on your local television station that she's invited several top news agencies to Robaku for a press interview tomorrow afternoon. She's promised to divulge a startling revelation regarding the tragedy." She added mockingly, "They were all very eager to accept the invitation. I'm afraid you're old news now, Zahra. And Eve Duncan gives so few interviews."

Her eyes were suddenly wary. "Revelation?"

"It's a good way to intrigue and start the buzz going, don't you think?"

"That sounds like a threat to me," Zahra hissed. "You'd both blow your credibility. No one would believe you. You wouldn't take the chance."

"I admit I hesitated, but Eve is an idealist. Once she finished the reconstruction of that skull, she said she couldn't live with herself if she kept silent. What could I do but throw my support behind her?" Jill paused. "And it's not a threat but a warning. Or perhaps an opportunity. I don't really want you if I can have Varak. He's the big story. You're small potatoes."

"What?" Jill could see her eyes flash. She'd thought that bruising Zahra's vanity would be the way to hit home. Then Zahra recovered quickly. "Varak is *dead*. There is no story where he's concerned."

"I think there might be. I've studied Varak for years, and I know what a complete sociopath he is." She tilted her head. "I have no idea why you're doing this, Zahra. I wonder if you realize what you've gotten yourself into by dealing with him. You're a strong, dominant woman, and he won't put up with it. It's only a matter of time before he kills you." She smiled faintly. "You've probably already had to talk yourself out of situations you found dangerous."

"I don't know what you're talking about," Zahra said through set teeth. "Varak is dead."

"No, he isn't. Not yet. But you'd be much better off if he was." Jill added bluntly, "Because I'll never stop going after him, and you'll be caught in the cross fire. Pity, since you've been doing so well lately.

But they'll burn you at the stake once they find out how you've been coddling Nils Varak." She paused. "But if you find a way to deliver him to me, I won't care if he's accidentally shot by you or one of your soldiers. Maybe you could set it up so that you'll truly be a heroine. All I want is the monster dead and the story finished. I might even be able to persuade Eve that Varak dead is the primary goal, and we don't want to spend years in courts just to tangle with your lawyers. As I said, you're ingenious, and I'm sure you could figure out how to come out of a scenario like that in fantastic shape. Consider it a challenge."

"I consider this insanity." Zahra got to her feet, her cheeks flushed. "And I'll have to ask you to go." Then she suddenly burst out, "You think you can do this to me? You'll lose. I always win." Her eyes were glittering with malice. "Just as I won from you before." She took a step toward her. "Did what they did to you hurt, bitch? I told them it had to hurt."

"Then they did what you told them to do," Jill said steadily. "I've already figured out that had to be Varak. Why do you think I want him so much? Give him to me, and he'll never bother either of us again. Take the challenge, Zahra."

She turned and strode out of the office.

Her phone. Jill had to have her phone.

She quickly stopped at the clerk's desk and picked up her belongings from the security basket.

Don't look to see if anyone is following.

Just hope that Zahra was now turning on the TV in that office to watch Eve Duncan and make sure Jill hadn't lied to her.

Eyes straight ahead.

Jill called Gideon as she walked out of the palace. "The Kiya statue. It has to be in full view, somewhere close to Eve, while the TV broadcast is going on."

Gideon cursed. "We don't have time, Jill."

"Make time."

———

Bitch! Bitch! Bitch!

Zahra's hands clenched into fists as she watched Eve Duncan's face on the TV across the office. Eve was sitting at her worktable, and Zahra's statue of Kiya was resting on the dais like a favorite ornament. Like it belonged to her. Zahra wanted to throw something at that image, which had no hint of the glamour or fascination that Zahra possessed. The only thing she could see in that woman was boring sincerity.

Maybe no one was watching her damned announcement.

But they probably were, and they'd probably watch her TV interview tomorrow, too. Jill Cassidy was right. Those news reporters were like hungry vultures.

She felt a rush of panic. Things had been going so well. She'd thought she had everything under control. Now she had to deal with the scandal that might come if Eve Duncan came forward, with Jill Cassidy standing beside her. That was going to be a media and diplomatic nightmare to straighten out. How was she going to handle it?

Her phone was ringing.

Varak. She hoped he hadn't seen that TV announcement. But the bastard always knew what was going on.

She answered the phone. "Don't blame me for this. It's not my fault. I just found out about it."

"It *is* your fault. I told you to fix it. What's that announcement the whore is going to make tomorrow?"

"What do you think? According to Cassidy, they're going to cause big-time trouble. I told her that no one would believe them, but she was raving about setting up permanent shop at Robaku to call attention to Eve Duncan and her reconstruction work." She added the one threat that had frightened her the most: "And getting permission from the U.N. to tear down the schoolroom and build some kind of chapel. There's no doubt that they'd find the treasure."

Varak was cursing. "If you'd gotten rid of them earlier, this would never have happened. You've stalled me and stalled me until we're down to this. I can't afford for even one person to believe them. It's my neck on the line, you stupid cunt."

Zahra felt the fury surge through her. It was too much. He was talking to her as if she were one of the whores she provided for him. As if she didn't have enough to worry about without these insults. "Then if you think I've done so badly, why don't you take care of it yourself?" she spat out. "Maybe I was wrong to keep you from being reckless enough to take us both down. Get rid of all of them for all I care. Do what you like!"

She cut the connection.

She was breathing hard, panting, as her anger continued to rise. She should probably call him back and try to pacify him, but she couldn't do it. It had gone on too long. The son of a bitch had actually almost strangled her the last time she'd seen him. Hadn't Jill Cassidy said something about how dangerous it was to deal with him? As if she didn't know that for herself. But she was smarter than Cassidy ever dreamed of being, and she could handle him.

If she wanted to do it.

Think. She slowly leaned back in her chair. The situation had turned critical. She could either face a nightmare of explanations and suspicions if Eve Duncan gave her interview tomorrow, or she could accept that in the end, Varak's solution was best. Eliminate those troublesome people at Robaku who were a threat to her and Varak. And who'd had the nerve to steal *her* Kiya statue, she thought angrily.

Or she could handle the problem in a way that was infinitely more pleasing and satisfying in her eyes. A little more difficult, but it would eliminate giving that son of a bitch anything he wanted.

Take the challenge, Jill Cassidy had said.

Zahra could meet any challenge.

She just had to decide which way she wanted to meet it.

But regardless, it would have to involve Varak. She reached for her phone to call him back.

"I was angry," she said the moment he answered the phone. "I'm still angry. But it's clear something has to be done. You've been nagging me about your share of the treasure? Well, I'm ready to talk about it. But not until you give me everything I need before you fly out of here."

ROBAKU

"You could have called me when you were on your way back here," Novak said curtly when he met Jill as she parked her car. "Would that have been too much bother?"

"No, but I knew that you'd have someone monitoring the front gates of the palace and would know when I left." She was walking quickly toward the museum. "And I didn't know what kind of high-tech listening devices Zahra's people might have. I took a risk even calling Gideon. I didn't want her listening in when I chatted with anyone."

"It wouldn't have been a 'chat,'" Novak said. "And they don't have anything that high-tech. Strictly low-grade stuff."

"I didn't know." She added wearily, "And I didn't want to talk to you anyway. Zahra is never easy, and she was particularly difficult today. I had to concentrate on doing what I had to do." She glanced at him, and said deliberately, "What I told you that I could do. Pressure, Novak."

"And did you do it?"

"I believe I did. I won't know until I see signs later. I lined up choices for her. I suggested she could kill Varak, which I'm sure she'd like to do. And I told her that schoolroom would be threatened by

Eve and me, so she might order Varak out of his rat hole to attack us. She'll be terrified that her precious treasury might be discovered. Or there's the possibility she's so besotted with the statue that she might get careless and go after it herself. But even then, she'd probably pull Varak into it in some way. Zahra might take one choice or none at all. But it might lead her to make her own choices, which might suit us as well. All we care about is getting Varak here." They had reached the museum, and she put her hand on his arm. "How did Eve's TV announcement go?"

"Fine. She was warm, concerned, businesslike, appealing." He grimaced. "And hating every minute of it. She doesn't care for the media."

"I know. But this time it wasn't my fault. It was her idea to get Gideon to set it up." She paused. "I did everything I could to talk her out of it. It paints a big bull's-eye on her chest."

"And you don't have one? Be serious."

He was right. After that conversation with Zahra, she'd put everyone here at Robaku at risk. "We knew what we were getting into from the beginning. Eve didn't."

"She knows now. She thinks you're doing the right thing. She's right." He was standing looking at her. "Though I hate to admit it." He suddenly kissed her, hard. "And I know you pulled it off with Zahra. We're going to find out before this day is over that you changed the story to suit yourself." Then he was releasing her and turning away. "I've got to get back to the village and make sure we've made Robaku look like a peaceful, helpless place that Attila the Hun would lust to get his hands on."

"Not too helpless," she called after him.

"Be quiet, Jill," he said over his shoulder. "You told us to do our job and let you do yours. You're officially on the sidelines now." He disappeared around the curve of the path.

But she didn't want to be on the sidelines. She was still on edge and needed to know what was happening. She opened the door and went into the museum to see Eve.

"I'm glad you're back." Eve looked up from working on the Mila reconstruction. "I wanted to get rid of Novak. He was pacing the floor in here after I threw out that TV crew. That was the last thing I needed."

"But he said you did very well."

She shrugged. "As good as can be expected." She smiled. "We had to scramble to get that Kiya statue displayed. Why did you want us to do it?"

"I'm not sure. Instinct. The sight of it might be the final thing that pushes her over the edge. It seemed right."

"And your instincts have proved to be very good as far as getting people to make that final commitment. I'm evidence of that." Her eyes narrowed on Jill's face. "How did you do this time?"

She smiled. "As well as can be expected." No, Eve deserved more than that. "I wish I knew. It might have worked. Everything seemed solid. I appeared to be striking the right notes. We'll have to see." She looked around the museum. "All those skulls in their pretty boxes are gone. Where are they?"

"I thought it would be better if we hid them somewhere in the jungle. Zahra knows they're here and wanted to get rid of them. She could have Varak target them."

"Target," Jill repeated. "That's what I told Novak you were now."

"Of course I am. Now stop talking about it." She looked back at Mila. "I want to finish this bit, then I want to call Michael and talk to him for a while. It will relax both of us."

"You told me that he...knew things. Won't he realize that something is wrong?"

"More than likely. But he'd realize it anyway. I'm not going to cheat either one of us today because I want to pretend everything is fine. I'll just tell him I don't want to discuss it, and he'll accept it."

"That's good." The bond between mother and son must be as intricate as it was strong, but Jill knew that this call might not have been made if Eve hadn't been aware how precarious was their position. "He's a wonderful boy."

"Yes, he is." Eve looked up and made a face. "Now stop fretting about us. I have no intention of dying today. I just don't want Michael not to have heard my voice when he's going to be worrying. Joe can't call him right now, so it's up to me."

"Where is Joe?"

"Varak," she said simply. "He went to keep an eye on the compound to see if there's any indication that Varak might be going to take action. He promised to report back to Novak as soon as he saw any signs." She met Jill's eyes. "And that should tell us if your talk with Zahra worked. I really hope it did because Joe was not at all pleased about my little TV show today."

"I hope so, too." That was a massive understatement. Jill dropped down in a chair and tried to relax her tense muscles. "I guess all we can do is wait to hear from Joe."

The call came from Joe two hours later.

Jill straightened in her chair as Eve took the call. Her gaze flew to Eve's face, trying desperately to read her expression.

But Eve was listening and only said one sentence before she ended the call. "Then I'll expect you."

She put down the phone, and her eyes met Jill's. "Joe's on his way back. You did it, Jill." Her eyes were shining, and the excitement and triumph were all there in her face. "Varak's on the move!"

───────◆───────

KIYANI PRESIDENTIAL PALACE
10:40 P.M.

Where the hell was Dalai?

Zahra strode into her quarters and tore off her dress and threw it on the bench. "Dalai, get in here. I need you!"

Dalai was suddenly in the room, her eyes wide with alarm. "I'm sorry, madam. I thought you'd be downstairs longer."

"You're not supposed to think. Just be here when I want you here. I need to change and be ready to get out of this place. Get me that scarlet pantsuit and the black boots."

"Right away, madam." Dalai flew toward the closet room.

This wasn't the time for the idiot girl to be this careless, Zahra thought. Everything tonight had to go precisely as she had planned. Dalai must not hesitate with performing even one order.

And Dalai wasn't the only one who had to perform faultlessly to Zahra's orders. She dropped down on her vanity stool, reached for her phone, and punched in Varak's number.

"I don't have time to talk to you now," Varak said impatiently when he picked up. "The team I sent to reconnoiter Robaku just got back. I've been getting their report."

"What was it?"

"It's going to be a snap. We'll be in and out in a heartbeat."

"Then you'll take time to talk to me. I agreed to this madness, but I won't go into an attack on Robaku blindly. I have to know what I have to deal with when all the smoke clears. It's got to look like the attack was made by the same terrorist group that blew up the U.N. headquarters. You can't be careless or messy, or I'll never be able to justify the deaths. Duncan is too famous."

"I thought that you'd agreed never to give me orders," he said softly. "When this is over, you might need another lesson."

Bastard. He couldn't resist the threat even in a situation where he might be getting everything he wanted. Zahra instinctively raised her hand to her throat. "When this is over, I'm never going to see you again. You can take your share of the gold and go straight to hell."

"So brave now that you're back in that fine palace. Perhaps I'll get a palace of my own now that you're doing the smart thing and giving me what you promised." His voice lowered. "But how do I know that your Kiya's treasure is worth my time? Maybe you've been lying to me. You've never actually let me go down there to see it."

And she wouldn't this time if there was any other choice. "I told you that I'll let you go down there tonight before you attack Robaku. You can check it out yourself."

"I wouldn't have it any other way. It had better live up to expectations."

"You said you were in a hurry. I'm trying to give you an update on what I've done to protect us. Do you want to hear it, or would you rather threaten me?"

"Both. But I'll listen as long as it includes the release of that damn gold you've been promising me all this time."

"I have no choice. I can't be careful any longer. And I have to get rid of you before someone finds out that Duncan is telling the truth at that press conference."

"How awkward. It would be a disaster for me, bitch."

"Don't worry, I'll get you safely out of the country. I've arranged to have an army transport truck be driven to Robaku and parked a few miles down the highway. You can have your men drive the truck to pick up your share of the treasure after you've eliminated the problem at the village. And I want you out of Robaku and on your way to the airport within an hour."

"But you claim there's such a lot of gold," he said mockingly. "And it would go faster if I didn't have to divide it. Perhaps I'll arrange to get a second truck."

She stiffened. "Don't even think about it. I have a private jet waiting at Jokan airport for you to get out of the country. If the pilot sees more than one truck driving up to be unloaded, then he has orders to take off and leave you to find your way through the jungle and out of Maldara on your own."

Silence. "You wouldn't do that. I'd still be a risk for you."

"I won't let you steal my share of Kiya's treasure," she said fiercely. "You caused me to lose the Great Beloved Wife statue. I won't be cheated of anything else. You deliver my Kiya statue back to me and clean up that village. Then you get out of my country."

Another silence. "I'll let it go for now. I can always come back."

"That would be madness. Even you wouldn't run that risk again."

"Wouldn't I? But I run through money so quickly, and the idea of your looking over your shoulder is so pleasant. I can just see—" He broke off, and said impatiently, "But I have no more time. I have to make certain I'll have no problem with Robaku tonight. Give me the code to that treasure room."

"So you can steal it all and go on the run? You'll get the treasure when I know that you've given me what I need."

"And how will you know that?" he asked sarcastically. "I can't see you risking your neck and dodging bullets to come and check."

"Of course not. I'll send Dalai to report back to me and open it for you. You've always found her accommodating." She saw that Dalai had come back in the room and was frozen in place at the door. "And if you do everything I've told you to do, then I might allow you a bonus. You can take her with you." She smiled maliciously as she saw the young girl go pale. "Plane flights can be so boring."

"I'll decide later. Just have her there ready to open that door when I'll need her."

"At two in the morning?"

"Two. If everything goes as planned." He cut the connection.

She set her phone on the vanity and looked at Dalai. "You kept me waiting. How many times have I told you that mistakes have consequences?"

"It won't happen again, madam." Her voice was trembling. "Please don't send me to him."

"What you wish isn't important. But you might be lucky. I'm not certain how things will work out tonight."

"But you're sending me to Robaku alone? You told him you aren't going with me."

"But I seldom tell the truth to Varak. That would be the height of foolishness. Eve Duncan still has Kiya's Great Beloved Wife. I saw it on that television broadcast. Varak knows how valuable it is. He said he'd get it back for me as part of our deal." Her lips twisted. "Oh, he'll go after it, but he'll also try to steal it from me. How could I trust a little rabbit like you to keep him from doing it? No, I'll have to be there in case he tries to steal it after he rids me of Duncan. That statue is *mine*." She met Dalai's eyes in the vanity mirror. "And you'd better not make any mistakes tonight, Dalai," she said coldly. "I won't tolerate them."

"I promise I won't make any mistakes." Dalai nodded at the clothes on the bed. "May I help you dress? Is that what you're wearing?"

"Why else would I tell you to bring them?" She gazed at her image in the mirror and was abruptly dissatisfied. "I have to look spectacular tonight. Do you understand? I have to look like the queen I am. Whenever anyone looks at me, they have to be impressed. It's going to be a special night."

She could see that Dalai was staring at her, puzzled. But she wasn't about to make explanations. She was the only one who counted, and everyone would realize that after this was all over. Whichever choice she made, she would make it a success. "Hurry. It's almost eleven. Do my hair... " She added, "And I want to use the ruby comb in it tonight."

Dalai's gaze flew to her face.

Zahra caught the glance. "That always alarms you, doesn't it? Why? You've never seen me actually use it in the way it should be used."

"It doesn't alarm me. Whatever you wish." She was heading for the closet room again. "I'll go get the comb out of its special container. I'll be right back."

———◆———

Dalai had to steady her hands as she dialed Jill. She had to hurry. Zahra seldom followed her into the closet room for any reason, but this was a strange night. She kept her voice to almost a whisper when Jill answered. "It will be two or shortly before. They're going after Kiya's treasure."

"It's been taken care of," Jill said. "Anything else?"

"Only to watch Eve Duncan. Zahra's angry about the statue. She won't stop until she gets it." She cut the connection and thrust her phone in her pocket. Don't stop. Keep moving. Nothing must look suspicious. Every motion, every word, must seem totally natural. She knelt at the mahogany jewelry box that held the special container and drew out the jeweled comb. So beautiful. But Zahra had never cared about the beauty. She had just wanted to play her deadly game when she had taught Dalai to make the poisonous liquid with which the prongs were usually coated.

She put the shimmering ruby comb on its tray and took a deep breath. Then she started for the closet door to go back into the bedroom.

Be natural. Don't let her see anything.

She could do this.

But Zahra was right.

This was going to be a very special night.

———◆———

"Two," Jill said as she turned back to Eve and Joe. "And we might have gone overboard about luring Zahra with that statue. Dalai is worried about Eve." She looked at Joe. "Can you persuade her to get out of here? If the statue is the bait for the trap, I could take her place here."

"It's not only the statue," Joe said grimly. "The two of you set Eve up, and now they want her dead." He turned to Eve. "Are you happy now?"

"No, but I will be if you stop growling and get out of here," Eve said. "You've arranged all kind of surveillance around this museum, Joe. You said Varak will reconnoiter before he strikes and will know exactly where I am. But he won't risk coming after me if he thinks it's a trap. He's got to feel as if he's in charge." She looked him in the eye. "Well, if I'm a target, let them come and try to take me. That way we'll know Varak won't skip out on us. That's what this is all about. Then you can whisk down and save me like Superman."

"Get out, Eve," Jill urged. "Sometimes things don't turn out as planned. He's right, we did this together. But you wouldn't have even been on this continent if it wasn't for me. Do you think I could stand the thought of—"

"Out." She turned her back on them and went to her worktable. "I don't care about what you think you can stand, Jill. I won't let Varak have even a chance of escaping tonight." She looked down at the half-finished reconstruction of Mila staring up at her from the dais. "He's never going to be able to do this to a child again." She sat down on her stool and began to smooth the clay beneath Mila's cheekbone. "So both of you clear out, and do whatever you have to do to make that bastard think that I'm as helpless as those kids were when he took his machete to them. Let's get this over with."

———◆———

"I'm going to stay here." Jill stopped abruptly only a short distance from the museum. "It's not as if I can do anything down at the village, Joe."

"You can keep me from pissing off Novak," Joe said curtly. "Not that I'd ordinarily care, but most of the action will probably be aimed at the village, and I'm leaving him in the lurch. He knows that there's no way I'll be anywhere but with Eve."

"And you shouldn't be. What does that have to do with keeping Novak from being pissed off?"

"He asked me to send you down to Hajif at the caves, where the villagers are sheltering. He wants the old man to keep his eye on you." His lips twisted wryly. "Which he knew would be a near-impossible task. If Eve hadn't wanted to get rid of you also, I wouldn't have even been able to get you out of that museum."

"You didn't get me out. There's no reason why I can't stay here. I might be needed."

"No, you won't," he said bluntly. "You'd probably only get in my way. I have no desire to watch over anyone but Eve, and you might distract me. Go down and let Hajif find you something to do."

She silently shook her head.

He muttered a curse. "I can take care of her myself. I don't need you. Shall I show you?" He took her wrist and pulled her off the path and into the jungle. He pointed at a large banyan tree a few feet away. "That's where I'll be situated. From the second branch I'll have a clear shot at anyone approaching the front of the museum. No one could get past me." His tone was low, intense. "And I'm a dead shot, Jill. Do you want to hear about my qualifications in the SEALs? What's more, I wouldn't hesitate for a second. All Varak has to do is show himself, and he's history."

"I know that."

"And there are two more of Novak's men who have sharpshooter credentials who will be stationed within signaling distance. You're not needed here, Jill. We can take him down."

She might not be needed, but she desperately wanted to be here.

Joe nodded slowly as he read her expression. "But it's not smart, you could get in our way."

She gave one last glance at the museum, then turned on her heel. "Heaven forbid I do that. By all means, go climb up your damn banyan tree and do all that SEAL stuff. Just don't let her get hurt while you're flexing your muscles."

She took off down the hill toward the village.

CHAPTER

19

H urry, Dalai!" Zahra was running past the brook toward the tall
boulders. "Can't you see that I don't need to have him angry
with me right now? Tonight is going to be difficult enough for me."

"I'm right behind you," Dalai said. "I don't see him. He hasn't
gotten here yet. You don't have to—" She inhaled sharply as Varak
stepped from behind the boulders. He was dressed in camouflage and
had an ammunition belt across his body, a gun on his shoulder, and
a holstered machete at his waist. He was carrying a large backpack.
He looked angry and impatient, and Dalai could feel the fear tighten
her throat. No matter how often she told herself that she must not
be afraid of him, it didn't help.

He barely glanced at her as he turned to Zahra. "I thought you
weren't going to be here." He smiled mockingly. "Don't you trust
me?"

"No." Zahra took a step toward him. "I want my statue. Dalai is
nothing. I decided you'd have no trouble refusing to give it to her
after you took it from Duncan." She met his gaze. "But you'll have a
lot of trouble if you try to cheat me."

"You flatter yourself." His lips twisted. "The only problem I've
ever had with you was surviving your vanity and stupidity. Now

show me how to get into that treasury room, then get out of here. The only thing I want to do is take a look down there and make sure you aren't cheating me. After that, I don't have much time. I've got to give Markel the signal to start the attack on the village while I take care of the museum."

"By yourself?" She frowned. "I told you not to be careless."

"There are half a dozen men here on the hill who will be on hand if I need them. But I won't need them. I have a few special surprises that I've planned for her, including the one you offered me." His gaze went to the museum in the distance. "Duncan's like you, a stupid woman who doesn't realize who she's dealing with. It will be a pleasure to teach her."

"I don't care how you do it as long as I get everything you promised me." She knelt before the third boulder and quickly entered the code. "Go down, take a look around to make sure that I didn't lie to you. Then come up and get rid of every single trace of anyone who might be a difficulty to me."

He started to move toward the ladder, then stopped. "I think you'd better come with me." He gestured down into the darkness. "I don't like the idea that you've changed your mind about sending pretty little Dalai here alone. I don't care for abrupt changes of plans."

She shrugged. "I'll go if you like. Do you think I have someone down there ready to knock you out and toss you in a trunk as I did Dalai one time?" She laughed. "You would have been amused. But I'd never try that with you." She'd pulled out her flashlight and was climbing down the ladder as she spoke. "Come along, Dalai, he's afraid of us."

Dalai turned on her own flashlight, took a deep breath, and followed her. It was worse than it had ever been, she thought. This place of horror and Varak, who was the giver of pain and terror. It would be all right. She could get through this. No one was really paying attention to her. Be the rabbit Zahra thought she was.

Varak stood and watched them both go down before he turned on his flashlight and ran down the ladder.

The beam of his flashlight illuminated the hallway; and then he was striding down the hall and into the treasury.

He stopped short. "Holy shit!"

"I told you I didn't lie." Zahra was behind him. "This is *mine*. Kiya meant it for someone like me, who was strong enough to use it as it should be used."

"You mean by giving it to me?" His beam was going from treasure to treasure, examining the jewels and the gold. "Yes, I'm sure she knew exactly what she was doing." He turned back to Zahra. "And there's so much. No wonder you were willing to give me half. But it would be very hard to choose." He paused. "Almost impossible."

She stiffened. "Then I'll make it easy. I'll stay down here with Dalai, and I'll choose the items I want while I'm waiting for you to bring me the Great Beloved Wife. You will come back, have your men quickly load the treasure I will give you, and get out. I will keep my share safely here at Robaku as I've always done." Her voice hardened. "And you will not betray me. Did I forget to mention that I told my Minister of Police that I feared for my life from those terrible terrorists? He insisted on having me monitored so that I would be able to be immediately traced in an emergency. If I don't call in every hour, they'll come after me," she said fiercely. "You said you'd have no trouble with an attack on this sleepy little village. You won't find my personal guard quite as easy to handle. You might end up with nothing."

He was silent. Then he shrugged. "Just commenting." He smiled. "I believe I can tolerate our arrangement." He suddenly turned to look at Dalai. "Did you really toss her in a trunk down here?" He watched as Dalai froze, her gaze fixed on him. "I believe you did," he said softly. "When you start choosing your half, save the trunk for me."

"If I get my statue," Zahra said. "And you make sure I'll have no more trouble with Robaku. Then you'll get everything I promised."

"I've already paid my dues to you. I did it the day I destroyed that schoolroom for you. Consider everything else as a bonus." He met her eyes. "And you know I'll do it well. You've watched me do it before. There won't be anyone left alive when I've finished here."

"And how you enjoy it." She chuckled. "You should pay me."

"Not amusing." He glanced around the room overflowing with treasure. "And if I don't get what I consider my fair share, I'll have to take it. Now show me how I get to that tunnel you said would take me to the museum from here."

The tunnel! Dalai froze. Why was he asking that? Dalai's eyes widened in panic as she whirled to Zahra. "The tunnel you had started when you had the museum built? But remember, you decided not to finish it. You said you liked the idea of linking them to have a way to get the treasure out, but then you realized thieves could also get into the treasure room through the museum."

"Of course, I remember," Zahra said coldly. "But necessities change. Varak said he needed a way to get into the museum undetected. The tunnel was over two-thirds done, and Varak said that he'll have no problem setting off an explosion that will allow him to blow the rest of it. He said one blast, and he'd be inside the museum." She smiled. "Won't that be an interesting surprise for Eve Duncan?" She turned to Varak. "I don't mind your blowing her up, but you bring me my statue intact. I'm making it easy enough for you."

"You forget that there's more than this little surprise to think about," Varak said sarcastically. "It's only a way to get in without being seen. I also have to worry about what happens once I hit that area with the second round of explosives. Where's that tunnel?"

"Behind that granite rock to the left of the ladder. Show him, Dalai."

Dalai was already moving toward the ladder. This was all going wrong, she thought desperately. Who would have thought Zahra would remember this old tunnel? But Dalai should have thought about it. Eve Duncan might die because she hadn't considered the possibility it might be used.

"Get out of my way." Varak was striding out of the treasure room and heading toward the ladder. "You're shaking. Why are you scared? It's no wonder I find you such a bore." He was working at loosening the rock behind the ladder with the pick he'd yanked from his backpack. "Maybe I should take you with me and show you something to be really afraid about." The rock came free, and he rolled it aside and peered into the damp darkness. "Stinking mess." He put on his backpack. "I'm going to have to crawl most of the way. You'd better not have lied to me, Zahra." He disappeared into the darkness.

Dalai watched for a moment before she whirled around and turned back to Zahra. "Did you lie to him? Can he get through?"

She shrugged. "He thinks he can. I wouldn't lie when it means my statue. I want him to get to the museum."

"But you lied to him about the Minister of Police. I wasn't sure he'd believe you."

"Neither was I. But it worked, didn't it? Not bad for a 'stupid' woman."

"Do you think that he'll actually get you the statue?"

She shrugged. "I believe he'll kill Duncan and take the statue from her. Whether he intends to give it to me won't be clear until it happens. But at least he will have done what I needed him to do as far as Duncan is concerned. Once he gets back here, I'll know what I need to do about him." She tilted her head as she gazed critically around the treasure room. "Pity. I might actually have to give him some of Kiya's treasures if he does everything he promised he'd do here. As he said, he's quite lethal, and he could succeed." She added cheerfully, "But I can always arrange to get all of them back later. All I'd have to do would be to hire someone like Varak to help me. As long as Varak stays away from Maldara and isn't causing me any problems, I could live with his having a moderate share . . . for a short time."

"There's no one 'like' Varak. He would take more than a moderate share."

Zahra's smile deepened. "Then I would have to make an adjustment."

"You mean, you would kill him," Dalai said quietly. "That's why you wore the ruby comb tonight."

She shrugged. "It's another alternative, another way to get rid of him. It would be easy enough. The bastard is so big and strong. Yet all I'd have to do would be to get close enough to him to just run those prongs over his throat." She reached out and stroked a gold-rimmed vase next to her. "Not quite as safe, but I could use this attack on Robaku to my political advantage. I've been considering—" She broke off, frowning as something struck her. "You don't sound like yourself, Dalai. Why are you asking me all these questions?" She started to turn to face her. "Haven't I told you that—" She stopped as she saw that Dalai had crossed the room and was staring down at the golden trunk. "What are you doing?" Then she thought she realized what was happening. "He frightened you." She shrugged. "It might not happen. The idea just intrigued him."

"As it intrigued you." Dalai's gaze hadn't shifted from the trunk. "It must have made you feel very strong and powerful." She lifted the lid and gazed down inside it. "Because being that afraid made me even weaker and more dependent on you than ever."

"You had to be taught your place." Zahra was frowning again. "And you're sounding very disrespectful. I won't permit that, Dalai. You know what I'll do to you."

"My place," Dalai repeated. "I've let you tell me what that is all these years. I believe I've learned it very well." She paused. "But not from what you told me. It was because I had to teach myself who I really am to survive you."

"What's *wrong* with you?" Zahra hissed. "I won't take this from you. Have you forgotten who I am? I'm the leader of this country. Your father sent you to serve me. I let you live in my palace. You're nothing, Dalai."

"So you tell me," Dalai said. "Nothing. Or rabbit." She paused. "Or slave. But I'm none of those things, Zahra."

"Zahra?" Her lips tightened, her expression incredulous. "Insolence. You do not address me in that fashion."

"No, I won't address you at all," Dalai said. "After I've finished with you, I will go away and not see you again. I will try not to ever think of you." She met her eyes. "And I believe I will succeed because I'm stronger than you think I am."

"Go away? Do you think I'd let you leave me?" Zahra's dark eyes were glittering, her lips curled. "Perhaps I will, but only to go to Varak. I'll let him teach you manners, you little slut. You shake when he looks at you."

"Yes, I do. But how will you send me to him when you said you might kill him? You must make up your mind, Zahra." Her smile had a tinge of mockery. "Because threats won't work anymore. I'm afraid of Varak, but I'm not afraid of you. I haven't been afraid of you for a long time."

"Of course, you are. You know what I can do to you. You jump when I snap my fingers."

"Because I knew it pleased you, and it kept me safe. Pretense. Only a game. You had to believe I would never betray you. You had all the power, and I had to wait until it was my time." She met her eyes. "I realized when I was lying in that trunk that I wasn't going to live if I didn't change and become as strong as you are. I'm afraid your punishment backfired, Zahra."

"And you think this is your time?" She laughed. "What a fool you are. I've never been more strong."

"And I've never had a time when I wasn't alone. It makes a difference." She shined the beam of her flashlight around the room. "Kiya's treasure. I've always hated it. But only because of what you did to me here. You said she was like you, but I think she stood on her own."

"Not alone?" Zahra's voice was suddenly suspicious. "Why aren't you alone? Why are you saying all this now?"

"Because you're not going to get your statue. You're not going to get to make a choice of alternatives. Varak is going to die, and everyone is going to know what you've done." She was looking down at the trunk again. "I could tell them, couldn't I? You've shared so much with me."

"You? No one will believe you," Zahra burst out. "Why would anyone pay attention to a little servant girl when she's muttering lies against me?"

"Perhaps when they hear from your own lips that they're not lies." She reached down into the trunk and pulled out a disk lodged against the ornate side of the gold interior. "Your voice is very well-known, Zahra. Jill Cassidy thought that there would be no problem having it identified by experts." Her smile was bittersweet. "It was her idea to put the recording device in this golden trunk. I wouldn't have chosen it because the fear is still with me. But she's kind, and she was upset when she heard about my hours in this cage."

"You and that bitch *bugged* my conversation with Varak?" Zahra's eyes were blazing. "It won't do you any good." She was moving toward Dalai, every step sleek, catlike. "Because you're going to give it to me. Who knows? I might forgive this madness if you don't make me more angry."

"No, you won't." Dalai was backing away, slipping the disk into her jacket pocket. "I've gone too far. We both know it. You'll have to stop me any way you can."

"I want that disk," Zahra said between clenched teeth. "Give it to me."

Zahra jumped toward her.

Dalai threw her flashlight at her, and it hit Zahra in the mouth. Then Dalai dived behind a huge urn as the flashlight rolled across the floor.

"Hiding, little rabbit?" Zahra was half kneeling as she moved across the dim room. "How stupid to throw that flashlight at me. How are you going to see me? But I still have my flashlight, and I'm catching glimpses of you. Frightened? Look at you, dodging behind all those trunks and statues in the dark. I'm closer to you now. I can hear you breathing. And you said you weren't afraid of me. Liar."

Dalai froze behind a carved chaise. She could hear Zahra breathing. But Zahra sounded excited, and Dalai realized that she was excited, too. She wasn't frightened as Zahra assumed. The blood was pumping through her veins, and there was no fear, only the rush of adrenaline. She felt... eager, her gaze on every move Zahra made.

She could see Zahra's shadow behind the glare of her flashlight. She was reaching up to her chignon.

The ruby comb, Dalai thought. She had been expecting it.

She watched in fascination. Zahra was loosening the comb in her hair, getting it ready for the strike. "You're right. You've gone too far," Zahra said softly. "You went too far the moment you thought you could stand up and be anything but the slave you are. Slaves should always kneel, Dalai. You should have remembered that."

Then she leaped. She was on top of Dalai. She hit Dalai's head with the flashlight. Then she struck Dalai again.

Dalai rolled away from her, grasping the flashlight and using all her strength to pull it away from Zahra. Then she was frantically searching in her jacket pocket as she watched Zahra pull the ruby comb from her hair.

She was aiming the prongs at Dalai's face! Dalai felt the prongs break the skin at her chin as she fought to push Zahra's hand aside. Strong. Zahra had always been so strong...

"Yes," Zahra said fiercely. Her eyes were gleaming down at Dalai. "That should be enough. You'll feel the poison any second. You're dead, Dalai. We both know it." But the comb was moving again, raking Dalai's throat, she could feel the blood flow... "But this is pure pleasure..." Zahra whispered: "I want more. I want to see you suffer. You thought you could hurt me? You betrayed me!"

Zahra was enjoying this too much, Dalai thought. If Dalai didn't move quickly, Zahra might decide to cut her throat. Dalai's hand closed on the switchblade knife in her pocket. Distract her. She gazed at Zahra frantically, pleadingly. "Please, don't do—"

She rolled to the side, taking Zahra by surprise. The switchblade was out and open.

Dalai reached out and plunged the pearl-handled knife into the hand holding the comb.

Zahra screamed.

"What are you doing?" Zahra was staring at her hand in disbelief. "Why did you—You fool! It's too late. You'll be dead in—"

"That's what you said." Dalai's heart was beating hard as she carefully edged away from the knife she'd plunged into Zahra's hand. She swallowed. Everything had gone so quickly, she was having trouble believing what she'd done. "And you might be right if you hadn't always let me prepare the poisons for the comb. But I couldn't take a chance that you would use the poison on Eve Duncan instead of Varak. I had to be in control." She stared into Zahra's eyes, then her glance shifted to the knife sticking upright in the hand clutching the comb. "You understand control, Zahra."

Zahra's eyes widened in horror as she realized what Dalai meant. "The comb had no poison? You switched the poison to that knife?"

"I had to be prepared. That's what I told myself. But it might have been a lie." She said wearily, "Maybe this was always how I intended it to end. I could have run. I could have hit you on the head. I could have just pretended that nothing had changed. But I let the words come. I let you go after me." She was slowly sitting up. "Because something *had* changed, and I couldn't ignore it."

"It *hurts.*" Zahra was staring dazedly down at the wound in her hand. "It's burning, you bitch. You did it. It's really the poison." She was suddenly trying to move toward her. "I'll *kill* you."

Dalai shook her head. "You're already too weak. Remember how you described what the poison would do to frighten me? All you can do is lie there and hate me. It won't be long now."

"I *won't* die," Zahra panted. "Weak people like you die. I'll live

through this. I'm like Kiya and Cleopatra, queens who ruled the world."
Zahra's voice was frantic with fear and anger as she felt the poison sear
inside her. "But I would have been greater than them. I have to be
greater. I won't let you take that from me. I won't let anyone take—"

Dalai shook her head. "You're not great, Zahra." She leaned closer
and looked into her eyes. "You're nothing. You should recognize that
word. *Nothing.* And soon you'll be less than nothing."

Zahra's eyes were filled with outrage and horror. Her mouth fell
open, and her eyes glazed. "*No!* Not me. I won't have it! This can't
happen to—"

She was dead.

Dalai stared at her for a long moment. So many years of fear and
torment...She should feel something, shouldn't she? She felt nothing but flatness and bewilderment. She got wearily to her feet. It
didn't matter what she was feeling. Maybe she'd know later.

Now she had to do something to help Jill or Eve Duncan. Varak
had seemed so confident that he could get through that tunnel. Dalai
had to call Jill and let her know. She was helping no one staying
down in this splendid golden treasury that Zahra had worshipped.

Hurry!

She reached for her phone as she started to run up the ladder.

She heard the explosions before she'd gone more than two rungs.

She climbed the rest of the rungs, panicked.

Then she was outside, staring desperately in the direction of the
museum. But she couldn't see it! It had disappeared.

All she could see was the thick layer of rolling black smoke reaching for the sky.

"Come back inside." Hajif was trying to draw Jill back into the cave.
"You're not supposed to be out here. All is going well. Mr. Novak
said that it should be over soon."

She could see that it was going well as she gazed down at the streets of the village. Varak's men had been sitting ducks for Novak's team waiting for them. But there was still violence and blood and all the hideous signs of war to which Jill had become accustomed.

The acrid scent of tear gas...

Gunshots.

Men running...

Explosions.

Men firing automatic rifles...

And men with machetes...

How she hated those machetes.

"Come back inside," Hajif said again. "Mr. Novak will not be—"

Kaboom.

The ground shook, throwing her to the ground.

Then another explosion.

Her eyes flew toward the hill.

Smoke. The entire hill was wreathed in thick, black, smoke.

"What is that smoke?" Hajif's gaze had followed Jill's to the top of the hill. "Was it a bomb? I don't see a fire."

Neither did Jill though she thought she could see a dull glow beyond those thick clouds of smoke. "I think...it's a military-grade smoke grenade. I've seen them before, in Pakistan. Varak must have launched it with a chemical explosive of some sort to keep feeding the smoke." She was struggling to get to her feet. "Probably oil or carbon base...I don't know why he—" She broke off as the reason came to her. "No one can see through that smoke. You'd be almost blind."

Smoke. Black. Impenetrable. Curling like thick shadow serpents into the sky from the hill.

From the museum.

That thick black smoke would completely obscure vision from only a few yards away.

And Joe's position in that banyan tree was more than twenty yards from the museum. He wouldn't be able to see anything.

Panic iced through her. "No!"

Then she was ripping off her tee shirt. "Keep everyone in the caves, Hajif." She wrapped the tee shirt over her mouth and nose as she tore away from him. She heard Hajif shouting behind her as she ran through the jungle and streaked up the path.

Through that impossibly thick smoke, she couldn't even see the banyan tree where, only hours earlier, Joe had shown her he'd set up to take his shot. She didn't know if he was still there in the jungle or heading toward that museum as she was doing.

She didn't care. She only knew what she had to do.

Get to Eve.

She reached the museum. The door had been thrown wide.

No fire. But smoke in every corner and pouring out the door.

And there was a gaping black hole where the back windows had been. A hole big enough for Varak to have been able to take Eve out of the museum and avoid that front entrance.

And no Eve.

Maybe Joe had already gotten her out...

But Mila's reconstruction was still on the worktable. Eve would never have left her there to be destroyed.

She grabbed the skull and took it with her as she tore back out of the museum.

Her eyes were stinging as she ran out into that thick cloud of smoke again. She shouted, "Eve!"

"Here she is!" It was a man's voice in the distance. "Come and get her, Jill. It *is* Jill Cassidy, isn't it? How could I ever forget your voice? I was hoping to see you here."

And how could she ever forget Varak's voice? Laughing as she struggled beneath the weight of his body as he beat her. Don't think of that moment of weakness. Make him speak again so she could locate him.

And so Joe could locate Eve.

"Say something, Eve," she called. "Has he hurt you? He's a coward and very good at hurting helpless women...or children." Her hand tightened on her gun. "Isn't that right, Varak?"

"Yes, because they're of no importance. Except when they're being stubborn. Your friend Duncan is proving to be very obstinate. She won't tell me where the Great Beloved Wife statue is hidden. Come and help me persuade her."

"Stay where you are, Jill," Eve called. "You know you can't do anything. Don't give him what he wants."

Jill was almost sure Eve's voice was coming from the dense jungle behind the museum. She started toward it. "You're alive. That means there has to be something we can do."

Are you listening, Joe? Do you hear us? All that training, all that intensity and boundless passion. Track him. Find him.

She was struggling to breathe. Her throat felt raw. But there was less smoke as she rounded the curve in the trail that led to the rear of the museum. She thought she could see darker figures among the haze. Eve?

"I see you, Jill," Varak said. "You're just a shadow in all this smoke, but I can make you out. And I don't see the gun in your hand, but I know it's there. Because you had one when we had our little party with you. It didn't do you any good then. It won't do you any good now. Because your friend, Eve, also had a gun, and I was forced to smash a few fingers and take it away from her. I admit I was tempted to use my machete on them. But perhaps later...right now all you have to know is that the barrel of the gun is pressed to her temple. That means you're going to come forward and toss your gun to me, or I'll press the trigger. I'll give you to the count of three. I want that statue, and I don't have time to play games. Unfortunately, I've had a call from Markel, and he says things aren't going as we hoped in the village. So it seems I've got to get out of here." His tone was suddenly harsh. "But I'm not going before I get that statue. It appears as if I'm going to need money. But I'd do it even if it weren't worth a fortune, just to keep it away from that bitch, Zahra. She worships it." He started the count. "One...Two..."

"Stop." She knew that the crazy bastard would do it. "I'm coming toward you. We can work this out. Don't hurt her."

Where are you, Joe?

He had to be close. He was a much better tracker than she was. There had to be a reason why he hadn't made his move, and it was probably that threat Varak had made.

She stopped a few yards from Varak. The smoke was still thick here, but she could see him. He had a scarf covering his mouth and nose, and it brought back the chilling memory of that night in the jungle. Forget it. Fear was her enemy, and it would only weaken her. She flinched as she saw that he hadn't been lying about the gun pressed to Eve's temple. She quickly tossed her gun on the ground beside him. "If things aren't going your way, you should let her go and run. If Eve Duncan dies, they'll never stop hunting you."

"I've been hunted for most of my life. I haven't been caught yet." He cocked his gun. "The statue, Eve," he said softly. "I know you have it. I saw it when you were bragging about that press conference on TV. Where is it?"

"I'm listening. I want to live," Eve said. "I have a family. I did hide that statue. But Jill might be right. Maybe we can make a deal."

She was playing for time, Jill knew. Banking on the belief that Joe was close. But Joe couldn't do anything as long as that gun was pressed to Eve's temple.

So get the barrel away from her.

Give Joe his chance. Give Eve her chance.

How?

Then, as she looked down at the reconstruction of Mila that she was still carrying, she realized she knew.

"But maybe we shouldn't give in to him, Eve. He's bound to be lying to us." Jill's voice deliberately rose hysterically. "I told you what he did to me. I can't let—" In midsentence, she hurled Mila's skull with full force at the hand in which Varak was holding the weapon and knocked his gun up in the air. The next instant, she dived to the ground next to him, reaching for the gun she'd just tossed to him.

She heard Varak swearing as he stomped on her hand and instinctively swung the weapon in his hand toward her to fire it.

Pain.

She gasped as the hot wave of agony spread through her side.

But he was turning away from her toward Eve again.

No!

But Eve was tearing away from him and dropping to the ground. "Now, Joe!"

A single shot from a Remington 700.

Varak's body whiplashed as the bullet struck him in the throat. His eyes bulged as he saw the blood spurting. "What the—" Then he started to fall to the ground.

But Joe's second bullet tore into Varak's left eye, jerking him backward.

And then the third bullet struck him in the center of his forehead, and his head exploded.

Jill saw him collapse a few yards away, the blood pouring from the wounds. So much blood...

Dead. Is that how monsters died?

Eve was kneeling beside Jill, her face pale. "Lie still." Her voice was shaking. "Why couldn't you have just waited? I could have stalled him. You're bleeding, dammit."

"Mila... I'm sorry about Mila. I couldn't think of anything else to do. All that... work..."

"What? Mila? Where did that come from? For heaven's sake, I think that she'd forgive you. I know I do." Her voice was suddenly fierce. "Providing you don't die on us. I won't have that, Jill."

"Of course, I... won't die." Jill's voice sounded strange, slurred, even to herself. "I'm just a little... tired..."

Darkness

—◆—

EMBASSY HOSPITAL

There was light streaming through that window, Jill realized as her eyes opened. Strange. It had been dark only minutes ago, but now it was light...

She saw Novak's face above her. And that hospital smell...

"Nairobi?" she whispered drowsily.

"No, we're done with Nairobi." He leaned forward. "Embassy hospital. But we do keep meeting this way. It's got to stop, Jill. I don't think I can take much more."

Then she was wide-awake. "Eve!"

"She's fine," he said. "You took the bullet. But you're fine. It was a flesh wound in your left side, and you have a cracked rib." He grimaced. "Well, maybe Eve's not so fine. She was with you most of the night after the doctors patched you up. She wouldn't let anyone else get near you. She only left when Quinn said that her son was on the phone and needed to talk to her. Then she graciously allowed me to sit with you."

"No one needs to sit with me. You shouldn't be here anyway. I know you've got stuff you need to do." She had a vague memory of smoke and explosives and men running... "Your team probably needs you. It must be a major disaster scene at Robaku."

"It is, but we've got it under control. I've been back and forth to Robaku all night." He paused. "And I *should* be here." His hand covered hers on the bed. "Stop giving me orders. This isn't your story anymore until you get out of that hospital bed. It's mine."

His hand was warm and safe, and she didn't want to move it. "You said I was fine." She had a sudden thought. "Dalai. Is she okay?"

"Other than trying to fight everyone in the emergency room to make them release her. They insisted on keeping her overnight to make sure those cuts on her face and throat didn't contain the same

poison that killed Zahra. Her room is down at the end of the hall."
He shook his head as she tried to sit up. "No, you don't get out of
that bed until the doctor says that you can. I'd say she's proved she
can take of herself."

"That doesn't matter. I brought her into this. She deserves my
support."

"And I can see that you're already planning on how to get down
that hall as soon as I leave this room. Relax, Jill. It's not going to
happen."

He wasn't going to budge. He was being his usual domineering
self. She fell back against the pillows. It wasn't worth fighting him
right now. Her throat still felt raw, her side was throbbing, and she
had to figure things out anyway. "You'll have to leave here soon.
You've programmed everyone not to be able to do without you. You
said you had it under control. What does that mean? What did you
do?"

"As soon as Varak's men were subdued, I had photos taken of the
scene and Varak's body removed and flown to Nairobi for complete
DNA and lab work. Then I brought U.S. Ambassador Sandow and
his staff to Robaku and started the real battle." His lips twisted. "To
keep us all from getting arrested. I had to call in my director to use
all his political connections to try to smooth the way until I could
get those DNA results. I'm lucky he didn't cut me loose. He still may
decide to do it."

"Not likely. You're the golden boy, and he'll know that if anyone
can clean up this mess, it will be you." She smiled. "And I might be
persuaded to write a story or two to sanitize your spotty image."

"I'll pass. You're right, as long as I can manage to make this appear
as a triumph for democracy and keep a civil war from erupting, I'll
dodge the flak." He paused. "That's going to be the prime danger,
Jill. The Kiyani legislature is already in an uproar about their president's being murdered. We gave them no details, but we're going to
have to do it soon. They're making threats to everyone in Maldara,

and Botzan is the main target. It doesn't help that Zahra had recently turned herself into a heroine." He met her eyes. "We're exploring options to keep them from turning this into a disaster."

It was clear there was meaning behind that last sentence. Options? What would keep this from becoming—

No! She immediately rejected the thought that had occurred to her. But she knew that it had occurred to Novak, too. She was silent a moment, trying to think of any other possible way to avoid it. But there wasn't any other option at this moment, dammit. "You know what you have to do," she said jerkily. "No more deaths. No more war. There can be no confusion or infighting. Zahra has to stay a heroine. She has to be the one who helped take down Varak in revenge for his attack on the U.N." Her lips twisted bitterly. "Varak killed her, and she died a martyr. You can stage that beautifully, Novak. You'll have to get a reputable journalist to break the story as soon as possible." She added fiercely, "But it won't be *me*. I won't lie and make Zahra Kiyani out to be anything but who she is. And when all this craziness is done, I'm going to be the one who discovers that disk that proves that a mistake has been made, and Zahra is actually a murdering bitch. Is that understood?"

"Understood," he said quietly. "It will save lives, Jill."

"Stop trying to soothe me. I know it's necessary. We can't let our trying to keep Varak from starting his slaughter all over again begin a war of its own. But it's a lie, and I hate it. So go away and do what you have to do. I'll look at it as one of those dark Grimms' fairy tales instead of a story that I can be proud of. I'll block it out and be fine with it in a few days."

"No, you won't," he said. "And I'm not fine about any of this. I don't want you to send me packing. You scared me to death," he said hoarsely. "I just want to sit here and make sure you're not going to fade away."

"Well, now you've had your time to do that," Eve said brusquely from where she was standing in the doorway. "Now get back to work, Novak. Joe said you know all those diplomats and politicians better than he does, and he needs you to keep them at bay until we get the results back on Varak's DNA. The situation is getting explosive. Right now, no one is sure that we didn't perform our very own coup."

"Maybe we did." He got to his feet. "My director said that it was only a question of semantics. However, you'll be comforted to know that Jill and I discussed a way we might avoid a civil war." He was heading for the door. "But there are a few more things that might be helpful. I think I'll give Gideon a call." He looked back at Jill, and said sharply, "Stay in that bed until you see the doctor."

Before she could answer, he was gone.

"If anyone can stop the tanks from rolling, he can," Eve said with a grin. "He might just roll back over them." She came across the room and dropped down in the chair Novak had vacated. "Joe says he's watched him, and he's incredible at pulling strings and manipulating situations. Rather like someone else I know."

Jill flinched. "Mine was a onetime effort. And I've tried to make up for it."

Eve's smile ebbed. "I'd say throwing yourself in front of a bullet for me might qualify. But it wasn't only a onetime effort. You pulled the strings that brought Varak to Robaku."

"And almost got you killed." She looked at Eve's bandaged hand. "Varak said he hurt your hand. Are you okay?"

"Just bruised. And don't be ridiculous. We all knew what the stakes were. We were all ready to pay them." She leaned forward. "I'm not going to thank you. That goes without saying. I just need to tell you that, in spite of the way we started out, I've been thinking of you as my friend for a long time now. I *keep* my friends, Jill. I have no intention of letting you slip away because you're still having guilt feelings. So get a grip and realize that we're in it for the long haul."

"I'll try to oblige." She found her throat tightening with emotion. "Though I'm not sure Joe wouldn't agree that the guilt is justified."

"You still have a cracked rib from the bullet you took for me. Joe might just think you walk on water right now."

Jill chuckled. "That won't last."

"You can never tell. Life has been nothing but surprises since I got to Maldara."

"But you'll be very glad to leave."

Eve nodded. "I want to go home." She paused. "But not quite yet. I'm going to take a quick trip to see Michael and Jane while Joe and Novak settle all the furor that happened at Robaku. Then I'm coming back to finish the reconstructions of those children. It shouldn't take me more than a few months, and I want to finish what I started."

"What *I* started."

"Whatever. You're doing it again, Jill. Stop it." She got to her feet. "Now I'm going to tell your doctor that you're awake. And then I'm going down the hall to see Dalai. I tried before, but she wasn't talking to me. She's kind of shut down. She seems very much alone."

"As soon as they let me up, I'll go and see what I can do," Jill said. Then she changed her mind and reached for her phone on the bedside table. "No, it's not me she needs."

CHAPTER

20

Y ou're putting me to a lot of trouble, Dalai." Gideon sighed as he opened the door of her hospital room. "Particularly since it seems I'm a busy man today, very much in demand. You could be a little more accommodating."

She stiffened, her gaze flying to his face. "I didn't mean to cause you trouble. I didn't ask to see you. Go away."

"That appears to be your theme song where I'm concerned." He came into the room and strolled over to the bed. "But I can't go away because Jill thinks that I have to make things right with you." He shook his head. "Which is unreasonable because you've told her that I was the injured party. But Jill has to make her stories end the way she wants them to, so I guess we'll have to go along with her." He gently touched her cut chin. "Zahra hurt you. I told you to let me know if that happened again. You persist in not listening to me."

She moved her head away from his touch. "It's nothing," she said jerkily. "And it shouldn't matter to you anyway."

"Ah, yes, because you used me." He shook his head. "I'm an in-credibly rich man, Dalai. Do you realize how many times I've been used since that first time I saw you when you came to Zahra? The two seem to go together. You become accustomed to it after a while. Sometimes it's even amusing watching the process."

"Amusing?" She looked at him in disbelief. "This was different. I could have killed you."

"Only if I was too stupid to protect myself."

"I could have killed you," she repeated.

"You appear to be stuck on that thought." He frowned. "So I guess I'm going to have to go at this from another angle. Yes, there was a slight possibility that you might have been to blame for getting me killed if everything had gone wrong. So you'll just have to do something to make up for it."

She tensed, her hands clenching on the sheet. Her eyes lifted to meet his own.

"No," he said quietly. "How could I do that to you when all I can see when I look at you is that big-eyed young girl who could have been my sister." He shrugged. "But I have no sister, and Varak killed my parents. We're both alone. But I believe we could manage to be friends. So I think we should stick together for a while until you become accustomed to life without Zahra."

She frowned suspiciously. "Are you pitying me again?"

"Perish the thought. I'm going to put you to work." He smiled. "Because it appears I'm going to be used again. This time by Novak, and I can't talk him out of it. He thinks he can quiet down all the uproar in the Kiyani government by arranging with the generals and bureaucrats to accept me as interim president until they can scramble and set up an election." His eyes were suddenly twinkling. "Since everyone would find me acceptable due to my charm, wit, and fat wallet. I told Novak to get me out of there fast, or they'd draft me for the duration."

"President..." She was looking at him in bewilderment. "Like Zahra?"

"Interim," he repeated. "And definitely not like Zahra. So will you come back to that place you must have hated, and we'll make the best of it for the time we have to be there? Then I think you might be ready to go to school or start a new life. Whatever you like."

"I have no money to start a new life. I have *nothing*."

"Not true. You have Kiya, the Great Beloved Wife. Novak is pulling strings to donate the Kiya treasury to the Kiyani people, but I bought the Great Beloved Wife in a separate deal at an enormous fee."

"And you think I would take that from you?"

"No, I'm not offering. I know better. But the interest on what the statue will bring in from tours and exhibits will be a tidy sum. You can consider it part of your salary."

"And what am I supposed to do for this salary?" she asked warily.

"Jill says that you've been very inventive surviving Zahra. I'm sure you'll find ways to make that hellish period in the palace bearable for me. You've listened and know everything that's going on in that government. You know where all the political bodies are buried. Maybe you'll even be able to get me out of that interim position sooner. Now that would earn a gigantic bonus."

"No, it would not," Dalai said flatly. But her eyes were shining with sudden interest. "No pity. But I could do this. I know these people. I've watched them all for Zahra and reported back to her. And I know their servants and every flaw in their lives." She frowned. "But it would be easier if you could make them accept me with respect. It made it more difficult for me when they saw the way Zahra treated me."

His lips tightened. "You mean as a slave."

"She did not say that word around anyone but me."

"But the implication was there."

"Always."

And it was incredible that she'd managed to rise above that stigma as well as all the other abuse Zahra had inflicted on her, Gideon thought. *But don't show sympathy or I'll never get her to accept help.*

He said lightly, "Then I guess we'll have to give you a fancy official title and your own staff to overcome it. What do you think?"

She stared at him for a long moment. "I think you're still trying to be kind to me." She was gazing directly into his eyes. "You cannot help yourself. It is your way, your character. And I need that kindness right now. But I will not need it for long." She lifted her chin. "Give me a little time, and you will see that I will get stronger and stronger. I don't know anything about this being friends. But you will learn to rely on me. It will be me who helps and lends *you* strength when you need it, Gideon."

Gideon nodded solemnly. "I don't have the slightest doubt that will be true." He turned to leave. "I'm already anticipating being deep in your debt."

"Wait." She moistened her lips. "I'm sorry I can't return your knife to you. You said it was a keepsake. Eve told me that Novak probably won't give it back because he thought Zahra's death shouldn't be connected to me."

"It was *your* knife, Dalai. I told you that I thought my father would want you to have it." He smiled. "I know he'd think it couldn't have been used for a better purpose. Neither do I."

She stared at him defiantly. "And neither do I."

He chuckled. "Then we won't worry about it, will we? Now I have to go and see Jill and tell her that we've come to an agreement. If that's all right with you?"

She nodded. "Yes, go talk to Jill." She suddenly smiled. "Because you're not at all sure about any of this except that you wish me to be safe and happy. But she will understand. When I told her that Zahra had told me once that she was like Kiya and I was only her slave, she said bullshit. She asked me how I didn't know that I wasn't the one who was like Kiya." She straightened, and her smile vanished. "Tell Jill that I've decided that she was right. I *am* like Kiya." She added quickly, "But I won't let that hurt you or anyone I care about. I just have to learn who she really was and how to control it."

"I'll tell Jill." He added gently, "And being like Kiya isn't all that bad. She changed the world for herself and generations after her. I'm looking forward to seeing what you can do." He lifted his hand. "I'll see you tomorrow, Dalai."

———————

"She *is* like Kiya, Gideon," Jill said thoughtfully. "She's a survivor. Her story has been a nightmare so far, yet here she is on the road to her own Great Journey." She tilted her head. "But I didn't mean for you to practically adopt her, Gideon. I just wanted you to do something to make her feel better."

"And I did it," he said lightly. "But I'm warning you that she'd be insulted if you mention adopting her. She's having enough trouble understanding the friendship concept. If there's any adoption going on, I have an idea that she'd be the one in control." He leaned forward and brushed a kiss on Jill's forehead. "Don't worry about it, this is right. It's what I should have done a long time ago. We'll work it out together. Maybe I should be grateful that Novak is pulling me into that mess in the Kiyani government. It will give Dalai something to challenge her." He straightened and turned to leave. "What's next for you? Are you going to be at that news conference tomorrow? I need a friend in the media to glorify all my good points."

"The media loves you. That's another reason why Novak is bull-dozing you through the legislative session. You're perfect, Gideon."

"True." His brows rose. "Does that mean you're deserting me?"

She shook her head. "It means I'm tired and need to move on," she said wearily. "It means I don't want to be around when all of Maldara is fawning over Zahra's memory. It means I've been fighting this battle for two years, and now that we're ending the story, I'm ready to skip the epilogue. I feel flat. I need something fresh and new to spark me."

"I'm fresh. I'm new. Just watch what I do to those stale old bureaucrats once I get my foot in the door." He added coaxingly, "It will be fun, Jill."

"I've been doing some research in my spare time on a project that will be fun, too. And you'll be too busy to miss me, Gideon. Maybe I'll come back for the coronation."

"Coronation was Zahra. I have no royal aspirations. Just a little fun for the shortest possible time, then I'm back in my plane and heading for the wild blue yonder." He grinned. "Don't lose touch, and I'll head your way."

She watched him walk out of the room before she turned and started packing up the few belongings Eve had brought to her. She was going to miss Gideon. He had been her friend and ally since this had begun. But it wasn't as if she was losing him entirely. People moved constantly in and out of her life. It was how she lived, how she worked. It didn't alter how she felt about them.

It wouldn't change how she felt about Novak.

Don't think about Novak right now.

It was hurting, and it wasn't as if she hadn't known that it was going to end like this. It was why she'd fought to keep it from beginning. It was too intense. He was too dominant. They'd both do far better alone.

Alone.

She wasn't really alone, she told herself. She had friends, she had her work, she didn't need a man like Novak, who would be a constant disturbance.

She didn't need Novak.

She would finish packing, check out of this hospital, and go say good-bye to Eve. Eve had said that their friendship was for the long haul, and she owed her that courtesy.

Then she would give Novak a call on her way to the airport. That would be the best way to handle it.

No, Novak would be furious. He would recognize it for the escape it was. She didn't care. It would be too easy to let herself delay the inevitable. She would take any way she could to avoid the pain of what had to be done.

She needed that escape, she thought wearily.

———————◆———————

"You're not going to get away with it," Eve said flatly when Jill walked into the museum two hours later. "Gideon blew the whistle on you with me. I squealed to Novak. He should be here any moment."

"So much for enduring friendship," Jill said. "I was going to call him. He's just ... busy."

"Absolutely. Novak is doing a hell of a lot to keep this country stable. He doesn't deserve having to face you running out on him right now. Don't be a coward. It's not like you. At least you should stick around until he has a chance to get his breath." She crossed the room and gave her a quick hug. "Ordinarily, I'd stay out of your business. But you've never made it a practice to stay out of mine, so why should I worry? We've gone way past that." She smiled. "Whatever you choose is fine with me. But you never ran out on me, and it's not fair to do it with Novak."

"You're damn right it's not," Novak said grimly from the doorway. "But that doesn't mean you didn't try to do it." He was across the room and pulling Jill toward the door. "And I could see it coming when you woke up in that hospital room." They were outside now, and he slammed the door shut behind him. "You were worried and concerned and wanting to set everything in order."

"Of course I was. I'd just returned to consciousness, and I wanted to make sure everyone was alive and well, dammit."

"No, there was more to it than that. I know you very well now, Jill. There was an edge. You were relieved when I was called away by Quinn. If Eve hadn't phoned me today, I would still have been here with you anyway. I would have tracked you down. I wasn't about to let you walk away."

"It seemed to be a good time to do it." She moistened her lips. "We have our own lives to lead, and they would interfere with each other. We both know that what we had was purely sex, sparked by the adrenaline from what we were going through."

"Do we?" He jerked her into his arms and kissed her. "I don't know anything of the sort. I don't know what's happening with us, but I'm not afraid to stay around to find out. But it's clear that you *are* afraid." His hands closed on her shoulders. "Not that I blame you. You haven't had the most stable life since your father tossed you out into the world. But it still makes me mad as hell."

"I can tell." She tried to shrug away from him. "I'm not afraid. I'm just being reasonable."

"And keeping your own personal story close to you, private and untouched. I know you don't want to let anyone come in and add anything to your life. But I'm not going to let you get away with that." His eyes were boring into hers. "Because I'm too selfish, and I won't let you go. And I won't let you lie to yourself and cheat us both. Remember the night you were so afraid Varak was going to cheat us? It's the same thing, Jill." His grasp tightened. "You're smart, recognize it. You don't have to commit. Just admit to yourself what you're doing."

She couldn't look away from him. Was it true? She wouldn't be questioning herself if there wasn't an element of truth in his words. And she'd thought she knew herself so well. She smiled with an effort. "And admit you're right?"

He went still. "That would also help a hell of a lot."

"I won't do it." She paused. "But I might admit that I was running away, and that's neither honest nor intelligent. That would also mean I thought there was a reason to be afraid of you. But you've never done anything to make me afraid. You never will." She suddenly kissed him. "So that means this is my problem, and I refuse to be afraid of it. I'll have to examine why it exists and face it."

His arms tightened around her. "*Yes.*"

She smiled and shook her head. "Not that easy, Novak. I told Gideon the truth about being ready for something new and fresh. I'm still going to leave Maldara. You're going to be busy here for a long time straightening out Varak's identity and preventing those bureaucrats in Botzan and Kiyani from starting another civil war. After you finish, if you still think there's something besides sex between us, come and see me. And who knows, maybe the sex will be enough."

"I don't believe that will be true." His eyes were narrowed on her face. "And just where am I supposed to find you?"

"I'll let you know. My first stop is Cairo to do more research." She found herself drawing closer to him. She wanted to touch him. The excitement was growing. Why be afraid to take a chance? Why not have it all? Novak was the most exhilarating man she had ever met. Share the sex. Share that wonderful mind. There was time enough to see what else might be waiting for them. "After that, I could let you know where I'll go from there."

"Research?" He tilted his head. "Just what are you doing, Jill?"

"I've been thinking about Kiya. I thought I'd try to find out her story. Or at least where she was buried."

"In Egypt?" He shook his head. "She died in Maldara according to the journal."

Jill shook her head. "No, not Cleopatra's daughter. We already know a good deal about her. The *first* Kiya. Akhenaten's Great Beloved Wife from the Eighteenth Dynasty. She had such a powerful influence, yet no one knows that much about her. Her life is surrounded by mystery, and we're not even certain where her remains can be found."

"You've found yourself a deeper mystery to dig into?" He shook his head ruefully. "And you can't resist the story."

"No, why should I?" It was all clear to her now, all hesitation gone. "The world is filled with millions of incredible, wonderful stories. And each one is an adventure to explore. But I'm inviting you along on this one, Novak. Do you know why?" Her brilliant smile lit her face as she went back into his arms. "Because I'm beginning to believe that if we're lucky, if we don't screw this up, in the end, you might be my very favorite story of all time."

AUTHOR'S NOTE

Kiya, daughter of Cleopatra VII, never existed except in my imagination. However, Queen Kiya, the Great Beloved Wife of the Pharaoh Akhenaten, was real and one of the most mysterious and intriguing figures in Egyptian history. No one is sure where she came from before arriving at his court, though some scholars believe she might have been a Mitanni princess. But once she was established in Cairo, Kiya was evidently a source of boundless controversy and excitement. From the richness of her monuments, there was no doubt she had an exalted status, and, at one time, Egyptologists thought she might have even been the mother of Tutankhamun. This proved to be unlikely, but her title of Great Beloved Wife certainly must have made her position at court very competitive with Akhenaten's beautiful chief wife, Nefertiti.

But Kiya disappeared from history during the last third of Akhenaten's reign. Her name and images were erased from monuments and replaced by those of Akhenaten's daughters. Why?

Exile? Death? Disgrace?

Or did Kiya just become bored with the court and go away on her own Great Journey to a far land?

You know which one I would choose.

But it's a mystery . . .

ABOUT THE AUTHOR

Iris Johansen is the #1 *New York Times* bestselling author of more than 30 consecutive bestsellers. Her series featuring forensic sculptor Eve Duncan has sold over 20 million copies and counting and was the subject of the acclaimed Lifetime movie *The Killing Game*. Along with her son, Roy, Iris has also co-authored the *New York Times* bestselling series featuring Kendra Michaels. Iris Johansen lives near Atlanta, Georgia.

"When two of the brightest minds around .... questions about war, peace, and Christianity, you get t..... ....ying a question-and-answer format, the authors seek to prompt readers of all kinds—whether philosophers, historians, statesmen, theologians, combatants, or individuals—to consider carefully the complex issues before them and to foster further investigation. When might war be right and peace be wrong, or vice versa? No question, regardless of difficulty, is off-limits for Charles and Demy, whose own perspectives are generously rooted in the natural moral law inscribed on the human heart, in a Christian worldview revealed in Scripture, and in the classic just-war tradition, which eschews both militarism and pacifism. War is hell on earth and the stakes are extremely high. This book provides much-needed theoretical and practical wisdom on this sadly perennial issue. In our post–Cold War, terroristic, and morally ambivalent era, it couldn't be more timely."

—**David Naugle**, Professor of Philosophy, Dallas Baptist University

"Charles and Demy have done a masterful job not only of posing the most important moral questions surrounding war but also of proposing trenchant and sophisticated answers to these questions firmly grounded in the natural-law tradition. As if that were not reason enough to purchase the book, the added benefit for theologians, church historians, ethicists, religious educators, and seminarians is that both authors, who write as evangelicals, find that the notion of natural law is resolutely affirmed in the work of the Protestant Reformers, who themselves were deeply concerned about issues of just governance, legitimate authority, civil society, and the common good, in addition to matters of faith, the church, and ecclesiastical culture. This book's treatment of these issues and far more is itself an excellent example of the equity that the authors think is characteristic of the just-war tradition. I highly recommend this book."

—**Stephen J. Grabill**, Senior Research Scholar in Theology,
Acton Institute for the Study of Religion

"As one who has written about just-war theory in the media during times of conflict, I find it refreshing to be able to recommend a book that explains that just war is not a theory that gives license to the use of violence, but one that attempts morally and responsibly to address the issue of the proper use of force. This book is well done and repays the time one gives to grapple with the difficult area of human conflict."

—**Darrell Bock**, Research Professor of New Testament Studies,
Dallas Theological Seminary

"The new threats to international peace and security have cried out for moral clarity, for a fresh appraisal of the relevance of the Christian just-war tradition. In *War, Peace, and Christianity*, J. Daryl Charles and Timothy Demy have answered the call admirably. Unlike most of what passes for 'biblical ethics,' their careful analysis refuses to use the Bible as a proof text for political propaganda. With great intelligence and common sense, the authors have assembled the insights of natural law, historical experience, political realism, and biblical theology. Those who hope to impose utopian schemes for world peace will find no comfort here. But those who seek justice as part of the command to 'love thy neighbor' will find much wisdom to light the way."

—**Joseph Loconte**, Senior Fellow and Lecturer in Politics,
The King's College, New York

"Far too much recent commentary emanating from the Christian community on matters of war and peace has been ad hoc, sentimental, and ill-informed, without any grounding in the church's profound and nuanced tradition of moral and practical reflection on the subject. Charles and Demy have sought to address this problem, answering even the most knotty questions with lucid and learned essays that provide Christians of various backgrounds—philosophers, historians, statesmen, theologians, combatants, and ordinary individuals—with an inviting point of entry into that rich tradition. The result is a book to be grateful for, one that has the potential to improve the quality of our thinking on these essential matters."

—Wilfred M. McClay, SunTrust Chair of Excellence in Humanities,
University of Tennessee at Chattanooga

"This is an important book. In an era when Christians are tempted to think that pacifism is the biblical and responsible position of a Jesus-follower, this volume makes a reasoned and erudite argument to the contrary. It makes available to readers a wealth of scholarship in a format that is inviting to the nonspecialist. I recommend this book for university courses in political science and ethics, to Sunday school classes on contemporary issues, and to thinking Christians considering one of our most urgent societal debates."

—Gerald R. McDermott, Jordan-Trexler Professor of Religion,
Roanoke College

"The questions about a Christian's response to war and violence have been with the world for two millennia. Unblinkingly, the authors confront those daunting questions and provide clearly reasoned, historically justified, and morally coherent answers. The book weaves natural law, just-war theory, the role of pacifism, history, and Christian belief into a volume that will be a resource and an inspiration for further reflection for decades to come. This work will take its place as a renowned apologetic for the Christian philosophical method of morally harnessing organized conflict, an enduring feature of our common human nature."

—David Forte, Professor of Law, Cleveland State University

"Warfare as I knew it in the 1980s and '90s has changed forever. My son, an Army Infantry officer on his third deployment to Iraq/Afghanistan, is dead center in the middle of this country's modern-day warfare—international terrorism. In light of the statement 'there will always be evil men, and thus there will also be the need to restrain evil men,' authors Charles and Demy tackle the tough questions: Are we justified in responding to and intervening in this global threat? What is our just-war theory toward rogue groups that target innocent people and our military? Does the United States of America have a moral obligation to militarily respond to global terrorism? Is all use of force just? What is the definition of classic just-war tradition and war against evil and injustice? This in-depth volume will answer these and many other pertinent questions that face our country today."

—Robert J. Keneally, Lieutenant Colonel (Retired),
United States Air Force

WAR, PEACE,
AND CHRISTIANITY

WAR, PEACE, AND CHRISTIANITY

QUESTIONS AND ANSWERS
FROM A JUST-WAR PERSPECTIVE

J. Daryl Charles and Timothy J. Demy

WHEATON, ILLINOIS

War, Peace, and Christianity: Questions and Answers from a Just-War Perspective
Copyright © 2010 by J. Daryl Charles and Timothy J. Demy
Published by Crossway
        1300 Crescent Street
        Wheaton, Illinois 60187

The views expressed in this book are solely those of the authors and do not represent or reflect the position or endorsement of any governmental agency or department, military or otherwise.

Cover design: Tobias' Outerwear for Books
Interior design and typesetting: Lakeside Design Plus

First printing 2010
Printed in the United States of America

Unless otherwise indicated, Scripture quotations are taken from the HOLY BIBLE, NEW INTERNATIONAL VERSION®. Copyright © 1973, 1978, 1984 Biblica. Used by permission of Zondervan. All rights reserved. The "NIV" and "New International Version" trademarks are registered in the United States Patent and Trademark Office by Biblica. Use of either trademark requires the permission of Biblica.

Scripture quotations marked ESV are from the ESV® Bible (*The Holy Bible, English Standard Version®*), copyright © 2001 by Crossway. Used by permission. All rights reserved.

Scripture quotations marked HCSB are from *The Holman Christian Standard Bible®*. Copyright © 1999, 2000, 2002, 2003 by Holman Bible Publishers. Used by permission.

Trade paperback ISBN:	978-1-4335-1383-1
ePub ISBN:	978-1-4335-2419-6
PDF ISBN:	978-1-4335-1384-8
Mobipocket ISBN:	978-1-4335-1385-5

Library of Congress Cataloging-in-Publication Data
Charles, J. Daryl, 1950–
    War, peace, and Christianity : questions and answers from a just-war perspective /
J. Daryl Charles and Timothy J. Demy.
      p. cm.
    Includes bibliographical references and indexes.
    ISBN-13: 978-1-4335-1383-1 (tpb)
    ISBN-13: 978-1-4335-2419-6 (ebk)
    ISBN-13: 978-1-4335-1384-8 (pdf)
    ISBN-10: 1-4335-1383-8 (tpk)
    1. War—Religious aspects—Christianity—Miscellanea. 2. Just war doctrine—
Miscellanea. 3. Peace—Religious aspects—Christianity—Miscellanea. I. Demy, Timothy J.
II. Title.
BT736.2.C44 2010
261.8'73—dc22

                                      2009035013

Crossway is a publishing ministry of Good News Publishers.

SH		21	20	19	18	17	16	15	14	13	12	11	10
14	13	12	11	10	9	8	7	6	5	4	3	2	1

For everything there is a season,
and a time for every matter under heaven:
. . . a time for war, and a time for peace.

ECCLESIASTES 3:1, 8 ESV

If war is ever lawful, then peace is sometimes sinful.

C. S. LEWIS

For both extremes a remedy must be found,
that men may not believe either that nothing is allowable,
or that everything is.

HUGO GROTIUS

Contents

Acknowledgments   15

Introduction   17

Part One: Just-War Tradition and the Philosopher

1. What is the role of natural-law thinking in just-war moral reasoning?   27
2. Is there a development of natural-law thinking in the classical philosophical tradition?   37
3. What about cultural relativism? Aren't "truths" relative to the culture in which they are held?   44
4. What is the relationship between law, natural law, and coercion?   48
5. Isn't "just war" a contradiction in terms?   51
6. Doesn't just-war thinking really serve as a justification or pretext for violence?   53
7. Don't just war and pacifism represent two opposing poles on the spectrum of force?   55
8. Aren't all wars, because of the tragic loss of human life, inherently unjust and immoral?   59
9. Aren't there different varieties of pacifism?   63
10. Don't pacifists and just warriors want the same goal, namely, peace?   66
11. Doesn't the sanctioning of force inevitably lead to violence?   70
12. Isn't it a weakness of the just-war tradition that it can justify a war that is unjust?   75
13. What is the difference between a preemptive war and a preventive war?   77

14. What about the statement "All is fair in love and war"?   78
15. Isn't there a "presumption against war" in the just-war
    tradition?   79
16. What is the relationship, if any, between human rights and
    just-war thinking?   82
17. What about warfare and the environment?   85
18. What are the shortcomings of the just-war tradition?   86
19. What good is the just-war tradition in a secular and multi-faith
    world in which not everyone accepts it?   88
20. Does the just-war tradition prevent or promote war?   89
21. Does just-war moral reasoning apply to the problem of
    terrorism?   90

Part Two: Just-War Tradition and the Historian

22. In the history of ideas, is just-war moral reasoning a uniquely
    religious or specifically Christian perspective on war and
    peace, or are there precursors?   97
23. What is the significance of these just-war parallels in pre- or
    non-Christian cultures?   103
24. Given the clear traces of an emergent just-war thinking in
    early Christian history, what were early Christian attitudes
    toward war and military service? Was pacifism pervasive and
    universal?   108
25. What were attitudes toward military service and war among
    particular early fathers of the church?   113
26. When in the early centuries A.D. does just-war moral theory
    begin to develop in the Christian historical tradition?   122
27. Why is legitimate authority so important in the just-war think-
    ing of Thomas Aquinas?   128
28. Isn't just-war thinking a pretext for crusading and imperi-
    alism?   130
29. What effect did the Protestant Reformation have on the
    church's understanding of war and military service?   135
30. What were Luther's views on war and military service?   137
31. What were Calvin's views on war and peace?   141
32. What about the "radical Reformation"? Not all Protestant
    Reformers shared the views of the high Reformers like Luther
    and Calvin.   143
33. Were the Crusades examples of the just-war tradition?   145
34. Isn't the just-war position really just a Western and European
    justification for war?   148

35. How was the American Revolution understood from the standpoint of war? 150

36. How are we best to understand the American Civil War, and what were prevailing attitudes toward war? 154

Part Three: Just-War Tradition and the Statesman

37. What are the core criteria for going to war in just-war moral reasoning? 159

38. What are the prudential criteria in just-war moral reasoning, and how do they differ from the core criteria? 171

39. What about last resort and exhausting all possible nonviolent alternatives? It seems as if just-war proponents will inevitably justify going to war. 174

40. If the criterion of just cause is not satisfied, does this render a war unjust? 177

41. What is the role of the United Nations in a nation's decision to declare war? 180

42. How does just-war moral reasoning apply in the context of international relations? 183

43. Why should governments and people of religious persuasion in particular respond to genocide and egregious human-rights violations? 186

44. Isn't the just-war position really a pretext for an uncritical nationalism? 189

45. What about humanitarian intervention? Short of all-out war, should nations intervene to prevent or retard egregious human-rights violations or catastrophic geopolitical developments, and on what basis? What about a nation's claims to sovereignty? 191

46. What is the nature of humanitarian intervention? How does this differ from war? 196

47. What are the different types of humanitarian intervention? 200

48. What about the case of former Yugoslavia? 203

49. What are *post bellum* ("postwar") contributions that just-war thinking can make? 205

50. Can the just-war tradition accommodate the "war" on terrorism? 208

51. What is a preemptive war? 213

52. What is a preventive war? 215

53. Can preventive war be accommodated in traditional just-war categories?   216
54. How does the concept of "supreme emergency" relate to the just-war tradition?   220
55. Can just-war thought accommodate a world with weapons of mass destruction?   224
56. What about the statement "One person's terrorist is another person's freedom fighter"?   228
57. What is the relationship between Islamic terrorism, Islamic resurgence, and Islam's conflict with Western culture?   231
58. Is the just-war idea limited to self-defense?   237
59. What are the implications of just-war thinking for *jus post bellum* ("justice after war"), and what might this suggest in contemporary geopolitics?   239
60. How much flexibility is there in the just-war tradition to grow and accommodate new challenges?   247

Part Four: Just-War Tradition and the Theologian

61. Doesn't Jesus' teaching in the Sermon on the Mount to "turn the other cheek" and not resist evil require pacifism on the part of Christian faith?   251
62. Doesn't Jesus set aside the law in favor of a new ethic?   254
63. Isn't retaliation counter to Jesus' teaching and thus unchristian in spirit?   259
64. Doesn't St. Paul in Romans 12 require nonretaliatory, nonviolent responses to evil?   262
65. What about "rendering to Caesar"? After all, Jesus seems to have exposed Rome's pretensions of sovereignty.   263
66. Hasn't Romans 13 been used to justify much evil by political regimes throughout history?   267
67. Isn't political power a "necessary evil," if not inherently evil, as portrayed in the Revelation?   271
68. Since Christians are called to be "peacemakers," shouldn't our highest human goal be to strive for peace around us?   275
69. Isn't war immoral since taking human life is a violation of the sixth commandment?   278
70 What is the relationship between peace and justice?   280
71. Doesn't love require us to forgive our enemies?   283
72. Shouldn't the Christian trust the eschatological judgment by God of evil rather than fight or go to war?   287
73. What is the relationship between mercy and justice? Aren't we commanded to show mercy to all people?   291

74. Isn't "turning the other cheek" rather than retribution the more Christian response to evil? 294

75 Is there a difference between retribution and revenge? Surely, a vengeful spirit is counter to loving one's enemy. 297

76. Aren't fighting and warfare a denial and contradiction of the Lamb of God, whose image projects sacrifice? 300

77. What is the church's role in a nation's decision to go to war? Should the church be involved in deciding what is just cause? 303

78. Why does God allow war? 306

79. Can a Christian legitimately serve in the military? 310

80. Is the just-war idea only a Christian construct, or can other religions embrace it also? 313

81. What is the view of war in Roman Catholic social teaching? 315

82. How does Islam view war and peace? 317

83. Is the concept of "supreme emergency" theologically valid? 324

84. Is the concept of just war merely for Christians? 327

Part Five: Just-War Tradition and the Combatant

85. Does deterrence really work? 331

86. What about nonlethal weapons? 334

87. Are mercenaries permitted within the framework of just-war thought? 336

88. How does the just-war tradition understand asymmetric warfare? 341

89. How relevant is the just-war tradition in a world of high-tech weapons? 342

90. How does noncombatant immunity affect conflict and war? 344

91. Aren't all wars "just" to the victor? 348

Part Six: Just-War Tradition and the Individual

92. Why do people, including those of religious faith, disagree so strongly about war and peace? 353

93. Don't charity and resort to force or going to war stand in blatant contradiction? 356

94. What about self-defense? Does Christian faith prohibit force in this context? 361

95. Doesn't Gandhi demonstrate the effectiveness and necessity of pacifism? 364

96. Isn't pacifism a legitimate position for the religious believer who takes seriously his or her faith? 367

97. In light of Jesus' call to "peacemaking," doesn't the New Testament require pacifism of the Christian disciple? 372

98. Aren't strife and conflict always sinful, the product of the human heart? 375
99. How did C. S. Lewis view war? 377
100. What about Dietrich Bonhoeffer's example? How are we to reconcile his attraction to pacifism with his willingness to participate in the attempt on Hitler's life? 381
101. What are common misunderstandings or misuses of just-war doctrine? 386
102. Aren't issues of war and peace matters of individual conscience for religious believers? 392
103. What should an individual do whose country is involved in an unjust war? 394
104. From the standpoint of religious conviction, doesn't going to war mean that fellow Christians from different countries will kill each other? 397

Recommended Reading 399
Index of Names 407
Index of Scripture 411

Acknowledgments

Many people are involved directly and indirectly in every publishing project. We are especially grateful for the enthusiasm and support of friends at Crossway. Allan Fisher shared our concern for the topic of this book from the beginning and embraced the project wholeheartedly. Thanks also go to Jill Carter for keeping us on track, to Josh Dennis for his management of design, and to Thom Notaro for his editorial skills and dedication.

We owe a great debt to James Turner Johnson, who has steadfastly articulated and upheld the moral substructure of the just-war tradition. The fruit of his work has been to bring clarity and understanding to the historical development of the tradition, as well as to bring much-needed wisdom from the tradition to bear on contemporary geopolitical affairs. His character and writings have been exemplary, bearing Christian witness in a hostile world.

I (Daryl) am supremely grateful to Professor Robert P. George, McCormick Professor of Jurisprudence at Princeton University and director of the James Madison Program in American Ideals and Institutions, and to Dr. Bradford Wilson, executive director of the James Madison Program, for the invitation to serve during the 2007–2008 academic year as William E. Simon Visiting Fellow in Religion and Public Life. That invitation provided the luxury of incomparable resources at the university, continual interaction with university faculty and students, and rich fellowship and exceptionally stimulating conversation. This volume is part of the fruit of research done during that fellowship year.

Special thanks must go to Madison fellows with whom I served. Robert Clinton (Southern Illinois University), David Ericson (George Mason University), Jack Barlow (Juniata College), and Paul Kerry (Brigham Young University) in particular helped sharpen my thinking through their friendship, their penetrating questions, and their thoughtful personal engagement.

I (Tim) have been blessed with friends without whose encouragement this work would not have been completed. Gary Stewart enthusiastically supported the work from the beginning and offered many valuable insights. Lynn Barnes and Carrie Wood were persistent in keeping me focused and adding daily support. I owe Tommy Ice, Wayne House, and Bob Allums thanks for their friendship and expertise.

At the U.S. Naval War College, I am grateful to the former provost, Dr. James Giblin, whose encouragement to pursue this work reaffirmed its need and relevance. Other colleagues likewise strengthened my efforts and helped minimize my shortcomings. Especially helpful were Professors Stan Carpenter, Doug Smith, Jay Hickey, John Meyer, Gene Andersen, Martin Cook, Dayne Nix, Gary Ohls, and Tom Grassey. Navy Chaplains Kyle Fauntleroy, Phil Gwaltney, and Michael Gore also provided helpful insights and counsel.

During two years of study at the University of Cambridge, I was challenged to review and evaluate my understanding of war, peace, and international relations. I am indebted to Professors Tarak Barkawi, Charles Jones, and Philip Towle for their intellectual stimulation. Cambridge friends of the Selwyn Club also provided many hours of discussion, sharpening my analytical and communication skills. In the midst of these studies I was privileged to use the facilities of Tyndale House, Cambridge, and benefited greatly from that experience and the spiritual refreshment it offered. Especially pertinent for this work were conversations and concerns shared with visiting scholar Peter Jones.

I owe special thanks to my wife, Lyn, a steadfast supporter and the wisest person I know.

From 1981 until 2008, I served as a Navy chaplain afloat and ashore with U.S. Navy, Coast Guard, and Marine Corps units. I owe a great personal and professional debt to hundreds of colleagues, shipmates, and members of the U.S. Armed Forces with whom it was a privilege to serve. They daily demonstrated exceptional professionalism and a commitment to upholding justice in war and peace. They did so with their words, their actions, and, sadly, sometimes their lives. You will not be forgotten.

Introduction

Although spirited and often contentious debates over war and the use of coercive force have characterized the post–Cold War era, a sturdy and philosophically robust reexamination of the rich tradition that qualifies both war and peace is urgently needed in our day. Fully apart from U.S. involvement in Iraq, Afghanistan, and the "war on terrorism," the new geopolitical challenges to security around the world call attention to the need for exploring the ethics of war, peace, and interventionary force.

Alas, the end of the Cold War did *not* bring an end to human suffering, cruelty, and catastrophe, nor did it usher in the new peaceful order that some had projected and for which many had longed.[1] If anything, it heralded new contexts in which human depravity might show itself—from Kuwait, Iraq, and Afghanistan to Bosnia-Kosovo-Herzegovina and Rwanda, to Burundi, Sierra Leone, and Liberia, to Somalia and Sudan. And these are wholly aside from the production of chemical, biological, and nuclear weapons by sundry unruly nations, drug trafficking on most (if not all) continents, and the breathtaking rise of a maturing international terrorism that is often religiously motivated and increasingly worldwide. These crises, at the very least,

---

[1] It is surely no overstatement to suggest that the end of the Cold War found policy makers poorly prepared to deal with geopolitical crises that have since arisen. In fact, it laid bare a severe lack of moral discourse related to these developments. Moreover, for those who viewed the Cold War as the consequence of defects in the international order, the post–Cold War period was thought, however briefly, to usher in an era of increased power and prestige for the United Nations. The tragic geopolitical reality is that catastrophe after catastrophe have visited the international community, leaving the UN to scramble for any sort of coherent and effective approach, and showing most nations to be relatively nonresponsive. As one Burmese human-rights activist recently lamented, "There are no countries in the world which have gained liberation through the help of the United Nations" (Ludu Sein Win, veteran Burmese and Rangoon-based journalist, cited in *The Irrawaddy*, April 2008, 5).

herald the need for reinvigorated debates about the merits and moral substructure of interventionary force.[2]

But the political or geopolitical challenge is perhaps not the greatest. More pressing may be the West's inability to make moral judgments that, in the end, bear upon serious statecraft and, ideally, translate into responsible policy considerations. In the aftermath of the Second World War, Hannah Arendt, whose postwar reflections on the "banality of evil" are well known, ventured to predict in an essay titled "Nightmare and Flight"[3] that the problem of evil would be *the fundamental question* of postwar intellectual life in Europe. Yet, strangely, already in the 1950s, even when atrocities associated with the Holocaust remained a permanent scar on the European psyche, concern with moral evil and the political problems that it causes had begun to disappear from Western political thought.[4] Thus, for an American president to speak of "evil" in the geopolitical context, as have several of our recent presidents, is to invite scorn of the *greatest* magnitude, both at home and abroad. For the moment, however, let us agree to put aside our own political sympathies; what was unforgiveable to most people was the fact that *someone in public office* would name evil and then contextualize it in the field of international relations.[5]

But how indeed might those who are responsible for policy propose to deal with the scale of humanitarian need that in our day is massive and frequently the result of unstable regimes?[6] And what moral and political resources might inform our response to such situations—situations that fall short of formal war per se but require some measure of interventionary force for humanitarian purposes?[7] Should governments respond and intervene to prevent—or retard the effects of—genocide, mass murder, enslavement of peoples or people groups,

---

[2]Surely the frequency of U.S. intervention, or assistance with intervention, in other countries since the end of the Cold War—from Haiti to Kuwait and Iraq, to Somalia and Zaire, to Bosnia-Kosovo—has been surprising (and indeed alarming) to many. Few would have anticipated the sheer density of geopolitical catastrophes that have occurred since the collapse of the Soviet Union.

[3]This essay is reproduced in Jerome Kohn, ed., *Hannah Arendt: Essays in Understanding, 1930–1954* (New York: Harcourt Brace, 1994).

[4]This post–World War II development, in our view, has been correctly observed by Nicholas Rengger and Renée Jeffery, "Moral Evil and International Relations," *SAIS Review* (Winter 2005): 3–4.

[5]The point, we should emphasize, is not whether making moral judgments can be done in a more nuanced or diplomatic fashion; it is only that international relations are generally ill-prepared to deal with moral categories. At the very least, such a state of affairs might invite thoughtful, multidisciplinary moral discourse that is not *severed* from geopolitical realities.

[6]This instability may be characteristic of new states, failed states, or those states on the verge of collapse.

[7]Here we are using the term *humanitarian* in its narrower sense, wherein intervention is undertaken to promote the welfare of humanity, especially through the elimination of gratuitous pain and suffering.

and egregious human-rights violations? Why or why not? If so, then when, by what rationale, and by what criteria? As it affects foreign policy, few questions will be more pressing in the years to come.

Because issues of war and peace are literally issues of life and death, the tragedy of war must be neither forgotten nor minimized. Surely, conventional wisdom is not far from the mark in reminding us that the horrors of war are the closest approximation to hell on earth. War changes lives forever in ways that are otherwise unthinkable; hereon both secular and religious viewpoints agree. As seen from a wider religious and Judeo-Christian perspective, war entails the death and killing of people who are fashioned in the likeness of their Creator and who therefore possess inherent dignity and incalculable worth. Yet, the very same *Weltanschauung* affirms that war is sometimes necessary.

Few (if any) world-and-life views eschew war in *all* circumstances, and no faith tradition is monolithic in its dogma and practice regarding war and peace. This is certainly the case with Judaism and Christianity, whose values have undergirded our own cultural tradition. Throughout its millennia-long history, the Judeo-Christian moral tradition has justified, rationalized, restrained, and informed war, the conduct of warfare, and the conditions for peace. In various times and by diverse means, it has both upheld and departed from biblical standards, and both ecclesiastical and secular leaders have appealed to its teachings for national guidance and support.

This volume is based on the wider social, moral-philosophical, and political assumption that the sturdiest, wisest, and most well-defined position (whether secular or religious in orientation) regarding war and peace is lodged in the mainstream of the classic just-war tradition. Some aspects of this rich tradition, based on natural-law moral reasoning, predate the Christian era, extending back not merely to classical Rome and Athens but to ancient Israel. Theoretical development of the tradition, at the same time, is firmly grounded in early Christian history and theology stemming from theologians and thinkers such as Ambrose and Augustine. Important medieval construal of qualifying war can be found in the thinking of Maimonides and Thomas Aquinas, both of whom—from Jewish and Christian perspectives respectively— are authoritative interpreters of law and its application. Significantly, both Maimonides and Aquinas, who are the beneficiaries of a renewal in Aristotelian thinking, wrestle with war as both prerogative and political duty; both individuals, moreover, view law as teleological and undergirded by divinely instituted moral predicates that are known through the "natural law."

Further aspects of the just-war tradition are developed or refined by seminal thinkers such as Vitoria, Suárez, and Grotius in the sixteenth and seventeenth centuries, against the backdrop of religious wars in Europe, as well as "new world" discoveries in the Americas. Refinement and application of the tradition during this early-modern period are critical to the emergence of international law, which imposes legal and moral sanctions on the community of nations. And yet other parts of the tradition are mirrored in the twentieth and twenty-first centuries, as seen, for example, in the accent on human rights, humanitarian concern, and emergent political-legal developments. At bottom, the tradition has always been multidisciplinary and far-reaching with regard to the social-political, legal, and philosophical net cast by it proponents.

At the same time, it also needs emphasizing that European warfare, in its various historical expressions, cannot be thought to mirror adequately the just-war tradition. Thus, for example, the Crusades, the Spanish Inquisition, the wars of religion during the sixteenth and seventeenth centuries, and wars associated with colonial expansion represent violent and unjust episodes in Western history that not infrequently failed to uphold the values and goals of the just-war tradition. Indeed, very often it was in reaction to such brutal and savage conflict that the just-war tradition responded.

To understand properly the mainstream of the classic just-war tradition is to appreciate the theoretical and moral-philosophical assumptions that undergird the tradition. As James Turner Johnson so aptly writes:

> The just war idea is not free-floating, to be given whatever content one may think appropriate in whatever context. Understanding its meaning means engagement with the tradition out of which it comes and entering into dialog with the classical statement of the just war idea within that tradition. . . . Just war tradition has to do with defining the possible good use of force, not finding exceptional cases

when it is possible to use something inherently evil (force) for the purposes of good.[8]

Misconstrued by many as a means to endorse any war by throwing a mantle of "just" or "justice" over a nation's intrusion, just-war thinking is best understood as an approach to *comparative* justice applied to the considerations of war or intervention. Justice in the present life is always approximate. To acknowledge the possibility of error or human fallibility in moral reasoning is not to give up on the ideal of justice. Nor is it to abdicate, as imperfect human beings, the social-political necessity of working for justice on behalf of those who need it. Justice, after all, is the moral tissue that holds "civil society" together. Philosophically, just-war thinking understands itself as a mediating position between the ideological poles of *Realpolitik* or militarism, on the one hand, and pacifism, on the other. This "mediating" posture might well be illustrated through our attempts at "criminal justice" in the domestic context: we neither acquiesce to violent crime, on the one hand, nor tolerate police brutality, on the other. Authentic justice is lodged somewhere in the "messy middle." That requires of imperfect men and women the resolution to work for justice (albeit imperfectly) in order to preserve the common social good; anything less is morally and socially deficient. In the words of Hugo Grotius, justice insists neither that everything is always permissible nor that nothing ever is.[9]

Moreover, just-war moral reasoning is rooted in a certain moral realism about human nature. Such realism influences how we construe power and the use of coercive force. Consequently, it encourages a healthy skepticism and uneasiness about the use and abuse of power without opting out of political reality altogether in favor of utopian fantasies. It understands that moral judgments, and subsequent actions, must proceed in a world of limitations, estrangements, and partial justice, thereby fostering recognition of the provisional nature of all political arrangements. Yet, it recognizes self-defense against—and, on occasion, active opposition toward—unjust aggressors and

---

[8] James Turner Johnson, *The War to Oust Saddam Hussein: Just War and the New Face of Conflict* (Lanham, MD: Rowman & Littlefield, 2005), 35–36.
[9] This logic forms the heart of Grotius's just-war thinking found in *The Law of War and Peace* (1625).

agents of oppression, while refusing to legitimate imperialistic crusades and the building of empires in the name of peace.[10]

In his seminal treatise *On War* (*Vom Kriege*), the noted Prussian military theorist Carl von Clausewitz observed that war and conflict are multidimensional, touching the psychological, intellectual, and spiritual dimensions of the human experience. "Theory becomes infinitely more difficult as soon as it touches the realm of moral values," he notes.[11] And indeed, religious and ethical sentiments are most assuredly part of the domain he termed "moral values." Although military forces of hundreds of thousands might clash in global conflict (as evidenced by the twentieth century), it is ultimately individuals acting as moral agents who determine the fate of nations. Rarely cited, however, are Clausewitz's further observations:

> Military activity is never directed against material force alone; it is always aimed simultaneously at the moral forces which give it life, and the two cannot be separated.
>
> . . . moral values can only be perceived by the inner eye, which differs in each person, and is often different in the same person at different times.[12]

Whether one is a combatant, noncombatant, political leader, philosopher, concerned citizen, or policy maker in the context of any given conflict, ethical values inform our social-political views, either in support of or in dissent against that conflict. Values, alas, always have consequences.

The present volume, in its affirmation of the classic just-war tradition, in no way represents an attempt to glorify or promote war; such, it needs pointing out, has been a persistent criticism of the last decade and particularly since 2003. Rather, it seeks to answer common and persistent questions about war and peace from within the moral logic that inheres in the just-war idea. In so doing, we have chosen to engage the reader through a question-and-answer format, hoping that such might stimulate readers to probe issues of specific social-

---

[10]So Jean Bethke Elshtain, "Just War and Humanitarian Intervention," *Ideas* 8, no. 2 (2001): 18–19. This wider logic of thought undergirds two very different volumes by Elshtain, *Augustine and the Limits of Power* (South Bend, IN: University of Notre Dame Press, 1991), and *Just War against Terror: The Burden of American Power in a Violent World* (New York: Basic Books, 2003).

[11]Carl von Clausewitz, *On War*, ed. and trans. Michael Howard and Peter Paret (1832; repr., Princeton, NJ: Princeton University Press, 1976), 136.

[12]Ibid., 136–37.

cultural, historical, and geopolitical concern. We do not consider any of the answers here to be exhaustive. Rather, they are starting points for necessary reflection on topics that are typically complex, usually culturally conditioned, and often having a long history.

This volume is a collaborative effort. It mirrors converging ideological perspectives and convictions of the two authors, even while one of us writes from the perspective of moral and political philosophy and the other approaches questions from a professional military vantage point. Both of us write as theorists as well as practitioners—one having done criminal justice research before entering the university classroom full-time, the other continuing to train officers in professional ethics and moral leadership at one of the nation's military war colleges. And both of us embrace the broader philosophical commitments of the just-war tradition in its classic expression, even though one of us grew up in the Anabaptist tradition (and still retains an appreciation for its religious commitments). Although in conversation one might detect different nuances in our individual understandings of social arrangements, moral philosophy, theology, or political views, we stand in essential agreement. This unity of perspective, in the end, has its roots in the depth and breadth of just-war moral reasoning.

To be sure, many secular and religious thinkers have sought in fresh ways to address the perennial concerns of war and peace in recent years; one need only consult the literature since 2003. But frequently this is done without an adequate social-political and philosophical grounding that joins past and present.[13] Our modest proposal is to join a centuries-long conversation, in the hopes that enduring resources— resources that imbue our own cultural tradition—might bear upon contemporary geopolitical challenges. And in a post-consensus cultural climate, such resources—for the politician, the educator, or the thoughtful layperson—are urgently needed.

---

[13]Notable exceptions are the writings of Michael Walzer, e.g., *Just and Unjust Wars*, 4th ed. (New York: Basic Books, 2006), and *Arguing about War* (New Haven, CT: Yale University Press, 2004); James Turner Johnson, e.g., *Just War Tradition and the Restraint of War: A Moral and Historical Inquiry* (Princeton, NJ: Princeton University Press, 1981), *The Quest for Peace: Three Moral Traditions in Western Cultural History* (Princeton, NJ: Princeton University Press, 1987), and *Morality and Contemporary Warfare* (New Haven, CT: Yale University Press, 1999); Oliver O'Donovan, e.g., *The Just War Revisited* (Cambridge: Cambridge University Press, 2003); Jean Bethke Elshtain, e.g., *Just War Theory: Readings in Social and Political Theory* (ed.) (New York: New York University Press, 1992), and *Just War against Terror*; and Brian Orend, e.g., *War and International Justice: A Kantian Perspective* (Waterloo, ON: Wilfrid Laurier University Press, 2000), *Michael Walzer on War and Justice* (Cardiff: University of Wales Press, 2000), and *The Morality of War* (Peterborough, ON: Broadview, 2006).

PART 1

JUST-WAR TRADITION AND THE PHILOSOPHER

Q. 1 What is the role of natural-law thinking in just-war moral reasoning?

Natural-law moral reasoning proceeds on the baseline assumption of a shared nature in all human beings, regardless of culture or location. Part of that "nature" is a moral intuition that discerns between good and evil and expresses itself at the most rudimentary level by eschewing moral evil and doing good (so, Thomas Aquinas). Thereby it provides a common moral grammar for all people—for people of religious or nonreligious persuasion—and facilitates moral discourse in a culturally and socially diverse context.

What needs emphasis is that human beings demonstrate this moral intuition on a daily basis at the most rudimentary level. In traveling, for example, we have the option of taking the plane, the car, the bus, or the train. And along the way, we might opt for yogurt, a hamburger, a burrito, or Chinese food. None of these decisions, as they concern travel or eating, is infused with moral meaning; each has legitimacy. If, however, we were to decide between eating a hamburger and eating human flesh, then our decision would take on considerable moral significance. And if the purpose of our travel were to eliminate human beings in the service of the Mafia, our travel would suddenly acquire a moral cast. Why? One need not be a religious person to discern the difference.

The fact that natural-law thinking goes against the stream of contemporary moral and political philosophy, as well as jurisprudence, says nothing about its efficacy or its viability. It is only to point out that human reflection on what T. S. Eliot called "the permanent things" is perceived as out of step with the contemporary *Zeitgeist*.[1] Perhaps the

---

[1]Already over two decades ago Harold Berman observed that in the past two generations, American public philosophy had shifted from a historically conscious and morally grounded theory of law to a more instrumental, pragmatic theory. Berman wrote: "The triumph of the positivist theory of law—that law is the will of the lawmaker—and the decline of rival theories—the moral theory that law is reason and conscience, and the historical theory that law is an ongoing tradition in which *both* politics and morality play important parts—have contributed to the bewilderment of legal education. Skepticism

cultural or ethical relativist might offer a rejoinder. Perhaps, one might argue, as does one criminologist in the journal *Criminal Justice Ethics*,[2] cannibalism has moral and social significance in a particular culture and therefore should be honored.[3] And perhaps killing relatively innocent human beings because they stand in the way of business is permissible. Recall the cultural relativist's insistence that morality is social and culturally constructed, that there are no objective or transcendent moral guidelines for humans universally. In general, then, it would appear that moral principle, if we may call it such, inevitably comes into conflict with self-interest, not only in the cases of cannibalism or Mafia business-as-normal. And this, as one political philosopher has well argued, is the perennial problem for a society that wishes to order itself meaningfully and justly.[4] But the fact of conflict does not in and of itself explain the presence of moral principle. When confronted with an option, why not opt for human flesh? And who is to say that killing for the Mafia is wrong? After all, it would seem that, at least in some cases, one man's murder is another man's business savvy.

While most social scientists are not in the habit of reading Aristotle, they would surely benefit from his musings on human culture. In *Politics*, Aristotle formalized what most human beings intuit: the community—and specifically, the political community (the *polis*)—is a "natural" human association—"natural" in the sense that it corresponds with our inherent nature. To argue that our nature is social—and thus moral—is to argue for what is self-evident; hence, the organic link between *Politics* and *Nicomachean Ethics*. By implication, Aristotle was arguing that the human propensity for an ordered community sets human beings apart from animals. Moreover, the capacity of language, as Aristotle well understood, is an inherently *moral* capacity, insofar as language can "declare what is advantageous and what is the reverse," just as it can "declare what is just and what is unjust." Herein human

and relativism are widespread." "The Crisis of Legal Education in America," *Boston College Law Review* 26 (1985): 348. It is difficult to disagree with Berman.

[2]See the symposium published in the Summer–Fall 1994 issue of *Criminal Justice Ethics* (13, no. 2) devoted to a critique of James Q. Wilson's book *The Moral Sense* (New York: The Free Press, 1993).

[3]Gilbert Geis, "Moral Innatism, Connatural Ideas, and Impuissance in Daily Affairs: James Q. Wilson's Acrobatic Dive into an Empty Pool," *Criminal Justice Ethics* 13, no. 2 (Summer–Fall 1994): 77–82. Geis is angry at and dismissive of Wilson's suggestion of innate moral intuitions, viewing such as an "absurdity." Geis chooses rather to side with the cultural anthropologist who, in assessing the social significance of cannibalism, believes that "Christianity spoils our feasts."

[4]Hadley Arkes, *First Things: An Inquiry into the First Principles of Morals and Justice* (Princeton, NJ: Princeton University Press, 1986), 3–8.

beings distinguish themselves from the broader animal kingdom.[5] And although in the last three decades arguments have been proffered by certain sociobiologists and primate philosophers that human morality has its genesis in evolution and that this "evolving" can be observed in nonhuman animals, such arguments are purely speculative and ignore very basic differences between humans and nonhumans. Chief among these is that we do not expect animals to offer *excuses* or *justifications* for their actions—a moral realm that presupposes reason plus expression through language. To be able to employ a language or grammar of morality is to possess moral agency—the freedom to choose particular types of action over others, which then can be deemed praiseworthy or blameworthy.

In religious terms, Christian theology distinguishes between a general and a more particularized mode of revealed knowledge operative among humankind. Accordingly, what unites all people is the former, a knowledge of moral "first things" that is prior to any knowledge they might acquire. This "prior" knowledge—what we can't not know, in the words of one social philosopher[6]—is precisely what one New Testament writer wishes to describe when he refers, in his letter to the Romans, to a moral law "written on their hearts" (Rom. 2:14–15). Pagan Gentiles, he notes, "do by nature the things required by the law"; thereby "they show that the requirements of the law are written on their hearts." Because of this "law" that is rooted in human "nature," nonreligious peoples' "consciences [are] bearing witness" and "their thoughts . . . accusing" them. This is none other than the language of the natural law. It is "nature" because it describes *the way things are*, and the fact that not everyone gives assent to the natural law does not assail its universal reality.[7] It is a "law" because *nothing can change our essential nature*. Since moral depravity is actual and total in extent but restrained in degree, the potential in humans to express depravity, devastating as it may be, neither eliminates our ability to choose to do good (freedom) nor releases us from the sense of moral obligation (culpability, the common good).

---

[5]Aristotle, *Politics* 1253a, cited in *The Politics of Aristotle*, ed. and trans. Ernest Barker (Oxford: Oxford University Press, 1981), 5–6.

[6]J. Budziszewski, *What We Can't Not Know: A Guide* (Dallas: Spence, 2003).

[7]For this reason Jacques Maritain can write that the rejection of natural-law thinking "proves nothing . . . , any more than a mistake in addition proves anything against arithmetic" (*Man and the State* [Chicago: University of Chicago Press, 1951], 90).

To employ the language and logic of morality is to presuppose *of necessity* that (1) there is a right and a wrong and (2) humans exercise a moral "freedom" with respect to particular choices. This freedom, in turn, means that people can be held responsible for their actions. Thus, for example, when people are rewarded or punished not for the moral quality of their acts but for the accident[8] of their racial background, it must be said that racial discrimination is wrong *of necessity* and not merely on the basis of perspective, circumstance, or social location.[9] This conclusion is a moral predilection that all people everywhere and at all times intuit, even when some people in some cultural locations refuse to honor it. Moral "first principles," it should be emphasized, cannot be proven or "demonstrated" through experiment since they are anterior to human experience and experiments. The proposition that "all men are created equal" cannot be "demonstrated"; it is a "necessary truth" based on the reality of human nature. For this reason, as one political philosopher observes of the moral skeptic:

> The person who seeks to deny the existence of morals will spend most of his days trying to flee from the perils of contradiction and the tangle of his own argument. He will discover, again, that for the man of reason the existence of morals must hold the place of a necessary assumption or a first principle in the ground of his understanding.[10]

Clearly, in the exercise of human moral freedom, there are differing degrees of culpability and guilt—among individuals and among nations. And these must be handled in differing ways according to a moral "system" that is consistent and coherent. Both "criminal justice" in the domestic context and classic just-war thinking draw from the same "system" of moral reasoning. Both proceed on the basis of certain fundamental baseline moral discriminations. For example, we discriminate between relative guilt and relative innocence, we discriminate between greater and lesser forms of evil and injustice, and we discriminate qualitatively between criminal and punitive acts. Moreover, both draw from the same canons of moral principle in the pursuit of justice: for example, sufficiency of cause for justifying intervention,

---

[8]"Accident" is used here not to mean "mistake," but in its philosophical sense, meaning a feature or property of a substance that is not essential to its existence.
[9]See Arkes, *First Things*, 51–54, for a creative and compelling development of this sort of thinking.
[10]Ibid., 84.

the rationale of a greater good or right intention in applying coercive force, proportionality with respect to means, and publicly legitimized authorization for applying coercive force.

The natural law is acknowledged both in the classical philosophical tradition and in the mainstream of the Christian moral-philosophical tradition, both of which generously inform the Western cultural tradition. In Thomistic thought we observe a particularly sophisticated development of natural-law thinking. Aquinas is careful to explain the link between human intuitions and the natural law and to establish the natural law as the basis for just, rightly ordered relations. Early-modern just-war thinkers build upon Thomistic thought, applying natural-law moral reasoning to questions of territorial sovereignty and international relations.

To the surprise of many, the notion of the natural law is resolutely affirmed in the writings of the Protestant Reformers, who thought deeply about issues of government, legitimate authority, civil society, and the common good, and not merely about matters of faith, the church, and ecclesiastical culture. However deeply entrenched a present-day bias against natural-law thinking would seem to be among Protestant thinkers,[11] it cannot be attributed to the sixteenth-century Reformers themselves. While it is undeniable that they sought to champion a particular understanding of grace and faith that in their estimation was utterly lacking,[12] their emphasis was *not* to the exclusion of modes of moral reasoning that were rooted in natural-law thinking.[13]

Both Luther and Calvin believed that the "golden rule," as it is expressed in both Plato and Jesus' teaching, was simply the restatement of a higher inviolable law, or norm, rooted in a moral universe, by which human deeds are judged. Calvin writes that "there is nothing more common than for a man to be sufficiently instructed in a right standard of conduct by natural law."[14] It is significant that even

---

[11]On the Protestant neglect of the natural law and its ramifications for moral discourse, see J. Daryl Charles, *Retrieving the Natural Law: A Return to Moral First Things*, Critical Issues in Bioethics (Grand Rapids: Eerdmans, 2008); and Stephen J. Grabill, *Rediscovering the Natural Law in Reformed Theological Ethics*, Emory University Studies in Law and Religion (Grand Rapids: Eerdmans, 2006).

[12]See in this regard Alister E. McGrath, *Iustitia Dei: A History of the Christian Doctrine of Justification*, 2 vols. (Cambridge: Cambridge University Press, 1986).

[13]It is accurate to insist that the Reformation controversies with the Catholic Church were foremost *theological and not ethical* insofar as the Reformers assumed the natural law as a moral-theological bedrock in their system and therein maintained continuity with their Catholic counterparts.

[14]John Calvin, *Institutes of the Christian Religion*, ed. John T. McNeill, trans. Ford Lewis Battles (Philadelphia: Westminster Press, 1960), 2.2.22.

Luther, for whom grace is so crucial, insisted that law and an uneasy conscience are the first point of contact between the Creator and all human beings. The uneasy conscience, as Luther understands it, is nothing more than the expression of an internal "law."

It goes without saying that the age of Augustine and Aquinas and that of early-modern thinkers differ greatly in the sort of dilemmas that needed addressing. Given the cultural synthesis of the Middle Ages, for example, medieval theorists developed their understanding of just war explicitly from religion and secondarily from natural law. This relationship is reversed in the Age of Discovery and the early-modern period, when new challenges to just-war thinkers emerge. These challenges concern people outside Christendom as well as a divided Christendom. Regarding the first: Does just-war thinking apply to non-Christian peoples? What about cultures and nations that find themselves outside Christendom? Do the very same just-war criteria apply? Why or why not?

Three early-modern theorists who provide an important adaptation of just-war principles on the basis of an appeal to natural law are Francisco de Vitoria (1480–1546), Francisco Suárez (1548–1617), and Hugo Grotius (1583–1645). By the year 1510, disquieting reports had reached Spain that Native Americans were being denied basic liberty and property. The immediate challenge confronting Vitoria was the Spanish vision to colonize the new peoples of the Americas. Spain was prepared to justify war with Native Americans to possess their land and seek their "conversion" to the Christian faith. Vitoria's task was to challenge the Spanish king on the basis of the unjust treatment of the American Indians. Against conventional thinking his argument was nothing short of scandalous: neither the king, nor the pope for that matter, could authorize war against the Indians. Neither religious nor economic nor political reasons alone make coercion and warfare just, Vitoria argues in *Reflections on the Indians and the Law of War*; Indians and Spaniards have equal rights. The only cause for war that is just is a wrong that is intuited through natural moral law, a wrong that is discernable to all people everywhere through reason. Going to war based on religious differences or "the spirit of discovery" is not justifiable. No war is just that inflicts upon a population unprovoked injustice. And even were the Indians to attack the Spanish, a just response would be only a defensive response that sought to minimize loss.

In Vitoria are to be found the beginnings of international law, that is, of principles governing all nations that are anchored in natural moral law. Vitoria's argument is significant because it acknowledges an international community of independent states or people groups that have rights, territorial sovereignty, and reciprocal duties as to conduct. Unlike just-war thinkers before him, Vitoria grounds the notion of just war not in Christian theology per se, but in moral obligation that is known through natural-law reasoning. What natural reason has established among the nations is that certain rights and privileges, rooted in justice, are inviolable. Nature establishes a bond between all men; man is not a wolf to his fellow man; he is another man. If principles of just war are applicable to non-Christian peoples, then the rationale, the very basis, for justice and peace could not be narrowly Christian. Human-rights violations and justification for going to war are the same for all people everywhere; they are rooted in moral realities that are unchanging and universally applicable.

Central to the work of Suárez are the emphasis on natural law and the matter of how states are to conduct themselves. Whereas civil law is alterable, based on customs and usage, the law of nature is universal and unchanging, governing how human beings as well as nations deal with one another. All aspects of justice flow from this reality. Under the rubric of charity, Suárez scrutinizes the role of the state in both defensive and offensive modes: "A required mode and uniformity as to it [warfare] must be observed at its beginning, during its prosecution and after victory."[15] This mode of moral conformity, Suárez was careful to maintain, is founded upon the natural law and is common to religious and nonreligious alike.[16]

Considered the father of modern international law, Grotius confronts the dilemma of just limits to war in much the same way as Vitoria and Suárez. The results of his work would be foundational for just-war thinking in the modern era. In his important work *The Law of War and Peace* (1625), Grotius argues that how nations relate to one another is governed by universally binding moral principles. These are "binding on all kings" (1.1.10) and "known through reason" (1.3.16). This argument has important implications for both the church and the state,

---

[15]Francisco Suárez *Three Theological Virtues* 3.8.1. We are here dependent on the English translation of James B. Scott, *The Spanish Origin of International Law: Lectures on Francisco de Vitoria (1480–1546) and Francisco Suárez (1548–1617)* (Washington, DC: Georgetown University Press, 1929), 77.
[16]Suárez *Three Theological Virtues* 3.8.2.

for it places limitations on both. It also places limitations on whether nations may go to war justly and how warfare is to be conducted. Given the reality of the natural law, such rules of military engagement are valid for all people. Historian Paul Christopher has well summarized the importance of Grotius's work, observing among his more enduring contributions: (1) international law, grounded in the "laws of humanity" that govern international relations, (2) advocacy of universal, natural laws that impose moral and legal restrictions on nations, and (3) clearly articulated rules of international law for the conduct of war that specify *jus ad bellum* and *jus in bello* requirements.[17]

Vitoria, Suárez, and Grotius understand justice to have deeper roots than mere religious confession. Justice is known through nature and is intuited universally as binding upon all people everywhere. Thus the "law of nature" becomes a "law to the nations" (*jus gentium*), holding people groups accountable to the unchanging demands of justice, which orders right relations. As an extension of antecedent Christian moral thinking, just-war principles find confirmation in the natural law and not solely an appeal to religious faith.[18]

Natural law presupposes both the existence of universal moral norms and a basic awareness of these in all humans. Natural law is assumed to exist among all peoples, based on a shared humanity. It is a "natural" system of ethics that neither depends on one's being religious nor contradicts religion. Something is forbidden because it is wrong *in sic*.[19] For this reason, natural-law thinking is foundational to just-war theory. The just-war thinker holds certain moral truths to be self-evident. This applies both to individual criminals, who need

---

[17]Paul Christopher, *The Ethics of War and Peace*, rev. ed. (Upper Saddle River, NJ: Prentice Hall, 1999), 81–103.

[18]A common objection among religious thinkers is that natural-law thinking is autonomous to a so-called Christian ethics and to the authority of Scripture. This view is utterly false and mirrors a fundamental misunderstanding both of law as an entity and of the natural law as the basis of human moral intuition. The Hebrew and Christian Scriptures *presuppose* the natural law (cf. Rom. 2:14–15, which describes this "law" as "written on [human] hearts"). Moreover, the "Ten Commandments" simply define the contours of the natural moral law as a moral code that applies to all of humanity and not exclusively to any particular culture or society.

[19]Some see common moral truths as self-evident without reference to God. Others (we) explain the shared sense of right and wrong as something that is revealed, therefore having a theological basis. In the latter understanding, it isn't a question of natural versus revealed/religious, but both natural and revealed (notwithstanding degrees of suppression of knowledge of the One who speaks in that revelation). For an example of the Reformers on this subject, see McNeill's note in Calvin's *Institutes of the Christian Religion* 1.3.1: "On verse 5 [of John 1], Calvin writes: 'There are two principal parts of the light which still remains in corrupt nature; first, the seed of religion is planted in all men; next, the distinction between good and evil is engraved on their consciences.'" Also *Institutes* 4.20.16: "It is a fact that the law of God which we call the moral law is nothing else than a testimony of natural law and of that conscience which God has engraved upon the minds of men."

restraint and punishment in the local community, and to nations that violate basic moral norms in the wider human community. The very premise on which just war rests is that there is a universal "moral sense" that informs human beings, in relative terms, as to what is good, just, and acceptable over against what is evil, unjust, and unacceptable. The question of *how* we decide, procedurally and internationally, to deal with these gross violations is a secondary—though by no means unimportant—matter, calling for wisdom and prudence.

The natural law might be construed as an imprint made on (human) nature itself. Justice represents the basic obligation of human beings as creatures. "Nature," confirmed through conscience, reveals to all people everywhere an awareness of basic moral reality that may not be transgressed. To wit: "You shall not murder," "You shall not steal," and "You shall not covet" are known *not only* through the Hebrew Scriptures in the form of the Ten Commandments (literally, the "Ten Words"), which were given to ancient Israel as the backbone of its covenant relationship to the Creator. Rather, these injunctions are known and intuited by all human beings, "written on their hearts" (Rom. 2:15), woven into the very fabric of creation. Cain knew this, and he fled (Gen. 4:1–16). But all people prior to the giving of the law on Mount Sinai knew it as well, including those who formalized the Hammurabi Code in the eighteenth century B.C. The relevant question is, *How* did they possess this basic moral knowledge?

The implications of natural-law moral reasoning extend further. The natural moral law makes us aware of a fundamental distinction between killing in self-defense and premeditated murder.[20] The fact that secular law, as is practiced in contemporary culture, even makes this distinction (unaided by scriptural revelation or theology) is witness to this universal fact. Just-war moral reasoning proceeds from this moral starting point. It distinguishes at the most fundamental level between justice and injustice, between "defense" and "aggression." Applying political prudence, it clarifies situations and conditions in which a state might go to war and what sort of response might or might not be permissible. Just-war thinking requires that responsibility and accountability, not the lust for violence or conquest, be sufficient cause for action. Political ethicist Jean Elshtain describes the heart of just-war thinking in a way that, in extended fashion, deserves repeating:

---

[20]See, e.g., Numbers 35, wherein this basic moral distinction is expanded in considerable detail.

> Just war argument sustains a worldview that construes human beings
> as innately and exquisitely social. It follows that all ways of life are
> laced through with moral rules and restrictions that provide a web of
> social order. For St. Augustine . . . God's natural law was written in
> human hearts; thus, unsurprisingly, all ways of life incorporate basic
> grammars of injunctions and prohibitions which regulate important
> things—the taking of life, sexual relations, the administration of
> justice. . . . What happens in families bears a reference to what sort
> of society one lives in overall; domestic peace and civic peace are
> related, are of a kind, rather than being entirely separate concerns.
> We can assess a people and a way of life by looking at what this
> people lifts up and loves; by what it shares in common and by what
> it rejects or thrusts aside.[21]

Seen in this way, just-war thinking is rooted in a certain view of
reality. It understands the individual to have overlapping social commitments and loyalties. These entail family, civil society, and the state.
While these realms are not identical, they are nevertheless related. All
need to be ordered. And all are ordered by just notions of "peace" that
have their foundation in universal moral standards or norms. Social
relations as well as political action in a just society will mirror some
measure of indebtedness to those enduring values.

The natural law, then, corresponds with the human beings' most
rudimentary moral intuitions, according to which human behavior must
be ordered. It facilitates "civil society," apart from (though in harmony
with) religious conviction, to determine what behaviors are acceptable
and unacceptable, what is morally just and unjust. While religious faith
may be viewed by its adherents as providing the highest expression and
fulfillment of human virtue, the natural law written on the human heart,
as it were, witnesses in all people to basic moral obligations and to the
basic distinction between good and evil. Murder, theft, lying, infidelity,
harming the innocent, and the like are readily intuited moral violations.
For this reason, there are basic prohibitions against these actions that
find expression to varying degrees in all cultures.[22] A moral order is
protected "on its border," so to speak, by negative commands; great
social good arises in a society from positive motivation, namely, from the

---

[21] Jean Bethke Elshtain, "Just War as Politics," in David E. DeCosse, ed., *But Was It Just? Reflections on the Morality of the Persian Gulf War* (New York: Doubleday, 1992), 54–55.

[22] The natural-law argument does not deny moral differences in various cultures. Rather, it assumes that there is one means by which all human beings, regardless of culture, arrive at moral principle. This distinction is developed more fully in the next question.

growth of virtues in its citizens. Natural law has the function of protecting these "borders." It will guard against the error of rationalism, on the one hand, which fails to take into account the sinfulness of humans, and the error of relativism, on the other hand, which denies the validity of moral norms. If natural law provides general moral guidelines, known to all through reason,[23] for what is just and unjust, then the problem of war and the just use of force furnish a useful example of how those guidelines might be applied.[24]

Q. 2 Is there a development of natural-law thinking in the classical philosophical tradition?

Despite the observation that all things change, Heraclitus (ca. 536–470 B.C.) believed that wisdom points to a wider "law" of the universe, a transcending *logos* or reason, to which human nature and human ethical striving are ordered. All human laws are informed by and issue from one "divine" law. Such, Heraclitus

---

[23]While it is fashionable today to speak of "reasonable" people who come to a "reasonable" consensus on moral-social issues and laws that affect those issues, "reason" can arrive at very different conclusions about critical moral issues; in fact, it can even justify and sanction what is intrinsically immoral. Hence, it is necessary to distinguish between right reason, which is naturally ordered toward truth, and an "Enlightenment" form of reason that is prejudiced against all revealed religion, tradition, and moral authority outside of the self and denies the very possibility of knowing objective truth. According to this latter variety, the only reference point in the individual for determining what is moral is personal preference and what he or she agrees to *negotiate* in the public square. But in abandoning the search for truth, we obscure through the resultant nihilism the true dignity of human reason, as John Paul II argued with considerable persuasion in his final major encyclical *Fides et Ratio* (nos. 46–47). For a trenchant analysis of how natural-law reasoning differs from the assumptions of the dominant jurisprudence and moral philosophy of our day, see Charles Rice, *50 Questions on the Natural Law: What It Is and Why We Need It*, rev. ed. (San Francisco: Ignatius, 1999), 40–171.

[24]Theologian and pacifist Stanley Hauerwas writes that if just war is based on natural law, which is "a law written in the conscience of all men and women by God," then "it seems that war must be understood as the outgrowth of legitimate moral commitments." "Should War Be Eliminated? A Thought Experiment," in John Berman and Michael Cartwright, eds., *The Hauerwas Reader* (Durham, NC: Duke University Press, 2001), 404. This statement, upon inspection, is both true and false, depending on how it is interpreted. It is true that just-war moral reasoning, not war itself (as is implied by the statement), issues out of natural-law assumptions, given the universal character of justice. It is false to imply, as this statement does, that war "must be understood as the outgrowth of legitimate moral commitments." War is the outgrowth of *human moral depravity*, not human moral commitments. To fail to make this basic moral distinction is to fail to distinguish the criminal act from the punitive or restorative act (which would render criminal justice in the domestic context, indeed in *any* context, absurd). For those who are thus minded, an ideological precommitment to absolute pacifism inevitably and inexorably leads to the morally dubious position that the use of force and reluctantly going to war for justified purposes are *necessarily*, and therefore *always*, moral "compromises" and hence always unjust (ibid.). This ideologically absolutist stance on coercive force, however, represents neither mainstream ethical reflection in the Western cultural tradition nor mainstream thinking in the Christian moral tradition. The contribution of the just-war moral tradition is that coercive force must be justified and severely qualified *if and where* it is to be applied. The natural law, properly construed, does *not* "justify violence."

taught, was intuited through wisdom: "Wisdom is the foremost virtue, and wisdom consists in speaking the truth, and in lending an
ear to nature and acting according to her. Wisdom is common to
all."[25] Heraclitus's attempt to understand a "natural moral law" as
unchangeable stands in noted contrast both to the demagoguery of
the Sophists and the capriciousness of the population. The Sophists of
Heraclitus's day, like the sophists of any era, refused to venerate the
"natural moral law," since they viewed laws as artificial constructs
that merely serve the interests of those in power. It is in this light that
we perhaps understand Socrates' and Plato's veneration of the *nomoi*,
the "laws"; so, legal historian Heinrich Rommen: "The philosophers
spoke of the . . . laws with great respect: the peoples who had no
polls were to them barbarians. Hence, it happened, too, that Socrates,
despite his distinction between what is naturally right and legally right,
pronounced the laws of Athens to be 'right' without qualification."[26]
Something in the classical philosophers' observations about human
nature strikes us as enduring, for Heraclitus's understanding of the
"natural law" would serve as a precursor to the Stoic notion of the
logos that pervades and unifies all of the cosmos while placing upon
all humans certain ethical obligations.

Natural-law thinking in Plato and Aristotle is characterized by a
high regard for the *polis*. All of life, for them, is therefore "political"
insofar as the city-state subsists in rightly ordered relationships. Our
natural inclinations and abilities should order the ideal society. Both
Plato and Aristotle reject a subjectivism about what is "good." The
good, for Plato, consists, for example, in knowledge and beauty and is
self-evident, independent of a human reference point. Aristotle differs,
however, on one point. He holds the good to be understood in terms
of human nature, for which an analogy is helpful. An acorn derives
from the genus oak *by nature*, from which all oaks, regardless of their
maturation point or variety or utility, are identified. Yet despite their
differences on what constitutes the good, we observe in both Plato and
Aristotle a care to preserve the social order. As a result, both place
strong emphasis on ethics, on what is just, and how human laws might

---

[25]Heraclitus, *Fragments* 112–14, reproduced in Charles M. Bakewell, *Source Book in Ancient Philosophy* (New York: Scribner's, 1907), 34.
[26]Heinrich Rommen, *The Natural Law: A Study in Legal and Social History and Philosophy*, trans.
T. R. Hanley (Indianapolis: Liberty Fund, 1998), 7.

reflect enduring moral norms. Significantly, both recognize that what is *legally* just may or may not be what is *naturally* just.

Plato acknowledges that laws might protect the narrower interest of a particular class and not all of society. Bona fide justice, by contrast, is thought to inform proper laws, since justice will seek to provide for and protect the common good.[27] While positive laws are arbitrary and subject to change, the demands and obligations of justice remain unchanging. In this way they mirror a higher moral standard. In the end, then, the *polis* or state exists as a teaching mechanism to test the moral character of its citizens. Its function is to make human beings virtuous to the extent that they embody justice. In this way, humans accord with the "law of nature." In a "naturally" ordered society, each person utilizes those abilities with which "nature" has endowed him.[28]

Even when direct appeals to nature as the foundation of unchanging ethical norms are not developed very explicitly in Plato, the basic argument found in his *Republic* is that there exists an order in both physical and human nature that is objective and universal. The proper use of reason, coupled with the ordering of impulses, becomes the source of human moral obligation. To violate this is to create disorder and unhappiness.[29]

In Aristotle we find perhaps the high point of the development of pagan ethical theory,[30] and certainly one that furnishes a stepping-stone toward natural-law thinking, even when it is incomplete. Aristotle believes that everything occurring in life has a purpose or proper place (*telos*), resulting in a "natural" order of all things.[31] The intrinsic nature (*physis*) of anything can be known by identifying its end, its *telos*. Given this order, we may determine what is "good" in its essence. Nature, then, serves as a guide for citizens, for politicians, and for statesmen.[32]

---

[27] This is a recurring theme in *The Laws*, esp. book 4.

[28] This is a distinctive feature of Plato's *Republic*.

[29] Cf. *The Laws* 889–90, wherein Plato argues that proper laws are to be derived from and find parallels in physical nature. Paul E. Sigmund, *Natural Law in Political Thought* (Cambridge: Winthrop, 1971), 8–9, summarizes the presence of "natural law" theory in Plato as follows: "To the extent . . . that Plato believed that there were universal principles inherent in nature which imposed a moral obligation on all men, he was enunciating a natural-law theory. Insofar as he viewed any given law as an inadequate representation of the eternal principles of justice, he was asserting a theory of natural (i.e., ideal) justice rather than one of natural law."

[30] Hence, the attention in Thomas Aquinas's own work to Aristotelian categories.

[31] Aristotle, of course, is a naturalist and no theist; the cosmos is to be understood as self-existing.

[32] It should be noted, however, that "nature" was used by Aristotle to justify the inferiority of women, children, and slaves (*Politics* 1254–55).

When this is transferred to social-political life, the aim of each member of the *polis* is to pursue what is virtuous and just and thereby embody good citizenship. Human beings are free to act in accordance with reason, that is, to do what *ought* to be done. Ethics, therefore, as Aristotle makes clear, is to act in accordance with our fundamental nature. Nature, consequently, where it is illumined by right reason, guides human beings in distinguishing between virtue and vice. The implication, in social-political life, is that laws can be legally justified yet morally unjust. Natural law therefore describes both how things *are* in their essence and how they *ought to be*. By analogy, morality can be compared with gravity to the extent that it is grounded in natural-law thinking. That is, there are moral first principles that are self-evident and needing no explanation.[33]

In *Nicomachean Ethics*, Aristotle acknowledges some human behaviors to be intrinsically wrong—for example, murder, theft, and adultery.[34] Moreover, a distinction between "conventional" justice, by which constant change is to be expected, and unchanging "natural" justice surfaces later in the same work.[35] Also found in *Nicomachean Ethics* is a clear distinction between natural law and positive or conventional law. What is legal is not inevitably moral; Aristotle is not inattentive to the difference.[36]

In Aristotle, as in Plato, justice is not the domain of private individuals. Freedom is legitimate only to the extent that one acts in accordance with nature. Justice expresses itself corporately in the city-state among the citizens; hence, the veneration of the *polis*.[37]

It can be reasonably argued, as Paul Sigmund has done, that Plato's and Aristotle's understanding and discussion of "nature," "natural justice," and "common law according to nature" lay the foundations for a theory of metaphysical natural law, although the formalizing of such theory remains for Stoic moral philosophers. Nature is to be viewed as harmonious and purposeful, while human

---

[33]From a Christian standpoint, Aristotle intuits properly; as a nontheist, however, he simply cannot make sense of first cause and guilt.

[34]Book 2.

[35]Book 5.

[36]Aristotle *Nicomachean Ethics* 5.7 (1097a–1135a).

[37]For this reason both are thought by political philosophers to be state socialists, and this denomination is not inaccurate. Nonetheless, much in their ethical thought coincides with Christian revelation, even though the state, potentially, can be deified.

nature is thought to exhibit an intelligible order from which ethical norms might be extracted.[38]

As a moral-philosophical outlook, Stoicism emerged at a time when the city-state had been eclipsed by a world empire, and that empire subsisted largely of two classes, aristocracy and the masses. The Stoic view of reality emphasizes the seriousness of life. Surrounded by a world of war, corruption, disease, sorrow, and natural disaster, Stoics believed that happiness is attainable not by the appetites or the pursuit of gain but by virtue and right reason. Wisdom, they believed, is clouded by human passions. Through knowledge one attains understanding as to human nature; proper use of reason and nature are one. To achieve happiness is to live rationally, and thus to live in accordance with nature.

Stoic ethics is to be understood against the backdrop of Stoicism's view of nature, the cosmos, and humankind's place therein. To conform to the good is to live in conformity with reason and "nature." In contradistinction to Epicurean thought, Stoics believed that the virtuous life is grounded not in pleasure, but rather in one's pursuit of what is good, of which pleasure is merely a by-product. Passion and human appetites are perceived as irrational and therefore "unnatural." In late antiquity, Stoicism affected broader cultural attitudes through its emphasis on individual moral attainment irrespective of class distinctions.[39]

Writing in the first century B.C., Cicero is considered to be the primary interpreter and transmitter of the Stoic understanding of natural law.[40] He speaks of the *lex nata*, the law within, which he regards as the foundation of law in general. This law of right and wrong, he observes, is universally valid and unbending. It is born within us, not learned or received by tradition, but imbibed from nature itself. Accordingly,

> true law is right reason in agreement with nature; it is of universal application, unchanging and everlasting; it summons to duty by its commands, and averts from wrongdoing by its prohibitions. . . . It is

---

[38]Sigmund, *Natural Law in Political Thought*, 12.

[39]While not all Stoic philosophers were thus minded, Seneca (first century) and Epictetus (late first and second century) opposed slavery and the laws that upheld it, based on the natural-law implications of human dignity and equality that presupposed freedom. See, in this regard, Vincent Cauchy and Michel Spanneut, "Stoicism," *New Catholic Encyclopedia—Vol. 13* , 2nd ed. (Detroit: Gale, 2003), 534–39.

[40]So Rommen, *The Natural Law*, 20.

a sin to try to alter this law, nor is it allowable to attempt to repeal
any part of it, and it is impossible to abolish it entirely. We cannot
be freed from its obligations by senate or people, and . . . . there will
not be different laws at Rome and at Athens, or different laws now
and in the future, but one eternal and unchangeable law will be valid
for all nations and all times.[41]

For Cicero, the inner law allows human beings to distinguish
between good and bad human ordinances, between just and unjust
laws, between what is honorable and what is dishonorable. Only a
madman, he notes, "would conclude that these are matters of opinion, and not fixed by Nature."[42] "The civil law," he contends, "is
not necessarily also the universal law."[43] Ruinous consequences were
for him proof positive that the "Laws of nature" have been violated.
Therefore, civil laws *must* find their roots in the deeper principles of
enduring moral judgment. Cicero was able to look past legal *forms*
to the moral *substance* of legislation. There is a marked difference
between expediency and moral rectitude.[44]

Although by the time of the Christian advent Stoic thought had
been in existence for three centuries, it was in the first century—the
period of the Caesars—that Stoic ethical *Massenpropaganda* blos-
somed.[45] This was spawned in no small measure by the excesses,
despotism, and moral bankruptcy that attended this era; social conditions served to create fertile soil in which both Stoic and Christian ethics emerged. For this reason, it is not coincidental that Stoic
themes and categories surface in the writings of the New Testament,
where one finds evidence of interaction between Christian and Stoic
life views. Both groups were active in the marketplace,[46] propagat-
ing their views for consumption by broader audiences. Both used
similar techniques—for example, diatribe, paraenesis, epistles, and
ethical catalogs—as well as a common moral vocabulary in advancing their message.

---

[41]Cicero, *On the Republic* 3.22, trans. C. W. Keyes, Loeb Classical Library (Cambridge, MA: Harvard University Press, 1928), 79.
[42]Cicero, *On the Laws* 1.16, trans. C. W. Keyes, Loeb Classical Library.
[43]Cicero, *De officiis* 3.17, trans. W. Miller (London: William Heinemann; New York: G. P. Putnam's Sons, 1928), 339, 341.
[44]Ibid., 401. Rather creatively, Hadley Arkes has pondered the implications of Cicero's "natural-law" thinking for our time. See his essay "That 'Nature Herself Has Placed in Our Ears a Power of Judg-ing': Some Reflections on the 'Naturalism' of Cicero," in Robert P. George, ed., *Natural Law Theory: Contemporary Essays* (Oxford: Oxford University Press, 1992), 245–77.
[45]By the first century, Stoics and Cynics were viewed as the popularizers of ethics.
[46]See in this regard Acts 17:18.

Perhaps the most lucid demonstration that comes to us of early Christian interaction with a Stoic worldview is St. Luke's brief but tantalizing portrait of the apostle Paul in Athens (Acts 17:16–34). Here, in the Socratic mold, Paul is seen dialoguing with the philosophers in the *agora*, the marketplace, prior to addressing the Council of the Areopagus. Significantly, in the Areopagus address Paul appeals to nature in contending for the God who has made himself known. Paul also exploits important Stoic themes—among these, cosmic unity, divine kinship, and divine offspring. He appears to be utilizing a wordplay on "knowledge" (*gnōsis*), not incidental in light of the Stoic primacy of knowledge and knowing as the foundation of the moral life.[47]

To observe that Paul is accommodating himself by employing moral categories that Stoics and Christians have in common is not to deny the radical difference between the two. It is only to point out that the Christian message will look for common ground in building bridges to the pagan mind. In the Areopagus speech, general revelation and "natural law" give way—that is, they serve as an introduction to—special revelation in Christ the "God-man" (see 17:31). The truth of the gospel is disclosed by the "apostle to the pagans": God has made himself known to all, and all are called to repentance, in anticipation of the great day of moral reckoning, on which the God-man, who was raised from the dead, will judge all (vv. 30–31). Herewith Paul exposes deficiencies in the Stoic worldview—for example, the Stoic understanding of divine *logos* as reason and knowledge rather than transcendence embodied in the God-man; Stoic rejection of the notion of a bodily resurrection; and Stoic absence of eschatological perspective, wherewith it rejects any notion of an afterlife or climactic future day of moral accountability.[48]

---

[47]See especially Acts 17:22–31.

[48]Two further transparent uses of Stoic categories by New Testament writers are worth noting. One is the prologue to the Gospel of John (1:1–5). There the writer presents Jesus as the eternal, preexistent *Logos*, through which all things were made and are constituted, and in which all things inhere—consistent with Stoic cosmology. The *logos*, however, is not pure reason, but is personal and preexistent, incarnated as flesh and blood within the constraints of the temporal world. The second instance is found in 2 Peter 1, where the writer employs a catalog of virtues (vv. 5–7), mirroring a debt to the technique of Stoic moralists who dominated ethical discourse at the popular level in the first century. It is a standard feature that "knowledge" begins or ends Stoic ethical lists. Thus, because in the Stoic scheme all virtues are corollaries of knowledge (*gnōsis*), philosophy can be viewed as both a means and an end. By this moral calculus, vice is equated with ignorance. It may well be that in 2 Pet. 1:5–7 the writer is exploiting this common epistemological assumption in his moral exhortation; hence, his strategic use of the catchwords "knowledge" and "knowing" throughout the epistle in addition to its inclusion in the catalog of virtues (1:5–7). In the 2 Peter catalog, moral progression occurs by adding *gnōsis* to *aretē*, virtue or moral excellence, which is rooted in the foundation of *pistis*, faith. Christian ethics differs from its Stoic counterpart in that it strips knowledge of its technical nuance so that it is not a goal or end in itself. Knowledge in the Christian ethical scheme is necessary to the extent that

Ethicist Gilbert Meilaender has made the observation that Stoic ethics strikes us as far too sane and austere, albeit heroic.[49] And indeed it is neither theocentric nor christocentric; it is rather an ethic based wholly on willpower and devoid of grace. Nevertheless, in the period of its blossoming at the time of the Christian advent, it preserves, in the words of Heinrich Rommen, the "seeds of the Logos" and provides the literary forms and linguistic vessels into which Christian writers would pour their own theological ideas. Out of this mixture there emerged in time a new, yet related, doctrine of natural law.

Q. 3   What about cultural relativism? Aren't "truths" relative to the culture in which they are held?

Since the mid-twentieth century, the argument from cultural relativism has held sway over the social sciences and much of wider academic thinking. It goes without saying that the issues of war and peace and military intervention become exceedingly problematic if in fact it can be shown that moral truths vary from culture to culture. For by this account, no nation, regardless of the so-called morality and justness of its cause, could rightly intervene. At best, we would have to consign ourselves to the conviction that rogue nations and other nations simply have to "learn to get along."

The issue, then, from the standpoint of the cultural relativist, is whether there are moral truths that are universal in character and scope. This question is no small matter and should not be easily dismissed. The importance of this matter can be readily illustrated from geopolitical events of both the present and the past. At the theoretical level, we are justified in asking whether there are *natural* rights—by which we refer to those endowments that are self-evident, based on a human dignity that is universally shared—and rights that are *arbitrary* and *posited* (i.e., "positive" rights). Do, for example, Armenians, Jews, Cambodians, Rwandans, Sudanese, and other beleaguered

---

reason, part of the image of God in human creation, is subordinated and conjoined to divine grace. On the convergence of Stoic and Christian moral categories, see J. Daryl Charles, *Virtue amidst Vice: The Catalog of Virtues in 2 Peter 1*, Journal for the Study of the New Testament: Supplement Series 150 (Sheffield: Sheffield Academic, 1997).

[49]Gilbert Meilaender, "Stoic or Christian?" in *Things That Count: Essays Moral and Theological* (Wilmington, DE: ISI Books, 2000), 298. In this essay Meilaender is reflecting specifically on the writings of the late second-century emperor and Stoic Marcus Aurelius.

people groups have a *right* not to be slaughtered? Why or why not? Do nations and people groups have the right not to be victimized by terrorist groups? Why or why not? If so, wherein is lodged this fundamental right? On what basis can we justify this right as natural and therefore due all people? Do individuals and groups of people have a *right* not to be carried off into modern-day forms of slavery—whether in the form of sex trafficking or forced labor? On what basis?

From the days of William Wilberforce, the great abolitionist reformer, to the present, voices in our own cultural tradition have arisen to argue that, in such matters, appeal must be made to moral first principles that govern all men and nations. In his important book *First Things*, Hadley Arkes cites one such example—that of Joseph Story, who in 1822 (a decade before Wilberforce's valiant and tireless efforts were finally successful in the British Parliament) set forth his argument against slave trading. This practice, Story believed,

> is repugnant to the great principles of Christian duty, the dictates of natural religion, the obligations of good faith and morality, and the eternal maxims of social justice. When any trade can be truly said to have these ingredients, it is impossible that it can be consistent with any system of law . . . that purports to rest on the authority of reason or revelation. And it is sufficient to stamp any trade as interdicted by public law, when it can be justly affirmed, that it is repugnant to the general principles of justice and humanity.[50]

But a critically important and very basic question confronts us. Can the moral obligations that issue out of the natural law and may or may not be expressed in the laws of some nations be counted as obligatory—morally binding—on other nations and the international community as a whole? And why or why not? And doesn't the principle of national sovereignty, enunciated since the Treaty of Westphalia, militate against the imposition of such binding moral obligations on all nations? Is this not a violation of national sovereignty? What if nation X, because of the lucrative nature of the slave trade or its violent cultural history, wishes to continue this practice, even to the present day?[51]

---

[50]Cited in Arkes, *First Things*, 134.
[51]Indeed, this very geopolitical dilemma faces us today at numerous levels and, in our opinion, will only increase.

Such a scenario creates a dilemma for positivists, who "posit" certain rights rather than root them in an unchanging foundation and moral climate of natural law. In this sense, legal positivists and cultural relativists share a common need, and that need is to deny the proposition that right and wrong, basic good and evil, have a universal character.[52] In effect, then, cultural relativism prevents us from holding other nations accountable when genocide, moral atrocity, or egregious human-rights violations confront the international community. No nation—indeed, no authority of any type—may intervene for the purposes of rectifying injustice and moral atrocity, since, in theory, moral atrocity cannot exist, based on the assumption that different cultures approve of human practices that have social meaning. This assumption extends to practices such as cannibalism, genocide, incest, mutilation, and "honor killings." One cannot judge or condemn these acts; one can only voice an opinion on the basis of personal or social *preferences*. Logically, this position prevents us from condemning the brutalities and moral atrocities of the twentieth century, during which period hundreds of millions of people lost their lives as a result of political and ideological practices that had their roots in social and cultural beliefs.[53]

Typically, anthropologists will cite the diversity of cultural customs and social practices in various societies as "proof" that there is no objective standard of moral truth. Furthermore, for another society to condemn or interfere with the unacceptable moral practices of a particular society is to be "imperialistic." It is, accordingly, "wrong" to stand in moral judgment over another society or nation. But here the cultural relativist finds himself caught in contradiction to the degree that, in expressing a particular belief or conviction, he himself resorts to moral judgment by assuming a nonrelative sense of the term *wrong* in order to condemn a particular position. It would seem, then, that cultural relativism is parasitic, for it requires the existence of an objec-

---

[52]Few have developed and exposed the implications of this sort of contradictory thinking more lucidly than Arkes, *First Things*, 134–58.

[53]The exact numbers, of course, vary and, by any measurement, boggle the mind. Consider, for a moment, the mind-boggling statistics that illustrate the disappearance of the distinction between evil and good in notable twentieth-century regimes. French historian Stephane Courtois, in his introduction to *The Black Book of Communism*, places the number of human deaths in the vicinity of 100 million, while Robert Conquest, *Reflections on a Ravaged Century*, estimates the total to be in the 170 million range (see question 95). Surely, all these human lives matter, a fact for which pacifists and separatists, who reject natural-law thinking as well as just use of force, lack any legitimate answer.

tive right and wrong in order to make pronouncements that themselves end up being moral judgments.[54]

What escapes the purview of many cultural anthropologists is the fact that even when people living in different societies may come to have differing moral practices and hold differing moral judgments, there is a universal disposition among human beings to raise questions and make determinations about what is good and bad, acceptable and unacceptable. The essence of this basic moral intuition is to do good and eschew evil. That is to say, "the moral order is protected on its borders by negative precepts, but in the interior positive precepts suggest the inexhaustible openness of the human good."[55] In this light, we discover that indeed many commonalities are to be found among various cultures.

While societies differ in many respects, several things may be said to account for these differences. One is that those differences may lie in a deficiency of moral reasoning, or an incomplete knowledge that contributes to the process of human moral reasoning. Thus, it is reasonable to argue, with Aquinas, that while moral truth may be the same for all, it is not equally known by all.[56] To require of others what we require for ourselves—what in Plato and Jesus is called "the golden rule"—is to reveal, to ourselves and to others, that we *do* in reality conceive of human nature and human action in universally wrong-and-right categories.[57] For example, there is no virtuous person alive who would accept the proposition that slavery for some human beings is a good thing.

Second, all societies operate on a basic presupposition of justice, and all demarcate between behaviors that are acceptable and unacceptable. There is, quite simply, no human society, past or present, that has tolerated *any and all* behaviors. Indeed, the first Neanderthal who is hit on the head by a neighbor and utters a version of "Why did you do that?" mirrors not only an awareness of the moral world in which

---

[54]Useful critiques of the assumptions of cultural relativism can be found in Bernard Williams, "An Inconsistent Form of Relativism," in Jack W. Meiland and Michael Krausz, eds., *Relativism* (South Bend, IN: University of Notre Dame Press, 1982), 171–74, and Gregory Koukl and Francis J. Beckwith, *Relativism: Both Feet Firmly Planted in the Air* (Grand Rapids: Baker, 1997).

[55]So Ralph McInerny, *Ethica Thomistica: The Moral Philosophy of Thomas Aquinas* (Washington, DC: Catholic University of America Press, 1982), 48.

[56]Thomas Aquinas *Summa theologiae* (hereafter *S.T.*) I-II Q. 94 (New York: Blackfriars, 1975). Here Aquinas's illustration is geometric: the fact that the three angles of a triangle together equal two right angles is true, regardless of whether it is known to be true by all people.

[57]Here we are making the moral argument on *ontological* grounds. The *epistemological* side of this question, which concerns the sources of moral knowledge and how this comes to human beings, is a very different question.

we all live but also the fact that there exist "necessary truths."[58] And these truths make justice, behavioral justification, discernment, and the very distinction between "acceptable" and "unacceptable" possible. The recognition and confirmation of a universal, shared moral sense in human beings lies no further away than the threshold of moral outrage, as one political philosopher emphasizes.[59] The temper of our moral reflex when we are slighted, that is, when we are on the receiving end of injustice, reflects the fact that a moral intuition, and therefore the ability to make moral judgments, is already in place.[60]

Yet a third consideration with regard to the human moral sense is very simply that moral knowledge can be ignored. People can choose to engage in malevolent acts that violate others, knowing full well that these acts are "wrong," prohibited, even abominable. Hence, Aquinas speaks of the human reason being obscured and the will hardened toward evil, so that doing good grows increasingly difficult.[61]

Q. 4   What is the relationship between law, natural law, and coercion?

In most human communities, law is seen to have authoritative force in directing or constraining human behavior. This authority is lodged not in the individual per se, or in social conventions, or in circumstances, or even in majoritarian thinking, important as a majority in the democratic context may be. Rather, its authority transcends all of these levels, deriving from what we might call "moral predicates" or "permanent things." By contrast, any individual who might advance authoritative claims over the masses would lack both moral and legal authority, just as any one social institution—whether a political party or the Rotary Club—doing the same would similarly *in sic* lack a source of moral authority that is transcending. The reason for this is not difficult to grasp: any individual, party, interest group,

---

[58]This is the sort of logic that is developed by Arkes in his important chapter "Necessary Truths" (pp. 51–84) in *First Things*.
[59]Ibid., 82.
[60]This reflexive reaction, it should be noted, unlike matters of conscience, which can vary considerably among people, is perfectly consistent (i.e., occurring virtually 100 percent of the time), eliciting the same reaction in all people everywhere. It is as if a moral law is at work within human beings.
[61]Aquinas *S.T.* I-II Q. 85. For this reason, John Paul II stressed that "the most dangerous crisis" that can befall society is "the confusion between good and evil," which ends up destroying human culture (*Veritatis Splendor* nos. 51, 93).

club, or institution cannot be said to represent the human community; only voluntary political arrangements that are broadly representative of humans *qua* humans can approximate such. And precisely for this reason, according to Thomas Aquinas, legitimate authority, which is broadly representative in its constitution, is a primary criterion for justifying war.

Permit us to further qualify our answer. It is not the mere power structure—be it local, state, federal, or dictatorial—that qualifies authority. Rather, power structures issue out of the moral authority of law itself, and the moral authority of law derives from its proximity to justice.[62] Law's legitimacy, then, is relative to its ability to secure or maintain justice. Given the potential of human beings to do evil, justice in the human community may on occasion need to be secured by means of coercive force.[63] Correlatively, for those in authority to fail to interdict or restrain evil when it bursts upon the human community (or beforehand, where sufficient knowledge thereof exists) is a failure of justice; indeed, one might argue, to fail to marshal a coercive resistance in such circumstances is to be an accomplice in that evil. To affirm the good, as Aquinas and all pacifists would do, needs qualification, since for the latter this would mean a universal prohibition of taking human life. The natural-law ethic, however, as it informs just-war moral reasoning, presupposes an institutional framework of political units that (1) meets the minimum criterion of legitimate authority and (2) permits the taking of life in certain situations that distinguish between innocence and guilt. Aquinas recognized three such situations: self-defense, capital punishment, and just war.[64]

We are well aware that not all coercive force need be equated with punishment or punitive sanctions, although in most cases of deviant behavior and criminality some such sanctions will be necessary. Nevertheless, criminal law proceeds on the assumption that criminal sanctions both deter—a matter that we discuss elsewhere—and serve a pedagogical function, insofar as punishment informs (1) the victimized party, who deserves redress, (2) society, which has been

---

[62] In general terms, Aquinas regards law as "an ordinance of reason for the common good" (*S.T.* I-II Q. 90). For this reason he can write that the natural law is "the light of natural reason, by which we discern what is good and what is evil" (Q. 91). Thus, through right reason we discern the good that must be pursued and the evil that must be eschewed (Q. 94).

[63] More generally, on the relationship between law and coercion and its moral-philosophical basis, see John Finnis, *Natural Law and Natural Rights* (Oxford: Clarendon, 1982).

[64] Respectively, on self-defense, *S.T.* II-II Q. 64; on capital punishment, Q. 62; and on just war, Q. 40.

scandalized by such offense, and (3) the offender who has violated the community, as well as (4) potential, future offenders, who might be tempted to scandalize the community. The goal of criminal justice and criminal law, then, is no less than the preservation of the community, or, simply said, the common good. And needing emphasis is the fact that the common good arises from the realities of our shared human nature and human need. For this reason, law in general and laws in particular must conform to moral predicates; they may not be merely posited according to time, circumstance, or social location. Where justice—as expressed by the laws that mirror it—is fluid, we call this phenomenon a travesty of justice. Why? Because justice must have a universal character to it; otherwise, it is not justice in the proper sense. Historically understood, the tradition of natural law does not exist to *limit the range* or application of positive law; rather, it exists to *guide* positive law, which is to say, to *establish the moral parameters* within which positive law can legitimately function.

If the "justice" in criminal justice is nonfluid, then society's retributive response to social-political evil must also be nonfluid, whether in the domestic or in the international context.[65] Retributive justice seeks to restore the just social balance that is or was normative. This order requires the apprehension, isolation, and punishment of criminals, who have violated the common good through a wrong use of moral freedom. Retribution, then, properly understood and distinguished from "retributivism," rectifies this imbalance, and in many cases this rectification can only proceed by means of coercive force applied by society. While the *lex talionis* ("the law of the tooth") is thought by many of our contemporaries to be a deficient measure of justice, much of this modern sentiment is rooted in a misunderstanding of both origins and principles that have undergirded it since antiquity. At least in biblical terms, the *lex* expresses *both justice and mercy*, insofar as it establishes *both upper and lower limits* of retribution on the basis of proportionality and propriety; hence, one speaks of "an eye for an eye," "a tooth for a tooth," and so on. Just as civilized societies do not cut off the hands of those who steal cookies from a cookie jar, nor do they (nor *should* they) slap the wrists of people who murder innocent human beings. Thus, proportionality lies at the very heart of

---

[65] If there is no objective moral truth and there are no transcendent moral referents, then there is no sure and reliable means for guaranteeing just relations between people (thus John Paul II, *Centesimus Annus* no. 44).

bona fide justice, and for this reason it constitutes the core of just-war moral reasoning.

Not only do legitimate authority and proportionality undergird justice rightly construed, but the use of force must also be rightly intended. Thus, for example, the Western legal and moral tradition generally has acknowledged the difference between homicide and murder.[66] Not all killing is morally wrong, even when all forms of killing are grievous. Our own cultural tradition, until relatively recently, has acknowledged exceptions on the basis of intention. For example, premeditated murderers forfeit their natural right to life, as do political tyrants, mass murderers, pirates/terrorists, and progenitors of genocide and egregious human-rights violations. Within this wider rubric of exception fits the category of justified war.

Justice without force, as someone has wisely quipped, is a myth, because there will always be evil men, and evil men will need to be hindered.

Q. 5   Isn't "just war" a contradiction in terms?

In its understanding of human nature, human relations, civil society, and the place of force, the just-war position perceives itself to be a mediating or moderating position between the ideological poles of militarism and pacifism.[67] Hence, "just-war theory" is something of a misnomer, and this for two reasons. First, it is not a theory but the expression of practical reason placed in the service of others who need justice. Second, it is not about just wars but rather about how we might make moral judgments in the face of social-political evil and grievous injustice. Ethicist Paul Ramsey, in our view, is correct in his admonition that we speak not of "just war"

[66]This very basic distinction has been part of the Western legal tradition from the beginning and finds detailed rationale in biblical literature; see, for example, the narrative account found in Numbers 35, which elaborates the function of strategically placed "cities of refuge" to which an involuntary manslayer might flee for adjudication.

[67]In chap. 11 ("The Uses of a Doctrine on the Uses of Force") of *We Hold These Truths: Catholic Reflections on the American Proposition* (New York: Sheed and Ward, 1960), John Courtney Murray offers a sustained critique of what he believes to be "false dichotomies" in our thinking about war and peace. Historic Christian moral reasoning, he insists, lies between "the two extreme positions" of "a soft sentimental pacifism and a cynical hard realism." To settle for either extreme, in Murray's view, is the "abdication" of human moral reasoning (pp. 265–66). Murray is particularly critical of those who make calls to "abolish war," whether in the name of Christian ethics or any other name, since they give little thought to responsible public policy and fail to wrestle with the common good.

but of "justified war," since virtue and justice are matters of moral discrimination, right intention, and directing the will according to human need.[68]

Properly viewed, therefore, just-war thinking is not concerned first and foremost with military tactics and strategy. Nor does it serve as justification for any or all military conflict. Rather, it is an *approach to statecraft* that views peace as not only possible but *morally obligatory* as a *by-product* of justly ordered human relationships. Peace, in this light, is not to be understood merely as the absence of conflict; it is rather the fruit or consequence—the by-product—of a justly ordered society. At its best, the just-war tradition has worked to forge moral and political links between the limited use of armed force and the pursuit of peace, security, justice, and freedom. This linkage rests on a foundational assumption: that morality and politics "do not exist in hermetically sealed compartments of life. Rather, the tradition insists that there is one indivisible human universe of thought and action, a universe that is . . . inescapably moral and inescapably political."[69]

The just-war position, then, is an account of ordering society in a manner that "places politics within an ethically shaped framework" and commits its citizens to debates "whenever and wherever a resort to force is contemplated."[70] As such, just-war moral reasoning can be formulated according to basic assumptions about human nature that guide our social and political arrangements. Just-war reasoning

- promotes skepticism and queasiness about the use and abuse of power while not opting out of political reality altogether in favor of utopian fantasies,
- requires action and judgment in a world of limits, estrangement, and partial justice,
- fosters recognition of the provisional nature of all political arrangements,
- advances respect for other peoples and nations, in terms of both autonomy and accountability,

[68] *War and the Christian Conscience: How Shall Modern War Be Conducted Justly?* (Durham, NC: Duke University Press, 1961), 16.
[69] George Weigel, "From Last Resort to Endgame: Morality, the Gulf War, and the Peace Process," in David E. DeCosse, ed., *But Was It Just? Reflections on the Morality of the Persian Gulf War* (New York: Doubleday, 1992), 19–20.
[70] So Elshtain, "Just War as Politics," 46.

- acknowledges the necessity of self-defense and intervention against unjust aggression and gross oppression while refusing to legitimize imperialistic crusades and empire building.[71]

Q. 6 Doesn't just-war thinking really serve as a justification or pretext for violence?

Far from preparing society for violence or encouraging violence, just-war moral reasoning, given its basic presuppositions about both *permitting* and *limiting* the use of force according to particular moral criteria (e.g., just cause, right intent, legitimate authorization, proportionality, noncombatant immunity), not only constitutes a legitimate response to the problem of social-political evil in a fallen world but also *preserves* social bonds and *guards* basic freedoms rather than threatening them. Given its inherently *moderating* assumptions about coercive force and its commitment to address moral evil, it undergirds the very foundations of civil society.[72] The potential misuse of coercive force, for unjust purposes, is not in and of itself an argument against its proper use; its potential for misuse only reminds us that human beings are moral agents.

One might object that just-war moral reasoning, as well as the natural-law thinking that supports it, offers invariable justification for war, violence, or military conflict. One ethicist raises a partially valid objection when he writes, "For if just war is based on natural law, a law written in the conscience of all men and women by God, then it seems that war must be understood as the outgrowth of legitimate

---

[71]These just-war assumptions are set forth variously in chaps. 4 and 7 and the epilogue of Jean Bethke Elshtain, *Women and War*, rev. ed. (Chicago: University of Chicago Press, 1995), as well as in Elshtain, *Just War against Terror: The Burden of American Power in a Violent World* (New York: Basic Books, 2003), chap. 3.

[72]Undergirding the writings of ethicist Paul Ramsey on war is the conviction that force and armed conflict are *both* permitted *and* limited from a moral standpoint, based on the requirements of charity. So, e.g., *War and the Christian Conscience: The Limits of Nuclear War* (New York: Council on Religion and International Affairs, 1963); *The Just War: Force and Political Responsibility* (New York: Scribner's, 1968); and *Speak Up for Just War or Pacifism* (University Park: Pennsylvania State University Press, 1988). The theoretical basis of charity's moral obligations, both in permission and limitation, are developed initially in *Basic Christian Ethics* (New York: Scribner's, 1954), 153–90 (chap. 5, "Christian Vocation"), and especially the discussion under the heading "A Christian Ethic of Resistance." Political ethicist Jean Bethke Elshtain has persuasively argued that the very moral principles and distinctions governing just-war reasoning are what are requisite for and undergird civil society. See, notably, chap. 4 ("The Attempt to Disarm Civic Virtue") of her *Women and War*, 121–59, and the introductory chapters of *Just War against Terror*.

moral commitments."[73] Therefore, "just" use of force and going to war for justified purposes are for some opponents of the just-war tradition necessarily—and therefore *always*—"the compromises we make with sin" and "cooperating with sin," and hence always unjust.[74]

In our view, however, John Courtney Murray's basic distinction between violence and force is critically important in assisting us in making necessary moral discriminations. He writes: "Force is the measure of power necessary and sufficient to uphold . . . law and politics. What exceeds this measure is violence, which destroys the order of both law and politics. . . . As an instrument, force is morally neutral in itself."[75] For this reason, as Murray and moral thinkers past and present have intuited, the just-war tradition is lodged squarely within the mainstream of the Christian moral tradition, even when the potential for indiscriminate violence, or for justifying indiscriminate violence, is always part of the human condition.

In its classical expression within the Western moral tradition, the use of force finds justification on four principal grounds: to protect the innocent, to recover what has been wrongfully taken, to defend against a wrongful attack, and to punish evil.[76] The just warrior, then, takes up arms and enters conflict only *reluctantly* for the express purpose of protecting innocent human beings and preventing greater evil. The just-war position is made necessary by the fact that we live in the period of the "already but not yet," that is, in the temporal order that is characterized by human fallenness and penultimate peace. Like the pacifist, the just-warrior is committed to "putting violence on trial," in the words of one theorist; and like the pacifist, he will also evaluate life from the perspective of those who suffer and those who are potential victims.[77] At the same time, unlike the pacifist, he will highly qualify peace and find deficient the world's definition of peace, fully

---

[73]Hauerwas, "Should War Be Eliminated?" 404.

[74]Ibid. Hauerwas follows John Howard Yoder, whose ideological pacifism and principled opposition to just-war thinking are a product of his Anabaptist theology. Representative of Yoder's work in this regard are *The Original Revolution: Essays on Christian Pacifism* (Scottdale, PA: Herald, 1971); *What Would You Do?* (Scottdale, PA: Herald, 1983); *Nevertheless: The Varieties and Shortcomings of Religious Pacifism*, 2nd ed. (Scottdale, PA: Herald, 1992); *The Politics of Jesus*, 2nd ed. (Grand Rapids: Eerdmans, 1994); and *When War Is Unjust: Being Honest in Just-War Thinking*, 2nd ed. (Maryknoll, NY: Orbis, 1996).

[75]Murray, *We Hold These Truths*, 288.

[76]James Turner Johnson, "Threats, Values, and Defense: Does the Defense of Values by Force Remain a Moral Possibility?" in Jean Bethke Elshtain, ed., *Just War Theory* (New York: New York University Press, 1992), 57–60. Johnson's essay originally appeared in William V. O'Brien and John Langan, eds., *The Nuclear Dilemma and the Just War Tradition* (Lexington: Lexington Books, 1986), 31–48.

[77]Elshtain, *Women and War*, 123.

aware that some forms of "peace" are oppressive, totalitarian, and therefore unjust.

Just-war moral reasoning serves as a necessary antidote to the famous dictum of Clausewitz—"To introduce the principle of moderation into the theory of war itself would always lead to logical absurdity"[78]—whose monumental tome *On War* shaped European military thinking prior to the First World War. For undergirding just-war thinking are a certain moral seriousness and moral realism that result in moderation and unity of ends and means. Just-war intentions, moreover, aim at securing a just rather than unjust version of peace, a critical distinction that mainstream just-war thinkers through the ages maintain. Thus, for example, according to Aquinas, "those who wage war justly aim at peace, and so they are not opposed to peace, except to the evil peace."[79] Aquinas is merely following Augustine, who distinguished between *justa pax* and *iniqua pax*.[80]

Q. 7 Don't just war and pacifism represent two opposing poles on the spectrum of force?

Most people tend to think about war and peace in terms of two opposing perspectives, which for them are the pacifist and the just-war position. However, in terms of ideological commitments, it is more accurate to understand just-war moral reasoning as a *mediating* position between two poles that are absolutist in their assumptions about the use of force: militarism/crusade/jihad, and pacifism.[81] Significantly, these two rivals—pacifism and political

---

[78]Carl von Clausewitz, *On War*, ed. and trans. Michael Howard and Peter Paret (Princeton, NJ: Princeton University Press, 1976), 14.
[79]*S.T.* II-II Q. 40.
[80]*The City of God* 19.12.
[81]John Courtney Murray, in his important book *We Hold These Truths*, 258, describes the just-war position as "a way between the false extremes of pacifism and bellicism." The important anthology edited by John Kelsey and James Turner Johnson, *Just War and Jihad: Historical and Theoretical Perspectives on War and Peace in Western and Islamic Traditions* (New York: Greenwood, 1991), also places the just-war position as intermediate to pacifism and jihad. Human-rights scholar David Little concurs, noting that "the Christian story is a story of shifting combinations of . . . three attitudes. . . . While pacifist and holy war or crusading appeals are undoubtedly mutually exclusive, the just war attitude serves to mediate between the two extremes." "'Holy War' Appeals and Western Christianity: A Reconstruction of Bainton's Approach," in Kelsay and Johnson, *Just War and Jihad*, 123. And James F. Childress's typology of force includes five positions—nonresistance, nonviolent resistance, limited violent resistance (discrimination and proportionality), limited violent resistance (proportionality only), and unlimited violent resistance—but implies that just-war principles be a moderating position. "Contemporary Pacifism: Its Major Types and Possible Contributions to Discourse about War," in

"realism"—find it necessary either to attack the just-war framework or to couch their arguments in its terms.[82]

Properly viewed, warfare can be examined according to three ideological starting points and logically possible positions. The first holds that war and coercive force are *always* justifiable, morally or legally. Resort to violence, whether in its religious form (jihad[83] or crusade) or in its secular counterpart (often referred to as *Realpolitik* or political realism), requires no justification. No moral restraints beyond political expediency or the "command of God" (in the case of religiously motivated terrorism) need be applied. In the political "realist" mindset, strategy and morality are severed. Or, morality in the strategic moment is relativized, even when in practice the moral agnostic would acknowledge that *some* decisions indeed *are* agonizing and problematic, or that there is such a thing as a shared moral judgment.[84] In its own contorted way, the crusading mindset, or jihad, seeks to be "integrated" to the extent that it understands all of life as a whole. That is, religious belief is not privatized or separate from the daily existence; it touches all. War, therefore, is simultaneously a religious *and* a political act. For the holy warrior and the jihadist, the cause is just by virtue of divine revelation; as such, duty is more important than making moral judgments or deliberating over coercive strategies.

The second position, in its pure form, stands at the opposite pole on the spectrum of force. It holds that violence and coercive force are *never* justifiable under any circumstances and that war must be avoided at *any and all* costs. To its great credit, it is sensitive to the violent tendencies that permeate human nature and society in general, refusing to baptize "Caesar" and the sword for its own purposes. Relatedly, it recognizes diverse—and in many respects, creative—avenues for political and social action. Also, in its religious form, the pacifist position takes seriously both the commitment to neighbor love and the demands of Christian faith. At least in the previous generation

George Weigel and John P. Langan, eds., *The American Search for Peace: Moral Reasoning, Religious Hope, and National Security* (Washington, DC: Georgetown University Press, 1991), 109–31.

[82] John P. Hittinger has correctly observed this dynamic and developed its implications in "Just War and Defense Policy," in David F. Forte, ed., *Natural Law and Contemporary Public Policy* (Washington, DC: Georgetown University Press, 1998), 333–60.

[83] Here we use the term *jihad* in its more derivative sense—divinely sanctioned warfare—and not in its narrower sense of "*striving* in the path of God."

[84] For a compelling but nonreligious argument against the moral agnosticism of the "political realist," see the chapter "Against Realism" in Michael Walzer, *Just and Unjust Wars*, 4th ed. (New York: Basic Books, 2006). Adopting a similar position though incorporating religious concepts is Jean Bethke Elshtain, "Reflections on War and Political Discourse: Realism, Just War, and Feminism in a Nuclear Age," *Political Theory* 13, no. 1 (1985): 39–57 (reproduced in Elshtain, *Just War Theory*, 260–79).

it has shown a willingness to self-sacrifice, counting the cost of one's convictions, even when it means paying the price of alternative service to others.[85] Furthermore, pacifism is keenly sensitive to the distortions of faith that come with an uncritical view of the state—a continual problem throughout the history of the church. Pacifists help sensitize nonpacifists to an all-too-human tendency to rationalize violence in the service of nationalism.

At the same time, ideological pacifism, because of its commitment to nonviolence and consequent refusal to resist evil directly through action, *in practice* bestows upon evil and tyranny an advantage in the present life. This, it will be remembered, was the critique of Reinhold Niebuhr, who noted somewhat caustically that had Christians demonstrated more love in his day, Hitler would not have invaded Poland.[86] Indeed, there did come a point at which Nazi evil reached a critical mass and warranted retribution by the nations. To deny the need for active resistance and retribution is ethically untenable—then or now. Precisely how pacifism is able to counter—or negate—totalitarianism has not yet been sufficiently demonstrated, as Michael Walzer has argued with considerable persuasion.[87] Justice without force is a myth, because there are always evil men, and evil men must be hindered.[88] Thus, reasoned political judgments are a necessary reality, which on occasion will require the application of coercive force. And why? Because the very goods of *human flourishing* are at stake—goods that need protecting.

Yet a further prominent feature of the pacifist position is its excessively pessimistic view of governing authorities and related detachment from civil affairs. As a consequence, it severs meaningful ways of contributing constructively to statecraft, and specifically, to security issues, whether in domestic or foreign affairs.[89] Historic religious

---

[85] An example is the generation of wartime pacifists like my (Daryl's) father, a Mennonite "conscientious objector" who, to his credit, performed alternative service in a veterans' hospital during World War II. Conscription, of course, was the reality of the Second World War. The fact that military service in our culture today is voluntary renders pacifism as policy not only dubious but unrealistic.

[86] See Niebuhr's critique of the pacifist position in *Christianity and Power Politics* (New York: Scribner's, 1940), 1–32.

[87] *Just and Unjust Wars*, 328–32.

[88] The reality is that society without coercive powers is an impossibility, whether locally, nationally, or internationally. And if coercive powers belong to the governing authorities, they cannot simultaneously be legitimate in domestic affairs but illegitimate in foreign policy. The same authority that restrains internal enemies of society also opposes external enemies. Elizabeth Anscombe's essay "War and Murder," in Richard A. Wasserstrom, ed., *War and Morality* (Belmont, CA: Wadsworth, 1970), 42–53, cogently argues for the necessity of coercive powers of government. Anscombe is perhaps best known for having "won" a debate with C. S. Lewis.

[89] If political authority is *inherently* evil, as many religious pacifists tend to believe, it follows that state, local, and federal government, not to mention school boards, unions, and all political interest groups, always and everywhere become vessels of corrosion and tyranny in the public sector.

pacifism, in its sixteenth-century Anabaptist form, like its counterpart today, rejected the views of Luther, Calvin, and Zwingli regarding Christian participation in the affairs of the state. The historic "peace churches"[90]—so designated not because other confessions are unconcerned with peace but because these churches refuse military service and participation in war, to the present day—prohibited Christian believers from bearing the sword or governing.[91]

Unlike both militarism and pacifism, which through their absolutist views of force sever morality and politics and encourage a false dichotomy between private and public morality, just-war moral reasoning weighs motives and takes into account the realities of human nature and protecting the common weal. It probes both whether the application of force is justifiable (*jus ad bellum* criteria) and how to proceed in the application of force (*jus in bello* criteria). And it understands that while "might never makes right" in and of itself, moral applications of force *can* serve what is right and at least approximate justice. It reckons with the reality that force has a neutral quality about it and therefore can be used for just or unjust purposes. Force, it acknowledges, is not per se an evil or expression of injustice; rather, it depends on the moral character of those who employ it. Rejecting the absolutism of both militarism and pacifism, just-war moral reasoning places itself between two extremes—a placement that Grotius summarizes thus: "Men may not believe either that nothing is allowable, or that everything is."[92]

Further, the just-war position commits itself to restoring justice to people and contexts in which evil and injustice would otherwise prevail. It thereby aims to achieve a greater good than otherwise would exist. Concomitantly, it refuses to acquiesce to the counsels

---

[90]The "peace churches" are primarily three confessional streams: Quaker, Mennonite, and Brethren. While Quakers today are principally of two types, Mennonites and Brethren are found in much greater denominational variation. The latter two groups are the descendents of what historians refer to as the "radical Reformation"—"radical" insofar as these sixteenth-century reformers were radically separate from the world and the world's institutions based on the assumption of an absolute dualism between the world and the spiritual domain. Herein they differed starkly from their Lutheran and Reformed counterparts. Thus, for example, in Article 6 of the Schleitheim Confession, a confession of faith adopted in 1527 as an authoritative summary of key doctrinal beliefs of the Swiss Brethren (the Anabaptist fathers of the radical Reformation), we read concerning the sword: "The sword is ordained of God outside the perfection of Christ." What follows in the confession is an explanation of why the Christian believer can neither apply the sword nor serve in the office of a magistrate. The reason for this is the belief that the Christian's true citizenship is in heaven and not on earth. Just as Christ did not utilize the sword, so his followers must live accordingly.

[91]While not all groups or individuals associated with the "radical Reformation" were pacifist, most were. One notable exception was the Anabaptist preacher Balthasar Hubmaier.

[92]Hugo Grotius, *The Law of War and Peace*, trans. R. L. Loomis (Roslyn, NY: Walter J. Black, 1949), 1.1.

of skepticism and cynicism that would have us believe that measured and guided coercive force cannot proceed under a moral imperative. While it shares with pacifism the ultimate objective of peace, unlike pacifism it understands, as does Aquinas, that "peace is not a virtue, but the fruit of virtue."[93] Therefore, peace must be highly qualified and justly ordered. The Mafia and tyrannical dictators, after all, know and impose a peace that is illicit.

Policy, it has been said, is the meeting place of political authority and morality. Just-war moral reasoning takes that responsibility seriously, not settling for the acquiescence of pacifist nonresistance or the bellicosity of "political realism" when it comes to public matters. It is an important function of morality to command and guide the use of power—that is, "to forbid it, to limit it, or, more generally, to define the ends for which power may or must be used and to judge the circumstances of its use."[94] At the same time, moral principle cannot be incarnated in public policy if those who are responsible for establishing policy—indeed, citizens themselves—have not learned how to engage in moral reasoning and make moral discriminations. And to insist on public moral principle yet be socially detached and not participate in those public institutions that potentially strengthen or undermine justice is to undercut our own moral authority. While those of pacifist conviction, particularly in its religious expression, may be tempted to decry society (as well as fellow Christians who are nonpacifists) from a position of social and communal detachment, it needs emphasis that they too benefit from the maintenance of a social-political order that is necessarily justly (and at times forcefully) ordered.

Q. 8   Aren't all wars, because of the tragic loss of human life, inherently unjust and immoral?

Empirically, there would appear to be but one adequate answer to this question. Whether one ponders the hundreds of thousands who have died in world wars or the "mere" several thousands who are casualties in lesser wars, localized wars, or the "war on terrorism," this question would seem to provide its own

---

[93]*S.T.* II-II Q. 29.
[94]Murray, *We Hold These Truths*, 273.

answer. After all, war is hell, as we've often heard, and nothing can offset this reality. As authors, we agree—to an extent, that is.

The pacifist surely presents a compelling case in arguing that, based on human loss, any war is immoral. Who among us can put a premium on human life? From the standpoint of loss, there is no explanation, no justification whatsoever, that might be deemed adequate. Period. In truth, everyone should become a pacifist tomorrow were this the only measurement of justice so-called. But there are other perspectives that need to be taken into consideration. We offer one.

On a daily basis, everywhere around us, law-enforcement officials engage in crime control, crime prevention, and crime interdiction. They operate on a decidedly different level than most theorists, yet like those theorists they maintain the highest regard for human dignity and human life. They do this, often unbeknownst to the public, at great cost and considerable effort. Most laypersons are unaware of the energy, planning, strategizing, and agonizing over how to deal with the problem, wherever it surfaces, of criminal behavior and, specifically, violent crime. Virtually any account of crime in our newspaper will suffice to illustrate.

Suppose a child in your neighborhood is kidnapped. And suppose the kidnapper has taken refuge in a house in the neighborhood. What does local law enforcement do? Commit itself in principle to nonviolent intervention and hope that the kidnapper will change his ways and release the child without any altercation? Or perhaps firebomb the house so that the criminal will surely be incapacitated or killed? Criminal justice, at least as we have known it, will—very predictably, mind you—weigh the options, examine the dangers attendant, consult with other law-enforcement agencies, and chart its response. Along the way this will include attempting to "negotiate," cordoning off the neighborhood, and perhaps a host of other measures. Why these measures? And why this predictability as a response?

What we in the broader public take for granted is assumed in responsible criminal justice. In our particular scenario, law-enforcement officials neither (1) expect that the kidnapper will suddenly have a change of mind and give himself up without incident nor (2) resort to firebombing the house, or whole neighborhood, for that matter, in order to be sure to kill or restrict the kidnapper. The concern for safety and justice is balanced by a concern for the victim, as well as concern for the neighborhood environment. This latter concern, we must remember, does not mean a renunciation of coercive—even lethal—force should it be required. At the same time, police always measure their calculated use of force against the possibility of harm to the victim. This response to evil is fairly straightforward and remains noncontroversial.

But if we agonize over criminal justice for those who are vulnerable to mass murder, genocide, or a holocaust, the stakes become far greater even while the moral principles do not change. This is not to suggest that one potential death—that of the kidnapped girl—is any less tragic than the slaughter of a million people. It does, however, test the moral fabric and resiliency of a society's body politic, whether the holocaust is our own or our neighbor's.

Not to intervene when we know, via diplomacy, political relations, and intelligence, that mass murder is imminent would be irresponsible. But it is more; it is to be an accomplice to that mass murder. How we think about—indeed, how we prepare for—such scenarios is not hypothetical; rather, it describes the world in which we live. What is our ethical duty to our neighbor, or a neighbor nation? If we suggest that all war is always and inevitably immoral, we turn our backs on those who might, on some rare occasion, need our intervention. For this reason, Reinhold Niebuhr in the late 1930s could write, "It is not possible to disavow war absolutely without disavowing the task of establishing justice." In his own day the dilemma reached critical mass in just a few years as the storm clouds of totalitarianism loomed on the horizon. Consequently, Niebuhr was left to confess:

> We cannot make peace with Hitler now because his power dominates the Continent, and his idea of a just peace is one that leaves him in security of that dominance. We believe . . . that a more just peace can be established if that dominance is broken. But in so far as Hitlerian imperial will must be broken first, the new peace will be an imposed peace.[95]

To pose the question What price was sufficient to justify going to war with Germany? is not to engage in some sort of specious moral calculus. It is rather a lesson that continually beckons us, even when we

---

[95]Reinhold Niebuhr, *An Interpretation of Christian Ethics* (New York: Harper, 1935), 103. This volume appeared two years after Hitler's accession to power.

as Western observers have never experienced personally the excesses of mass murder and genocide. But the dilemma of moral justification for military intervention is one that stared Niebuhr in the face. Certainly no "hawk" himself, Niebuhr was convinced that "even the most chastened Germany would not be willing, except as she is forced, to accept certain provisions for the freedom of Poland and Czechoslovakia and the freedom of small nations generally."[96] And in this vein, Niebuhr was convinced that a pacifist refusal to actively resist evil in practice bestows on evil and tyranny an advantage in the present life. Pacifism, he believed, tempts us to make no moral judgments at all when they are desperately needed; in that sense, then, evil does gain the upper hand.

In his significant statement "Why the Christian Church Is Not Pacifist," Niebuhr sides with Ambrose, Augustine, and Aquinas, who believe that genuine love *can* be—even when it *will not always* be—called upon to actively and directly oppose the forces of evil, given the sinful will to power that is rooted in human depravity. Responding somewhat sarcastically to the pacifists of his day who advocated nonintervention in foreign affairs, he writes: "If we believe that if Britain had only been fortunate enough to have produced 30 percent instead of 2 percent of conscientious objectors to military service, Hitler's heart would have been softened and he would not have dared attack Poland, we hold a faith which no historic reality justifies."[97] It was difficult then, and is now, to argue with Niebuhr's logic.

Niebuhr sensed, and surely the Jews of his day knew, that there are sorrows and evils that are far worse than the physical deaths and ravages of war. Simply said, there are, in fact, some human goods that are of such a high value that enormous sacrifices are justifiable in their defense. This, of course, is a moral and not mathematical judgment. Truly civilized society ascribes to human dignity and justice the highest place in its hierarchy of values. If this hierarchy disintegrates and justice is subverted, society is eclipsed. Peace and stability themselves are the fruit of justice. For this reason, peace is incompatible with a tolerance of evil. And for this reason, as Niebuhr well understood, it will never be possible this side of the *eschaton*, to disavow war absolutely without disavowing the task of justice, over

---

[96]D. B. Robertson, ed., *Love and Justice: Selections from the Shorter Writings of Reinhold Niebuhr* (Philadelphia: Westminster Press, 1992), 52.

[97]Niebuhr, *Christianity and Power Politics*, 6.

which human beings have been made stewards in a fallen world. A belief in human dignity, given the human propensity for moral evil, requires such a view.

Q. 9   Aren't there different varieties of pacifism?

For several decades it has been customary for people to distinguish between several types of pacifism.[98] Indeed, one writer distinguishes between no fewer than twenty-one varieties of pacifist conviction.[99] Not coincidentally, this trend has run parallel with the development of nuclear weapons and their capacity for mass human destruction. The broader assumption among those who are ideologically pacifist is that the capacity for producing weapons of mass destruction automatically trumps or negates the human capacity for moral reasoning and moral discernment.

During the period of the Cold War, Soviet imperial doctrine dictated a policy of maximum security and minimum risk in its belief that, because of the dialectic pattern of human history, the capitalist world in time must disintegrate and pass from the world stage. Therefore, at every turn military preparedness and national security were thought to be necessary both for the maintenance and consolidation of its power base and for advancement in the international theater. To this end, a premium was placed on the development and the threat of nuclear weapons. The question that this presented to American foreign policy during these years was America's degree of preparedness in the face of any given potential threat. While theologians such as John Courtney Murray, ethicists such as Paul Ramsey, and theorists such William V. O'Brien argued on the basis of just-war moral reasoning that it indeed was possible to face the threat of Soviet advancement (i.e., to maintain just-war principles in an age of nuclear possibilities), they constituted a distinct minority. The bulk of religious and ethical discourse was in denial of the possibility that just-war thinking and the nuclear age were compatible, if for no other reason than that the advances in weapons technology made just war impossible.

---

[98] So, for example, Yoder, *Nevertheless*; and Childress, "Contemporary Pacifism," 109–31.

[99] Yoder, *Nevertheless*. In his 1971 edition, Yoder identified seventeen varieties; in the 1992 revision, four more are added. At the same time, Yoder acknowledges the presence of an ideological precommitment: war and coercive force can never, under any circumstances, be used for just purposes (139–43).

Logically, this sort of thinking could only lead to the conclusion that war now had become a moral absurdity; no justification might possibly be adequate in the face of present developments. This moral position was variously called "nuclear pacifism" or "relative pacifism," by which it was argued that the sheer destructive nature of modern weaponry, *in practice*, renders a just war an implausibility. Nuclear pacifism, then, had come to distinguish itself from absolute pacifism to the extent that it did not view war or the use of force as intrinsically evil. Nuclear pacifists, rather, were content to affirm that war in the present had *become* evil owing to the means and proportions. This view was by no means limited to the periphery of American religious life. Much to the contrary, it had come to represent the mainstream, as evidenced, for example, not only by Pope Paul VI's infamous "Never Again!" speech before the United Nations in the mid-1960s but also by the myriad denominational statements and declarations published during the 1980s decrying nuclear buildup.[100]

One critic of both militarism and his own church's nuclear pacifism was William V. O'Brien. He belonged to a minority of religious thinkers who believed that limited war in a nuclear age is neither unrealistic nor a "dangerous heresy," but in fact a foundation for any realistic policy of deterrence and defense. While reacting to the excesses of *Realpolitik*, O'Brien also rejected any ethic that failed to take seriously the political realities of the present, and in this way he mirrored the "moral realism" of ethicist Reinhold Niebuhr a generation earlier. War, as understood by O'Brien, is a political "given" in the present order. Therefore, he argued, the elimination of war is utopian at best and wrongheaded at worst. The first order of business, then, morally speaking, is to limit and contain it by means of time-tested just-war moral reasoning.[101]

The church, as O'Brien saw it, must not be a pacifist church. Typical questions of his day—questions such as "Would Jesus submit to the draft?" and "Would Jesus go to war?"—"seem to me extremely irrelevant," he wrote in *War and/or Survival*. More important for him were those questions that wrestled with the character of justice. What is justice? What does justice require of us ethically? And what does justice require when the rights of people, created in the image of God,

---

[100]See n. 113 for representative documents that were published by most denominations.
[101]See, for example, chap. 8 ("The Laws of War"), in William V. O'Brien, *War and/or Survival* (Garden City: Doubleday, 1969).

are being denied? Addressing those of religious persuasion, O'Brien argued that an informed interaction with the mainstream of the historic Christian tradition must condition our moral analyses of war.[102] And this would entail owning up to our political responsibilities in a world of social-political evil, totalitarian oppression, and egregious human-rights violations.

The 1983 pastoral letter of the U.S. Catholic Bishops, *The Challenge of Peace*,[103] which served as a focal point for much contemporary debate over war, was a case in point and cried out for a thoughtful response. The document, in O'Brien's view, was "seriously flawed" for two principal reasons. At one level, it failed to acknowledge the threat that totalitarianism posed to the free world during the Cold War era. O'Brien chided the bishops for their inability to establish just cause in their deliberations, and thus, their inability to grasp just-war principles. Moreover, the bishops seemed to believe that *no* cause could justify going to war in *any* situation. Thus, he concluded, they have a dilemma. On the one hand, they wish to acknowledge the threat of evil in the world. On the other hand, they cannot bring themselves to say that such a threat should be deterred. On the one hand, they pay lip service to the just-war tradition; on the other hand, they alter the tradition and render it incapable of establishing justice. Their deterrence, in the end, is "disembodied."[104] O'Brien's exhortation to the church—and specifically, to his own bishops—was to forsake idealism and aim at moral realism. For their idealism was a consequence of their nuclear pacifism, which wrongly proceeded on a presumption against coercive force, weapons, and war rather than against injustice and evil, as historic just-war moral reasoning has always done.[105]

In his important book *The Just War Revisited*,[106] moral theologian Oliver O'Donovan acknowledges the popularity—and the usefulness, for purposes of sociological typology—of speaking of varieties of pacifism. At the same time, he insists that ideologically there is but one

---

[102]Ibid., 265.

[103]Washington, DC: United States Catholic Conference, 1983.

[104]William V. O'Brien, "The Failure of Deterrence and the Conduct of War," in O'Brien and John Langan, eds., *The Nuclear Dilemma and the Just War Tradition* (Lexington: Lexington Books, 1986), 155.

[105]O'Brien's criticism of the bishops' statement is found in two essays: "The Failure of Deterrence," 154–97; and "The Challenge of War: A Christian Realist Perspective," in Judith A. Dwyer, ed., *The Catholic Bishops and Nuclear War* (Washington, DC: Georgetown University Press, 1984), 37–63. For a summary elsewhere of O'Brien's thought, see J. Daryl Charles, *Between Pacifism and Jihad: Just War and Christian Tradition* (Downers Grove, IL: InterVarsity, 2005), 74–76.

[106]*The Just War Revisited*, Current Issues in Theology (Cambridge: Cambridge University Press, 2003).

pacifism; it is a pacifism that at bottom does not believe that temporary judgments in the present life, carried out by temporal authorities, are necessary (based on divine institution).[107] Peace, so construed, is a gift of God that becomes severed from the realm of the political. It is a pacifism that begins with the presumption against violence and war, not against injustice and evil.[108]

The proper response, it seems to us, must be that of Aquinas, indeed of the mainstream of classic just-war thinking through the ages. To engage in political ethics and policy making, to wrestle with our temporal duties as citizens of not only the eternal but also the temporal order, is not to fiddle while Rome burns. No, we must in the end reject the "eschatological humanism" of Tertullian and other religious isolationists, for whom there exists a rigid separation between our spiritual and our temporal duties. In its place, we should opt, rather, for an "incarnational humanism" that takes seriously our mandate to "occupy" faithfully in the affairs of the present life.[109] This occupation entails—even when it is not limited to—responsible involvement in social institutions that support and sustain the culture.

Q. 10 Don't pacifists and just warriors want the same goal, namely, peace?

The heart of just-war moral reasoning historically has been its opposition to—and, hence, a basic presumption against—injustice and oppression. Recent reinterpretations of just-war thinking, however, particularly in religious circles, have tended instead to proceed on a presumption against war itself. This mutation—and indeed we are justified in describing this shift as a mutation—has led to what James Turner Johnson, perhaps the foremost contemporary authority on the just-war tradition, properly calls "the broken tradition."[110] What Johnson is reiterating is simply that the main-

---

[107]Ibid., 7.

[108]See the next question, which further probes the difference in starting points between pacifism and the just-war position.

[109]These terms are used by Murray, *We Hold These Truths*, in his provocative chapter "Is It Basket Weaving? The Question of Christianity and Human Values," 175–96. Murray contends that there is a place for all that is "natural, human and terrestrial" without compromising our Christian faith. This includes helping to preserve justice and the civic order.

[110]James Turner Johnson, "The Broken Tradition," *The National Interest* (Fall 1996): 27–36.

stream of classic just-war moral reasoning historically has stood first and foremost against injustice and oppression, not force per se.

Understanding this shift and the manner in which it proceeds requires that we consider how cultural attitudes regarding war and the military develop and evolve. Ponder for a moment how the last fifty years have molded the way in which we as Americans—and as authors we write in the American context—think about war and peace, especially in the church and in the academy. Our national experience as a result of the way World War II ended (at least in the Pacific theater) and the American experience in Vietnam in particular have powerfully combined to shape our national ethos, whether we are Catholic, Protestant, or Orthodox. Add to this the proliferation of nuclear as well as chemical/biological weapons in the last forty years and their potential for mass destruction, and many religious people believe that the proportions of modern warfare are so inherently evil that war or the use of military force is *intrinsically* immoral. Thus, already in 1960, Roman Catholic theologian John Courtney Murray could write that the use of force was no longer considered a moral means for the redress of violated legal rights. The justness of the cause, he worried, had become "irrelevant," and

> there simply is no longer a right of self-redress; no individual state may presume to take even the cause of justice into its own hands. Whatever the grievance of the state may be, and however objectionable it may find the status quo, warfare undertaken on the sovereign decision of the national state is an immoral means of settling the grievance and for altering existent conditions.[111]

What Murray conceded is applicable to the present day. There exists today—perhaps less so among laypersons but overwhelmingly so in academic circles and in many religious quarters—*a presumption against war and force in general rather than a presumption against injustice.*[112]

Evidence of this shift abounds. We see it perhaps most notably in denominational statements during the 1980s that resulted from the

---

[111]Murray, *We Hold These Truths*, 256.
[112]In addition to Johnson, "The Broken Tradition," 27–36, see also his "Just Cause Revisited," in Elliott Abrams, ed., *Close Calls: Intervention, Terrorism, Missile Defense, and "Just War" Today* (Washington, DC: Ethics and Public Policy Center, 1998), 3–38, esp. 21–28; and J. Daryl Charles, "Presumption against War or Presumption against Injustice? The Just War Tradition Reconsidered," *Journal of Church and State* 47, no. 2 (Spring 2005): 335–69.

escalation of Cold War tensions prior to the collapse of the Soviet empire.[113] War, it was solemnly maintained, could not possibly be justified, regardless of the gulf between democratic self-government and totalitarianism. *Both* superpowers, it was argued, were immoral in "threatening" the world. These various denominational pronouncements illustrate quite helpfully the critical distinction that we are making. In each of these documents, the authors assume that *peace is the starting point* for thinking about justice and that force cannot be a moral entity. The concerns stated in these documents bring to mind the words of C. S. Lewis, who against the backdrop of the Second World War critiqued the "semi-pacifism" of his own day:

> War is a dreadful thing, and I can respect an honest pacifist, though I think he is entirely mistaken. What I cannot understand is this sort of semi-pacifism you get nowadays which gives people the idea that though you have to fight, you ought to do it with a long face and as if you were ashamed of it. It is that feeling that robs lots of magnificent young Christians in the Services of something they have a right to, something which is the natural accompaniment of courage.[114]

The just-war tradition, however, proceeds on a different assumption. Without justice, peace itself can be illegitimate. Again, in the words of Aquinas, "peace is not a virtue, but the fruit of virtue."[115] The animating spirit of just-war thinking, properly understood, is that "social charity comes to the aid of the oppressed."[116] Therefore, if we

---

[113]For example, see the 1986 statement by the United Church of Christ, "Affirming the United Church of Christ as a Just Peace Church"; the United Methodist bishops' statement, *In Defense of Creation* (Nashville: Graded Press, 1986); the 1987 report by the Episcopal Diocese of Washington, D.C., *The Nuclear Dilemma: A Christian Search for Understanding* (Cincinnati: Forward Movement, 1987); and the statement in 1988 by the two hundredth General Assembly of the Presbyterian Church (USA), *Christian Obedience in a Nuclear Age* (Louisville: Office of the General Assembly, Presbyterian Church [USA], 1988). The important 1983 statement by the U.S. Catholic Bishops, *The Challenge of Peace: God's Promise and Our Response* (Washington, DC: United States Catholic Conference, 1983), also proceeded on a presumption against war rather than evil (par. 70). Consequently, the bishops were taken to task by several Roman Catholic just-war scholars for their failure to keep the two distinct. See, e.g., O'Brien, "Failure of Deterrence," 37–63; Johnson, "The Broken Tradition," 27–36; and Johnson, "Just Cause Revisited," 3–38, for representative criticisms. O'Brien saw *The Challenge of Peace* as seriously flawed for two important and related reasons: its inability to identify and establish just cause and its failure to acknowledge the threat that totalitarianism posed during the Cold War era. Both of these resulted in the bishops' only "paying lip service" to the just-war tradition. However, Roman Catholic social teaching on war and peace as spelled out in the Catechism of the Catholic Church remains in basic continuity with the classic Christian position on war. It reiterates both *jus ad bellum* and *jus in bello* criteria without obscuring the differing assumptions of pacifist and just-war thinking.
[114]C. S. Lewis, *Mere Christianity*, rev. and amplified (San Francisco: HarperSanFrancisco, 2001), 119.
[115]*S.T.* II-II Q. 29.
[116]So Ramsey, *Speak Up for Just War or Pacifism*, 109.

categorically rule out the *possibility* of war or coercive force, we then categorically rule out just intervention, which *may* on occasion be a requirement of love rightly construed. The just-war tradition, hence, strongly qualifies "peace" by acknowledging that if this "peace" is not justly ordered, it may well be illegitimate, even oppressive. Peace, it must be emphasized, is not merely *the absence of conflict*. As thinkers such as Aquinas and Suárez argue, those who wage war in just manner are not opposed to peace, unless, of course, it is an evil peace.[117]

Most of the denominational statements that were issued during the Cold War share a common weakness.[118] The authors of these sundry statements mistakenly assume that the just-war tradition begins with a presumption *against war*; however, this reveals a basic misunderstanding of the tradition. In its moral justification, the classic just-war position issues out of a presumption *against injustice and evil*. Properly understood, the tradition understands itself as a *mediating* or moderating position between two poles that are absolutist in their attitudes toward coercive force. On the one hand, the militarist—whether secular (i.e., the "political realist") or religious (the jihadist or crusader)—views war and coercive force as justifiable under any circumstance. No moral restraints beyond political expediency or the "command of God" need be applied. On the other end stands the pacifist. Given the suffering and bloodshed caused by violence and war, the pure or "principled" pacifist believes that war and coercive force are *never* permissible; war is to be rejected under any and all circumstances.

By contrast, the just-war position proceeds on the assumption that coercive force per se is not evil and that its application depends on the moral character of those employing it. Correlatively, it understands that there *are* occasions arising from gross injustice in which, reluctantly, we may need to apply coercive force, even if this means going to war, for the protection and preservation of a third party. Resort to war is sometimes, though not always, unjust. Those who attempt to blend pacifist and just-war assumptions do justice to neither.[119] Moreover,

---

[117]Aquinas *S.T.* II-II Q. 40 and Suárez *On War* 1.

[118]See n. 113.

[119]One of the reasons we emphasize the distinction between a presumption against *injustice* and a presumption against *war* is that much contemporary debate, two decades *after* the Cold War, nevertheless remains locked into a Cold War mindset. Religious pacifists of the 1980s deemed war *inherently* unjust if for no other reason than the destructive capacity of nuclear weapons. A rethinking of international security, based on both conventional and nonconventional threats, as well as the increase in regional crises, is required.

in the end the pacifist will reject the validity of just-war criteria, given the ideological conviction that coercive force and war can *never* serve a just end; for the pacifist, "last resort" can never be fulfilled.

Q. 11 Doesn't the sanctioning of force inevitably lead to violence?

For those who have great difficulty with the use of force in the service of charity and justice, this is a logical and compelling question. And given the violent impulse in human nature, one might seem justified in arguing that force always and irrevocably leads to violence and thus *becomes* illegitimate whether or not it was originally so intended. According to classic just-war moral reasoning, however, force *may* be applied for moral purposes and in morally defensible proportions when and where it is highly qualified. As we have sought to emphasize in a prior question, the moral difference between force and violence lies at the heart of just-war moral reasoning, mirroring a basic moral intuition that is commonly overlooked by the ideological pacifist.

But let us back up one step in order to probe the logic of the pacifist, for whom force can never serve just purposes. If force in fact *cannot* be morally qualified, as the ideological pacifist will argue, then one will have to acknowledge that the entire criminal justice system is wrongheaded and that "criminal justice" as we understand it, whether in the domestic or an international context, is bound for failure and should be eliminated immediately as an utter waste of time and resources. In other words, if we follow such thinking to its logical and inevitable conclusion, then we are *required* to permit violent crime to occur around us and to eliminate any and all attempts at law enforcement. *No* crime prevention or interdiction—at *any* level—is morally permissible, since force can *never*, under *any* circumstances, be morally guided and serve just purposes.

But as we all know, and as every child intuits (and indeed hopes), morally guided force *can* in fact be applied in the face of imminent evil. Ponder, for example, the proverbial wisdom embodied in the following moral exhortations:

> Rescue those being led away to death;
>> hold back those staggering toward slaughter.
> If you say, "But we knew nothing about this,"
>> does not he who weighs the heart perceive it?
> Does not he who guards your life know it?
>> Will he not repay each person according to what he has done?
>>   (Prov. 24:11–12)

The thrust of this saying, irrespective of cultural or situational location, is patent: to do nothing in the face of moral evil is to be an accomplice to that evil. The reason why this exhortation belongs to ancient proverbial Wisdom Literature is that *it accords with human nature* and thus applies universally, irrespective of where people find themselves. It corresponds to what is requisite of all human beings everywhere and at all times. It accords, very simply, with what is just.

But how, we might ask, can one honor and obey such a command without morally guided force? While not every situation, to be sure, calls for this sort of response, there will be occasions in which one may be required to act with force, as suggested in the wording of this proverb ("Rescue those being led away to death"; "hold back those staggering toward slaughter"). All people, whether or not they possess religious faith, are morally obligated to do justly. This ability to perform justice is rooted in the knowledge—a universal knowledge—of what is good and what is required of human beings *qua* human beings.[120] And where doing justly *may* require that morally guided force is necessary, we recall the aforementioned necessary distinction between force, which we may define as the degree of power necessary and sufficient to *uphold* law and politics, and violence, which exceeds this measure, in the end destroying the order of both law and politics.[121] Hereby we maintain that force is a morally neutral entity and can be used for just or unjust purposes.

Perhaps the reader will permit both of us authors to speak from personal experience. One of us (Daryl) spent part of the 1990s doing criminal justice research in Washington, D.C., before entering the classroom full-time. The other of us (Tim), in addition to nearly three decades of service as a Navy chaplain, teaches military ethics at one of the nation's military war colleges. These cumulative experiences,

---

[120]See, for example, Mic. 6:8.
[121]So Murray, *We Hold These Truths*, 288.

we readily admit, have helped to shape the way in which we conceive justice issues, as well as policy considerations. As a result, our view of justice is not merely academic, nor is it confined to narrowly religious notions of pietistic faith, on the one hand, or a politically beholden agenda, on the other. Rather, it readily and necessarily interacts with political, social, and moral-philosophical dimensions of human nature that, upon reflection, show themselves to be timeless and universally shared.

If we are to assume, with some, that force inevitably leads to violence and that, by extension, war and killing are *never* morally justified, let us consider the alternatives, drawing parallels from the realm of criminal justice. If force is inevitably immoral, then we are left with two attitudes toward criminal behavior. One is to see the world as a jungle and unqualified brute force as the necessary means by which to keep an upper hand. In such a world, might *does* make right, and moral considerations fall by the wayside. We can only trust in police brutality. The other response is to allow crime to occur, without any forcible restraints. (We grant that this is only a theoretical possibility, since no communities exist, to our knowledge, that in practice adopt such an attitude toward policy.) But the point to be emphasized is this: we are not limited to the two opposing positions—either police brutality or tolerating crime.

There is a third choice, a mediating position located *somewhere in the middle* that requires discernment and hard work in its application. In a relatively free society we trust in police, law-enforcement officers, security agencies, and public authorities to arrest and punish the criminal element in our midst; we do this for the good of both the community and the criminal, and we do this because it is morally necessary. We do not expect our public servants—law-enforcement officers, for example—to enter harm's way and to do this merely by pacific, "nonviolent" means. Even the ideological pacifists among us do not (normally) object when force is needed to restrain violent criminals in our communities. At least, by way of illustration, they do not object when armed policemen foil an attempted robbery of the bank in which they, as pacifists, have money—savings—held in "safe-keeping."

While force is not *always* necessary on the part of the public authorities to preserve the social order, it is regularly needed because of human willfulness and depravity. And in more extreme situations, where criminals with violent psychopathic behavior threaten the community with catastrophic violence, law-enforcement officers and agencies plan and strategize, using any and all means, before deciding on an assault to incapacitate or eliminate the criminal. Let it be reiterated: they do this for the good of the community, and ultimately for the good of the offender himself, not to mention the good of would-be criminals who might be inhibited (or emboldened) by the community's commitment (or lack thereof) to maintain law and order. And in so doing they apply force that is *proportionate to the perceived threat*. Both just-war thinking and criminal-justice thinking lead us beyond a choice between crime and police brutality, between passive acquiescence and militarism, between "softer" and "harder" forms of idealism.[122]

At this point, we anticipate a certain objection coming from some of our readers. When the issue is actual war, the pacifist seems to have a legitimate point. Aren't all wars *inherently* unjust, exuding the worst degree of brutish violence that humans can know? As Augustine worried, warfare breeds the temptation to unleash unjustified violence. And certainly a great temptation for those engaged in battle is the killing of the innocent. The assumption, however, that war itself is uncontrollable is untenable. According to just-war moral reasoning, a justified war entails reciprocal and proportionate use of force that is directed for the purpose of achieving a higher political and social goal. At bottom, then, just-war thinking proceeds on the assumption that there are *limitations* on what may and may not be done. Conducting warfare entails—indeed, *requires*—control and measured response at every turn within the government and the military. Any force that is initiated is used with great deliberation. Military activity, therefore, carries with it an intrinsic imperative toward control and restraints, and such is "to conserve both moral and material forces and ensure that these are always responsive to direction."[123] The degree to which this is always carried out is another matter. Nevertheless, to argue that military force cannot be controlled and morally guided is simply

---

[122]Inis L. Claude Jr. argues convincingly for this *via media* in "Just Wars: Doctrines and Institutions," *Political Science Quarterly* 95, no. 1 (1980): 83–96.

[123]Michael Howard, "*Temperamenta Belli*: Can War Be Controlled?" in Elshtain, ed., *Just War Theory*, 24. This essay originally appeared in Michael Howard, ed., *Restraints on War: Studies in the Limitation of Armed Conflict* (Oxford: Oxford University Press, 1979), 1–15.

false.[124] For this reason, we normally speak not of "military violence" but of "military *force*."

With Augustine, we surely acknowledge that the fruit of war cannot be guaranteed, because the aims of a justified war are always *approximate*, just as law-enforcement officers cannot guarantee that no innocent bystanders will be hurt at the scene of a crime. At the same time, we also wish to reiterate that just-war moral reasoning is guided by moral strictures and limitations such as noncombatant immunity. Political ethicist Jean Elshtain, however, puts the matter in perspective:

> Although civilian casualties should be avoided if at all possible, they occur in every war. . . . The demands of proportionality and discrimination are strenuous and cannot be alternately satisfied or ignored, depending on whether they serve one's war aims. The norms require that a war-fighting country ask itself critical questions about each criterion.[125]

The just-war tradition maintains the moral distinction between guilt and innocence, between combatant and noncombatant, between involuntary manslaughter and murder—distinctions that are rooted in scriptural teaching and the natural law.

Much contemporary pacifism is grounded in a basic horror and revulsion at the notion of violence and bloodshed. While these are unquestionably horrible, policemen and emergency medical technicians, to their credit, voluntarily engage horror and bloodshed as a public service every day as part of their normal work. Violence and bloodshed, hence, are not the worst of evils. The *worse evil* is *not to engage* social-moral evil when it manifests itself and innocent people are its victims. Properly understood, just-war thinking sanctions neither an illicit peace nor unqualified violence; rather, it places *both* on trial, as it were, requiring that force be motivated by charity and utilized in the service of justice. One does not cease to be a moral being when one takes up arms. Any policeman, regardless of his political preferences, will verify this truth.

---

[124]Few have made this argument as lucidly as Howard in his essay "*Temperamenta Belli*," 23–35.
[125]Elshtain, *Just War against Terror*, 66.

Q. 12 Isn't a weakness of the just-war tradition that it can justify a war that is unjust?

Clearly, the possibility exists—indeed, it will always exist—of human beings and nations attempting to justify a war or conflict where just cause fails. This is noncontroversial, even when pacifists press the argument that to be intellectually and morally honest, just-war proponents must concede the potential for some wars to be mistakenly declared "just," or the fact that untold suffering of innocent people has been caused by unjust wars. But in itself, this potential for unjust war is no argument against the moral validity of the just-war position. For the very logic of moral reasoning that *prohibits* some wars will also, out of intellectual honesty, need to recognize that some wars *may* be just. Thus, the argument based on fallibility of human judgment, that wrong judgments are possible, carries no weight. The same sort of reasoning might be applied to criminal justice—that is, domestic—policy; yet few pacifists would therefore argue that criminal justice as we know it should be *entirely* jettisoned simply because the system has problems or incidents of injustice.

But let us extend further the pacifist logic. Perhaps one might argue, as John Howard Yoder and others have done, that *no war* has ever fully met just-war criteria and that no state or government has ever backed down from war as a result of political or external pressure.[126] How might one respond? Since modes of reasoning as well as weapons may be used for just or unjust purposes, the just-war proponent simply acknowledges this possibility. At the same time, this possibility does not relieve him of the need to discriminate between justice and injustice, between guilt and innocence, between a justly ordered peace and an unjust peace, between justifiable and unjustifiable means. Just-war theorists reckon with an imperfect world, in which imperfect humans must consensually make moral discriminations in less-than-perfect ways. In the present life—that is, on this side of the *eschaton*—such imperfect deliberation will need to continue. Law-enforcement officers who protect our cities do this every day. The alternative is to embrace an idolatrous condition of "peace" that is simply utopian in its character, whether it has religious or nonreligious justification.

---

[126]This is the overriding assumption of Yoder's book *When War Is Unjust: Being Honest in Just-War Thinking*, 2nd ed. (Maryknoll, NY: Orbis, 1996).

We return to what is a recurring theme in this volume, namely, that peace is a cherished commodity in need of strong qualification. Here we stand in alignment with classic just-war moral reasoning throughout the centuries—from Ambrose and Augustine to Aquinas, Calvin, Grotius, and the Catholic Catechism in the present day. Peace is not merely the absence of conflict, strife, or war, and it may in fact be just or unjust, as mafioso, thieves, and terrorists well know. A recurring theme of modern Western cultural life is that peace is to be preserved at any cost.[127] Among human beings and human societies, however, that peace will need to be justly ordered—the *tranquillitas ordinis* described by Augustine and Aquinas. The possibility of war, therefore, need not shake our faith, nor should it deter us from giving ourselves wholeheartedly toward working for justice in the most highly qualified manner. This we shall do, even in an imperfect and frequently unjust world.

Proponents of just-war thinking do not see themselves as dodging the so-called difficult questions about war and warfare. If anything, they see a duty to *pose* the hard questions, knowing that the moral tradition, in its essence, is concerned to formulate and apply those conditions that individuals and societies, in good conscience, must apply to the problem of war.[128] In short, the tradition requires that we engage in moral discrimination at a variety of levels. Part of war's tragedy, we readily concede, is that perfect justice eludes us. At the same time, just-war thinking reckons with the moral burden that conflict is justified by the ultimate goal of restoring to a political community or society that condition of civil peace and those fundamental human rights that produced the (just) cause for war in the first place. That is to say, *a worse evil would be enshrined if war were not initiated in the first place.*[129] Surely, the challenges that accompany our imperfect attempts to apply justice are great, as any law-enforcement officer will

---

[127]In religious terms, the Old Testament metaphors that so powerfully weigh on our imaginations—e.g., the lion lying down with the lamb and humans beating their swords into ploughshares and spears into pruning hooks—are intended to foreshadow a future, eschatological reality; they represent ultimate, not penultimate, reality. The ideal, it must be reiterated, should not be mistaken for the real. Stated in other words, human beings have not been promised a world without strife, conflict, or war, nor may it be argued that these elements can be abolished; such are utopian designs and not a proper construal of biblical religion.

[128]Few have stated this rationale with greater force and clarity than William V. O'Brien, in *The Conduct of Just and Limited War* (New York: Praeger, 1981), 330–32.

[129]For a persuasive restatement of "just cause" in the broader sense, see Mark Evans in "In Humanity's Name: Democracy and the Right to Wage War," in Evans, ed., *Just War Theory: A Reappraisal* (Edinburgh: Edinburgh University Press, 2005), 71–89, esp. 73–78.

attest. But they are even greater where no enduring canons of justice are thought to exist.

Q. 13   What is the difference between a preemptive war and a preventive war?

The concepts of preventive and preemptive war differ markedly. To consider the manner in which they differ is to view them as part of a predictive continuum of response. Preemption is a response to a *perceived immediate and credible threat* of attack and war; prevention is a response to a *perceived future threat* of attack and war. Michael Walzer calls this continuum a "spectrum of anticipation."[130] Both preventive and preemptive war are sometimes placed under the category of "anticipatory attacks"; as such, neither concerns actions of operational preemption that occur within an ongoing conflict. Decisions for preventive or preemptive wars are strategic-level considerations, not operational- or tactical-level matters.[131] Anticipatory wars, and especially preventive wars, are "hard cases" for the just-war perspective. (Other such cases include nuclear deterrence and humanitarian intervention.)

Philosophically, Immanuel Kant allows for both preemptive and preventive war, although he argues that such instances should and will be increasingly rare as international society develops, and the rule of law and economic interchange and interdependence become normative in supporting peace.[132] In both the preemptive and the preventive war, there exists the conviction on the part of the initiator of the military action that to fail to act would result in its own nation or forces being attacked. Therefore, the "defender" initiates armed conflict, seeking to gain an advantage. What has changed in recent warfare is the matter of technology, as well as timing.

Historically, preemption and prevention have been thought of within the framework of large ground forces moving across geographic borders. In such instances, one had to reckon with a time delay and

---

[130]Walzer, *Just and Unjust Wars*, 75.
[131]Karl P. Mueller et al., *Striking First: Preemptive and Preventive Attack in U.S. National Security Policy* (Santa Monica, CA: RAND, 2006), xii.
[132]Neta C. Crawford, "The Justice of Preemption and Preventive War Doctrines," in Evans, ed., *Just War Theory*, 30–31.

buildup of forces. In contemporary warfare, the timeline for pre-conflict buildup has been significantly reduced. Depending on the nations involved, there may be only a few minutes between a state of war and a state of peace. New weapons and asymmetrical warfare have also blurred some of the distinctions between what is considered preemptive and preventive. While preemption and humanitarian intervention received a fair amount of attention in political and philosophical literature prior to the Iraq war, preventive war did not, and much that has been written since then is partisan and polemical, focusing on the specifics of that conflict rather than the theory.[133] However, such is not true in all cases, and some thinkers anticipate a rise in preventive war, especially unregulated preventive war. They argue that serious thought needs to be given to this issue by citizens, policymakers, strategists, and all others concerned with the use of force.[134]

Q. 14 What about the statement "All is fair in love and war"?

In casual conversations, statements such as "All is fair in love and war" are common and often accepted as part of daily life and an unfortunate necessity. However, they can also be flawed and wrongheaded, running contrary to moral reality. Frequently, they are little more than bumper-sticker philosophies that mirror an ethics of expedience rather than serious reflection on enduring ethical norms. Acceptance of this slogan presupposes a worldview in which there are no absolutes or ethical norms—that is, anything goes. It is, quite literally, antinomianism (lawlessness). Accepting such a perspective as a world-and-life view results in consequences that destroy both the individual and society. If there are no objective moral values and absolutes that transcend individual or collective subjectivity, then there is no way to declare an act right or wrong, good or bad, lawful or unlawful.

In addition, this slogan also fails to distinguish between the actions of individuals and states. It equates activities within a romantic rela-

---

[133]Randall R. Dipert, "Preventive War and the Epistemological Dimension of the Morality of War," *Journal of Military Ethics* 5, no. 1 (2006): 33.
[134]See Thomas M. Nichols, *Eve of Destruction: The Coming Age of Preventive War* (Philadelphia: University of Pennsylvania Press, 2008).

tionship with actions of warring factions or nations and gives moral equivalence to both sets. It implies that both realms are governed by the same category of human activity.

Ethically, it is fallacious to believe that anything (or everything) is permissible in romance, and it is equally erroneous to believe that there are no boundaries in warfare. In its essence, this slogan succinctly states the very opposite values of the just-war tradition. Accepting the slogan denies every tenet within the *jus ad bellum* and *jus in bello* categories, and it ignores standards of ethics, theology, law, and human rights. Its acceptance leads logically to individual calamity and the collapse of nations and the international order.

Q. 15 Isn't there a "presumption against war" in the just-war tradition?

Although its roots extend further back than the previous generation, the phrase "presumption against war" derives from the U.S. Catholic bishops' 1983 pastoral letter *The Challenge of Peace*. In this document the bishops attempt to represent Roman Catholic teaching on just war as beginning with a general presumption against war. With this as a starting point, the *jus ad bellum* criteria were then to be used to determine whether the presumption should be overruled in particular cases, or left to stand so that a party would not enter into a state of war. Amid Cold War fears of escalation to a nuclear level during the 1980s, many Protestant denominations also accepted this presumption and published statements in accord with this belief.

In affirming this presupposition, the bishops—as well as the many Protestants who also accepted it—shifted the tradition away from an emphasis against injustice per se and a view of the use of force as morally neutral. Reviewing the concept, James Turner Johnson takes exception to the bishops' thinking: "To cast the just war idea as beginning with a general presumption against war was to make it something different from what the classic idea had been."[135]

---

[135]James Turner Johnson, *The War to Oust Saddam Hussein: Just War and the New Face of Conflict* (Lanham, MD: Rowman & Littlefield, 2005), 27.

Drafted in the Cold War context, which was characterized by debate over nuclear weapons and the concept of mutual assured destruction, the bishops' formulation of peace attempted to offer a mediating position between pacifists and just-war proponents. In an environment in which there was a fear of nuclear war, the presumption focused on *jus in bello* matters (proportionality and discrimination), giving them priority over *jus ad bellum*. Critics such as Johnson and William V. O'Brien have contended that rather than providing a middle way, the concept represents a clear departure from the just-war tradition without acknowledging it as such.[136] It is a mutation of the historic position insofar as it understands coercive force as an evil—though perhaps lesser evil—in and of itself. But this assumption is false and as such furnishes the wrong starting point for thinking about war. Force per se is not evil; it is, rather, a morally neutral entity that depends on the moral character and intentions of those who employ it.

Historically, the roots of this presumption might be seen in response to aspects of warfare as displayed in the Franco-Prussian War (1870) and World War I. Especially in the latter, the dimensions of war appeared nationalistic, senseless, out of control, and wasteful of human life on a scale beyond comprehension. These perceptions, coupled with the total-war thinking of some in the Second World War and the fear of nuclear war closer to our time, led to a view of war that *in principle* rejected its use as an instrument of justice.

The thinking of ethicists in recent decades has further encouraged a strong presumption against war and coercive force. One case in point is the construal of just-war theories by James F. Childress in 1978. Childress argues that the killing and harm done in war is a prima facie wrong.[137] In response, critics such as James Turner Johnson contend that this position logically leads to what some have called a "just war pacifism," a position that the Catholic bishops appear to assume. Notes Johnson,

As the bishops have developed and applied it ["just war pacifism"] in various contexts since 1983, they have transformed the tradi-

---

[136]This has been a regular feature in the writings of Johnson, who further argues that the presumption is one of several departures from the historic just-war perspective. See, e.g., "The Broken Tradition," 27–36; "Just Cause Revisited," 3–38, esp. 21–28, and, more recently, "Just War, as It Was and Is," *First Things* 149 (2005): 14–24. See as well O'Brien, "Failure of Deterrence," 37–63, and "The Challenge of War," 154–87.
[137]James F. Childress, "Just War Theories: The Bases, Interrelations, Priorities, and Functions of Their Criteria," *Theological Studies* 39 (September 1978): 427–45.

tional just war categories from moral concerns to guide the practice of statecraft into a series of moral obstacles that, as described and interpreted, are arguments against the use of moral force's ever being justifiable.[138]

But there is a further, logical flaw in a presumption against war or coercive force. Not only is it fundamentally at odds with the classical idea of justified war, but the nature of the judgment upon which the claim is made is also inadequate. Rather than flowing from a deontological moral principle (a "categorical imperative," as Kant put it), the "presumption against war" is a product of prudential judgments about the nature of modern war.[139] By making a prudential argument about modern warfare the basis of the presumption, one grounds his argument for war and peace in a condition that is certain to change, rather than in an unchangeable moral principle and moral wisdom. "It gives pride of place to judgments about contingent conditions over obligations inherent in moral duty."[140]

As traumatic and horrible as the instances and experiences of war have been since World War II, the conflicts have not been models of total war as in the two world wars. Rather, they have been limited and regional in which the proximate causes have been mostly political, ethnic, and religious. They have been exactly the kind of wars classic just-war tradition addressed. Even in the case of a global "war on terror," classic just-war moral reasoning is well suited as a framework, based on the fact that its constitutive criteria address head-on what is morally abominable in terrorism's justification.[141]

The distinction between a presumption against *war* or coercive force and a presumption against *injustice* is very real and has enormous implications for morally responsible public policy. For this reason, it needs reaffirmation in contemporary discussions of war and peace, since it mirrors mainstream Christian reflection on war and peace as developed and articulated through the centuries.[142]

---

[138]Johnson, *The War to Oust Saddam Hussein*, 50. For a historical argument against Johnson, specifically in relation to Aquinas, see Richard B. Miller, "Aquinas and the Presumption against Killing and War," *The Journal of Religion* 82, no. 2 (April 2002): 172–204.
[139]Johnson, "The Broken Tradition," 33.
[140]Ibid., 34.
[141]See the related question below.
[142]See also Charles, "Presumption against War or Presumption against Injustice?" 335–69.

Q. 16 What is the relationship, if any, between human rights and just-war thinking?

Thus far we have assumed the moral necessity of both coercive and noncoercive (i.e., humanitarian) intervention in extraordinary cases. Both coercive and noncoercive responses are guided by the same moral criteria—standards that constitute the heart of just-war moral reasoning. We have proceeded on the assumption that the realm of humanitarian concerns confronts us—indeed, it confronts all nations—with universal aspirations and fundamental rights that inhere in our being *human*. Because they mirror the natural law, humanitarian values transcend human religious, ethnic, and ideological differences; they are a common fund, true and applicable to everyone, everywhere, and at all times. What all human beings share by means of this common moral fund invariably is brought into bold relief by cases of oppressive suffering, egregious human-rights violations, and massive dimensions of injustice.

But this sort of thinking presupposes that there is something inviolable in basic human rights and human values. An inescapable question confronts us: Can we in the current cultural climate assume this much? Can we make the fundamental claim that all people everywhere and at all times have certain inalienable rights? This ascribes to justice a transcendent status. It requires of us the presumption of universal moral norms. But such a presumption flies in the face of the contemporary *Zeitgeist*. In our own cultural context, modern and postmodern skepticism have bred within us an intractably relativistic and nihilistic mindset, causing us to deny the universality of norms and values. Simultaneously, totalitarian statism, rogue regimes, and international terrorism together through their violence and inhumanity deprive people of those basic rights and values that heretofore have been thought inviolable. The question, then, of the source and rationale for human rights must not be ignored.

A recent collection of essays with the provocative title *Does Human Rights Need God?*[143] probes one relevant aspect of this question. Some contributors to this volume argue, in accordance with the traditional view, that the notion of human rights makes little sense apart from

---

[143]Elizabeth M. Bucar and Barbra Barnett, eds., *Does Human Rights Need God?* (Grand Rapids: Eerdmans, 2005).

a theistic framework. Others maintain that respect for human rights can issue out of a secular worldview, with religion in some cases even serving as an obstacle to human rights. One contributor believes that only Christianity offers the best account of our moral commitment to human rights, although another contributor, of Christian conviction, believes that the language of "human rights" is more indebted to the Enlightenment legacy. Yet another contributor appeals to theism and the Hebrew Scriptures for any sustainable basis of human rights. Contributors who are Muslim and Confucian purport to share partial common ground with the Judeo-Christian account, though on theologically diverse grounds. Another contributor, who himself is a Christian theist, situates human-rights thinking within an understanding of the natural law, by which basic human goods and human aspirations are intuited in a way that does not rely expressly on religious authority. Finally, a counterpoint is presented by two contributors who observe historically the manner in which religion—and particularly fundamentalist religion—either restricts or denies human freedoms and rights. At bottom, this volume raises the question, both implicitly and explicitly, of whether any normative concept of human rights requires "some sort of theological or religious grounding," in order to be "coherent, valid, or otherwise sustainable."[144] This, we think, is by no means an idle question.

Is explicit belief in revealed religion—if we grant that Judeo-Christian religion affirms the inherent dignity of the human being—necessary to conceptualize and affirm basic human rights? We as coauthors do not pretend to be neutral in our understanding of human rights, human responsibilities, and human participation in "civil society" as traditionally understood. Such, in our view, flourishes best as a result of a theistic framework. At the same time, we affirm the significance of the natural law, which is guided by right reason and by which one need not be a theist in order to intuit and believe that there are basic human goods that need protecting. For this reason, one of this nation's charter documents asserts, "We hold these truths to be self-evident, that all men are created equal, that they are endowed by their Creator with certain unalienable rights, that among these are

---

[144]Ibid., 3. Significantly, while all the contributors to this volume affirm *that* human rights are non-negotiable, there is no consensus as to *why* this should be. In fact, the force of the volume is to give the impression that human rights do *not* require theism per se, an assumption that is problematic, given the transcendent character of rights and the *imago Dei*, yet remains outside the scope of our present discussion.

life, liberty and the pursuit of happiness."[145] And while the natural
law implies the existence of a God, as it did for the framers of this
document, human rights may still be recognized and defended without resorting explicitly to revealed religion. Hereby we wish only to
argue that general revelation—that is, human wisdom—is accessible
and sufficient for all people to have a minimum knowledge of their
humanity and their surrounding world.[146]

But what about the potentially negative role of religion? Many
in our day will argue that religion can be an impediment to the experience of bona fide human rights and aspirations, as evidenced by
our contemporary world. One need only consider widespread violation of human rights in Latin America, Africa, the Middle East, and
Southeast Asia as powerful evidence. In fact, we would not deny that
even *Christians* have contributed to abuses historically. But the fact
that misguided or hypocritical religion has served to mislead others
through a false or inadequate representation of truth, goodness, and
justice does not itself constitute a legitimate reason to deny universal and transcendent norms for truth, goodness, and justice. What's
more, the secularist account of human rights, so-called, shows itself
repeatedly to be an inadequate philosophical grounding of human
rights, as we attempted to argue in an earlier question. In truth, what
is thought to be a modern invention (i.e., human rights) is in reality
an outlook that grows out of a Judeo-Christian anthropology that
undergirds the broader Western cultural tradition.[147] Human rights,
consequently, are the outgrowth of an inherent human dignity, and
the sanctity of human personhood, an intrinsic sanctity, does not—
indeed, cannot—grow out of natural causes. Human rights extend
to all human beings by virtue of their being *human*, or in religious
terms, by virtue of their creation in the *imago Dei*.[148] Therefore, what
is considered humane and inhumane, just and unjust, has universal
applicability and uniform measurement. Discerning what is humane

---

[145]Compounding things, an earlier draft said "sacred and undeniable."

[146]A pertinent question is whether human rights may be defended *consistently and cogently* without
reference to the human dignity we know through natural revelation.

[147]That such an assertion is hotly contested in a postmodern, post-Christian era does not eliminate
the historical and documentary evidence of this reality.

[148]The so-called sanctity of human life consists in humans' uniqueness and worth, which extend not
only to those deemed "fit" or socially useful, but also to the weaker among us. Human "weakness"
is particularly acute at both ends of the life spectrum. We do not kill the aged or infirm because they
function less efficiently than most people in society; as humans they have intrinsic value. Similarly,
whether early human life is found inside or outside the womb speaks only to the location of life that
has come into being and bears not one iota on the *nature* of the human being—a being that is simultaneously material *and* immaterial in its constitution.

and inhumane, just and unjust, constitutes the very logic of just-war moral reasoning.

A state's authority exists for the purpose of preserving and defending the rights of its members. Its authority is legitimate to the degree that it carries out this mandate. Just-war thinking arises out of certain fundamental convictions—for example, that justice is due all human beings, that approximate (versus absolute or perfect) justice is discernible, and that this approximate justice is worth attaining and preserving. This mode of reasoning applies equally to domestic or international concerns.

Q. 17   What about warfare and the environment?

The destructiveness of war reaches far beyond the pain, suffering, and death of combatants and noncombatants (and animals). It also has short-term and long-term effects on the environment. Ecological concerns are part of the ethical and operational considerations of leaders and commanders in any conflict in the West. International law addresses environmental protection in both *jus ad bellum* and *jus in bello*.[149] The traditional Hague and Geneva conventions and treaties contain provisions pertaining to the protection and destruction of the environment. Additional international attention, provisions, and protocols have arisen in the legacy of the war in Vietnam, as well as the Gulf War. Concerns during and after the former pertained, among other things, to defoliation from the use of the herbicide Agent Orange. During and after the latter war, questions were raised regarding atmospheric and marine pollution on two counts: (1) the intentional polluting by Iraq of the Persian Gulf through Saddam Hussein's releasing millions of gallons of oil into the water and (2) Iraq's setting fire to Kuwaiti oil fields.

One clear convergence of environmental concern and the just-war tradition is in proportionality wherein a military action or operation substantially affects the environment as well as the enemy. Whether intentional or otherwise, the world's militaries, in enormous measure, have real and potential effects on the environment during war

---

[149]Sonja Ann Jozef Boelaert-Suominen, *International Environmental Law and Naval War*, The Newport Papers 15 (Newport, RI: Naval War College Press, 2000), 45–77.

and peace. These effects suggest a sobering responsibility on the part of a nation's social, military, and political structures to consider the ramifications of military activity and to evaluate that activity both politically and ethically.[150]

A Judeo-Christian view of the environment fully recognizes and accepts responsibility for maintaining and using natural resources. Care for the earth and its inhabitants is an inviolable measure of stewardship stemming from the creation mandate in Genesis 1. At the same time, to be concerned for the environment is not to suggest that there will not be occasions that require going to war.

Q. 18   What are the shortcomings of the just-war tradition?

The just-war tradition is not a monolithic perspective with unanimous assent to all of its aspects by advocates through the centuries. Rather, it is a consensual perspective that has undergone continuous refinement as new circumstances and fresh challenges have arisen. In recent decades there has been a resurgence of just-war thinking. The fruit of this resurgence, predictably, has been a variety of perspectives in both secular and religious spheres.

A perusal of the literature on just-war theory over the last forty years, by both proponents and critics, reveals a common interpretative pattern. More often than not one encounters a critique of the core criteria of the framework and criticisms of the application of the criteria.[151] Concerns about applicability of the framework to emerging aspects of contemporary warfare also force just-war proponents to answer new questions and wrestle with new scenarios. For example, does the tradition privilege the state over the individual? Does the tradition need to be replaced completely? Or what about the increasing trend to place children as enemy agents in harm's way, given the traditional view that children have noncombatant status?[152]

Just-war proponent Mark Evans notes five of the major objections to the just-war position that are worthy of our consideration:

---

[150]See in this regard Thomas G. Grassey, "The Natural Environment and the World's Militaries," unpublished paper, Naval War College, Newport, RI, 2006, 11–12.
[151]See for example, Kateri Carmola, "The Concept of Proportionality: Old Questions and New Ambiguities," in Evans, ed. *Just War Theory*, 93–113.
[152]See, e.g., Charles Jones, "War within Reason," *Cambridge* 57 (February 2006): 10; and Helen Brocklehurst, "Just War? Just Children?" in Evans, ed., *Just War Theory*, 114–33.

- What counts as a "war" is far from clear-cut, and therefore appropriate applicability of the just-war theory will always be contestable.
- Going to war, in which people will inevitably die or suffer serious injury, can never be morally justified.
- The nature of actual decisions to go to war and decisions taken in the conduct of war are such that the criteria of just-war theory are not in fact going to be respected.
- Just-war theory is too abstract to deal with the brutal concrete particularities of conflict; reality is always far too messy.
- Judgments about "right" and "wrong" and "good" and "evil," which just-war theory enjoins us to make, are actually unhelpful in orienting appropriate responses to the events in question.[153]

Each of these objections, in our view, can be reasonably answered, and in his argument Evans offers a reasoned response to each. Nevertheless, the objections show that the just-war position has not been without serious criticism.[154]

From our perspective, it is not a matter of defects in the just-war framework itself, but rather one of understanding how the tradition itself has been misunderstood or misapplied, as well as addressing new concerns appropriately from within the framework. As an example, we might cite the dilemma of nuclear weapons during the Cold War and, more recently, the challenges of escalating global terrorism. Unlike some critics, we do not think the tradition needs to be replaced; rather, we would argue that it needs continuous refinement and expansion based on its classical commitment to reason within the parameters of wisdom and revelation of moral principles that are accessible to all people. Evans is correct when he concludes: "For all of its problems, the theory seems to raise all of the questions it is appropriate to raise about the morality of war and it organises them in an integrated structure that it seems *hard* to better. But it is not obviously pointless still to try to do so."[155] Indeed, as contemporary geopolitical events have shown us, there is an urgent need to reflect on and develop the

---

[153]Mark Evans, "In Defence of Just War Theory," in Evans, *Just War Theory*, 204–10.
[154]See also in this regard Gabriella Slomp, "Carl Schmitt's Five Arguments against the Idea of Just War," *Cambridge Review of International Affairs* 19, no. 3 (September 2006): 435–47.
[155]Evans, "In Defence of Just War Theory," 220.

post bellum implications of just-war thinking, that they might stand alongside the traditional *jus ad bellum* and *jus in bello* considerations of the tradition.[156]

Q. 19 What good is the just-war tradition in a secular and multi-faith world in which not everyone accepts it?

Every religion and faith perspective, including secularism, agnosticism, and atheism, has a particular perspective on war and peace. While those views may not be fully articulated or even internally consistent, all people perceive the world around them by means of a world-and-life view that is supported by certain assumptions about the cosmos, first causes, human nature, and morality. These operating assumptions, in turn, determine how one views war and peace. Just-war advocates are the first to acknowledge that their position is not universally held. At the same time, they recognize that amid competing views of war, the just-war position represents an ideal that is applicable to and normative for all people groups. Disregard for its principles and values does not negate its validity. For those who accept the tradition, it provides guidance and a framework within which leaders, citizens, and military forces can make the necessary ethical decisions about potential and actual conflict. In that sense, it is a "tradition with teeth" insofar as laws, military operations, and rules of engagement are grounded in a tradition of permanent values and principles.

As we attempted to argue in a previous question about the natural moral law, just-war thinking is rooted in a particular view of reality. This view of reality is characterized by the conviction that human relationships and human communities must be justly ordered. Within that ordered community there will exist overlapping social commitments and loyalties, whether they are directed to family, to vocation, to civil society, or to the state. While these realms are not identical, they are nevertheless related, and all need to be ordered. And all are ordered by just notions of peace that have their foundation in universal moral standards or norms. Any meaningful degree

---

[156]On *post bellum* implications and applications of just-war thinking, see J. Daryl Charles and David D. Corey, *Justice in an Age of Terror: The Just War Tradition Reconsidered*, American Ideals and Institutions (Wilmington, DE: ISI Books, forthcoming), chap. 10 ("*Jus Post Bellum*: Extending the Implications of Just-War Thinking to Post-War Reconstruction").

of social relations or political action in a society that is relatively just will mirror, in some measure, an indebtedness to transcendent values. A society in which permanent values are not on display cannot endure for long.

Q. 20   Does the just-war tradition prevent or promote war?

At its base, just-war thinking reckons with the problem of evil and injustice in the world. With Hugo Grotius, it maintains parameters in understanding what is a moral and just response to that evil and injustice: we are never to think either that no response is ever permitted or that any and every response is. In order to rectify the effects of social-political evil, morally guided application of coercive force is both permissible and restrained. As a consequence, just-war moral reasoning seeks to prevent unjust wars and promote justice when war becomes a necessity, so that the ensuing peace is characterized by a just political order internally, internationally, and among states. As a moral tradition it recognizes just causes for and just limits within war. The intent of the just-war perspective is to provide a moral and ethical framework within which decisions regarding the appropriate time for war and actions within war can be evaluated. Ends and means are thereby united by a moral substructure.

By attempting to limit and restrain war, the tradition aims to minimize the evils and effects of war. Advocates of the just-war position, which represents the *mainstream* rather than the fringes of our wider cultural tradition, understand that not all war is avoidable and that there are indeed situations in which it is morally and politically necessary to enter a state of war. It was within this understanding that C. S. Lewis wrote on the eve of World War II, "If war is ever lawful, then peace is sometimes sinful."[157] Similarly, James Turner Johnson observes:

> It is a mistake to think of peace simply as the absence of war. . . .
> As the classic just war theorists well understood, the fundamental
> responsibility of those with sovereign authority is to serve a just and

[157]C. S. Lewis, letter to the editor of *Theology*, cited in *God in the Dock: Essays on Theology and Ethics*, ed. Walter Hooper (Grand Rapids: Eerdmans, 1970), 326.

peaceful order. This is their particular burden. The justified use of force is one of the tools they must have available. To think otherwise is to forget the kind of world we live in.[158]

In the present age, war will never be eradicated; thus, the just-war tradition avoids the utopian error of thinking—or hoping—that war might be abolished. It reckons with the stubborn reality of human nature and human fallenness, which is not only the normative teaching of historic Christian theology but the empirical evidence on display in all of human civilization. In this way, basic human discernment and just-war moral reasoning acknowledge that, where the lamb and the lion are presumed to lie together in the present age, the lamb will need constant replacement. While the elimination of conflict is an ideal goal toward which we all strive, it must be sought in conjunction with a peace that is just and not one that is illegitimate.

Q. 21 Does just-war moral reasoning apply to the problem of terrorism?

A response to terrorism can be made by using the ethical model of the just-war framework, particularly because of its commitment to uphold the principles of proportionality and discrimination.[159] This is a relatively recent field of discussion within the tradition, given the fact that the magnitude of terrorism only in the last decade has reached global proportions.

Terrorism is an asymmetric type of war. That is, those who practice it do so in part because they do not have the weapons or forces to engage nations in open combat on land or by sea. The fact that this war is asymmetric and nonconventional does not make terrorist actions or goals justifiable. Christopher C. Harmon states well the challenge that terrorism poses:

> Terrorism presents moral challenges because it is a kind of political depravity. One might say that if terrorism is not wrong, then nothing in politics or war can be condemned and all should be permitted. ... The use of terrorism is no indication of the justice of the avowed

---

[158]Johnson, *The War to Oust Saddam Hussein*, 67.
[159]See the discussion of just-war criteria in part 4.

cause. The choice of terrorism may or may not be made out of desperation but it is, quite simply, an evil choice.[160]

Acts of terrorism are especially reprehensible because they target the innocent and noncombatants. Even when religious justifications and language are used by its proponents, terrorism remains a moral abomination; indeed, we do a disservice to all if we capitulate and accept the terrorist's basic ideas and assumptions. Jean Bethke Elshtain reminds us that *"a person who murders is not a martyr but a murderer. To glorify as martyrs those whose primary aim is to murder civilians because they deem the end glorious is to perpetuate a distorted view of the world."*[161] Terrorism expert Christopher Harmon concurs:

> Terrorism is violence which no moral person can like, or ethically approve. The essence of terrorism includes immoral kinds of calculations: singling out victims who are innocent; and bloodying that innocence to shock and move a wider audience. To this doubly immoral path of political action, terrorists sometimes add the deliberate use of weapons that are nonselective in their killing range. By attacking citizens in peacetime with such indiscriminate means as car bombs and grenades, terrorists become the moral equivalent of war criminals in time of war. . . . The terrorist admits of no contradiction between speaking warmly of "the people" but also fighting "for them" with bombs of compressed gas and nails that kill and burn passers-by. Such acts are abhorrent to nearly any civilization or any time and place. Indeed, one could well argue that if terrorism is not immoral, then nothing is immoral.[162]

Yet, regardless of what the terrorist does, responses to those acts can be made—indeed, must be made—within the just-war framework, which is committed to calculated and therefore restrained and appropriate responses. For example, terrorists may not adhere to the ethical principles of discrimination and proportionality, but those who fight them must do so. Thus, Elshtain writes: "A robust politics of democratic argument turns on making the right distinctions. America's war against terrorism would collapse into a horror were we to fail to distinguish between combatants and noncombatants in our

---

[160]Christopher C. Harmon, "Terrorism: A Matter for Moral Judgment," *Terrorism and Political Violence*, 4, no. 1 (Spring 1992): 17.
[161]Elshtain, *Just War against Terror*, 10; emphasis hers.
[162]Christopher C. Harmon, *Terrorism Today* (London: Frank Cass, 2000), 190.

response."[163] James Turner Johnson concurs: "The reference point for thinking morally about responses to terrorism should be the just war tradition."[164] Despite its morally despicable nature, terrorism does not grant us the license to combat it by abandoning longstanding ethical norms. For example, the law of proportionality and the distinction between combatants and noncombatants must be upheld, just as they are in the realm of criminal justice.

For those who adopt a just-war framework, there are concerns and questions that must be asked in waging war against terrorism. Moral reflection that occurs after the fact is simply insufficient; it must inform our response from the start. What are particular issues that need our consideration? In a real world of evil, war, and terror, civil society will ask the sort of questions posed by Johnson, whom we cite at length:

> Is the good accomplished proportional to the means used? Are there any other means of dealing with the problem that have a reasonable hope of success? Both historically and logically, these concerns are secondary to those termed "necessary"; yet they are nonetheless important additional guidelines for moral policy and decisions regarding potential uses of force. In particular, these prudential criteria remind us that the use of military force is neither the preferred nor the only option for dealing with terrorism. As awesome a weapon as the cruise missile is, for example, its availability does not diminish the importance of other weapons in the struggle against terrorism: policies aimed at cutting off terrorist capabilities, removing their support, eliminating conditions in which they tend to flourish, gathering and sharing intelligence about individual terrorists and terrorist organizations, and bringing them to justice. A moral policy on dealing with terrorism should incorporate such approaches along with the possibility of resort to moral force.[165]

In addition to the questions raised by Johnson, particular tactical issues such as preemption, civilian casualties, positive identification of terrorists, and targeting terrorists who often hide amidst the civilian population (utilizing schools, houses of worship, and hospitals as

---

[163]Elshtain, *Just War against Terror*, 20.
[164]James Turner Johnson, "In Response to Terror," *First Things* 90 (February 1999): 13.
[165]Ibid.

cover) must be addressed repeatedly as military operations and other efforts against terrorists continue.

Augustine, one of the early seminal just-war thinkers,[166] worried that the greatest danger in war was not the physical harm that it causes but rather the passions that it inspires. That is a serious reminder to all who enter armed conflict in any form. As the struggle against terrorism continues and changes, it is wise to keep in mind the famous dictum of the military theorist Carl von Clausewitz that war is never final.[167] If Clausewitz was right, the memory of past conflict, motivation for future conflict, and methods of a new type of conflict are almost certain as terrorism is confronted by nations in the twenty-first century.

The present struggle against terrorism is one that will likely be protracted, achieving near-global proportions. While being attentive to ethical restraints, we must not allow ourselves to fall prey to the relativist distortion—fashionable in many elitist circles—that "one man's terrorist is another man's freedom fighter." Such statements play into the hands of nihilism, irrespective of its garb, and collapse the basic distinction between good and evil, justice and injustice. By it very nature, terrorism is morally indefensible. Regardless of one's religious perspective, terrorism is an abuse of human rights and produces a toxic effect wherever it is manifest, whether or not people are personally targeted, injured, or killed.[168] Within the just-war tradition, we would argue, there exist both the flexibility and the repository of moral principles to confront the threat that terrorism poses.[169] One of the primary challenges is to apply those principles consistently and judiciously in an environment wherein expediency often prevails over ethical wisdom.

---

[166] Augustine's views on war and peace are not systematic; rather, one must piece them together as they surface in assorted writings. This is not to suggest, however, that he has little to say on the subject; to the contrary, he thought deeply about such matters.

[167] Carl von Clausewitz, *On War*, ed. and trans. Michael Howard and Peter Paret (Princeton, NJ: Princeton University Press, 1976), 80.

[168] Harmon, *Terrorism Today*, 14.

[169] It should be acknowledged that not all observers agree that just-war thinking is sufficient to combat terrorism. For example, Neta C. Crawford sees value in tradition but identifies numerous difficulties in its ability to handle the terrorist threat. See her essay "Just War Theory and the U.S. Counterterror War," *Perspectives on Politics* 1, no. 1 (March 2003): 5–25.

PART 2

JUST-WAR TRADITION AND THE HISTORIAN

Q. 22 In the history of ideas, is just-war moral reasoning a uniquely religious or specifically Christian perspective on war and peace, or are there precursors?

Religious faith is not requisite to intuit and implement justice at any level—whether in personal relationships, in a family, in a neighborhood, in a nation or society, or among different nations—even though just-war moral reasoning has been nurtured and refined in the soil of the Western cultural tradition, of which the broader Christian tradition constitutes an important part.[1] The awareness of the natural moral law in *all human beings* by virtue of our shared humanity, what has been described as a type of "law written on the heart,"[2] witnesses to the most basic realities of living in a moral universe. Thus Thomas Aquinas could insist that the foundational moral principles are the same for all with regard to rightness and awareness and that the human moral sense reduces to doing good and eschewing evil, from which all other moral precepts derive.[3] Different people and different cultures use different means to describe what we call "the natural law." For example, in addition to St. Paul reference to the "law written on their hearts," one may speak of the "golden rule" in Plato and Jesus, the *Tao* in Chinese culture, the Ten Commandments, *dharma* in Hindu thought, what the founders of the American republic referred to as the "laws of nature" (mirroring "nature's God") and "self-evident truths," and what one political philosopher describes as "what we can't not know."[4] Human beings,

---

[1]Political historian John Hittinger observes: "The religious traditions which have accepted and developed the just war tradition represent a large part of Western society. Perhaps their numbers or influence are diminishing, but they [nevertheless] keep alive the discourse and the ideal. . . . Surely, this is an important task." "Just War and Defense Policy," in David F. Forte, ed., *Contemporary Public Policy* (Washington, DC: Georgetown University Press, 1998), 340.

[2]This is the language of the New Testament; see esp. Rom. 2:14–15; also Gen. 1:26–27.

[3]Thomas Aquinas *Summa theologiae* (hereafter *S.T.*) I-II Q. 94 a. 4. It is because of this basic awareness of right and wrong, justice and injustice, that the apostle Paul can argue that whether Jew or Gentile, whether religious or pagan, all people possess a minimum awareness of what is good, right, and just, in the end rendering them "without excuse" (Rom. 1:20).

[4]J. Budziszewski, *What We Can't Not Know: A Guide* (Dallas: Spence, 2003).

based on their shared humanity (or, in theological terms, the "image of God"), are endowed with a moral sense that allows them to discern the basic contours of justice. Because it mediates right relations, justice is therefore the moral tissue that binds any civil society.[5]

It is this consensus that makes it possible to identify principles of justice and precursors to just-war moral reasoning that antedate the Christian era. Several examples are instructive, one of which, it needs emphasis, bears direct relationship to Christianity. The Hebrew Scriptures offer a narrative testimony to the Creator's self-disclosure to humankind in general and to a covenant people in particular. What is striking about this narrative account is the centrality of the moral code that is revealed—an encoding in the form of the "Ten Words" that are understood to be universal in their application and to undergird a Mosaic code that is historically conditioned in its application to the life of ancient Israel, the covenant people.

Given the amount of material in the Old Testament devoted to war, some commentary is necessary. Much of the warfare in the early period of Israel's founding is unique to Israel's establishment as a theocracy. This establishment was to serve as a testimony to Yahweh's presence with Israel as a covenant people, who ultimately would bear the messianic seed for the salvation of the world. It needs emphasizing that, excluding the initial conquest of Canaan (in which context we are to understand holy war, the "ban," and Yahweh's directives), Israel did not embark on wars of conquest against the surrounding nations, even when she was directed to go to war for self-defense. Just-war principles, however, do surface in the Old Testament narrative. One example is recorded in Deuteronomy 20, from which instructions several moral conditions might be culled—for example, the assumption that Israel's enemies, not Israel herself, were provoking war; instructions on negotiating terms of peace; attempts to avoid combat and bloodshed; noncombatant immunity (discrimination) as applied to women and children; and protection of the environment (over against a scorched-earth military policy).[6]

---

[5] Our concern is less to describe with precision *how* this moral sense develops or is refined than to acknowledge its presence and functioning in human beings by means of moral reasoning and moral discernment.

[6] Certainly, to the modern mind there are difficulties with this text that elude any easy explanation. The point to be made, however, is that qualifications for going to war and proceeding in war are consistent with just-war moral reasoning. For an attempt to assess how to interpret warfare in the Old Testament, especially in light the nature of *true theocracy*, see, for example, Steven B. Cowan, "War in the Old Testament," *Areopagus Journal* (November–December 2006): 16–18. See also, Peter C.

Chinese culture that antedates Christianity contains intriguing evidence of just-war moral reasoning. Sun Tzu, a fifth-century B.C. philosopher-soldier, states that because war is a matter of vital importance to the state, "it is mandatory that it be thoroughly studied." At the same time, he states, "weapons are tools of ill omen." The first of the essentials requiring examination, according to Sun Tzu, is the "moral influence." War, he writes, is "a grave matter; one is apprehensive lest men embark upon it without due reflection."[7] Wisdom will view armed conflict as "a regrettable necessity" rather than a love of violence, since "violence would be against the Tao, and he who is against the Tao perishes young." And because "soldiers are weapons of evil," they are "not the weapons of the gentleman." However, when "the use of soldiers cannot be avoided, . . . the best policy is calm restraint. . . . He who delights in slaughter will not succeed in his ambition to rule."[8] In addition, rules of engagement were recognized that required just cause to begin a war, notification of pending attacks, humane treatment of prisoners and the injured, noncombatant immunity for innocents, and a commitment not to prolong war. So, for example, *The Wisdom of Laotse*: "Generally in war the best policy is to take a state intact; to ruin it is inferior to this. . . . To capture the enemy's army is better than to destroy it. . . . The worst policy is to attack cities." According to wisdom, "The slaying of multitudes should be mourned with sorrow. A victory should be celebrated with the Funeral Rite." In general, wisdom will oppose all attempts at over-reliance upon force of arms, for "such things are likely to rebound." Therefore, "a good general effects his purpose and stops" to consider wisdom. This wisdom will not rely wholly on strength of arms, nor will it glory or boast therein.[9]

Perhaps pre-Christian Chinese reflection on war represents an isolated case and is not representative of human cultures in general. Does this "consensus" regarding rules of military engagement exist elsewhere? During the fourth century B.C. the Hindu civilization of India codified in the *Book of Manu* humanitarian rules that were to regu-

---

Craigie, *The Problem of War in the Old Testament* (Grand Rapids: Eerdmans, 1978), and Eugene H. Merrill, "The Case for Moderate Discontinuity," in Stanley N. Gundry et al., *Show Them No Mercy: 4 Views on God and Canaanite Genocide*, 61–94 (Grand Rapids: Zondervan, 2003).
[7] Sun Tzu, *The Art of War* 1.1, reproduced in *War and Peace*, Classical Selections on Great Issues, series 1, vol. 5 (Washington, DC: University Press of America, 1982), 301.
[8] *The Wisdom of Laotse* 30–31, in *War and Peace*, 562–63.
[9] Ibid., 562–67.

late warfare conducted by "honorable warriors." According to these rules, noncombatant immunity was granted to several categories of people, including civilians, unarmed soldiers, and those who were fleeing.[10] Roughly concurrently with the *Book of Manu*, Plato and Aristotle question what is sufficient warrant for going to war, even when they view war as a necessary evil. In Plato's *Republic*, the ravaging of enemy territory and property is outlawed, while immunity is granted to women, children, and those men who are deemed innocent.[11] In *The Laws*, Plato acknowledges that only the commonwealth, that is, a properly constituted authority, can declare war or peace.[12] The goal of going to war, according to Aristotle, is that we may live at peace, not war itself. War must be conducted with the virtue of nobility and grandeur, he writes, and is justified under the following conditions: as a result of aggression, to address a prior wrong, and when injustice is underway. Going to war is justified in the case of self-defense, defending our own, and aiding our allies.[13]

If what we are arguing is valid, that basic principles of justice are universally intuited, then one might expect to find this sort of "consensual" thinking about war and peace codified elsewhere, even in unexpected places. In the first century B.C. the Roman Stoic philosopher Cicero (106–43) develops criteria that justify going to war, including just cause as applied to provocation, formal declaration of war by delegated authority, and last resort in the event of the failure of diplomatic and peaceful efforts to avert conflict.[14] Wars that are unjust, according to Cicero, are those undertaken without proper cause, such as "when war is fought out for supremacy and when glory is the object of war." The sole justification for going to war is "that we may live in peace unharmed."[15] Moreover, "no war is just, unless it is entered upon after an official demand for satisfaction has been submitted or warning has been given and formal declaration made."[16] Cicero advocates restraint in war even with those who have

---

[10]*The Law of War*, vol. 1, ed. Leon Friedman (New York: Random House, 1972), 3.

[11]*The Republic* 4 (471a-b).

[12]*The Laws* 12 (955b-c).

[13]Aristotle *Nicomachean Ethics* 10 (1177b) and *Politics* (1425a-b).

[14]Writing at the time of Rome's disintegration, Augustine extends the principles of war enunciated by Cicero. He and Christian thinkers after him mainly restrict just cause to three principal conditions: defense against aggression, the righting of wrongs, and the restoration of peace. Cicero includes as just cause the vindication of honor, which Christian moral thinkers reject. But most notably, the latter root justice in the concept of Christian charity and neighbor love.

[15]Cicero, *De officiis* 1.11, trans. W. Miller (London: William Heinemann; New York: G. P. Putnam's Sons, 1928), 41.

[16]*De officiis* 1.11, trans. Miller, 37.

committed wrongs against Rome: "There is a limit to retribution and punishment."[17]

In the early republic, Rome developed a relatively elaborate protocol by which to handle grievances against another city or state. According to this protocol, ambassadors would travel to the offending territory and demand reparations. They would then return to Rome and wait thirty-three days for a response. If none was forthcoming, they made a second diplomatic visit to threaten war. If reparations were still refused, the Roman Senate would be informed of the failure in negotiations, at which point the Senate voted whether or not to resort to force. In the event that the Senate deemed the situation as just cause for going to war, the ambassadors traveled a third time to the enemy's territorial border to declare war, which was formally announced by throwing a javelin into enemy soil.[18] This approach to the declaration of war, as described by historian Alan Watson, has significant consequences:

> First, the Romans have the psychological advantage of knowing, even before the fighting begins, that they have the verdict of the gods. Their war is just. Second, this conclusion is not shaken even by a Roman defeat. A defeat in the just war [the *bellum justum*] shows that the Romans were unable to execute the god's judgment. Execution of judgment is not the affair of the gods.[19]

Watson's rehearsal of the manner in which early-republic Rome sought to justify war, developed in the important volume *International Law in Archaic Rome: War and Religion*, is important at several levels. Given the limited primary sources of this period that are available, it helpfully sheds important light on early Roman understanding of war and peace. In addition, it illuminates the secular responsibilities of the priestly college, the *jus fetiale*, in its role as ambassadors of the state. Watson elucidates the social-political and legal substructure of early Roman thinking about war and peace—thinking, for example, that governed the making of treaties, deter-

---

[17]*De officiis* 1.11, trans. Miller, 35. It must be emphasized that whether or not Rome embodied the principles as articulated by Cicero is not our concern.
[18]On this protocol set within the wider context of Roman deliberations over justice, see Alan Watson, *International Law in Archaic Rome: War and Religion* (Baltimore: Johns Hopkins University Press, 1993). On the protocol itself, see as well Paul Christopher, *The Ethics of War and Peace*, rev. ed. (Upper Saddle River, NJ: Prentice Hall, 1999), 13–14.
[19]Watson, *International Law in Archaic Rome*, 27–28.

mining just cause for war, undertaking war as a last resort, declaring war, and demanding reparations. The extent to which justice was ever mirrored by Roman *imperium* and whether or not Roman deliberations about war and peace were just, it needs reiteration, are not our present concern. We only wish to point out, as Cicero illustrates, that some form of moral reasoning appeared in deliberation over war. Whence did this come? And why, in any culture, does it surface? Do law and politics of any era, whether or not they mirror a democratic form, have transcendent moral predicates—predicates that can be observed in different cultures and at different times based on a shared humanity—that permit justice to have an abiding, universal character, as Aristotle believed?

Within the Western cultural tradition, both secular and religious thinkers and institutions have been transmitters of the just-war tradition. Within the Judeo-Christian moral tradition, a tradition central to our own cultural context, one can observe a particularly heightened emphasis on discerning and applying justice as it pertains to both the individual and the community. This derives from two intersecting baseline convictions: (1) the covenantal nature of humanity's relationship to the Creator (a Creator whose essence is understood to consist of goodness, moral perfection, and justice), and (2) the attendant moral obligations to one's neighbor that issue out of this covenantal relationship. The frequently unacknowledged debt to Christian moral reflection has been astutely pointed out by just-war historian James Turner Johnson:

> Today we have versions of just war thinking in international law . . . , in military codes of conduct, in the thought of political philosophers like Michael Walzer, and even in the language of policy. But there are reasons to maintain a specifically Christian perspective on this issue, not only for informing the behavior of individual Christians who may be involved in the use of force as ordinary police or soldiers or in community roles, up to the highest level of government, but also as a way of contributing to a vigorous public debate aimed at understanding the justifications and limits of the use of force in the nation and the world today.[20]

---

[20] James Turner Johnson, "Can Force Be Used Justly?" Abraham Kuyper Lecture of the Center for Public Justice, Gordon College, November 1, 2001.

Thus, one does find precursors in various cultures to an explicitly Christian perspective on war and peace.[21] Although just-war moral reasoning is refined in the Christian moral tradition over the centuries, it does not find its sole provenance in Christian religious conviction.

Q. 23 What is the significance of these just-war parallels in pre- or non-Christian cultures?

One's answer to this question derives fundamentally from how human beings construe justice, the ultimate test of which is how to approach the problem of human evil and the dilemma of war. Our prior assertion that religious faith is not requisite to *intuit* and implement justice—which is a social quality described by classical, pre-Christian moral philosophy as being a "cardinal" virtue—is corroborated by the fact that wisdom and moral intuition are accessible to pre- and non-Christian cultures. Christians are not the first to wrestle with moral duty, right and wrong, and demarcating justice and injustice. To argue for unchanging moral norms throughout human civilization, in nonreligious terms, is simply to posit a moral universe that is characterized by certain moral laws, without which all human behavior is random or unpredictable and no one can work for justice in a *shared* sense.[22] Thus, we are confronted with two rudimentary questions: namely, (1) whether the ethical norms that inform justice are fluid and thus changing over time in human history, and (2) how human beings discern basic ethical norms, regardless of whether or not we agree precisely on those norms.

It is significant that numerous ancient cultures—including Mesopotamia, Egypt, and ancient Israel—possessed as part of their cultural repertoire a corpus of "wisdom literature." In the ancient Hebrew Scriptures—what we call the Old Testament—this corpus included the books of Job, Proverbs, and Ecclesiastes, and portions of the Psalms.

---

[21]See also Christopher, *The Ethics of War and Peace*, chap. 1, and J. Daryl Charles, *Between Pacifism and Jihad: Just War and Christian Tradition* (Downers Grove, IL: InterVarsity, 2005), 31–34.

[22]The inability of some religious conservatives to distinguish lower-order from higher-order beliefs, by which we distinguish convictions and obligations that are unique to the religious community from those that apply ethically to all people universally, may help explain why some have difficulty entering into meaningful moral discourse in the public square. They lack a moral grammar with which to bridge the gap between believer and unbeliever. For a helpful discussion of the importance of first- and second-order beliefs, see Brendan Sweetman, *Why Politics Needs Religion: The Place of Religious Arguments in the Public Square* (Downers Grove, IL: InterVarsity, 2006), esp. chap. 1.

Therein one reads statements of a peculiarly generalized nature—
statements such as:

> It is to a man's honor to avoid strife,
>   but every fool is quick to quarrel. (Prov. 20:3)

> Hatred stirs up dissension,
>   but love covers over all wrongs. (Prov. 10:12)

> Better is a patient man than a warrior,
>   a man who controls his temper than one who conquers a city.
>   (Prov. 16:32)

as well as the following:

> Bloodthirsty men hate a man of integrity
>   and seek to kill the upright. (Prov. 29:10)

> He who oppresses the poor shows contempt for their Maker,
>   but whoever is kind to the needy honors God. (Prov. 14:31)

> There is a time for everything,
>   and a season for every activity under heaven:
> a time to be born and a time to die,
>   a time to plant and a time to uproot,
> a time to kill and a time to heal,
>   a time to tear down and a time to build . . . ,
> a time to love and a time to hate,
>   a time for war and a time for peace. (Eccles. 3:1–3, 8)

> Defend the cause of the weak and fatherless;
>   maintain the rights of the poor and oppressed.
> Rescue the weak and the needy;
>   deliver them from the hand of the wicked. (Ps. 82:3–4)

> If you faint in the day of adversity,
>   your strength is small.
> Rescue those who are being taken away to death;
>   hold back those who are stumbling to the slaughter.
> If you say, "Behold, we did not know this,"
>   does not he who weighs the heart perceive it?
> Does not he who keeps watch over your soul know it,
>   and will he not repay man according to his work?
>   (Prov. 24:10–12 ESV)

In the prior question we suggested, based on the assumptions of natural-law thinking, that all human beings are endowed with a moral sense that allows them to discern the basic contours of justice, in accordance with the natural law. Throughout most of human civilization, then, one can identify common assumptions—a consensus, if you will—as to what constitutes good and evil, just and unjust, principle right and wrong. For this reason, mainstream Christian thinkers throughout the ages—champions of the so-called "permanent things"[23]—lived in the conviction that basic moral principles, assumed by and standing in agreement with biblical revelation, are accessible to all people by virtue of God-given reason. It is out of this conviction that C. S. Lewis presses the ever-relevant argument regarding the *Tao*—the term he chose to depict the "law of nature"—in both *Mere Christianity* and *The Abolition of Man*. Not only does the natural moral law not contravene the ethics of Christ, Lewis insists, but as an ethical standard it simply cannot be circumvented insofar as it is the source from which all moral judgments spring. Thus, for Lewis, the *Tao* is pre-Christian, indeed, one might say *pre-religious*. Basic virtues such as reliability, faithfulness, justice, mercy, and generosity form the backbone of all civilized societies and are intuited as true, based on a shared humanity, independent of human or religious experience.

Lewis, of course, is well aware that Christians—and Protestants in particular—object to natural-law thinking on the mistaken assumption that it detracts from Christianity.[24] But Lewis rejects this view. Leaving little room for misunderstanding, he offers the reader further rationale in *Christian Reflections*:

> The idea that Christianity brought an entirely new ethical code into the world is a grave error. If it had done so, then we should have to conclude that all who first preached it wholly misunderstood their own message: for all of them, its Founder, His precursor, His apostles, came demanding repentance and offering forgiveness, a

---

[23]Representative of this sort of thinking are G. K. Chesterton, T. S. Eliot, Evelyn Waugh, Charles Williams, Dorothy Sayers, and C. S. Lewis. See in this regard the delightfully informative volume edited by Andrew A. Tadie and Michael H. Macdonald, *Permanent Things: Toward the Recovery of a More Human Scale at the End of the Twentieth Century* (Grand Rapids: Eerdmans, 1995), which offers snapshots of the aforementioned thinkers, who persisted in emphasizing the "permanent things" through their writings.

[24]On the ignorance or near-wholesale rejection of natural-law thinking among recent generations of Protestants, see J. Daryl Charles, "Protestants and Natural Law," *First Things* (December 2006): 33–38, and Charles, *Retrieving the Natural Law: A Return to Moral First Things*, Critical Issues in Bioethics (Grand Rapids: Eerdmans, 2008), 111–55.

demand and an offer both meaningless except on the assumption of a moral law *already known* and *already broken*.[25]

It is no more possible, Lewis believes, "to invent a new ethics than to place a new sun in the sky. Some precept from traditional morality always has to be presumed. We never start from a *tabula rasa*: if we did, we should end, ethically speaking, with a *tabula rasa*."[26]

As an example of Lewis's argument, we return briefly to Sun Tzu's *The Art of War*, referenced in the previous question and considered the earliest of known treatises on the subject.[27] It is not insignificant that Sun Tzu lived during a period of relatively large, well-trained armies. As to the remarkably detailed planning and conduct of military operations found in this work, one military historian writes:

> His [Sun Tzu's] purpose was to develop a systematic treatise to guide rulers and generals in the intelligent prosecution of successful war. He believed that the skillful strategist should be able to subdue the enemy's army *without engaging it*, to take his cities *without laying siege* to them, and to overthrow his State *without bloodying swords*. . . . He did not conceive war in terms of slaughter and destruction; to take all intact, or as nearly intact as possible, was the proper objective of strategy.[28]

So, for example, in "Waging War," the second section of *Art*, we learn that "operations of war require one thousand fast four-horse chariots, one thousand four-horse wagons covered in leather, and one hundred thousand mailed troops."[29] Such proportions strike the modern imagination as mind-boggling. Thus, his reflections on how to approach and engage in military conflict might legitimately be given the subtitle "Wisdom and War," and they strike the modern reader as unusual to the extent that they offer profound insight into a perennial dilemma. Thus, for example:

---

[25]C. S. Lewis, "On Ethics," in *Christian Reflections*, ed. Walter Hooper (Grand Rapids: Eerdmans, 1967), 46; emphasis added.
[26]Ibid., 53.
[27]A precise dating of *The Art of War* eludes most historians. Based on descriptions of armies, leadership, weaponry, and tactics (e.g., allusion to the crossbow, which revolutionized warfare strategy), it is safe to assign the work to the period of ca. 400–320 B.C. On introductory matters surrounding its writing, see Sun Tzu, *The Art of War*, trans. (with intro.) S. B. Griffith (Oxford: Oxford University Press, 1971), 1–12.
[28]S. B. Griffith, a retired Brigadier General (U.S. Marine Corps) and translator of *Mao Tse-tung: On Guerilla War*, in his introduction to *The Art of War*, x; emphasis added.
[29]Sun Tzu *The Art of War* 2.1.

- There has never been a protracted war from which a country has benefited.
- The supreme art of war and apex of skill is to subdue the enemy without fighting.
- War is a grave concern to the state.
- Of the fundamental factors by which war must be appraised, the first is moral influence.
- With many calculations, one can win a war; with few, one cannot.
- Weapons are ominous tools to be used only when there is no alternative.
- Neither rewards nor punishment should be excessive.
- Treat captives well and care for them.
- Generally in war the best policy is to take a state intact; to ruin it is inferior to this.
- To capture the enemy's army is better than to destroy it.
- When the enemy cannot be overcome by any other means, only then shall victory be gained in the shortest possible time, at the least possible cost to human lives, and with the fewest possible casualties.
- Do not thwart an enemy returning homeward. Show him there is a road to safety and so create in his mind the idea that there is an alternative to death.
- The *Tao* is the way of humanity and justice. Those who excel in war first cultivate their own humanity and justice and maintain their laws and institutions.[30]

It is supreme irony that Sun Tzu's reflections on war were translated and introduced to the Western world by a French missionary. Cognizant that war not only is a matter of vital importance to a state but also furnishes a mirror of that state's cultural values, Sun Tzu provides the first known attempt to formulate a rational—that is, moral and intellectual—basis for the planning and conduct of military operations. Surely, we are justified in asking, whence comes this wisdom? And whence derives the moral commitment to "benevolence" and "righteousness"?

---

[30]Ibid., 1.1–4; 1.13; 1.27; 2.1; 3.1–3; 3.10; 4.15; 7.30–31.

Q. 24 Given the clear traces of an emergent just-war thinking in early Christian history, what were early Christian attitudes toward war and military service? Was pacifism pervasive and universal?

Patristic study in recent decades reveals significant disagreement among historians regarding the position of the early church toward war and military service.[31] This disagreement is noteworthy insofar as it challenges the conventional view of the early church. In his singularly important book *Christian Attitudes toward War and Peace*, Roland Bainton begins the chapter titled "The Pacifism of the Early Church" with the following assertion:

> The three Christian positions with regard to war . . . . matured in chronological sequence, moving from pacifism to the just war to the Crusade. The age of persecution down to the time of Constantine was the age of pacifism to the degree that during this period no Christian author to our knowledge approved of Christian participation in battle.[32]

And because, according to Bainton, the history of the early church is to be viewed as "a progressive fall from a state of primitive purity," the conclusion would seem unavoidable that "if the early Church was pacifist then pacifism is the Christian position."[33] For the last fifty years, Bainton's portrait of the early church as uniformly and universally pacifistic has held sway in most versions of early Christian history. Even among those who are not pacifistic by background or conviction, the degree to which Bainton's account is accepted as normative is remarkable.

---

[31]For reasonably balanced assessments of Patristic witnesses that have appeared in the last two decades, see, e.g., David G. Hunter, "A Decade of Research on Early Christians and Military Service," *Religious Studies Review* 18, no. 2 (1992): 87–94; Frances Young, "The Early Church: Military Service, War and Peace," *Theology* 92 (1989): 491–503; Louis J. Swift, *The Early Fathers on War and Military Service* (Wilmington, DE: Michael Glazier, 1983); and John Helgeland, Robert J. Daly, and J. Patout Burns, *Christians and the Military: The Early Experience* (Minneapolis: Fortress, 1985). Similarly, several essays and book chapters might be adduced: e.g., John Helgeland, "Christians and the Roman Army A.D. 173–337," *Church History* 43, no. 2 (1974): 149–63, 200, an expanded version of which appears in *Aufstieg und Niedergang der römischen Welt* (hereafter *ANRW*), II.23.1, 724–834; and chap. 1 of James Turner Johnson, *The Quest for Peace: Three Moral Traditions in Western Cultural History* (Princeton, NJ: Princeton University Press, 1987), 4–66 ("Christian Attitudes toward War and Military Service in the First Four Centuries").

[32]Roland H. Bainton, *Christian Attitudes toward War and Peace* (New York: Abingdon, 1960), 66.

[33]Ibid.

Bainton, of course, is by no means the sole voice to have concluded categorically that the early church was pacifist. The writings of John Cadoux,[34] Jean-Michel Hornus,[35] and Anabaptist theologian John Howard Yoder,[36] in addition to those sympathetic to Yoder's "radical critique of Constantinianism,"[37] have exercised an inordinate influence on Christian thinking to the present day about the early church's attitude toward war and peace. Taken together, their testimony would seem univocal: the early church was pacifist, and the pacifist position is authentically Christian.

That there was a general avoidance of military service by Christians in the first century is readily acknowledged by all, and for reasons that are clearly understandable. As a small, relatively marginalized social group, the earliest Christians would have been inclined initially to abstain from many social-cultural, commercial, and political activities in the expectation of the imminent coming of the kingdom of Christ.[38] It was not solely or inevitably pacifism and the abhorrence of war that motivated the earliest Christians,[39] though for some it was. Rather, among the earliest believers one finds the predominance of a conspicuously *otherworldly* expectation—the expectation of the coming of Christ's kingdom rather than acceptance of Caesar's already-present earthly kingdom.[40] Evidence coming to us from the second and third centuries, as generations of believers needed to adjust their eschatological expectations,

---

[34]For example, C. John Cadoux's two massive volumes published in the early 1900s, *The Early Christian Attitude to War: A Contribution to the History of Christian Ethics* (London: Headley Bros., 1919), and *The Early Church and the World* (Edinburgh: T&T Clark, 1925), the former having been reissued in 1982. Cadoux proceeds, like Bainton, on the assumption of the church's "progressive fall" in moral purity through the first four centuries as an explanation for Christians' increasing involvement in both civil and military affairs.

[35]*It Is Not Lawful for Me to Fight*, rev. ed. (Scottdale, PA: Herald, 1980), translating the French original that appeared in 1960.

[36]Representative works of Yoder include *Nevertheless: The Varieties and Shortcomings of Religious Pacifism*, 2nd ed. (Scottdale, PA: Herald, 1992); *The Original Revolution: Essays on Christian Pacifism* (Scottdale, PA: Herald, 1971); *The Politics of Jesus*, 2nd ed. (Grand Rapids: Eerdmans, 1994); *What Would You Do?* (Scottdale, PA: Herald, 1983); and *When War Is Unjust: Being Honest in Just-War Thinking*, 2nd ed. (Maryknoll, NY: Orbis, 1996).

[37]So, e.g., Stanley Hauerwas, *The Peaceable Kingdom: A Primer in Christian Ethics* (South Bend, IN: University of Notre Dame Press, 1983); *Should War Be Eliminated?* (Milwaukee: Marquette University Press, 1984); *Against the Nations* (Minneapolis: Winston, 1985); "Taking Time for Peace: The Moral Significance of the Trivial," in *Christian Existence Today* (Durham, NC: Labyrinth, 1988), 253–66; and "Why the 'Sectarian Temptation' Is a Misrepresentation: A Response to James Gustafson (1988)," in John Berman and Michael Cartwright, eds., *The Hauerwas Reader* (Durham, NC: Duke University Press, 2001), 107–25 (reproduced from the introduction to *Christian Existence Today* [Durham, NC: Labyrinth, 1988], 1–19).

[38]See, e.g., Matt. 24:1–25:46; Acts 1:9–11.

[39]See Matt. 8:5–13; Luke 3:14; 7:1–10; Acts 10:1–11:48.

[40]Johnson, *The Quest for Peace*, 42.

indicates that there was a mixture of participation and pacifism. James Turner Johnson observes:

> Beginning with the second century, though, there is increasingly hard evidence [of military participation]. . . . [and] this evidence presents a picture not of a single doctrine, but of plurality; not of universal rejection of war and military service, but of a mixture of acceptance and rejection of these phenomena in different sectors of the Christian world.[41]

Where it was apparent, opposition to military service in the early church was further predicated on a rejection of idolatrous practices within the Roman army. These practices included taking an oath to the emperor who was appointed as *Pontifex Maximus*, and participation in a military system that included oaths to the standards of the legion and a religious system within the military. The discovery of *Feriale duranum*, a calendar of Roman army religious celebrations for the year A.D. 226, indicates festivals for the imperial cult and the army that included sacrifices and other activities that Christians would have viewed as idolatrous.[42] The structure of the Roman military also would have made Christian worship therein difficult, and for precisely this reason Tertullian denounces military service as a Christian (*On Idolatry* 19.2). For soldiers in the Roman army who converted to Christianity it was unlikely that they were able to leave the army since enlistments were for twenty years. And, as is well known, those who deserted the legions were under a death sentence. Christians in the army would have had to associate and worship, when possible, with other Christians in urban areas and forego worship when serving on the frontiers of the empire.[43]

In spite of pagan religious practices in the Roman army, Christians were already serving in the military by the mid- or late second century, and in at least one legion they may have constituted a majority. Bearing on our discussion is a noteworthy event mentioned in passing in Tertullian's *Apology*[44] that occurred in the early 170s[45] and is confirmed by

---

[41]Ibid., 17.

[42]Helgeland, Daly, and Burns, *Christians and the Military*, 48–55. These pages also include a translation of *Feriale duranum*. See also Helgeland, "Roman Army Religion," in *ANRW*, II.16.2, 1470–1505.

[43]Johnson, *The Quest for Peace*, 42–43.

[44]Tertullian *Apology* 5 (. . . *illam Germanicum sitim Christianorum forte militum precationibus impetrato imbri discussam contestatur*).

[45]Historians differ as to the exact date; the range is from A.D. 171—so, e.g., Philip Carrington, *The Early Christian Church*, vol.2, *The Second Christian Century* (Cambridge: Cambridge University Press,

both Christian[46] and Roman sources.[47] That the event is recorded by multiple non-Christian sources serves to strengthen its authenticity. It concerns the famed "Thundering Legion" (*Legio Fulminata*)[48] of the Roman Army during the reign of Marcus Aurelius, the "most grave of emperors," according to Tertullian.[49] The incident occurred along the Danube in the Balkans, where the noted Twelfth Legion was defending against the invasion of barbarian hordes.[50] The Roman army had been suffering from a desperate lack of water owing to a drought in the region. According to the account of Eusebius, upon seeing the enemy approaching, soldiers knelt on the ground in prayer. Their supplication was followed by a thunderbolt from heaven that both put to flight enemy troops and sent rain to refresh the parched Twelfth Legion. Tertullian, writing several decades later, says that Marcus Aurelius himself gave the Christians credit for this miracle,[51] as does Eusebius,[52] although pagan accounts attribute it variously.

What is of interest in this story, regardless of its embellishments and varied accounts,[53] is the information that Christians were already serving in the army.[54] If there were Christian believers serving in the Twelfth Legion during the reign of Marcus Aurelius, it is reasonable to assume that they had been enlisting previously. Commenting on those who record the incident, historian John Helgeland writes:

1957), 224–25—to 174, so, e.g., Robert M. Grant, *Augustus to Constantine: The Rise and Triumph of Christianity in the Roman World* (San Francisco: Harper & Row, 1970), 91.

[46] Eusebius *Ecclesiastical History* 5.5.

[47] *Marcus Aurelius* 24.4 and *Dio* 72.8–10. The event is further depicted on the column (arch of triumph) of Marcus Aurelius in Rome, erected in the mid-170s. And on coins minted by Marcus Aurelius, Jupiter is depicted hurling thunderbolts at Germanic hordes.

[48] The Latin word describing the legion, *fulminata*, is a perfect passive participle, meaning literally "thunderstruck," not "thundering," thereby suggesting the authenticity of the event.

[49] *Apology* 5. What is significant in the account of Tertullian, considered to be one of two chief pacifist early church fathers, is that there is not so much as a hint of suggestion that the presence of Christians in the army was wrong and reprehensible. Historian Louis J. Swift presses this point firmly in "War and the Christian Conscience—I: The Early Years," in *ANRW*, II.23.2, 845.

[50] The Twelfth Legion had been stationed in Cappadocia (present-day eastern Turkey) before the war, where there were known to be many Christian recruits.

[51] *Apology* 5. Pagan accounts give credit variously to the emperor himself, an Egyptian magician, and pagan gods.

[52] *Ecclesiastical History* 5.5. Writing shortly after the Edict of Milan (A.D. 313), Eusebius uses the words "report has it . . . " to describe the incident involving the Twelfth Legion.

[53] Perhaps the most detailed discussion of the sources and circumstances surrounding the "Thundering Legion" is that found in John Helgeland, "Christians and the Roman Army," *ANRW*, II.23.2, 766–73.

[54] Until the decade of the 170s we find no explicit references in Patristic literature to Christians serving in the military. This silence need not be interpreted as opposition to military service by Christians on principle. Interpreters as divergent as Stephen Gero, "*Miles Gloriosus*: The Christian and Military Service according to Tertullian," *Church History* 39, no. 3 (September 1970): 285–98, and James Turner Johnson, *The Quest for Peace*, 4–66, point to social factors that adequately account for this shift in the second century.

Apollinaris, Tertullian and Eusebius tell the story without the slightest hint that these soldiers were wrong in joining that legion, or for remaining in it if they were converted while serving. All three churchmen recount the story to prove to Romans that Christians did their part in defending the empire. Since it is difficult to imagine Christians appearing all of a sudden with Marcus on the Danube, Christian participation in the army at Melitene must have taken place long before 173.[55]

Evidence, therefore, is fairly strong that from A.D. 173 onward there were significant numbers of Christians in the army, and "the numbers of these Christians began to grow, despite occasional efforts to purge Christians from the army, through the second and third centuries into the age of Constantine. We may estimate the number of Christian soldiers at the beginning of the fourth century in the tens of thousands."[56]

Summarizing Christian perspectives on military service in the early centuries, Johnson writes,

> This alternative picture [to pacifism] is one that highlights the initial eschatological separatism of the earliest stages of the Christian movement, in which not violence as such but close involvement in the affairs of the world was to be shunned, followed by a gradual adjustment to such involvement in the wake of the realization that the new age was not immediately at hand—an adjustment that took place in different ways and at different rates among Christians in various parts of the empire, and one that did not compromise earlier moral purity but instead sought ways to direct it into life within the world at large.[57]

If we adopt this interpretation of the development of early Christian attitudes toward war and military service,

> it is not necessary to hypothesize a revolutionary change in these attitudes in the time of Constantine, along with the associated negative implications such a hypothesis requires regarding the laxity and moral complacency of the fourth-century Church. Rather we are led to think of a gradual consolidation of a positive moral acceptance

---

[55]Helgeland, "Christians and the Roman Army," 773.
[56]Johnson, *The Quest for Peace*, 44–45.
[57]Ibid., 61.

of participation in affairs of the state, including military service and war, which paralleled a rejection of violence in other parts of the Church that also rejected Christian involvement in the wider society in ways well beyond those associated with the military.[58]

From the standpoint of historical accuracy, it is crucial to stress that this perspective challenges at the most basic level what noted church historians and ethicists have accepted as axiomatic. A more nuanced and composite reading of Patristic texts yields the conclusion that emerging attitudes among religious believers toward military life did not constitute a "falling away" from early Christian teaching or apostolic purity, as has been popularly and broadly assumed. If indeed the first-century Christians avoided war and the military because of their eschatological expectations and social status, it is only natural that with the change of those expectations over time and a realization of the need to "occupy" the world, there would then arise the need for pluralistic interpretations of the role of Christians in society. This would be true of all vocations, including the military.

Both the subsequent pacifism and the acceptance of military service that led eventually to increased just-war theorizing were movements away from the position of the first-century Christians, who avoided the issue because it was not pressed upon them and because they thought the world of Caesar would soon pass away.[59]

Q. 25 What were attitudes toward military service and war among particular early fathers of the church?

The conventional approach to understanding just-war thinking is to assign it to the period of Augustine (354–430), who in the pacifist account is thought to develop its origins. This profile, however, is somewhat simplistic, for two reasons. First, it generally opts for a selective reading and exegesis of Patristic texts that antedate the bishop of Hippo, texts that do not confirm a *uniform and universal* rejection of military service among Christian believers. Second, it tends to give too much credit to Augustine as a theorizer or

---

[58]Ibid., 16–17.
[59]Ibid., 46.

systematician, since nowhere in his writings does he formally develop just-war theory per se. Rather, one must cull his various writings and piece together his views on war and peace and military service.[60] Not only is just-war thinking found in Augustine, but it also occurs in the teaching of his spiritual mentor, Ambrose (340–396). And indeed, well before their time, Christians who wrestled with their duties to organized society had begun serving in the Roman legions—a portrait that already is suggested in the pages of the New Testament.[61] We learn of this directly and indirectly from the early church fathers, even from Tertullian and Origen, about whose pacifist views much has been written.

While the later Tertullian, who is characterized by an increasing sectarianism, exhibits an increasing hostility toward the powers, such is not true of him earlier. This shift has caused one historian to remark, "It is difficult to believe that the man who wrote the *Apology* [A.D. 197] is the same man who wrote *On the Military Crown* about fourteen years later," even when the later document is a product of his sectarian, Montanist perspective.[62] In his *Apology*, for example, which was written for a pagan audience to demonstrate that Christians could be found everywhere in the empire and in fact contributed to its well-being, Tertullian acknowledges the necessity of war and claims that Christians even contributed by praying for brave armies, for a faithful Senate, for the peace of the world, and for peace within the empire, acknowledging the need to defend territorial borders against invading barbarians.[63] Moreover, he stresses that Christians participate responsibly in society. He can write unabashedly that, like normal people throughout the empire, Christians frequent the marketplace, the inns, and the public baths; they eat the same food, wear the same attire, and have the same customs.[64] What's more, "We sail with you and fight [in the military] with you and till the ground with you, we conduct business with you. We blend our skills with yours, [and] our efforts

---

[60]This is *not* to suggest that Augustine has little to say on the subject. Much to the contrary. It only means that his views are spread throughout a vast array of writings, including sundry epistles and his magisterial *City of God*.

[61]In addition to the fact that neither John the Baptist nor Jesus nor the apostles call soldiers away from their at times "violent" vocation, it is altogether striking that the military metaphor and attendant imagery are used so frequently by the writers of the New Testament (e.g., Rom. 6:13, 23; 1 Cor. 9:6–7; 2 Cor. 2:14–16; 6:4–7; Eph. 6:10–18; Phil. 2:25; Col. 2:15; 4:10; Philem. 1–2; 1 Thess. 5:8; 1 Tim. 1:18; 2 Tim. 2:3–6; Rev. 2:10, 12, 26–27; 4:11; 5:6–14; 7:12; 9:9–11, 16–19; 13:1–18; 16:14; 17:14; 19:11–16).

[62]Helgeland, "Christians and the Roman Army," 150.

[63]*Apology* 30, 32.

[64]Ibid., 42.

are at your service."[65] Through the *Apology*, Tertullian is attempting to refute the accusation of Christians' social detachment. Thus, he offers a list of assorted activities and vocations in which Christians can be found and gladly participate. Tertullian both concedes Christians' presence in the Roman legions *and* emphasizes the peaceful character that governs their relationships.[66]

In Tertullian's treatise *De corona* (*On the [Military] Crown*), the only Patristic work that is devoted to the ethics of military service and war,[67] the reader learns that Christians served in the Roman army in North Africa. In fact, it is conceded that under certain conditions a Christian might be able to serve as a magistrate, provided that he avoid certain idolatrous contexts.[68] (And we know from Eusebius that before the fourth century there were Christian governors in the provinces.) What's more, Tertullian can pray for "'security at home,' for 'brave armies,' and for protection of the imperial house."[69]

In his work *De idololatria* (*On Idolatry*), Tertullian writes for the purpose of describing specific vocations that are thought to imperil one's faith. Included in this list are Roman civil service and military service. Both, he believes, are forms of pagan sacrifice. As to the latter, we know from military history that higher ranks in the Roman legions sacrificed to the emperor. And while lower ranks traditionally did not participate directly in this practice, they were present at such ceremonies, swore allegiance to the emperor, and wore badges that bore the emperor's effigy.[70] Tertullian adopts a very literal rendering of Jesus' words: "One soul cannot be owing to two masters—God and Caesar."[71]

---

[65]Ibid.

[66]He writes, for example: "Who else, therefore, are understood [by Isa. 2:3–4] but we, who, fully taught by the new law, observe these practices. . . . For the wont of the old law was to avenge itself by the vengeance of the glaive [sword], and to pluck out 'eye for eye,' and to inflict retaliatory revenge for injury. But the new law's wont was to point to clemency . . . [and] to convert to tranquility . . . and to remodel the pristine execution of 'war' . . . into the pacific actions of 'ploughing' and 'tilling' the land" (*Adversus Judaeos* 3, reproduced in *Ante-Nicene Fathers* 3.154). In several of his writings, Tertullian applies future, eschatological promise concerning "swords into plowshares," foretold by Old Testaments prophets, to the present age in Christ.

[67]The occasion of this writing is the recounting of one Christian soldier who appeared bare-headed in the camp, holding in his hand his military crown. Having refused to wear it on his head, he was imprisoned (*De corona* 1.3) and (presumably) led off to his death (which Tertullian does not describe). We do learn from the account, however, that other Christian soldiers were a part of that company, since Tertullian chastises them for paying tribute to the emperor as "laurel-crowned Christians" and serving "two lords," unlike their martyr brother in the faith (1.6).

[68]*On Idolatry* 17.

[69]*Apology* 30, 32, reproduced in *The Fathers of the Church*, trans. E. J. Daly (Washington, DC: Catholic University of America Press, 1962), 86, 88.

[70]Christopher, *The Ethics of War and Peace*, 17–18. See also Helgeland, "Christians and the Roman Army," 149–63.

[71]*On Idolatry* 19. Tertullian was opposed to a Christian's wearing garlands *anywhere* simply because of the close connection between military garlands and pagan deities, and thus, the fear of idolatry

But the danger of idolatry, according to Tertullian, is widespread, and one cannot be too careful. His list of forbidden occupations is not limited to the state. The danger of idolatry should also prevent Christians from becoming teachers and students, since both require studying the classics of Greek and Roman literature. In addition, trades such as gold- and silversmithing as well as woodcarving are also to be avoided, since these vocations so frequently entail making pagan idols for clients. And not only vocations, but our lifestyles are potentially idolatrous. So, for example, fancy hairstyles and outer adornments are to be eschewed.[72]

The other chief pacifist among the early church fathers is Origen (185–254). Consideration of the context in which his views were formulated is important. In the third century, Origen sought to defend Christianity in the light of attacks made by the pagan philosopher Celsus. Celsus pressed the argument that Christians who did not serve in the Roman legions would contribute to Rome's collapse at the hands of barbarian hordes. Origen's response is noteworthy. He concedes that some believers are in fact soldiers, although most are not, since killing is not the way of Christ.[73] More importantly, he maintains, Christians support the empire in equally valid ways through their prayers for its leaders. In this way, the forces of evil are also combated. Significantly, like Tertullian, Origen acknowledges the possibility that the military might "fight in a righteous cause."[74] What's more, Origen wishes to affirm that Christians "are cooperating in the tasks of the community." In fact, he insists, none contribute more on behalf of the emperor than do Christians, and "though we do not become fellow-soldiers with him . . . , yet we are fighting for him and composing a special army of piety through our intercessions to God."[75] Unfortunately, in all of his writings, this is the only work—*Against Celsus*—in which Origen addresses the issue of war. And even here the concern is not the ethics of war per se. Like Tertullian, Origen also prohibits Christians from bearing the sword. Yet it should be noted that, like Tertullian, he neither denies to government the moral duty of self-defense nor denies

---

(*De corona* 11.6; 12.1). He was also keenly aware of the *sacramentum*, the military oath taken upon enlistment and then twice a year by every soldier.

[72]Tertullian *De cultu feminarum* 2.9; 3.1.

[73]Origen, *Contra Celsum* 3.7, trans. H. Chadwick (Cambridge: Cambridge University Press, 1980), 509.

[74]Ibid., 8.73.

[75]Ibid.

that Christians actually served in the military. In fact, he acknowledges the difference between just and unjust wars, citing as just causes battles "fought for one's country."[76]

A pagan rhetorician at the time of his conversion in the year 246, Cyprian eventually became Bishop of Carthage in North Africa. During the persecution of Diocletian in the mid-third century Cyprian fled and worked underground and was martyred in 258. He writes of his own day that "roads are blocked by robbers, the seas are beset with pirates," and wars are

> spread everywhere with the bloody horrors of camps. The world is soaked with mutual blood, and when individuals commit homicide, it is a crime; but it is called a virtue when it is done in the name of the state. Impunity is acquired for crimes not by reason of innocence but by the magnitude of the cruelty.[77]

Characteristic of Cyprian's writing is his noting the restraint of Christian virtue: believers do not hate; they do not retaliate; they repay with kindness; they depart from rage, discord, and contention because of their faith in Christ. Despite his lament of the degree of savagery of his own day,[78] he stops short of condemning Christian participation in the military and in fact acknowledges Christian acquaintances who are serving in the Roman army.[79]

Clement of Alexandria (150–ca. 215), a Greek contemporary of Tertullian, offers statements that might be interpreted in differing ways. On the one hand, he can write, "In Peace, not in war we are trained," yet, on the other hand, Clement's frequent use of military imagery would seem to suggest a positive view of military life. In contrast to Tertullian and Origen, he doesn't proscribe military service from the standpoint of faith. Moreover, in an intriguing bit of commentary on the beatitudes, and on peacemaking in particular,[80] he speaks of war and peace in the context of our battle against the flesh, against carnal dispositions of the mind. "Peacemakers," he notes, are those who teach "faith and peace" and who "war against sin."[81] Elsewhere, Clement observes, "But for a man, bare feet are quite in

---

[76]Ibid., 4.82, 83.
[77]Cyprian, *Treatise* ("to Donatus"), trans. R. J. Deferrari (New York: Father of the Church, 1958), 12.
[78]*Treatise* 9.16.
[79]Cyprian *Epistle* 39.
[80]Matt. 5:9.
[81]Clement *Stromateis* 4.7.

keeping—except when he is on military service."[82] Hereby he intimates that military service is part of normal civic life and therefore a valid profession. In his writings, Clement does not offer any commentary on the ethics of war or military service per se. His advice to soldiers who convert to Christ stands in notable contrast to that of Tertullian. He exhorts Christians, regardless of their station, to manifest Christian witness in their vocation. So, for example, farmers are to acknowledge in the field the God who gives yield, while sailors are to call upon their heavenly Pilot, and soldiers are to honor their supreme Commander in performing justice.

A leading presbyter in the church at Rome at the beginning of the third century, Hippolytus was persecuted, was exiled, and died a martyr in the year 235. His *Apostolic Tradition*, wherein appear statements regarding the military, is written in order to enunciate requirements of church membership. In this context, it is said that a soldier who possesses authority must not execute people, and if commanded to do so he must disobey the order.[83] Whether Hippolytus is addressing prisoners of war or Christians being persecuted is unclear. Furthermore, no baptized believer, he believes, can enter military service without denying God. Like Tertullian, Hippolytus understands certain lifestyles and types of work automatically to negate Christian faith and therefore any membership in the church—for example, acting, prostitution, participating in the games, and teaching pagan classics.[84] Of Christians and military service he writes:

> A soldier of the civil authority must be taught not to kill men and to refuse to do so if he is commanded, and to refuse to take an oath. If he is unwilling to comply, he must be rejected for baptism. A military commander or civic magistrate who wears the purple must resign or be rejected. If an applicant or a believer seeks to become a soldier, he must be rejected, for he has despised God.[85]

Dionysius of Alexandria, a disciple of Origen who became Bishop of Alexandria in 247, informs us that the martyrs of his day included "men and women, both young men and old, both maidens

---

[82]*Paedagogus* 2.12, accessed at www.newadvent.org/fathers/02092.
[83]Hippolytus *Apostolic Tradition* 16.17.
[84]Ibid., 16.10–22.
[85]Ibid., 16.17–19, trans. B. S. Easton (Hamden: Archon Books, 1962), 89.

and aged matrons, both soldiers and private citizens."[86] Moreover, he offers a noteworthy account of a certain group of soldiers. "These men," he writes, "had taken up their position in a mass in front of the [military] tribunal. A certain person was on trial as a Christian, and he was about to deny [the faith]." As a result, these soldiers "ran quickly up to the bench of judgment and declared themselves to be Christians" too.[87]

Though not addressing Christians in the military per se, Lactantius is usually cited by most historians as an unremitting pacifist who opposes warfare on the grounds of both bloodshed, which he believes to be wholly inconsistent with Christian virtue, and idolatry. "Why would the righteous person carry on war and mix himself with the passions of others when his mind is engaged in perpetual peace with others?" he asks. The Christian, by contrast, "considers it unlawful not only himself to commit slaughter, but [also] to be present with those who do it."[88] In fact, Lactantius's pacifism is such that he believes "it makes no difference whether you put a man to death by word . . . or . . . by the sword."[89] Lactantius believes that if human passions are restrained, then no one will use violence militarily "by land or by sea." Indeed, no one will lead an army to carry off and lay waste the property of others. For what does it say of the interests of any nation, if it acts to the detriment of another state or nation? To extend one's borders violently, to increase the power of the state, to improve the revenues of one's nation—all of these things, insists Lactantius, are not virtues; rather, they are "the overthrowing of virtues."[90]

In the aftermath of the mid-third-century Diocletian persecution, Lactantius recounts the treatment of soldiers who refused to sacrifice to the emperor. Diocletian "ordered not only all who were assisting at the holy ceremonies, but also all who resided within the palace, to sacrifice. And further, by letters to the commanding officers, he ordered that all soldiers should be forced to the same impiety, under pain of being dismissed from the service."[91] According to Lactantius,

---

[86]Dionysius *Fragments* 2.1 (*Ante-Nicene Fathers* 6.96).
[87]Ibid., 2.8.
[88]Lactantius *Divine Institutes* 18, accessed at www.ccel.org/ccel/schaff/anf07.iii.ii.v.xviii.
[89]Ibid., 6.20.
[90]Ibid., 6.6.
[91]Lactantius *On the Deaths of the Persecutors* 10, accessed at www.ucalgary.ca/~vandersp/Courses/texts/lactant/lactpers.

Diocletian's simple wish was to exclude Christians from the imperial court and from the army.[92] Notwithstanding Lactantius's opposition to violence, he acknowledges that killing might be of necessity if a man were compelled to go to war.[93] In addition, he issues near-unqualified support for Constantine's battles, which he believed to be divinely inspired.[94]

Basil, in the mid-fourth century, seems to underscore a distinction between murder of innocents and killing in the context of military conflict, even when he recommends that those in the latter category abstain from communion for a period of three years: "Our predecessors did not consider killing in war as murder but, as I understand it, made allowances for those who fought on the side of moderation and piety."[95] Notwithstanding his concern for holiness, Basil acknowledges that one can be a committed Christian and serve as a soldier: "I have become acquainted with a man who demonstrates that it is possible even in the military profession to maintain perfect love for God, and that a Christian ought to be characterized not by the clothes he wears but by the disposition of his soul."[96]

The conventional portrait of the early church that comes to us is that the early Christians were uniformly pacifistic, followed by the church's fourth-century "compromise" with the Roman Empire. Beginning with Constantine's rule, it is typically argued, Christians "prostituted" themselves to secular authority. This portrait, however, does not bear up under close scrutiny. It errs both in its oversimplifying early Christians' relation to the state and in its attributing to fourth-century Christians an overly uncritical attitude toward governing authorities. As Augustine painstakingly argues in his magisterial *City of God*, there are civic duties that are required of the Christian believer, even in a culture that is (quite literally) crumbling.

The limited evidence we have of early Christian attitudes toward war is inconclusive. Both strands—pacifist and nonpacifist—can be detected. Clearly, many Christians did oppose military service, and this for any number of reasons. These included otherworldly escha-

---

92 Ibid., 11.
93 *Divine Institutes* 5.18.
94 This is vividly on display in chaps. 37–52 of *On the Deaths of the Persecutors*. See esp. chap. 44.
95 Basil *Letter* 188 (*Nicene and Post-Nicene Fathers*, Second Series, vol. 8). It should be noted that soldiers who killed in battle were *not* excommunicated by the early church.
96 Ibid., 106.

tological expectations of the first generations of believers that tended to produce cultural separation rather than integration, opposition to bloodshed, opposition to any sort of death sentence, the ubiquitous nature of the imperial cult, the idolatrous perception by Christians of soldiers' oath taking (the *sacramentum*) and the military standards, and ceremonial sacrifice to the emperor among officers, to name but a few.[97] However, opposition to military service was not universal. Nor was opposition due to explicit prohibitions in the New Testament, as evidenced by the fact that soldiers in the New Testament are never called to abandon their profession. Even historian Roland Bainton, who with his Quaker background has contributed substantially to a pacifist reading of the early church, concedes from the existing evidence that while "ecclesiastical authors before Constantine condemned participation in warfare," this was not the case regarding military service "in time of peace" and military service in general.[98]

In summarizing early Patristic evidence as a whole, historian John Helgeland makes the following observations:

> Although the Church Fathers did not encourage violence, they were not unanimous in their views on the necessity of war; both [the earlier] Tertullian and Origen prayed for the emperors' success in waging war in defense of the empire. The sermon on the mount seems to have determined the Fathers' ethics concerning murder on a person-to-person basis, but not their thoughts about war. There is practically no evidence from the Fathers which would support the argument that the early church denied enlistment on the ground that killing and war were opposed to the Christian ethic.[99]

To these observations we would add—with notable emphasis—that soldiers were *not* excommunicated from the church on the basis of military service with its attendant duties. What's more, Tertullian is the lone early Patristic writer to argue that army life as a whole is idolatrous and thus problematic for Christian believers.[100] We

---

[97]On the many potential conflicts that awaited the religious believer upon entering the military, see Adolf Harnack, *Militia Christi: Die Christliche Religion und der Soldatenstand in den ersten drei Jahrhunderten* (Tübingen: Beck, 1905).

[98]Bainton, *Christian Attitudes toward War and Peace*, 66, 81. The assumption, however, that a distinction existed among Christians between "peacetime" military service and participating in military conflict lacks any Patristic evidence.

[99]Helgeland, "Christians and the Roman Army," 764.

[100]It needs reiteration that for Tertullian the chief problem is idolatry and not bloodshed. Both in *De idololatria* (*On Idolatry*) and *De spectaculis* (*On the Shows*), this burden is clearly central, and similar arguments press to the fore in *De corona* (*On the [Military] Crown*). Indeed, in Tertullian's view, idolatry

know of no controversy in the church during the early centuries that required the entire church to adjudicate over military service. Nor do we find quarrels between churches or groups of churches over such matters—only scattered dissent here and there of individuals. If we may judge from the silence of the rest of Patristic writers, such was not perceived to be a major problem.

Not only is the modern reader struck by a conspicuous *absence* of the subject of war and military service in Patristic literature, but in sifting through the evidence one becomes distinctly aware that among Patristic writers attitudes varied. Thus, based on the full weight of Patristic evidence, it is fair to contend that the early church was not absolutist on either pacifism or military service.[101] One way of viewing the shift from pacifism to *conditional* acceptance of military conflict, rather than simply attributing it to uncritical attitudes of church fathers in the wake of "Constantinianism," is to view it as the consequence of social location, a growing awareness of civic responsibility and stewardship, and Christians' wrestling with vocational callings in their social and cultural context. These callings invariably might include law, public administration, service to the state, or protecting the community. We should, therefore, be surprised were we to find agreement on the issue of military service and war among early Christians everywhere and at all times.[102]

Q. 26 When in the early centuries A.D. does just-war moral theory begin to develop in the Christian historical tradition?

Early Christian just-war thinking begins to emerge not only in Augustine, as is typically thought, but in the writings of his spiritual mentor, Ambrose, Bishop of Milan. In the writings of both fathers, two elements are striking. One is the concern that

---

would appear to be more deplorable than murder, constituting the highest offense against God (*De spectaculis* 2.9: "summa offensa penes illum idololatria"). And significantly, Tertullian seems unwilling to separate idolatrous acts from idols themselves, for "polluted things pollute us" (8.10).

[101]This is the verdict of historians as diverse as Hans von Campenhausen, *Tradition and Life in the Church*, trans. A.V. Littledale (London: SPCK, 1968); Helgeland, "Christians and the Roman Army," 725–73; and James Turner Johnson, *The Quest for Peace*, 3–66.

[102]On the lack of agreement among Patristic voices of the first three centuries, see more recently J. Daryl Charles, "Patriots, Pacifists, or Both? Second Thoughts on Pre-Constantinian Early-Christian Attitudes toward Soldiering and War," *Logos: A Journal of Catholic Thought and Culture* 13, no. 2 (Spring 2010).

Christians not remain aloof from affairs of the state and this world as they wait for the *eschaton*. The other is the fact that both individuals renounced the right to self-defense. What is significant about Ambrose is his location and his position. Before he became a bishop, he served as a Roman governor in the northern military outpost of Milan. While it is tempting, in light of his background, to portray Ambrose as something of a crusader, that would be wholly inaccurate. He acknowledges, for example, in his preaching and teaching that the continuous assaults on the Roman Empire by barbarian hordes were part of a larger pattern of divine judgment on Rome's paganism. Nevertheless, he admonishes Christians under his watch *not* to extract themselves from civic affairs as they await the coming age. Of interest is the fact that his advice comes in the form of outlining duties of the clergy who have been entrusted with shepherding the flock. The language of these duties, curiously, is the language of *virtue*—justice, temperance, and wisdom. The virtuous life, as Ambrose understands it, has both vertical and horizontal dimensions; it applies to our serving society as well as to our serving God, to bodily usefulness as well as to godliness.[103]

One might ask why the emphasis on temporal duties. Doubtless Ambrose is responding to a version of Tertullian's perennial question "What does Athens have to do with Jerusalem?" Tertullian's answer, of course, represented the sentiment of many in the early church: absolutely nothing. For since the world is an ash heap, destined to go up in smoke, why—to change the metaphor—rearrange chairs on a sinking ship? Ambrose, like Augustine after him, seems to have two aims in mind: to rebut those pagan contemporaries who laid Rome's demise at the feet of otherworldly Christians, and to exhort the Christian community *not* to retreat from the affairs of the present life while awaiting the next.

Right conduct in war is one of several practical illustrations Ambrose uses to underscore duties that are part of our temporal lives. Cardinal virtues such as justice, temperance, courage, and wisdom, for Ambrose, are integrated in the Christian's life; indeed, faith *maximizes* the expression of these virtues. Ambrose's discussion of these virtues contains moral criteria that are applicable to the question of whether or not to go to war—what is known in the just-war tradition as *jus ad bellum*. It is clear, Ambrose argues, that the cardinal virtues,

---

[103] Ambrose *On the Duties of the Clergy* 2.6; 2.7.

as the philosophers teach them, are compatible with the Christian virtues as they come to us through the teaching of Scripture. And why? Consider, for example, the virtue of courage, which "in war preserves one's country from the barbarians, or at home defends the weak or comrades from robbers." This moral quality, Ambrose maintains, is "full of justice." Furthermore, "to know on what plan to defend and to give help, how to make use of opportunities of time and place, is the part of prudence and moderation." In addition, "temperance itself cannot observe due measure without prudence. To know a fit opportunity, and to make return according to what is right, he argues, belongs to justice."[104]

Ambrose not only wrestles with the moral criteria for entering into conflict but also believes that justice is applicable *in the midst of* military conflict itself, what the just-war tradition refers to as *jus in bello* (Latin for "justice in war"). So, to illustrate, he maintains the need for justice in dealing with those who have been defeated and in granting noncombatant immunity to those deemed innocent.[105] Through Christian reflection on justice, Ambrose lays the ground rules for how conflicts between competing duties are to be arbitrated, as well as how conflict between parties, even nations, is to be handled.

There is considerable continuity between Ambrose and Augustine in terms of the moral criteria that bear on whether and how to engage in the use of coercive force. From a layperson's perspective, it must be conceded that Augustine's views on war and Christian faith do not come to us neatly packaged. One must glean his views from multiple sources—for example, from letters written in reply to inquiries about the viability of Christian faith, as well as from his reflections in *The City of God*, written as a response to pagan challenges to the faith.[106]

---

[104]Ibid., 1.27.129, reproduced in *Nicene and Post-Nicene Fathers*, Second Series (New York: Christian Literature Co.; Oxford: Parker and Co., 1896), 10:22.

[105]Ibid., 2.7.32–39. Ambrose firmly believes that it is not virtuous to gain victory by unjust means such as excessive cruelty. For this reason he condemns in the strongest terms the lack of restraint exercised by the Emperor Theodosius who lay siege to the city of Thessalonica (late fourth century) to quell an insurrection. As evidenced by his letter to Theodosius (*Epistle* 51.6–12, "To Theodosius," reproduced in *Nicene and Post-Nicene Fathers*, Second Series, 10:450–53), Ambrose is doubly pained. He mourns the injustice of the slaughter, and his prior friendship with the emperor makes this travesty all the more difficult.

[106]Augustine lived in a period not unlike our own—a time of social disintegration and upheaval. Christianity became the official religion of the empire (formally in A.D. 383), though several emperors had professed Christian faith since Constantine, whose Edict of Milan in 312 ended the persecution of Christians. Thus, an inquiring mind and hunger to know truth made Augustine well suited to the challenges of his era. Before his conversion he was a student of philosophy and thus was able to interact with the moral philosophy of Plato, Aristotle, and Cicero. He was also a champion of Christian orthodoxy in an era of great theological controversy.

Augustine evades any attempt on our part to find a neat, systematic, and single coherent treatment of war in his writings. But what he does say is very significant.

Several aspects of Augustine's application of Christian faith to the realities of fallen culture are worth pondering. Like his spiritual mentor Ambrose, Augustine rejects self-defense,[107] with one exception: the soldier who acts in self-defense and in defense of others.[108] The reason for this is his conviction that it is better to suffer harm than to harm another. But this is not all. He also recognizes that a magistrate, like any head of a household, bears the responsibility to provide for and protect his own. Moreover, like Ambrose, Augustine believes *the obligation of Christian love* is to defend and protect the *innocent third party*, which is to say, whoever stands in need based on external aggression. Not to apply what he calls "benevolent harshness"[109] to the evildoer is as wrong as to cause evil.[110] By this phrase he means *just retribution that is rooted in charity with the aim of securing peace.*

This understanding of Christian social ethics in the service of society beckons us at the most fundamental level. For Augustine, justice and charity are not at odds. Justice is concerned with a right ordering of society for the sake of social peace, what Augustine calls the *tranquillitas ordinis*. He acknowledges the existence of both a just peace (*justa pax*) and an unjust peace (*iniqua pax*); the distinction is critical. For this reason, peace *requires* the ordering of justice. Even robbers, he observes, have order and maintain a certain "peace" within their own orbit in order to plunder the innocent.[111] Peace as a good, even in its relative state this side of the *eschaton*, must be guarded, since it furnishes the environment in which we contemplate life's mysteries.

---

[107]Aquinas's principle of "double effect" counters the Augustinian reticence toward self-defense. Aquinas argues that the act of self-defense may have two effects, one being the preservation of one's life (a natural intuition), the other being the slaying of the attacker. Thus, in light of one's intention, this act of preserving a life is not illegitimate. At the same time, an act may be rendered illegitimate if it is not proportionate to the intended end. *S.T.* II-II Q. 64 a. 7.

[108]*Epistle* 47 ("To Publicola"), trans. J. G. Cunningham, *Nicene and Post-Nicene Fathers* (NPNF), ed. Philip Schaff (Grand Rapids: Eerdmans, 1956). Augustine's thinking in the matter of self-defense seems to have evolved somewhat. Earlier, in *On Freedom of the Will*, he had expressed strong reservations.

[109]*Epistle* 138 ("To Marcellinus"), NPNF, 485.

[110]In *On the Duties of the Clergy* 1.24.115; 3.4.27, Ambrose poses questions such as: "In the case of a shipwreck, should a wise person take away a plank of wood [on which to float] from an ignorant sailor [who cannot swim]?" Augustine uses the examples of highway robbery, assassination, and soldiering to develop his argument in *On Freedom of the Will* 1.5 and *Contra Faustum* 22.70.

[111]*The City of God* 19.12.

While ultimate peace that is consummated in the kingdom of God does not require restraints, penultimate peace does.[112]

As Augustine conceives of it, charity is lodged at the center of human experience and must motivate all that we do. It motivates human virtue, is self-sacrificing, and expresses itself toward one's neighbor. It orders all human actions, even the use of coercive force and going to war. Furthermore, it is willing to order itself toward justice in society. As a social force, this "rightly ordered love"[113] is foremost concerned with what is good—for the perpetrator of criminal acts as well as for the society victimized by criminal acts. When "men are prevented, by being alarmed, from doing wrong, it may be said that a real service is done to them."[114]

Based on the wedding of justice and charity, Augustine renders legitimate an exception to the prohibition of killing. It is legitimate precisely when it involves the public good—for example, in the case of the soldier or public official who is carrying out his public trust by establishing a justly ordered peace.[115] For this reason, Augustine can write elsewhere to Boniface, a governor of a northern African province, "Do not think that it is impossible for anyone to please God while engaged in active military service."[116] Surely, the modern reader worries that Augustine is being uncritical of the political authorities. What about military commands that are inherently unjust? In the event that military commands do contravene the divine will, Augustine is clear, citing the importance of proper motives and being vigilant to the fact that idol worship, no stranger to the military, might endanger Christian confession. He answers that Christian soldiers can soldier but *not sacrifice to pagan deities*. Actions are subordinated to intentions. Soldiers, of course, are not the only ones who wrestle with such tensions; the same applies to anyone who confesses Christ yet wishes to exercise his stewardship as a magistrate.[117]

We appreciate Augustine's treatment of war and peace only to the extent that we understand the reasons why he pens *The City of God*. A major emphasis in *City* is that one can simultaneously be a devout Christian and a good citizen. Properly viewed, Augustine's treatment

---

[112]Ibid., 15.4; 19.112, 27; 22.24; *Epistle* 189.
[113]*The City of God* 15.22 and *Contra Faustum* 22.78.
[114]*Epistle* 47, NPNF, 293.
[115]Ibid. Augustine argues similarly in *The City of God* 1.21.
[116]*Epistle* 189 ("To Boniface"), NPNF, 553.
[117]*Sermon* 62.13.

of war is a subset of his discussion of citizenship. This emphasis, it should be remembered, is necessary if pagans are laying Rome's demise at the feet of disinterested or apathetic Christians and challenging the basis for Christian belief. At the same time, it is also exceedingly important if many Christian believers are viewing Rome's collapse— and with it, the disappearance of the vaunted *pax Romana*—as a sign that the end is near, that the *eschaton* is imminent. Certainly, if Christians are by nature reticent to involve themselves in culture, they are severely tempted to withdraw at a time of cultural upheaval. But our temporal responsibilities, as Augustine views them, are not to be abdicated. Christians, after all, are citizens of two kingdoms, even when our ultimate allegiance is to one of them.

In this light, war, which for Augustine is both a plague and at times a necessity, is not merely a legal remedy to punish or restrain injustice, though it entails that. It can also be morally justified, so long as the criterion of justice informs our considerations in both going to war and proceeding in war.[118] The implication of this social reality, as Augustine understands it, is that the moral principles governing whether or not to go to war (*jus ad bellum*) and how to proceed amidst war (*jus in bello*) apply not merely to Christians (or even Romans); they are applicable to humankind universally. Even when the ideals of justice and peace are only fully reserved in the *civitas Dei*, the heavenly city, they are still important goods that need protecting in the *civitas terrena*, since the two cities co-mingle.

From Augustine's collective writings it is possible to glean several just-war principles. These include just cause,[119] proper authority, formal declaration, the aim of securing a just peace, retribution as distinct from revenge, and discrimination between innocence and guilt. Given the present reality of evil, humans may justify going to war; however, they do so only reluctantly. Augustine serves to remind us that political judgments are at bottom moral judgments. Christian justification for coercive force is neighbor love that must be willing on occasion to protect the innocent third party. The law of love obliges us to use force in the aid of others. Love according to Augustine is dynamic, active,

---

[118]Ibid., 18.13; see also 19.12–13.

[119]According to Augustine, war is justified only under certain conditions—e.g., defending against an unjust oppressor, protecting or rescuing innocent victims in hostile territory, defending an ally, and repelling an assault while traveling (*The City of God* 19.15). Both offensive and defensive action can be wrongly motivated (22.6); nevertheless, both can be justifiable (*Quaestionum in Heptateuchum* 4.44 and *Contra Faustum* 22.71–72).

and able to distinguish between the person and the sin. Therefore, love on occasion may be required to be physically coercive.

Lest one be tempted to think Augustine a crusader, he is not; neither is he an uncritical, passive slave of the state. When political power forces one to do what is wrong, then "by all means disregard the power through the fear [of God]," since the ruler might threaten "with prison, but God [threatens] with hell."[120] War is not to be taken lightly and is a last resort, for it is "a higher glory still to stay war itself with a word than to slay men with the sword."[121] Augustine is under no illusions regarding Rome's own record of aggression, for "peace and war had a competition in cruelty."[122] He is keenly aware that there is no such thing as a Christian polity; Christian wisdom and political power are distinct. Augustine, in the end, is a distinctly "chastened" patriot,[123] which is to say that he is simultaneously committed *and* detached, cognizant of his earthly responsibilities yet confessing his ultimate allegiances.[124]

Q. 27 Why is legitimate authority so important in the just-war thinking of Thomas Aquinas?

As noted above, political authority exists for the purpose of preserving the moral-social order and guarding the greater good of the community. Where authority is used for that purpose, it is legitimate, regardless of its particular form. According to Aquinas, war can only be waged by sovereign authorities, and with good reason. Given the frequency with which princes, nobles, and criminals all engaged aggressively in combat, and this for *private* ends, it is not difficult to understand why this emphasis presses to the fore.

---

[120]*Sermon* 62.13.

[121]*Epistle* 229, NPNF, 581.

[122]Given his sarcastic tone, Augustine seems to be pressing the argument in this part of *The City of God* that external aggression should be added to the Roman pantheon, since as a veritable goddess she contributed greatly to the empire's growth (*The City of God* 4.15). For this reason we reject the viewpoint of Frederick H. Russell, *The Just War in the Middle Ages* (Cambridge: Cambridge University Press, 1975), 19–25, who argues that Augustine prepared the way for a "holy war" or crusader mindset that took root in the Middle Ages.

[123]Jean Bethke Elshtain, *Women and War*, rev. ed. (Chicago: University of Chicago Press, 1995), 252, 268, uses the notion of a "chastened patriot" to describe mediation between warring and pacifist positions.

[124]On the emergence of early-Christian just-war thinking in Ambrose and Augustine, see also Charles, *Between Pacifism and Jihad*, 37–45.

For medieval thinkers, the fear is chaos and the longing is for order. Hence, one finds in Aquinas the strong distinction between *duellum*, the private quarrel or duel, and *bellum*, war. Insofar as war is a *public* matter, *bellum* must be adjudicated by political-legal means and not private citizens.

For this reason, proper authority is situated at the center of just-war moral reasoning, alongside just cause and right intention. In a day when private wars, piracy, and vandalism were often justified, Thomas's emphasis on order and proper authority is not misplaced. Once private warfare becomes normative, all matters degenerate into revenge. But because the magistrate represents the people, he is thus responsible for protecting the common weal against anarchy and tyranny. Public goods require public authority to act on behalf of the community. An act of temporal judgment must be imbued with authority, and war as an act of judgment is a public, not private, act of vengeance. Only governments may make war, just as only police, law-enforcement officers, and magistrates may arrest criminals. This representation of the community is the heart of politics—a necessity that Aquinas grasps. Inherently "modern" questions such as the *process* by which governing authorities come into power are not a concern of Thomas in his discussion of war. However, his emphasis on protecting the common good presupposes that those authorities are not despotic in nature.

Why do we have a harder time justifying armed rebellion or revolution than war, our revulsion of armed conflict notwithstanding? It is because people in society rely on powers that are external to themselves. We may apply the same sort of thinking to the problem of terrorism. In addition to the fact that it purposefully (1) violates noncombatant immunity (discrimination) by striking at innocents and (2) defies proportionality, what is most striking is that it wages war by disordered means. That is, it is self-authorized rather than representative of—and duly authorized by—a political community, which alone renders it illegitimate. Terrorism, in the end, forces us to recognize how indispensable politics and government are. It is the essential nature and structure of government to judge, to establish a just order, and to harness its power in the interests of right judgment and law.[125]

---

[125] Oliver O'Donovan, *The Just War Revisited*, Current Issues in Theology (Cambridge: Cambridge University Press, 2003), 18–32, offers a lucid argument in support of this reality.

As it turns out, justice in war stands in corresponding relation to the exercise of justice in the domestic context (i.e., criminal justice). The difference is that it represents an emergency situation and therefore necessitates powers that belong to no individual person. But Christian moral thinkers such as Oliver O'Donovan are right to maintain that justice in war is carried out by the very same principles as justice in ordinary situations.[126] Justice, after all, is of the same character everywhere and in all situations.

Q. 28 Isn't just-war thinking a pretext for crusading and imperialism?

Throughout this volume we proceed on the baseline assumption that just-war moral reasoning constitutes a mediating position between the two opposing poles of militarism and pacifism.[127] This position represents mainstream Christian thinking on war and peace. The concern that just-war thinking might serve as a pretext for crusading or imperialism might appear legitimate, and perplexing, given the church's willingness to condone violence throughout its history. To illustrate, what of the role played by Aquinas in the thirteenth century to enunciate the core criteria of just-war thinking? Surely, this would seem to be a prime example.

In response, it should be emphasized that the crusading spirit was past when Aquinas was codifying a Christian understanding of war and force.[128] He was no crusader, even while we are justified in calling him an interventionist. But, one is likely to object, what about the existence of military religious orders in his day? Aquinas takes up the matter of these orders in a different context than his discussion of the generic question Is it permissible to go to war? in *Summa theologiae*. His own rationale for military religious orders is quite simply that their establishment was necessary "because of the failure of secular princes to resist unbelievers in certain lands"; these orders, he further observes, were not autonomous but rather accountable to a

---

[126]Ibid., 19.
[127]In parts 1, "Just War Tradition and the Philosopher," and 4, "Just War Tradition and the Theologian," we set forth this assumption explicitly.
[128]See chiefly his treatment of war in *S.T.* II-II Q. 40.

higher authority.[129] In addition, one should be mindful that Thomas's father and several of his brothers were knights. "Knights are rapacious," Aquinas lamented in at least one sermon—a confession that, given his own lineage, is not insignificant.[130] One should also recall his imprisonment by his own family for fifteen months in order to dissuade him as a young man from joining the Dominican friars. Thus, we must resist viewing Aquinas as encouraging or advancing a crusading spirit.[131]

Several early-modern moral thinkers also demonstrate the profound difference between just-war moral reasoning and the crusading spirit. One of these is the Spanish theologian Francisco de Vitoria (1480–1546), who lived during the period of new-world conquest. Because of Spain's influence in the sixteenth century as the intellectual center of Europe, as well as its most dominant military and colonial power, the question of Spanish treatment of indigenous people raised critically urgent questions as to the character and moral underpinnings of justice. The essence of Vitoria's argument—an unpopular one in his day—is this: the king has no right, even if he were lord over the whole earth—which he is not—to claim ownership of the Native Americans' land.[132] Vitoria argues against conventional thinking that the emperor is *not* the ruler of the world: *Imperator non est dominus orbis*. In fact, he maintains, *the church* is not subject to him, nor are *other nations*. In fact, neither the king nor the pope, for that matter, could authorize war against the Indians. Neither religious nor economic nor political reasons alone make coercion and warfare just. Therefore, war with the Indians to acquire their land is unjust, he argues in *Reflections on the Indians and the Law of War*; Indians and Spaniards have equal rights. The only cause for war that is just

---

[129]Ibid., II-II Q. 188. Even in religious wars the same three core criteria—proper authority, just cause, and right intent—are normative, with the goal being the public good and the advancement of justice, *not* proselytizing (ibid., Qq. 64 and 66; see also *Quodlibet questionae* 2.16).

[130]Aquinas, *Sermon* 41, cited in Edward A. Synan, "St. Thomas Aquinas and the Profession of Arms," *Medieval Studies* 50 (1988): 424.

[131]In accordance with the early church fathers, Aquinas supported disqualification of clergy and spiritual leaders from military involvement, considering their spiritual duties of mediating the Christian sacraments to the wider church as a "higher" calling that required separation (S.T. II-II Q. 40).

[132]Five centuries removed, we fail to appreciate how revolutionary Vitoria's work was at the time. The words of one fourteenth-century Spanish lawyer tell us much about the religious and political environment of the time: "If anyone asserted that the Emperor is not the monarch of the entire world, he would be a heretic; for he would make a pronouncement contrary to the decision of the Church and contrary to the text of the Gospel which says: 'A decree went forth from Caesar Augustus that a census should be taken of all the world,' as St. Luke has it, and so Christ, too, recognized him as emperor and master." Cited in the introduction to Francisco de Vitoria, *De Indis et de Iure belli reflectiones*, ed. Ernest Nys, trans. J. P. Bate (repr., New York: Oceana; London: Wildy and Sons, 1964), 76.

is a wrong that is intuited through natural moral law, a wrong that is discernable to all people everywhere through reason. Going to war based on religious differences or "the spirit of discovery" is not justifiable.[133] No war is just that inflicts upon a population unprovoked injustice. And even were the Indians to attack the Spanish, a just response would be only a defensive response that sought to minimize loss.[134]

Against the crusading mindset, Vitoria enumerates specific causes that might warrant going to war, placing himself in line with just-war thinkers of the past: defense against aggression, recovery of that which has been stolen, and punishment for wrongdoing. He is adamant in rejecting the prevailing view of his day. Force is *not* justified in the case of difference of religion, in promoting conversion to the faith, as a response to rejection of the faith, or to defend the magistrate's sense of vainglory. The Spaniards could forcefully require right of passage denied by the Indians, however, but only with "moderation and proportion," so as to "go no further than necessity demands, preferring to abstain from what they lawfully might do rather than transgress due limits."[135] As applied to the Indians, specific situations that might justify coercive intervention are identified by Vitoria. For example, the Indians may not persecute those who convert to Christian faith. Indian chiefs, moreover, may not exercise tyranny. Other just causes include self-defense, defending allies, quelling sedition, defending public safety, and preserving general peace against tyrants or aggressors.[136]

---

[133]Vitoria *De Indis* 2.15.

[134]Vitoria's criticisms of Spain's unjust treatment of American Indians strike us as all the more radical given the practice of slavery in Spain and Portugal. In Vitoria's day, Spanish slaves consisted of blacks, whites, Moors, and Jews. What Vitoria was willing to acknowledge was utterly unpopular, for Spain had been guilty of numerous crimes against the Indians.

[135]Vitoria *De Indis* 3.2. Consistent with traditional just-war thinking, Vitoria also affirms *in bello* requirements of proportionality and discrimination between guilty and innocent (*De Indis* 10, 34–39). Regarding the former: retribution is to be "proportionate to the offense, and vengeance ought to go no further." As to the latter: "The deliberate slaughter of the innocent is never lawful in itself" and is forbidden by natural law. "It is never right to slay the guiltless, even as an indirect and unintended result." "The basis of a war," Vitoria observes, "is a wrong done. But a wrong is not done by an innocent person. Therefore war may not be employed against him." Vitoria is not unmindful of collateral damage and acknowledges that preventing harm to *all* innocents in war is impossible. Such a situation might include the storming of a fortress in a just war with the knowledge that innocent people are inside. Prudence in such a case is therefore necessary, always with the aim of avoiding potential abuses.

[136]Ibid., 10–19. Vitoria must confront the delicate matters of justice as well in his wrestling with justice toward the Indians. Can the fact of Indians' vices, morals, and questionable practices be just cause for war? No, says Vitoria, even though their idolatrous practices (for example, cannibalistic rites in parts of Mexico and South America) were considered abominable and savage. The Spanish should be allowed to carry on trade in the New World, and the barbarians may not impede such commercial activity. If the Indians *do* attempt to impede them, the Spanish should seek to reason with them

Without question, the history of Spain's adherence to these principles, of course, is not a happy one. As the record bears out, more often than not peace was subverted by conquistadors who had no intention of acting justly. What is striking about Vitoria's work is that it constantly challenges the authorities to consider moral alternatives. Rendering evil for unwarranted provocation is unacceptable in Vitoria's view, for it causes justice to go into hiding.[137]

Another early-modern figure deserving our attention is the Dutch legal theorist Hugo Grotius (1583–1645), considered the father of international law. Grotius is remarkable for several reasons, not least of these being his important work *The Law of War and Peace* (1625). In it he argues how relations between nations must be governed by universally biding moral principles, at the heart of which stands the natural law. Grotius lived and wrote in the context of the Thirty Years War that had ravaged much of Europe prior to the Peace of Westphalia in 1648, causing him to brood much over the horrors of war and the ways of peace. It was the bitterness of this strife, rending church and state and leaving no international authority, that inspired him to reflect on war and peace. Weary and committed as he was to peace, he did not exclude the possibility of war, however. Rather, the ravages of war led him to refine just-war thinking in such a way that it should become the handmaiden of authentic justice, in the end securing an enduring social peace. In *The Law of War and Peace* he probes when, how, and by whom war might justly be conducted. Thus, Grotius was anything but a crusader.

Given his abhorrence of war's ravages, his chief objective was to prevent war in the first place. Nevertheless, in those situations where people are unable to prevent war, they must aim to minimize its devastation. Grotius self-consciously places himself between what he called two "extreme" positions—militarism and pacifism: "For both extremes a remedy must be found, [in order] that men may not believe either that nothing is allowable, or that everything is."[138] Human reason and social necessity do not prohibit all force; only that

---

without violence. If the Indians use violence, then the Spanish may repel them forcibly. If the Indians seek to destroy them, the Spanish may resort to war. See section 3 of *De Indis*, wherein these matters are treated in considerable detail.

[137]See also "Just-War Thinking in the Late-Medieval and Early-Modern Period," chap. 3 of Charles, *Between Pacifism and Jihad*, esp. 56–60.

[138]Hugo Grotius, *The Law of War and Peace*, trans. R. L. Loomis (Roslyn, NY: Walter J. Black, 1949), 1.1.

which is morally repugnant, such as human oppression. This mediating position, between militarism and pacifism, for him is wisdom. It is wisdom insofar as it recognizes that peace is not the mere absence of conflict but the fruit of a justly ordered society, and because government, with all its faults, has a critical role in restraining evil in the present world.[139] Given these assumptions, Grotius sets forth in considerable detail moral criteria that are applicable to all nations in discerning whether to use coercive force (*jus ad bellum*) and how such might be applied (*jus in bello*).[140] The importance of a thinker such as Grotius lies not only in his ability to discern the moral obligations of justice, but also in the fact that he lays the foundation for just relations among nations—a foundation that is applicable to our own day and qualifies Grotius, among political scientists, as the "father of international relations."[141]

From Augustine onward to the present, the development of just-war thinking in Christian tradition emanates from these two fundamental burdens: when resorting to force is justified and how to use and apply force morally, or, in two words, permission and limitation.[142] Justice, regardless of its context, demands both permission and limits. And those limits have upper as well as lower restrictions. This is decidedly *not* the case for militarism, crusade/jihad, or the imperialist spirit.[143]

---

[139]Ibid., 2.9.

[140]For a war to be just, Grotius believed, six criteria are necessary: just cause, sovereign authority, proportionality, formal declaration of war, reasonable chance of success, and last resort (ibid., 2.1–3.1). For an excellent—and quite accessible—discussion of Grotius's just-war criteria as they apply in a more contemporary context, see Christopher, *The Ethics of War and Peace*, 81–103.

[141]For further discussion of Grotius's contributions, see Charles, *Between Pacifism and Jihad*, 62–66.

[142]Ethicist Paul Ramsey, in the introduction of *War and the Christian Conscience: How Shall Modern War Be Conducted Justly?* (Durham, NC: Duke University Press, 1961), uses these two terms to demarcate just-war thinking.

[143]It bears reiterating that the concern of some that just-war thinking might serve as a pretext for the crusading or imperialist spirit is legitimate to the extent that they sincerely wish to avoid condoning violence, as the church on occasion has done. But it is illegitimate when that concern itself is a pretext for a secular fundamentalism or a particular political viewpoint in current American cultural life. Strangely, the present is a moment of conspicuous paranoia in American politics, as a spate of recent alarmist books on "American theocracy" indicates—titles such as *American Theocracy: The Peril and Politics of Radical Religion, Kingdom Coming: The Rise of Christian Nationalism, Thy Kingdom Come: How the Religious Right Distorts the Faith and Threatens America*, and *The Baptizing of America: The Religious Right's Plans for the Rest of Us*. The terms *theocracy* and *theocrat*, as one observer has correctly noted, are currently being lobbed by bomb-throwing columnists, cultural commentators, and political "centrists" in a way that is troubling. On their account, which casts religious conservatives as mullahs and proto-fascists, America is poised to fall into the hands of a new breed of ayatollahs (one writer even speaks of an "Evangelical Taliban"). This sort of alarmist rhetoric calls into question the intellectual honesty of those employing it. In their view, orthodox religion has no business being in the marketplace, and issuing apocalyptic warnings about "theocracy" seems to be the most effective way of keeping it out. See in this regard Ross Douthat, "Theocracy, Theocracy, Theocracy," *First Things* 165 (August–September 2006): 23–30.

Q. 29 What effect did the Protestant Reformation have on the church's understanding of war and military service?

In a very generic sense, one of the effects of Protestant Reformational thinking was its accent on work, vocation, and calling. The Reformers emphasized that the Lord bids each one of us to a particular calling and therefore appoints to us duties that accord with our particular giftings and abilities, over which he has made us stewards. This accent struck at the heart of the clergy-laity divide, which was characteristic of broader medieval life but which in seed form was manifest early in the Patristic era.[144]

Each person, according to early Protestant thought, has "his own kind of living assigned to him by the Lord as a sort of sentry post so that he may not heedlessly wander about throughout life."[145] Divine callings extend to any number of vocations. They extend from magistrates to laborers to heads of households; nothing, provided it is not proscribed by the natural law as mirrored in the Ten Commandments, falls outside of divine "assignment." Monks and magistrates alike can serve God. Whatever is done out of a motivation to honor God and serve others is legitimate in and of itself. The Protestant Reformers' double emphasis that God gives every person diverse abilities and that these giftings correspond to one's calling served as a powerful impetus toward renewal both in the church and in broader culture. All work, in light of creation, is valuable service.

For the average layperson, this conviction has important implications. Work is not to be judged by its outer appearance, that is, by its sense of social usefulness or prestige. Rather, all work is dignified in God's sight, based on creation. Therefore, we must resist social pressure, cultural currents, even theological trends that might cause us to view some lines of work as inferior. No line of work, no type of vocation, falls outside of Christian calling; any task, when approached in faith, is to "be reckoned very precious in God's sight." In addition,

---

[144]Whether we consider Tertullian, for whom "Athens" and "Jerusalem" remain irreconcilable, or Eusebius, who drew a distinction between what is "perfect" and "permissible," or medieval life in general, we can appreciate the "protest" by Protestant Reformers to the extent that they viewed all vocations as dignified. One social critic characterizes the "sacred" versus "secular" dualism in terms of "Catholic" and "Protestant" forms of distortion. See Os Guinness, *The Call* (Nashville: Thomas Nelson, 2003), 32–41. While this portrayal has its weaknesses, it is nonetheless useful.

[145]John Calvin, *Institutes of the Christian Religion*, ed. John T. McNeill, trans. Ford Lewis Battles (Philadelphia: Westminster Press, 1960), 3.10.6.

this renewal of thinking about work and vocation invigorates daily life for each person, regardless of the task to which he or she is called. Calvin thus could write, "A man of obscure station will lead a private life ungrudgingly so as not to leave the rank in which he has been placed by God."[146] Every person, thus conceived, "will bear and swallow the discomforts, vexations, weariness, and anxieties in his way of life, when he has been persuaded that the burden was laid upon him by God." From this awareness arises a very important consolation in the Christian's life, as Calvin sees it: "No task will be so sordid and base, provided you obey your calling in it, that it will not shine and be reckoned very precious in God's sight."[147]

Among Christians—be they Roman Catholic, Orthodox, or Protestant—the nature of calling and vocation has not infrequently been perverted by a dualistic type of thinking between "spiritual" and "secular" forms of work. Among the church fathers, numerous examples of the former beckon us, perhaps the most famous being Tertullian (late second century), whose famous question "What does Athens have to do with Jerusalem?" epitomizes the sacred-secular dichotomy that remains in some Protestant evangelical circles yet today.

Because the Protestant Reformers assumed the natural law as a moral-theological bedrock in their system, they maintained ethical continuity with their Roman Catholic counterparts.[148] It is accurate, and critically important, to insist that the Reformation controversies with the Roman Catholic Church were foremost *theological and not ethical*. Where Protestant Reformers represent a shift is, for example, their desire to redefine the medieval distinction between clergy and laity. The implication of this reality is simple yet far-reaching: because all vocations rank the same before God in terms of dignity, *all realms of human activity* are valid realms of service and productivity, whether as teachers, medical scientists, politicians and magistrates, economists, legal theorists, manufacturers, craftsmen, or soldiers and law-enforcement officers. There is no difference between monk or

---

[146]Ibid.
[147]Ibid.
[148]The protest of the magisterial Protestant Reformers in the sixteenth century, it needs emphasis, was foremost *theological* and not ethical in its constitution. That is, they retained, with their Catholic counterparts, the affirmation of the natural law as part of God's general revelation to believer and unbeliever alike, and thus, a reflection of a moral universe. See Stephen J. Grabill, *Rediscovering the Natural Law in Reformed Theological Ethics*, Emory University Studies in Law and Religion (Grand Rapids: Eerdmans, 2006); Charles, "Protestants and Natural Law," 33–38; and Charles, *Retrieving the Natural Law*, 111–55.

magistrate. Christians can carry out obedience to God, whether as butchers or bakers or candlestick makers, whether as magistrates or silversmiths or soldiers.[149]

Q. 30 What were Luther's views on war and military service?

Luther has much to say about the military vocation, and his views are on display in several of his writings.[150] Perhaps none of these mirrors his understanding of vocational calling so clearly while simultaneously showing a markedly pastoral side as does *Whether Soldiers, Too, Can Be Saved*,[151] written to a knight and personal friend, Assa von Kram. Therein Luther extends a previous conversation with von Kram in which issues of personal conscience were discussed. As the title suggests, not a few laypersons in his own day struggled to reconcile their work in the marketplace of daily life with their Christian faith, and among these, many soldiers struggled to reconcile their profession with Christian faith.[152] Luther acknowledges that not a few soldiers either are offended by their vocation or have strong doubts. In fact, some "have completely given themselves up for lost that they no longer even ask questions about God and throw both their souls and their consciences to the winds."[153]

Luther's argument, as developed in response to his friend, consists of several planks. He finds it necessary (1) to distinguish between an office or occupation and the person filling it; (2) to ground the purpose

[149]This emphasis, revolutionary as it was in the sixteen century, cannot be called new. Humans were created to do work *before the fall*, that is to say, prior to the curse that was found. Therefore, work of any sort is *not* a curse but rather that for which we have been created and in which we are satisfied.

[150]See particularly the treatises *Temporal Authority: To What Extent It Should Be Obeyed*, *On War against the Turk*, and *Whether Soldiers, Too, Can Be Saved*.

[151]See *Luther's Works* (hereafter *L.W.*), ed. Jaroslav Pelikan and Helmut Lehmann (Philadelphia: Fortress, 1967), 46:91–129.

[152]It is helpful to recall that Duke Frederick, the founder of the University of Wittenberg, not only provided Luther with a home in which to live but also was a major financial supporter of Luther during his tenure as a professor. The dualistic, clergy-versus-laity mindset that not only characterized Luther's day but can surface in any era tends to minimize Frederick's role. Such thinking may be inclined to view benefactors of any era, particularly if they are magistrates or governing authorities, as performing less than a spiritual service. And what shall we say of another magistrate, the mayor of Wittenberg, whose financial contributions allowed Philip Melanchthon's home to be renovated, or Lucas Cranach, the banker who translated and printed Luther's *Ninety-Five Theses*? While the clergy-laity divide can be found in any generation, it goes without saying that attitudes regarding vocation have changed dramatically since the sixteenth century, as John Paul II's 1981 encyclical on human work, *Laborem Exercens*, makes abundantly clear.

[153]*L.W.* 46:93.

and use of the sword in Pauline and Petrine theology; (3) to reconcile the seeming incompatible use of lethal force with being a Christian; and (4) to harmonize the epistolary material of the New Testament with the teaching of Jesus in the Gospels, since often the two are set in opposition. These are necessary qualifications before Luther treats individual tactical questions regarding going to war. Each of the qualifying arguments requires some comment.

Because his friend is concerned to maintain a clear conscience, Luther wishes to demonstrate that faith and fear are antithetical. If his friend worries—or truly believes—that military service is disobedience, then he will be unable to serve in his vocation with courage, boldness, and a good conscience. Thus, the first order of business, according to Luther, is to be sure of those forces that mold the conscience and Christian conviction, and to be cognizant of what the Scriptures teach. In this way, insists Luther, the knight (not to mention others who with him enter military conflict) is sure to lose neither God's favor nor eternal life.

In the first place, Luther distinguishes between an occupation and the person who fills it, that is, between a work or duty and the man who performs it. One can do this only if one affirms the role of the magistrate and the function of the sword as being divinely instituted for the purposes of punishing evil and protecting the good (Rom. 13:1–4; 1 Pet. 2:13–14).[154] The very fact that this has been ordained by God is "powerful and sufficient proof" for Luther that war and those necessities that accompany wartime "have been instituted by God." "What else," Luther asks, "is war but the punishment of wrong and evil?" "Why does anyone go to war, except because he desires peace and obedience?"[155]

But there is a problem. An occupation can be good and right in and of itself and yet effect wrong because of the character of the person filling it. Luther uses two types of illustration: a judgeship and a marriage. The office of a judge, which "is a valuable divine office," can be used for good or bad. And a marriage, which per se is "precious

---

[154]Luther believes that God has established two kinds of government among human beings. The one is spiritual and has no sword; rather it relies on the Word to change and make righteous. The other is by means of the magistrate, who administers justice through the sword. And even though this is not a form of righteousness that leads to eternal life, Luther acknowledges that the aim of the governing authorities is the preservation of temporal peace among men. God advances both forms of justice, the internal and the external.

[155]L.W. 46:95.

and godly," nevertheless has "many rascals and scoundrels" who are part of it. Luther applies the same logic to being a soldier: of itself the occupation is valuable and necessary, but at the same time it is dependent on what kind of person fills it and to what end it is directed.

Relatedly, can a soldier, who must go to war, engage in killing? Is this work "sinful or unjust"? And should it produce a bad conscience before God? Must a Christian always and only do no harm? Clearly, for Luther, this office "can nevertheless become evil and unjust." Surely, slaying would not seem to be a work of charity, and yet Luther argues that in fact it *may* be. He maintains, just as Augustine did, that charity wills *what is best both for society and for the wrongdoer.* Luther uses an analogy to make the point. A doctor, who is good and performs an important service, in extreme cases might be required to amputate a limb that is diseased. Based on what meets the eye, this would appear cruel and merciless. However, for medical reasons this extreme action is necessary to save the rest of the body and work for the greater good. The soldier, says Luther, performs a similar valuable service in punishing the wicked by lethal force, even when "it seems an un-Christian work completely contrary to Christian love." Yet, in pondering how the work of the soldier "protects the good and keeps and preserves wife and child, house and farm, property, and honor and peace," Luther sees how valuable this occupation really is.[156]

Luther is under no illusions. He acknowledges that war is a great plague; this is undeniable. He does, however, remind his readers that they should consider how great the plague is that is actually prevented by war. In the end, he argues, one must look at the office of the soldier—an office that exists to "keep the peace"—and see it as "useful to the world as eating and drinking or any other work."[157]

But what about abuse? What about those who kill needlessly and defile the office of soldier? Luther recognizes this possibility and states that this is the fault of the person, not the office. And there are many who soldier for precisely the wrong reasons, for example, mercenaries. Wrong motives and wrong character notwithstanding, just wars *may* be necessary in a world of injustice and unjust peace. In support of his conviction that the profession of military service is honorable and necessary, Luther, like Augustine and Aquinas before

---

[156]*L.W.* 46:94, 95, 96.
[157]*L.W.* 46:96–97.

him and just-war theorists thereafter, cites John the Baptist. When soldiers came to him with questions, the Baptist did not condemn their vocation or call them out of military service. Rather, he exhorted them toward justice and contentment. That is, he denounced *abuse* of the office but not the office itself. The abuse, Luther insists, does not affect the office.

On a second occasion in *Whether Soldiers*, Luther finds recourse in John the Baptist, noting two things about the text of Luke 3. The Baptist "confirms the right" of soldiers to their pay and to their duties as soldiers.

Despite his relatively high view of the political authorities, Luther cannot be accused of being a crusader type, even when in his day the Ottoman Empire had extended as far as Hungary. He condemned Christian attempts, usually by popes, to incite war in the name of Christ. We should recall, too, his response to the Peasant Revolt. The peasants, it should be remembered, were sympathetic to his teachings. Yet, despite the excesses of both the church and the authorities, Luther advocated suppressing the peasants when they decided to turn violent. In *Against the Robbing and Murdering Hordes of Peasants*, he writes: "If [the ruler] does not fulfill the duties of his office by punishing some and protecting others, he commits as great a sin before God as when someone who has not been given the sword commits murder."[158]

Consistent with Ambrose, Augustine, and Aquinas before him, Luther believes that bearing the sword is not inconsistent with Christian discipleship. It is not, he writes in *Temporal Authority*, for the purpose of "avenging yourself or returning evil for evil, but for the good of your neighbor and for the maintenance of the safety and peace of others."[159] Luther allows little room for misinterpretation: "In what concerns you and yours, you govern yourself according to love and tolerate no injustice toward your neighbor. The gospel does not forbid this; in fact, in other places [i.e., other than Matt. 5:39] it actually commands it." And on behalf of others, Luther stresses, a Christian *may and should* seek retribution, justice, protection, and help, doing all that is possible to achieve it.[160]

---

[158]*L.W.* 46:53.
[159]Ibid., 45:96.
[160]Ibid., 45:96, 101.

Q. 31   What were Calvin's views on war and peace?

In his *Institutes of the Christian Religion* Calvin develops more explicitly than Luther the link between Scripture and natural moral law—a link that he believes to be critical to the preservation of civil society.[161] The enactment of justice through civil law is predicated on the moral law, which God has woven into the fabric of creation. If the moral law of God forbids all Christians to participate in killing, then how can it possibly be, asks Calvin, that a magistrate, who is responsible to wield the sword (Rom. 13:3–4), might be a pious individual? If, however, we understand that in the infliction of punishment the magistrate is not acting *of his own accord*, but in fact is executing justice as God requires of him, then the issue is not an embarrassment to the Christian. Not all forms of killing, Calvin maintains, are punishable. For example, it is not murder for the one governing to utilize the sword in obedience to heaven. There is "no valid objection to the infliction of public vengeance, unless the justice of God be restrained from the punishment of crimes."[162] Citing Romans 13:4, Calvin speaks approvingly of Moses and David, who with integrity obeyed the Lord.

If we raise the objection that "the New Testament contains no precept or example, which proves war to be lawful to Christians," Calvin responds in Augustinian fashion. If Christian faith condemns participation in all wars, then the soldiers who inquired of the Baptist about their souls "ought rather to have been directed to cast away their arms, and entirely renounce the military profession." But much to the contrary, the advice given to them is to perform their work with the proper motivation. "An injunction to be content with their wages," observes Calvin, "was certainly not a prohibition of the military life."[163]

But given Calvin's seemingly uncritical view of the powers, someone is likely to raise the charge of unnecessary cruelty and lay it at Calvin's feet. "I am not an advocate for unnecessary cruelty," Calvin insists. Contrarily, it behooves the magistrate to be on his guard

---

[161] Much of Calvin's discussion of war and duties of the state is found in 4.20.1–12. See also Daniel Pellerin, "Calvin: Militant or Man of Peace?" *The Review of Politics* 65, no. 1 (Winter 2003): 35–59.
[162] *Institutes of the Christian Religion*, trans. John Allen (Philadelphia: Presbyterian Board of Publication, 1844), 4.20.10.
[163] Ibid., 4.20.12.

against the twin errors of undermining justice, on the one hand, and excessive cruelty, on the other. He must not, "by excessive severity, wound rather than heal; or, through a superstitious affectation of clemency, fall into a mistaken humanity, which is the worst kind of cruelty, by indulging a weak and ill-judged lenity, to the detriment of multitudes."[164]

Calvin extends the moral reasoning of preserving civil society beyond mere criminal justice. Because it is sometimes necessary for those in authority publicly to take up the sword against individuals or parties who perpetrate evil, Calvin observes, "the same reason will lead us to infer the lawfulness of wars which are undertaken for this end." Kings and nations too "have been entrusted with power to preserve the tranquility of their own territories, to suppress the seditious tumults of disturbers, to succour the victims of oppression, and to punish crimes." If they are to be "the guardians and defenders of the laws," argues Calvin, it is incumbent upon them "to defeat the efforts of all by whose injustice the discipline of the laws is corrupted."[165] There is no difference between robbers who plunder private citizens and robber nations who do the same on a larger scale.

As noted above, Calvin—more so than Luther—argues for the coercive powers of the state on the basis of the natural law, but in his view, many religious people fail to see the importance of law as a basic concept. Laws, he writes, are the "strong nerves of civil polity," or, in the words of Cicero, "the souls of states," without which governing cannot subsist.[166] Calvin is aware that many religious believers deny that a state is (and must be) well constituted by laws, which have their basis in the "law of the nations" (i.e., the natural law). But this rejection or suspicion on the part of pious folks is "dangerous" to the extent that it fully misses an important part of creation. For this reason, Calvin finds it necessary to discuss the nature of law, making a threefold distinction between moral, ceremonial, and judicial law, in order to demonstrate what type of law remains abiding and what is obsolete.

What lies behind all moral norms is abiding and universally present: "It is a fact that the law of God which we call the moral law is nothing else than a testimony of natural law and of that conscience which God

---

[164]Ibid., 4.20.10.
[165]Ibid., 4.20.11.
[166]Ibid., 4.20.14.

has engraved upon the minds of men." This law of nature must be "the goal and rule and limit of all laws."[167] What we call the Ten Commandments delineates the contours of the natural moral law. The moral law forbids stealing—everywhere, at all times, and for all people. This was true of the Jews, it was true of the Romans, and it is true today. The same can be said of adultery, false witness, and murder.[168]

Civil law, in turn, is predicated on the natural moral law and the revealed truth of Scripture. It is "the dictate both of natural equity, and of the nature of the office," therefore, that "princes are armed, not only to restrain the crimes of private individuals by judicial punishments, but also to defend the territories committed to their charge by going to war against any hostile aggression."[169]

Can the sword be abused or unjust? By all means, says Calvin. Here the authorities "ought to be very cautious." If retribution is to be inflicted, it is "not to be precipitated with anger, exasperated with hatred, or inflamed with implacable severity."[170] Rather, those bearing the sword should "commiserate our common nature even in him whom they punish for his crime."[171] In addition to just cause, Calvin cites right intent and last resort as moral criteria for going to war: "the evident object of war ought to be the restoration of peace, [and] certainly we ought to make every other attempt before we have recourse to the decision of arms." Otherwise, he notes, the authorities "grossly abuse their power."[172]

Q. 32 What about the "radical Reformation"? Not all Protestant Reformers shared the views of the high Reformers like Luther and Calvin.

While it is true that not all Protestants shared the views of the magisterial Reformers on military service and war, most did.[173] One notable exception is the sixteenth-century Ana-

---

[167]*Institutes*, trans. Battles, 4.20.16.
[168]Ibid.
[169]*Institutes*, trans. Allen, 4.20.11.
[170]Ibid., 4.20.12.
[171]Ibid., quoting Augustine.
[172]Ibid.
[173]Among contemporaries of the Reformers, Erasmus is a most interesting profile. He was pacifist to the extent that he believed Christian influence should restore and restrain the internal workings of the state, resulting in the ideal of abolishing war. Yet, in the international context he believed that war

baptist movement, which rejected the views of Luther and Calvin (and the Swiss Reformer Zwingli, who stood in basic agreement with them) regarding Christian participation in the affairs of the state. The separation and pacifism of the early Anabaptists, it should be emphasized, did not occur in a social or political vacuum; indeed, there were very good reasons for it. It is against the background of their rejection and persecution by both Catholics and Protestants that the position of the Swiss Brethren (as the earliest Anabaptists came to be known) on civil society and its use of the sword is best understood. Writes one historian: "They became separatists in part because of the persecution suffered at the hands of civil authorities backed up by . . . Reformers and Catholics; separation from the affairs of these regimes was thus an attempt to distance themselves from the evil use of power that was, in part, directed toward them."[174]

Where historic Anabaptists differ from many contemporary Anabaptist pacifists, however, is in their general orientation toward the political powers. Anabaptist writers today, particularly Anabaptists within the academy, tend to have a more negative, apocalyptic view of governing authorities. That is, they tend to have deep suspicions of the Pauline teaching in Romans 13 that political power is divinely instituted, and that coercive force—"the sword" of Romans 13:4—is a necessary expression of that authority for the preservation of the moral-social order.[175] As evidenced by the sixth of seven articles of the Schleitheim Confession, penned in 1527 as a brief summary of Anabaptist beliefs, historic Anabaptism affirms that the sword is ordained by God in the hand of the authorities for the twin purposes of punishment and protection, even when it is believed that Christians cannot participate in those tasks:

> We are agreed as follows concerning the sword: The sword is ordained of God outside the perfection of Christ. It punishes and puts to death, and guards and protects the good. In the Law, the sword was ordained for the punishment of the wicked and for their

---

waged against the "Turks" was justifiable. For a thorough examination of the seeming inconsistencies in Erasmian thought, see José A. Fernández, "Erasmus on the Just War," *Journal of the History of Ideas* 34, no. 2 (1973): 209–26.

[174]Johnson, *The Quest for Peace*, 164.

[175]Arguably the most influential Anabaptist theologian of the latter twentieth century, John Howard Yoder, views Revelation 13 and not the classic text of Romans 13 as normative of the state. This animates in particular his important work *The Politics of Jesus*, 2nd ed. (Grand Rapids: Eerdmans, 1994), though it is a recurring subtheme in numerous of his writings.

death, and the same [sword] is [now] ordained to be used by the worldly magistrates. (Art. 6)[176]

Notwithstanding the early Anabaptists' absolute separation, while the Schleitheim Confession expressly forbids the Christian believer to use violent force, it does *not* reject violence per se in the hand of the magistrate.[177]

The writings of Menno Simons (1496–1561) have provided broader theological justification for Anabaptist beliefs to the present day. Simons articulates a two-kingdom approach to Christian loyalties, by which it was understood that the spiritual and the temporal are separate, with believers' allegiance being to the heavenly order.[178] This separation, in turn, precludes participation in any form of activity that might be construed as compromise from conflation of the two realms. Hence, Anabaptists since the sixteenth century, for religious reasons, not only abstain from political involvement and embrace nonviolence, but also abstain from all forms of civil service and most forms of public service, including military service.[179]

Q. 33 Were the Crusades examples of the just-war tradition?

The Crusades do not reflect the tenets of the just-war tradition in its classical expression, although aspects of the tradition were debated during the centuries in which the Crusades occurred. In November of 1095, the ecclesiastical Council of Clermont, representing much of Western Christendom, declared: "Whoever for devotion alone, not to gain honour or money, goes to Jerusalem to liberate the Church of God can substitute this journey

---

[176]We are dependent on the translation of "The Schleitheim Confession of Faith" by J. C. Wenger in *Glimpses of Mennonite History* (Scottdale, PA: Mennonite Publishing House, 1940), 206–13.

[177]One of us (Daryl) writes with an understanding of Anabaptism from the inside, having grown up in the Mennonite tradition.

[178]This two-kingdom understanding is not to be confused with that of Luther, for whom it meant something very different, and who acknowledged dual allegiances in the present life.

[179]In identifying civil and public service, we refer to vocations that *directly* have to do with maintaining civil society—e.g., government, politics, and government-related work—as well as vocations that are viewed as *indirectly* contributing to our social structures—e.g., economics, social science, physical science, security, law and legal theory, and corporate interests. This stands in stark contrast to the Anabaptist commitment to provide social assistance through relief, charity, and welfare, which is almost always done privately through their churches and not through public or governmental vehicles. To their great credit, Anabaptists provide social assistance in a variety of ways today that have made them a model to the body of Christ, along with Catholic Charities.

for all penance."[180] With these words a new era of violence and war-fare emerged in Europe and the Middle East—one using holy war to further Christianity. Although war was not new in Christian history, linking it with penance and spiritual vitality was unique. Subsequently, the idea emerged that a "holy" war (the term *crusade* was used only later) was acceptable and justifiable when it was understood as directly commanded by God and proclaimed by the papacy.[181]

When Pope Urban II preached the crusade, calling upon Christians in the West to aid Christians in the Byzantine East and recover Jeru-salem from Islamic control,[182] the crowds are said to have responded with cries of *Deus lo volt!*—"God wills it!" These words became a common battle cry during the bloody centuries of the Crusades, cen-turies during which Christians slaughtered both non-Christians and Christians, and Christians were slaughtered by non-Christians.

Crusade historian Jonathan Riley-Smith defines the Crusades as "war-pilgrimages proclaimed by the Popes on Christ's behalf and waged for the recovery of Christian territory or people, or in their defense."[183] Throughout the era of the Crusades one encounters both adherence to the tenets of the just-war tradition—for example, just cause—and neglect of the tradition. This was true of both theologians and practitioners. The result was what we might surmise: a mixture of ideas and responses as to the role of faith and force. This has led students of the medieval era such as Frederick H. Russell to conclude the following:

> The crusade as a juridical institution existed only in the Middle Ages, and was a *sui generis* synthesis of the pilgrimage, the vow, the holy war and the just war that has continued to defy attempts at neat analysis. Within the just war the crusade coexisted uneasily at best, partly because there was no clear precedent to serve as an

---

[180]Cited in Christopher Tyerman, *The Crusades: A Very Short Introduction* (Oxford: Oxford University Press, 2004), 12.

[181]In this regard, see the commentary offered by Alex J. Bellamy, *Just Wars: From Cicero to Iraq* (Cambridge: Polity Press, 2006), 44–45.

[182]In our own day, one cannot but notice the moralistic posturing by writers—many of them Chris-tian—over the impact of the Crusades. As historian Robert Louis Wilken helpfully reminds us, out of ignorance many conveniently overlook the fact that the Crusades were part of a response against the occupation of lands that had been Christian for centuries before the arrival of Islam. This inconvenient perspective, it needs reiterating, does not comport well with the cultural *Zeitgeist*—both within and outside the academy—as the fear of perceived imperialism is far greater than the will to resist evil on behalf of the persecuted and oppressed.

[183]Jonathan Riley-Smith, "Rethinking the Crusades," *First Things* (March 2003): 20. For an excellent and standard work on the subject, see Riley-Smith's *The Crusades: A Short History* (New Haven, CT: Yale University Press, 1987).

unambiguous guide. . . . From their informed vantage points ecclesiastical writers certainly were aware of the Church's directive role in the various crusades within and without Europe, but they were reluctant to consider the crusading movement explicitly in legal or theological commentaries.[184]

This mixed response illustrates that the just-war tradition was both forgotten and refined over time in the midst of many historical variables and circumstances. In this sense we may speak of a "fluid" tradition, even when its guiding moral principles remain nonfluid and transcend any particular era.

Arguably the most significant aspect of the just-war tradition considered during the era of the Crusades was the medieval debate over just cause for war. Building on earlier Roman and Christian thought, medieval just-war thought accepted as just cause for war (1) defense against wrongful acts in progress, (2) punishment of past wrongful acts, and (3) recovery of property lost as a result of wrongful acts. These three reasons were intermingled with religious ideas of the prince as the minister of God to carry out justice (based on interpretation of Rom. 13:4) and the defense of religion as an aspect of just cause and one of the many things to be defended, along with defense of individuals and defense of property. The shift to defense of religion as an element in defensive war resulted in a blurring of offensive and defensive acts of war. James Turner Johnson observes:

> Defense of religion, moreover, could entail military action even when the other party was not itself attacking or threatening attack: "The enemies of the Church are to be coerced even by war," wrote the canonist Gratian, quoting from Augustine, who had used this argument to urge the use of the Roman army against the Donatist schismatics (Gratian, *Decretum 2.23.8.48*). This line of reasoning blurred the distinction between offensive and defensive use of force more thoroughly than that between preemptive and reactive resort to force.[185]

This blurring of ideas permitted coercive use of force against enemies of the church, whether they were within Christendom but deemed her-

---

[184]Russell, *The Just War in the Middle Ages*, 294–95.
[185]James Turner Johnson, *The Holy War Idea in Western and Islamic Traditions* (University Park: Pennsylvania State University Press, 1997), 53.

etics or outside Christendom, such as Muslims or other non-Christians. Consequently, for some, the medieval notion of a crusade or holy war blended into "just war."[186]

Roughly concurrent with the Crusades were important developments in political theory. One significant debate concerned varied interpretations of Augustine's *City of God* as to the proper roles of princes and popes in maintaining the political community. Eventually, the right of the prince as the leader of secular society to make war for religious as well as political reasons achieved ascendancy. This, then, set a pattern that lasted for several hundred years until the conclusion of the Thirty Years War (1648).[187]

Political ramifications of the Crusades still echo in today's world, and in the twenty-first century they become a rhetorical rallying point for Muslim extremists, gaining prominence not previously held in Islamic and Arab historiography.[188] While the Crusades are only one episode in the long history of warfare, they provide a useful case study for how issues of faith and force overlap and what unfortunate consequences follow from an improper alliance of the two.

Q. 34 Isn't the just-war position really just a Western and European justification for war?

Though notions of justified intervention predate Christian reflection on war and peace, the just-war tradition is firmly and historically rooted in Christian moral-political thought and in the history of warfare in the West. The tradition arose not in a cultural or moral vacuum, but in the crucible of violence, upheaval, and injustices that gave rise to values that contributed to the foundations of Western civilization. Thus, it is accurate to observe the historical particularity of this tradition, even when it must be stressed that the values underlying the tradition are universal in application and affect all people in all ages. James Turner Johnson writes:

---

[186]Ibid., 53–54. See also 174–75, where Johnson compares nonreligious just wars with their religious counterpart (e.g., the Crusades).

[187]So ibid., 55.

[188]This is the view of Bernard Lewis, *Islam and the West* (New York: Oxford University Press, 1993), 12–13.

> The just war idea is not free-floating, to be given whatever content one may think appropriate in whatever context. Understanding its meaning means engagement with the tradition out of which it comes and entering into dialog with the classical statement of the just war idea within that tradition. . . . Just war tradition has to do with defining the possible good use of force, not finding exceptional cases when it is possible to use something inherently evil (force) for the purposes of good.[189]

Therefore, thinking about warfare within the just-war tradition means wrestling with ideas and values that are upheld because they are considered greater than any individual, nation, philosophical perspective, or era.

It is also important to remember that the history of European warfare and the history of the just-war tradition are not identical or even complementary. The Crusades, the Spanish Inquisition, the wars of religion during the sixteenth and seventeenth centuries, and wars associated with colonial expansion are but a few of the many violent episodes in European history that often failed to uphold the values and goals of the just-war tradition.[190]

It is important for the average reader, who may be unacquainted with the early-modern contributions of Vitoria, Suárez, or Grotius to the just-war tradition, to grasp the impact of these developments to law and international relations. These contributions are felt to the present day and include, at the most basic level, an approach to international law that is grounded in universal "laws of humanity," rooted in the natural, by which international relations might be governed, and concomitantly, in rules of international conduct of war that are clearly defined according to *jus ad bellum* and *jus in bello* requirements. Summarizing the significance of early-modern Christian just-war thinkers for the present day, one student of the tradition writes:

> The just war theory has repudiated religious and ideological causes for going to war. . . . All people have equal rights by virtue of their common humanity. Justice insists that we treat equals equally. Reli-

---

[189]James Turner Johnson, *The War to Oust Saddam Hussein: Just War and the New Face of Conflict* (Lanham, MD: Rowman & Littlefield, 2005), 35–36.

[190]For recent evaluation of religion and European warfare, see Michael Burleigh, *Earthly Powers: Religion and Politics in Europe from the French Revolution to the Great War* (New York: Harper-Collins, 2005), and *Sacred Causes: Religion and Politics from the European Dictators to Al Qaeda* (New York: HarperCollins, 2006).

gious differences and causes are therefore as irrelevant to the pursuit of justice as are differences of race or culture or economic status. Justice cannot allow for morally irrelevant considerations.[191]

In its motivation, just-war moral reasoning struggles to discern the moral obligations of justice where it may apply and to provide a framework for just relations among nations that is applicable everywhere and at all times.

Q. 35 How was the American Revolution understood from the standpoint of war?

Christianity played a prominent role both in helping to shape the worldview of many during the Revolutionary period and in providing spiritual and intellectual strength for the varying responses to the war. When the American colonies declared independence from the British, there were mixed responses among Christians in the colonies. No unanimity existed among colonial Christians regarding the validity of the war theologically or politically, nor was there to be found a wider consensus about participation in the ensuing political and military struggles. Generally, just-war thinking was not a prevailing perspective among American colonial Christian clergy or laity. Nor was it prominent in the political thought of non-Christian political activists.[192]

American colonists struggled less with the theoretical problem of war than they did with the issue of rebellion. Given the broader theological concerns about rebellion against the backdrop of a monarch who was perceived as divinely appointed, they drew upon the historical precedent of the English Revolution (ca. 1639–1688) and a political philosophy derived principally from the writings of John Locke. In Locke's thinking, the concept of sovereignty was rooted in the people of the state rather than the monarchy. Lockean perspectives on sovereignty, coupled with a strongly Puritan heritage, helped con-

---

[191]Arthur F. Holmes, "A Just War Response," in Robert G. Clouse, ed., *War: Four Christian Views*, rev. ed. (Downers Grove, IL: InterVarsity, 1991), 182.
[192]On the intellectual sources and traditions for the war, see Bernard Bailyn, *The Ideological Origins of the American Revolution*, rev. ed. (Cambridge, MA: Harvard University Press, 1992).

dition colonial Christians for revolution.[193] When hostilities erupted, most Protestant evangelical clergy supported the colonial war effort,[194] a fact that has led George Marsden to note:

> As soon as we look at the rationale offered to justify the Revolutionary War, we should be struck by a most revealing feature of its justification. The American revolutionaries, despite the Christian profession of many of them and the Christian heritage of almost all of them, seem generally not to have felt any need to provide an elaborate rationale for resorting to violence and killing. . . . [They] seem to have regarded the resort to warfare as almost a matter of course. . . . But for the participants, the idea of shifting the resistance from an essentially nonviolent resistance to an essentially violent base required no special theoretical justification.[195]

Historian Mark Noll has identified four categories of religious response to the war. The first response was the patriotic response. Infused with the political values of the Whig worldview and religious values and heritage of Puritanism, many colonists readily joined the patriots seeking independence. Noll writes of their willingness to do so:

> The nurture Christians provided to the Revolution extended beyond the fact that many believers saw history, human fallibility, and public virtue in much the same way as the Whigs did. It took but little effort to align the Puritan belief in a higher law ordained by God and standing in judgment over all men with the Whig world view in which the positive law of particular nations was subservient to natural human rights and the laws of reason. The fact that the heir of the Puritan discovered this higher law in the written pages of Holy Scripture did not lessen his natural bent toward the Whig conception of proper government.[196]

---

[193]See Timothy George, "War and Peace in the Puritan Tradition," *Church History* 53, no. 4 (December 1984): 492–503.

[194]George Marsden, "The American Revolution: Partnership, 'Just Wars,' and Crusades," in *The Wars of America: Christian Views*, ed. Ronald A. Wells (Grand Rapids: Eerdmans, 1981), 22–23. See also Mark A. Noll, "The American Revolution and Protestant Evangelicalism," *Journal of Interdisciplinary History* 23, no. 3 (Winter 1993): 615–38; and Mark Valeri, "The New Divinity and the American Revolution," *The William and Mary Quarterly* (3rd Ser.) 46, no. 4 (October 1989): 741–69.

[195]Marsden, "The American Revolution," 12.

[196]Mark A. Noll, *Christians in the American Revolution* (Washington, DC: Christian University Press, 1977), 150–51.

Christian patriots participated in the fighting throughout the war and many clergy served as chaplains and soldiers.[197] Others preached sermons in the churches and the public forum supporting the soldiers and rallying public support for the revolutionary cause.[198]

A second response to the war was the reforming response. With the patriot response, it stood in support of the war. While it, too, drew from the Whig worldview and Puritan heritage, it differed to the degree that it presented a more critical spiritual and theological voice within the patriotic perspective. The sermons and views of the "reformers" were not subjugated to political concerns but rather were directed chiefly toward spiritual rebirth and the renewal of society (and notably, the eradication of slavery) in the midst of the war effort.[199] Noll writes of these particular leaders:

> Where other Calvinistic ministers felt no qualms about intermingling the verities of political liberty and the truths of Christian freedom, these individuals preserved a distinction between the two. All of them proved in the end to be faithful, in one degree or another, to the cause of colonial Patriotism. None of them, however, allowed that loyalty to displace a more intense loyalty to the Christian faith as they understood it. Nor did it push aside their deeply felt obligation to speak specifically Christian truth into Revolutionary society.[200]

These colonists supported the war but worked hard to maintain a viewpoint that did not allow theology to be consumed by politics.

The third colonial Christian response to the war belonged to those who remained loyal to Great Britain. Some of these loyalists stayed in the colonies while others departed willingly or unwillingly for Canada, England, or other parts of the British Empire.[201] Loyalists as well looked to their religious and political heritage, often Anglicanism and Methodism, for guidance in determining a proper response to the war. In all, 20–30 percent of the American colonists are thought to

---

[197]See Eugene Franklin Williams, *Soldiers of God—The Chaplains of the Revolutionary War* (New York: Carlton, 1975).
[198]See Ellis Sandoz, ed., *Political Sermons of the American Founding Era, 1730–1805*, 2 vols. (Indianapolis: Liberty Fund, 1991).
[199]Noll, *Christians in the American Revolution*, 80–81.
[200]Ibid., 102.
[201]See Mary Beth North, *The British-Americans: The Loyalist Exiles in England 1774–1789* (Boston: Little, Brown and Co., 1972); and North Callahan, *Royal Raiders: The Tories of the American Revolution* (Indianapolis: Bobbs-Merrill, 1963).

have supported the loyalist position.[202] Writes one American religious historian:

> Christian Loyalism during the Revolution was made up of many components. Christians who chose to resist the Patriotic tide did so as much for political, social, and cultural reasons as for explicitly religious ones. In this respect, however, they did not differ greatly from Christian Patriots who, more often than not, pledged allegiance to Patriotism for other than Christian motives. Neither Patriots nor Loyalists were reluctant to use religion as a means to enhance the appeal of political positions assumed for other than religious reasons.[203]

Loyalists were no less fervent in their views than others, and they often upheld their convictions in the midst of extreme hostility and great sacrifice.

The final response to the war was that of Christian pacifists. Looking beyond the political allegiances of the patriots and loyalists (and also drawing their scorn), these individuals condemned the war and participation therein regardless of political orientation. The most vocal pacifists were the Quakers, but others such as Mennonites, the Church of the Brethren, Moravians, and Schwenckfelders, in addition to individual members of other denominations, were among their ranks. Not infrequently, these pacifists ministered to the wounded and prisoners. Observes Noll: "The testimony of Christian pacifism was neither the most prominent nor the most vocal of Christian responses to the American Revolution, but without an understanding of its nature and expression, the history of Christians in the American Revolution is incomplete."[204]

Both preceding and during the American Revolution, many colonists believed that they had just cause to rebel and that they were acting in self-defense and self-preservation, at least politically. One may speak of a mood of reluctance among many of the clergy, with only a minority exhibiting a genuine crusading zeal.[205] While we may detect some alignment among colonial America with just-war principles in general, evidence that it was being articulated is difficult to find.

---

[202]Noll, *Christians in the American Revolution*, 103.
[203]Ibid., 122.
[204]Ibid., 147.
[205]Melvin B. Endy Jr., "Just War, Holy War, and Millennialism in Revolutionary America," *The William and Mary Quarterly* (3rd Ser.) 42, no. 1 (January 1985): 19.

Q. 36   How are we best to understand the American Civil War, and what were prevailing attitudes toward war?

Throughout the Civil War, leaders on both sides of the conflict claimed just cause for their engagement in the conflict. At the same time that aspects of the *jus ad bellum* tradition were claimed, frequently throughout the war, the *jus in bello* principles of discrimination and proportionality were not upheld. Americans in both the North and the South were experiencing war at a level that was different from earlier American conflicts.[206]

America's founders and framers had envisioned a nation that was to be different from European nations in terms of a unified spirit and a freedom from internal and external strife and warfare. Those hopes were shattered early as the colonies became embroiled in struggles with Native Americans, the French, and finally, the British. Three quarters of a century after gaining independence, and several wars later, Americans again turned to war, this time against each other. The long and bloody fratricidal struggle deeply affected Americans, changing the nation and shaping the values of its citizens for succeeding generations.

Political, moral, and theological debates about slavery were present from the colonial era onward. Throughout the first half of the nineteenth century one detects the presence of a reforming spirit that was directed at societal problems. Chief among these were prisons, asylums, and slavery. Fueled by a theological optimism that the eradication of these problems would hasten the physical kingdom of God, some reformers and Northern clergy soon focused on the abolition of slavery as the greatest need of the age. As a result of the mix of tensions between state and national leaders over rights, the westward expansion of the nation, and dissent over slavery in new territories and states, sharp disagreement eventually erupted into open violence. The result was a national bloodbath in which both sides claimed divine support, divine judgment, and divine victory.[207]

---

[206]Harry S. Stout, *Upon the Altar of the Nation: A Moral History of the Civil War* (New York: Viking, 2006), xiii-xiv.

[207]Ronald D. Rietveld, "The American Civil War: Millennial Hope, Political Chaos, and a Two-Sided 'Just War,'" in Ronald A. Wells, ed., *The Wars of America: Christian Views* (Grand Rapids: Eerdmans, 1981), 82–88.

Not only did the war split the nation ideologically and geographically, it also did so theologically and ecclesiastically. Several denominations divided along ideological and geographical boundaries. Once hostilities commenced, churches in the North and South supported their respective armies through prayer, sermons, chaplains, and organized philanthropy. Intense religious fervor and times of spiritual revival and renewal occurred in both armies.[208] Because both sides appealed to theology for support of their perspectives, it was only inevitable that these appeals created such intense theological debate that one is justified in speaking of a *theological* as well as a political crisis across the land. Thus Mark Noll: "From the historical record it is clear that the American Civil War generated a first-order theological crisis over how to interpret the Bible, how to understand the work of God in the world, and how to exercise the authority of theology in a democratic society."[209]

What was the particular influence of the clergy in sustaining and promoting prevailing war views? James H. Moorhead describes it in the following manner:

> Clergy of North and South found scriptural grounds for ardently supporting their respective causes. They preached that message unabashedly. America in the mid-nineteenth century was a culture drenched in the images of the Bible. The ministers' ability to justify war in the name of the sacred Book did much to mobilize popular support and to maintain that loyalty until bullets and disease had claimed more than six hundred thousand lives.[210]

In supporting the war effort, advocates in the North and South often turned the arguments and rhetoric into that of a crusade more than a just war. Both sides were confident that their cause was God's cause, that God would bring them victory rather than defeat, and that they were fighting in accordance with the will of God.[211] In consequence, just-war principles were set aside as war ravaged the nation,

---

[208]There has been much work done on the subject of religious faith in the military during the war. See, more recently, Steven E. Woodworth, *While God Is Marching On: The Religious World of Civil War Soldiers* (Lawrence: University Press of Kansas, 2001); and Benedict R. Maryniak and John Wesley Brinsfield Jr., *The Spirit Divided: Memoirs of Civil War Chaplains*, 2 vols. (Macon, GA: Mercer University Press, 2006–2007).

[209]Mark A. Noll, *The Civil War as a Theological Crisis* (Chapel Hill: The University of North Carolina Press, 2006), 162.

[210]James H. Moorhead, "Preaching the Holy War," *Christian History* 11, no. 1 (1932): 38–41.

[211]Stout, *Upon the Altar of the Nation*, 139–49.

leaving scars that are still visible in American society and culture. As divided Americans entered the conflict, both sides believed their cause was just. At the end of the conflict those beliefs were still strongly held in the North and South. "Winners and losers alike would concede almost anything, it seemed, except the idea that their internecine war was ultimately meaningless or unjust."[212]

Interpretations of the war continue in abundance nearly a century and a half later. Perhaps because it was a *civil* war, it has continued to draw the attention and imagination of Americans in ways that other wars have not. In particular, the leadership and spirituality of Civil War political and military leaders has been the focus of considerable scholarly attention. For those who wish to study the Civil War in order to understand its significance for issues of war and peace, Harry Stout's words provide a poignant reminder: "There are no ideal wars. Peace is the only ideal, and every war is at some level a perversion of it. In a less-than-ideal world, however, in which we sometimes labor under a moral imperative to war, we cannot afford to do less than demand a just war and a merciful outcome."[213]

Like the American Revolution, the Civil War was not caused by religion. Yet, it is impossible to ignore the role that religious faith played in intensifying political, popular, and military support for it.

---

[212]Ibid., 458.
[213]Ibid., 461.

PART 3

JUST-WAR TRADITION
AND THE STATESMAN

Q. 37 What are the core criteria for going to war according to just-war moral reasoning?

Because politicians and pundits alike often speak of "just war" without an awareness of the moral tradition that lies behind this designation, we must qualify not only the "just-war" usage but also the assumptions that undergird this usage. Just-war thought in its classic expression, we should emphasize, is not first and foremost about military tactics and strategy; nor is it about justifying military operations that already have been undertaken. Rather, properly viewed, it is a *morally guided approach to statecraft* that (1) qualifies the administration of coercive force and (2) views peace as the result of justly ordered relationships. Not all use of force is just; frequently it is not. And not all use of force creates conditions for bringing about peace and justice. Therefore, the use of force must be highly qualified. Peace is *not* to be understood as the absence of conflict; it is rather the *fruit or by-product* of a justly ordered society.

The ordering of society—and the just maintenance of that order at its various levels—is the task of policy. A proper understanding of the nature of policy is useful in clarifying the role that just-war moral reasoning plays in the overall enterprise of justice. With one moral thinker, then, we may say that policy is "the hand of practical reason" that is "set firmly upon the course of [human] events."[1] Policy, furthermore, is "the meeting place of the world of power and the world of morality, in which there takes place the concrete reconciliation of the duty of success that rests upon the statesman and the duty of justice that rests upon the civilized nation that he serves."[2] Perhaps the linkage between "the world of power" and "the world of morality" strikes the reader as unusual or unseemly. Nevertheless, our own

---

[1]John Courtney Murray, "Morality and Modern Warfare," in Kenneth W. Thompson, ed., *Moral Dimensions of American Foreign Policy* (New Brunswick, NJ: Transaction, 1994), 27. (Murray's essay was originally published in 1959 by the Council on Religion and International Affairs.)
[2]Ibid. See as well John Courtney Murray, *We Hold These Truths: Catholic Reflections on the American Proposition* (New York: Sheed and Ward, 1960), 272.

understanding of policy proceeds on the assumption of this linkage, without which civil society ceases to be civil.

Surely, one is tempted to argue that no aspect of policy and the ordering of human affairs has evolved more than the problem of war and military intervention. And indeed it is difficult to argue otherwise. At the same time, it needs emphasis that as long as a civil society remains civil—by which we mean that as long as a nation (1) seeks to embody justice and to attend to the duties of justice, and (2) does not proscribe moral principle in the ordering of human affairs—then that nation will be informed by and profit from the political-moral resources of previous generations that will aid it in its present challenges.[3] At its best, the just-war tradition has worked to forge moral and political links between the limited use of armed force and the pursuit of peace, security, justice, and freedom. This linkage rests on a foundational assumption, namely, that morality, politics, and governing "do not exist in hermetically sealed compartments of life" and that there is "one indivisible human universe of thought and action," which is inescapably moral and political.[4] Set forth in part 1 of this volume in our discussion of natural-law thinking, this linkage can scarcely be overstated, particularly in a cultural climate of moral pessimism and deeply ensconced secularism, a climate that is abetted by religious syncretism and moral vacuity.

The present volume, then, represents an attempt to stand in continuity with classic just-war proponents who variously have argued that the cluster of issues lying at the heart of war and peace—for example, the character and conditions of justice, the nature of politics, the importance and role of political authority, and the dualism of dignity and depravity that constitutes human nature—are most responsibly and realistically addressed by the just-war tradition.[5] As we have argued elsewhere in this volume, characteristic of the tradition is a moral realism that escapes the ideological poles of militarism, on the one hand, and pacifism, on the other. This moral realism is best

---

[3]So political historian John P. Hittinger, "Just War and Defense Policy," in David F. Forte, ed., *Contemporary Public Policy* (Washington, DC: Georgetown University Press, 1998), 333, who argues cogently in this regard.

[4]George Weigel, "From Last Resort to Endgame: Morality, the Gulf War, and the Peace Process," in David E. DeCosse, ed., *But Was It Just? Reflections on the Morality of the Persian Gulf War* (New York: Doubleday, 1992), 19–20.

[5]Many people may be surprised that just-war thought is a significant ethical component in the education received at the U.S. military academies and war colleges.

understood in light of basic just-war assumptions, which are ever in need of clarification and reiteration.

At the same time, we find it necessary to point out two general distortions in the popular perception of just-war thought. One is to erect unrealistic expectations of just-war reasoning, as if it is an exact science or a ready-to-order, cookie-cutter solution that automatically and perfectly fits particular geopolitical crises. In truth, just-war thought provides a moral framework and moral parameters within which a principled analysis of policy options might be considered to govern a just response to catastrophic geopolitical developments. Moral wisdom and prudence are needed for their application and implementation. A second problem is the tendency to invert primary and secondary just-war criteria, so that analysis of military intervention and coercive force begins with secondary or prudential considerations that, in fact, derive from—and thus can only be understood in light of—*primary* or core moral criteria. By drawing a distinction between primary and secondary elements, just-war advocates do not intend to ascribe insignificance to the latter; they only wish to underscore an order of priority in moral reflection, as the following discussion will hopefully clarify.

Historically, two groups of criteria serve as guidelines or moral norms that help determine the *relative* "justness" or "rightness" of action according to just-war moral reasoning. These criteria assist us in determining whether to go to war (the historic *jus ad bellum* criteria) and how to conduct war (the *jus in bello* criteria). Although many discussions of just war contain longer lists of the former that are probably familiar to us, all criteria derive from—and issue out of—three core criteria that constitute the heart of just-war moral reasoning: just cause, proper authority, and right intention. While identified by a host of just-war thinkers ancient and modern, the core criteria are accentuated by Thomas Aquinas[6] and have served as a basis for all subsequent just-war thought up to the present.[7]

---

[6]Thomas Aquinas *Summa theologiae* (hereafter *S.T.*) II-II Q. 40.
[7]We follow just-war historian James Turner Johnson, who in assorted writings has distinguished between primary and secondary criteria. The core of the *jus ad bellum* requirements consists of those three enunciated by Aquinas—just cause, legitimate authority, and right intention—which are presently under discussion. See as well J. Daryl Charles, *Between Pacifism and Jihad: Just War and Christian Tradition* (Downers Grove, IL: InterVarsity, 2005), 130–36.

1. *Just cause*. To establish the justness of a cause is to make funda-mental moral distinctions—for example, between innocence and guilt, between the criminal and the punitive act, between retribution and revenge, between egregious human-rights violations ("crimes against humanity") and the need for humanitarian intervention to restore basic human rights. In principle, just cause is motivated by two chief concerns: to rectify injustice or to prevent injustice; hence, Aquinas can argue that "those who are attacked are attacked because they deserve it on account of some wrong they have done."[8] While there is a sense in which all violence is tragic, even more tragic is the permit-ting of human oppression, gross injustice, and crimes against human-ity.[9] Human beings, wherever they are found, have a basic human responsibility toward their neighbor. When an innocent third party, our "neighbor," is being attacked, assaulted, or oppressed, we are mor-ally obligated to respond. Any nation or people group must be able to identify an injury or injustice inflicted from the outside. Not every injustice, of course, necessitates coercive force or war. When, however, a nation invades and annexes as its own another nation, people group, or territory, the most basic human rights to sovereignty are violated. A military response is deemed just in restoring those inalienable rights.[10] Just cause, then, wrestles with an appropriate response where gross injustice and moral culpability are established. It seeks to defend the basic order of justice that has been violated.

Just cause for attack, writes Thomas Aquinas, arises out of the fact that "those who are attacked should be attacked because they deserve it on account of some fault." Citing Augustine, Aquinas identifies a just war as "one that avenges wrongs, that is, when a nation or state has to be punished either for refusing to make amends for outrages done by its subjects, or to restore what it has seized injuriously."[11] Sufficient justification for war, according to Hugo Grotius, includes reclaiming stolen or occupied territory, oppressive injury or harm (even in another nation) that requires punishment or prevention of humanitarian abuses, threat to or rescue of nationals, terrorism, and

---

[8]*S.T.* II-II Q. 40 (New York: Blackfriars, 1972).
[9]Jean Bethke Elshtain, *Just War against Terror: The Burden of American Power in a Violent World* (New York: Basic Books, 2003), esp. in chap. 3 ("What Is a Just War?"), presses this distinction quite forcefully.
[10]Aquinas does not distinguish between offensive or defensive wars, although later just-war thinkers do.
[11]*S.T.* II-II Q. 40.

preventive attack.[12] War, for Grotius, is justifiable only "to continue the work of peace."[13] Sufficient warrant may also arise from humanitarian abuses, that is, when another state or people group "inflicts upon his subjects such treatment as no one is warranted in inflicting."[14] Grotius, it should be observed, developed a lengthy list of *unjust* causes alongside those situations that were deemed just.[15]

Just-war moral reasoning proceeds on the assumption that human beings are equipped to discern basic justice and injustice. We must reject the implication or thinking, found in some circles, that because we can never know whether a cause is *absolutely* just, therefore we cannot discern basic justice. This assumption is both true and false. It is true insofar as it recognizes that in an imperfect world people will not have perfect moral faculties. But it is false in that it denies—or suggests—that human beings cannot distinguish fundamentally between justice and injustice.[16] This sort of thinking has significant ramifications, for to assume that a cause cannot be identified as just or unjust in the end paralyzes the moral agent in a state of nonaction.[17]

2. *Right intention.* Morally guided force will seek to advance a greater good and secure a greater peace then heretofore had existed. Aquinas insists that belligerents should have a right intention "so that they intend the advancement of good, or the avoidance of evil." "It may happen," he notes, "that the war is declared by the legitimate authority, and for a just cause, and yet be rendered unlawful through a wicked intention."[18] Unjust war is perhaps best illustrated by what does *not* constitute right intention. Such scenarios include a sovereign's pride or reputation, vengeance, national aggrandizement, blood-thirst

---

[12]Hugo Grotius *The Law of War and Peace* 2.1–3.1. Below we rely on the translation of R. L. Loomis (Roslyn, NY: Walter J. Black, 1949).
[13]Ibid., 1.1.
[14]Ibid., 2.25.7.
[15]Ibid., 2.22. While Grotius lays a theoretical foundation for military intervention, there is no present consensus in just-war doctrine supporting a right to military intervention not narrowly considered self-defense. Nevertheless, William V. O'Brien writes: "The substance of the just cause in just revolution is to remove a government that *is intolerable to its subjects* . . . [and] this just cause is a kind of self-defense of the people." In such a scenario, according to O'Brien, "resistance to a *violently oppressive or genocidal* . . . government may literally be justified as self-defense." "Just War Doctrine's Complementary Role in the International Law of War," in Alberto R. Coll et al., eds., *Legal and Moral Constraints in Low-Intensity Conflicts*, International Law Department Studies, vol. 67 (Newport, RI: Naval War College, 1995), 189; emphasis added.
[16]This type of thinking weakens *The Challenge of Peace*, the significant 1983 pastoral letter by U.S. Catholic bishops. See, e.g., paragraph 92 of the document, which would seem to be grounded on notions of "comparative justice" and moral equivalence.
[17]In theological terms, this is a denial of the *imago Dei* and our rational moral self, which sets apart the human creature.
[18]Aquinas *S.T.* II-II Q. 40.

or lust for power, and territorial expansion.[19] For war to be just, its aim must be a greater good, and that greater good is a justly ordered peace. Where the magistrate or political sovereign is acutely aware of his responsibility to protect the common weal of his population or another, chances are greater that just criteria have been met for going to war. The establishment of a just peace rules out the possibility of territorial domination, revenge, or other wrong motives. Within just-war thinking, the goal of war is *to stop the strongman*, not to kill. Thus Oliver O'Donovan: "It is not essential to war-making that you kill, merely that you should intend to remove by all necessary means the forces that oppose you. The scale of loss of life, important as it is in any concrete moral decision, does not define the distinctive nature of war as such."[20]

A just response acknowledges the greater goal of a just peace and goes beyond sentiments of hatred and vengeance that are so typical of human behavior. It is cognizant that anything apart from just cause negates the morality of the response.

3. *Proper authority*. To address matters of sovereignty, to declare a war, and to wage war, there must exist a public authority that has responsibility for the people. Aquinas writes that

> it is not the business of a private person to declare war. . . . More-over it is not the business of a private person to summon together the people, which has to be done in wartime. And as the care of the common weal is committed to those who are in authority, it is their business to watch over the common weal of the city, kingdom or province subject to them.[21]

War, then, is necessarily an act by "the authority of a sovereign by whose command the war is to be waged."[22] As Aquinas observes, private acts of justice—*duellum* over against *bellum*—are rooted in vengeance; only public acts of justice are legitimate. Therefore, only governments may make war, "for the same reason that only police and magistrates may arrest and only judges sentence, namely, that they

---

[19]So, e.g., Augustine *Contra Faustum* 22.74, and Aquinas *S.T.* II-II Q. 40.
[20]Oliver O'Donovan, *The Just War Revisited*, Current Issues in Theology (Cambridge: Cambridge University Press, 2003), 21.
[21]*S.T.* II-II Q. 40.
[22]Ibid.

require representative persons, acting for the community, to perform them."[23] Summoning or representing the people does not legitimately belong to the private sphere. To the magistrate, rather, belongs the responsibility to watch over the common weal. This is the very nature of the *polis*, the political community. Justice requires representative consensus, even when it does not require perfection.

Such accords with a classical view of authority insofar as those who govern exist first and foremost to preserve the common good.[24] The "sword" in the hand of the magistrate, moreover, is to be wielded against both internal and external enemies, against criminal individuals as well as unjust states. Both can undermine justice at the elementary level. Coercive force—not always or even regularly requisite—will be necessary if a justly ordered peace is to be preserved; the preservation of inherently public goods *requires* it. Force is neither to be misused through indiscriminate application nor to be considered inherently evil. Political historian John Hittinger has expressed well this foundational moral sentiment:

> There are [certain moral] goods worth the risk of war and . . . "peace at any price" is unacceptable. . . . The pacifist misses this complex reality of the possibility and political conditions for human flourishing [while] . . . [t]he realist approach, by which the conduct of war is bound by no moral limit, undermines the very moral and political legitimacy of the regime.[25]

Justice in war is a moral and legal judgment. Though beyond the mere confines of domestic criminal justice, and thus extraordinary rather than ordinary in character, war requires—like criminal justice—representative authority for its enactment. Perhaps the best way to illustrate the nature of public authority that must stand behind war making is to note three distinct ways in which a belligerent party may lack authority. Authority is lacking where (1) the cause of belligerence lies *outside* its sphere of authority from the very beginning, (2) authority has collapsed from *within* for whatever reason, and (3) a claim to authority is not authorized as being representative of a people. These conditions illustrate why terrorism (along with piracy and other forms

---

[23]O'Donovan, *The Just War Revisited*, 21–22.
[24]Moreover, this is the view of authority that one finds in the historic Christian tradition as mirrored in the teaching of the New Testament (see Rom. 13:1–7; 1 Tim. 2:2; 1 Pet. 2:13–14).
[25]"Just War and Defense Policy," 342.

of nonstate criminal action) is a moral abomination. It simply cannot lay claim to authority, whether past or present in form.

As a function of proper authority, the ability to declare and go to war is not merely a legal formality. It is rather the meeting place of morality and political prudence in a government's attempt to redress social-political evil. In this regard, both militarism and pacifism miss the essence of political responsibility. The former rides roughshod over any moral considerations, focusing purely on what it believes to be military necessity. By its ignoring moral considerations, it undermines the very legitimacy of politics. The latter tends to devalue the political realm either by its disengagement or by its attempts to undermine policy.[26] Its failure is a failure to recognize the role that politics plays in preserving the peace. The former abuses political power; the latter negates it.

As it applies to authority, just-war moral reasoning performs two moderating functions. On the one hand, it holds in check excessive claims to state sovereignty by conceiving of justice and rights in universal—that is, international—terms. On the other hand, it affirms the right of government *qua* government to adjudicate over justice and rights in a way that private individuals and nonstates are not permitted to do. This very attempt to balance the claims of justice and power—an intuition that lies at the heart of just-war thinking—is itself one the greatest moral safeguards that we have against totalitarian schemes.[27]

For the political realist (i.e., the militarist), the very notion of limitations placed upon war and warfare would surely seem utterly absurd. According to just-war moral reasoning historically, justified use or means of armed force—that is, the measure of *jus in bello* requirements—has been guided by moral parameters concerned not merely with the elimination of evil but with the ultimate good of the community as well. Put otherwise, these criteria suggest that the *means* must be commensurate with the goal. Justice, properly construed, cannot order a just end and at the same time appropriate any means,

---

[26]Certainly the average layperson of pacifist conviction does not purpose to undermine policy. Nevertheless, one observes a strong commitment to political radicalism at the academic level, whereby both the religious and the nonreligious not infrequently support oppressive regimes—often Marxist or totalitarian—while being highly critical of democratic society. For a penetrating critique of this aspect of academic pacifism in the last half of the twentieth century, see Guenter Lewy, *Peace and Revolution: The Moral Crisis of American Pacifism* (Grand Rapids: Eerdmans, 1988).

[27]Both the rights of and the restraints on governments are discussed with considerable insight in O'Donovan, *The Just War Revisited*, 18–32.

even an unjust one, to achieve its end. Two words—permission and limitation—characterize this measure.[28] Thus, the application of force is morally justified to the extent that it is conditioned by the reasons for and the manner in which that force is applied. Two principal criteria reflect the *in bello* tradition and natural extension of the prior *ad bellum* qualifications.

4. *Proportionality*. The principle of proportionality has to do with the shape of the act of retributive judgment being administered and rests on several basic assumptions. It begins with the baseline recognition that a moral loss through injustice has occurred (just cause) prior to the consideration of whether and how force is justified to restore what was lost. As a moral property, it seeks to balance the good that an application of force will create over against the evil that will result from not forcibly intervening.[29] Force is an entity that can be *regulated*, and the degree of force applied is not to be greater than what is needed to render the enemy compliant. In principle, all-out war would be counter to the very reason for being of the armed forces in nontotalitarian nations. It is for this very reason that we speak of "military force" and not "military violence."

Just-war thinking distinguishes itself from crusading or militarism by its commitment to *limit* war. This is a moral stricture that is all but ignored by the religious or secular militarist, who is willing to enter into total war. The motivation behind this spirit might be nationalist or religious, or it could be both. Any necessary means is thought justifiable in order to obliterate the enemy. By contrast, for the just-war proponent, to wrestle with proportionality of response is to discern not only what is reasonable in terms of economy of force in a given situation but also what is a truthful approximation of the wrong done. After all, punishment is measured strictly by desert.[30]

In war as in criminal justice, this principle remains constant. Responses that are proportionate to the crimes committed are a reflec-

---

[28]The reconciliation of permission and limitation was the great burden of Hugo Grotius as he agonized over the devastation of the Thirty Years War. In this light, he exhorts, "For both extremes [militarism and pacifism] a remedy must be found, that men may not believe either that nothing [ever] is allowable, or that everything [always] is." *The Law of War and Peace*, 1.1. Ethicist Paul Ramsey, as well, spoke in terms of permission and limitation in articulating the just-war tradition; see, e.g., his introduction to *War and the Christian Conscience* (Durham, NC: Duke University Press, 1961).

[29]So James Turner Johnson, "The Just-War Idea and the Ethics of Intervention," in J. Carl Ficarrotta, ed., *The Leader's Imperative: Ethics, Integrity, and Responsibility* (West Lafayette, IN: Purdue University Press, 2001), 118–19.

[30]Thus O'Donovan, *The Just War Revisited*, 58.

tion and requirement of justice. The retributive response in warfare, according to Grotius, must be commensurate with the evil being redressed. Thus, for example, a draconian response to lesser abuses is illegitimate. Wisdom must cause kings and those with representative authority to assess the cost of war as it affects not only the enemy but also other nations and people groups. Proportionality is governed by a just moral, social, and political aim toward which war must be directed.[31] That the limitation of war and its execution is a *moral mandate* lies at the heart of just-war moral reasoning.[32]

   5. *Noncombatant immunity or discrimination.* The same moral reasoning that leads to determinations about going to war contributes to conduct in war. Ends and means are related. This linkage is all but lost on the crusader/militarist/political "realist," who can justify war but fail to apply any restraints in prosecuting war. The most basic moral prohibition, even in war, is the taking of innocent life. This proscription, as we noted, is part of the natural moral law and confirmed in legal codes both ancient and modern. Guilt is predicated on intention. A justified war is one that, in Thomistic terms, is waged against those who deserve it. The noncombatant—including civilian populations, wounded soldiers, prisoners, women, children, and noncombatant males—may not be held "guilty" as may a government or military representatives of that regime. Because of human dignity, respect for life is not to be forgotten.[33] Inflicting any suffering or injury that is not *directly related* to morally legitimate strategic purposes is strictly prohibited. A fundamental flaw of both militarism and totalitarianism is their indiscriminate attitude toward human life. Accordingly, all and any may be sacrificed for the greater political end. At the same time, it must be acknowledged that the principles of proportionality and discrimination are difficult to apply with precision at all levels of the spectrum of military force.

---

[31]Grotius *The Law of War and Peace* 2.20, 24.

[32]This fundamental commitment undergirds the writings of all classic just-war theorists and comes to expression quite succinctly in Hittinger, "Just War and Defense Policy," 333–60.

[33]The ideological pacifist will object, of course, that because of human dignity, war and retributive justice are *never* morally justified. To this objection, we would simply say that it is *precisely because* we treat people as moral agents, that is, as those made in the divine image, that they are held accountable for their actions. In this light, then, retributive justice that is proportionate and appropriate is not only tolerable, but requisite, based on the *imago Dei*. Most parents intuit this moral reality as it applies to their children.

But what if, for example, a war must be waged in locations where the belligerents and civilians are closely intermixed and the belligerents have intentionally carried on their work in this way? Here the moral imperative approximates that of law enforcement in the domestic, criminal justice context. Law-enforcement officers must plan and calculate in order to avoid needless killing. However, where the threat has reached critical mass in their judgment, there comes a time when action must be taken against belligerents, even if it means a threat to the lives of others. Military activity—that is, the realm of *in bello* considerations—is based on deliberation and intent. Therefore, just-war thinking makes a distinction between deliberate and unintended liability. If, to use a frequent example from the Iraq wars, a strategic target locates itself in an area that is densely populated with civilians, the same moral principles apply that would guide law-enforcement officers in any city who are attempting to prevent or interdict a crime threat. In cases of potential catastrophe in our cities, law-enforcement officers and agencies must weigh the necessity of preventing evil over against the possibility of collateral damage, and they do not take this burden lightly.

In the military context, the fact that there are (or may well be) civilian casualties does not in and of itself render a war or a military intervention unjust. Human beings cannot require both justice and perfection; if we could, we would need to give up on criminal justice in the domestic context. Even the ideological pacifist will acknowledge that law-enforcement agents *at some point* must use force—even *lethal* force—in the event that a bank, in which both pacifists and non-pacifists have committed their life savings to "safe-keeping," is being robbed. Or, at another level, perhaps the pacifist has fewer qualms about the authorities and law-enforcement officers' using lethal force to intercept terrorists who are about to blow up a public works facility on which millions of people in a city are dependent. But such are no idle comparisons or analogies; in a fallen world, the common good is dependent on such scenarios.

In the international context, we might illustrate through events of the Second World War. For tactical purposes, a city's communications network, railroad system, ammunition plants, and factories are bombed. In these operations, civilians are killed. These deaths are simultaneously grave and yet unavoidable; what needs emphasis is that these individuals were not targeted.[34] Was it moral to stop the Germans by means of bombing strategically? Does strategic bombing, given the possibility of innocent deaths, require *no* bombing? Should Allied forces, in the end, *not* have resisted Hitler and the German *Wehrmacht*, in the awareness that civilian lives would be lost?[35]

Michael Walzer, in our view, is correct to point out a tendency among those who operate at one pole of the coercive force continuum. The ideological pacifist, he observes, will make noncombatant immunity into a stronger and stronger rule, "until it is something like an absolute rule: all killing of civilians is (something close to) murder; therefore any war that leads to the killing of civilians is unjust; therefore every war is unjust"; hence, Walzer concludes, pacifism "reemerges from the very heart of the theory that was originally meant to replace it."[36] However, the refusal to make distinctions regarding human deaths suggests, as Walzer emphasizes, a "doctrine of radical suspicion." This radicalism is "a radicalism of people *who do not expect to exercise power or use force, ever, and who are not prepared to make judgments that this exercise and use require.*"[37]

Just-war advocates do not intend or wish deaths. At the same time, they do not, with absolute pacifists, require on putatively moral grounds the nonuse of lethal force. In the task of resisting social-political evil, we simply cannot have it both ways; it needs reiteration that we cannot require both justice *and* perfection, since working for justice is always an *approximate* endeavor. The ambiguities that attend our imperfection demonstrate why just-war moral reasoning must be applied with political prudence insofar as military intervention always entails imprecise calculation and different situations call for different solutions within the wider sphere of moral parameters.

---

[34]Hittinger, "Just War and Defense Policy," 350–51, develops the implications of this kind of scenario quite helpfully.

[35]There has been much written on the history and ethics of the bombing campaigns in World War II. For a starting point, see Stephen A. Garrett, *Ethics and Airpower in World War II: The British Bombing of German Cities* (New York: St. Martin's, 1993); Christopher C. Harmon, *"Are We Beasts?" Churchill and the Moral Question of World War II "Area Bombing,"* The Newport Papers, 1 (Newport, RI: U.S. Naval War College Press, 1991); and Tami Davis Biddle, "Dresden 1945: Reality, History, and Memory," *Journal of Military History* 72, no. 2 (April 2008): 413–49.

[36]Michael Walzer, *Arguing about War* (New Haven, CT: Yale University Press, 2004), 13.

[37]Ibid., 14; emphasis added.

Q. 38 What are prudential criteria in just-war moral reasoning, and how do they differ from the core criteria?

While the three core criteria of just cause, right intent, and proper authority constitute the heart of just-war thinking, together they give rise to other related conditions. As we have already argued, to distinguish between primary and secondary conditions is not to suggest that the latter are insignificant. It is only to recognize that they are derivative; that is, they *issue out of* primary or core considerations (rather than vice versa) that weigh the obligations of justice, express political prudence, and require discernment in terms of their application, given their imprecision. In contrast to primary criteria, the secondary criteria establish prudential tests as to whether or not the use of force in a given situation is wise. Because these secondary criteria are frequently the primary focus of most contemporary discussions of just war, they are to be understood and assessed in the light of historic just-war moral reasoning:

1. *Last resort.* Going to war can be justified only on exceptional conditions. Thus, only when the core conditions of just-war moral reasoning have been met without any solution is war to be undertaken. To grapple with last resort is to reckon with the gravity of acts of force, even though that is a factor only when the other principle conditions have been considered. Have all reasonable efforts to utilize nonmilitary (e.g., diplomatic, economic, and political) alternatives been exhausted? The operative word here is *reasonable*, since those who oppose all war in principle will *never* see diplomatic possibilities as having been exhausted.[38]

Because of the priority given to last resort in contemporary discussions of just war, there is much confusion as to its proper place in just-war moral reasoning. James Turner Johnson makes an important clarification:

> The criterion does not mean always postponing use of military force until every possible means short of force has been tried. If one comes into a situation late in the day, as is almost by definition the case when a conflict has created urgent humanitarian needs, working

---

[38]Given the attention in our own day to last resort, this criterion receives further qualification in the following question.

the gradualist way might simply postpone what is necessary until still later, perhaps making the situation worse and requiring a more robust, costly, and dangerous intervention when force is finally brought in.[39]

Properly understood, last resort leads us to deliberate not over fore-stalled timing per se but rather over what sort of action should be taken. All possibilities are considered, including the military option.

2. *Reasonable chance of success.* Although situations of gross injustice arise that cry out for just intervention, there are some that, sadly, will hold little likelihood of success. While there may be a moral justification for a seemingly hopeless intervention or resistance, just-war reasoning seeks to balance a potential greater good against the costs and losses of war that would incur. Does the desired just goal equal or surpass the losses that war will produce? What is the ultimate cost of war and loss imposed on both sides? Does the cost indicate that the war effort is worth the endeavor? These questions do not represent a crude sort of utilitarianism or consequentialism; rather, they mirror an assessment of gains based on inherent dangers, projected losses, and a reasonable chance of securing victory. They suggest whether or not the cause is hopeless, and thus, politically and militarily unwise.

3. *Proportionate means.* Integral to just-war moral reasoning is its fundamental commitment to moral restraint in the use of force. The principle of proportionality lies at the heart of justice in general and military necessity in particular. In the domestic context, the criminal justice system is effective to the extent that its response to crime is swift, consistent, and proportionate to the acts that have been com-mitted. According to James Turner Johnson, proportionality of means is the prism through which to regard the just-war condition that force should serve the greater end of peace.[40]

It should be said that, while the principle of proportionality shows itself even in antiquity among non-Christian cultures, it has not been a formal object of discussion in classic just-war doctrine until rela-tively recently. In recent decades it has been the focus of fierce debate,

---

[39]Johnson, "The Just-War Idea and the Ethics of Intervention," 123.
[40]*The War to Oust Saddam Hussein: Just War and the New Face of Conflict* (Lanham, MD: Rowman & Littlefield, 2005), 18.

perhaps most notably during the Cold War era. Given the destructive propensity of modern weaponry, some have largely assumed that just-war theory is obsolete and that the least destructive means should be employed.[41] To the contrary, just-war moral reasoning is all the more required—and adequate, we believe—to guide responsible use of force. In the domestic context, law-enforcement officers take appropriate measures in fighting crime. That is, they utilize those weapons, tactics, and strategies that are appropriate (or, proportionate) to the menace confronting the community.

4. *Peace as the ultimate aim*. A justified war will be one that has a greater good in view and not mere avenging of wrong. Such is the lens through which to measure right intention. Does going to war proceed with the ultimate goal of establishing a just peace and political-social stability? Does the likelihood of achieving a greater good guide the prospects of going to war? This moral value is perhaps best expressed by Augustine: "For peace is not sought in order to the kindling of war, but war is waged in order that peace may be obtained. Therefore, even in waging war, cherish the spirit of a peacemaker, that, by conquering those whom you attack, you may lead them back to the advantages of peace."[42] The ideal expressed in the just-war tradition, as one theorist wisely notes, "is far from a celebration of wrath, violence, and enmity; it is an ideal in which the use of force serves to overcome these and to create peace"—an ideal that "has to do with defining the possible good use of force, not finding exceptional cases when it is possible to use something inherently evil (force) for the purposes of good."[43]

5. *Formal declaration of war*. When nations formally and publicly state their intentions, several things ensue. One is to ensure that war is removed from the private domain. Another is the possibility of the opponent's surrender. A further benefit is that a formal announcement communicates a warning to the offending nation. This in itself may ultimately prevent war.[44]

---

[41]The writings of Paul Ramsey, William V. O'Brien, and more recently, James Turner Johnson have sought to counter this widespread though mistaken assumption.
[42]Augustine, *Epistle* 189, trans. J. G. Cunningham, *Nicene and Post-Nicene Fathers* (NPNF), ed. Philip Schaff (Grand Rapids: Eerdmans, 1956), 554.
[43]Johnson, *The War to Oust Saddam Hussein*, 22, 36.
[44]Grotius *The Law of War and Peace* 3.3.

Q. 39 What about last resort and exhausting all possible non-violent alternatives? It seems as if just-war proponents will inevitably justify going to war.

It is difficult to overstate the difference between the just-war position and that of the militarist. It shall need reemphasis that the just-war tradition understands itself as a mediating position between the two poles of pacifism and militarism. Whether in its secular (*Realpolitik*) or religious (holy war) form, militarism needs no moral justification for resorting to violence or going to war.

Last resort means that going to war is not a consideration until all other *reasonable* nonmilitary (e.g., diplomatic, economic, judicial, and political) means have been exhausted and proven unsuccessful. As we have sought to emphasize, the operative word here is *reasonable*, since those who oppose all war in principle will *never* see diplomatic possibilities as having been wholly exhausted. Moreover, we have identified last resort as a secondary or prudential rather than core criterion of just-war moral reasoning. Emerging initially in the framework of early-modern just-war thinkers such as Vitoria, Suárez, and Grotius, last resort is subordinated to—and therefore, issues out of—just cause.[45]

To be sure, there is no little controversy that swirls around contemporary discussions of last resort, and even among just-war theorists there exists considerable disagreement as to what degree of exploring nonmilitary alternatives is reasonable. While the dilemma of probing nonmilitary alternatives is legitimate, much confusion arises from a failure to make the necessary distinction between primary and prudential criteria. For many, whether pacifist or nonpacifist, this distinction is often lost. Often the categories of primary and secondary are inverted so that considerations about what is morally justified are guided not by just cause or right intention or competent authority, but by secondary criteria—criteria that per se *depend on the primary criteria for their legitimacy*.[46]

---

[45]Few have argued this distinction with greater moral clarity than James Turner Johnson. See, e.g., his essay "Just Cause Revisited," in Elliott Abrams, ed., *Close Calls: Intervention, Terrorism, Missile Defense, and "Just War" Today* (Washington, DC: Ethics and Public Policy Center, 1998), 3–38.

[46]Johnson, *The War to Oust Saddam Hussein*, 57–61, helpfully illustrates how, in the contemporary context, this inversion expresses itself. See also Johnson, *The Just War Tradition and the Restraint of War* (Princeton, NJ: Princeton University Press, 1981), and *Morality and Contemporary Warfare* (New Haven, CT: Yale University Press, 1999).

But consider, for a moment, the idea of exhausting all alternative courses of action. After all, such seems the eminently reasonable and right thing to do, and virtually every level of social relationship bears out this sentiment: parents intuit it, neighbors do, as do most employers. Thus, we must pose the critical question, When, or at what point, does it become clear that *all* alternatives have truly been exhausted? Depending on one's ideological perspective, last resort may never reach fulfillment, since there is always *one more* strategy or attempt that can be implemented. For this reason we stress that alternative actions be *reasonably* explored. Taken literally and not reasonably, as Michael Walzer points out, last resort would render all war morally impossible. That is, we can "never reach lastness, or we can never know that we have reached it."[47] But as one defense analyst perceptively notes, in cases where rogue nations or terrorists and the use of weapons of mass destruction are part of the threat and moral equation, last resort comes into clearer relief; namely, it is secondary to just cause, given the potential threat to innocent masses. To defer action when arsenals already exist or are being used to threaten others might in fact induce an aggressor, or give him the needed time, to use his weapons. In such a scenario, the cost would be thousands, even hundreds of thousands, of lives.[48]

Correlatively, to limit just cause in that sort of situation to a *defense against armed attack*—be it an attack with conventional weapons or biological weapons—would be morally suspect and does not always fit the actual circumstances of a conflict.[49] Is it morally justifiable to wait until damage, destruction, and death have occurred before determining an armed response against an aggressor? In such a scenario, buying time could literally cost thousands of lives. There is a reason, then, why this criterion does not appear in classic just-war theory but surfaces first in the early-modern period, even though its basic concerns are always close to the heart of just-war thinking. This reason has to do with the logic of last resort when it is not tethered and subordinated to *just cause*: when the possibilities are endless for "peaceful" resolution, just cause can *never* be identified. What's more, the "peaceful" resolution in the end may in fact be unjust. Hence, in

[47]Michael Walzer, *Just and Unjust Wars*, 4th ed. (New York: Basic Books, 2006), xiv.
[48]Brad Roberts, "NBC-Armed Rogues: Is There a Moral Case for Preemption?" in Abrams, ed., *Close Calls*, 86–87.
[49]Johnson, "Just Cause Revisited," 18, presses home this point in the contemporary context.

several questions throughout this volume we attempt to clarify the operating assumption of the classic just-war tradition, which begins with a fundamental presumption not against force or war but against evil and injustice.

Given the changing configuration of geopolitics in the world since the Cold War, and particularly the dilemma that terrorism poses, we should amplify the difficulties that an inversion of last resort, from secondary to primary, creates. In conventional international conflict, for example, established diplomatic channels are employed, and international organizations typically play a mediating role. But terrorism, because it is committed by nonstate actors who possess no recognized competent authority and therefore possess neither sovereignty nor moral authority, precludes the possibility of diplomatic, economic, judicial, or political alternative actions. How does a nation-state deal with terrorists? In fact, it might be reasonably argued that an attempt to establish any direct or formal contact with terrorist groups is to grant them a sense of legitimacy that would aid their illegitimate cause.[50]

In addition to terrorism, military intervention for humanitarian purposes renders the criterion of last resort inadequate in and of itself where it is not subordinated to just cause. One need only consider examples of genocide that have occurred during the last fifteen years or so. Should other nations not have intervened in venues such as Bosnia/Kosovo? And what about Rwanda? Clearly, diplomatic, economic, or nonmilitary strategies—that is, nonmilitary alternatives—become next to irrelevant on the eve of the slaughter of innocents whose numbers boggle the human mind. Did nations lack moral justification for coercive intervening in Rwanda? There is a moral obligation that falls on any and all who have the wherewithal to protect potential victims from atrocity—a moral obligation that in the end cannot be adequately addressed by last resort alone. Not infrequently, nonmilitary means are insufficient to address political-social evil such as enslavement, genocide, and egregious human-rights violations.

While the phenomena of terrorism, piracy, international drug cartels, and genocide might seem to pose unique challenges to just-war thinking, the tradition nevertheless offers guidance and

---

[50]On the ability of just-war theory to address terrorism, see the helpful essay by Anthony Clark Arend, "Terrorism and Just War Doctrine," in Abrams, ed., Close Calls, 223–36.

political-moral wisdom by which to offer morally responsible and just counterresponses.[51]

Q. 40 If the criterion of just cause is not satisfied, does this render a war unjust?

A common perception of just-war doctrine is that it is used to validate wars that have been undertaken or to justify prior decisions about going to war. Our biggest aid in determining what should or should not be undertaken, however, does not come from history, as Oliver O'Donovan wisely cautions, since historical judgments are always prejudiced and never come neatly packaged.[52] Rather, the most important element in proper discernment is the art of moral reflection, seasoned with responsible political judgment that is attentive to particular human inclinations—for example, nationalistic pride, self-righteousness, popular sentiment, desire for domination, shortsightedness, apathy, and moral cowardice.

The fact that we might believe strongly in the relative justness of a cause counts neither for nor against the validity of that cause. For this reason, in the words of the ancient proverb, wisdom lies in a multitude of counselors. Moral intuition is acutely aware that counsel may be wise or unwise, appropriate or inappropriate, reflective of good or evil motives. A wider circle of counselors has the cumulative effect of helping us to discern whether particular advice is wise or not. This is true both at the personal level and at the level of politics and public policy. Wise counsel will help us avoid the pitfalls of haste, self-delusion, and improper motives. These are particularly critical in the face of decisions of enormous import that loom before us. For this reason, then, even sincere belief per se in the justness of our cause is not adequate to the task of establishing just cause in going to war.

---

[51]International drug dealing is akin to terrorism as a nonconventional security threat that requires just application of force for the purposes of peace, even when it is not a direct threat to national security. In addition, one might cite limited military strikes (short of formally going to war) on a hostile nation as further evidence that just cause (as opposed to last resort) is primary. Consider, for example, the Israeli air strike on the Iraqi nuclear reactor in Osirek in 1982 in order to remove (at least for the short term) Iraq's nuclear capability; or, imposition of a no-fly zone over Kurdish sectors of Iraq, which was guilty of genocidal treatment of the Kurdish population.
[52]O'Donovan, *The Just War Revisited*, 13.

For a war to be just, Aquinas insists, three things are necessary: the justness of the cause, sovereign authority, and right intention.[53] It is significant that this discussion of just war in the *Summa* begins with the question, "Is it always sinful to go to war?" The implication is that it *may* be sinful and it *may not*. Aquinas then lists common objections or arguments so as to illustrate the centrality of the three core criteria. Surely, the task of politics—then and now, regardless of its form—is to serve as the transmission between morality and policy. This requires, then, that moral judgments must inform the implementation of specific policy initiatives. In the case of armed conflict, which is not the usual but rather the unusual or extraordinary domain of politics, it is incumbent on legitimate authority to establish the justness of the cause. Where evidence thereof fails, the just cause fails, and the war itself is unjust. Aquinas, as did later just-war thinkers such as Suárez and Grotius, knew that princes and sovereigns were capable of pursuing bad causes wholeheartedly.

Grotius, in particular, is painstaking in distinguishing between just and unjust cause in validating war. Given his abhorrence of war, in the context of the Thirty Years War that lay waste to much of Europe prior to the Peace of Westphalia in 1648, his overarching concern was to prevent it in the first place. However, where it cannot be prevented, minimizing its devastating effects is paramount. Of the six criteria enumerated by Grotius for a war to be just,[54] the principle of just cause is understood to be motivated by two concerns: to rectify or to prevent injustice. For war to be just, a response must be proportionate to the injustice itself. It must further aim at some greater good. Not every injustice necessitates coercive force or war. Specific reasons for just cause included reclaiming stolen or occupied territory, oppressive injury or harm (even in another nation) that requires punishment or prevention of humanitarian abuses, threat to or rescue of nationals, countering terrorism, and preventive attack. War, for Grotius, is justifiable only "to continue the work of peace," and we do not go to war except "with the desire to end it at the earliest possible moment."[55] What is especially noteworthy in Grotius is the attention that he gives to particular scenarios that render a war *unjust*.[56]

---

[53]*S.T.* II-II Q. 40.
[54]*The Law of War and Peace* 2.1–3.1.
[55]Ibid., 1.1.
[56]Ibid., 2.22–23.

Ultimately, it is not the task of individuals, interest groups, civic organizations, lobby groups, or the church to make or implement policy decisions, even when all of these should be integrally involved in moral discourse about war and peace. "The evaluation of these [just-war] conditions for moral legitimacy belongs to the prudential judgment of those who have responsibility for the common good,"[57] and as such the state is the final arbiter of just or unjust cause. In the Western context, this responsibility is distributed throughout the body politic, with a "division of labor" in terms of the decision-making process.

In the democratic context, perhaps one is tempted to ask whether the citizenry, in a collective sense, might not in fact be best suited to determine just cause and whether or not to go to war. This suggestion, especially in a democratic context, would seem eminently reasonable. Should such monumental moral judgments be entrusted to the public? Fully aside from the fact that in contemporary Western societies the public is relatively fickle and subject to the whims, social currents, and ideological slants of those who control information (by which we refer not to government but chiefly to the electronic and print media and sources that control public information), there is a more fundamental reason to reject this view. Classic just-war doctrine places authority not with the people but with those who represent the people. Public goods require public authority to act *on behalf of the community*. For this reason, in Aquinas's thinking *authority* causes the related just-war criteria to cohere. Only the state is entrusted with the power to order society, a conviction that lies at the heart of Western political theory as well as the primary religious traditions that undergird it.[58]

But the reasoning behind Aquinas's position need not be relegated merely to the dustbin of historical memory. It has enormous implications for our own day. Both of us can attest—Tim in military policy and Daryl in criminal justice policy—to the fact that the public normally does not possess information, intelligence, data, and pertinent facts to which governing authorities are privy. This is particularly true regarding matters of national security, and necessarily so, since it is impossible for the citizenry at large to be cognizant of both policy implications and tactical considerations vis-à-vis domestic or national

---

[57]Catechism of the Catholic Church, par. 2309.
[58]Rom. 13:1–7; 1 Tim. 2:1–2; Titus 3:1; and 1 Pet. 2:13–17.

security, as military services and governmental agencies are. These practical ramifications notwithstanding, the more important reason lies in the role of government, whose chief function is to order and protect society.

We conclude with an application of just-war thinking to the above question.[59] What about the possibility that a decision to go to war is mistaken, based on wrong intelligence or a mistaken reading of the evidence? The general position we take on the question of wrongly declaring "just" what is *unjust* is that even sincere belief in the justness of our cause is not adequate to the task of establishing just cause in going to war. But because justification for going to war is based on (1) moral reflection on the existing pattern of evil or injustice and (2) the *intention* of fostering an enduring, justly ordered peace, and because weighing just cause is (3) an *approximate* rather than exact science, we would take the position that mistakes do not occur easily where just-war moral reasoning is taken seriously. For this reason, over time a nation can *warrant or induce* war, even in the absence of *conclusive* evidence, because it uncovers a pattern of deception that not only hides severe human-rights violations internally but also destabilizes geopolitical relations externally.[60] This, we grant, would be the exception to the rule.

Q. 41   What is the role of the United Nations in a nation's decision to declare war?

Frequently in our day, discussions of proper authority in the context of war and peace have focused on the United Nations. Many people proceed on the assumption that the condition of last resort is not satisfied until it is acknowledged by the international community, represented by the UN. But this assumption is questionable on several counts, not least of which is the fact that

---

[59]Throughout this volume we attempt to avoid political partisanship and wish rather to focus on the moral wisdom resident in the just-war tradition. In illustrating through the 2003 Iraq war, we are aware of the potential for inviting charges of political partisanship, though these charges, in our view, do not hold up.

[60]In this regard, see the fascinating essay by Davis Brown, "Iraq and the 800-Pound Gorilla Revisited: Good and Bad Faith and Humanitarian Intervention," *Hastings International and Comparative Law Review* 28, no. 1 (2005): 1–24.

it runs counter to Article 51 of the UN Charter that acknowledges a nation's right to self-defense.

It is debatable whether an international body, which gives voice to oppressive regimes as well as democratic and relatively free nations, has the moral authority to determine whether the requirements for going to war are justly satisfied. In addition, the UN's primary mission of maintaining peace and humanitarian work would seem to stand in conflict with the task of determining whether just cause is present for a nation to go to war. Furthermore, the UN presently lacks the capability to conceive of—let alone implement—a coercive intervention in the political and domestic affairs of many nations around the world, and certainly of any major power. Then there is the problem of the double standard that consistently plagues the UN as a body. It refuses to violate the borders of some nations but not others; it refuses to acknowledge the right of self-determination to some territories that it grants to others; and it sanctions human-rights violations of some nations but not those of others. Finally, the UN simply does not possess the collective wherewithal—both in terms of moral resolve and in terms of resources—to enforce what it mandates.[61]

To probe the role of the UN, then, in the matter of war is to necessitate a reexamination of the just-war criterion of competent authority.[62] If just-war thought rests on a moral foundation that endures for the ages, then the issue, properly viewed, is how the UN fits into the overall moral substructure of just-war tradition rather than vice versa, namely, trying to fit just-war thought into the agenda of the UN as a council of nations that, in historical perspective, is a relatively recent geopolitical development. The UN, it should be remembered, is not a world government, and thankfully so. Formally, decisions by the Security Council, the UN's inner sanctum, are *recommendations*, and through its diplomatic efforts it seeks to persuade nations to comply with its resolutions, stopping short of implementing force. Because the UN possesses no sovereignty, it lacks the moral force of a competent authority in two ways: the absence of public accountability and the absence of a command-and-control system for the use of force.[63]

---

[61]This was graphically on display through Iraq's ignoring seventeen UN resolutions before March of 2003. If a person strongly believes in the moral authority of the UN, then a nation's blatant disregard for those resolutions cannot be dismissed (regardless of their number).

[62]This is precisely what Eugene Rostow does in his important essay "Competent Authority Revisited," in Abrams, ed., *Close Calls*, 39–63.

[63]Roberts, "NBC-Armed Rogues," 98.

Hence, Security Council resolutions are not needed for a nation to exercise self-defense or go to war. (None of this means that working with the UN is unimportant or that it should not be sought; it means only that the UN's legitimacy is limited.)

Thus, while working with the UN is politically prudent to the extent that it represents the wider community of nations, there is no *moral obligation* on the part of a nation contemplating war to receive consent from this body since (1) the UN does not technically "wield the sword" as a national government does and, (2) given its commitment to *avoid war* and its constituency (democratic and nondemocratic nations), it runs the risk of fostering *unjust peace*. Precisely as its predecessor, the League of Nations, it runs the risk of being irrelevant to the concerns of justice, particularly when rogue nations have (potentially) greater representation in its process than democratic ones. In response to the person who believes that the U.S., or any other nations, for that matter, should be accountable to the UN, Eugene Rostow, we think, has put the matter in proper perspective:

> It is plausible to claim that the Security Council of the United Nations should be treated as the ultimate guardian of the soul of the state system, the only body that could possibly give an authoritative verdict on the morality of using force. But seventy years of experience with the Council of the League of Nations and its successor, the United Nations Security Council, offers no ground for optimism or even hope about the capacity of the Security Council to make such decisions consistently and rationally.[64]

That the UN, based on its track record, "offers no ground for optimism" is in many respects to state the matter charitably, since as a collective body it has abetted injustice and moral atrocity in ways that deprive it of moral authority.[65]

---

[64]Ibid., 63.

[65]Consider the following scenario. In recent years, we learned that in the conflict between Israel and the militant Muslim group Hezbollah, which is committed to Israel's annihilation and by all accounts initiated recent bouts of conflict, UN "peacekeeping" forces have made a startling contribution: they have openly published on a daily basis real-time intelligence as to the location, equipment, and force structure of Israeli troops in Lebanon. UNIFIL, the United Nations Interim Force in Lebanon, present on the Lebanon-Israeli border since 1978, is of course officially "neutral." This "neutrality," nevertheless, has resulted in UNIFIL publishing new information, at times only thirty minutes old when posted, and never more than twenty-four hours old. Specific military intelligence that UNIFIL posted could not have been secured from any non-UN source, and the same sort of intelligence has not been provided by the UN about Israel's enemies. An independent review of UNIFIL Web-site postings during recent conflict revealed daily reports showing where Israeli soldiers were located, positions from which they

Q. 42 How does just-war moral reasoning apply in the context of international relations?

In a previous question we observed a shift in thinking from medieval to early-modern presuppositions. An important adaptation of just-war principles for the early-modern period because of changing geopolitical developments is made by theorists such as Francisco de Vitoria and Hugo Grotius, discussed above, as well as Francisco Suárez. What makes their collective contributions noteworthy is their appeal to the natural law. Justice, as they understand it, has a deeper basis than mere religious belief, even when nature and religious belief do not contradict one another. Justice is known through nature and intuited universally as binding on all people everywhere. Thus, the law of nature becomes a law to the nations (*jus gentium*), holding all people accountable to the unchanging demands of justice.

Let us consider this shift in emphasis in more detail. The eras of Ambrose and Augustine and Aquinas, and even of the Protestant Reformers to an extent, differ greatly in the sorts of dilemmas that need addressing. Given the cultural synthesis of the Middle Ages, medieval theorists developed their understanding of just war explicitly from Christian religion and secondarily from natural law. This relationship is reversed in the Age of Discovery and early-modern period, which present new challenges to just-war thinkers. These challenges concern people outside Christendom, as well as a divided Christendom. Regarding the first: Does just-war thinking apply to non-Christian peoples? What about cultures and nations that find themselves outside Christendom? Do the very same just-war criteria apply? Why or why not? Such are the questions that demand answers.

In the work of Vitoria, Grotius, and Suárez we find the beginnings of international law, that is, principles governing all nations that are anchored in natural moral law. Vitoria's argument is significant because it acknowledges an international community of independent states or people groups that have rights, territorial sovereignty, and reciprocal duties as to conduct. Unlike just-war thinkers before him, Vitoria grounds the notion of just war not in Christian religion per

---

were firing, and Israeli movement strategies. On the nature of this development, see Lori L. Marcus, "What Did You Do in the War, UNIFIL?" *The Weekly Standard* (September 4, 2006).

se, but rather in moral obligation that is known through natural-law reasoning. What natural reason has established among the nations is that certain rights and privileges, rooted in justice, are inviolable. Human "nature" establishes a bond between all humanity; man is not an animal to his fellow man; he is another person. If principles of just war are applicable to non-Christian peoples, then the rationale, indeed the very basis, for justice and peace could not be construed as narrowly Christian. Human-rights violations and justification for going to war are the same for all people everywhere; they are rooted in moral realities that are unchanging and universally applicable.

An overriding concern in Suárez's work is how states are to conduct themselves; hence, there is an accent on the natural law. Whereas civil or municipal law is alterable, based on customs and usage, the law of nature is universal and unchanging, governing how individuals as well as nations deal with one another. All aspects of justice flow from this reality. Suárez scrutinizes the role of the nation-state in both defensive and offensive modes: "A required mode and uniformity as to it [warfare] must be observed at its beginning, during its prosecution and after victory."[66] Going to war and implementing war, Suárez maintains, "is common to Christians and to unbelievers," since it "is founded upon the natural law."[67]

Roughly contemporary to Suárez, Grotius confronts the dilemma of just limits to war in much the same way as Vitoria and Suárez. The results of his work would be foundational for just-war thinking in the modern era. As we saw, in his important work *The Law of War and Peace*, Grotius argues that how nations relate to one another is governed by universally binding moral principles. These are "binding on all kings" and "known through reason."[68] This argument has important implications for both the church and the state, for it places limitations on both. It also places limitations on whether nations may go to war justly and how warfare is to be conducted. Given the divinely instituted natural law, such rules of military engagement are valid for all people.

---

[66]Francisco Suárez *The Three Theological Virtues* 3.8.1, an English translation of which is found in James B. Scott, *The Spanish Origin of International Law: Lectures on Francisco de Vitoria (1480–1546) and Francisco Suarez (1548–1617)* (Washington, DC: Georgetown University Press, 1929), 77.
[67]Ibid., 3.8.2. Justification for going to war, according to Suárez, may be fourfold: defense of one's territory, recovery of what has been wrongly taken, enforcement of rights, and vindication (*Disputationes* 13.1).
[68]*The Law of War and Peace* 1.1.10; 1.3.16.

The enduring nature of Grotius's contributions, easily lost on the contemporary reader, needs reiterating, particularly amidst a generation unaccustomed to engaging in moral reasoning. Grotius's legacy includes international law, grounded in the "laws of humanity," that govern international relations; advocacy of universal, natural laws that impose legal and moral restrictions on nations; and clearly articulated rules of international law for the conduct of war that specify *jus ad bellum* and *jus in bello* requirements.

Viewed collectively, it is impossible to overstate the significance of Vitoria, Suárez, and Grotius for the development of just-war thinking as it applies to the community of nations. One commentator, quite aptly, we think, has summarized the contribution of these early-modern just-war theorists:

> The just war theory has repudiated religious and ideological causes for going to war. . . . All people have equal rights by virtue of their common humanity. Justice insists that we treat equals equally. Religious differences and causes are therefore as irrelevant to the pursuit of justice as are differences of race or culture or economic status. Justice cannot allow for morally irrelevant considerations.[69]

For much of its history, the Western cultural tradition has assumed, based on reason and revelation, that human goods need preserving and fostering, and that this can occur only in the context of a properly ordered community. Such cannot transpire apart from justice, which entails rendering to all human beings *qua* human beings what is their due. Natural justice is maintained—and enforced, when necessary—by the *polis*, the political community. In the modern era the reality of international affairs sets forth the need, as far as is possible, to work through the channels of existing international relations. Justified intervention does not overlook the dilemma of national sovereignty, but neither does it presume that sovereignty to be absolute. Overriding this sovereignty is a matter of extreme gravity, whether that intervention is military or humanitarian. In either case, moral as well as prudential criteria must coalesce in a moral judgment that justice has been egregiously denied human beings in such a manner as to morally

---

[69]Arthur F. Holmes, "A Just War Response," in Robert G. Clouse, ed., *War: Four Christian Views*, rev. ed. (Downers Grove, IL: InterVarsity, 1991), 182.

obligate others to intervene.[70] A basic distinction between regimes that are civilized and those that are barbaric is the degree to which their politics, their understanding of law, and their approach to military affairs mirror totalitarian tendencies.[71]

Q. 43   Why should governments and people of religious persuasion in particular respond to genocide and egregious human-rights violations?

Created in 1945 and determined to "save succeeding generations from the scourge of war, which twice in our lifetime has brought untold sorrow to mankind," the United Nations from the beginning resolved itself "to reaffirm faith in fundamental human rights, in the dignity and worth of the human persons, in the equal rights of men and women and of nations large and small."[72] From its very inception, the UN General Assembly passed numerous resolutions to prevent human-rights violations by its own member nations. Among the most significant was the passage in 1948 of the Universal Declaration of Human Rights,[73] which contained provisions for the right of every person from birth onward to life, liberty, fundamental human rights, and security of person. Article 5 of the Declaration specifies: "No one shall be subject to torture or to cruel, inhuman or degrading treatment or punishment."

Also passed by the General Assembly in 1948 was the Convention on the Prevention and Punishment of the Crime of Genocide,[74] which defined genocide as "acts committed with intent to destroy, in whole or in part, a national, ethnic, racial or religious group." Significantly, the parameters of the convention extended beyond genocide per se; also included were conspiracy to commit genocide, direct and public incitement to commit genocide, attempts to commit genocides, and complicity in genocide. The convention codified, in a universal and comprehensive manner, the moral obligation of nations

---

[70]See also question 41, "What is the role of the United Nations in a nation's decision to declare war?" and further questions related to humanitarian intervention.
[71]So Paul Ramsey, *The Just War: Force and Political Responsibility* (New York: Scribner's, 1968), 146; and Hittinger, "Just War and Defense Policy," 348–49.
[72]From the Preamble to the UN Charter.
[73]General Assembly Resolution 217 A.
[74]General Assembly Resolution 260 A.

to prevent genocide and protect basic human rights, representing a post-Holocaust commitment on the part of the human community collectively to prohibit—and intervene to prohibit—the deliberate systematic murder of a people group. For this reason the twofold failure of the world to prevent genocide in Rwanda in the mid-1990s,[75] as well as genocide, enslavement, and displacement of people in Sudan since 1990, constitutes one of the greatest moral indictments of our time. As one human-rights advocate reminds us, genocide doesn't just happen.[76] Why, then, do relatively free nations, with the wherewithal to intervene, turn a blind eye to genocide when and where it shows signs of emerging?

On an ongoing basis, news arrives in the mail (though rarely through the broadcast media) of the persecution of Jews and Christians by Muslims, as well as conflicts between other faith traditions on several continents. Textbooks in Saudi public schools inform students that the Crusades never ended and that jihadic holy war is considered by some Muslim scholars as necessary for the spread of Islamic faith.[77] Islamic nations in Africa, the Middle East, and Southeast Asia have been fertile soil in which a militant Islamic ideology has been nurtured in the last two decades, making conditions ripe for egregious human-rights violations among non-Muslims and nonmilitant Muslims. Increasingly, the face of militant Islam raises important questions about basic human-rights violations that require our engagement with the moral principles that undergird just-war moral reasoning.

But the prospect of jihadic terrorism is not the only development that warrants our consideration. With the collapse of the Soviet empire, many—from the layperson to the policy maker—considered the use of military force as a question lacking urgency. Alas, the end of the Cold War did not bring an end to human suffering, cruelty, and catastrophe. If anything it heralded new contexts in which human depravity might show itself. Precisely those human catastrophes *since* the end of the Cold War—from Kuwait, Iraq, and Afghanistan to Bosnia-Herzegovina and Rwanda, to Burundi and Liberia, to Somalia and

---

[75]Most estimates range between 800,000 and 1.25 million people slaughtered. For a rather sobering in-depth account of how this remarkable brutality was prepared, and then subsequently ignored by the international community, see Linda Melvern, "A Conspiracy to Murder: The Rwandan Genocide," a Parliamentary lecture accessed at www.lindamelvern.com/parliament_lecture.htm.
[76]Nina Shea, "Genocide Doesn't Just Happen," *National Review Online*, June 1, 2007.
[77]See, e.g., Hassan Fattah, "Don't Be Friends with Christians or Jews, Saudi Texts Say," *The New York Times* (May 24, 2006), parallel accounts of which appear in the July 17, 2006, newsletter published by the Center for Religious Freedom.

Sudan—herald the need for reinvigorated debates about the merits and moral substructure of humanitarian intervention and armed conflict. Consider, for example, in the brief period since the Cold War, Iraq's occupation of Kuwait and genocidal treatment of its own people, notably the Kurdish population; the starvation of civilians in Somalia; exile and enslavement of Christians as well as nonmilitant Muslims in Sudan; the slaughter of between three-quarters of a million and 1.25 million people in Rwanda; genocide in Bosnia/Kosovo; the need for massive humanitarian efforts in Burundi, Rwanda, Liberia, Sudan, and Afghanistan; the production of chemical and biological weapons in Libya and Iraq; drug trafficking on several (if not all) continents; the breathtaking rise of maturing international terrorism worldwide; and the talibanization of Afghanistan, Pakistan, portions of central and southeast Asia, and northern and western Africa.

It seems to us that these diverse crises force laypersons, educators, politicians, and policy makers alike to reflect on the morality of war, the use of force, and military intervention. Should we intervene? Why or why not? How? When? By what criteria and in what measure? At the most basic level, genocide and gross human-rights violations confront people of faith with fundamental questions of justice. Do religious believers have responsibilities toward others that transcend narrowly defined spiritual conversion? Do they in particular have a vested interest in helping to safeguard human rights wherever possible? And in what specific ways can religious believers work for justice? Should they perhaps not be especially sensitized to the violation of basic human rights worldwide and willing to oppose crimes against humanity and social-political evil that has caused human suffering? If we choose to do nothing, why? If we choose to act, how should such interdiction proceed?

Regardless of their source, and whether they arise out of religious fervor or secular-materialist antipathy toward all religion, egregious human-rights violations, crimes against humanity, and genocide make the human community morally culpable at several levels. Not only are these unspeakable acts crimes that are committed by specific and direct perpetrators; they also implicate those people groups, societies, or communities that either sanction or tolerate and stand by as the crimes are being committed. Moreover, they implicate neighboring nations or people groups that might have the wherewithal to prevent them. And, of course, they implicate all of us who would simply turn a blind eye and relegate the duty of intervention to others.

Because genocide and crimes against humanity do not happen overnight, both nations and individuals are morally culpable. Religiously, it will not suffice either to say that God will render justice in the next life to victims of genocide (the pacifist argument) or to say that we did not know (the West's argument). Both responses are an abdication of moral responsibility in the here and now.

Q. 44 Isn't the just-war position really a pretext for an uncritical nationalism?

In our responses to many of the questions posed thus far, we've tried to show that just-war moral reasoning both *permits and limits* the use of force. Another way of describing its basic moral logic is that as a doctrine it "both *condemns and condones* collective violence depending upon the circumstance, the situation and ends sought."[78] As a mediating position between pacifism and jihad/crusading/militarism it avoids the twin temptations of believing that everything is always justified and that nothing ever is. In a world that is violent and frequently characterized by a reflexive nationalism, just-war thinking represents a necessary antidote, for it understands itself as being subordinated to the demands of charity, justice, and human dignity, all of which seek to protect the innocent from gross injustice and moral evil.

With its inherent commitment to constraining collective violence and unbridled militarism, just-war moral reasoning proceeds on several assumptions that undercut the nationalist spirit. It assumes the existence of universal moral dispositions; it distinguishes between guilt and innocence, between just and unjust action, and between aggressor and victim in a fallen world; and it applies force in measured ways that are appropriate to the injustice perpetrated. All this, as one political ethicist argues, is necessary if we are to possess a vision of civic virtue.[79]

---

[78]Jean Bethke Elshtain, *Women and War*, rev. ed. (Chicago: University of Chicago Press, 1995), 128; emphasis added.
[79]Ibid., 151–52.

But what about patriotism? Is the patriotic impulse in itself a good or bad thing? And if we presume that it can be either, to what extent is it healthy, and at what point does it cloud our moral thinking? Certainly, as authors in the North American context, we cannot fail to take note of the patriotic spirit for which Americans are known and which remains incomprehensible, if not odious, to much of the surrounding world. Is this nothing more than the age-old, aggressive, warlike ethos of nationalism masquerading as a kinder, gentler species that we call patriotism? Surely, there are excessive elements of the patriotic tendency that, when shading into nationalism, are lamentable. At the same time, properly conceived, patriotism should be understood as an authentic part of the repertoire of civic ideals to be legitimately celebrated. Citizens, after all, if they take their citizenship seriously, offer much to society that is constructive; the natural result of that service, within the context of community, will be a sense of gratitude, even moderated pride. For this reason, and we think rightly, Jean Elshtain identifies the proper balance in recognizing civic responsibility when she speaks of a "chastened patriotism." Chastened patriots, she observes, are men and women who have learned from the past. Listen to Elshtain's description of what this posture entails:

> Rejecting counsels of cynicism, they modulate the rhetoric of high patriotic purpose by keeping alive the distancing voice of . . . remembrance and recognition of the way patriotism can shade into the excesses of nationalism; recognition of the fact that patriotism in the form of armed civic virtue is a dangerous chimera. The chastened patriot is committed and detached: enough apart so that he and she can be reflective about patriotic ties and loyalties, cherishing many loyalties rather than valorizing one alone. . . . A civic life animated by chastened patriotism bears implications for how we think of peace and war, and for the pitfalls in how each has been construed.[80]

On this account, "chastened patriots," then, are poised between unacceptable extremes. They resist placing duty and loyalty to the nation above all other duties and loyalties, while resisting the temptation to dismiss all civic duty as jingoism or nationalism.

---

[80]Ibid., 253.

Q. 45   What about humanitarian intervention? Short of all-out war, should nations intervene to prevent or retard egregious human-rights violations or catastrophic geo-political developments, and on what basis? What about a nation's claims to sovereignty?

The inner logic of just-war thinking, given its funda-mental commitments, permits force to be used for the purposes of redressing or preventing massive human-rights violations against a people or people groups. The realm of humanitarian inter-vention remains one of the great neglected dimensions of just-war thinking that needs exploration.[81] Indeed, since the end of the Cold War era, the sheer number of international crises that are regional in character has increased exponentially. They thrust the matter of humanitarian intervention in our faces, whether or not we care to be burdened by them.

At the theoretical level, much philosophical discussion of interven-tion tends to revolve around the issue of state sovereignty and what one observer calls "the permissibility question."[82] Less attention has been paid to the other side of the coin, the question of when interven-tion might be morally obligatory. The difficulties with the notion of national sovereignty are readily clear. In our own day, sovereignty may be interpreted in such a way that it grants a nation or territory immunity from intervention by the international community, regard-less of how oppressive its treatment of its own people. James Turner Johnson describes the dilemma that we will increasingly need to face in the post–Cold War period:

> Thus, Slobodan Milosevic, on his first appearance before the International Tribunal for the Former Yugoslavia, denied the authority of that court to indict or try him, claiming sovereign immunity because he was head of state when the acts in ques-tions occurred. Similarly Saddam Hussein justified his resistance to weapons inspections, as well as other resolutions adopted after

---

[81]On the long history of Western interventions, especially in the nineteenth century, see, Gary J. Bass, *Freedom's Battle: The Origins of Humanitarian Intervention* (New York: Alfred A. Knopf, 2008).
[82]So Kok-Chor Tan, "The Duty to Protect," in Terry Nardin and Melissa S. Williams, eds., *Humani-tarian Intervention*, Nomos 47 (New York: New York University Press, 2006), 84.

the 1990–1991 war to punish and constrain Iraq, by claiming they infringed on Iraq's sovereignty.[83]

Johnson observes that "regime change," while the terminology may be fairly new, in itself is not all that new in the context of international politics. He invites us to consider examples such as Tanzania's deposing of Idi Amin in Uganda, Vietnam's deposing of Pol Pot and the Khmer Rouge in Cambodia, and the United States' removal of Manuel Noriega in Panama.[84]

This and related questions—for example, war crimes and justice, short- or long-term intervention short of war, and postwar nation building—belong properly to the domain of just-war thinking, and broadly to what we might call *post bellum* considerations.[85]

Certainly, external sanctions are necessary for the imposition and restoration of justice where war crimes have been committed by nations and/or leaders unwilling to observe any moral restraints. These sanctions not only hold such parties accountable, but they also serve as a deterrent to potential evildoers. In addition, for justice to be confirmed, the extent to which individuals in war are guilty of war crimes must be verified and publicly identifiable. Consider the testimony of one man who has witnessed catastrophe at multiple levels. In a highly significant address in 1997 at the U.S. Holocaust Museum, South African Justice Richard Goldstone, who had been Chief Prosecutor of the International Criminal Tribunals for the former Yugoslavia and Rwanda, had this to say:

> The one thing I have learned in my travels to the former Yugoslavia and in Rwanda and in my own country is that where there have been egregious human rights violations that have been unaccounted for, where there has been no justice, where the victims have not received any acknowledgement, where they have been forgotten, where there's been a national amnesia, the effect is a cancer in the society. It is the reason that explains, in my respectful opinion, spirals of violence that the world has seen in the former Yugoslavia for centuries and

---

[83]Johnson, *The War to Oust Saddam Hussein*, 62.
[84]Ibid., 63.
[85]These considerations are developed in greater depth elsewhere in chap. 10 ("*Jus Post Bellum*: Extending the Implications of Just-War Thinking to Post-War Reconstruction") of J. Daryl Charles and David D. Corey, *Justice in an Age of Terror*, American Ideals and Institutions (Wilmington, DE: ISI Books, forthcoming).

in Rwanda for decades, to use two obvious examples. . . . So justice can make a contribution to bringing enduring peace.[86]

Sanctions are necessary to prevent ideals of justice from disappearing into mere endless discussions. The regulations found in the Geneva, Hague, and Nuremberg Conventions prohibit certain actions, based on international law, that are not required by military necessity. These accord roughly with the *jus in bello* tradition.

Can coercive force be used for the purpose of peacekeeping missions? Can humanitarian intervention be achieved apart from full-scale military operations? Just-war thinking lends itself to these complex situations, as post–Cold War crises around the world have graphically shown. While such situations are complex and evade any precise guidelines, thereby generating enormous national debate, they nevertheless raise unavoidable questions of morality and justice that are addressed by just-war moral reasoning. Given the commitment of justice and charity to defend and protect the third party, the occurrence of serious human-rights violations and crimes against humanity in another nation or people group requires a moral and measured response among those who are in a position to prevent or alleviate suffering.

Intervention, in whatever form, requires the use of power. The proper question, however, as James Turner Johnson points out, is not whether the political community should exercise power, but rather what kind of power it should exercise, when, and for what reasons. And rightly used, military force might back up or assist humanitarian policies whose principal expression is not military.[87] This is true even of situations in which we have no national interests at stake— catastrophic situations that are the implied responsibility of surrounding nations.[88]

This, of course, raises the sovereignty question. What about a nation's claims to sovereignty? Without question, the case against intervention has a hard core. After all, there exists within the international community a bias against interfering in the internal affairs of other nations.[89] According to the conventional explanation, state sovereignty constitutes one of the hallmarks of modern international

---

[86]The transcript of this address appeared in *The Washington Post*, February 2, 1997, C4.
[87]Johnson, "The Just-War Idea and the Ethics of Intervention," 108–9.
[88]Bosnia and Somalia might be cited as relevant examples.
[89]So Article 2 of the United Nations Charter.

relations since the Treaty of Westphalia (1648). And indeed the two main players in international politics over the last hundred years, Marxism and liberalism, have both tended to take a dim view of intervention, though in a qualified way and for entirely different reasons.[90] While this presumption against interference is present, international law as developed by Hugo Grotius takes account of both national sovereignty *and* natural law. That is to say, also presupposed in the concept of sovereignty is that the rights and authority of the state derive from its *individuals* who make up the state.

Therefore, the principle of state sovereignty contains (whether or not it is recognized) a human-rights component.[91] This would mean, for example, that individual citizens have the right (1) to live in a state of their choice, (2) to express differing or dissenting opinions, (3) to live relatively securely and without fear of state intrusion, and (4) to earn a living and provide for one's family. All of these things are fundamental to what it means to be *human*. Our definition of *sovereignty*, therefore, must also entail *responsibility*, not merely *privacy*.[92] A nation's "right" to persecute or oppress its people does *not* have precedence over human rights and the law of nature. Expressed differently, a sovereign's failure or unwillingness to respect the rights of the citizenry means a forfeiting of the rights of sovereignty. Thus Grotius:

> The fact must also be recognized that kings, and those who possess rights equal to those of kings, have the right of demanding punishment not only on account of injuries committed against themselves or their subjects, but *also on account of injuries which do not "directly affect them but excessively violate the law of nature or of nations in regard to any persons whatsoever."*[93]

Our response to the question What about humanitarian intervention? depends fundamentally on whether we believe that we have a

---

[90]For a discussion of the rationale provided by these two political systems, see Stanley Hoffmann, "The Politics and Ethics of Military Intervention," *Survival* 37, no. 4 (Winter 1995–1996): 29–51, esp. 33–36.
[91]Stanley Hoffmann, "Sovereignty and the Ethics of Intervention," in Hoffmann et al., *The Ethics and Politics of Humanitarian Intervention* (South Bend, IN: University of Notre Dame Press, 1996), 13.
[92]Here we offer the crucial distinction pressed by Catherine Lu in her important essay, "Whose Principles? Whose Institutions? Legitimacy Challenges for 'Humanitarian Intervention,'" in Nardin and Williams, eds., *Humanitarian Intervention*, 195–99.
[93]*The Law of War and Peace* 2.20.40; the English translation here provided by F. W. Kelsey, in Grotius, *Law* (Indianapolis: Bobbs-Merrill, 1962), 504; emphasis added.

duty, a moral obligation, to defend and protect the innocent.[94] While we might argue that a failure to intervene and save lives is less problematic morally than the indiscriminate taking of lives based on military intervention, nonintervention is nevertheless problematic and must not be ignored. The moral standards or criteria by which to measure the justness and appropriateness of humanitarian intervention are those that constitute just-war moral reasoning. So, for example,

- massive human-rights violations constitute a *just cause* for intervention because of the inalienable quality of basic human rights;
- a state or coalition of states possesses *legitimate authority* to intervene in cases where human-rights violations are severe enough to warrant overriding the principle of nonintervention, since national sovereignty is not absolute;
- a state may intervene with humanitarian intervention based on its *right intention*, namely, to protect the innocent and the oppressed.[95]

It is certainly true that intervention may reflect self-interest even as it claims just cause, and that its intrusion may trigger negative effects in the target nation, especially if force is used. Yet, the fact that outside intervention interferes with the agenda and operations of a state government is not *ipso facto* evil, since that agenda and those activities may themselves be evil and cause massive suffering for its people. Conversely, it is also true that nonintervention may be morally and politically worse than intervention.

To intervene or not to intervene? That, as Michael Walzer insists, should always be a hard question.[96] It should be a hard question for a variety of reasons: because the prospect of intervening force should always generate hesitation; but also because there is no pat formula to every crisis in the world; but also because domestic brutality and civil war

---

[94]Two very compelling arguments in support of the view that humanitarian intervention is a moral duty are offered by Tan, "The Duty to Protect," 84–116, and Carla Bagnoli, "Humanitarian Intervention as a Perfect Duty: A Kantian Argument," in Nardin and Williams, eds., *Humanitarian Intervention*, 117–40. Although people and nations certainly lack a *perfect* sense of duty and justice to identify the precise need for intervention, we would argue that a consensus regarding our duty and relative justice can be achieved. Otherwise, neutral nations that are committed to nonengagement and nonintervention would be morally superior, which is not the case.

[95]These core just-war criteria are discussed at some length by Joseph Boyle, "Traditional Just-War Theory and Humanitarian Intervention," in Nardin and Williams, *Humanitarian Intervention*, 31–57.

[96]"The Politics of Rescue," *Dissent* (Winter 1995): 35. Walzer is lamenting the fact that most people have a strong presumption *against* intervention, and for understandable reasons.

and political tyranny and genocide and religious persecution are part of the world in which we live; and because we are moral agents who must give account of our actions. Therefore, it seems to us that the task before us, in crafting wise policy, is not to be interventionist or noninterventionist; rather, it is to discriminate morally so that we might engage in *jus ad interventionem* when and where human need calls for it.[97] In the present world, there *will* be victims of tyranny, oppression, ethnic hatred, and genocide who will urgently need our help. And stepping into a situation to help innocent people and prevent greater suffering qualifies as an expression of neighbor love, to use Augustine's categories.

While nonviolent intervention is always morally preferable to violent, noncoercive responses will simply not be adequate for the moral challenges of genocide, enslavement, systematic starvation, and widespread, egregious human-rights violations. Human decency, then, based on the natural moral law and our common humanity,[98] not to mention Christian charity, would oblige us to intervene in cases where outrageous social-political evil is taking place. The moral rationale of Grotius is enduring: if the wrong is obvious and in some cases a tyrant were to inflict upon the population such treatment as would be wholly unwarranted, the exercise of the right to resist that is vested in human society is not annulled.[99]

Q. 46 What is the nature of humanitarian intervention? How does this differ from war?

The realm of humanitarian concern confronts us with universal aspirations and basic rights that inhere in our being human. Humanitarian values, because they mirror the natural

---

[97]The need for policy that is the product of morally and politically astute discrimination is brilliantly argued in Hoffmann, "Sovereignty and the Ethics of Intervention," 12–37.

[98]Thus, e.g., Samuel Pufendorf, *The Whole Duty of Man, According to the Law of Nature*, trans. A. Tooke (1691), ed. I. Hunter and D. Saunders (Indianapolis: Liberty Fund, 2003), 238: "Nothing is more agreeable to the Laws of Nature than the mutual Peace of men with one another, preserved by the voluntary Application of each Person to his Duty; living together in a State of Peace, being a peculiar Distinction of Men from Brutes . . . [and] here common Prudence and Humanity do admonish us to forbear our Arms there, where the Prosecution of the Injuries we resent is likely to return more Hurt upon us than ours, than it can do Good."

[99]*The Law of War and Peace* 2.25.8. Michael Walzer's line of reasoning regarding humanitarian intervention, in *Just and Unjust Wars*, is similar to that of Grotius. He notes, "The violations of human rights within a set of boundaries is so terrible that it makes talk of community or self-determination . . . seem cynical and irrelevant" (90). See also Gareth Evans, *The Responsibility to Protect: Ending Mass Atrocity Crimes Once and For All* (Washington, DC: Brooking Institution Press, 2008).

law, transcend human religious, ethnic, and ideological differences. What all human beings share in common invariably is brought into bold relief by cases of great injustice, suffering, and egregious human-rights violations. Christians and other people of faith should be at the forefront of addressing human suffering and defending the truly oppressed. For this reason, a basic principle, which lies at the heart of just-war moral reasoning, should guide any truly humanitarian relief assistance: Humanitarian action should be proportionate to the degree of suffering wherever it may occur.[100]

In our own world, humanitarian intervention may take differ-ent forms and apply to diverse situations and seem justifiable for a number of reasons. At the same time, intervention by definition is *extraordinary*, that is to say, a *departure* from the normal pattern insofar as it is imposed from the outside.[101] And because it is extraor-dinary, that is, because it "breaks the normal pattern" as it were of territorial sovereignty, it raises the important question of authority and thus requires moral justification. At the most fundamental level, who decides whether intervention is necessary? On what basis? For what purposes? And according to what moral measurement and criteria?

Perhaps more than ever before, today in the post–Cold War era nations such as ours will need to rethink policy options because of the need for humanitarian intervention. With the collapse of the Soviet empire two decades ago, many—from the politician and policy maker to the average layperson—assumed the use of military force or military intervention to be a question lacking urgency. Yet we would argue that it is precisely those developments *since* the end of the Cold War that induce the need for reexamining intervention.[102]

Traditionally, because it is extraordinary in nature, intervention has been conceived of primarily in terms of abrogating a state's sov-ereignty by military force. International relations today suggest that a wide variety of means, short of military coercion, might be employed to apply pressure where outrageous injustice or oppression is occur-ring. Intervention might be diplomatic, political, social and/or eco-nomic, or a combination thereof. Writes one policy analyst:

[100]So Larry Minear and Thomas Weiss, *Mercy under Fire* (Boulder: Westview, 1995), 63.
[101]Few have argued this more lucidly than John Langan, "Humanitarian Intervention: From Concept to Reality," in Abrams, ed., *Close Calls*, 109–24.
[102]See question 43, in which the extraordinary variety and seriousness of post–Cold War geopolitical catastrophes has been rehearsed.

Intervention can . . . take the form of omission (e.g., embargoes and boycotts) that disrupt the normal flow of communications and commerce. . . . [It] can be overt, with the intervening government taking responsibility for the actions it carries out or subsidizes or endorses; or it can be covert, with the intervening government unwilling to acknowledge its involvement in operations that may be of dubious legal status at home as well as in the targeted country. The form and the legal status of intervention will also depend to some extent on the perceived legitimacy of the sovereignty involved.[103]

A social-political scenario in which intervention is necessitated may or may not give the appearance of stability to the outside. Indeed, in our media age, it is increasingly common that a nation under consideration will use media voices—both electronic and print—to influence worldwide opinion against the possibility of intervention. In fact, from the perspective of international law, the nation's condition may even appear to be normal, with no external aggression apparent to indicate any moral rupture of its internal life. Recent geopolitical events involving, for example, Bosnia, Somalia, and Rwanda, as well as Cambodia and Uganda before that, suggest that the condition of a nation or people group in question may well be worse than expected or assumed from the outside. And as the world is learning, intervention in our day is far more likely to be *late* than premature. This has serious implications for rethinking policy.

Andrew Natsios, who served as Director of Foreign Disaster Assistance with the U.S. Agency for International Aid (AID) from 1989 to 1993, calls attention to the moral ambiguity that characterizes the post–Cold War period. Policy makers are beset by troubling ethical issues brought on by a rising tide of ethnic and tribal conflict that parallel the failure (or unwillingness) of states to prevent egregious human-rights violations. "Complex humanitarian emergencies," according to Natsios, may be defined according to five general characteristics: (1) ethnic, religious, or tribal conflict that includes widespread atrocities against the civilian population; (2) the deterioration of governmental authority; (3) macro-economic collapse; (4) widespread health and nutrition problems, coupled with food shortages; and (5) massive population movement of displaced people.[104] Natsios has identified,

---

[103]Langan, "Humanitarian Intervention," 111.
[104]"Complex Humanitarian Emergencies and Moral Choice," in Abrams, ed., *Close Calls*, 126.

in 1996 alone, no fewer than twenty-three "complex emergencies" that involved nearly 40 million people who were at risk of death from violence, epidemics, or starvation.[105] These sorts of numbers, it seems to us, are compelling, indeed deeply disturbing. Neither laypersons nor policy makers can ignore these dimensions of evil.

For this reason, charity and human decency will cause us to think through morally serious policy options that have adequate moral justification and realistically address possible contemporary scenarios. While agreement may elude us as to the specifics (i.e., how, when, where) of various policy options, *that* human beings are morally obligated to intervene and come to the aid of victims of gross injustice should be beyond controversy. The current unpopularity among the American public and American politicians regarding international intervention may or may not represent moral principle. We freely grant the impossibility of the U.S. responding to all—or even most—catastrophic emergencies or crises around the world. Without question, the common complaint that the U.S. is not to "police the world" has legitimacy. And, in truth, our resources for responding to crisis situations are limited. What's more, not all situations will call for the same solution, and some of these situations may exact a far greater cost—human or otherwise—than is justifiable. Finally, there is no guarantee of a beneficial or peaceful outcome in every potential intervention. These and other moral concerns will need reflection and adjudication.

On the other hand, an attitude of detachment that is suspicious of intervention may in fact serve as a smokescreen for our inability to make moral judgments and to engage social-political evil head-on. The noninterventionist impulse may stem from true humility, but it may also reflect cowardice, selfishness, and moral obtuseness.[106] Those who have struggled, particularly at the policy level, with a moral rationale and possible strategies for intervention understand the excesses at both ends of the ideological spectrum—among noninterventionists and interventionists.

What form should a morally responsible policy of intervention take? There is no pat answer to this question. While acknowledging the reality—and necessity—of vigorous debate and disagreement on

---

[105]Ibid., 127.
[106]We agree strongly with Langan, "Humanitarian Intervention," 118, who has pressed this point in his analysis of potential interventionist policy.

details, we believe that responsible policy will be informed by the very same principles that guide just-war moral reasoning: for example, justness of intervention, working through proper existing political authority (as far as possible), right intention (i.e., aiming for a greater good than presently exists), and proportionality (to the suffering being endured by victims of abuse). Prudentially, it will also utilize all possible resources for assistance; these include political/diplomatic, economic, social/cultural, and military. In addition, it will involve nongovernment organizations (NGOs) and various relief assistance organizations, depending on the scale of relief necessary.[107]

In the end, there is much that can be done in the name of humanitarian intervention short of full-scale military intervention.

Q. 47 What are the different types of humanitarian intervention?

In the previous two questions we have attempted to emphasize the urgency of the debate over humanitarian intervention in the post–Cold War era. In our argument we have stressed that the *duty* to intervene, based on just-war reasoning, is morally beyond debate.[108] What we have *not* argued thus far is what specific type of intervention might be called for in the present day. We presume that humanitarian intervention is not limited to—even when it enlists the support of—the military, insofar as "humanitarian" presupposes nonviolent activity that is economic, political-social, even private (i.e., nongovernmental) in its character. Furthermore, we have presumed that different kinds of international crises require different kinds of response and have different kinds of thresholds for intervention. Hence, the question of *diversity* in humanitarian response must be addressed. Our views are necessarily informed by primary as well as secondary just-war criteria (already distinguished in a previous question) that remain relevant to the issues at hand.

---

[107]For a helpful discussion of tactical considerations leading to humanitarian intervention, see Robert L. Phillips, "The Ethics of Humanitarian Intervention," in Phillips and Duane L. Cady, *Humanitarian Intervention* (Lanham, MD: Rowman & Littlefield, 1996), 1–29.

[108]Even John Paul II, who generally stood in opposition to the use of force and specifically was opposed to U.S. military intervention during the Gulf War, argued that in extraordinary cases nations have "a duty to intervene." "Address to the Diplomatic Corps," *Origins* 22, no. 34 (February 4, 1993): 587.

How does one distinguish between various social-political evils? One's answer, of course, will determine how one will respond, and if necessary, intervene. Consider recent geopolitical catastrophes. The Kurdish sector of Iraq, Rwanda, and Bosnia, we may argue, are examples of genocide, whereas Somalia constitutes a case of mass starvation; and Sudan and Liberia have mirrored a condition of civil war, though Sudan, out of militant Islamic ideology, has actively pursued the enslavement of—while desiring genocide for—part of its population. Do all of these crises require the same interdictory response on the part of relatively free nations? Do all, some, or none justify intervention? And why?

What are specific reasons that warrant humanitarian intervention? Military historian Paul Christopher identifies the following different categories: disaster relief, protection of refugees, prevention of genocide, curtailment of human-rights violations, or similar responses to other human suffering. What is the factor that unites all of these circumstances? According to Christopher, it is that "the intervening nation uses its armed forces in a coercive role to cause some effect in the internal affairs of another nation and, after this humanitarian objective is achieved, the intervening force withdraws."[109]

Reflecting on the duty of nations to intervene from an explicitly Christian standpoint, Drew Christiansen and Gerard Powers, who have served as foreign policy consultants with the United States Catholic Conference, offer a typology of humanitarian intervention that identifies justifications for intervening, causes of crises needing interdiction, objectives to be pursued in intervening, and suitable means by which to execute intervention.[110] According to their schematic, justifications for and causes of intervention include genocide, mass starvation, human-rights abuses, refugee crises of undemocratic regimes, repression by totalitarian regimes, civil war or ethnic conflict, failed states, and interstate conflict. Legitimate objectives in intervention include replacing offending governments,[111] rebuilding the politi-

---

[109]Paul Christopher, *The Ethics of War and Peace*, rev. ed. (Upper Saddle River, NJ: Prentice Hall, 1999), 193. Christopher issues two cautions. He admonishes us, on the one hand, to relativize the rights of national sovereignty in discussions of intervention. Nations should not be permitted to conceal human-rights violations under the guise of "sovereignty." On the other hand, the legitimacy of the need to intervene must be critically examined and found morally compelling. Different modes of governing and different religious or social customs are to be tolerated. Crimes against nature are not.

[110]"The Duty to Intervene: Ethics and the Varieties of Humanitarian Intervention," in Abrams, ed., *Close Calls*, 190.

[111]For both moral and prudential reasons, Christiansen and Powers argue that a state's sovereignty may not be overridden except in exceptional, extreme cases (194–95).

cal/economic/social order, containing conflicts, encouraging political settlements, protecting civilian populations, providing humanitarian aid, and restoring justice. Finally, acceptable means are predicated on the nature of the crisis and may be nonviolent (e.g., diplomacy, humanitarian relief, civil or legal measures), coercive (e.g., diplomacy, arms embargoes, economic sanctions), or military (e.g., peace keeping or enforcement, protection, or deterrence) in nature.

Christiansen and Powers rightly argue for a wider application of just-war moral reasoning, emphasizing that such an approach does not merely apply to fighting in war per se but rather is a mode of moral analysis that informs noncoercive measures as well. Just-war reasoning, as developed within the Christian moral tradition, has always been situated in a broader political ethic, whereby means and ends are always related. It is here that, after a proper assessment of just cause, legitimate authority, right intention, and our duty to innocent civilians has been made, the significance of prudential concerns such as last resort, probability of success, and proportionality come into play, since secondary just-war criteria wrestle with strategic considerations.[112]

Given the freshness of debates over the U.S. war with Iraq, we might consider the Iraqi people in order to illustrate the importance of extending just-war thinking to postwar scenarios. Regardless of the reader's political sympathies, it is safe to say that the one area that received the *least* consideration by political and military strategists was the *post bellum* (postwar) dimension of nation building. Twenty-five years ago, remarkably, Iraq's per capita income was $3,600 annually, roughly that of Spain at the time. Per capita income as of October 2003 barely reached the $600 mark. Between 1980 and 2001, Iraq tumbled fifty places in the United Nations Humanitarian Development Index.[113]

Diplomatic efforts, the "extended hands" of the military, the private sector, nongovernment organizations, and even the church all play a crucial and collective role in reconstructing any semblance of a civil society in war-torn or politically decimated regions. The reconstructive task, however, begins with education. Education has something of a humanizing effect, particularly in cultures that have known

---

[112]A strength of the Christiansen-Powers essay is its sensitivity to those who are suffering worldwide. To what degree do we have a *duty* to intervene and defend the innocent who are oppressed? This question requires further moral reflection on the part of not only policy makers but the Christian community itself.

[113]Ana Palacio, "The Rebirth of a Nation," *The Wall Street Journal* (October 27, 2003), A22.

totalitarian tendencies and repressive rule. Thus, basic exposure to ideas, to history, to other cultures, to literature, to law, to science and technology—all of these are critical. At a very practical level, job skills will need to be learned in order that Iraqis can be productive, utilizing their remarkable creativity. A future generation of leaders must be educated—leaders who will not simply emigrate to the West where they might live the rest of their lives in relative ease and affluence. Part of the educational task is political-legal and economic. The legal system, for example, is all but nonexistent in these countries, and much of this is due to monarchical or dictatorial practices. Basic notions such as the rule of law, which free societies take for granted, are meaningless, for "law" has been entirely arbitrary, while graft, corruption, and injustice have largely been the norm. Very often, socialist practices were the nearest thing to official policy in the past. Learning to be self-motivated, to serve others, to make basic wise economic decisions—these require a fundamental change in the way people think. Government restricted what jobs were available, where people could work, and how much they could earn. And in the end, government siphoned off from the people what resources they had in order to maintain power. Overcoming the past, then, is particularly challenging but essential if a people are to become self-governing and a relatively just society. Nothing less than justice is required to allow formerly oppressed people to flourish.[114]

Ultimately, military intervention and coercive measures more often than not appear to be the only plausible way of preventing or retarding gross humanitarian suffering and oppression. Nevertheless, in many instances a combination of military and humanitarian (i.e., noncoercive) measures will be suitable to the need at hand.

Q. 48   What about the case of former Yugoslavia?

The case of former Yugoslavia has surely been an acid test for post–Cold War international relations. And it strikes us as a rather complex acid test, at that. It has challenged our

---

[114]To be sure, we must be careful not to foist upon a rebuilding nation *our* own culture. They must learn to flourish in theirs. We do, however, facilitate *what is due all people*—the choice to be free from social-political tyranny. Justice, after all, is universal and therefore cannot rightly be construed merely as "Western" or "American."

understanding of war, peace, state sovereignty, and military as well as humanitarian intervention, and our responses to genocide and crimes against humanity. In addition, one is justified in asking why European nations provided so very little resolution to a dilemma that was in their backyard. The failure of the European community of nations to stabilize the region forced the United Nations' involvement; however, UN operations from that point forward might be deemed largely ineffective. Only a few years prior to things reaching critical mass, a Winter Olympics had been held in this former nation (in the city of Sarajevo)—a memory not too distant for most of us. What happened, and why, so quickly?[115]

While some have laid the blame at the feet of NATO policy, this is far too easy an answer. NATO policy has been directed more by American initiatives than by those of European powers, who far and away stand to gain or lose most by these directives, given their location. In the most tangible sense, the former Yugoslavia did not affect national interests of the U.S. Tragically, and inexplicably, the leading European powers—hereby we mean Germany, France, and the British—used the same rationale: the Balkans do not represent our security interests. Thus, civil war—if we may depict it as such—ensued.

Alas, as we all realized by the mid-1990s, this was no civil war. In time, the world was forced to acknowledge the sovereignty and secession of Croatia, Slovenia, and Bosnia-Herzegovina, with Serbia and Montenegro then forming a single state themselves. Certainly it is reasonable to ask, Where was the United Nations in all this? The cold reality began setting in that the "Balkan War" was in fact no civil war but rather international in its character, marked by Serbian and Croatian aggression against independent states. This, of course, implicated all NATO powers, whether they wished it or not.

If the "Balkan War" was in fact no civil war but an international development, then from the perspective of international law and the just-war tradition specifically, *NATO intervention and beyond* was legitimate and thus should be evaluated on the basis of the *jus ad bellum* criteria. As to the matter of authority, one political observer is correct to stress that we must reject the view that ultimate authority rested with the UN Security Council at this point. This was not

---

[115]For an in-depth study of the tragedy, see P. H. Liotta, *Dismembering the State: The Death of Yugoslavia and Why It Matters* (Lanham, MD: Lexington Books, 2000).

the case, since the Security Council members involved—Russia, Germany, and France—had forfeited any moral authority by their indifference to the conflict.[116] Moreover, the very charter of the UN, which is "peacekeeping" in its mission, requires that UN forces, which are lightly armed, be deployed in regions only at the invitation of the host country. But what happens when there are nations or people groups that are predisposed against "peacekeeping" and the UN's neutral policing?[117] When sovereignty of nations (or emerging nations) and the law of nations collide, what is just? National sovereignty, even emergent sovereignty, never trumps the law of nations, which is to say, the natural law. Sovereignty cannot justify genocidal practices.

In retrospect, a "peacekeeping" operation that is minimally armed and ideologically "neutral," assigned to a region in which there is quite literally no peace to keep, can only serve to benefit those who are committed to aggression, provocation, and egregious human-rights violations. While we authors are not in a position to recommend policy, based on common sense and fundamental principles of justice (what Grotius referred to as the "law of nations") it would seem that short of American intervention, European alliances—and we have principally in mind the NATO alliance—will need strengthening in order to avoid another Bosnia. One of the lessons of the former Yugoslavia is a discomfiting one: along with Rwanda, it reminds us that moral passivity is unacceptable—unacceptable because of the massive dimensions of chaos, killing, and destruction that result from the failure to intervene. Where men and nations lack the political will to prevent injustice, particularly in their backyard, we only invite further calamity.

Q. 49 What are *post bellum* ("postwar") contributions that just-war thinking can make?

In *Just and Unjust Wars*, Michael Walzer has written that there can be no justice in war if there are not, ultimately, responsible men and women.[118] While the militaristic cynic and the

---

[116]Rostow, "Competent Authority Revisited," 55.
[117]According to Article 51 of the UN Charter, those who wish to exercise their "right of self-defense" may do so "until the Security Council has taken the measures necessary to maintain international peace and security."
[118]*Just and Unjust Wars*, 288.

ideological pacifist would deny such, this truth needs emphasis. And nowhere is the truth of this statement on display more graphically than in the aftermath of war. Standard accounts of just-war theory focus on two categories of moral analysis—*jus ad bellum* and *jus in bello* considerations. Scant attention is generally paid to yet a third—and critically important—dimension of justice, namely, justice after war—*jus post bellum*.[119] If, in fact, part of the moral efficacy of just-war thinking is right intention and a concern for the proper ends, then *jus post bellum* considerations are requisite.

Recent geopolitical developments such as Bosnia/Kosovo and the Iraq War reveal the need to think through this third area more thoroughly. With regard to any conflict, however, we must ask, What is the overall aim for such conflict to be declared just? While the militarist thinks primarily in terms of victory or conquest and destruction of the enemy, just-war proponents seek to bring about, and help establish, a state or condition that is qualitatively *better* than what existed prior to war. At the bare minimum, we might cite, in positive terms, several things as requisite in the aftermath of war: the restoration or imposition of basic human and political rights that either did not exist or were eradicated from social life, compensation for victims who suffered from the prior regime, and affirmation of political sovereignty as well as territorial integrity. Negatively, justice requires that initiators of the aforementioned suffering and oppression be held accountable for the crimes they perpetrated, which violated basic justice.[120] Brian Orend, in thinking through the nature of the *post bellum* task, utilizes the metaphor of radical surgery to describe an extreme yet necessary measure undertaken in the interest of a future greater good. He writes that if

> just war, justly prosecuted, is like radical surgery, then the justified conclusion to such a war can only be akin to the rehabilitation and therapy required after surgery, in order to ensure that the original intent is effectively secured—defeating the threat, protecting the

---

[119]Notable exceptions to this are Nathan Oren, ed., *Termination of War: Processes, Procedures and Aftermaths* (Jerusalem: Hebrew University Press, 1982); Walzer, *Just and Unjust Wars*, chap. 7; Brian Orend, *Michael Walzer on War and Justice* (Cardiff: University of Wales Press, 2000), chap. 6; Orend, "Terminating Wars and Establishing Global Governance," *Canadian Journal of Law and Jurisprudence* (July 1999): 253–96; and Gary J. Bass, "Jus Post Bellum," *Philosophy & Public Affairs* 32, no. 4 (2004): 384–412.

[120]See Walzer, *Just and Unjust Wars*, 109–23, and Orend, *Michael Walzer on War and Justice*, 138–39.

rights—and that the "patient" in this case can only be the entire society of states.[121]

In this vein, James Turner Johnson argues that the just-war criteria of right intention and the aim of peace presuppose a readiness to engage in postwar nation building:

> In some cases, nation-building may be a necessary adjunct to the provision of humanitarian relief or protection of relief efforts or the endangered population. In such cases, the idea of military intervention should include the possibility of not only fighters but engineers, communications teams, military police, and civil affairs units, or of civilian teams that would fulfill these functions and others necessary to the rebuilding of a stable civil order.[122]

Even post–World War II Germany, one might argue, required Allied support and reconstruction, for it was not Germany *qua* Germany that was intolerable, but Nazi Germany. Writes Walzer, "Pending the establishment of a post-Nazi and an anti-Nazi regime, the Germans were to be placed in political tutelage." Why? It was a consequence of their failure to overthrow Hitler themselves. "The forfeiture of independence, however, entails no further loss of rights; the punishment was limited and temporary; it assumed, as Churchill said, the continued existence of a German nation."[123] In the words of Gary Bass, "The threat of Nazism and German militarism was something with deep roots in German institutions, and the Allies could hardly just walk away. At a bare minimum, Germany needed to be reshaped."[124] Indeed, to walk away from any nation in a postwar scenario is to invite anarchy and thus to contradict the very essence of original just-war principles.

Civil society—utilizing diplomatic efforts, the "extended hands" of the military, the private sector, nongovernment organizations, even the church—plays a crucial role in reconstructing any semblance of a civil society in war-torn or politically decimated regions. Despite the great challenges that reconstruction poses, as postwar Germany illustrates, there is nonetheless great hope. Aside from fundamental secu-

---

[121] Orend, *Michael Walzer on War and Justice*, 139.
[122] Johnson, "The Just-War Idea and the Ethics of Intervention," 124.
[123] Walzer, *Just and Unjust Wars*, 115.
[124] Bass, "Jus Post Bellum," 397.

rity issues, the reconstructive task begins with education. Education, as noted earlier, has a humanizing effect, particularly for people who have known totalitarian, repressive rule. Exposure to ideas, history, literature, other cultures, law, science, and technology is critical. On a practical level, citizens need to learn job skills to make productive use of their gifts and creativity. What's more, a future generation of leaders must be raised up as part of the recovery.

In many war-torn or decimated countries, because of monarchical or totalitarian rule, the legal system is all but nonexistent, and where it does exist, the practice of law has been arbitrary, creating a climate in which graft and injustice have been the rule. Overcoming the past in this regard is particularly challenging yet essential if a people is to become self-governing. All of the important components in a nation's rebirth—education, learning job skills, the rule of law, self-government, and so on—will contribute to the overall development of that people. Learning to be self-motivated, to serve others, to make basic wise economic decisions—these require a fundamental change in the way people think, since in the past government siphoned off from the people what resources they had in order to consolidate and maintain power.

Thus, to emphasize *post bellum* nation building is to take seriously the aims of justice and peace that have been declared before conflict is entered. Nothing less than justice is due a formerly oppressed people in order that they might flourish. From the standpoint of humanitarian intervention, the failure of a victorious nation to provide assistance in postwar reconstruction of another nation calls into question its claim to have waged a just war.[125]

Q. 50 Can the just-war tradition accommodate the "war" on terrorism?

If, in the words of one political philosopher, "politics is not the nursery,"[126] then politicians, theorists, and strategists who wish to respond to international terrorism and the "war on

---

[125]Here we stand in agreement with Bass, whose argument for reconstructive efforts even in former genocidal states ("Jus Post Bellum," 396–404) is compelling.
[126]So Elshtain, *Just War against Terror*, 1–2.

terror" (sometimes called the "Long War") confront a particularly challenging expression of a fallen world. Terrorism is a complex security issue with many far-reaching consequences, both intended and unintended. The just-war tradition, in our view, is well situated to accommodate this challenge, but such an accommodation rests on the actions and agency of those waging the war under its rubric. What's more, those who act must be consistent in applying the categories and principles of the tradition. A *just* "war on terror," it needs emphasis, *is* viable, provided that it is consistently carried out in accordance with the components and premises of the just-war tradition. Terrorism is simply one point on a continuum of armed conflict, and the just-war tradition has the flexibility to address any aspect of that continuum.

This point warrants accentuation. The problem is not the just-war tradition as a viable ethical construct for engaging terrorism but rather the *consistent appropriation* of the principles and categories within the construct. It is a question of application, not logical and ethical validity. At the same time that we stress the importance of consistency, we wish to keep in mind the categorical difference between combating terrorism in generic terms and the present "war on terror." The latter has specificity and historical context that the former lacks.

Any political or ethical issue, including war, must be evaluated by its principles, policies, and practices. Moral principle serves as the intellectual foundation from which policies (including laws and governing documents such as international law and rules of engagement) are established. From these policies stem individual and community practice and conformity or nonconformity. In the end, this continuum of *principle leading to policy leading to practice* expresses itself in the following way: justice informs and serves as a basis for just-war moral reasoning, whose governing principles inform a so-called "war on terror" by relatively free societies, which assume a modicum of responsibility in addressing evil in the world. We grant that the ideological pacifist will not be predisposed (or equipped) to counter terrorism of any sort, whether domestic or international. We do, however, presuppose a willingness on the part of the citizenry to implement criminal justice, whether in its domestic or foreign context.

Once the validity of fighting terrorism within a just-war framework is established, it is incumbent on the military structure to consistently apply the policy (i.e., the tradition as articulated in the law of land warfare and specific rules of engagement). But we must add a caveat: as the "war on terror" continues, it may or may not conform to the just-war tradition. If the traditional categories of *jus ad bellum, jus in bello,* and more recently, *jus post bellum* are consistently followed in terms of application, there will be conformity with the broader tradition. At the same time, we must stress that there is flexibility and elasticity in the tradition that enables it to address new challenges, all the while being faithful to the moral principles that underpin the tradition. The major contemporary proponents of just-war thinking—we have in mind Walzer, Johnson, Elshtain, O'Donovan, and Evans—uphold its validity in addressing terrorism and its ability to offer ethical guidance.

But perhaps we assume too much at this point. After all, definitions of "terrorism" and the "war on terror" are separate entities. To illustrate: there are more than one hundred definitions of terrorism in governmental, political, and scholarly literature,[127] each grounded in the focus and function of the author, agency, or organization studying the phenomenon; nevertheless, there is overlap and a core consensus of opinion. Despite this considerable diversity, all definitions agree that terrorism involves violence or the threat of violence. This fact remains uncontested, even when it is true that while all terrorism is violence, not every form of violence is terrorism. One definition in the international arena drawn from the first International Conference on Terrorism (1973) and considered valid in our own day is that terrorism is "the deliberate and systematic, murder, maiming, and menacing of the innocent to inspire fear for political ends."[128]

According to conventional wisdom, four elements or premises are thought to constitute terrorism. As an act it is (1) premeditated and not random violence, (2) political in essence rather than criminal, (3) aimed at civilians rather than military targets or combat-ready troops,[129] and (4) an attempt to capture the media spotlight (or divine

---

[127]So C. A. J. Cody, "Terrorism, Morality, and Supreme Emergency," *Ethics* 114 (July 2004): 772. Philip Jenkins, on the opening page of his volume *Images of Terror: What We Can and Can't Know about Terrorism* (New York: Aldine de Gruyter, 2003), also laments that defining terrorism is next to impossible. While we grant diversity of opinion in terms of definition, we reject the view, implied by Jenkins, that terrorism is foremost a *sociological* pathology rather than a moral delinquency.

[128]Christopher C. Harmon, *Terrorism Today* (London: Frank Cass, 2002), 1.

[129]This is a violation of the principle of discrimination and one of the key reasons that terrorism stands outside ethical permissibility in the just-war tradition. Discrimination prohibits a just-war proponent's use of terrorism.

approval if it is religiously motivated). Terrorism, then, is thought to be a violent political reaction to the status quo. However, the subsequent "war on terror" instigated by the United States and others in the aftermath of the 2001 terrorist attacks has challenged conventional thinking, since it has been carried out as a deliberate response to the attacks of 9/11 and to a perceived threat of international terrorism that is ideologically rooted in militant Islamic jihadism.[130] The current "war" may or may not include efforts against nationalist terrorism, state-sponsored terrorism, or macro-terrorism.

Although the just-war tradition was formulated for conventional warfare, it has been utilized and developed over the centuries such that it can address any type of warfare. This, however, does not mean that it *approves* of all types of warfare. For any theory of war to be viable it must be comprehensive, internally consistent, compatible, and applicable in a viable manner; that is, it must be realistic and stand up to moral scrutiny. While just-war theory is not static, its revisions or reapplications must maintain internal coherence and consistency for it to remain valid and viable. Within the traditional just-war categories of *jus ad bellum* and *jus in bello*, and more recently *jus post bellum*, are the various criteria such as right intention, proportionality, and discrimination. Elshtain, Johnson, Walzer, and others have shown that military operations against terrorism do fall within the categories and that all of the criteria *can* be met, confirming the unity and validity of the theory.

Because there are similarities between military action against terrorists and police action against criminals (the goal of both being justice), it is certainly reasonable, as some have done, to question whether the military is the appropriate agency to conduct counterterror operations. If not, it could be argued that *last-resort* instrumentally has not been achieved. That is, there might be other agencies or organizations that are better suited to the task. If there are and these structures are not being used, then one might argue that the tradition is an invalid construct for justifying counterterrorism. (This does not solve the issue of which agency or entity *is* appropriate. It simply argues that others *might* be more appropriate.)

---

[130]On the character of terrorism since the early 1990s, we refer the reader to Walter Laqueur, *The New Terrorism: Fanaticism and the Arms of Mass Destruction* (New York: Oxford University Press, 1999), and Mark Juergensmeyer, *Terror in the Mind of God: The Global Rise of Religious Violence*, rev. ed. (Berkeley: University of California Press, 2003).

In his classic text *The Just War* (1969), predating Walzer's secular perspective of the tradition, Paul Ramsey asks, "Can counter-insurgency abide by the distinction between legitimate and illegitimate military objectives while insurgency deliberately does not?"[131] This question about insurgency warfare is a corollary to questions about terrorism and counterterrorist operations. Both insurgency and terrorism are on the "low-conflict" end of the spectrum of war, and both are asymmetric types of warfare. This similarity is important because it offers a parallel model for addressing terrorism within the just-war tradition, since counter-insurgency has been recognized as a valid response, even though difficult, within the tradition.[132] The phenomenon of terrorism reminds us that the tradition speaks to warfare across the spectrum—from low-intensity insurgency to high-intensity nuclear warfare, with conventional force-on-force conflict being the median. At the same time, no one who has seen firsthand, or even secondhand, the effects of terrorism can fail to be moved by its violent and destructive nature. Trauma, tragedy, and tears are always its fruit. Harmon reminds us, "Terrorism never loses its essential nature, which is the abuse of the innocent in the service of political power."[133]

Decisions about engaging in any war are difficult and the "war on terror" is no exception. A viable theory does not guarantee correct understanding or application. Johnson points out:

> As the classic just war theorists well understood, the fundamental responsibility of those with sovereign authority is to serve a just and peaceful order. This is their particular burden. The justified use of force is one of the tools they must have available. To think otherwise is to forget the kind of world we live in.[134]

Such sentiments certainly underscore reality—politics isn't the nursery. However, within the framework of the just-war moral reasoning, it *is* possible to conduct a "war on terror" and to target acts of terrorism justly, whether or not we choose to view this conflict as "war" in the strictest sense.

---

[131]Ramsey, *The Just War*, 433.
[132]O'Donovan, *The Just War Revisited*, 64–66.
[133]Harmon, *Terrorism Today*, 29.
[134]Johnson, *The War to Oust Saddam Hussein*, 67.

Q. 51 What is a preemptive war?

A preemptive war is one in which a nation initiates military action against an enemy in order to eliminate an immediate and credible threat of serious harm. It is action undertaken when war is understood to be inevitable. By striking first, the preempting nation expects to eliminate or reduce the enemy threat. The just-war tradition and international law permit self-defense in response to an assault, and those arguing for preemption normally do so on the basis of self-defense. The June 1967 Six-Day War is frequently presented as an instance of a preemptive war.[135] Just-war proponents contend that a state not only has a right to self-defense, but also has a moral obligation to defend its citizens, and preemption is an extension of that obligation.[136]

Both secular and religious contemporary just-war theorists such as Michael Walzer, Neta C. Crawford, and James Turner Johnson have upheld and addressed the viability of preemption within the just-war tradition. Walzer believes "states may use military force in the face of threats of war, whenever the failure to do so would seriously risk their territorial integrity or political independence. Under such circumstances it can fairly be said that they have been forced to fight and that they are the victims of aggression."[137] It is certainly worth noting that preemptive wars are rare. One study found that of all inter-state wars between 1816 and 1995, only three were considered preemptive: World War I, Chinese intervention in the Korean War, and the 1967 Arab-Israeli Six-Day War.[138]

The difficulty in pursuing preemption is that of probability and certainty. One can never know with absolute certainty the intentions of another party; consequently, acting preemptively becomes a matter of judgment and the validity of one's military intelligence, as well as the use of that intelligence. And Johnson adds, "The justification of preemption is inherently difficult to demonstrate publicly because

---

[135]See Walzer, *Just and Unjust Wars*, 82–85.
[136]For current thought on preemption and ethical considerations, see Henry Shue and David Rodin, eds., *Preemption: Military Action and Moral Justification* (Oxford: Oxford University Press, 2007).
[137]Ibid., 85.
[138]Dan Reiter, "Exploding the Powder Keg Myth: Preemptive Wars Almost Never Happen," *International Security* 20, no. 2 (Autumn 1995): 6.

enemy from changing the balance of power or otherwise behaving in a manner that the preventer would judge to be intolerable."[147] Preventive war aims to forestall the maturation of the menace; it is waged "not out of strong conviction that a dangerous threat is brewing in a target state, but rather because it is suspected that such a threat might one day emerge."[148]

While it is conventionally thought that the 1981 air raid by Israel of the Iraqi nuclear reactor in Osirek, near Baghdad, constitutes a textbook example of preemptive use of force, in the narrower sense this event demonstrates decidedly *preventive* measures undertaken to avert a future—and more catastrophic—warfare scenario. Based on intelligence and the belief that Iraq was intending to target Israel with nuclear weapons, Israel sent six jets toward Baghdad to take out a nuclear reactor. This air strike effectually removed the possibility that Iraq would use nuclear capabilities against Israel, even when one might argue that the evidence was not "beyond doubt."

Most just-war proponents consider preventive war to be beyond the scope of the tradition and its limits of permissibility. In part, they reject it because it abandons the *jus ad bellum* criterion of last resort and the *jus in bello* criteria of proportionality (since there is nothing to which a proportional response is made) and discrimination (since those being attacked are not actively engaged in hostilities even though they are likely uniformed personnel).

Q. 53   Can preventive war be accommodated in traditional just-war categories?

The preventive war is one that "is undertaken when a state believes that war with a potential adversary is possible or likely at some further date and that, if it waits, it will lose important military advantages. In this case the threat is not imminent or even certain to materialize."[149] Preventive war cannot be accommodated in traditional just-war categories as they are currently articulated. It violates the standard categories of *jus ad bellum* and *jus in bello*—

---

[147]Ibid., v–vi.
[148]Ibid., vi.
[149]Crawford, "The Justice of Preemption and Preventive War Doctrines," 25–26.

and more recently *jus post bellum*—in such a way that any attempt to place it within the framework requires substantial modification of the whole. Preventive war fails in meeting particular criteria, thus eroding and invalidating the unity of the framework.

Most just-war proponents and jurists condemn preventive war—theorists on the ground that it is a clear violation of just-war tradition, and jurists on the basis of international law. However, this condemnation has not been universal. Historically, relatively few of the major just-war writers address preventive war, although Grotius in *The Laws of War and Peace* (1625) permits preventive war in rare cases; even so, the validity can still be questioned.[150] Other early-modern theorists permitting preventive war under extreme circumstances include Emmerich de Vattel and Immanuel Kant, though neither Vattel nor Kant stands strictly in the just-war tradition. For Kant, preventive war is permissible but not desirable because he believes it fails in an overall sense to promote international and perpetual peace.[151] More recently, Michael Walzer has contended that there are times when preemptive war is morally permissible, but preventive war is inherently more problematic, though every case must be analyzed individually.[152]

Other major just-war thinkers such as Ramsey[153] and Johnson[154] also reject preventive war. Ramsey concedes the possibility that a preventive war is defensive in every sense except for the initial aggressive act of resorting to armed force.[155] If so, then the entire concept of aggressor must be clarified. Advocates of preventive war, some within the just-war perspective and others outside of it, include Allen Buchanan, Robert Keohane, and Randall Dipert.[156]

For the just-war theorist, prevention hinges on whether or not every component of the *jus ad bellum* and *jus in bello* criteria is followed or met. Have there been any exceptions? The traditional answer has been no. While the criteria do not constitute a mere checklist, each

---

[150]As does Randall R. Dipert, "Preventive War and the Epistemological Dimension of the Morality of War," *Journal of Military Ethics* 5, no. 1 (2006): 33.
[151]Crawford, "The Justice of Preemption and Preventive War Doctrines," 31, evaluates Kantian reasoning.
[152]See Walzer, *Just and Unjust Wars*, 85.
[153]Ramsey, *The Just War*, 68.
[154]James Turner Johnson in his various works argues for the validity of preemption but sees preventive war as unjust. See, more recently, *The War to Oust Saddam Hussein*, 52–53, 114–22.
[155]Ramsey, *The Just War*, 64.
[156]Allen Buchanan and Robert O. Keohane, "The Preventive Use of Force: A Cosmopolitan Institutionalist Perspective," *Ethics & International Affairs* 18, no. 1 (2004): 1–22. See also Buchanan, "Institutionalizing the Just War," *Philosophy & Public Affairs* 34, no. 1 (2006): 2–38, as well as Dipert, "Preventive War and the Epistemological Dimension of the Morality of War," 32–54.

component must be present for warfare to be morally and ethically viable under the perspective.

In our view, therefore, preventive war fails to uphold the just-war perspective on several counts. It assumes that today's potential rival will certainly become tomorrow's adversary. It requires the ability to know an adversary's capability and intention, an assumed perfect knowledge of which may be false, misinterpreted, or premature. The initiator discards the criterion of last resort for "preventive defense" and assumes that all other diplomatic and economic pursuits will fail and are therefore unnecessary.

Consequently, preventive war may well become the first choice rather than the last or reasoned choice within the initiator's frame of reference. It makes "last resort" the first resort. Correlatively, it could also fail the criterion of *right intent* (i.e., proper motivation). The initiator might believe that war is being commenced for reasons of self-defense when in fact it was anchored in reasons other than self-defense, such as imperialism or economics. At the very least, such would be the perception of others—especially if the conflict is geographically removed from the initiator.

Also, within *jus ad bellum* requirements, preventive war fails to meet the criterion of *just cause* in that it assumes a certain future breach of justice that has not yet occurred. Further, it may also fail on *limited aims* depending on how far-reaching or global the threat is considered to be. Although most concerns about preventive war fall under the *ad bellum* category, there are also the *in bello* issues of discrimination and proportionality that are problematic with preventive war.

Questions arise concerning proportionality because there has been no offense to which a proportionate response and action can be measured. The offense is assumed but not realized. On the other hand, it could be argued that a preventive war favors proportionality by minimizing future deaths at the cost of present deaths incurred in the preventive action. This, it will be remembered, was part of the rationale in the 1981 preemptive strike by Israel against the Iraqi nuclear reactor at Osirek. (As noted already, there is considerable debate as to whether this action should be classified as a preemptive strike or a preventive action.) The Israelis intentionally destroyed the reactor the week before it was fueled and went "hot" so as not to endanger the surrounding community and to prevent what they believed would be a future threat with much more lethality. [157]

The Israel-Iraq historical illustration aside, preventive war has difficulty meeting the criterion of discrimination. Discrimination becomes an issue because those likely killed by the initiator in the preventive war, though military personnel, are not *actively* engaged in hostilities, and being in a uniform does not in itself make people legitimate targets. Because the adversary has not yet made an aggressive move, nearly all those killed or injured by the preventive war would be noncombatants. (Even in the case of Osirek, the one fatality was a French contractor.) Thus, preventive war erodes the combatant and noncombatant distinction. Also, as a corollary to this erosion, the preventive war could expand occasions for use of preventive force such as assassinations, torture, and violation of prisoner of war rights and status, creating further moral and legal problems.

Beyond the traditional categories, preventive war is problematic in that it increases instability and insecurity, thus eroding peace, part of the objective of just-war theory (though secondary to justice). Although preemption can fit within traditional just-war categories, it is an ethical, logical, moral, and legal slippery slope toward prevention. In a world of asymmetric war and threats of terrorism, the preventive impulse is strong and understandable, but one that must be resisted in the application of just-war theory. Neta Crawford observes: "The psychological reassurance promised by a preventive offensive war doctrine is at best illusory, and at worst, preventive war is counterproductive. Preventive wars are imprudent, because they bring wars that might not otherwise happen and increase resentment."[158]

While some might desire to extend the logic of justified preemption as authority for preventive wars, this can only be done if *all* threats are immediate and grave.[159] Even then one must come back to a fundamental purpose of the just-war perspective, namely, the reduction of war. Preventive war as a doctrine, even if legally legitimate, is likely

---

[157]There was, however, considerable debate within the Israeli government prior to the decision, and Ariel Sharon, part of that government, stated, "This was perhaps the most difficult decision which faced any [Israeli] government during all the years of the state's existence." Ariel Sharon, cited in Barry R. Schneider, "Radical Responses to Radical Regimes: Evaluating Preemptive Counter-Proliferation," McNair Paper Number 41, May 1995, Institute for National Strategic Studies, 13.

[158]Crawford, "The Justice of Preemption and Preventive War Doctrines," 47.

[159]Ibid., 43.

to increase rather than decrease warfare around the globe and, consequently, undermines the moral argument of just-war proponents.

Q. 54   How does the concept of "supreme emergency" relate to the just-war tradition?

The issue of "supreme emergency" raises concerns that intersect with both *jus ad bellum* and *jus in bello* spheres. These concerns have to do with legitimate authority, proportionality of means, and discrimination (noncombatant immunity). The phrase *supreme emergency* was originally used by Winston Churchill to refer to the crisis and British struggle against Nazism in the early part of World War II. On December 16, 1939, as First Lord of the Admiralty, he wrote to the Cabinet:

> The final tribunal is our own conscience. We are fighting to re-establish the reign of law and to protect the liberties of small countries. Our defeat would mean an age of barbaric violence, and would be fatal, not only to ourselves, but to the independent life of every small country in Europe. Acting in the name of the Covenant, and as virtual mandatories of the League and all it stands for, we have a right, indeed are bound in duty, to abrogate for a space some of the conventions of the very laws we seek to consolidate and reaffirm. Small nations must not tie our hands when we are fighting for their rights and freedom. The letter of the law must not in *supreme emergency* obstruct those who are charged with its protection and enforcement. It would not be right or rational that the aggressive Power should gain one set of advantages by tearing up all laws, and another set by sheltering behind the innate respect for law of its opponents. Humanity, rather than legality, must be our guide.[160]

This historical event illustrates well the struggle of applying ethics in times of war. Although Churchill voiced "supreme emergency" in the context of discussions about Great Britain invading neutral Norway, from which Germany obtained much of its iron ore, it was later applied to the "area bombing" of German cities in which thousands

---

[160]Winston S. Churchill, *The Second World War*, vol. 1, *The Gathering Storm* (Boston: Houghton Mifflin, 1948), 547; emphasis added.

of noncombatants were killed. These actions instigated a passionate ethical debate that continues even to the present, in part because the bombing was seen to violate the just-war principles of proportionality and discrimination.[161]

Michael Walzer's discussion of "supreme emergency" in *Just and Unjust Wars* has strongly influenced its acceptance in just-war thought. According to Walzer, the core of "supreme emergency" is that "there is a fear beyond the ordinary fearfulness (and the frantic opportunism) of war, and a danger to which that fear corresponds, and that this fear and danger may well require exactly those measures that the war convention bars."[162] In short, there is a time and place for emergency ethics when and where it becomes right (and perhaps, mandatory) to do "wrong."

Prior to World War II, British Prime Minister Stanley Baldwin captured the essence of "supreme emergency" when he wrote about terror bombing: "If a man has a potential weapon and has his back to the wall and is going to be killed, he will use that weapon, whatever it is and whatever undertaking he has given about it."[163] For a situation to be one of supreme emergency there must be both the imminence of danger and extremity of danger. While all war is horrible and its lethal and destructive elements are enormous, not all wars involve struggle over ultimate values or the complete destruction of a society. Furthermore, that a nation is about to be defeated in and of itself does not necessarily constitute a supreme emergency since the issue at stake is not loss of territory or political and governmental structures; rather, "supreme emergency" concerns extreme developments such as moral and physical extinction and the loss of entire social and cultural structures. Nor does "supreme emergency" apply to individuals, combatants or others, since the individual soldier is not exempted from moral prohibitions. Such applies only to the state.

---

[161] The literature on this subject is vast. For an excellent earlier overview, see Christopher C. Harmon, *"Are We Beasts?" Churchill and the Moral Question of World War II "Area Bombing,"* The Newport Papers, 1 (Newport, RI: U.S. Naval War College Press, 1991). Other representative works include Stephen A. Garrett, *Ethics and Airpower in World War II: The British Bombing of German Cities* (New York: St. Martin's, 1993); Frederick Taylor, *Dresden: Tuesday, February 13, 1945* (New York: HarperCollins, 2004); Max Hastings, *Bomber Command*, rev. ed. (London: Pan, 1999); and A. C. Grayling, *Among the Dead Cities: The History and Moral Legacy of the WWII Bombing of Civilians in Germany and Japan* (New York: Walker, 2006).

[162] Walzer, *Just and Unjust Wars*, 251. See also, Brian Orend, "Is There a Supreme Emergency Exemption?" in Evans, ed., *Just War Theory*, 134–53.

[163] Cited by Walzer, *Just and Unjust Wars*, 252.

Proponents of "supreme emergency" reserve it for unique moments in history, although they do so with great sobriety. In the words of one theorist:

> Faced with some ultimate horror, their options exhausted, they will do what they must to save their own people. This is not to say that their decision is inevitable (I have no way of knowing that), but the sense of obligation and of moral urgency they are likely to feel at such a time is so overwhelming that a different outcome is hard to imagine.[164]

Supreme emergency is paradoxical because in such a circumstance moral values and constraints are still valid and yet must be overruled, in that not doing so would result in the destruction of such values. Walzer writes:

> There are no moments in human history that are not governed by moral rules; the human world is a world of limitation, and moral limits are never suspended—the way we might, for example, suspend *habeas corpus* in a time of civil war. But there are moments when the rules can be and perhaps have to be overridden. They have to be overridden precisely because they have not been suspended. And overriding the rules leaves guilt behind, as a recognition of the enormity of what we have done and a commitment not to make our actions into an easy precedent for the future.[165]

Again, Walzer notes,

> "Supreme emergency" describes those rare moments when the negative value that we assign—that we can't help assigning—to the disaster that looms before us devalues morality itself and leaves us free to do whatever is militarily necessary to avoid the disaster, so long as what we do doesn't produce an even worse disaster.[166]

Anytime "supreme emergency" is invoked, it is done with the knowledge that moral values and ethical norms are being broken, not permanently suspended, and with great guilt and remorse. Also, only when a nation or community is faced with a defeat such that enemy triumph

---

[164]Ibid., 254.
[165]Michael Walzer, *Arguing about War* (New Haven, CT: Yale University Press, 2004), 34.
[166]Ibid., 40.

will entail "a loss of value greater than men and women are morally obliged to bear" is there a state of supreme emergency.[167]

One of the strongest arguments against "supreme emergency" is that it limits the option of employing such emergency ethics to the state alone (the legitimate authority). "Supreme emergency" is not understood to be an option for individuals, substate actors, terrorists, or groups; it is solely the prerogative of the nation-state, itself a representation of the political community.[168] Yet in a time when many are questioning the continued validity of the Westphalian system, some find it difficult to limit it to the state alone.

Supporters of "supreme emergency" limit its application to the state in part because "the survival and freedom of political communities . . . are the highest values of international society."[169] However, if this premise is not accepted, then the limitation is in question. Such is the position of C. A. J. Coady, who writes:

> What is needed, at the very least, is an argument that locates the survival and freedom of states as the highest human value and one that is capable of justifying the overriding that supreme emergency requires. I doubt that any such argument exists . . . [hence] the attempt to restrict the supreme emergency exemption to states is unpersuasive. Either it applies more generally or it does not apply at all.[170]

If the exemption is broadened, it also diminishes the rarity of its use and further erodes the category of supreme emergency, opening it further to exploitation by terrorists and others. Coady believes that "supreme emergency" also "undervalues the depth and centrality of the just-war prohibition on killing the innocent."[171]

Ultimately, one must decide whether any prohibitions in ethics generally and in warfare specifically are absolute. The "supreme emergency" question forces one to consider the very nature of ethics and ethical systems. Whether one accepts or rejects the notion of emergency ethics or supreme emergency, it is important to remember the narrowness of its definition and use. Walzer's caution is well worth

---

[167]Ibid., 47.
[168]"Supreme emergency" is strongly rooted in communitarian ethics; cf. Walzer, *Arguing about War*, 42–46.
[169]Walzer, *Just and Unjust Wars*, 254.
[170]C. A. J. Coady, "Terrorism, Morality, and Supreme Emergency," *Ethics* 114 (July 2004): 785, 787.
[171]Ibid., 788.

heeding: "As hard cases make bad law, so supreme emergencies put morality itself at risk. We need to be careful."[172] For this reason, William V. O'Brien equates a just war with a "*limited* war."[173]

Q. 55 Can just-war thought accommodate a world with weapons of mass destruction?

Any theory of war or philosophical-theological framework that fails to address the concept of weapons of mass destruction is incomplete. The just-war tradition provides a framework for thinking about issues of war and peace that is broad enough to encompass and evaluate the entire spectrum of weapons and the full range of military operations. It should be emphasized that consideration of nuclear and other weapons of mass destruction has been part of dialogue and debate within the just-war tradition since their inception, which spans several generations.[174] Discussions about weapons of mass destruction are usually carried forth in relation to the *jus in bello* criteria of proportionality and discrimination. Michael Walzer has also tied nuclear weapons—and more specifically, nuclear deterrence—to the concept of "supreme emergency." Walzer writes:

> Supreme emergency has become a permanent condition. Deterrence is a way of coping with that condition, and though it is a bad way, there may well be no other that is practical in a world of sovereign and suspicious states. We threaten evil in order not to do it, and the doing of it would be so terrible that the threat seems in comparison to be morally defensible.[175]

While not all just-war proponents would agree with Walzer's perspective, his words demonstrate the seriousness of a world with weapons of mass destruction.

---

[172]Walzer, *Arguing about War*, 33.
[173]Hence the title of his book, *The Conduct of Just and Limited War* (New York: Praeger, 1981).
[174]Here we refer the reader to the cumulative writings of Paul Ramsey, William V. O'Brien, and James Turner Johnson, who for a span of the last forty years have applied just-war moral reasoning to the nuclear age. See as well Walzer, *Just and Unjust Wars*, 269–83, and more recently, Darrell Cole, *When God Says War Is Right: The Christian Perspective on When and How to Fight* (Colorado Springs: Waterbrook, 2002), 127–36.
[175]Walzer, *Just and Unjust Wars*, 274.

The bombing of Hiroshima and Nagasaki at the end of World War II introduced a new era in the history of warfare in which nuclear weapons were added to the arsenal of weaponry options for the superpowers. Following the Second World War, the U.S. and the Soviet Union entered a nuclear arms "race" for the purposes of deterring one another from nuclear attack and, from the perspective of the U.S. and its NATO allies, to prevent a Soviet attack in Western Europe. Delivery systems for nuclear weapons spanned air, land, and sea domains and created a strategic environment in which the threat of their use became part of a national defense strategy. Although those weapons were never used by either the Soviets or the Americans, Cold War nuclear brinksmanship helped shape the course of post–World War II life. This did not, however, change the nature of warfare, given the fact that conflict and proxy wars of the two superpowers continued on several continents.[176]

It was in this context that debates about the ethics and morality of nuclear weapons occurred. Theologians, philosophers, political scientists, and religious and political leaders debated the viability of nuclear weapons throughout the Cold War years.[177] During that era, many thinkers, including just-war proponents, tended to distinguish between the possession of nuclear weapons, which were deemed acceptable as a deterrent until nuclear disarmament could be achieved, and the use of nuclear weapons, which was thought ethically untenable. The use of nuclear as well as biological or chemical weapons was understood to violate both discrimination and proportionality. Unless directed upon military forces in a tactical setting, their use would be outside the just-war tradition (although this also was subject to great dispute).[178]

Among religious thinkers, this general predisposition against the use of nuclear weapons has been called "nuclear pacifism," which we

---

[176]For an overview of the Cold War, with its strategic implications, see John Lewis Gaddis, *The Cold War: New History* (New York: Penguin, 2005). For more specific information on strategic thought regarding nuclear weapons during the era, see Steven E. Miller, ed., *Strategy and Nuclear Deterrence* (Princeton, NJ: Princeton University Press, 1984); and Michael Mandelbaum, *The Nuclear Question: The United States and Nuclear Weapons, 1946–1976* (Cambridge: Cambridge University Press, 1979). On proxy wars, see Odd Arne Westad, *The Global Cold War: Third World Interventions and the Making of Our Times* (Cambridge: Cambridge University Press, 2005). Finally, on nuclear weapons and the nature of war, see the brief but enlightening discussion in Max Boot, *War Made New: Technology, Warfare, and the Course of History 1500 to Today* (New York: Gotham Books, 2006), 307–8.
[177]See William V. O'Brien, "Just War Conduct in a Nuclear Context," *Theological Studies* 44 (June 1983): 191–220.
[178]See, e.g., "Paul Ramsey (1913–1988): Nuclear Weapons and Legitimate Defense," in Gregory M. Reichberg, Henrik Syse, and Endre Begby, eds., *The Ethics of War: Classic and Contemporary Readings* (Oxford: Blackwell, 2006), 614–24.

critique elsewhere in this volume by contrasting a presumption against force or war with a presumption against injustice or evil. The classic just-war tradition is characterized by the latter. The contributions of several just-war thinkers—particularly Paul Ramsey, William V. O'Brien, and James Turner Johnson—need underscoring. In the 1960s and '70s, Ramsey advocated policy prescriptions that he believed were imperative for the free world's security. These recommendations were based on both moral principle and political prudence. In his view (which was a minority view among religious perspectives), the U.S. needed to develop a rationale for the just use of conventional (including nuclear) military forces, given the Soviet threat. Falling prey to both pacifists' calls for disarmament and militarists' threats of mutually assured destruction would be both immoral and unacceptable. Further, U.S. policy should be clear, he argued, that we would not use nuclear weapons in a first strike but as a tactical response against aggression by the enemy. This response, moreover, would be governed by rules of "just conduct." Nuclear capability itself, Ramsey insisted, is not immoral and should be maintained for use in *counterforce* warfare, were that alternative regrettably necessary. Counterforce warfare has as its aim a just peace, not mutual destruction of societies. What's more, *intention* and not amount of destruction dictates what in the end is just use of force.[179]

In an era of nuclear pacifists, who theoretically might not rule out the use of coercive force as a potential moral instrument but *in practice* assumed that our present nuclear capabilities require of us a pacifist position, the work of O'Brien possesses a trajectory similar to that of Ramsey. O'Brien is keenly aware of the shortcomings of nuclear deterrence. Most military strategists, he complains, brushed aside the morality of limited war. At the same time, O'Brien belonged to a minority of religious thinkers who believed that limited nuclear war is not a "dangerous heresy," but in fact a foundation for any realistic policy of deterrence and defense.[180]

O'Brien's first major work on just war, *War and/or Survival* (1969),[181] argues for a moral realism that might counter the distor-

---

[179]Ramsey's rationale for the justified use of nuclear force is laid out most succinctly in *The Limits of Nuclear War* (New York: Council on Religion and International Affairs, 1963).

[180]See his essay "The Failure of Deterrence and the Conduct of War," in William V. O'Brien and John Langan, eds., *The Nuclear Dilemma and the Just War Tradition* (Lexington: Lexington Books, 1986), 154–97.

[181]Garden City: Doubleday, 1969.

tions of militaristic thinking. While reacting to the excesses of militarism, O'Brien also rejects any ethic that fails to take seriously the political realities of the present. Therefore, he argues, the elimination of war is utopian at best and wrongheaded at worst. The first order of business, morally speaking, is to limit and contain it.[182] For O'Brien, only the just-war tradition possesses the moral fiber to furnish the necessary framework.

James Turner Johnson is the leading contemporary authority on the historical development and application of the just-war tradition. Johnson has produced numerous serious and meticulously researched works on just-war theory since the mid-1970s. These works range from the historical development of just-war thinking in the Christian tradition, to a comparison of war and peace in Western and Islamic traditions, to the moral complexities of nuclear war, to nonconventional terrorist activity. Behind Johnson's work is a commitment to bring just-war perspectives to bear on contemporary perceptions of war. He believes that the issues of technology and modern weaponry are more the symptoms than causes of moral dilemmas today. More important, in his view, is how we understand force in political life, and how the use of force reflects moral values.

Just-war thinking can constructively assist governments, leaders, and policy makers by bringing ethical considerations to bear on a host of dilemmas—including the design and use of weapons. These considerations extend even to types of weapons that are not conducive to conventional warfare. Because much weapons technology can be adapted to purposes other than the original intent of those weapons when first designed and manufactured, it is necessary to consider not only how weapons are actively used (discrimination and proportionality), but also how they are designed. Thus, just-war proponent Oliver O'Donovan, who has argued for a ban on the design of specific technical features of a weapon, writes:

> It may seem a simple matter to name a class of weapon for prohibition, but weapons technology is fluid. In ruling something out, a ban presents an incentive to technology to overcome the new handicap it has imposed. . . . Weapons technology has terrorised the twentieth century by running ahead of moral, political, and legal control. It is easy to deplore its past role; but the practical question is always

---

[182]See esp. chap. 8 ("The Laws of War") in ibid.

how to bring it under control. . . . Prohibitions are unhelpful, unless accompanied by a serious attempt to apply moral reasoning to the task of weapons design.[183]

But there is another side to the weapons argument that is suggested by just-war moral reasoning. Conventional notions of international law do not adequately address the problem of weapons of mass destruction and what happens when rogue nations or terrorist groups in the post–Cold War era threaten national and international security. While the average layperson may be unaware, limited nuclear wars that perhaps were dismissed during the Cold War now invite serious reflection.[184] Questions not only of deterrence but also of preemption arise. For example, must a nation wait until catastrophe strikes before reacting, or is preemptive action morally permissible? Could it possibly be morally required? Aggression today threatens far more than the mere sovereignty of the state, and the resources of the just-war tradition, in all of its width and breadth, will be needed for morally appropriate responses.

Q. 56 What about the statement "One person's terrorist is another person's freedom fighter"?

The statement in question mirrors the distorted thinking of moral-equivalence debates that arose during the era of the Cold War and Marxist insurgency around the world. It essentially is like saying, "One person's rapist is another person's romantic." Although both rape and romance may involve sexual activity, they are qualitatively different actions that distinguish themselves by intention, means, and purpose. One (rape) is about power, and the other (romance) is about love.

So also are there distinctions between terrorism and freedom fighting. Both involve violence, but the means, targets, and methods are different. Terrorism targets the innocent and noncombatants, and its intention is "to cause to tremble" (from the Latin *terrere*). For present purposes, we shall adopt either of the following two definitions of

---

[183]O'Donovan, *The Just War Revisited*, 93–94.
[184]See in this regard Roberts, "NBC-Armed Rogues," 83–107.

terrorism in our attempts to make necessary moral discriminations: (1) the deliberate and systematic murder, maiming, and menacing of the innocent to inspire fear for political ends; (2) the unlawful or unthreatened use of force or violence against individuals or property to coerce or intimidate governments or societies, often to achieve political, religious, or ideological objectives.[185]

Words communicate meaning and value. Bumper-sticker statements and ideological sloganeering such as the above represent a worldview in which ethics, and actions based upon those ethics, are relative rather than absolute. Such statements are built upon an ethical relativism that rejects a normative understanding of truth. However, there are moral, ethical, and legal differences between a terrorist and a "freedom fighter." Yet, because of their rhetorical effect, slogans such as this one are accepted without critical reflection even while they "undercut the natural human antipathy for terrorist methods, and permit terrorist propaganda far more credence than it deserves."[186]

We believe terrorism to be morally, psychologically, and theologically indefensible. The immediate question is whether so-called oppressed or marginalized peoples are morally self-responsible. Should they be held accountable for their actions? Why or why not? The difference between morally justifiable resistance and armed rebellion or terrorism needs heightening.

In the most fundamental way, terrorism represents a disjunction at several levels.[187] It wages war by disordered means, in defiance of proportion and discrimination (noncombatant immunity). It thereby shows itself as a moral abomination through its total disregard for human dignity and personhood. Furthermore, it operates in defiance of legitimate authority, that is, by military organisms that are neither governments, nor *putatively* governments, nor subject to governments. Thus, terrorism is the waging of war by illegitimate means and ends, thereby placing the entire population—or entire populations—in a position of being a hostage or a hostage-shield, given the high degree of noncombatant death and destruction.[188] Because terrorists have

---

[185]Respectively, Christopher C. Harmon, "Terrorism: A Matter for Moral Judgment," *Terrorism and Political Violence* 4, no. 1 (1992): 2; and Timothy J. Demy and Gary P. Stewart, *In the Name of God* (Eugene, OR: Harvest House, 2002), 30–33.

[186]Harmon, *Terrorism Today*, 186.

[187]O'Donovan has argued thus—and persuasively, in our view—against terrorism in *The Just War Revisited*, 30–32.

[188]Here, O'Donovan's attempt to distinguish between terrorism and insurgency, while thoughtful and helpful, is not entirely persuasive. See the chapter "Counter-Insurgency War," in ibid., 64–77.

no interest in the welfare of communities for which they presume to speak or which they plunder and destroy, they dispossess themselves of any claim to moral authority, with recourse only to intimidation and manipulation in the most drastic and inhumane sense.

But perhaps the reader has lingering questions about terrorists' legitimacy, doubting that a punitive response by government is justified. All of criminal justice, as our cultural tradition has believed and practiced it, is based on the fundamental distinction between *intention* and *effect*, between guilt and innocence, between justice and injustice. Biblical norms for justice are taken for granted in contemporary notions of criminal justice, even when they are less readily conceded. For example, if you killed a person by accident, and the judges so determined this in the presence of multiple witnesses, your flight to the "city of refuge" prevented the avenger from slaying you.[189] If, on the other hand, witnesses confirmed that the act was premeditated, your own life was required. Murder and homicide are not the same. Criminal negligence, weighed on the scales of justice, is always less offensive than intended criminal acts. By its very nature, terrorism is intended violence against innocent human beings, and irrespective of its garb, it is the deliberate violation of established moral norms— norms that are known to all people through the natural law, that is, by virtue of creation and conscience.

If crime confronts any society with difficult moral judgments, then the phenomenon of terrorism thrusts this difficulty in our faces. At the same time, it forces us as nothing else does to recognize the indispensable nature of government, as Oliver O'Donovan has well argued.[190] Precisely for this reason, Aquinas listed legitimate authority first in his justification for going to war. Regardless of one's religious perspective, terrorism is a moral abomination against all people, whether or not they are personally targeted, injured, or killed.

Terrorism expert Christopher Harmon puts it this way: "One could well argue that if terrorism is not immoral, then nothing is immoral."[191] In an age that shies away from making moral judgments, the slogan "One person's terrorist is another person's freedom

---

[189]See Num. 35:6–34; Deut. 4:41–43; 19:1–21; Josh. 20:1–9.

[190]O'Donovan, *The Just War Revisited*, 32.

[191]Harmon, *Terrorism Today*, 190. The literature on terrorism is vast and rapidly growing. In addition to Harmon's important work, for introductions to the subject along with attendant ethical considerations, see Bruce Hoffman, *Inside Terrorism* (New York: Columbia University Press, 1998).

fighter," which screams at us for moral definition, needs to be seen for what it is.

Q. 57 What is the relationship between Islamic terrorism, Islamic resurgence, and Islam's conflict with Western culture?

In its essence, Islam is theocratic, and it has always been such from its inception. Hence, Islamism is nothing short of a rejection of both the reality and the intent of the secular state, and it understands itself as an important source of social resistance to the modern state.[192] From the Islamic point of view, the process of secularization has pushed religion out of the public sphere. The secular state therefore is viewed as a contradiction to all for which Islam stands.

This perspective has enormous ramifications for politics, law, and statecraft. Compare the theocratic vision with another model. Throughout Christendom and in broader Western culture, God and Caesar have been thought to coexist, based on Jesus' distinction between the two realms in his teaching. In Islam, however, God *is* Caesar in that "he alone is the supreme head of state, the source of sovereignty and hence also of authority and of law. The state is God's state, the law is God's law. The army is God's army—and, of course, the enemy is God's enemy."[193] Thus, during the 1970s, Hasan al-Banna, a founding member of the Muslim Brotherhood in Egypt, could criticize Jesus' distinction between Caesar and God: "Caesar and what is Caesar's are to the one and only victorious God," he declared.[194]

Reference to "the enemies of God," while seeming excessively militant to the average Westerner, needs to be understood within the broader framework of Islamic theology. Conceptually, as we have observed, it has its roots in a theocratic understanding of the world,

---

[192]This is not to argue that Islam is opposed to state power; only to the state's secularism. Islamic ideology calls for an Islamization of the entire culture *through* state power. Thus, Seyyed Vali Reza Nasr, *Islamic Leviathan: Islam and the Making of State Power* (Oxford: Oxford University Press, 2001), 15–17.

[193]So Bernard Lewis, "Islamic Revolution," in *From Babel to Dragomans: Interpreting the Middle East* (Oxford: Oxford University Press, 2004), 305.

[194]Hasan al-Banna, *Five Tracts of Hasan al-Banna*, ed. C. Wendell (Berkeley: University of California Press, 1978); see esp. 80–82 for a development of this argument.

which consists in the division between the *dar al-Islam* ("house of Islam") and the *dar al-harb* ("house of war"). Those enemies, moreover, might be internal or external to the "house of Islam." Given the fact that according to Islamic law, the penalty for apostasy is death (since apostasy is a denial or rejection of ultimate allegiance and authority), Islam is conceived not merely as a religious community but as a *polity*.[195] In our own day, not incidentally, resurgent or "fundamentalist" Islam[196] can be seen to have a markedly legalist quality. That is, its burden is to counter the abandonment of the sharia, the systematized law of Islam, and to resist what Muslims view as "infidel" laws and cultural practices. Because its critique covers "the whole range of social and political modernization," its declared purpose, in the words of Bernard Lewis, is

> to undo all the political, legal and consequent social changes that have been introduced during the period of Westernization, and to restore the full panoply of the Islamic state and the Islamic holy law. Only when the neopagan apostates who rule in Islamic lands have been deposed, and their laws and institutions abrogated and annulled, will the true Islamic life become possible, and the true mission of Islam be accomplished.[197]

In wrestling with this question, we proceed on the assumption that Islamic fundamentalism need not be radical or militant in nature. Correlatively, we do not equate religious fundamentalism with terrorism, even when that is the popular caricature. We further assume that any "war on terrorism" is not merely about security or military response, though it entails that; rather, it requires understanding the theological environment in which radically militant values are shaped. For this reason, former British Prime Minister Tony Blair was correct to note in a recent issue of the journal *Foreign Affairs* that the roots of the current wave of global terrorism and extremism are deep, reaching down through decades—indeed, centuries—of alienation, victimhood, and political oppression in the Arab and Muslim world. In such an environment, political radicals become religious radicals and vice

---

[195]Lewis, "Islamic Revolution," 306.

[196]We do not hold the view that militant or radical movements represent all or even most of Islam in the present day, or that "fundamentalist" Islam is necessarily militant or radical in nature, or that radical Islamic groups are homogenous. The great geopolitical question is whether more tolerant and "moderate" factions within Islam or more militant ones will emerge as dominant.

[197]Lewis, "Islamic Revolution," 309.

versa.[198] At the same time, we must emphasize that Islamic radicalism does not stem solely—or even primarily—from desperation or poverty or particular social conditions, as some theorists maintain. What is undeniable is that radicals come from a variety of socioeconomic and educational backgrounds. Many of those individuals implicated in mass murder over the last decade are university trained and have even studied in the West.

The authors of the recent definitive study *Islamic Radicalism and Global Jihad* argue that even though violent confrontation between Islamic radicalism and the West has been one of the defining features of the twenty-first century, radicalism's ideology has evolved over time. Moreover, they emphasize—rightly, in our view—that this radicalism cannot be understood apart from Islam's basic theological-philosophical foundations and its long-term goals and vision.[199]

> Islam, since its earliest days in the seventh century, has had a political valence. The teachings of Islam, especially the Qur'an, provide much of the vocabulary for expressing political ideas, since politics and religion are seen as part of the same sphere, unlike the secular and religious dichotomy that dominates contemporary Western political theory. Islamist groups—both violent and nonviolent—are able to use this vocabulary to their advantage in order to make the case for reform, justice, and social change.[200]

The profile of a group such as Al Qaeda is a requisite case in point. Al Qaeda represents two things simultaneously, and this reality cries out for understanding: it is (1) a violent Islamic organization with a small core of strategic leadership yet worldwide tentacles and (2) part of a large and growing political-religious movement of Islamic revival.[201] As suggested by its name (which means "the base"), its ideological trajectory can be readily identified. In the words of Michael

---

[198]Tony Blair, "A Battle for Global Values," *Foreign Affairs* (January–February 2007), accessed at www.foreignaffairs.org/20070101faessay86106/tony-blair/a-battle-for-global-values.
[199]Devin R. Springer, James L. Regens, and David N. Edger, *Islamic Radicalism and Global Jihad* (Washington, DC: Georgetown University Press, 2009). See esp. chaps. 1 and 2, in which basic ideological commitments of Islam are set forth against the backdrop of more recent geopolitical developments.
[200]Ibid., 8. To say, as the authors do, that Islam "has had a political valence" throughout its history is the equivalent of saying that children are inclined toward play. Despite this wild understatement of Islam's fundamental *equation* of God and Caesar, the authors usefully observe the importance of a *vocabulary* that facilitates revolutionary change.
[201]So Michael Radu, "Al Qaeda Confusion: How to Think about Jihad," a July 2007 electronic publication of the Foreign Policy Research Institute, accessed at www.fpri.org/enotes/200707.radu.alqaedajihad; site discontinued.

Radu, a fellow of the Foreign Policy Research Institute, Al Qaeda was established

> as a vanguard, elite organization, not dissimilar, conceptually, from the previous Marxist Leninist self-selected vanguards of the proletariat (Shining Path in Peru, Red Brigades in Italy, etc.) seeking to reestablish Islam's historic (and mostly mythical) supremacy and purity throughout the world via unification of the *umma*, the Islamic community, under a single political and religious leadership and state. . . . The means to accomplish this is jihad, strictly defined by the followers of this ideology as warfare.[202]

Because Al Qaeda's ideology is rigorously antinationalist, it is attractive to alienated or poorly integrated young Muslims living in Western nations and, in a strange way, appeals to Muslim elites wherever they may be situated. Tactically, Al Qaeda's strategy appears to be to exacerbate geopolitical situations in which chaos, conflict, or confusion already exist.[203] What bothers many people in the West is the seeming inability of moderate Muslims to denounce and counter Islamic terrorism. How may we account for this relative silence?

At the same time, a fairly wide range of Middle East scholars stand in relative agreement that there exists throughout nonviolent Islam worldwide considerable sympathy for radical groups. Why is this? In the Islamic context, extremism often begins with religious doctrine. But in short order, it is disseminated by offshoots of the Muslim Brotherhood and by Wahhabist extremists in madrassas of the Middle East and Asia, to be exported worldwide.[204] The reason for this broad-based sympathy is the general perception shared by most Muslims that Islam is in a state of crisis—even victimhood—owing to Western domination and thus needs revival.[205] Precisely *how* to go about this revival generates no little disagreement, but *that* a revival is needed is accepted by virtually all Muslims, moderate or militant. Today, then, in myriads of

---

[202]Ibid.

[203]See the particularly prescient commentary on this strategy offered by Radu, ibid.

[204]The fact that Blair, "A Battle for Global Values," perceptively identifies this development is salutary, although he stops short of drawing conclusions.

[205]Surely, multiple factors might be cited as to *why* there is a resurgence of radicalism. Among these, for example, are a weariness of Western domination, a desire for purity of faith, the collapse of Marxist and communist ideologies, the Soviet defeat and pull-out of Afghanistan, and information technology (of which Muslim societies, ironically, in their loathing of the West, have been beneficiaries). On the ideological roots of the Islamic resurgence, see Springer, Regens, and Edger, *Islamic Radicalism and Global Jihad*, 8–51; here the authors perform the important service of highlighting the intellectual "fathers" of this resurgence, particularly those of the twentieth century.

countries around the globe, terrorists—even when their active cadres are relatively small—seek to exploit the widespread sense of alienation and grievance that characterizes the broader Muslim world.[206]

This, then, in addition to the fear of reprisal from militant Muslims, may account for the seeming inability of Muslim moderates to denounce terrorism and radicalism. While there are indeed moderating influences and perspectives within Islam, maintaining solidarity with the wider brotherhood is of utmost importance, given the widespread perception of victimhood and deprivation attributable to the West. Muslim moderates are caught between the radicals and the masses; and those who dare to offer public criticism tend to pay dearly for their dissent. In the view of one esteemed student of Middle Eastern culture, the relationship between militant and nonmilitant versions of Islam is one of urgency. If the leadership of militant groups can persuade the broader world of Islam to accept their views and their leadership, then a dark, protracted struggle lies ahead.[207]

Part of the critique of world politics that undergirded the late Samuel Huntington's controversial "clash of civilizations" hypothesis in the early 1990s was the belief that conflict in the years ahead would not be primarily politico-ideological or economic but "cultural."[208] Thereby Huntington wished to underscore the roots of human conflict—roots that are products of many centuries. In his view, "civilizational" or cultural differences have resulted in some of the *most violent* conflicts over the centuries simply because cultural features are less mutable than political or economic practices. Moreover, because of the secularizing and modernizing tendency in much of the world, "fundamentalist" religion has moved in to fill the void sensed by many. And with the disappearance of the Cold War fault line, a new one has emerged to take its place, namely, the cultural division between Islam and the West.

Huntington's thesis, of course, was controversial when it appeared, and it remains so today. In a day like ours, when diversity, otherness, and inclusiveness tend to trump questions of philosophical substance and truth (both in academic and in popular discourse), historians, political philosophers, and social critics are squeamish about affirm-

---

[206] A useful resource that sheds light on the mindset of Muslim victimization is Bernard Lewis, "The Roots of Muslim Rage," in *From Babel to Dragomans*, 319–31.

[207] Bernard Lewis, "The Rise of Terrorism" (chap. 9), in *The Crisis of Islam*, 137–64.

[208] Samuel P. Huntington, "The Clash of Civilizations?" *Foreign Affairs* 72, no. 3 (1993): 22–49.

ing a clash of civilizations and cultures. At least in the nonjudgmental West, to affirm such a thesis is to invite scorn of the highest order, and not infrequently, induce heartburn.[209]

In the prior question we refrained from making predictions. And we shall maintain this fundamental posture. Nonetheless, we also believe that profound and irreversible changes have occurred—and are occurring—throughout Islam. As it applies to terrorism, there would seem to be emerging in the Muslim world a network of jihadist groups that, while not hierarchically related, nevertheless are unified ideologically. As described by one policy analyst, Al Qaeda has transformed into a network of "franchises" that agree ideologically but operate independently, resulting in a more dangerous geopolitical situation because of its de-centralization.[210] Hence, we find significant the remarkably blunt acknowledgment by a German-Turkish author who straddles the Islam-versus-West cultural fault line:

> Politicians and religious scholars of all faiths are right in pointing out that there are many varieties of Islam, that Islamism and Islam should not be confused, that there is no line in the Koran that would justify murder. But the assertion that radical Islamic fundamentalism and Islam have nothing to do with each other is like asserting that there was no link between Stalinism and Communism.[211]

We return to the question we posed above, which was intended to probe the interrelationship of Islamic fundamentalism, Islamic terrorism, and Islam's cultural conflict with the West. The base from which radicalized movements within Islam are drawing manpower is growing in the Middle East, Africa, Asia, and Europe. The potential for destruction in utterly massive proportions doubtless gives terrorists hope, whether through weapons of mass destruction or "soft

---

[209]So, for example, Springer, Regens, and Edger, *Islamic Radicalism and Global Jihad*, 228, caution the reader, "The first element of a proposed strategy emphasizes the necessity of moving beyond the rhetoric of a clash of civilization, emotions and values." And humanitarian scholars, it goes without saying, are extremely uncomfortable with the vocabulary of clash and conflict; thus, for example, the reader learns from Peter J. Hoffman and Thomas G. Weiss, *Sword and Salve: Confronting New Wars and Humanitarian Crises* (Lanham, MD: Rowman & Littlefield, 2006), 145, that "Samuel Huntington's 'clash of civilizations' is fraught with contradictions."

[210]Lowell E. Jacoby, "Five Years after 9/11: What Needs to Be Done," a February 2007 electronic publication of the Foreign Policy Research Institute, accessed at www.fpri.org/enotes/200702.jacoby. fiveyearsafter911; site discontinued.

[211]Necla Kelek, as cited by Peter Schneider, "The New Berlin Wall," *The New York Times* (December 4, 2005).

kill" techniques such as penetrating the infrastructure of information technology through cyberterrorism or penetrating the infrastructure of our public works and utilities. Our basic orientation in posing the above question is not alarmist but rather realist; we wish to discern the deeper significance of militant Islam. In this vein, we find compelling the assessment of one student of Islamic terrorism, who contends that

> just as Stalinism (and Pol Pot or Mao) was made possible by the mass of usually peaceful and naïve believers in the Marxist Utopia, Al Qaeda and its nebula are permanently feeding up from the growing Islamic revivalist movement. To separate the two should be the goal of Muslims and non-Muslims alike, since they are all targets of jihadism. To deny the intimate link between the two is to deny reality. By making artificial distinction between the two, one only postpones and avoids the real struggle.[212]

It is impossible at present to deny the fundamentalist religious component in worldwide Islam. The question that remains is what element within Islam will shape the views of the masses. Whether moderation or extremism will prevail is unclear. Some observers have argued that in the West especially, moderate forms of Islam such as Sufism offer a potential for a viable Muslim experience coupled with Western political values. Certainly there is much within this tradition that appeals to Western considerations.[213]

Q. 58 Is the just-war idea limited to self-defense?

The right of self-defense against attack is a fundamental principle of international law and is deeply embedded in the just-war tradition. Indeed, self-defense has been understood to be not only a right of political leaders but also a duty. A war of aggression is not a just war and is contrary to just-war thinking and international law. For this reason, from the beginning of Christian reflection on the

---

[212]Radu, "Al Qaeda Confusion."
[213]See Stephen Schwartz, *The Other Islam: Sufism and the Road to Global Harmony* (New York: Doubleday, 2008), and Seyyed Hossein Nasr, *The Heart of Islam: Enduring Values for Humanity* (San Francisco: HarperCollins, 2002).

problem of war, self-defense has been central to just cause for going to war and remains at the heart of the classic just-war doctrine.[214]

While one normally thinks of the just war as one of self-defense of the political community, the tradition also allows for preemption within that framework. This is by no means merely a contemporary development in thinking. Early-modern theorists such as Vitoria and Suárez, in wrestling with the complexities of "New World" discovery, and Grotius, in agonizing over Europe's decimation through religious wars, well recognized the difficulty of competing claims of justice. And on occasion, they realized, armed conflict may take on the appearance of being offensive when in truth its design is defensive. In their deliberations over what justice requires, they confronted a possible scenario and asked: Can stages of preparation for war, though not actual war themselves, be a violation of just-war principles? That is to say, is there such a thing as malicious preparation for war that qualifies as just cause for reprisal or prevention? Grotius understood the delicacy of this moral continuum and argued that a "defensive war" may be justified against a wrong not yet perpetrated.[215] He acknowledged such, all the while aware of the need to trust in divine providence for "protection against uncertain fears."[216]

Several applications of Grotian just-war moral reasoning require our consideration. One is how to confront the possibility of a belligerent state or potential enemy that is actively engaged in acquiring or producing nuclear capabilities and weapons of mass destruction.[217] In thinking through contemporary scenarios, one is forced to concede that just cause does not merely concern a *rationale* for the beginnings of conflict (though it does concern this); it also agonizes over the *timing* or precise point at which this conflict is considered actual or immediately threatening.

More recently there has been much discussion and debate about the legitimacy of humanitarian interventions. Just-war reasoning, as we argue elsewhere in this volume,[218] supports the idea of humanitar-

---

[214]For this reason, Oliver O'Donovan overreaches when he argues that "when self-defence, of state, community or individual, has the last word, paganism is restored" (*The Just War Revisited*, 9). The cumulative weight of classic Christian thinking, with some exceptions, affirms the morality of self-defense at various levels. Allowing for those voices within the Christian tradition that demur, what we *may not* insist is that such is a restoration of paganism.

[215]*The Law of War and Peace*, 2.1.

[216]Ibid.

[217]One of the strengths of O'Donovan's volume, *The Just War Revisited*, is his attention to this dilemma; see, e.g., 48–58, 78–94.

[218]See the previous questions on humanitarian intervention in part 3.

ian intervention.[219] What happens when the state no longer serves as the sole or primary guarantor of human security?[220] It is not only self-defense that the just-war idea upholds but also the defense of the helpless—those who are unable to marshal any self-defense.

Q. 59 What are the implications of just-war thinking for *jus post bellum* ("justice after war"), and what might this suggest in contemporary geopolitics?

Despite the frequency of military intervention and post-conflict scenarios around the world during the last two decades, one looks in vain for a protocol to guide *post bellum* operations and strategy. In their assessment of the U.S. role in post-conflict activity, James Carafano and Dana Dillon are correct: post-conflict aims must be part of American pre-conflict planning and should exhibit as much forethought toward fighting for peace as toward fighting battles, since winning the peace is *the* goal of winning a just war. Or, in their words, successful post-conflict operations will "starve the seeds of future conflict."[221]

But there is a problem. Even when the U.S., to the present day, has a relatively long history of involvement in postwar activity, there is a problematic pattern, particularly in recent times. Not infrequently, the U.S. will aspire to leave behind "a free-market, liberal state committed to the rule of law, a strong civil society, and peaceful intentions." While the intention may be correct, more often than not the goal has not been achieved. Not infrequently U.S. post-conflict operations have started with what might be viewed as a "clean slate" solution. This clean slate usually entails abolishing most of the vestiges of the previous regime, both military and civilian. For example, the de-nazification of postwar Germany and the de-baathification of Iraq are mirrors of this tendency.[222] What is needed in the reconstruction of a society,

---

[219]James Turner Johnson, *The War to Oust Saddam Hussein: Just War and the New Face of Conflict* (Lanham, MD: Rowman & Littlefield, 2005), 122–26.

[220]See Patrick Hayden, "Security Beyond the State: Cosmopolitanism, Peace and the Role of Just War Theory," in Evans, ed. *Just War Theory*, 157–76.

[221]James J. Carafano and Dana R. Dillon, "Winning the Peace: Principles for Post-Conflict Operations," *Backgrounder* #1859, accessed at www.heritage.org/research/nationalsecurity/upload/sr-7wcover.pdf.

[222]Ibid.

however, entails far more; it encompasses education, political and legal rehabilitation, economic infrastructure, and more.

But to insist that postwar activity be more proactive is far more easily said than accomplished. And most moral and political philosophers who on theoretical grounds might argue for *jus post bellum* have difficulty appreciating the practical challenges in the implementation of policy initiatives. Consider, for example, the matter of predicting accurately, in a pre-conflict context, what might be needed in a post-conflict scenario. Prewar estimates of postwar necessities are not necessarily a reliable measuring tool. The needs of Iraq illustrate our point. Given that Iraq, in its prewar state, was roughly "the size of California, has porous borders, is awash with arms, and has a diverse population of about 25 million (with at least 10 million in eight major cities),"[223] we might ask what sort of defense analyst (let alone, what sort of thinking politician) would confidently estimate the security and reconstruction challenges. Few analysts (or moral or political philosophers, for that matter) would have had a clue.

In addition, despite Germany's remarkable postwar example of reconstruction and progress, whatever the U.S. has learned over the years about rebuilding a post-conflict society has not been incorporated into mainstream military thinking in any systematic way. By way of illustration, Carafano and Dillon note that the U.S. army did not even have a field manual on occupation management before 1940; only in 1942 were staff positions created to advise military leadership about civil affairs in occupied territory.[224] Unquestionably, geopolitical developments since the Cold War have taught the U.S., and hopefully other nations, about the reality of post-conflict responsibilities. Most assessments, however, would suggest either that the U.S. did not do enough post-conflict planning before the Iraq war or that it did not apply what it has learned over the years. At the same time, it is only fair (and accurate) to point out that most people are oblivious to the fact that reconstruction funds, based on the Marshall Plan, were not made available until 1949, that is, four years after the formal termination of the war. What's more, the amount that the U.S. contributed was a relatively small part of the overall reconstruction investment that

---

[223]Ibid.
[224]Ibid.

was needed for Europe at the time[225] and therefore does not provide a strong precedent for postwar Iraq.

Although *jus post bellum* is presently lacking prescriptive categories both at the theoretical level and in international law, this third column of just-war reasoning needs development for establishing and guiding parameters of *post bellum* reconstruction and nation building. What might a commitment to "justice after war" entail? What specific realms constitute part of an intentional postwar reconstruction project? To ask such questions is to ponder what social, political, legal, economic, educational, and security spheres are necessary for *any* nation or people group to become self-sustaining, regardless of whether its people, in the strictest terms, are postwar, post–civil war, post-genocide, near collapse (owing to political and/or economic destabilization), or otherwise.

In attempting to underscore the importance of *jus post bellum*, we operate on the assumption that in most potential postwar situations, there is sufficient time in which to consider—and plan for—these dimensions. At the same time, we also allow that in some extreme situations, such as preventing genocide in future Rwandas, *there will not be sufficient time* for planning a full-scale reconstruction project. The fact that inadequate time is available because mass killing is underway or ready to explode does *not* excuse those nations that have the wherewithal to prevent the mass killing from intervening.[226] Nevertheless, Brian Orend is correct to insist that a failure to construct *jus post bellum* in a prescriptive sort of way is, at the bare minimum, to permit an unconstrained war termination and to prolong the warring process.[227] Ad hoc postwar arrangements likely cannot address the deeper societal needs that contributed to a nation's collapse in the first place.

What particular principles of post-conflict or postwar priority might be essential to a reconstructive project? Once the transition has been justly guided, what specific aims—both short- and long-term—are requisite? Any strategies are to be guided by the assumption that the aim of "just regime change" is "a minimally just political community."[228] Orend identifies a number of constitutive elements

---

[225]The discussion of Carafano and Dillon (ibid.) is quite helpful in this regard and demonstrates insight into the practical realities of policy that most philosophers and social theorists miss.

[226]In current literature very little commentary is capable of looking past Iraq to the broader moral issues.

[227]*The Morality of War* (Peterborough, ON: Broadview, 2006), 161; see also Orend, "Justice after War," *Ethics & International Affairs* 16, no. 1 (2002): 43–44.

[228]*The Morality of War*, 197.

that are part of a more comprehensive strategy. These elements are both immediate and long-term in their implementation:

- Maintaining strict adherence to just-war principles through-out the entire process
- Purging the old regime and prosecuting war criminals
- Disarming the society
- Providing sufficient security for people to return to (or initially experience) peaceful lives
- Incorporating and working with the locals in the broader reconstruction project
- Encouraging nonstate actors such as voluntary organizations and "civic groups" to flourish
- Helping to rebuild the economy rather than burdening the people economically
- Assisting with education
- Avoiding an exit that is too hasty[229]

At the conceptual level, the United Nations General Assembly document *Responsibility of States for Internationally Wrongful Acts* has attempted to formulate the broader notion of nation building and reconstruction following war or collapse, according to four broader categories—reparation, restitution, compensation, and satisfaction.[230] Together these components are viewed as essential in helping to refashion the infrastructure of a nation torn by war:

- *Reparation* is the responsibility of a state to make amends for injury to another state caused by a wrongful act; reparation may be moral or material and will also take the form of restitution, compensation, and satisfaction.[231]

---

[229]Ibid., 204–7. In his essay "Justice after War and the International Common Good," in Charles Reed and David Ryall, eds., *The Prince of Peace: Just War in the Twenty-First Century* (Cambridge: Cambridge University Press, 2007), 219–36, John Langan ponders the responsibilities that attend the termination of war. Rather than focusing on the actual events that terminate hostilities, he considers the altered network of relationships between combatants and among nations. This sort of emphasis is very much needed, although Langan stops short of proposing specific recommendations.

[230]United Nations General Assembly Resolution *Responsibility of States for Internationally Wrongful Acts* 56/83 (December 2001), Articles 31–37. More recently, Pamela Y. Willsborgstede, in "Defining a Framework for Reconstruction," a paper presented to the U.S. Army War College in 2004, has developed the implications of the UN document with great sensitivity.

[231]The language of "reparations," however, needs qualification in our day, given the negative associations with the terms that tend to assign guilt and blame. Nevertheless, it is consistent with traditional just-war thinking, which understands justice as requiring redress of injury or harm that has been

- *Restitution* involves reestablishing the situation that existed prior to the wrong, materially where possible; the burden is not disproportionate to the wrong caused or the benefit derived.
- *Compensation* is payment for damage cause by the wrong if such damage was not made good by restitution; damages must be financially assessable.
- *Satisfaction* redresses injury that cannot be repaired via compensation or restitution; satisfaction includes recognition of guilt, regret, formal apology, or another appropriate mode of response; satisfaction should be proportionate to the injury and may not take the form of humiliation of the responsible state.

Roger P. Alford believes that reparations in particular are a pivotal part of *post bellum* reconstruction. Reparations are made more necessary and more difficult by the simple fact that suffering does not allow itself to be measured adequately.[232] By what currency or in what measure should the repair or redress of injury, injustice, harm, and loss (both material and immaterial) be levied? Moreover, while an important aspect of justice is backward looking (i.e., to the injustice and harm done), it also looks forward to the potential of the particular nation or people group becoming a contributing member in the community of nations. In this regard, it needs emphasizing that victorious nations typically do not "look forward" so much as extract vengeance. There is all the more reason, then, for the principles of just war to mediate the reconstruction; to assist any vanquished nation in its wholesale reconstruction is to truly affirm right intention and the greater peace. Hence, victors may waive their right and claims to compensation in the best interests of those vanquished.

The above fourfold scheme, proposed in the UN document, while conceptually delineating the contours of justice, might be faulted for its seeming inability to prescribe, in adequately social, cultural, educational, political, legal, and economic terms, what is needed for a nation's rehabilitation. *Reparation, restitution, compensation,* and

---

induced by an aggressor. This redress is an essential component of international law, as stated in the Hague Conventions of 1907 and the 1949 Geneva Conventions, for it addresses the matters of wrongdoing or unlawful action.

[232]Roger P. Alford, "On War as Hell," *Chicago Journal of International Law* 3, no. 1 (2002): 207–18.

satisfaction, after all, are judicial terms; that is to say, they speak to the matter of redress and thus are *reactive* in their constitution.

Both compensation and satisfaction, which are governed by the principle of proportionality, speak to the matter of punishment, which is necessary at two levels. Victims must be vindicated or compensated for loss, or costs, they have suffered and endured, while compensatory justice in the form of war-crimes trials are necessary for those who initiated or are chiefly responsible for aggression or injustice.[233] By it basic character, the principle of proportionality requires that the burden of justice be weighed (and balanced) against the costs and benefits of its imposition and the degree of previous injustice or moral atrocity. Thus, for example, moral accountability for war crimes or "crimes against humanity" is proportionate to the nature of the crimes that were committed. That accountability is required is a foregone conclusion, and punishment is a mirror of both our belief in moral agency and our understanding of intrinsic human dignity. Already in part 2 we advanced the argument that punishment per se is neither immoral nor inappropriate. Indeed, it is a necessary therapeutic component in bringing healing to a society that has been ruptured by gross violations of human rights. Proportionality, it should be recalled, has both upper and lower limits.

Satisfaction is a form of accountability that typically is measured in social and economic terms. However, in cultural contexts such as Afghanistan and Iraq, or other nations in which genocide or widespread violation of human rights has occurred, this element needs not only moderation but reinterpretation. People who have experienced grievous loss through mass murder, atrocity, or denial of the most basic human rights—that is, those who are authentic victims—are in desperate need of some authority both to acknowledge the factuality of that loss and to accept responsibility for helping mitigate the effects of that loss.

In addition to the retrospective component of justice, what also needs forethought is the *proactive* and forward-looking element in justice, which is requisite for rebuilding a society or nation. More effectively addressing this positive component of rehabilitation is an important volume published by the Center for Strategic International Studies, *Winning the Peace* (2004),[234] which frames post-conflict reconstruction according to "four pillars" of infrastructural necessity:

---

[233]Orend, "Justice after War," 47.
[234]Robert C. Orr, ed., *Winning the Peace: An American Strategy for Post-Conflict Reconstruction* (Washington, DC: Center for Strategic International Studies, 2004).

- security
- governance and participation
- economic and social well-being
- justice and reconciliation

These "pillars" are identified in the light of developments in Iraq, Afghanistan, the Balkans, and Sierra Leone, where failed, defeated, or war-torn states can be seen to undermine the stability of the entire region of which they are a part. The military component is only the initial part of securing peace and stability, while the difficult (and more long-term) questions remain.

Recent U.S. experience in postwar scenarios leads Carafano and Dillon to propose a cluster of principles of post-conflict operation that, in their words, help to avert the "disease and unrest" formula. By this they refer to symptoms of a humanitarian crisis that arise from the absence of basic and immediate needs—for example, security, health measures, food and water supplies, and protection from exposure to the elements. At this point, then, after having taken massive population-wide precautions against these immediate postwar dangers, the focus can then turn to the matter of handing over the reins of political authority to indigenous leadership and assisting the rebuilding of the nation's infrastructure. Carafano and Dillon argue that there is a rhythm or pattern of reconstruction that emerges with the implementation of the following principles:

- Principle #1: The reconstructing authority (and in the case of the U.S., beginning with the office of president) must articulate a specific and credible plan of national restoration with clear objectives, which may or may not involve regime change. This is essential both for sustaining public support and for the allocation of resources.
- Principle #2: The reconstructing authority must eliminate undesirable influences in the previous regime while preserving government as a whole. Formal governmental institutions are responsible for providing basic services and sustaining the infrastructure of the nation under rebuilding. Where they have been destroyed and do not exist, the task is more formi-

dable; nonetheless, these institutions must be rebuilt or created quickly in the post-conflict process.[235]

- Principle #3: The reconstructing authority must formulate a vision of the end state and a clear plan that spells out the particulars of transfer of authority and the plan's overall implementation.
- Principle #4: Postwar activity should be multilateral wherever possible.
- Principle #5: Post-conflict activity, in the case of the U.S., should involve different U.S. agencies and require interagency cooperation.
- Principle #6: At all levels of operation, unity of effort is essential.
- Principle #7: Lessons learned need to be documented and implemented for the sake of ongoing operations in the future.[236]

These principles, of course, have chiefly to do with the logistical implementation of change and reconstruction, particularly in the early stages of the process. Long-term conceptualization of the rebuilding process, however, necessitates the identification of particular social and political values on which a society must be built in order that its members might be self-governing and flourish. In the conclusion of *Arguing about War*, Michael Walzer ponders the long-term "political arrangements" that would be necessary to the health of the international order if we wish to avoid the extremes of a radical decentralization of sovereign states, on the one hand, and an all-powerful central regime, on the other. As Walzer sees it, several nonnegotiable elements are constitutive of any relatively stable political order:

- the capacity to promote peace
- distributive justice
- cultural pluralism
- individual freedom

---

[235]In the case of totalitarian regimes, certain elements, laws, or practices may be more deeply embedded in the governmental structure than they are in democratic regimes. At the same time, change that is too radical in the basic structure of government may negatively affect postwar reconstruction.
[236]Carafano and Dillon, "Winning the Peace," 6–9.

With these elements guiding reconstruction, a form of pluralism might be restored—or created—that fortifies "an increasingly dense web of social ties" and builds on "the institutional structures that now exist, or are slowly coming into existence."[237] For Walzer, political success and social stability are anchored in the coexistence and interlocking of specific cultural values. Chief among these, in Walzer's view, are religious pluralism, peace, equality, and autonomy.[238] These values in particular are important insofar as they protect ethnic and religious minorities and guard personal liberties. For this reason, Walzer is convinced of the need for a fundamental change in the present international climate, wherein the "politics of difference" ensures the lingering possibilities of ethnic cleansing and genocidal civil war. On the one hand, the danger of an overly centralized regime attempting to prevent such abuses (if in truth it wishes to do so) is the *totalizing* tendency of a "tyranny without borders." On the other, the danger of overly decentered and multicentered regimes is that *no one will stop* the evil. In the end, Walzer laments the fact that in the present international climate, true reform is rarely sought for its own sake; even among Western nations, it would seem, few people are "sufficiently interested."[239]

Q. 60 How much flexibility is there in the just-war tradition to grow and accommodate new challenges?

An ethical framework for thinking about the issues of war, peace, and justice will need to be consistent, noncontradictory, and comprehensive. It must be consistent so that the principles and components of the system pursue the same goals and ends throughout. For example, if justice is the goal, then it must be central in all three stages of consideration: (1) as preparations for going to war are considered (*jus ad bellum*), (2) as the war plans are executed (*jus in bello*), and (3) in the aftermath of war when peace and reconciliation are pursued (*jus post bellum*). A framework must be noncontradictory in that the various components and principles

---

[237]Walzer, *Arguing about War*, 186–87.
[238]The context in which Walzer describes these values (chap. 12, "Governing the Globe," of *Arguing about War*, 171–95) is a discussion that considers alternatives to international anarchy, on the one hand, and a global empire, on the other.
[239]*Arguing about War*, 189, 191.

must not undermine one another ethically. Finally, a system must be comprehensive so that it is able to address ethically the spectrum of warfare and developments that arises as warfare changes. Historically, the just-war tradition has shown itself to be capable of these challenges.

As a broader moral framework, the tradition has served as a guide for the better part of two millennia, with the core of its moral reasoning being consistent from Ambrose to Aquinas, to Luther, to Grotius, to our own day. The central tenets of the tradition have been developed and refined in response to both unique and persistent issues of war. As the geopolitical contexts of wars have changed, along with tactical developments in the technology and weaponry of warfare, the tradition has accommodated such changes. Indeed, just-war proponents recognize that there is a moral obligation to wrestle with new issues and problems. But a strength of the just-war tradition is precisely this: that it is an ongoing moral, legal, ethical, and religious dialogue that spans the centuries. Just as the tradition responded to the challenge of conflating church and state, just as it adapted to evolving geopolitics of the early-modern period, and just as it addressed the challenges of a nuclear age and weapons of mass destruction during the Cold War, so too it is demonstrating an inherent strength, resilience, and elasticity to speak to the formidable challenge that terrorism thrusts at us.[240] Those who prepare for war, military conflict, or humanitarian intervention must do so *not* because they desire conflict, but because they desire peace and justice. For this necessity, the just-war tradition continues to provide a necessary framework for ethical and prudential decision making.

---

[240]So, e.g., Elshtain, *Just War against Terror*; Neta C. Crawford, "Just War Theory and the U.S. Counterterror War," *Perspectives on Politics* 1, no. 1 (March 2003): 5–25; Cole, *When God Says War Is Right*, 127–49; and Charles, *Between Pacifism and Jihad*, 149–68. Though the views of these four authors are not uniform, thereby showing that the tradition is not static, they nonetheless demonstrate an essential unity of perspective.

PART 4

JUST-WAR TRADITION
AND THE THEOLOGIAN

Q. 61 Doesn't Jesus' teaching in the Sermon on the Mount to "turn the other cheek" and not resist evil require pacifism on the part of Christian faith?

Since most religious pacifists ground their convictions in a purported nonviolent "love ethic" of Jesus that is understood to be the teaching of Matthew 5:38–42, from an interpretative standpoint it is imperative that the meaning of Jesus' teaching in the Sermon on the Mount be assessed. It is significant and yet perhaps not all that surprising that these verses have fostered widespread misunderstanding throughout the centuries.[1] Certainly the matter of retaliation challenges Christian ethics as have few issues, past or present.

We focus our attention on the part of the sermon that is thought to engender or require nonviolence. Matthew 5:38–42 is one of six case illustrations of Jesus' teaching on the law (5:17). With the other five, it is Jesus' affirmation of the ethical requirements of Old Testament law—requirements that are enduring. And in similar fashion, it begins with the formula that Jesus has already used four times in this body of teaching—"You have heard that it was said, . . . But I tell you . . ." While some students of the biblical text interpret these particular words as referring to Mosaic law, such a reading does not fit the context. To introduce his teaching, Jesus has just reiterated that the law as revealed in the old covenant, continually reaffirmed by the prophets, is not to be set aside (5:17); it is binding. Jesus cannot be contradicting himself. What the context *does* require, however, is that contemporary notions—indeed, contemporary distortions of the law—need adjustment. One such illustration of contemporary error concerns retaliation.[2]

As it applies to the illustration recorded in 5:38–42, what needs emphasis is that Jesus is not setting aside the idea of restitution itself,

---

[1] For a fuller examination of these verses, see J. Daryl Charles, "Do Not Suppose That I Have Come . . .": The Ethic of the 'Sermon on the Mount' Reconsidered," *Southwestern Journal of Theology* (Spring 2005): 47–72.
[2] See the related question on retaliation below.

nor the "law of the tooth" (the *lex talionis*) as a *standard* of public justice.[3] To the contrary, the story of Zacchaeus[4] is a reminder that Jesus affirmed the Old Testament measure for restitution, which is a timeless moral principle. The apostle Paul, furthermore, implies the same in his teaching on what we owe others; the natural moral law is affirmed, and neighbor love is said to be the *fulfillment* (not a *setting aside*) of the law.[5] In the Sermon on the Mount, Jesus is challenging his listeners to consider their attitudes so that they respond properly to *personal* injustice or insult. That insult (personal injury) rather than assault (public injury) is at issue here is suggested by the mention of the right cheek being struck. And it is clarified by the further illustration, "If someone wants to . . . take your tunic, let him have your cloak as well" (5:40). Handling insults and matters of clothing (a basic human need) are not the realm of statecraft and public policy. In truth, all four illustrations of nonretaliation—turning the other cheek, offering the shirt off your back, carrying someone's baggage an extra mile, and lending to the one asking—correspond to the private domain. These are issues of personal inconvenience or abuse, not matters of public policy; they bespeak insult and not assault.

Thus, Jesus' injunction not to resist evil (5:39), contextually, must be located in the realm of personal injury, not state policy. Matthew 5–7 is not a statement on the nature and jurisdiction of the state or the governing authorities; rather, it concerns issues of personal discipleship. Its affinities are most closely with Romans 12:17–21, not Romans 13:1–7. In the sphere of the personal and private, justice does *not* call for retribution. In the sphere of the public, where the magistrate is commissioned to protect and defend the common good, justice demands retribution. This is the unambiguous teaching of the New Testament and not the supposed "compromised" thinking of imperialism or Constantinianism, so called.

But because this material is widely used to justify the pacifist position, our interpretation of these verses needs accountability. Misinterpreting these verses was common among religious folk in Ambrose's

---

[3]See the very thoughtful and thought-provoking volume by William I. Miller, *An Eye for an Eye* (Cambridge: Cambridge University Press, 2006), who demonstrates an appreciation for the historical roots of the *lex talionis* and its meaning in antiquity. Miller acknowledges, correctly, that the "law of the tooth" was first and foremost a measure of reciprocity, a principle of compensation, and not merely a law of punishment. Consequently, in its essence one finds not inhumanity, as moderns typically think, but *humanity*, since it presupposes both *upper and lower* limits for making restitution.

[4]Luke 19.

[5]Rom. 13:8–10; cf. 3:31. James insists, as well, that charity will keep the law (2:8–11).

and Augustine's day, as was true in Aquinas's day, and in Luther's day as well. Indeed, it continues to characterize religious attitudes down to the present. But mainstream Christian interpretation counters the widespread misunderstanding: the fathers of the church of every age are of one mind. All make the distinction between personal and public grievances, between matters of the heart and matters of state. While Aquinas and Luther differ with Ambrose and Augustine on the question of self-defense, as we have seen, all agree that the Christian must resist evil to protect others, although the *forms* of this resistance will differ and depend on the particular situations.

In his fascinating essay "Why I Am Not a Pacifist," C. S. Lewis considers Jesus' injunction regarding "turning the other cheek," which he believes cannot be intended to rule out protecting others. "Does anyone suppose," he asks, "that our Lord's hearers understood him to mean that if a homicidal maniac, attempting to murder a third party, tried to knock me out of the way, I must stand aside and let him get his victim?"[6] If Jesus is calling for *absolute* nonviolence based on Matthew 5:38–39, then we would be under obligation to *turn the cheek of a third party*. Lewis prefers to accept the plain reading of this text. Jesus' audience consisted of "private people in a disarmed nation," and "war was not what they would have been thinking of" by any stretch of the imagination.[7] Lewis's understanding proceeds on a plain reading of the text.

Against the view of mainstream Christian moral thinkers, Anabaptist theologian John Howard Yoder insists that Jesus' rebuke of Peter in Gethsemane—"Put your sword in its place. For all who take the sword will perish by the sword" (Matt. 26:52 ESV)—is certifiable proof of Jesus' renunciation of all violence.[8] But is it? The point of Jesus' emphasis is that *the Father*, not Peter, is to adjudicate. Consider Jesus' rhetorical question in the given context: "How then would the Scriptures be fulfilled, that say it must happen in this way? . . . But this has all taken place that the writings of the prophets might be fulfilled" (26:54, 56). The point of Jesus' rebuke is not *violence versus nonviolence*; rather, contra Yoder, it is *providence versus interference*. If Yoder's assertion were correct, then, at the very least, Jesus' use of

---

[6] "Why I Am Not a Pacifist," in *The Weight of Glory and Other Addresses*, rev. ed. (New York: HarperCollins, 2001), 86.

[7] Ibid., 50. Moreover, it should be observed that Jesus does not offer "the other cheek" when struck by an official during his own trial before the high priest (John 18:19–24).

[8] *The Politics of Jesus*, 2nd ed. (Grand Rapids: Eerdmans, 1994), 98.

the whip to beat people or animals or both in the temple would be utterly contradictory.

In the end, the Christian *is* called to resist evil *when and where it is possible*,[9] as saints past and present always have understood. And the apostle Paul states in no uncertain terms that the magistrate exists precisely for this divinely instituted function:

> For rulers are not a terror to good conduct, but to bad. Do you want to be unafraid of the authority? Do good and you will have its approval. For government is God's servant to you for good. But if you do wrong, be afraid, because it does not carry the sword for no reason. For government is God's servant, an avenger that brings wrath on the one doing wrong. (Rom. 13:3–4 HCSB)

Even when Jesus forbids the sword as a means to advance the kingdom of God, the New Testament does not teach an absolute or principled pacifism. Nor does it forbid the Christian from "bearing the sword"— or serving as a magistrate, for that matter—in the service of society and the greater good of the community. There is simply no suggestion in the New Testament that military service—*in any form*—is incompatible with Christian faith.

Q. 62 Doesn't Jesus set aside the law in favor of a new ethic?

Given the emergence of the Christian "sect" in the first century, certainly *the* controversial question for most first-century Jews would have been whether Jesus was advancing a new teaching. And most importantly, was this Jesus setting aside the Torah? In Matthew's Gospel, Jesus' attitude toward the law is center stage, and necessarily so. This is one of the important editorial perspectives of the Matthean narrative.

Matthew may be addressing two sides of one problem. In the fledgling Christian community some might be inclined to believe that the commandments that embody moral law are no longer valid or that the ethical standards of the kingdom of God, as inaugurated through Jesus, have somehow changed. And at the same time, on "the other

---

[9]Otherwise stated, to permit evil to occur when one has the wherewithal to resist or prevent it is to be an *accomplice* of that evil.

side of the street," where there is now a synagogue and debates are raging between the schools of Hillel and Shammai, the "fence around the law"—that is, the oral tradition[10]—has obscured the true meaning of the commandments. In a day when the Pharisees' claims to authority lay in their possession of the "oral Torah," it was those who abrogated the law who were to meet the force of Jesus' fury. Both stringent Pharisaical interpretation of the law and total freedom from the law were needing adjustment, if not rejection. The burden of Matthew 5:17–48 is the former.

The prohibition "Do not think . . . ," introducing 5:17, is a rhetorical device in a polemic against popular opinion.[11] What was this opinion? In Matthew's eyes, it was that Jesus' coming was to abolish "the Law or the Prophets." To a Jew, setting aside or abrogating the law constituted *the* mark of a heretic. Hence, the very opening words of Jesus' teaching in 5:17–20 would seem to be polemically and apologetically charged, and reflect a debate. Properly construed, Jesus' imperative carries the following sense: "Do not begin thinking—do not even consider the possibility—of abrogating the teaching of the law and the prophets." Jesus statement, then, is aimed at dealing with a fundamental misunderstanding of his mission.

It is significant that the teaching of the Sermon on the Mount is framed within two references to the law and the prophets. Matthew's use of the combination phrases "the Law or the Prophets" (5:17) and "the Law and the Prophets" (7:12; 22:40), as well as the reverse form "all the Prophets and the Law" (11:13), is meant to underscore a broader and notably prophetic dimension of the law. Frequently in the Old Testament the prophets "freed," as it were, the Torah from cultic manipulation by upholding a correct interpretation that emphasizes the *spirit* of the law. Such seems to be implied in 7:12 and is stated explicitly in 22:40.[12] Matthew's generic use of "the law" is illuminated not merely by its frequency,[13] but also by the struggle with Pharisaical Judaism mirrored throughout the Gospel narrative. The central charge

---

[10]E.g., Matt. 15:2; Mark 7:3, 5.

[11]See Dieter Betz, *The Sermon on the Mount* (Minneapolis: Augsburg Fortress, 1995), 173–97.

[12]"The law" in Matthew signifies the Pentateuch, which contains the revelation of God's will, the deposit of God's revelatory utterances to his people—utterances made binding by specific commandments and ordinances. The law, as Israel's standard for good works and the object of constant reaffirmation by the prophets, was accepted by the Christian community as binding, even when it needed recontextualization in Jesus' day ("You have heard that it was said. . . . But I tell you . . . ," 5:21–22, 27–28, 31–32, 33–34, 38–39, 43–44).

[13]Matt. 5:17, 18; 7:12; 11:13; 22:36, 40; 23:23.

leveled against the emergent Christian community was precisely this: it is not in continuity with Judaism *at its core*—namely, the Torah and the prophets. How were the disciples to rebut this charge?

Jesus' reference to "the Law and the Prophets" is intended to be an *ethical* imperative. "Good works" are accentuated in Matthew's Gospel, as suggested in 5:16 (". . . so that they may see your good works and give glory to your Father in heaven," HCSB) and in 7:12 ("whatever you would want men to do to you, do also to them," ESV). Taken together, then, "the Law and the Prophets" constitutes the moral law of God and that standard by which the disciple is to live his or her life.[14]

In addition to context, a key to properly interpreting Jesus' words "Do not think that . . ." lies in the relationship between "fulfill" and "abolish." Antithesis is the common thread found in 5:17, 18, and 19. The nature of the actions in verse 17 is that they are mutually exclusive. Although the verb "fulfill" carries the sense of "prediction" elsewhere in Matthew,[15] in 5:17 it connotes the sense of doing, performing, and obeying. Far from contravening the commandments delineated in 5:21–48, Jesus is calling for a heartfelt obedience to the commandments that love would fulfill.[16] The essence of Jesus' teaching is to affirm, confirm, and uphold the law. For the believer, it is to be obediently practiced, even when proper understanding of the law requires reinterpretation, given the distortions of the "traditions of the elders" (i.e., the oral "fence around the law") associated with contemporary rabbinic teaching.[17] In Matthew 5 we have to do with the law's outworking, its expression, and hence its continued validity. This teaching is in keeping with Matthew's emphasis throughout on "doing" the will of God.

---

[14]While to the modern reader the question of whether particular commandments are "fulfillable" is provocative, it was not a question for Matthew. What was commanded could and should be done. The contemporary reader is apt to miss the significance of *torah* for the first-century Jewish mind. Firmly rooted in the notion of covenant, it constituted the visible expression of one's relationship with God, a supreme gift of divine grace. A proper understanding of law can be gleaned both from the Psalms and Wisdom Literature of the Old Testament. Wisdom Literature in particular establishes a strong link between wisdom, covenant, and the law. The latter offers instruction to the wise and practical advice to the faithful and in no way is perceived as a burden; rather, it is a gift from God. The God of *torah* is the God of grace and love, an understanding that is affirmed by the New Testament itself. As an ethical guide, the law, with its commandments, is "holy, righteous and good" (Rom. 7:12). It is "perfect" and gives "freedom"; in its keeping, the Christian will be "blessed in what he does" (James 1:25). While St. Paul is severely critical of works-righteousness, that is, being "under the law" (e.g., Gal. 3:23 ESV) and doing "works of the law" (e.g., 2:16 ESV), he is adamant that love upholds and fulfills the law (Rom. 3:31 and 13:8–10).

[15]See n. 13.

[16]A list of commentators who understand Jesus to be canceling Old Testament moral precepts is lengthy. For a survey of the literature, see Charles, "Do Not Suppose That I Have Come . . . ," 55 n. 37.

[17]Matt. 15:1–9; Mark 7:1–13.

Is this rabbinic mystic Jesus setting aside the Torah that Moses had given? Such concerns would have been circulating at the local synagogue. Matthew's aim is transparent: the ethical demands of the law, reiterated by the prophets, are *not* to cease. Indeed, it is precisely because Israel sinned and abrogated the law, with its ethical demands, that the covenant had to be renewed.[18] The declaration by Jesus "Do not think that I have come to abolish the Law or the Prophets" is intended to negate and replace a false supposition, a popular caricature. At the same time, it formally establishes the direction of Jesus' teaching and it validates Jesus' authority in the eyes of both critics and disciples. In Jesus' assertions about the character of the law that follow, our Lord draws upon distinctly Jewish and apocalyptic imagery to underscore the binding force of the law as an ethical standard.

Jesus' declarations recorded in 5:18–19 employ the language of hyperbole. His use of terms variously translated "jot," "tittle," "iota," "dot," and "least stroke," as well as "commandments," "least," "great," "teach," and "break" is aimed at suiting the meticulous expectations of the rabbis.[19] Relying on the language of apocalyptic—notably, the passing of the heavens and earth (also used in Matthew 24)—Jesus affirms the abiding nature of the ethical standard.[20] Even the smallest aspects of ethical obligation remain, apocalyptically speaking, until a new heaven and earth appear. Why, in Matthew's eyes, is Jesus so adamant about the law's detail as well as permanence? Hyperbolic speech utilizes exaggeration for the sake of effect, and the effect is to emphasize durability. From Matthew's vantage point, to construe Jesus' "coming" as abolishing the law (as an ethical guide) is to misconstrue his coming altogether. The ramifications of loosing, annulling, or relaxing one of "the least" of these commandments—and

---

[18]If law is perceived as the basis for one's justification before a holy God—that is to say, what one does to merit divine grace—rather than the measure of God's unchanging ethical standard, then one is forced to treat Matt. 5:17 and Jesus' teaching about the law not unlike Marcion, who maintained that Jesus taught the exact opposite of what is recorded in Matthew. His reconstruction, hence, is rooted in radical discontinuity: "Why do you think that I came to fulfill the law. . . . I did not come to fulfill but to abolish." What many Christians share in common with Marcion, if less radically, is a reading of Matthew through the lens of a misunderstood Paul. But without law, there is no righteousness, no ethical standard. Without law, one is left with lawlessness. And while most people do not embrace the radical discontinuity of the heretic Marcion, many Christians—including "orthodox" Christian interpreters—fail to discern the law's protective and provisional function. Viewed ethically, the new covenant is not new; the ethical standard remains the same.

[19]Cf. Matt. 23:4, 8.

[20]This interpretation agrees with Wis. 18:4; Bar. 4:1, 4; Ezra 9:37; and Philo's *Life of Moses* 2.136, all of which speak of the permanent force of the law.

teaching others the same—are sobering. They entail a loss of rank in the kingdom of heaven (5:19).[21]

For Matthew, teaching and doing go hand in hand and are indivisible. For the disciples, this relationship cannot be overstated. What is transmitted to others, both in word and in deed, matters enormously; hence Jesus' vehement denunciation of this fundamental "disconnect" in scribal instruction and Pharisaical religion recorded later in the Gospel.[22] The flaw in the religious practice of Jesus' contemporaries is foremost *ethical*.

The least-versus-greatest contrast is a prominent theme in Matthew's Gospel, in accord with the reversal motif already noted. Its application in 5:19 to those of the teaching profession is clarified—and magnified—in 23:1ff., where it takes the form of prophetic woe cries directed at the teachers of the law.[23] Elsewhere in the Gospel narrative, Jesus ascribes greatness to the humble (18:4; 23:11), the "last" (20:16), and those who serve others (20:26). Through teaching and practice, the law is upheld and affirmed. In this way there can be no question as to the validity of the disciple's ethical guide. Jesus' statements in Matthew 5:17–19 constitute a straightforward and unambiguous affirmation of the law. The conflict between Jesus and the Pharisees, it should be emphasized, is an intra-Jewish conflict and has to do with the *interpretation* of the Torah, not its *validity*.

Jesus' pronouncement recorded in Matthew 5:20—"For I tell you, unless your righteousness surpasses that of the Pharisees and the teachers of the law . . ."—functions both to summarize the preceding statements and to introduce the case illustrations that follow. The formula "For I tell you" represents a *kelal*, an exegetical key, to Jesus' interpretive approach, not unlike that of rabbinic practice.[24] Herewith Jesus moves from principle to practice, calling for a better

---

[21]Elsewhere in Matthew's Gospel, Jesus employs the notion of rank in the kingdom of heaven, in keeping with the theme of divine reversal (18:4; 20:16; 23:2–12). Among teachers of the law, "light" commandments such as tithing on herbs and spices (Matt. 23:23) were set in contrast to "heavy" commandments such as profaning the divine name (26:63–65) and profaning the temple (12:6; 21:12–13; 26:62). Absurdly scrupulous in their tithing on mint, anise, and cummin, which were used for medicinal as well as culinary purposes, Pharisees neglected the more "weighty" matters of social ethics—e.g., justice and mercy (23:23–24). The result was an *ethical monstrosity* in and of itself. The Old Testament, it should be noted, does not teach an either/or ethic; both "small" and "weighty" requirements of the law are to be regarded. Stressing the former, however, to the neglect of the latter, is morally absurd.
[22]Matt. 23:3.
[23]E.g., Matt. 23:13, 15, 23, 25, 27, 29.
[24]See Israel Abraham, *Studies in Pharisaism and the Gospels* (New York: KTAV, 1967), 24; and N. J. McEleney, "The Principles of the Sermon on the Mount," *Catholic Biblical Quarterly* 41 (1979): 554.

righteousness, which is to exceed what establishment religion has promulgated. The emphasis in later Judaistic literature on avoiding the *appearance* of a lack of deeds, that is, an external form of "righteousness," would seem to square with the portrait we find in Matthew. The righteousness of the kingdom, by contrast, is virtuous in character (5:3–12) and expresses itself in a social morality performed from the heart (5:21–48). Pharisaical religion marks a departure from both the religion of the Old Testament and Christian discipleship. The judgment to befall Jerusalem in A.D. 70, portended by Jesus,[25] is not because Palestinian Judaism observes the Torah and the teaching of the prophets too closely. To the contrary, Jerusalem lacks the surpassing righteousness, and John the Baptist has sent a message of warning to that very effect. Repentance entails a change not in beliefs but in *deeds*.

Q. 63 Isn't retaliation counter to Jesus' teaching and thus unchristian in spirit?

Of the six situations—commonly called "antitheses" by biblical commentators[26]—that illustrate a proper and improper understanding of the law, none is more perplexing than Jesus' teaching on the *lex talionis*, the "law of the tooth" (Matt. 5:38–42). The *lex talionis* accords with the classic notion of justice that extends from antiquity—for example, the essence of which is present as early as the eighteenth century B.C. in the Code of Hammurabi—whereby humans are to render to everyone what is their due. The law's teaching on reciprocation affirms the *lex talionis* and appears in Exodus 21:24, Leviticus 24:20, and Deuteronomy 19:21. In Exodus 21 it is embedded in the context of how to redress injuries that are not serious. Where there is serious injury, however, "you are to take life for life, eye for eye, tooth for tooth, hand for hand, foot for foot, burn for burn, wound for wound, bruise for bruise" (Exod. 21:23–25). And

---

[25]This appears in Matthew 24.
[26]Betz, *The Sermon on the Mount*, 200, traces use of the term *antithesis* back to the second century and Marcion, for whom there existed radical discontinuity and no bridge between the Old and New Testament, by way of Adolf von Harnack's work *Marcion: Das Evangelium vom fremden Gott*, 2nd ed. (Leipzig: Hinrichs, 1924).

in Leviticus 24, retaliation is part of a discussion of how to deal with
those who profane what is sacred:

> If anyone takes the life of a human being, he must be put to death.
> Anyone who takes the life of someone's animal must make restitu-
> tion—life for life. If anyone injures his neighbor, whatever he has
> done must be done to him: fracture for fracture, eye for eye, tooth
> for tooth. . . . You are to have the same law for the alien and the
> native-born. I am the LORD your God. (vv. 17–22)

Deuteronomy 19 provides perhaps the clearest context for retaliation in the Old Testament. There it is part of instructions on how
to deal with wrongful death. Cities of refuge are established so that
Israel might distinguish between involuntary manslaughter and premeditated murder. Those accused of crimes are not to be convicted
on the basis of a lone witness: "A matter must be established by the
testimony of two or three witnesses" (v. 15). Justice lies in the hands
of "priests and judges who are in office at the time" (v. 17) and not
individual citizens.

Jesus' teaching on retaliation consists of five principal parts, all
admonitions, that are intended to be illustrative, following his encap-
sulation of the *lex talionis* ("eye for eye, and tooth for tooth," Matt.
5:38):

- Not resisting an evil person
- Turning the other cheek if you are struck on the right cheek
- Allowing a person to have your cloak if he is suing you over
  your tunic
- Going an extra mile when someone forces you to go one
  mile
- Giving and lending to the person who wishes to borrow from
  you

While some would interpret these statements as a repudiation of
Mosaic law,[27] that is emphatically not the case, as dictated by (1) the

---

[27]So, for example, the representative views of William Barclay, *The Gospel of Matthew*, rev. ed.
(Philadelphia: Westminster John Knox, 1975), 165: "But Jesus obliterated the very principle of
the law. . . . Jesus abolishes the old law of limited vengeance and introduces the new spirit of
non-resentment and non-retaliation"; John P. Meier, *Law and History in Matthew's Gospel: A
Redactional Study of Matt. 5:17–48* (Rome: Pontifical Biblical Institute, 1976), 157, who views
Matt. 5:38–42 as "the clearest and least disputable case of annulment in the antitheses"; and

context of Matthew 5 as established in verses 17–20 (reiteration of the permanent validity of the law's ethical requirements) and (2) the hermeneutical approach utilized by Jesus in all six case illustrations of 5:21–48 (simultaneous affirmation of the law and clarification of proper motives).[28] A measurement of justice, the *lex talionis* is embedded both in Old Testament law and throughout the ancient world as a legal principle; it gives concrete expression to the natural moral law that all people everywhere, based on reason and revelation, intuit (cf. Rom. 2:14–15). As a standard, it exists both to levy proportionality in society's response to specific crimes and to limit the upper reaches of that response. Both aspects—proportionality and limitation—inhere in the abiding character of justice—a cardinal virtue that is universal in scope and therefore uniform, extending via general revelation from pre-Israelite moral codes (e.g., the Hammurabi Code) through Israel's Torah, through Plato and Aristotle, through the teaching of the New Testament, and up to the present, where it informs the foundations of Western legal theory and practice (regardless of whether Western culture at present would acknowledge this legacy).

The Old Testament concept of restitution, showcased notably in the holiness code of Leviticus but reaffirmed by Jesus (e.g., in the incident involving Zacchaeus recorded in Luke 19), demonstrates reciprocity and proportionality, upon which retaliation—properly understood—rests. All moral standards for criminal justice as we comprehend it must rest on the foundation of reciprocity and restitution, without which "justice" is meaningless.[29] Far from negating the *lex talionis*, Jesus is adjusting its application among his contemporaries, who have misappropriated its application to situations that require restitution and compensation.[30]

Frank Thielman, *The Law in the New Testament: The Question of Continuity*, Companions to the New Testament (New York: Crossroad, 1999), 51–52, 56: "Here we find that in each case Jesus replaces a Mosaic command. . . . In cases where the Mosaic law in question is a pragmatic attempt to legislate a less than ideal situation, Jesus nullifies the command altogether by demanding a change in the situation itself so radical that, if it takes place, the legislation becomes unnecessary. . . . The difference between Jesus and the Mosaic law on this point is clear: the Mosaic law permits retaliation; Jesus forbids it."

[28] Matt. 5:17–20 serves as a necessary introduction to the six "case illustrations" of 5:21–48.

[29] Yet a third element, consistency, must accompany these components if the criminal justice system is to work effectively (see in this regard Eccles. 8:11).

[30] The strength of William Miller's fine study *An Eye for an Eye* is that the author grasps the essence of the *talion*, namely, that it was a humane method of compensation that established upper and lower limits rather than an inhumane form of punishment, as is widely held.

Q. 64 Doesn't St. Paul in Romans 12 require nonretaliatory, nonviolent responses to evil?

A common tendency in teaching and preaching is to sever the material in Romans 12 from that found in Romans 13. This detachment is unfortunate, for there is a very important linkage that must inform responsible Christian interpretation. Chapter 12 begins a listing of practical exhortations following Paul's theological argument up through the end of chapter 11. This listing unites several smaller groupings of ethical admonitions. They include being wholly dedicated to the purposes of God (vv. 1–2); rightly appreciating various gifts and callings in the body of Christ (vv. 3–8); and striving to manifest love in all relationships—to the brethren (vv. 9–13) and to the world (vv. 14–21). An important part of our relationships with unbelievers is how we handle personal abuse (vv. 17–21).

An overview of chapter 12 reveals a strong accent by the apostle on personal relationships. What does charity look like in our interactions with believers? With unbelievers? Two tendencies are typical. One, among the brethren, is to depreciate—perhaps take for granted—the unique gifts found among members of the Christian community. The second tendency is worthy of note for our present purposes. The tendency of the Christian when located among unbelievers is quite naturally to respond vindictively to personal insult or injury. Here the Apostle to the Gentiles addresses both spheres, church and world, with very concrete recommendations in the form of admonition: specifically, shunning a retaliatory mode, doing what is right, striving for peace as far as is possible, avoiding a vengeful spirit, taking comfort in the fact of divine justice, and doing practical things to diffuse animosity. In sum, Christians living in the imperial seat are to do good to those who mistreat them, not repaying evil for evil (12:17, 21).

But in our reading of the epistle to the Romans, a shift in focus goes almost unnoticed. There is no transition statement beginning the material in chapter 13. The apostle merely continues his thought, retaining several important themes such as one's neighbor, charity and respect, justice and vengeance, evil, and wrath. Several bridges unite the material of 12:17–21 and what follows: the accent on evildoing, the contrast between good and evil, and reference to vengeance and God's wrath. Catchwords that appear in 13:1–7 are "servant" (literally "deacon," used twice in 13:4, and "liturgist" in 13:6), "wrath," "wrongdoer," and "authority" (six times in 13:1–6). These serve as accent marks on what the apostle wishes to reinforce among his readers.

What needs emphasis here is the contrast between justice as *pro-scribed* in chapter 12 and justice as *prescribed* in chapter 13. "Vigilante justice" is outlawed in the economy of God, since personal insult and injury are part of the cost of discipleship. The believer, therefore, is exhorted not to take justice into his own hands. In the hands of the governing authorities, however, justice is *required*. Moral-social order depends on it, and not to wield the sword is to be delinquent in terms of the role set apart by the Almighty for the magistrate.[31]

Finally, what needs accentuation in our answer to this particular question is an element that surfaces throughout this entire volume; it is the matter of coercive force. Whereas the principled pacifist believes that force can *never* serve just and moral purposes, the just-war theorist acknowledges that force per se is not an evil, but rather depends on the moral character of those who employ it. Human beings are moral agents and thus can properly apply or misapply power in the service of their cause. The combined teaching of Romans 12 and Romans 13 is that there exist different authority spheres; that is, there is a well-defined difference between the private and the public sector. In the private realm, we are not commissioned to take justice into our own hands; justice, after all, is committed by God to the public or civil realm. In the public realm, not only is justice permissible; it is *required*. And we must not miss the specific teaching lodged in the end of Romans 12, namely, that the morality of human acts is based on intention. Precisely this element lies at the heart of just-war moral reasoning.

Q. 65 What about "rendering to Caesar"? After all, Jesus seems to have exposed Rome's pretensions of sovereignty.

Those who are suspicious of Christian involvement in cultural institutions in general and politics in particular would seem justified in their cultural detachment. After all, Jesus'

---

[31] What disturbs many of us today is the remarkable uncritical attitude that the apostle seems to have had toward government. Why no checks and balances? Why no warnings against the apocalyptic "beast"? Why no denunciation of the Roman *imperium*, which, after all, waged a "cruel peace" as far as its tentacles could reach? While these questions are legitimate, they remain outside our present focus.

own posture toward the political authorities of his day would appear to be uniformly negative. This disposition is evident in many of his statements, and in his personal encounters with authority he desacralizes political power and Rome's pretensions. "You would have no authority over me at all unless it had been given you from [my Father] above," he reminds Pilate as he is being unjustly sentenced (John 19:11 ESV). In the end it would seem, at least in the political sphere, that the religious believer should aim for *detachment* since the call to "render to Caesar the things that are Caesar's," which is juxtaposed to the commandment to render "to God the things that are God's" (ESV),[32] would seem *in practice* well-nigh impossible.

While this portrait of apparent detachment in the pages of the New Testament is compelling, it needs some moderation. Indeed, it needs strong adjustment on several counts. While the religious believer must take seriously the matter of ultimate allegiances, he or she must not make the mistake of taking on—and living under—a "messianic complex." To do so would be to misinterpret all of Jesus' exhortations toward faithfulness that are directed to his followers. Such is not to deny that Christ's followers will need to endure persecution, even death, if this is part of a greater cost of ultimate allegiances; it is only to underscore the difference between Lord and disciple, between Master and student, or in theological terms, between the eternal and the temporal.

Placed in human communities, human beings must take seriously the ethical imperative to render to "Caesar"—who is representative of authority—without *unduly* rendering to him an *ultimate* allegiance. Consider the context in which this statement by Jesus is uttered. A composite group of Pharisees (legalists) and Herodians (cultural libertines) is seeking to trap Jesus through his statements.[33] The tricky issue of taxes is raised. Given the relatively oppressive percentage at which Rome was taxing its territories, the question, from a Jewish standpoint, would have seemed legitimate. But this is not at all the point at hand.

Using the imperial image found on a coin, Jesus tells those in his audience that they are to give back to Caesar what belongs to him, without neglecting to give back to God what belongs to him. Several

---

[32]See Matt. 22:15–22; Mark 12:13–17; and Luke 20:20–26.
[33]Herodians are not mentioned in Luke's account, as they are in Matthew's and Mark's.

things are hereby implied. One is that taxes as taxes are not illicit and thus should not per se be viewed as an injustice or an impediment to faith.[34] Second, Jesus is hereby suggesting that human existence consists of particular realms—realms that are separate to the extent that they correspond to various human responsibilities or loyalties.

Both first-century Jews and twenty-first-century Christians probably wrestle with the same temptation, and that is to flee the world, or fight against the world's institutions, or piously (and indifferently) remove themselves from social institutions while shouting "prophetic" denunciations from the sidelines. It would seem that a perennial tendency among Christians of any era, with Tertullian, is to adopt a view of society that Athens has little or nothing to do with Jerusalem (and vice versa). Thus, they end up fleeing the world in order to be preserved for the great and future day. But this only marginalizes faith and the Christian community in the surrounding culture.[35]

Thus, responsible participation in the various institutions of culture includes—even when it is by no means restricted to—politics, government, public administration, and law enforcement. As a moral dilemma, the use of coercive force and going to war are ultimately a matter of policy, and policy is determined, at least in the free-world context, by representative government. For this reason, citizens of relatively free societies bear the moral responsibility for policy that is enacted. As someone has wisely said, policy is the meeting place of the world of power and the world of morality. This, it goes without saying, implicates religious believers, whose very presence in the culture should serve as a moral force. It falls to them especially, as people of moral principle, to uphold the work of justice. While nations differ greatly in terms of the degree to which citizen participation is permitted, in the free world responsible citizenship entails, among other things, that politics and policy making are part of the cultural mandate for those who profess religious faith.

But, of course, we immediately can hear the objection, and a seemingly reasonable one at that. *There is no Christian politics.* Or, *look how beholden are many Christians to a political party.* Or, *the church*

---

[34]The question of the *amount* of this percentage is strictly secondary to the broader concern.

[35]For this reason, theologian John Courtney Murray distinguished between an "*eschatological* humanism," by which one flees the culture, and an intentionally "*incarnational* humanism," by which one seeks to leaven the culture. This viewpoint is developed in *We Hold These Truths: Catholic Reflections on the American Proposition* (New York: Sheed and Ward, 1960) and is found as well in the writings of John Paul II.

has a long history of being corrupted by political power. Certainly, there is an important element of truth in these protests—an element that we do not wish to obscure or deny. And every generation of Christians doubtless has wrestled, to a greater or lesser extent, with the potential for the church to be co-opted by politics, political authorities, or the state. Indeed, it is a fact that Jesus relativizes the powers, as we have already emphasized; he desacralizes their claims to ultimacy and sovereignty. And, without question, much of his teaching is directed toward the problem of divided loyalties. But it does not follow, therefore, that politics is inherently evil and that all Christians always and in every place will fall prey to compromise. Nor does it follow that because Jesus desacralized political power, he denied its reality or efficacy. Rather, an important balance is found in his admonitions: he acknowledges the *coexistence* of political power and heaven's authority, while carefully keeping the two distinct.[36]

But *what about* compromise? After all, human beings—religious believers included—are easily tempted with political power, as the very temptation of Jesus himself in the wilderness would indicate.[37] In response, we can only acknowledge that *anything in this life*, material or nonmaterial, has the potential to become an idol, in the end a mirror of distorted allegiances. But compromise is *not* inevitable, even when it is always possible, and that is why we argue for *the moral necessity of politics* while at the same time rejecting the tendency toward despair or cynicism and disengagement.

Many religious believers, because of their perceived minority status, tend to develop a world-and-life view that is decidedly dualistic, in which sacred and secular domains are viewed as distinct rather than integrated. This flawed mindset has the unfortunate consequence of producing a truncated, compartmentalized approach to living, whereby different spheres of life are isolated, and faith becomes privatized rather than having public ramifications. For the dualist, a reorientation is in order, namely, a rethinking of the nature of "secular" vocations, including politics, government, public service, and the

---

[36]In this regard, the differences between Islam and Christianity are instructive. There is a reason that the former is known as "the religion of the sword," as political ethicist Jean Elshtain observes: "Not that Christianity has no knowledge of the sword. But within Christianity the sword always has to justify itself. The arguments within Islam begin in another place, asking . . . what is honorable in fighting rather than whether fighting in itself is forbidden." Jean Bethke Elshtain, *Just War against Terror: The Burden of American Power in a Violent World* (New York: Basic Books, 2003), 159.

[37]Matt. 4:1–11; Mark 1:12–13; Luke 4:1–13.

military. Hereby we are *not* arguing that church and state and family and community affairs are to be equated or that they blend into one another, in the end losing their distinctions as mediating structures in the culture. Rather, we only wish to contend that a holistic, unified view of life is necessary for the religious believer in order that a false sense of the "sacred" might not result in social-cultural isolation.

Doubtless there are professing Christians who would interpret the New Testament in such a way as to make it read that *nothing is owed Caesar*. As we have noted elsewhere in several questions, this is the Tertullian error. And it is a perennial error at that, even when it may arise out of entirely different motives.[38] Nevertheless, this understanding of "Caesar" and what is owed to public authorities is false and transcends our particular political preferences. Although Reinhold Niebuhr's rationale for justice and coercive force is not without its problems, in his own day Niebuhr reflected deeply on the relationship between faith and politics. While he is sensitive to the idolatry in any era that issues out of confusing faith and politics, he notes an opposite idolatry as well, and that is to see little or no relevance between the two spheres. This latter mindset is particularly problematic because "it denies the seriousness of political decision and obscures our Christian responsibilities for the good order and justice of our civil community."[39] Therefore, it would seem that it is incumbent upon us to resist both the nationalist and the isolationist tendency as it relates to "Caesar."

Q. 66 Hasn't Romans 13 been used to justify much evil by political regimes throughout history?

With this question, which is often raised by those who believe that Christians, wittingly or unwittingly, have sanctioned injustice "in the name of God," we begin to understand more clearly our own ideological precommitments. To grapple with the ethics of war and peace and to examine the morality of force is

---

[38]For example, an attitude of detachment might not only grow out of religious separatism; it might even serve as a smokescreen for a mistaken sense of absolute *autonomy*, whereby we are tempted to live as if we would have *no authority over us* whatsoever.

[39]Reinhold Niebuhr, cited in D. B. Robertson, ed., *Love and Justice: Selections from the Shorter Writings of Reinhold Niebuhr* (Philadelphia: Westminster Press, 1992), 60.

to reveal our assumptions about political power and about authority in general. To do such is in no way to suggest that religious believers need to be immersed in a vocation of politics; nor does it require that they study legal or political theory. It does mean, however, at least for those professing Christian faith, that they must take seriously the injunctions regarding authority found in their own faith tradition, not least of which is the crux text of Romans 13.

This task, however, is complicated by several factors. In the Protestant tradition, there has been no little controversy as to how to view the powers. Mainstream Reformers such as Luther, Calvin, Zwingli, and Bullinger held a relatively high view of political authorities, believing that all vocations, including the soldier and the magistrate, were honorable. "Radical" Reformers such as the Swiss Brethren, and Menno Simons afterward, by contrast rejected this view of political authority, choosing to view the powers from a critical distance and calling fellow Anabaptists to "absolute separation" from the world; at the very least, a believer could *not* serve as either magistrate or emissary of the state. These distinctions remain for the most part in Christendom today nearly five centuries later.[40]

Like the Gospel narratives and the book of Acts, the assorted epistles of the New Testament neither forbid nor idolize military service. Thus, if we might hope to find authoritative evidence of how to view military service and war, we encounter none. What we do encounter is a surprisingly uncritical view (at least according to contemporary modern standards) of the political authorities. Texts in Romans 13[41] and 1 Peter 2[42] are thought to create particular difficulties, given the church's speckled history and its tendency to justify abuse. Anabaptists and other pacifists are keenly aware, and with some good reason, of ways in which this text has been misused. But the variegated interpretive history of Romans 13, with its abuse, is not our focus. *Abusus non tollit usum*. The fact that a text can be misinterpreted says nothing about its meaning and its potential faithful application.

---

[40]In the tradition of my (Daryl's) own upbringing, the Mennonite tradition, it is illegitimate, based on theological rationale, to seek vocational service in any form of public administration, government, or the military. Moreover, aside from the realm of sociology (which permits—indeed, invites—critique of the culture), fellow Anabaptists generally are not to be found serving as lawyers, legal theorists, economists, and public-policy analysts, or in other similar public vocations.

[41]Rom. 13:1–7.

[42]1 Pet. 2:13–17.

What *may* be said, and what frequently goes unnoticed, is the contrast in Pauline thought between the personal and the political, that is, between the contexts of Romans 12 and Romans 13.[43] Following Pauline admonitions on how Christians relate to Christians, Romans 12 ends with a list of exhortations aimed at Christian interaction with the world around them. A telling barometer of how believers relate to others is how they handle insult, persecution, and personal abuse. In this vein, Paul's exhortations are straightforward and may be summarized as follows: avoid a retaliatory mode. As far as possible, strive for peace, seeking to do good to those who mistreat you. Believers are not to take justice into their own hands, for justice has a proper context in which it is displayed.

A shift in context helps illuminate the Pauline teaching that ensues in chapter 13. Whereas force and vengeance are prohibited in 12:17–21, they are both permitted and sanctioned in 13:1–7. Paul's argument is not that force and retribution, represented by the *jus gladii* ("right of the sword"; see 13:4), are inherently immoral. In the realm of the private relationships, justice is illegitimate and *pro*scribed; in the hand of the governing magistrate, however, it is *pre*scribed. And because the powers operate on the basis of *derivative* authority, they are to be *respected*—a watchword in 1 Peter (cf. 2:13–17). This "respect," which is not to be construed as an *ultimate allegiance*, is fully aside from whether the office is inhabited by honorable individuals. It is the clear and unambiguous teaching of the New Testament that the authorities exist for one purpose, and that is to preserve the moral-social order. The use of power—and by extension, force—is thus the essence of politics and governing. Governing is not governing without power. Therefore, given the tenor of Pauline instruction in Romans 13, which simultaneously *desacralizes and affirms* political power, the necessity of a moral and just application of force should be beyond controversy.[44]

---

[43]See also question 64.

[44]Observe the Pauline thrust here in relation to the "sword": "For rulers hold no terror for those who do right, but for those who do wrong. . . . But if you do wrong, be afraid, for he [the magistrate] does not bear the sword for nothing. He is . . . an agent of wrath to bring punishment on the wrongdoer" (Rom. 13:3–4). As we have done elsewhere in this volume, we call attention once more to the critical distinction between force and violence. Force is that measure of power that is necessary and sufficient to facilitate and uphold law and politics. What exceeds that measure is violence, which destroys or undercuts the proper function of law and politics. See in this regard Murray, *We Hold These Truths*, 288–89.

Not only Romans and 1 Peter but the so-called Pastoral Epistles as well suggest a proper view of the powers. Observe the tenor of Paul's admonition to Timothy. Among the first duties of the Christian community when it is assembled is to intercede with prayer on behalf of "all those in authority" (1 Tim. 2:1–2).[45] The purpose of this intercession is civil or domestic tranquility, which, by Paul's reasoning, helps to preserve human dignity and further the spread of the gospel (2:2–4). When we consider who may have been on the imperial throne, who presided in the Roman Senate, and who were the local political authorities at the time of Paul's writing, the apostle's instructions strike us as nothing short of scandalous.

That politics and government require power to operate, however, is not an assumption shared by all. The Tertullians in every age believe that because politics and governing do not relate to the spiritual side of life, they are therefore unimportant at best or perhaps inherently evil at worst. Religious believers, hence, should invest themselves in pursuits that are spiritual and radically otherworldly. The point to be stressed here is simply that if Christians are convinced that politics and power are inherently corrupt, a necessary evil, then they surely will not involve themselves in the political process or in social institutions that need the leavening influence of religious faith. While one might be tempted to applaud the motivation to maintain faithfulness amidst the culture, more often than not the fruit of this separatist mindset is to call believers *away* from responsible cultural engagement rather than back toward those social institutions that need their participation. That cultural influences can *potentially* contribute to the compromise of one's faith is no argument against cultural involvement. Moral compromise with the opposing values is *not* inevitable.[46]

Even when Jesus forbids the sword as a means to advance the spiritual domain, the New Testament cannot rightly be construed either

---

[45]This seemingly uncritical perspective is all the more remarkable if Paul's letter, as assumed, is being written from Ephesus, which was a haven of the emperor cult.

[46]Perhaps the most eloquent expression of the "necessary evil" view of governing powers is the important work by John Howard Yoder, *The Politics of Jesus*, first published in 1972 (2nd ed. 1994). Therein (and in his other works) Yoder argues that Revelation 13, not Romans 13, represents the normative New Testament teaching on the state. For this reason, the Christian is not to participate with the powers, since they are inherently and intractably hostile toward God. Yoder's assumptions about the political powers are extended to the early church. The reason for Christians' acquiescence to the state in the fourth century and their increasing involvement in the affairs of the state from Constantine onward, including the military, is readily explained: the church was "co-opted" by the empire. This account of the first four centuries, as we have noted in part 2, has been popularized by historian Roland Bainton and others and has achieved a remarkably wide currency over the last four decades in wider Christendom.

(1) to forbid the Christian from "bearing the sword" in the service of society and the common weal or (2) to teach that government is a necessary evil, though authority, like all realms of human endeavor, is susceptible to abuse. Oliver O'Donovan well explains why:

> Non-governmental organizations . . . can never claim the representative status that entitles a government to judge; and without judgment a state of ordered peace among and within the nations cannot command the authority of the law. It is the essential structure of government to harness representative status and power to the service of judgment and law. That structure is the provision of common grace, and without it our best efforts at making peace are doomed to be swept away.[47]

Q. 67 Isn't political power a "necessary evil," if not inherently evil, as portrayed in the Revelation?

We must recapitulate. As we observed in the previous question, what is disturbing to many of us today is the remarkably uncritical attitude that the Apostle to the Gentiles, writing to believers in Rome, seems to have had toward government and political realities. Putting ourselves in the shoes (sandals) of believers living in the imperial seat during the mid-50s of the first century helps us partially to fathom how utterly scandalous Paul's teaching concerning the authorities might have struck them. Recall, too, that we should assume a worst-case scenario at the time that the apostle penned his letter: the individual sitting on the imperial throne in time would orchestrate a ferocious persecution of Christians that would become infamous. In this light, one would rather expect Paul to adopt the markedly more pessimistic view of the powers that seems to animate the apostle John in his apocalyptic visions. Based on a reading of the New Testament Apocalypse it would truly appear that people such as Anabaptist theologian John Howard Yoder are correct: Revelation 13, not Romans 13, better approximates political reality and life for the average person in the shadow of a fallen world.

---

[47]Oliver O'Donovan, *The Just War Revisited*, Current Issues in Theology (Cambridge: Cambridge University Press, 2003), 32.

Let us momentarily reconsider Yoder's argument as well as its implications, both for religious communities and for maintaining a civil society. In *The Politics of Jesus*, he argues that Romans 13:1–7 is not the "center" of the New Testament's teaching on the state. Rather, that center is located in Revelation 13, with its depiction of the "beast" and the war that is foisted upon believers. Such, according to Yoder, more closely approximates political reality. Consequently, the Revelation mirrors a call to follow the Lamb, Christ, and to die. The saints do not in their lifetime "overcome"; they are rather killed by the sword.[48] Consistent with his Anabaptist forebears, Yoder maintains that Christians, therefore, are not to participate in the affairs of the state.[49] To do so is to collaborate with evil.

Yoder's argument is extended backward to the church fathers, who are seen as having "compromised" and "collaborated" with the powers in the age of Constantine and beyond. Christians, the argument goes, became co-opted by the empire, and with the end of formal persecution the church lost its prophetic posture. Gone was the pristine beauty and purity that characterized earlier generations of believers. Precisely in what way does the church "collaborate"? For Yoder, we are "accomplices" if we fail to comprehend the fallenness of the powers of this age. The "normative" understanding of the powers found in the New Testament, as Yoder sees it, is their *inevitable and intractable* hostility toward the people of God, such as we find in John's Apocalypse. In John's visions, the powers are at war with Christ, the Lamb, and the Lamb is at war with the powers. But the Lamb overcomes the powers by his death and the cross. Therefore, Christian believers are to view the powers as enemies of the faith.[50]

Because Yoder's argument amplifies a partial truth, particularly as it applies to the principalities and powers of this age,[51] there is something in the vision he articulates that is quite appealing in its desire for purity and its idealism. And were Revelation 13 representative of *all* authority (including political power), Yoder's argument

---

[48]Moreover, Yoder is adamant that the "sword" of Rom. 13:4 is merely symbolic of legal function and was not intended to bespeak the death penalty or war as (literal) punishment for temporal evil.

[49]See, for example, Article 6 of the Schleitheim Confession, adopted in 1527, which is representative of early Anabaptist views and prohibits believers from participation in affairs of the state. In all fairness, Anabaptist views on the state did not occur in a vacuum. They grew out of the sixteenth-century Anabaptist experience of persecution from both the Catholic and the Protestant side.

[50]The principal parts of Yoder's argument are to be found in chaps. 6, 8, 10, and 12 of *The Politics of Jesus*.

[51]See Eph. 1:21; 2:2; 1 Pet. 3:22.

would be forceful and immensely significant. Nevertheless, in spite of the *potential* for political corruption, his argument shows itself to be deficient at several levels.

At one level, Yoder's "radical critique of Constantinianism"[52] fails to recognize the diversity of Christian opinion among early Christians. Believers of the first several centuries were not uniformly (and universally) pacifist, as we have already observed,[53] even when there were good reasons for them to be so as a social minority. In addition, the Anabaptist and pacifist critique fails to wrestle sufficiently with the responsibilities of our dual citizenship, as Augustine painstakingly sought to maintain. An important subtheme in Augustine's writings is that, while it is certainly true that we are called to an ultimate allegiance, we nonetheless remain citizens of the earthly kingdom, and our citizenship entails responsible occupation, as Jesus described it, not abdication or disengagement. Augustine is very clear on this point: when the two allegiances collide, we have a higher allegiance, but not every decision or priority or sphere of life will entail conflict or an either/or decision. There are times, circumstances, and occasions that require us to respond in good faith by working *through and not outside of* particular social institutions for the purposes of helping to transform them, as well as people's lives.

There is a further problem—a hermeneutical issue—raised by Yoder's argument. Jewish and Jewish-Christian apocalyptic literature as a *literary genre* is predicated on an absolute antithesis between the spiritual and the temporal, between good and evil. Apocalyptic literature, however, is *not* intended to represent everything that the New Testament has to say about the powers, or even most of what it says. A major part of apostolic teaching in the New Testament is that governing authorities play a distinct and divinely instituted role in promoting justice and preserving the moral-social order. Hence, in our "theology of the powers" we are constrained to take into account the *combined* teaching of the New Testament, particularly as it surfaces in the Epistles, and harmonize with that of the Old Testament.[54]

---

[52]This is a recurring theme in many of Yoder's writings, not only in *The Politics of Jesus*.

[53]See questions 24 and 25.

[54]A related weakness is to presume *ethical discontinuity* between the Old and New Testaments, a presumption that erects a false dichotomy between Yahweh and Jesus, between judgment and mercy, between justice and love, as if justice and judgment govern the Old scheme of things ethically while love is the benchmark of the New. Such an interpretive flaw has disastrous implications for both theology and ethics and proceeds from a *misreading* of Scripture.

While responsible interpretation does not argue that Romans 13 says *everything* about government that is true, neither do the apocalyptic visions of John.

A final weakness of Yoder's pacifist position in light of his extreme pessimism over against governing authority is the very selective manner in which it views stewardship and tending the world. As responsible citizens and stewards of the culture, religious believers have the same privileges and responsibilities as others. Unless a particular vocation clearly and expressly violates moral principles—which military service, public administration, politics and political science, law and legal theory, law enforcement, and policy work do *not*—it is appropriate, then, for people of faith to occupy these vocations, seeking to contribute in meaningful ways to a broad array of social, political, and cultural structures. Even religiously grounded pacifists, after all, benefit from law and order that serve to furnish peace and stability in society. The presumptuous attitude, at least to our way of thinking, of "Let the Gentiles do the dirty work!" on the part of some toward the messy business of law enforcement, community protection, and criminal justice is quite unfortunate and misguided. Why should we assume that *someone else* will protect our homes and bank accounts, offer security to our public buildings, guard our cities and borders, and wrestle with policies that affect these realms? In our opinion, the accompanying mindset of civic disengagement that mirrors these sorts of assumptions is simply unsatisfactory. People who profess religious faith will need to consider the moral consistency of their position.

According to the Anabaptist model, Christians may not—indeed, *must not*—serve as magistrates or soldiers. But the list does not end there. Neither should they be policy makers, or legal theorists, or economists, or tax collectors (accountants?), or policemen, or security guards, or drivers of Brinks trucks, or public clerks, or any type of civil servant. In the end, the Anabaptist call to remove ourselves from the world is interpreted rather literally, so that, for fear of being "compromised" by "the powers," we do not involve ourselves in mainstream institutions of society. In its place, we build our "prophetic" communities on the sidelines of the culture.

But there is a decided difference between being "aliens" in the culture (as per 1 Pet. 2:11), out of allegiance to Christ, and *deliberately* pitching our tents on culture's periphery. The former is our calling; the latter, however, is our choice. The view of theological and cultural separatists, then, that political power is a necessary evil at best or inherently evil at worst, as in the apocalyptic vision of St. John, does not represent mainstream Christian teaching in any age; rather, it represents a deviation.[55] This is not to suggest that the church will not have to confront the powers in a prophetic spirit out of its commitment to faithfulness; indeed, there will be occasions that call for such action. It simply means that we need not resort to sectarian teaching to do so. It also means that our confronting the powers, when it does or must occur, will have a conspicuously hollow ring to it if in our sectarian isolation we are not integrally involved in tending the common good.

Q. 68 Since Christians are called to be "peacemakers," shouldn't our highest human goal be to strive for peace around us?

C learly, Christian from the beginning have been known as a pacific people. Their lifestyles are generally characterized by a contentment and simplicity that engender social harmony. Indeed, this would appear to be the meaning of Jesus' pronouncement,

> Blessed are the peacemakers,
> for they shall be called the sons of God. (Matt. 5:9)

Consider the other virtues listed alongside "peacemaking" in the beatitudes: poverty of spirit, mercy, humility, the ability to mourn with others, uprightness, purity, and the ability to endure persecution—all of these are postures of the heart, not particular actions to be taken or avoided. Peacemaking, in similar fashion, corresponds foremost to an inner disposition and not an external act or behavior.

It is the collective witness of the New Testament, indeed of all Scripture, that peace is present only in the context of right relation-

---

[55]We have attempted through this question to address the religiously grounded opposition to political power. There is a secular equivalent view, frequently assumed or advanced in academic circles, by which it is thought that power itself is evil, based on the *will to power* in human nature. To be human is bad enough, but to be powerful is to be doubly corrupt.

ships—that is to say, where justice has been affirmed. Such is the very centerpiece of biblical theology, especially of Pauline theology: "Therefore, since we have been justified [declared righteous] through faith, we have peace with God through our Lord Jesus Christ" (Rom. 5:1). One might well argue—correctly, we think—that without justice there is no peace. And what is true in the spiritual dimension also applies to the political. For this reason, Augustine accentuates the need, on the earthly plane, for a justly ordered peace, what he called a *tranquillitas ordinis*. Thomas Aquinas agrees, observing that "peace is not a virtue, but the fruit of virtue."[56] As we have already observed, justice and charity do not stand at odds; they are not polar opposites. Justice is concerned with a right ordering of society for the sake of social peace. Peace, of course, can be both just and unjust, legitimate and illegitimate. As one social commentator well notes, "Many horrors and injustices can traffic under the cover of 'peace.'"[57] Even thieves, Augustine emphasizes, maintain a certain peace and order within their own orbit for the sake of plundering the innocent.[58] And even Rome herself was guilty, in Augustine's view, of imposing a "cruel peace" in the name of the vaunted *pax Romana*. As a social good, then, peace is a relative entity on this side of the *eschaton* and not to be confused with the ultimate peace that lies beyond the present world.

This distinction between the ultimate and the penultimate, between temporal and eschatological peace, is critically important and must not be underestimated. The aspiration to peace, to be sure, is a universal human longing and is by no means confined to religious conviction. It is the goal of Marxists and non-Marxists, naturalists and supernaturalists, Hindus, Buddhists, Jews, and Christians, secularists as well as theists. While Christians by character are known for the peaceable nature they mirror and the inner peace they experience through faith, they do not uncritically adopt a utopian vision of "world peace"—a "peace" that needs severe qualification.

Tellingly, the apostle Paul, who develops the contours and implications of Christian theology more than any other New Testament writer, does *not* declare that "the greatest of these [theological virtues] is peace." The greatest, rather, is charity, which exists in concert

---

[56]Thomas Aquinas *Summa theologiae* (hereafter *S.T.*) II-II Q. 29 (New York: Blackfriars, 1975).
[57]Elshtain, *Just War against Terror*, 50.
[58]*The City of God* 19.12.

with faith and hope.[59] Strikingly, too, the writer of Hebrews offers a subtle commentary on peace that is primarily intended to point to the superiority of Christ. But, secondarily, there are important theological insights to be gleaned. In the writer's comparison between Melchizedek and Christ, there is an important lesson. Of the former, he writes, "First, his name means 'king of righteousness'; then also, 'king of Salem' means 'king of peace'" (Heb. 7:2). For reasons not only of biblical theology but political and social stability, this order is not incidental: first justice (or righteousness), then peace. This suggests that one (peace) is a by-product, the fruit, of the other (justice or righteousness). The order, again, is important in both the spiritual and the political realm—justice first, then peace. That is to say, out of a right ordering proceed right relationships. Without the former, there is no authentic latter. One need not be a politician or public officeholder to see the truth in this political reality.

The biblical concept of shalom, the peace of the kingdom of God established in its fullness, is that future eschatological reality to which various images in Old Testament prophetic literature point. Such images—for example, lions and lambs coexisting, swords becoming plowshares (Isa. 2:2–4; Joel 3:10; Mic. 4:3)—are familiar to us and are employed by both religious communities and secularists.[60] Consider the words of the prophet Micah, which resonate so powerfully with the human spirit:

> Nation will not take up sword against nation,
>   nor will they train for war anymore. (Mic. 4:3)

A common feature of utopian visions, whether religious or secularist in character, is that they seek, directly or indirectly, to impose a vision of "order" on society that is premature, and usually totalitarian in its implementation. Martin Luther's quip, for this reason, always needs to be kept in mind: If in the present life the lion is to lie with the lamb, the lamb will need constant replacement. There is both theological and political wisdom in this remark.

Politically speaking, the ideal must not be mistaken for the real. Human beings are not guaranteed a world without war and strife; nor

---

[59] 1 Cor. 13:13; cf. 1 Thess. 5:8.
[60] One thinks, for example, of the United Nations, which employs these images without qualification.

may it be argued that in the present life strife, self-interest, quarrel-
ing, and warring will cease. There will always be evil men, and thus
there will also be the need to restrain evil men. Peace, as most people
understand it, can be a false security that hides a waning of religious
commitment, a decline in general morality, or an increase in material
decadence. For this reason, for example, the First World War was frequently and mistakenly referred to as "the war to end all wars." An
authentic social peace, by contrast, is based on the proper ordering of
relationships. Socially, peace among human beings in the present must
be justly ordered; otherwise, it is no peace at all and may even serve
unjust ends.[61] The presence or possibility of war, given human nature
and the omnipresence of evil, need not, therefore, shake our faith or
render us passive spectators.

Q. 69 Isn't war immoral since taking human life is a violation of the sixth commandment?

For many religious believers, it is a given that the taking
of *any* human life is immoral. This conviction tends
to be rooted in a particular understanding of the sixth commandment.[62] An accurate translation of the commandment, however, is
more nuanced, as indicated by the Hebrew verb used: "You shall
not murder [*ratsah*]." The distinction between murdering innocent
life and generic killing not only forms the heart of this commandment but is maintained throughout the Torah—a distinction that is
assumed and preserved by Jesus,[63] as well as the writers of the New
Testament.[64] Not all forms of killing are proscribed in the Hebrew
and Christian Scriptures. While murder is proscribed by the Creator,
based on humans' creation in the image of God,[65] there is no absolute
sanction against the taking of life. As indicated by a number of Old
Testament narratives,[66] not all forms of killing or manslaughter are the
equivalent of murder. Moreover, capital punishment was prescribed

---

[61]So Thomas Aquinas: "Those who wage war justly aim at peace, and so they are not opposed to
peace, except to the evil peace." *S.T.* II-II Q. 40.
[62]Ex. 20:13; Deut. 5:17.
[63]Matt. 5:21.
[64]Rom. 13:9; James 2:11.
[65]Gen. 1:27; 9:6; Ex. 20:13; Deut. 5:17.
[66]E.g., Gen. 9:1–17; Num. 35:6–33; Deut. 4:41–43; 19:1–13; Josh. 20:1–9.

by Mosaic law for various crimes, just as killing in self-defense was not considered a criminal offense.

While life is an endowment and thus is sacred (hence the sixth commandment), it is not to be valued above the soul. Therefore, loss of life as punishment for crimes against humanity is not the moral equivalent of murdering the innocent. This fundamental distinction is present in Genesis as part of God's covenant with Noah[67] and forms the basis of traditional notions of criminal justice.[68] Consider the function of the "cities of refuge" in ancient Israel, which illustrate with great clarity the moral difference between manslaughter and murder. The most detailed instructions are set forth in Numbers 35.

In the Numbers narrative, the six cities of refuge are designated as such "so that a person who kills someone unintentionally may flee there" (v. 11 HCSB) and "so that the one who kills someone will not die until he stands trial before the assembly" (v. 12 HCSB). These cities exist for both the Israelite and the foreigner or temporary alien (v. 15). Murderers, according to these instructions, are to be put to death (vv. 16–21). What distinguishes the murder is intention: "if anyone in hatred pushes a person or throws [an object] at him with malicious intent and he dies," or "if in hostility he strikes him with his hand and he dies," in such cases the perpetrator is a murderer (vv. 20–21 HCSB). Moreover, what distinguishes the murder is its context: the scenario being described is not war or military conflict; it is within the course of normal civilian and civic life. In addition, the argument proceeds on the assumption that the land "where you live," that is, your home life, is "defiled" by the bloodshed that arises from murder.

---

[67] Gen. 9:6.

[68] This remains true, even when there are increasing calls among behavioral theorists to eliminate the traditional concept of criminal justice based on guilt and punishment for a more medical-biological model that seeks prevention. As representative of the literature, see Roy D. Masters, ed., *The Sense of Justice: Biological Formulations of Law* (Newbury Park, CA: Sage, 1992); Adrian Raine, *The Psychopathology of Crime: Criminal Behavior as a Clinical Disorder* (San Diego: Academic Press, 1993); Raine, *Crime and Schizophrenia: Causes and Cures* (New York: Nova Science, 2006); and Raine with José Sanmartin, *Violence and Psychopathy* (New York: Kluwer Academic, 2001); Roy D. Masters and M. T. McGuire, eds., *The Neurotransmitter Revolution: Serotonin, Social Behavior and the Law* (Carbondale: Southern Illinois University Press, 1994); W. Wayt Gibbs, "Seeking the Criminal Element," *Scientific American* 272, no. 3 (1995): 100–107; Robert Plomin et al., "The Genetic Basis of Complex Human Behaviors," *Science* 264 (June 17, 1994): 1733–39; Nicolas Rose, "The Biology of Culpability: Pathological Identity and Crime Control in a Biological Culture," *Theoretical Criminology* 4, no. 1 (2000): 5–34; and Richard E. Redding, "The Brain-Disordered Defendant: Neuroscience and Legal Insanity in the Twenty-First Century," *American University Law Review* 56, no. 1 (2006): 51–127. For an assessment of this broader trend, see J. Daryl Charles, "Blame It on the Knife (or My Criminal Brain): Second Thoughts on Biogenetics, Moral Self-Responsibility and 'Civil' Society," unpublished paper, Duke University conference on science and religion, March 13, 2008, a modified version of which appears in "My Criminal Brain Made Me Do It," *National Catholic Bioethics Quarterly* 9, no. 3 (Autumn 2009): 485–515.

The presence of war or international conflict is utterly foreign to the context of the narrative.

In continuity with the Christian moral tradition, the Catechism of the Catholic Church affirms both capital punishment and just-war thinking. "Legitimate defense of person and societies," the catechism asserts, is "not only a right but a grave duty for someone responsible for another's life, the common good of the family or of the state."[69]

Jesus' teaching regarding the body and soul seems to imply the distinction between the murder of innocents and generic killing, even when it is not his aim to elaborate on the distinction: "Do not fear those who kill the body but cannot kill the soul. Rather, fear him who can destroy both soul and body in hell" (Matt. 10:28 ESV).[70] "Thou shalt not kill" thus cannot rightly be interpreted to rule out all killing, including war. The purpose of war, furthermore, is to address an injustice, to stop the strongman, as it were, not to *kill* as such. For these reasons, killing in war is not the equivalent of murder. Finally and most importantly, the use of force in resisting or punishing evil is not entrusted to individual people. It rests with governing authorities, whose responsibility it is to protect the moral-social order. In this way, justice and retribution show themselves to be moral entities rightly distinguished from vengeance.[71]

Q. 70   What is the relationship between peace and justice?

Much contemporary thinking about peace and justice is flawed in terms of how it understands the relationship between the two. One fruit of this misunderstanding is the emergence of false dichotomies and false dilemmas. As it applies to the problem of war, a common fallacy is to suppose that war and peace are two "discontinuous and incommensurable worlds of existence and universes of discourse, each with its own set of rules."[72] Peace,

---

[69]Catechism of the Catholic Church, par. 2266.

[70]For this reason C. S. Lewis argues in his brief but brilliant essay "The Humanitarian Theory of Punishment," in *God in the Dock: Essays on Theology and Ethics* (Grand Rapids: Eerdmans, 1960), 287–94, that retribution, precisely *because human beings deserve it on the basis of moral agency*, verifies our worth as having been made in the image of God. Secular accounts of justice, by contrast, wholly miss this human insight.

[71]Rom. 12:17–13:10; 1 Pet. 2:13–14; cf. 1 Tim. 2:1–4.

[72]So, Murray, *We Hold These Truths*, 269.

accordingly, is that realm of morality in which an absence of conflict is to be found. War, by contrast, is thought to be a realm of evil that has nothing to do with peace. This is the sort of thinking that finds its way to bumper stickers, posters, and similar sloganeering, not to mention "Christian ethics" primers. So, we hear things like, "war should be abolished" or "weapons of mass destruction must be banned" or "[we are] pro-troops but anti-war." The assumption is, among other things, that war subsists in the realm of injustice while peace is the state of actualized justice. This, however, is utterly false.

Because justice is a cardinal virtue, we must ponder both its character and its order of priority for civil society, which in turn will shed light on its relationship to peace. Justice, despite the prostituted manner in which it is used in contemporary parlance, is not a fluid entity. Indeed, it is universal and unchanging. As developed philosophically both in the Judeo-Christian moral tradition and in pre-Christian philosophy (e.g., Plato's *Republic*), it is a cardinal virtue. Historically, justice has been defined as that which is due each person—a definition affirmed from Aristotle to Cicero to Aquinas.[73] Moreover, the language of justice fills the entire Bible, making it clear that it is the hallmark biblical ethics. And properly so, since justice describes how people associate with one another and thus how society functions. It is the very essence of justice to discriminate between righteousness and wickedness and between guilt and innocence;[74] to erect protection for those without a voice;[75] to seek to prevent injustice from arising or spreading;[76] to rectify situations in which injustice has established itself;[77] and finally, to render to each his due, out of which the principle of proportionality issues.

What this means in light of the question at hand is severalfold. It means the existence of set standards for behavior in society—if, that is, society is to remain civil. It also means that in order for justice to be established, human beings will need to participate in that process. Justice does not fall from heaven unapplied; rather, it is by divine mandate that humans are to implement and realize norms of justice, as much as it lies within their power. In addition, justice requires that

---

[73] Aristotle *Nicomachean Ethics* 5.1–11 (1129a–1138b); Cicero *De officiis* 1.5.15; Aquinas *S.T.* II-II Q. 58.
[74] E.g., Gen. 18:25; Isa. 5:20–24.
[75] E.g., Ex. 23:6–9; Lev. 19:9–10.
[76] E.g., Lev. 19:11–14.
[77] E.g., Isa. 10:1–2.

people receive what is due them, what they are owed. Nowhere is this element more important than in the realm of criminal justice, which breaks down when the translation of justice is uneven, inconsistent, and not impartial.

Aquinas's treatment of war in *Summa theologiae* is instructive and upholds the basic assumption in just-war moral reasoning that peace is only legitimate to the extent that it is rightly ordered. Beginning his discussion of war with this very distinction in mind, he asks, "Is it always a sin to fight in war?" As he frequently does, he addresses typical objections that cause someone to answer incorrectly. He identifies two common objections that he says are lodged in a misunderstanding of two biblical texts—Matthew 5:38–39 (not resisting evil but turning the cheek) and Romans 12:17–21 (not returning evil for evil). In response, he is at pains to show that coercive force per se is not a category of injustice but rather is necessary to the civic peace, the *tranquillitas ordinis* of Augustine.[78] Hence, when we speak of just war, we do not mean a war that, narrowly speaking, is just. Rather, we refer to warfare undertaken that is in conformity with the demands of charity, justice, and human dignity and that, in a morally measured way, seeks to protect the innocent third party from gross injustice and social evil.[79] A "peace" that is not justly ordered is not a legitimate one; otherwise, the very deliberate "peace" that exists among the Mafia is to be desired by all people and may be viewed, in religious terms, as a foretaste of heaven.

For the religious believer, one's foundation for acting and doing— that is, one's social ethics—is as sturdy or weak as one's grasp of theology. Both politically and spiritually, peace never comes except with a price, and that price is the sacrifice of procuring (and maintaining) justice. This is not only the message of the New Testament, but it is also the reality behind political stability in all relatively free societies. From a spiritual standpoint, righteousness or justice—concepts interchangeable in the Scriptures—always precedes peace. This order is not incidental. One is a by-product, a consequence, a fruit, of the other. First justice, then peace. The order or priority is critically important in the

---

[78]See Aquinas *S.T.* II-II Q. 40 a. 1; also Q. 7 a. 3–4, as well as Q. 18.
[79]This is the weakness of Reinhold Niebuhr's "Christian realism" insofar as Niebuhr, while willing to acknowledge that force must hinder totalitarianism, cannot ground the use of that force in a *positive* moral vision. Force, as Niebuhr understood it, is merely a "necessary evil."

spheres of theology and law and politics. First, right order; then, right relationship. Without the former, there exists no legitimate latter.

Q. 71 Doesn't love require us to forgive our enemies?

As authors who take matters of public policy and personal faith seriously, both of us must admit to being greatly dismayed at the depressingly irresponsible comments in the aftermath of 9/11 that issued forth from many religious leaders. Religious pronouncements, of course, ran the gamut from "America got what it deserves" to "Let us forgive our enemies." Both excesses, in the context of the events themselves, should be seen for what they were—theologically vacuous and unable to take seriously the role of governing authorities in preserving civil society and confronting moral evil.

Here we consider one of these statements—"Let us forgive our enemies"—a pious-sounding pronouncement that surely was uttered from many pulpits across the land. What about *forgiving our enemies?* On what should a theology of forgiveness rest? Surely, to forgive is the distinctly Christian thing to do, is it not? Not only does this question confront us with the nature of forgiveness as it touches our daily lives, but it raises further (and perhaps uncomfortable) questions. For example, are *nations* called to forgive? Were the Armenians called to forgive the Turks for genocidal activity? Were Allied forces called to forgive Germany sixty-plus years ago? Why or why not? What about forgiveness *in principle* for those who, regardless of historical location, commit mass murder and wreak public mayhem? *Are* we called to forgive in an unqualified manner? On what basis? If not, why not? And what would this forgiveness entail?[80]

Without question, forgiveness has a prominent place in the teaching of Jesus. However, given contemporary notions of forgiveness, it behooves us to distinguish between forgiveness as *inner psychological or emotional release* of a party who has committed wrong (what typically passes as forgiveness) and forgiveness as *declared external*

---

[80]A fuller treatment of the matter of "forgiveness" in the context of terrorism is found in chap. 5 of J. Daryl Charles, *Between Pacifism and Jihad: Just War and the Christian Tradition* (Downers Grove, IL: InterVarsity, 2005), esp. 108–12.

"release" by the offended party of a guilty party who has *acknowl-edged personal guilt* and *directly requests* to be forgiven. It is critically important that we distinguish between what authors Avis Clendenen and Troy Martin call an "intrapsychic" and an "interpersonal" under-standing of forgiveness.[81] Because these two models are worlds apart, this distinction is absolutely crucial.

While Christian faith requires of us not to harbor unforgiveness—by which we mean, most accurately, *resentment*—toward others, to focus on human emotional responses misses the essence of authentic forgiveness, which is concerned foremost not with our psychological state but rather with *reconciled relationships.* Forgiveness, accord-ing to scriptural teaching, concerns the latter. It is predicated on rec-onciliation with the Creator, whom all humans have offended. This reconciliation is individual and personal, and proceeds on the basis of repentance, contrition, and confession. Nowhere in Scripture are humans commanded to forgive parties of wrongdoing who have not (1) acknowledged the guilt of their actions, (2) demonstrated penitence for these actions, and (3) requested forgiveness from the offended party for the wrongs committed. This pattern, it cannot be stressed enough, is predicated on the divine model vis-à-vis human beings.

Our attempt to clarify the true meaning of forgiveness, of course, runs into difficulties, since the cultural climate around us has foisted upon us a sentimental understanding of forgiveness in which mercy trumps justice, consequences for wrongdoing are denied, and moral self-responsibility is absent. Added to this is, of course, a religious version of "therapeutic culture" to which we all are prone, which is called, among other things, "cheap grace." The point to be made is that love and mercy do not annul justice; as St. Paul reminds us, they fulfill it.[82]

Take an illustration from daily life. You *can forgive* a thief who, hav-ing been caught stealing your car, is apprehended by law-enforcement authorities and in contrition wishes to return or replace your car and ask for your forgiveness. (Though, don't hold your breath!) In your response, what have you done? In a qualified way you have "released" that person based on his willingness to own up to his action. That willingness is measured by certain demonstrable evidence, specifically,

---

[81]Avis Clendenen and Troy Martin, *Forgiveness: Finding Freedom through Reconciliation* (New York: Crossroad, 2002), 14–20.
[82]Rom. 13:10.

a commitment to (1) face you directly, (2) acknowledge moral responsibility, and (3) provide restitution. You *cannot forgive* a car thief, however, who remains unrepentant, apprehended or otherwise. Yes, you can struggle to make sure that hatred or resentment does not dwell within. But true forgiveness, biblically speaking, proceeds on the prior reality of repentance and contrition, followed by restitution.[83] In its very constitution, forgiveness is interpersonal and direct. Thus, only the offended party can grant forgiveness. Others who have not been directly victimized cannot. Finally, and most importantly, forgiveness *does not set aside the consequences* of the ethical violation. Offenders incur a debt that must be paid, a fact that is true in all realms of life and at all levels; again, this is based on the divine pattern.

The concept of forgiveness suffers when it is not rooted in moral reality. Moral reality, in turn, is established by justice, which cannot be fluid; justice is not justice if it is not everywhere and for all people the same.[84] This is why, as a biblical-theological concept, forgiveness is tethered to the principle of restitution. To make restitution is to *restore by making things right*, as any next-door neighbor of yours will be more than happy to tell you. In Old Testament law, restitution is always required *in proportion* to the sin committed; so, for example, an ox for an ox, a tool for a tool, property for property, indeed, a life for a life. In the New Testament—and recall Jesus' vigorous *affirmation* of the ethical requirements of the law[85]—this principle remains in effect; hence, the significance of the Zacchaeus narrative (Luke 19). What is striking about St. Luke's account is that Zacchaeus's repentance does not remain merely at the abstract level of a changed heart, as it does for so many contemporary Christians. Rather, the point of the story is that he demonstrated *tangible evidence* of a profound inner change. In his particular situation, justice was expressed in returning *fourfold* what he had stolen monetarily. One might even argue hereby that Christian faith will cause an individual to go *above and beyond* in demonstrating heartfelt contrition.

---

[83]Murder is the one crime that provides no possibility for restitution and therefore is a unique category.

[84]For this reason, we speak of a "miscarriage of justice" or a "travesty of justice" to depict unjust standards. By means of this sort of language we concede that justice cannot mean one thing for one party and something completely different for another. Even nonreligious people intuit the moral "wrongness" of uneven standards.

[85]Matt. 5:17–20.

Of course, in the realm of criminal justice, offenders rarely take the initiative and return goods to the offended party. But sometimes the initiative might be reversed, as in Jesus' teaching on confrontation recorded in Matthew 18, wherein the other party is at fault but has not shown repentance before you take the initiative. Even if the other party is obstinate and will not acknowledge guilt, you still go through a process of confronting him with his guilt. In the end, if he still refuses to accept moral responsibility, he is to be treated as an outcast. Which is to say, forgiveness or release is *not* granted.

As it concerns matters of public policy, a crucial implication of forgiveness needs to be brought into relief. While individuals are required to forgive, states and nations are not. While persons receive mercy from other persons, the role of the magistrate is not to forgive and issue mercy where justice is due. Rather, the authorities function to mete out *justice* where justice is due, since justice, as a *cardinal* virtue, constitutes the moral fiber of social relationships. Otherwise, society falls apart and becomes ungovernable, since standards themselves become impossible apart from the moral fiber of justice. In such an environment, it needs emphasis, criminals will thrive because there are no restraints and evil is permitted to abound. In short, a world without justice is hell. Coercive force, therefore, will always be necessary as an instrument of restraining evil, not merely to get us all to pay our taxes!

A distorted view of forgiveness, whether it is rooted in therapeutic culture or in bad theology, has disastrous results when applied to broader society and public policy. Mercy and charity, we must remember, do not cancel out justice. They remain wedded to each other, even when that wedding seems to be fraught with tension and must be applied in the proper context. This means that charity will always seek to honor what is just, true, and proportionate, including the need for punishment as moral retribution (and here we make a necessary distinction between retribution and revenge).

While mercy may be expressed by individuals toward individuals, it is not the prerogative of the state to forgive evil. Christian teaching throughout the ages has affirmed the morality of force that is applied for just purposes in the social setting. Christian theology does *not* teach that when people do evil deeds, they are automatically struck down by God, even when this might be a divine prerogative. In most societies, evildoers are not permitted the liberty of continuing their practices in freedom. They are apprehended, usually coercively, and restrained for their own good, as well as for the greater good of the surrounding population.

This assertion should not strike us as controversial; it is both baseline Christian theology and the common-sense realization of the natural law. And it is this expressly *social* purpose—the common weal—that the governing authorities must serve. They exist to reward the good and restrain as well as punish evil. For human beings to fail to respond to or prevent evil when they have knowledge or the power to do so is to be an accomplice in that very evil. Even a *religious justification for nonengagement*, namely, that God in his providence will make evil right in the end (which, in fact, he *will* do), or a religious justification for acquiescing to evil, namely "forgiving our enemies," does not release us from the obligation to resist and counter evil in the present life.

Q. 72 Shouldn't the Christian trust the eschatological judgment by God of evil rather than fight or go to war?

This question requires that, from a theological vantage point, we consider the ramifications of our dual citizenship—in the heavenly kingdom and in the earthly. In a day when the culture was literally crumbling around him, Augustine penned his magisterial *City of God* for the purpose of responding to pagan challenges to the faith. One cannot read *City* without the realization that Augustine is burdened by the possibility of Christian disengagement. This is particularly the case in his treatment of war, which seems to be part of a broader subsection on citizenship. Augustine's reflections leave little room for misunderstanding. We are citizens of two kingdoms, and when these two realms clash (which is inevitable), our allegiance is always and irrevocably to the spiritual. But there is an attendant danger, and this danger consists in the possibility that Christians might be so focused on the future life and the purely spiritual aspects of Christian commitment that they fail to take their earthly responsibilities seriously enough, thereby *abdicating rather than occupying*. Historic Christian faith, it should be emphasized, grounds our earthly duties not only in the doctrine of redemption but also in a theology of creation. Redemption has meaning only in the light of creation realities,[86] at the center of which lies stewardship.

The tendency toward abdication, of course, intensifies in times of social-cultural upheaval. But the temptation to flee the culture, because it is "going to hell in a handbasket" anyway, is ever present and one with which every generation of the faithful has to struggle. Writing in the 1930s, a period of social and political upheaval in its own right, H. Richard Niebuhr presented the argument for Christian "inactivity" in foreign affairs. This inactivity, as he sees it, is rooted in the conviction that the unfolding of history is the judgment of God on the nations of the world. This judgment, nevertheless, produces a good outcome, based on the reality of divine providence. Christians' inactivity, moreover, has a precedent: the "grace to do nothing" was practiced by the early Christians as well.[87] Through our inactivity we demonstrate repentance, Niebuhr argues, as well as an attitude that refuses self-righteously to judge our neighbor.

The other of the famous Niebuhr brothers, Reinhold, though appreciating much in Richard's commentary, nevertheless takes his brother to task for advancing Christian inactivity.[88] While Reinhold commends Richard for taking seriously Jesus' words and for his sensitivity to sin, he sees problems. Pure disinterestedness in moral-social evil, Reinhold warns, is an ideal that no nation—indeed, no individual—can achieve. Sooner or later, he is convinced, justice will entail "the assertion of right against right, interest against interests," until some kind of social peace and order is achieved. Love and repentance, he cautions his brother, "can do no more than qualify the social struggle in history"; they will never abolish the struggle, which inevitably will become violent.[89]

We must be wary of a utopian tendency. The hope of attaining a moral society without coercion, cautions Reinhold, "is an illusion which was spread chiefly among the comfortable classes of the past century." Absent from this mistaken view is any responsibility for the political consequences of not confronting evil actively. Yes, Rein-

---

[86]See Genesis 1 and 2.
[87]H. Richard Niebuhr, "The Grace to Do Nothing," *The Christian Century* (March 23, 1932): 378–80.
[88]This took place a week later in the same venue. See Reinhold Niebuhr, "Must We Do Nothing?" *The Christian Century* (March 30, 1932): 415–17.
[89]Ibid.

hold shares his brother's conviction of the providence of God, but he questions why the resultant attitude is passivity rather than action. And, yes, he concedes that providence *does* work through catastrophe, but "ethically directed coercion," he argues, seems the better—and moral—alternative. As long as the world is fallen and a place where the real and the ideal meet, human progress will depend on "the judicious use" of force in the service of the ideal. In practical terms, this means that coercion *may* be necessary to dissuade totalitarian regimes from imposing their designs on other nations and people groups.[90]

Akin to Richard Niebuhr and standing in sharp contrast to Reinhold, Anabaptist theologian John Howard Yoder, whose work was reviewed in a previous question, has been perhaps the most eloquent spokesperson in the latter half of the twentieth century for the view that Christians should await eschatological judgment rather than involve themselves in the temporal order to resist injustice and evil actively. As we have already noted, Yoder's argument presupposes a fallenness—intractably and inevitably so—of the (political) powers, and thus a "collaboration" with them when Christians participate in politics, government, or civil service. Recall in this vein his belief that Revelation 13, not Romans 13, is normative for Christian ethics. Yoder sides with Richard Niebuhr in his belief that authentic Christian discipleship will cause us to endure hardship and persecution, even totalitarian hardship, as we await the redemption of all things. Christian discipleship, he maintains, is in accordance with the way of the crucified Lamb, not the victorious Lion. Against the imperialistic tendency in the church of any age, this will entail laying down any visions of "reigning" in the present life.

Roughly contemporary to Yoder was the evangelical theologian Carl Henry, whose writings and work spanned the 1940s to 1990s. In contrast to Yoder's Anabaptist model of ethics, Henry proceeded from a more "Reformed" model in his attempts to articulate a vision of Christian social ethics that sought to address weaknesses in early-to-mid-twentieth-century evangelical thought life. In 1947, Henry published a brief but highly significant manifesto of sorts titled *The Uneasy Conscience of Modern Fundamentalism*. Therein Henry sought to call his fellow evangelical Protestant brethren to a deeper commitment in demonstrating the social relevance of their faith. While Prot-

---

[90]Ibid.

estant mainline churches, in his view, had disengaged themselves from Christian orthodoxy and displaced it with a predominately political program, many evangelicals, Henry worried, had fallen prey to the view that a transformation of earthly institutions was reserved only for the *eschaton*. This, in turn, caused evangelical types to neglect the existential needs of society around them and focus almost exclusively on spirituality, the devotional life, and conversion strategies. His point was not that these elements of Christian discipleship are unimportant. Rather, conservative Protestants "needlessly invited criticism and even ridicule" by their inclination to "parade secondary and sometimes even obscure aspects of our [theological] position as necessary."[91] For Henry, the resultant "uneasy conscience" with respect to the cultural mandate needed a response: the time had come to demonstrate the credibility of one's convictions.

Fundamentalism's failure to "work out a positive message within its framework," coupled with its "doom-and-gloom attitude toward society and world history," caused Protestant conservatives "to revolt against the Christian social imperative" itself. Most embarrassingly, for the first time in recent church history, Henry argued, evangelical Christianity stood "divorced from the great social reform movements" in a manner that ensured the loss of apostolic authority.[92] Henry's critique, it needs to be emphasized, was not merely negative; it also had a constructive agenda.[93] What is relevant for our purposes here, however, is his observation that Christians must be active in the present rather than abdicating responsible participation in social institutions as they await the dawning of a new age. Henry was not about to deny the orthodox confession that the kingdom of God has a futuristic component. But *what about the present*? What can the church demonstrate in the *here and now*? Henry was painfully aware of a pharisaical spirit that could be detected among fundamentalists, rendering their presence in society ethically unsound.[94]

Collectively, theologians like the Niebuhr brothers, Yoder, and Henry—each of whom carried a deep burden for the church's wit-

---

[91] Carl F. H. Henry, *The Uneasy Conscience of Modern Fundamentalism* (Grand Rapids: Eerdmans, 1947), i.
[92] Ibid., 36.
[93] The essence of this agenda was twofold, as Henry saw it: (1) to develop a comprehensive, all-inclusive world-and-life view, and (2) to become more competent in various fields of academic study, with the ultimate goal of understanding the culture.
[94] Ibid., 63.

ness to the world—remind us of the tension that exists between the "already" and the "not yet." Respectful of the deep divisions and differences that exist within Christendom, we nevertheless take our stand with the mainstream of the historic Christian church. It is the witness of the church consensually and the conviction of many voices, from Ambrose and Augustine to Aquinas, to the Protestant Reformers, to Vitoria and Suárez and Grotius, to Catholic social teaching up to the present day that charity *may* be called upon, in the present, to manifest what ethicist Paul Ramsey called a "preferential ethics of protection." While not all situations may call for a forceful response, violent aggression *will* call for a response, rooted in charity and justice, that is proportionate to the offense. Not to respond is to be an accomplice in that evil.

To resist violent aggression and gross injustice is an expression of responsible politics and social ethics, and it is consonant with biblical teaching. Nowhere in the New Testament do we find teaching to the effect that *in human history* good ultimately triumphs over evil. It is always conditional and provisional, requiring that we make moral judgments; such is the implication of the "already but not yet" understanding of the kingdom of God. On occasion these moral judgments will necessarily be on behalf of other people or people groups who are being victimized. When and where this occurs, their victimization will require a just and measured response.

Q. 73 What is the relationship between mercy and justice? Aren't we commanded to show mercy to all people?

In several previous questions we have observed the symbiotic relationship between love or mercy and justice. For the Christian, this relationship is a question of theological importance; for society, it is a question of supreme ethical significance. Where a wedge is allowed to exist between justice and mercy, our understanding of both poles will suffer deformation.

Consistent with both pre-Christian philosophical thinking and the Christian moral tradition, justice is a cardinal virtue insofar as it defines our capacity to fulfill our moral duties to fellow human beings; it is, simply put, a moral condition of right relations. Whether retributive (punitive), redistributive, or restorative in character,[95] justice alone constitutes the bedrock of right relations, and therefore, of civil society. Mercy[96] presupposes the abiding nature of justice, although it is not obligatory in the sense that justice is. Our model for both justice and merciful action is divine and covenantal:

> The LORD, the LORD, the compassionate and gracious God, slow to anger, abounding in love and faithfulness, maintaining love to thousands [of generations], and forgiving wickedness, rebellion and sin. Yet he does not leave the guilty unpunished; he punishes the children and their children for the sin of the fathers to the third and fourth generation. (Ex. 34:6–7)

In contrast to justice, which is static, the wonder of mercy lies in its voluntary aspect. This is expressed by Christian faith in the fact that, "because of his great love for us, God, who is rich in mercy, made us alive with Christ even when we were dead in transgressions—it is by grace you have been saved. And God raised us up with Christ and seated us with him in the heavenly realms in Christ Jesus" (Eph. 2:4–6).

In Christian theology, mercy is best appreciated against the bold relief of covenantal obligation and redemption. In the divine economy, justice is not set aside; rather, justice is satisfied by transferring punishment to Christ. This punishment, however, is not eliminated, only transferred. One feature of mercy that is frequently misunderstood is the relationship it has to justice. Specifically, mercy does not set aside the consequences of guilt.[97] Consequences, as it turns out, for every moral violation still must be paid in the earthly realm, whether for speeding, for stealing, or for strangulation. In fact, criminal justice is impossible if standards of justice are not fixed and implemented consistently. In the ethical domain, justice requires that payment be made and that it be proportionate to the offense; this is why the principle of *restitution* plays such an important role in the case illustrations of the Pentateuch. Biblically speaking, the only category of ethical offense for which no restitution exists is premeditated murder, which is why it is a capital offense.[98]

---

[95]So Thomas Aquinas *S.T.* II-II Q. 58.
[96]The Hebrew *hesed* is normally rendered "mercy" or "lovingkindness" in the Old Testament.
[97]Again, see Ex. 34:7.
[98]Gen. 9:5–6; Num. 35:1–33, esp. vv. 29–33.

The relationship between mercy and justice, and the need that consequences of moral evil not be eliminated, is further clarified by the tragic experiences of suffering people around the world. Recall the words of South African Justice Richard Goldstone, delivered in 1997 at the U.S. Holocaust Museum. Goldstone, who served as Chief Prosecutor of the International Criminal Tribunals for the former Yugoslavia and Rwanda, reflected on the character of human holocaust by observing that "where there have been egregious human rights violations that have been unaccounted for, where there has been no justice, where the victims have not received any acknowledgement, where they have been forgotten, where there's been a national amnesia, the effect is a cancer in the society."[99]

Notice that Goldstone was not calling for "mercy" as many today might understand it. Authentic justice in a broken world, rather, is *retributive* as well as *reparative* and *reconstructive*. Goldstone went on to delineate what civil society, as we construe it, and political communities must do in the light of moral atrocity. Justice, he maintained, will expose the truth of specific guilt and avoid a general or nebulous collective guilt that sidesteps accountability. If there is one recurring tendency in our world today, it is the failure of moral self-responsibility at virtually every level. Further, justice will insist on recording the truth of moral atrocity in the historical record for coming generations. This will have a pedagogical effect, allowing us and those after us to learn from it. And it will also serve to counter any attempts by the guilty, or those sympathetic with them, to fabricate excuses or avoid guilt. (Witness in our day, for example, the existence of Holocaust denial.)

Correlatively, where and when it is possible, we must publicly acknowledge the great loss endured by the victims of evil who, as broken and terrified people, seek and need the rectifying components of justice. There is perhaps no greater fear or dread on the part of victimized people anywhere than to believe that moral atrocity aimed at them will be left unaddressed and unpunished. Finally, free societies need to apply the deterrent of criminal justice, since human nature and potential criminals are deterred by the fear of apprehension, punishment, and negative consequences.[100]

---

[99]The text of Goldstone's address appeared in *The Washington Post*, February 2, 1997, C4.

[100]A similar though fuller discussion of the relationship of justice and mercy is found in J. Daryl Charles, *The Unformed Conscience of Evangelicalism: Recovering the Church's Moral Vision* (Downers Grove, IL: InterVarsity, 2002), chap. 9 ("Toward a Biblical Ethic: Principles in Polarity," 204–25).

Q. 74   Isn't "turning the other cheek" rather than retribution the more Christian response to evil?

R eligious pacifism throughout the church's history stems largely from a particular understanding of the Sermon on the Mount, and Matthew 5:38–39 in particular. The standard pacifist interpretation of these verses, already alluded to in a previous question, does not make the critical hermeneutical distinction between private and public justice, a distinction that is lodged in the literary context and is grounded in the reality of private-versus-public spheres of authority (as seen in Rom. 12:17–21 and 13:1–7, side by side). The pacifist interpretation of Matthew 5:38–39, mistakenly in our view, applies Jesus' ethical teaching on matters of the heart to the realm of the state and public policy. We are by no means the first generation of Christians, however, to conflate the two; this confusion can be detected in the church of all eras.

In a prior question we observed two salient features in the writings of Ambrose and Augustine. One is the concern that Christians, especially in times of social upheaval, might remain aloof from the affairs of society as they wait for the arrival of the *eschaton*, the last day. Augustine is acutely aware of this tendency among people of faith. In a letter written to his friend Marcellinus, a Roman official in Carthage who needed assistance in defending the Christian faith before influential pagans, Augustine's response is highly instructive. A specific charge needs rebutting, namely, that Christianity is incompatible with sound political rule and civic responsibility. Specifically, what about the problem of punishing criminals? Marcellinus's critics say that

> the preaching and teaching of Christ are not at all suitable for the morals of a republic. They have in mind the precept that we should not return evil for evil to anyone, but turn the other cheek to anyone who strikes us, give our tunic to anyone who takes our coat, and walk a double journey with anyone who would force us to go with him (Mt. 5:39–41).[101]

---

[101] *Epistle* 138 ("To Marcellinus"). We are relying on the English translation provided by Michael W. Tkacz and Douglas Kries, in Ernest L. Fortin and Douglas Kries, eds., *Augustine: Political Writings* (Indianapolis: Hackett, 1994), 205.

Augustine's advice is multifaceted and instructive. At the most basic level, he says, a righteous man privately should be willing to endure insult and abuse rather than respond with malice. Matthew 5:38–39, he points out, refers to a *disposition of the heart* and not the external act. Christ's teaching frees a man from an evil that, initially, is not external and foreign but inner and personal. Therefore, in many situations at the private level, overcoming evil with good will be effective in changing human behavior. Hence, a godly person should be prepared "to endure patiently the malice of those whom he seeks to make good."[102]

How do we respond, however, to those who are a menace to the community and who stubbornly refuse to be set straight? With those, Augustine maintains, we take up very different measures, and we apply to them a "benevolent harshness." The reason? "Their welfare rather than their wishes must be considered. . . . He whose license for wrongdoing is wrested away is usefully conquered, for nothing is less prosperous than the prosperity of sinners, which nourishes . . . and strengthens the evil will."[103]

It might be tempting, however, to accuse Augustine of being naïve with regard to political realities. Was he merely giving justification to abuses of the empire since, according to pacifist interpretation of the fourth and fifth centuries, the church had "compromised" and was now an "accomplice" to the powers? Despite the critique of "Constantinianism" offered by Roland Bainton, John Howard Yoder, and those sympathetic with them, Augustine is under no illusion regarding Rome's own record of aggression. Neither does he turn a blind eye to the injustices of the Roman *imperium*, for "peace and war had a competition in cruelty." But at the same time, Augustine appears to have little patience for the idea that Christianity will passively tolerate evil in the present, based on a distorted understanding of Jesus' Sermon on the Mount. For even pagans, he insists, are capable of displaying notable civic virtue without having religious faith. How much more should such be exhibited by those professing Christian faith?

Like Augustine before him, Aquinas responds to the common objection that war or the use of force is contrary to Jesus' teaching in the Sermon on the Mount not to resist evil. And like Augustine,

[102]Ibid., 206–7.
[103]Ibid., 208–9.

he notes that "a man avenges the wrong done to God and neighbor" because of charity. He cites Augustine: "Those whom we have to punish with a kindly severity, it is necessary to handle in many ways against their will. For when we are stripping a man of the lawlessness of sin, it is good for him to be vanquished."[104]

The ideological pacifist, of course, will counter that retribution amounts to an uncivilized, even barbaric, response by society to crime or moral evil. How might we response? One's answer, we think, depends fundamentally on whether a society can distinguish between the criminal act and the punitive act. Keeping in mind this important distinction and the fact that military service, even going to war, may be an expression of charitable motives, we may appreciate part of the reason that Luther finds it necessary to address religious believers of his own day in the treatise *Whether Soldiers, Too, Can Be Saved*.

Not only should the Christian, in Luther's view, *not* shun military serve, but he should consider it a *duty* and means by which to order peace and justice. Luther writes:

> The married state [by analogy] is also precious and godly, but there are many rascals and scoundrels in it. It is the same way with the profession or work of the soldier; in itself it is right and godly, but we must see to it that the persons who are in this profession and who do the work are the right kind of persons, that is, godly and upright.[105]

Having collapsed the popular stereotype of "spiritual" work, Luther observes that service to and through the state can be a "work of love" done "for the sake of others." Consistent with Ambrose, Augustine, and Aquinas before him, Luther believes that bearing the sword is not inconsistent with Christian discipleship. It is not for the purpose of "avenging yourself or returning evil for evil, but for the good of your neighbor and for the maintenance of the safety and peace of others."[106]

A troubling issue that we authors encounter, whether in the classroom, in private conversations, or in the chaplaincy, turns out to be

---

[104] Aquinas *S.T.* II-II Q. 40, citing Augustine *Epistle* 138.

[105] See *Luther's Works* (hereafter *L.W.*), ed. Jaroslav Pelikan and Helmut Lehmann (Philadelphia: Fortress, 1967), 46:94. Elsewhere (*L.W.* 5:102) Luther comments on how great it may seem when a monk renounces everything and goes into a cloister to carry on a life of asceticism, fasting, prayer, etc. And, by contrast, it appears so insignificant when a maid cooks and cleans and does other housework. Yet, Luther contends, God's command and blessing are there as well; even seemingly insignificant work is to be praised as a true service to God.

[106] Ibid., 45:96.

perennial among Christians. It is the seeming contradiction between the requirements of charity and the demands of the state. How does one reconcile the tension that arises from Jesus' admonition to turn the other cheek, on the one hand, and obeying and supporting the governing authorities, on the other, particularly when those authorities must wield the sword? Don't the personal and the political stand in conflict?

We shall need to keep in mind our remarks in a prior question about Romans 12 and 13. There is no contradiction in Pauline thought between the personal and the political. Both domains are to be guided by charity. The specific applications of that charitable action to them differs enormously, however, based on the divinely mandated context by which justice is *proscribed* and *prescribed*. While rendering "justice" is illegitimate in the private realm, and hence Paul warns sternly against revenge, it is both *permitted and required* and therefore legitimate in the public domain, over which the magistrate has been set. Therefore, when it comes to handling personal insults, abuse, and persecution, we are to "turn the other cheek" and "not resist an evil person" (Matt. 5:39). Giving other people our cloak or walking an extra mile or lending to those who wish to borrow (5:40–42) are *not* issues of statecraft and public policy, however much such actions might inconvenience us personally. When it is a question of defending others, however, then we are obligated to act on their behalf. On occasion, this will necessitate the application of coercive force, whether at the local, national, or international level. We do not "turn the other cheek" when moral atrocity occurs; to do so would be to assist in that very evil itself. In such a situation, charity indeed calls us to courage and a commitment to resist evil.

Q. 75 Is there a difference between retribution and revenge? Surely, a vengeful spirit is counter to loving one's enemy.

Both implicitly and explicitly, we have sought in several previous questions to emphasize the critical distinction between the criminal act and the punitive act. If this difference is not acknowledged, then it becomes impossible for a society to distinguish between retribution and revenge. At its base, the moral outrage expressed through retributive justice is first and foremost rooted in moral principle, not mere emotional outrage and hatred. Recall Augustine's words to Marcellinus: retribution is a form of "benevolent harshness."[107] The governing authorities, by punishing criminal behavior, mirror a concern for the welfare of the population and for those doing the wrong. Any parent knows the truth of this principle. Indeed, *not to act against the will of a wrongdoer* is, for Augustine, to nourish and strengthen the will toward evil. It needs reemphasis, especially in our culture, that it is *virtuous and not vicious* to feel anger at moral evil. In truth, something is very wrong with us if we *don't* express anger and moral outrage at evil. And yet, moral outrage alone is not enough.

Perhaps our readers will not grant, at first blush, a difference between retribution and revenge. Allow us to qualify further how the two are to be distinguished; conceptually, they are worlds apart. Whereas revenge strikes out at real or perceived injury, retribution speaks to an objective wrong. Whereas revenge is wild, "insatiable," and not subject to limitations, retribution has both upper and lower limits, acknowledging the moral repugnance both of draconian punishment for petty crimes and of light punishment for heinous crimes. Vengeance, by its nature, has a *thirst* for injury and delights in bringing further evil upon the offending party. The avenger will not only kill but rape, torture, plunder, and burn what is left, deriving satisfaction from his victim's direct or indirect suffering. Augustine described this inclination, rooted in the flesh, as a "lust for revenge."[108] Retribution has as its goal a greater social good and takes no pleasure in punishment. In this vein, consider the words of C. S. Lewis:

> We may [in wartime] kill if necessary, but we must never hate and enjoy hating. We may punish if necessary, but we must not enjoy it. In other words, something inside us, the feeling of resentment, the feeling that wants to get one's own back, must be simply killed. . . . It is hard work, but the attempt is not impossible.[109]

In addition, whereas revenge, because of its retaliatory mode, will target both the offending party and those perceived to be akin, retribu-

---

[107]*Epistle* 47.
[108]*The City of God* 14.14 and *Contra Faustum* 22.74.
[109]*Mere Christianity* (New York: Simon & Schuster, 1996), 109.

tion is targeted yet impersonal and impartial, not subject to personal bias. For this reason, Lady Justice is depicted as blindfolded. The difference between retribution and revenge is the difference between Romans 13 and the end of Romans 12; it is the difference between bona fide justice and vigilante "justice." The governing authorities are commissioned to "bear the sword," and they do so "not in vain." Why? St. Paul says in order to reward good and punish evil.

Understood properly, retributive justice serves a civilized culture, whether in domestic or international context. It isolates individuals, parties, or people groups who endanger the community—locally, nationally, or internationally—for their wanton disregard for the common good and a just peace. It controls the extent to which a citizenry is victimized by criminal acts. It rewards the perpetrator proportionately with consequences befitting the crime. And it forces both the offender and potential offenders to reflect on the grievous nature of the crime. Each of these elements is critical in preserving the social order.

For those who might refuse to recognize any difference between retribution and revenge, the consequences for social ethics are enormous. If society refuses to make this moral distinction, which the cardinal virtue of justice is committed to do, then it is *impossible* to denounce moral evil—anywhere, in any form, at any time. Indeed, if one is to be consistent, one's attempt to obliterate the distinction between retribution and revenge will logically lead to advocating the abolition of the *entire* judicial and criminal-justice system. And how can we denounce and respond to moral atrocity? Viewed in this light, the Nuremberg trials were wrongheaded, since Nazi war crimes—indeed, *any crimes against humanity*—cannot in principle be denounced, much less can mass murderers be put on trial and sentenced. In the end, one man's torture is another man's good time.

The impulse toward retribution, it needs reiterating, is not some lower or primitive impulse; rather, it corresponds to the divine image within us. To treat men or nations, however severely, in accordance with the belief that they should have known better—and they *do* know better—is to treat them as responsible human beings, endowed with human dignity and moral agency. So, for example, a society *unwilling* to direct retributive justice toward those who murder in cold blood is a society that has deserted its responsibility to uphold the sanctity of human life. Civilized society will not tolerate murder—at *any* level;

an uncivilized one will. And despite its flaws, we cannot dispense with criminal justice, whether at the domestic or international level. And in the end, the "root cause" of the criminal's or the terrorist's pathology becomes relatively immaterial, since neighbor love requires that we interdict, punish, and incarcerate. This corresponds to the criterion of just cause.

In the end, to affirm retribution, which is integral to the history of Judeo-Christian moral thinking and foundational to any self-governing society, is not to abandon one's belief in mercy and forgiveness. But it is to acknowledge the difference between criminal and punitive acts, as well as between private and public recourse. Retributive justice, then, is a moral necessity for a civilized culture. In responding retributively to moral evil, we channel our energies in several directions. We respond to victims who have been wronged. We respond to wider society, which has been scandalized by the wrong done in its midst. We also respond to the offending party by declaring that moral evil will not be tolerated. And, finally, we respond to potential offenders, who might be tempted to engage in the same evil. Understood correctly, retributive justice performs a multifaceted and indispensable moral good.[110]

Q. 76 Aren't fighting and warfare a denial and contradiction of the Lamb of God, whose image projects sacrifice?

This question represents an important plank in the argument of religious pacifists. Perhaps none has framed the matter more compellingly than Anabaptist theologian John Howard Yoder. In various writings, but particularly in *The Politics of Jesus*, Yoder argues that Christian faith requires us to follow the way of the crucified Lamb. Christ himself did not resort to force or violence; rather, he endured suffering and death for others. Thus, as those called to follow in Christ's steps, we too foreswear any recourse to violence and entrust ourselves to God, who will pronounce judgment in the

---

[110]We recommend highly the very succinct yet penetrating examination of the difference between retribution and revenge found in David A. Crocker, "Retribution and Reconciliation," *Philosophy and Public Policy* (Winter/Spring 2000): 1–6. For a discussion of this distinction in its application to the context of criminal justice and civil society in general, see J. Daryl Charles, *Between Pacifism and Jihad*, 143–47, and Charles, *Retrieving the Natural Law: A Return to Moral First Things*, Critical Issues in Bioethics (Grand Rapids: Eerdmans, 2008), 305–11.

future life. Hence, following the Lamb entails not the sword but the cross, not power but patience. Jesus himself chose suffering servant-hood rather than violent lordship, and he calls us to a similar path. Faithfulness, then, according to Yoder's argument, results in a willing-ness to accept defeat rather than complicity with evil.[111]

Throughout the history of the Christian church, there have been believers in every age who have shared Yoder's convictions about power and about the powers. Compelling as Yoder's argument is, it isolates one aspect of theological truth. What needs further consider-ation is the complementary theological portrait of Christ in Scripture: he is also the divine Warrior.[112] How, then, can Christians reconcile God the Warrior with God the Crucified One?[113] Given the fact that biblical images mirror to us the reality of God's character, how are we to understand properly the character of God? At the theological level, the responsibility of the Christian community is to reconcile the "lambness" and the "lionhood" of Jesus the Lord.

The first order of business might be to account for a seeming dis-crepancy between the God of the Old Testament, who condones not all wars but certainly some, and the God of the New. Some pacifist theologians must resort to arguing that the New Testament reveals a *new* ethical understanding of God that stands in bold contrast to that of the Old. Whereas the God of the Old Testament is a God of war, justice, and wrath, in the New he represents peace, forgiveness, and charity. A variant of this view is to contend that Israel's theocracy required God to be a warrior, whereas the warlike tendencies that are on display in the old covenant do not apply to the God of the new covenant, supremely revealed in Jesus Christ, the Lamb of God.

In stark contrast to this dualism, the mainstream of the historic Christian tradition posits a very different interpretive approach and commends itself to us: namely, to see *ethical continuity* between the two covenants. In the words of author Darrell Cole, God's warlike character cannot simply be spiritualized away in an effort to deny God as Warrior while affirming God as Pacifist.[114] And if the New Testament presup-

---

[111]See in particular chap. 12 ("The War of the Lamb," 233–50) of Yoder, *The Politics of Jesus*.
[112]In the Old Testament Yahweh is often depicted as the divine warrior, and in the last book of the New Testament, Revelation, Christ assumes this portrait.
[113]This question forms the backbone of discussion in chap. 2 of Darrell Cole, *When God Says War Is Right: The Christian's Perspective on When and How to Fight* (Colorado Springs: Waterbrook, 2002), 27–51.
[114]Ibid., 30.

poses the theological and moral foundations of the Old, as mainstream biblical scholars in the Christian tradition have assumed, then we are not at liberty to assume discontinuity between the Testaments. Otherwise, we are left with the God—or Gods, rather—of Marcion.

What needs emphasis is that Christ, as depicted in the New Testament book of Revelation, is *both* Lamb *and* Lion, the Crucified One *and* the Conquering Lord, the one who offers himself as a sacrifice *and* the one who vanquishes his enemies. What are the implications for the people of God as they reflect on these New Testament images? One is to understand that justice and love are *not* diametrically opposed. It is the nature of justice, which is a cardinal virtue, to fulfill one's moral duties to others, thereby showing itself as a moral tissue that holds society together. And this is precisely what charity aims to do as well. The divorce of justice and charity in the minds of most people is tragic, not infrequently leading to a sloppy sentimentalism or unbridled antinomianism. Even among so-called Christian ethicists, it is not uncommon to find justice and charity standing in opposition to one another. Justice, according to the stereotype, is assumed to be cold, harsh, unbending, and inflexible, while charity is thought to manifest precisely the opposite characteristics, having the person's best at heart. Thus, it is thought, that a society of those who would love their neighbor must dispense with justice as mediated by the courts and the state. Unhappily, this false dichotomy persists in the minds of all too many religious people, with the result that love, viewed as the highest Christian virtue, is disengaged from the moral content of the Christian life.[115]

We may freely and humbly grant the partial truth that Yoder and other pacifists wish to stress, namely, that we as Christians indeed shall need to count the cost of Christian faith, following the Lamb wherever faithfulness may lead. Both in the book of Revelation and in human history, this entails the likelihood of enduring persecution from the world, even the potential for martyrdom—a reality that early Christians understood quite readily, and Christians in Muslim cultures today also readily intuit. But to argue that Christian faith entails fol-

---

[115]So, e.g., Timothy P. Jackson, *Love Disconsoled: Meditations on Christian Charity* (Cambridge: Cambridge University Press, 1999), 174, 176, can write, "Love . . . is the greatest good; it does trump in cases of conflicting values"; and, "Charity is beyond both certainty and morality." More seriously, esteemed New Testament scholar Richard Hays, in *The Moral Vision of the New Testament* (San Francisco: HarperSanFrancisco, 1996), 324–25, can make the rather remarkable statement, "This extraordinary change of emphasis [i.e., Jesus' teaching as recorded in Matt. 5:38–48] constitutes a paradigm shift that effectually undermines the Torah's teaching about just punishment for offenders."

lowing Christ should not be construed to mean that Christians enact the life and mission of Christ himself. There is a difference between suffering for what is right—the lot of every Christian believer—and suffering to atone for the sins of the world.

Furthermore, in our attempts to develop biblical theology responsibly, the portrait of God as the crucified Lamb, as we have suggested, needs to be balanced with the complementary biblical image of God as Lord of Hosts and Conqueror. While conquest in the Revelation is portrayed as a future eschatological reality, the New Testament as a whole witnesses to the fact of our *dual citizenship*, over which we are stewards. As argued in a previous question, we are to render to Caesar what belongs to Caesar, without ascribing to Caesar ultimacy. These two responsibilities, while they *may* collide, are not always and inevitably in opposition, as the Tertullians and separatists of any age will maintain.

Even when some of the early Christian fathers saw particular sayings of Jesus—notably drawn from the Sermon on the Mount—as prohibiting Christians from engaging in warfare or military service, these New Testament passages should not be interpreted merely as prohibitions against the use of force or warfare that Christians are ethically bound to honor. For if *flat prohibition* of violence is the teaching of Christ, then *everyone* has the same duty. The implication of this presumption, of course, for our own day is patent: *none* may legitimately serve as policemen, law-enforcement officers, security guards, soldiers, National Guardsmen, judges, legal theorists, politicians, and policy analysts in our day. While the New Testament indeed teaches charity, nowhere does it prohibit the use of force as a means of advancing justice, retarding evil, and maintaining communal order; rather, it is the vengeful spirit at the personal level that is denounced.

Q. 77 What is the church's role in a nation's decision to go to war? Should the church be involved in deciding what is just cause?

From the vantage point of democratic society, one might wonder whether the empowered people themselves should not decide, on a collective basis, whether to go to war. In the democratic context, should it not be the *citizenry* that makes determinations about just cause? And if that is the case, then should the *church* not play a decisive role in that decision?

According to political philosophy that has been nurtured in the Western cultural tradition and informed by Christian theological presuppositions, the state has a clearly defined role in its representation of the people. It is divinely ordained to perform one primary function: it preserves the moral-social order and protects the political community. Belonging to the attendant responsibilities of the state, therefore, is the duty to adjudicate over matters of justice, whether in a domestic or an international context. This is not only Western political philosophy; it is the clear teaching of the New Testament as well (Rom. 13:1–7; 1 Pet. 2:13–17; cf. 1 Tim. 2:12).

Citizens, whether individually or collectively, are incapable of rendering judgments that belong to the domain of the state. *In sic* they lack the required intrinsic authority. To implement law and order, authority is necessary; after all, rendering a public judgment is a public and not private act. The public nature of the magistrate's office fundamentally distinguishes war (*bellum*) from dueling (*duellum*), piracy, or terrorism. At the civic level, only policemen and law-enforcement agencies can sanction criminal justice. This is because they are authorized by government—whether local, state, or federal—to do so. And only governments can declare or prosecute war. Government is representative of the political community; this is why citizens are not permitted to "take justice into their own hands." For citizens to make claims that are reserved for the state would be counter to the purpose of government and to usurp the state's role. For this reason, as Thomas Aquinas emphasized,[116] proper authority is the cornerstone from which all other just-war criteria derive their significance.[117]

From a purely practical standpoint, individual citizens, regardless of their abilities and competencies, rarely if ever have access to information, intelligence, and data that are essential to determinations of the state. The public, even with its best efforts (television and the Internet notwithstanding), simply does not have the benefit of tactical resources and information that are supplied by various government agencies, the military, and the intelligence community. And for good

---

[116]*S.T.* II-II Q. 40.
[117]See the questions on just-war criteria in part 4.

and necessary security reasons, much of this information is restricted and not in the hands of the public. Moreover, public opinion is easily swayed in democratic societies because of the influence of both the electronic and the print media, which operate in stark contrast to their counterparts in military dictatorships or totalitarian regimes, where they serve as vehicles of state propaganda. To entrust the citizenry, even in a democratic society, with national interests, let alone war-making potential, would be catastrophic.

Thus, it is useful to take note of the admonition contained in the Catechism of the Catholic Church, which reads:

> The evaluation of these conditions [i.e., just-war conditions] for moral legitimacy belongs to the prudential judgment of those who have responsibility for the common good. . . . Public authorities, in this case, have the right and duty to impose on citizens the *obligations necessary for national defense*.[118]

We are struck by the inclusion of these words in the catechism. To appreciate the wisdom not only of Western political theory but of divine purpose, one need only rehearse those chapters in human history wherein the church and the state were essentially one. Against this background, the influence of early-modern just-war theorists such as Francisco de Vitoria, Francisco Suárez, and Hugo Grotius is monumental. We illustrate with Vitoria.

By the early sixteenth century, the struggle between expansionists and missionaries in the "new world" was growing bitter. By the year 1510 troubling reports were reaching Spain that Native Americans were being denied basic rights to liberty and property. The immediate—and considerable—challenge confronting Vitoria, a professor of theology at Spain's leading university, was the Spanish expansionist vision. Because Spain was prepared to justify war with Native Americans to possess their land, seek their "conversion" to Christianity, and colonize them, its treatment of indigenous people, in war and in "peace," created the need for urgent discussions of justice. Neither the king nor the pope, argued Vitoria, could authorize war against the Indians. Neither religion nor economics made coercion and warfare just. Going to war on the basis of religious differences or "the spirit

---

[118]Catechism of the Catholic Church, pars. 2309–10; emphasis added.

of discovery" was not justifiable.[119] While Vitoria's position hardly strikes us as remarkable today, it was nothing short of revolutionary in his own time—for the simple fact that the church at that time was determining, to a greater or lesser extent, matters of state.[120]

But we return to the original question: Should the citizenry—particularly the church—be involved in deciding just cause for going to war? And what are the alternatives if we do not heed the words of the Catholic Catechism that (1) the evaluation of conditions for going to war belongs to those responsible for the public good and (2) public authorities have both the right and the duty to impose on the citizenry the obligations necessary for war? One alternative is anarchy, whereby the citizens bypass government (and the church's moral teaching) and re-create a vision that ultimately descends into the abyss. Another option, however, has a very different trajectory. Here we have in mind two possibilities. One belongs to a bygone era in our own cultural tradition, in which popes and princes (or kings) were scarcely distinguishable. But a second possibility brings us back to the present day, in which fundamentalist and jihadic Islam aspires to a global culture that eradicates the separation between church and state.

The alternative to a separation of church and state—properly understood—is holy war.

Q. 78   Why does God allow war?

Certainly, this is a question that plagues humankind, and not only those who profess religious faith. If God exists, why would he allow the untold suffering, misery, and evil that result from war? From our perspective, this important question very much resembles the perennial conundrum, Why does God allow evil? Assuming that this question represents the sincere wrestling with ethical dilemmas of a theist and not an atheist (who might wish to keep God and theists at bay), we may defer to the mainstream of the Christian theological-philosophical tradition. This tradition probes the mystery of evil by employing multiple lenses: conceptually it seeks

---

[119]Francisco de Vitoria, *De Indis et de iure belli reflectiones*, ed. Ernest Nys, trans. J. P. Bate (repr., New York: Oceana; London: Wildy and Sons, 1964), 2.5.
[120]See also "Just-War Thinking in the Late Medieval and Early Modern Period," chap. 3 of Charles, *Between Pacifism and Jihad*, esp. 56–60.

to understand this dilemma as, for example, (1) the result of wrong moral choices, (2) the effects of the natural moral law, (3) spiritual warfare, (4) evidence that a greater good is being worked out, or (5) a vehicle through which the love of God potentially can be made manifest to those who suffer. We find wisdom in the collective understanding of this multiperspectival approach to the problem of evil, while confessing, with generations past and present, that evil in the end remains a mystery.

But assuming this basis, we nevertheless wish to probe the particular problem of war, respecting the fact that religious believers differ enormously in their understanding of war and peace and the use of coercive force. They approach the question with radically divergent assumptions, as many of the questions in this volume doubtless illustrate. Some approach the dilemma of war in the mode of the social scientist, who attempts to identify the roots causes of crime or human pathology in light of psychological, sociological, economic, and political variables. These individuals are inclined toward discussions of human conflict and war that are divorced from purely theological considerations such as creation, human depravity, redemption, and divine providence. Their notion of God tends to be somewhat vague and amorphous, not infrequently mirroring that of surrounding culture. Consequently, it is the *love* of God that is accentuated above all other divine attributes. The notions of divine wrath, judgment, and punishment are utterly foreign to this outlook, typically overshadowed by the emphasis on God's benevolence, compassion, and condescension. Human happiness, rather than cruelty and suffering and the effects of sin, are understood to be those commodities to which human beings are entitled in this life. More often than not, this point of view argues for both the possibility and the necessity of war's *abolition* from the human experience, given its attendant horrors. Participation in war itself is therefore presumed to be sin.

But another religiously informed view of war requires our consideration—one that is equally prominent. This category of believer—what we might label the pietist—is inclined to evaluate war in relation to divine providence, at the same time assuming little or no connection between external, social applications of the faith and the internal, devotional life. This particular person frequently demonstrates little interest in theology or systematic study of the Bible, at least in the context of subordinating his interpretation to the mainstream of historic Christian faith. Correlatively, there is little concern for the intellectual or rational component of Christian faith; rather, the experiential, subjective aspect of faith is of paramount importance. Even when the problem of war might pose a severe challenge to this person because of the sheer enormity of the issues raised, it lies outside of spiritual experience.

Where *does* God enter the picture in these religious views? For many Christians, it is in the form of the common question, Why does God allow war? or How can God allow war? From a human vantage point, this question is entirely understandable. Yet, we would suggest that in order to begin thinking about war—and evil or wider suffering, for that matter—we must wrestle with what Scripture reveals about the divine nature and human nature. We must affirm, as a bedrock of faith, God's sovereign reign over all things. Not only is he Creator, but he is the "Lord of Hosts," or in the words of the Apostles' Creed, the Lord "Almighty," who rules and sustains all things. If this is true, then we are obliged to confess that nothing lies outside his providential rule, knowledge, and dominion. Not even war lies outside of God's control. Biblical revelation, after all, nowhere promises that human beings will be exempt from the experience of war. If anything, it implicitly promises war's existence (cf. Matt. 24:6–7; James 4:1–2). Therefore, the presence of war should not shake our faith.

Equally emphasized in biblical revelation is human depravity. Properly understood, war belongs to the wider category of consequences of sin that attend the present age. Because it is a part of human fallenness in the present world, war therefore is to be understood as a permanent fixture in the present life—not because we wish it, but only because it coincides with human fallenness. On this side of the *eschaton* or future life, we reconcile ourselves to its presence; in the next life, however, the effects of sin are no more.

Theologically, this spiritual reality has enormous implications for Christian social ethics. Crucially, it means that any stress on eliminating war is utopian and wrongheaded, *not because Christians do not wish for peace*, but because such a view of human nature is deluded and mistaken. It might be argued that the reason we expect God to abolish war in the present life is that we desire peace and that we sense a right to live in peace. But do we pause to ask what the purpose and function of peace in the present life might be? The desire for peace is human and natural, but it must be qualified—indeed, tempered—by the greater purposes of God (cf. 1 Tim. 2:1–5), namely, that we live holy lives. Far too often, let it be said, many people desire peace for selfish, materialistic reasons. The result is that we surround ourselves with a sense of false security. Witness, for example, the current tenor of religious belief and the moral dullness that characterize Western culture. One is surely justified in questioning whether we have a right to expect God to preserve a state of peace merely to allow us to engage in a state of obstinate and perpetual unbelief.[121]

World peace is *impossible* given the human condition. Luther illustrated this well when he quipped that if we believe that the lamb and the lion must lie together in the present age, then we shall need constantly to replace the lamb. This reality has significant ramifications for how society is ordered—ramifications that ideological pacifists cannot fully appreciate. Among those needing emphasis is this: punishment and judgment of sin are not fully postponed until the next world; they are temporal realities as well, for whatever a man sows he will reap. St. Paul, we think, captures part of this reality in affirming the need of governing authorities to exercise wrath on the evildoer (Rom. 13:4).

The ethical dilemma of war raises a host of complex questions, not the least of which concerns the suffering of innocent human beings. Yet, we should remember that theologians and philosophers have agonized for millennia over these issues; we are not the first to do so. The teaching of the classic Christian moral tradition is that Adam's sin affects us all; we all share in the plight of the human race, which is to say, all have sinned and fall short of divine standards. Therefore, *no one* is innocent—no one, that is, apart from the Son of God, who suffered innocently and vicariously on our behalf.

What might we then conclude? In times that try our souls (e.g., in times of war), we are brought to the deepest place of soul-searching, spiritual awareness, and heartfelt repentance. It is in those times especially that we acknowledge the providence of God and the sinfulness of human beings. In the end, difficult as is the question of why God allows war, it recedes as a result of a shift in our theological perspec-

---

[121]In this regard, see Martyn Lloyd-Jones, *Why Does God Allow War* (repr., Wheaton: Crossway, 2003), 81–101, for a penetrating examination of the character of God and the perplexities of human nature as they affect the issue of war.

tives once we enter into centuries-long conversation with prior generations of Christians and place our questions alongside our own study of
Scripture. What did the church in prior generations believe and teach?
What insights might historic Christian reflection on war, suffering, and
evil afford us today as we wrestle with perennial issues?

Perhaps, by means of divine grace and our awareness of human
frailty, we might begin to ask slightly different questions. We might
even ponder questions so scandalous as: Why doesn't God allow
humankind to self-annihilate? Or, why does his grace restrain evil?
Or, why does God redeem what is evil and transform it into good?
Or, what is God's greater purpose (the deeper wisdom alluded to in
passages such as 1 Cor. 2:6–10)? While the mystery and tragedy of
being human do not go away, the human perspective is altered—
indeed, transformed—as we begin to think biblically, theologically,
and historically.[122]

Q. 79   Can a Christian legitimately serve in the military?

There is no express prohibition of military service taught
in the Bible or in historic Christian doctrine. Although
throughout history some Christians have abstained from military
service, one does not find a mandate to that effect. Rather, an individual's choice in such matters should be shaped by the wider moral
parameters of scriptural revelation. Per se the military profession as
a form of service to society is not prohibited. Just as a Christian may
legitimately serve in any branch of the government or with the police
force, fire departments, or emergency services of the state and local
communities, so too is military service a viable and honorable profession. In principle, it functions as an extended police force, concerned
to monitor internal as well as external developments that bear upon
the maintenance of civil society and the common weal.

Christian believers, it needs reiterating, are not without
resources—past or present—to assist them in putting "secular" callings in proper perspective. One of the contributions of the Protestant
Reformation was the emphasis by magisterial Reformers on redefining

---

[122]Elsewhere, the theological implications of this question are probed, however insufficiently, in Charles,
Between Pacifism and Jihad, 24–28.

the distinction between clergy and laity, between the sacred and the secular. By way of illustration, the question of dignity in vocation is addressed rather pointedly in Martin Luther's 1525 treatise *Whether Soldiers, Too, Can Be Saved.*

Writing to a knight and friend, Luther makes the candid observation that in his day many soldiers struggle to reconcile their profession with Christian faith. Emphasizing the need for a good conscience, Luther underscores the distinction between the occupation and the person filling it, between the office and the officeholder. The question reduces in Luther's mind to whether Christian faith is compatible with the work of the magistrate or the task of military service, which may involve going to war and killing, "as military law requires us to do to our enemies in wartime."[123] Luther begins by stating a baseline assumption:

> The very fact that the sword has been instituted by God to punish the evil, protect the good, and preserve the peace [Rom. 13:1–4; 1 Pet. 2:13–14] is powerful and sufficient proof that war and killing along with all the things that accompany wartime and martial law have been instituted by God. What else is war but the punishment of wrong and evil?[124]

This view is a product of Luther's understanding of two realms, the sacred and the secular, that are nonoverlapping and have their own authorities. The church, therefore, exercises no sway over government; neither does government over the church. Every Christian, contends Luther, is a citizen of both domains, with responsibilities in each.[125] This is a departure from medieval thinking, which had tended to conflate the two.

Not only should the Christian *not* shun military serve, in Luther's view, but he should consider it a duty, since it is a critically important means by which to order peace in a just and ordered fashion. In this way, the Christian contributes to upholding the common social good. The strong clergy-laity divide that still lingered in his own day, in the end, was unacceptable. Luther writes:

---

[123]Martin Luther, "Whether Soldiers, Too, Can Be Saved," in *Luther's Works*, ed. Jaroslav Pelikan and Helmut Lehmann (Philadelphia: Fortress, 1967), 46:95.
[124]Ibid.
[125]Ibid., 45:81–129. This conviction is decidedly Augustinian in flavor: the Christian has two citizenships that must be reconciled.

It looks like a great thing when a monk renounces everything and goes into a cloister, carries on a life of asceticism, fasts, watches, prays, etc. . . . On the other hand, it looks like a small thing when a maid cooks and cleans and does other housework. But because God's command is there, even such a small work must be praised as a service to God. . . . For here [i.e., concerning secular and mundane vocations] there is no command.[126]

Consistent with Ambrose, Augustine, and Aquinas before him, Luther believes that bearing the sword is not inconsistent with Christian discipleship. This is true even while needing the qualification that retributive justice is not for the purpose of "avenging yourself or returning evil for evil, but for the good of your neighbor and for the maintenance of the safety and peace of others."[127] The gospel of Christ, Luther insists, does not forbid this; in fact, in other places (i.e., other than Matt. 5:39) it actually commands it. And on behalf of others, Luther stresses, a Christian *may and should* seek retribution, justice, protection, and help, doing all that is possible to achieve the common good.[128]

But surely, many of the earliest believers struggled with the very same question. Acts 10 recounts the crucial role played by the Roman centurion Cornelius in the purposes of God as the church was experiencing a crucial period of expansion. Several things stand out in this fascinating narrative, in which Luke describes the apostle Peter's encounter with an officer in the Roman legions. Cornelius is said to be a devoted man of faith, a God-fearer, one who generously gives to the poor, and a man of prayer (Acts 10:2). After Peter's encounter with Cornelius and the remarkable manner in which God uses this servant of the state to expand apostolic vision, there is no indication that Peter admonishes Cornelius to leave military service. The same, in fact, can be said of every encounter with a soldier, recorded in the New Testament, that the apostles and Jesus and John the Baptist had. Where soldiers do appear, they tend to exemplify faith and receive commendation.

Both Christian history and the biblical text permit us to draw several conclusions. As it applies to law enforcement and military service,

---

[126]Ibid., 4:341; 5:102.
[127]Ibid., 45:96.
[128]Ibid., 45:96, 101.

just-war moral reasoning provides a framework within which Christians (and others) can make ethical decisions regarding the proper use of coercive force for the purposes of safeguarding the common weal. A Christian who serves in the military does so in the hope that his or her service might ultimately promote justice, peace, and the preservation of human rights in a world that is marred by sin. To the extent that a citizen attempts to act in faith and in accordance with biblical teachings when given the opportunity, that person may be understood to walk in Christian obedience with ethical impunity and thus is free of guilt. By the same token, it is also the responsibility of the citizen and Christian to reject and resist illegal, immoral, and unlawful activities or orders. For this reason, C. S. Lewis asserts, "A Christian may lawfully be a hangman; but he must not hang a man whom he knows to be innocent."[129]

Q. 80 Is the just-war idea only a Christian construct, or can other religions embrace it also?

Just-war precepts as they are commonly articulated are a product of Christian moral teaching coupled with Western legal and political thought. At its core and in its refinement, the tradition historically has been molded by Christian ethical reflection. At the same time, as we have already argued, many of the values and ideas contained within the just-war idea are shared across cultures and religious systems, given the nonfluid, universal character of justice.[130] No religion eschews war in all circumstances or promotes it in every instance. In every religion there is some construct for war and peace. While many voices inside and outside of Christianity would question whether war can ever be just, many other voices across the religious spectrum assert that war for just purposes is possible as a last resort.

While just-war thinking in the classic Christian tradition is the most detailed qualification of war (as both *permissible* where necessary and *restrained*), it is not the only religious representation of war.

---

[129]"Conditions for a Just War," a letter to the editor of *Theology* (May 1939), cited in *God in the Dock: Essays on Theology and Ethics*, ed. Walter Hooper (Grand Rapids: Eerdmans, 1970), 326, and reproduced in Leslie Walmsley, ed., *C. S. Lewis: Essay Collection and Other Short Pieces* (London: HarperCollins, 2000), 767–68.
[130]By way of comparison, one might examine side by side the Code of Hammurabi and the Mosaic code to observe the "universality" of the character of justice.

In fact, even in Buddhism and Hinduism, religions often associated with pacifism, there are teachings that support the necessity of war at times. Tenzin Gyatso, the fourteenth Dalai Lama and Tibet's exiled spiritual and political leader, has endorsed the idea of just wars as an unfortunate necessity and cited World War II, the Korean War, and the Vietnam War as honorable from a moral standpoint.[131] Within Theravada Buddhism there are also principles that bear similarities to the just-war tradition. Although the higher principles of Buddhism condemn war and support nonviolence, there are exceptions when external aggression is justified.[132] Strands of thought that resemble just-war thinking can also be detected in Judaism and Sikhism, although no religion is monolithic in its followers' views of war and peace.[133]

Paul Robinson notes that, historically, when different rules of war and systems meet, "they tend after a period of time to converge . . . . However, before the convergence takes place, there is often a rise in particularly atrocious violence."[134] He argues that states and soldiers have usually considered that their values in war apply only to those who share the same values; as a result, this has led to atrocities with others.[135] One must concede the unfortunate fact that this is true, even when it is contrary to the normative values of the just-war thinking.

Just-war principles are normative for all people, regardless of their faith perspective or lack of it. This is one of the exceedingly important contributions of early-modern thinkers such as Vitoria, Suárez, and Grotius: just-war thinking is conceived in terms of the broader community of nations. Just-war theory repudiates ideological and religious rationales for going to war. Arthur Holmes explains:

> All people have equal rights by virtue of their common humanity. Justice insists that we treat equals equally. Religious differences and cause are therefore as irrelevant to the pursuit of justice as are differences of race or culture or economic status. Justice cannot allow for morally irrelevant considerations.[136]

---

[131]"Dalai Lama endorses just wars but not in the case of Tibet," World Tibet Network News, November 6, 2005, accessed at http://www.tibet.ca/en/wtarchive/2005/11/6_1.html on October 25, 2006; site discontinued.

[132]Elizabeth J. Harris, "Buddhism and the Justification of War: A Case Study from Sri Lanka," in Paul Robinson, ed., *Just War in Comparative Perspective* (Burlington, VT: Ashgate, 2003), 100.

[133]See George Wilkes, "Judaism and Justice in War," 9–23, and Gurharpal Singh, "Sikhism and War," 126–36, respectively in Robinson, *Just War in Comparative Perspective*.

[134]Paul Robinson, ed., "Introduction," in *Just War in Comparative Perspective*, 4.

[135]Ibid.

[136]Arthur F. Holmes, "A Just War Response," in Robert G. Clouse, ed., *War: Four Christian Views* (Downers Grove, IL: InterVarsity, 1991), 182.

Although not all nations and people groups affirm or adhere to the tradition, the moral values and guidelines that underpin the tradition are universal in their ramification and application.

Q. 81 What is the view of war in Roman Catholic social teaching?

Given the splintered nature of Protestantism, for which no definitive and authoritative position on matters theological or ethical exists (apart from Protestants' liturgical confession of the Apostles' Creed), we are led to inquire into the official position on war of the Roman Catholic Church. Fully aside from anti-Catholic bigotry that has characterized multigenerational thinking, Protestants perhaps will bemoan the perception that there is no unified thinking on ethical issues among Roman Catholics either. Whether or not this perception is valid depends largely on one's perspective. Undoubtedly, there exists among professing Catholics a wide range of views on significant ethical questions. This is particularly the case with respect to war.

This perception notwithstanding, we have only to consult the Catechism of the Catholic Church, which we adduced in previous questions and which in its 1992 publication (and 1994 English version) helpfully and definitively sets forth the church's *official* position on matters doctrinal and ethical. The catechism, then, is particularly helpful, given the mind-boggling diversity of ethical opinion that calls itself Catholic. Take, for instance, the high visibility of documents such as *The Challenge of Peace* (1983) and *The Harvest of Justice Is Sown in Peace* (1993), which were published by the U.S. Catholic Bishops' Conference. Both documents represent something of a deviation from classical just-war thinking to the extent that they conflate the baseline assumptions of the pacifist and the just-war positions, beginning with a presumption against *war and coercive* force rather than a presumption against *evil and injustice*, which is the basic operating assumption of classical just-war thinking. Both documents are deficient in their inability to state unambiguously that coercive force per se is not evil, and that force takes on the moral character of those employing it, based on intention. By contrast, the Catholic Catechism, which "faithfully and systematically present[s] the teaching of Sacred Scripture, the living Tradition in the Church and the authentic Magisterium,"[137] serves not only as an authoritative exposition of Catholic social ethics, but also as a more faithful representation of the *historic* Christian position on war and peace.

The very structure of the catechism is instructive. Divided into four parts, it sets forth historic creedal commitments at the outset, before developing the implications of doctrine for the ethical, spiritual, and sacramental life of the church. The longest section of the catechism, part 1 reaffirms—and thus understands itself as remaining in continuity with—historic Christian belief. One cannot probe a "Christian" view of humanity, poverty, oppression, or war without affirming the creedal faith that Christians everywhere and at all times have confessed. The classic Christian position on war, namely, that in a fallen world, resort to arms and coercive force *may* be justified, is sustained in the catechism. In accordance with just-war moral reasoning, this conviction is predicated on certain moral conditions and criteria.

Following Augustine and Aquinas, the catechism cites moral as well as prudential guidelines for determining *jus ad bellum* and *jus in bello* conditions, that is, conditions for going to war and for conduct in war. Under the heading "Avoiding War," the catechism states, "All citizens and all governments are obliged to work for the avoidance of war." The catechism continues, "However, 'as long as the danger of war persists and there is no international authority with the necessary competence and power, governments cannot be denied the right of lawful self-defense, once all peace efforts have failed.'"[138] While it does not develop the implications of this assertion, the catechism is rich with suggestions for moral reflection.

Relying on Aquinas's treatment of criteria for war's justification, the catechism reiterates prudential tests that constitute "strict conditions for legitimate defense by military force" and that require "rigorous consideration." These are said to render "moral legitimacy" to the prospect of armed conflict—that is, the *jus ad bellum* conditions—and include conditions such as the following: damage inflicted by the aggressor on the nation or community of nations must be lasting,

---

[137]Catechism of the Catholic Church, introduction, 4.
[138]Ibid., par. 2308.

grave, and certain; all other means of putting an end to it must have been shown to be impractical or ineffective; there must be serious prospects of success; the use of arms must not produce evils and disorders graver than the evil to be eliminated, given the inordinate power of modern means of destruction.[139] Also reiterated in the catechism are the *jus in bello* requirements of noncombatant immunity, including the humane treatment of wounded soldiers and prisoners, and proportionality. Disproportionate means of warfare such as extermination and genocide are decried in the strongest terms.[140]

What is significant about the catechism's qualification of these conditions is a concluding statement that religious activists among us might be inclined to ignore, even disavow: "The evaluation of these conditions for moral legitimacy [of justified war] belongs to the prudential judgment of *those who have responsibility for the common good.*"[141] This statement, it would seem to us, serves as an important reminder to Christians that in the end it is *not* the task of the church to make policy decisions, even when believers should be involved in policy conversations. Decisions remain the domain of political officeholders.[142]

Q. 82 How does Islam view war and peace?

It is customary in our day for Muslim spokespersons to argue that Westerners have an inaccurate and distorted understanding of war and peace—particularly, the concept of jihad—in Islamic ethics. This, it goes without saying, has been a standard argument since September of 2001. At the same time, it is impossible for serious students of the international scene to ignore the fact that conceptions of war and peace have been the subject of intense and ongoing debate among Muslims themselves. While the literature on Islam and the state has burgeoned in the last decade, the observation made by distinguished Muslim political scientist and Middle East scholar Sohail Hashmi in his important essay "Interpreting the Islamic Ethics of War and Peace" remains valid to the present day: Muslims

---

[139]Ibid., par. 2309.
[140]Ibid.
[141]Ibid.; emphasis added.
[142]See also Charles, *Between Pacifism and Jihad*, 81–82.

are "hopelessly divided" on *the* Islamic ethics of war and peace.[143] Nothing to date would suggest otherwise.[144]

Most Muslim scholars would acknowledge that the idea of jihad, which denotes "struggle" or "striving" in Islamic thought, is adapting to changes in international relations and that we are witnessing a period of reinterpretation and redefinition vis-à-vis contemporary events. Understandably, many Muslims are disturbed that the notion of jihad is typically associated with the sword (considered to be the "lesser" jihad) and are quick to point out that "striving" is foremost a spiritual reality, a "struggle in the way of Allah," which is perpetual.[145] Militant jihadists argue that the internal-struggle interpretation (i.e., the struggle for piety and purity) was itself influenced by Western forces. But while Muslims debate the literal-versus-spiritual understanding of the notion, it needs emphasis that Qur'anic traditions of war are based on verses mirroring particular events that are foundational to the establishment of Islam in the early seventh century. For this reason, Muslim political scientist Bassam Tibi writes: "All Qur'anic verses revealed between 622 and the death of the Prophet in 632 relate to the establishment of Islam at Medina through *violent struggle* against the hostile tribes surrounding the city-state."[146] Tibi rather forthrightly concludes that most debate among Muslims about war and peace "is based on literal readings of the Qur'anic verses pertaining to early Medina," since "Muslims believe in the absolute eternality of the Qur'an and the Hadith" (the prophetic sayings and deeds of Muhammad).[147]

Despite differences among Muslim interpreters, the common foundation for all Islamic understandings of war and peace is a worldview predicated upon a very important distinction. It is the distinction between "the house of Islam" (*dar al-Islam*) or the "house of peace"

---

[143]Sohail H. Hashmi, "Interpreting the Islamic Ethics of War and Peace," in Terry Nardin, ed., *Ethics of War and Peace* (Princeton, NJ: Princeton University Press, 1996), 146.

[144]We treat this important subject elsewhere in part 3, "Just-War Tradition and the Statesman."

[145]James Turner Johnson, *The Holy War Idea in Western and Islamic Traditions* (University Park: Penn State University Press, 1997), 19, describes the nuances of jihad in the following way: "The jihad of the sword, the 'lesser' form of striving according to one tradition associated with the Prophet Muhammad, is but one form alongside other, greater ones: the jihad of the heart (moral reformation), that of the tongue (proclaiming God's word abroad), and that of the hand (works in accord with the will of God). . . . This jihad may be directed within the community at other Muslims (in special cases such as apostasy, heresy, or rebellion) or outside the community at non-Muslim political communities that pose a threat to Islam." This overview is confirmed by Youssef H. Aboul-Enein and Sherifa Zuhur, *Islamic Rulings on Warfare* (Carlisle, PA: Strategic Studies Institute, 2004), 4–5, who identify six different categories of jihad.

[146]"War and Peace in Islam," in Nardin, ed., *Ethics of War and Peace*, 128; emphasis added.

[147]Ibid.

(*dar al-Salam*)[148] and the non-Muslim world, the "house of war" (*dar al-harb*)[149]—a distinction that was the hallmark of Islamic ethics long before the intrusion of Europe into the Muslim world.[150] Though not everyone of the "house of Islam" is Muslim, an essential condition of tolerance for non-Muslims is their acceptance of the supremacy of Islam and the primacy of the Muslims.[151]

One must grant that much of the tension that arises from Muslim interpretation today is legal or juristic and not merely religious or philosophical. A central question is the place of Islamic law—sharia—in relation to contemporary geopolitical developments. Because of the fundamental cleavage between *dar al-Islam* and *dar al-harb*, the centrality of war in Islamic theology, and the conviction of Muslims that war receives its authorization via divine legislation, it is inevitable that war and peace are understood as an expression (and extension) of Islamic law. That is, they are part of a system of divine command and moral obligation derived from divine command.

Historically, the establishment and spread of Islam at Medina and beyond were accomplished by waging war. For this reason, it is not coincidental that the sword became the symbol of Islam in Western culture. Moreover, Islamic militancy was reinforced by the sense of superiority of Muslims over their enemies.[152] The period of Europe's ascendancy, from the sixteenth century onward, signaled in broader terms the beginning of the modern period and Islam's attendant decline. Yet, despite its fundamental incompatibility with the world's international system, Islam's worldview, based on two irreconcilable "houses," remains unaltered.

Islamic notions of war and peace derive from two principal ethical sources, the Qur'an and the Hadith. Concomitant with the fundamental distinction between *dar al-Islam* and *dar al-harb*, Islam at its core understands itself as commissioned to subjugate all of humanity.[153] Where non-Muslims submit to this mandate (*da'wa*) of conversion,

---

[148]Qur'an, Jon. 10:25.

[149]The expression "house of war" was coined during the period of Islamic military expansion.

[150]This is maintained by a wide array of Islamic scholars—for example, Bernard Lewis, "Politics and War," in Joseph Schacht and C. E. Bosworth, eds., *The Legacy of Islam*, 2nd ed. (Oxford: Clarendon, 1974); Marshall G. S. Hodgson, *The Venture of Islam*, 3 vols. (Chicago: University of Chicago Press, 1974); and Bassam Tibi, "War and Peace in Islam," 128–45.

[151]Bernard Lewis, "Europe and Islam: Muslim Perceptions and Experience," in *From Babel to Dragomans: Interpreting the Middle East* (Oxford: Oxford University Press, 2004), 122.

[152]This point is emphasized by both Hashmi, "Interpreting the Islamic Ethics of War and Peace," 146–66, and Tibi, "War and Peace in Islam," 128–45, who as Muslim scholars disagree on the matter of commonalities between Islamic and Western war ethics.

[153]So, e.g., Saba' 34:28: "We have sent you forth to all mankind."

peace is the order; where it is resisted, Muslims stand under a moral obligation to impose the faith:

> In Islam, peace requires that non-Muslims submit to the call of Islam, either by converting or by accepting the status of a religious minority (*dhimmi*) and paying the imposed poll tax, *jizya*. World peace, the final stage of the *da'wa*, is reached only with the conversion or submission of all mankind to Islam.[154]

It is significant that the resort to force to disseminate Islam is not technically considered "war" (*harb*), a term that is used to depict force deployed by *non*-Muslims. Rather, Islamic jihad expresses itself in acts of "opening" the world to Islam (*futuhat*).[155] The difference is that unbelievers present obstacles to the faith by not submitting to Islam peacefully, thereby creating conditions and assuming responsibility for war. Bernard Lewis writes:

> It is the moral and religious duty of Muslims to share their good fortune with the rest of the world, not selfishly to keep God's final revelation for themselves, but to strive unceasingly to bring it to all human kind, *if possible in peace, if necessary by war*. This is one of the basic obligations of the Muslim faith.[156]

Similarly, Tibi summarizes Islam's orientation toward war and peace as stemming from no pacifist or nonviolent presumption against war. Islam enters into warfare in obedience to Allah and to spread Islam; war is made necessary by the refusal of unbelievers to submit. "World peace," then, "is reached only with the conversion or submission of all mankind to Islam."[157]

While students of the just-war tradition and Islamic jihad acknowledge points of commonality between the two ethical traditions,[158] perhaps no issue highlights the differences between the Christian and

---

[154]Tibi, "War and Peace in Islam," 130.

[155]Ibid.

[156]"Europe and Islam," 122; emphasis added.

[157]Tibi, "War and Peace in Islam," 130–31. This is not to argue that no Muslims personally subscribe to nonviolent resistance. See, e.g., Ralph E. Crow, Philip Grant, and Saad E. Ibrahim, eds., *Arab Nonviolent Political Struggle in the Middle East* (Boulder: Lynne Rienner, 1990). It is only to point out a fundamental trajectory within Islam that most of its adherents share.

[158]Scholars such as Hashmi, for example, point to the *jus in bello* conditions of proportionality and discrimination in Islamic ideology ("Interpreting Islamic Ethics of War and Peace," 161–62). Aboul-Enein and Zuhur argue that radicals of our day have been deceived in their selective reading and interpretation of the war verses in the Qur'an, obscuring the presence of "justice, moderation and restraint" that is thought to predate our era (*Islamic Rulings on Warfare*, 6–30).

Islamic ethical tradition as much as war and peace. The distinction between just and unjust wars based on moral and prudential criteria is foreign to Islam, despite contemporary arguments about medieval Muslim casuistry to the contrary. James Turner Johnson acknowledges Islam's religious understanding of war as being "radically at odds with modern Western culture's separation of church and state."[159] And Tibi is forthright:

> The Western distinction between just and unjust wars linked to specific grounds for war is unknown in Islam. Any war against unbelievers, whatever its immediate ground, is morally justified. . . . The usual Western interpretation of jihad as "just war" in the Western sense is, therefore, a misreading of this Islamic concept.[160]

One problematic verse from the Qur'an undermines potential claims that there is a pacifist strain in Islam: "Fighting is prescribed for you, even though it be hateful to you; but it may well be that you hate something that is in fact good for you, and that you love a thing that is in fact bad for you: and God knows, whereas you do not."[161] As Hashmi acknowledges, there is no equivalent in Islamic texts to Aquinas's question 40 from the *Summa*, "Are some wars permissible?"[162] Tibi agrees, emphasizing that Muslims do not view the use of force to propagate Islam as an act of war; rather, war results from *resistance* to "bringing the entire world into the 'house of Islam.'"[163] Precisely for this reason, he reminds us, Muslim historians tend to depict Islamic conquests not as "wars" but as "openings" of the world to Islam.

Some Muslim scholarship emphasizes that there was considerable disagreement among medieval exegetes on the question of when it is permissible to suspend jihad. The basis for this controversy was the seeming discrepancy between "verses of peace" and "verses of the sword." So, for example, in the Qur'an's eighth chapter, one reads, "If they incline toward peace, incline yourself toward it, and

---

[159]*The Holy War Idea in Western and Islamic Traditions*, 1.
[160]Tibi, "War and Peace in Islam," 131. Tibi is in conversation *inter alia* with the work of another Muslim scholar, Majid Khadduri, whose *War and Peace in the Law of Islam* (Baltimore: Johns Hopkins University Press, 1955), 63–64, had argued that jihad constituted *bellum justum*.
[161]2:216, as cited in Hashmi, "Interpreting the Islamic Ethics of War and Peace," 150.
[162]Ibid.
[163]"War and Peace in Islam," 141.

trust in God . . . [for] He alone is all-hearing and all-knowing."[164] In the ninth chapter, by contrast, the faithful are commanded to "slay the polytheists wherever you find them, and take them captive, and besiege them, and lie in wait for them at every conceivable place." The text continues, "Fight against those who . . . do not believe in God nor in the last day, and do not consider forbidden that which God and His Messenger have forbidden, and do not follow the religion of truth, until they pay the *jizya* with willing hand, having been subdued."[165] One might argue, of course, as Muslims do, that one needs to read the Qur'an in Arabic in order to understand it properly, since translations possess less "authority" than the original. And compounding the problem of interpretation is the Muslim doctrine of "abrogation," by which it is taught that later pronouncements of the prophet Muhammad abrogate or void his earlier pronouncements.

Given the disagreement, whether past and present, over how to interpret the peace and war verses,[166] it is no wonder that Islamic fundamentalists view themselves as a vanguard of the obedient, seeking to help restore Islam to a global superiority and establish, by any means necessary, an Islamic order. In the meantime, "Muslim states adhere to public international law but make no effort to accommodate the outmoded [theocratic] Islamic ethics of war and peace to the current international order."[167] Given the fact of Islamic understanding of non-Muslims as "minorities" or "infidel" unbelievers, responsible participation in international affairs is virtually impossible; at the most basic level, Islamic ideology appears to be incompatible with basic human rights.[168]

In contrast to Islamic ethics, by which war is understood in relation to divine revelation and therefore a measure of "holy" obedience, the concept of war in the Western cultural tradition generally has been developed and refined, with some exceptions,[169] wholly *apart* from expressly religious grounds. This is for several important reasons. One is the fact that Christian faith presumes for church and state a highly

---

[164]8:61.

[165]9:5, 29.

[166]As evidence of differences in Qur'anic interpretation, Tibi, "War and Peace in Islam," 134–40, identifies and discusses three divergent patterns of Islamic thinking about war and peace. Similarly, see multiple contributions to the volume edited by John Kelsay and James Turner Johnson, *Just War and Jihad: Historical and Theoretical Perspectives on War and Peace in Western and Islamic Traditions* (New York: Greenwood, 1991).

[167]Tibi, "War and Peace in Islam," 140.

[168]See Ann E. Mayer, *Islam and Human Rights: Tradition and Politics* (Boulder: Westview, 1991); and Bassam Tibi, "Universality of Human Rights and Authenticity of Non-Western Cultures: Islam and the Western Concept of Human Rights," *Harvard Human Rights Journal* 5 (1992): 221–26.

[169]One might cite as exceptions the Crusades and the Thirty Years War.

qualified separation of spheres and sovereignty; hence, the significance of Jesus' words, "Render to Caesar the things that are Caesar's, and to God the things that are God's" (Matt. 22:21; Mark 12:17; Luke 20:25 ESV). Islam knows no such distinction or equivalent, since "Caesar" and Allah are the same. Thus, we are witness here to two fundamentally antagonistic theories of statecraft.[170] In the Western cultural tradition, which to a greater or lesser extent has been informed by Christian assumptions, grounds for going to war emanate from nonsectarian ethical principles—for example, the natural law, territorial sovereignty, self-defense, and so on. A further reason for the contrast between the two ethical systems is two-pronged: war is related neither to the Christian's personal self-understanding nor to the Christian's sense of mission to the world—unlike Islam, which is under a divine mandate to "subjugate" the *dar al-harb* where no peaceful submission occurs. Propagation of religion is *never* justification for going to war, according to Christian moral thinkers from Ambrose to Aquinas to Vitoria and Suárez (during the Age of Discovery) and Grotius (amidst the Thirty Years War).

The fruit of Western cultural thinking about war and peace—a mode of reasoning with pre-Christian precursors and yet guided and refined by a Christian understanding of the world and human nature—is a highly qualified notion of war and its justification. This high level of qualification is not merely a result of the human desire for an absence of conflict. Rather, a peace that is *justly ordered* is understood as necessary—indeed, optimal—to the flourishing of human societies.

Therefore, given the radically different worldviews that animate the ethical systems of Islam and the West, which in turn inform their respective understandings of political philosophy and thus of war and peace, we are not optimistic that current or future cross-cultural discourse on the ethics of war and peace will yield any sort of "growing convergence," salutary as this goal might be. Rather, it is likely that confrontations between Islam and Western culture will persist, and that they will do so in rather dramatic form, as students of both cultural traditions have warned.[171] Unless, that is, a fundamental transformation occurs within one of those two ethical systems.

---

[170]Johnson, *The Holy War Idea in Western and Islamic Traditions*, helpfully and thoroughly develops the differences between the two ethical systems throughout his book.

[171]So, e.g., Samuel P. Huntington, "The Clash of Civilizations?" *Foreign Affairs* 72 (1993): 22–49; Bassam Tibi, *Der Krieg der Zivilizationen* (Hamburg: Hoffmann and Campe, 1995); and Tibi, "War and Peace in Islam," 142. On the character of recent dialogue between Muslim and Christian spokes-

Q. 83 Is the concept of "supreme emergency" theologically valid?

The issue of "supreme emergency" raises issues of theological, ethical, and philosophical gravity, yet leaves us with no fully satisfactory answer.[172] According to what is called "supreme emergency" in policy circles, there are times when the very existence of a civilization is at risk, and it thus becomes necessary or even mandatory to abrogate the normative ethical restraints of war and act in order to save a civilization from decimation and extinction. At bottom, "supreme emergency" is not about saving a military force or sparing a nation from military defeat or capture; rather, it concerns something much larger. It entails the conviction that because of a grave and catastrophic threat to a nation's way of life—the threat of massacre, enslavement, or annihilation—the laws and rules of war can be temporarily suspended without moral guilt in order to survive, since conventional diplomatic or military means fail to counter the threat.

When "supreme emergency" is invoked, the *jus in bello* rules of noncombatant immunity from intentional attack and the use of proportionality in the actions of warfare against legitimate military targets are most likely to be violated. Invoked by Winston Churchill during World War II, and subsequently acted upon in the area bombing campaigns of that war, the concept is most prominently articulated and defended by just-war advocate Michael Walzer.[173] The monumental ethical challenges posed by a condition of supreme emergency are captured by Brian Orend:

> What we have in the supreme emergency exemption is probably the most controversial, and consequential, amendment to just war theory ever proposed. The stakes regarding its acceptance into just war theory are enormous, and disturbingly relevant to an era hardly unacquainted with genocide and weapons of mass destruction.[174]

persons in the aftermath of Pope Benedict XVI's controversial Regensburg address (September 2006), see J. Daryl Charles, "Regensburg Left Behind," *Touchstone* (September–October 2009): 34–39.

[172]See also question 54, "How does the concept of "supreme emergency" relate to the just-war tradition?"

[173]Michael Walzer, *Just and Unjust Wars: A Moral Argument with Historical Illustrations*, 4th ed. (New York: Basic Books, 2006), 251–68. See also, Brian Orend, "Is There a Supreme Emergency Exemption?" in Mark Evans, ed., *Just War Theory: A Reappraisal* (Edinburgh: Edinburgh University Press, 2005), 134–53.

[174]Orend, "Is There a Supreme Emergency Exemption?" 135.

In dealing with the threat to civilization by Nazi Germany, Winston Churchill recognized the moral burden of having invoked "supreme emergency" and, in consequence, regretted some of the later bombings of World War II.[175] Not only does the burden of "supreme emergency" translate into present and future consequences, but the concept, if invoked, might also be used to justify terrorism, torture, or the deployment of weapons of mass destruction.[176]

Orend identifies five positions or perspectives on "supreme emergency" that range from outright rejection to qualified embrace: (1) a denial that such a thing as supreme emergency exists; (2) Churchill's Second World War consequentialism in a time of supreme emergency; (3) strict (absolute) respect for *jus in bello*, regardless of supreme emergency; (4) Walzer's paradoxical "dirty hands" position (i.e., that it is simultaneously right and wrong to act as required in a situation of supreme emergency); and (5) acknowledgment of supreme emergency as a moral tragedy but prudential strategy.[177] Decisions about the viability of the "supreme emergency" concept or its applicability in a given circumstance, like all ethical decisions, stem from one's own ethical framework. It should be acknowledged that just-war advocates are not in agreement regarding how to view "supreme emergency." Some accept the notion while others reject it.

From the vantage point of Christian faith, the doctrines of divine providence and sovereignty—which entail divine decrees, the divine will, and divine omniscience—bear upon one's ethical decisions and thus how catastrophe is understood.[178] Affirming these doctrines, coupled with the belief that humans are moral agents and thus morally self-responsible, yields the conviction that every event and decision has

---

[175]For a fuller analysis of Churchill and supreme emergency, see Christopher C. Harmon, *"Are We Beasts?" Churchill and the Moral Question of World War II "Area Bombing,"* The Newport Papers, 1 (Newport, RI: U.S. Naval War College Press, 1991).

[176]However, the concept as it applies to countering terrorism is routinely rejected, partially because terrorists are nonstate actors. See C. A. J. Coady, "Terrorism, Morality, and Supreme Emergency," *Ethics* 114 (July 2004): 772–89; Michael Walzer, *Arguing about War* (New Haven, CT: Yale University Press, 2004), 51–66; Darrell Cole, "Death before Dishonor or Dishonor before Death? Christian Just War, Terrorism, and Supreme Emergency," *Notre Dame Journal of Law, Ethics and Public Policy* 16 (2002): 81–99; and Daniel Statman, "Supreme Emergencies Revisited," *Ethics* 117 (October 2006): 58–79.

[177]Orend, "Is There a Supreme Emergency Exemption?" 139–51.

[178]Providence may be defined as follows: God, because of his sovereign exercise of authority over all creation, is continually involved with all created things in such a way that he (1) keeps them existing and maintaining the properties with which he created them; (2) cooperates with created things in every action, directing their distinctive properties to cause them to act as they do; and (3) directs them to fulfill his purposes (thus Wayne Grudem, *Systematic Theology: An Introduction to Biblical Doctrine* [Grand Rapids: Zondervan, 1994], 315).

significance, even when the interplay of divine providence and human moral agency remains a mystery.

This mysterious interplay undergirds not only numerous narratives but also the wider teaching of the Old and New Testaments. People of faith are to act responsibly, knowing that their actions are part of the wider divine plan of human history. Thus, for example, Joab, a leader of King David's army, declares in the midst of war preparations, "Be of good courage, and let us be courageous for our people, and for the cities of our God, and may the LORD do what seems good to him" (2 Sam. 10:12 ESV).

Christians are not fatalists, nor do they believe that God is the author of evil. Rather, they affirm the plan and power of God while assuming moral responsibility for situations and events in which they find themselves. Thus John Calvin writes:

> Now it is very clear what our duty is: thus, if the Lord has committed to us the protection of our life, our duty is to protect it; if he offers help, to use them; if he forewarns us of dangers, not to plunge headlong; if he makes remedies available, not to neglect them. But no danger will hurt us, say they, unless it is fatal, and in this case is beyond remedies. But what if the dangers are not fatal, because the Lord has provided you with remedies for repulsing and overcoming them?[179]

Presuming the moral obligation not to choose evil over good, or not to choose evil as a means toward good, we as Christians are forced to reconcile our belief in both divine sovereignty and human moral agency. There are occasions in which the burden of determining what is good in difficult circumstances may be enormous. Certainly, it is not possible to foretell every proper and theologically appropriate response to future circumstances, including future catastrophic circumstances. What, then, are we to make of "supreme emergency" in theological terms? Our answer allows for the possibility that there could arise a situation that might be properly labeled a supreme emergency, just as such a cataclysm confronted Churchill and much of Europe several generations ago. Yet, we are well aware of the fact that there is no consensus within Christian theology as to whether or not such a condition or circumstance either permits or requires the abrogation of regular ethical

---

[179]*Institutes of the Christian Religion*, ed. John T. McNeill, trans. Ford Lewis Battles (Philadelphia: Westminster Press, 1960), 1.17.4.

norms. Perhaps it is this lack of clear scriptural consensus that makes our attempts to interpret Dietrich Bonhoeffer's actions so difficult.[180]

In the end, we are generally disinclined toward abrogation, even in circumstances labeled "supreme emergency." James Turner Johnson properly warns:

> Clearly, the supreme emergency idea—the idea that under certain extreme conditions, all restraints on the conduct of war may be ignored—is fundamentally threatening to the conception that basic moral restraints ought to be observed even in war. . . . it opens a can of very toxic worms: it becomes a rationale for warfare in which anything goes, whether toward noncombatants or toward combatants.[181]

If Christians are to take seriously the doctrines of divine providence and sovereignty, they must consider how those doctrines can be applied to "supreme emergencies." Even when we take seriously the above warning by Johnson, we allow that it is possible both to uphold these pivotal doctrines and still to accept *any* of the five options regarding "supreme emergency" set forth by Orend. As authors we are inclined to favor either the third option (strict respect for *jus in bello* regardless of supreme emergency) or the fifth option (supreme emergency is a moral tragedy but prudential strategy), although we freely acknowledge that strong disagreement would exist among Christians. Regardless of those disagreements, what we strenuously maintain is that providence and sovereignty are never to be discarded in discussions of "supreme emergency." Such doctrines do permit belief in the possibility of a supreme emergency, but they also make the discussions more complex.

Q. 84   Is the concept of just war merely for Christians?

Although it has been shaped to a large degree by Christian values and a Western cultural heritage, just-war thinking is not the repository of Christians only.[182] All people, regardless of cultural and religious heritage, can also adhere to its principles,

---

[180]See question 100, "What about Dietrich Bonhoeffer's example?"
[181]James Turner Johnson, *The War to Oust Saddam Hussein: Just War and the New Face of Conflict* (Lanham, MD: Rowman & Littlefield, 2005), 35.
[182]This and related questions are discussed in part 1, "Just-War Tradition and the Philosopher."

based on the natural moral law. Although not everyone will necessarily accept its tenets, those tenets are considered applicable to all and for all people. In the midst of conflict, this means that even if opposing governments or forces or nonstate actors such as terrorists do not adhere to just-war principles, those who accept the tradition still act in accordance with the tradition. Just-war advocate Jean Bethke Elshtain identifies this tradition as a reflection of "Augustinian realism" insofar as, among other things, it "resists sentimentalism and insists on ethical restraint."[183] Thereby Elshtain simply wishes to emphasize the baseline assumption that the world is less than perfect and filled with tragedy:

> Estrangement, conflict, and tragedy are constant features of the human condition, and just war thinking laced with Augustinian realism offers no assurances that can ever make the world entirely safe. Augustinian realism is skeptical about the exercise of power even as it recognizes the inescapability of power.[184]

The just-war tradition is by no means the only Christian position on matters of war and peace. However, we believe it to be the one that most accurately reflects the totality of the teachings of the Bible and the history of the Christian moral tradition. If Christians are going to take theology and the call of Jesus Christ to a life of discipleship seriously, then thinking about issues of war and peace must be part of that process. The Christian world-and-life view is one that understands itself as speaking directly or indirectly to every sphere of human existence. While Christians of serious faith in every generation have disagreed on matters of war and peace, the just-war tradition represents mainstream consensual reflection on this ethical conundrum. Theologian Carl F. H. Henry has written: "Not to be fortified with good ideas is to be victimized by bad ones."[185] To the extent that the just-war tradition can be upheld by Christians and non-Christians alike in severely qualifying human intervention in the face of egregious moral evil, they will have done much to fortify themselves with a good and worthy idea.

---

[183]Elshtain, *Just War against Terror*, 70.
[184]Ibid.
[185]Carl F. H. Henry, *Twilight of a Great Civilization* (Westchester, IL: Crossway, 1988), 91.

PART 5

JUST-WAR TRADITION AND THE COMBATANT

Q. 85 Does deterrence really work?

At the academic level, this is a question that generates no little controversy and disagreement. At the practical level, by comparison, the matter of deterrence is relatively noncontroversial. The reason for this discrepancy would seem to have more to do with one's assumptions about human nature than with war and peace per se. If you talk to social scientists, for example, you'll find that most—though, by no means all—of them believe deterrence has little effect on human behavior.[1] And there is a reason for this conclusion. Those who are skeptical generally have a more secular and optimistic understanding of human nature: humans, it is generally believed, are basically good rather than inherently flawed. As a corollary of that view, punishment is thought to be injurious to a person's psyche.

Most economists, by contrast, answer the question Does deterrence work? in the affirmative. They observe the wide range of human activity in the realm of economics, business, and finance. Here, alas, humans are remarkably predictable and act accordingly. When handling money, material goods, and services, they operate as if there is some law—or cluster of laws—that directs them. While economists are not necessarily more religious than social scientists, their view of human nature is much more inclined toward a moral realism with regard to human behavioral patterns. In their projection of future market trends, coupled with their estimation of human psychology and behavioral motivation, they are characterized by a realistic understanding of human behavior.

The same can be said of "just warriors." Given the fallenness that is part of human nature, the ethics of the just-war position can be summarized in its two basic assumptions: it *sanctions* the use of coercive force in the face of evil to alleviate human suffering, and it

---

[1]Among criminologists in particular one would not expect to find this sentiment; nevertheless, it is strangely so. Economists, by contrast, are rather unified in observing the effects of deterrence on human behavioral patterns.

establishes moral limits as to what is a just response. Together, these two assumptions raise the important question of deterrence—a question that bears on human nature regardless of whether it applies in a domestic or an international context.

At the most fundamental level, people usually intuit that punishment and retribution deter evildoing. The retributive element would be viewed by virtually all citizens—with some exceptions—as a necessary instrument for preserving the social order. Does punishment deter? While many social scientists are inclined to say it does not, most parents, regardless of religious belief, will say without hesitation that it does deter. In fact, in all likelihood they will automatically attempt to implement "the law of deterrence" with their own children, whether consciously or unconsciously. As seen through the lens of parental control, the only case in which punishment—that is, pain or deprivation—does *not* deter is the child who has never known moral restrictions. For that individual, few things in this life will inhibit evildoing. And, of course, that child will end up being a "menace to society," and society will need protection from that individual.

The upshot of our hypothesizing here is that while social-scientific studies tend to report that punishment and retribution have little or no observable deterrent effect on people, econometric studies performed by economists, for whom *theory must be validated by practice*, tend to point in the opposite direction. To understand the disparity in results, one need only consider the presupposed model of human nature that undergirds the methodology of each. While there exists a strongly "positive" view of human nature in the social scientists, and thus a strong bias against punishment and negative reinforcement, economists operate on a very different assumption. They are well aware that *the greater the cost*, the greater the effect on behavioral responses, which in turn affects the market. Alas, this reality in the end determines the flow of goods.

The difference between the social scientist's understanding of human nature and that of the economist might be summarized as follows: the latter is guided by a moral realism, while the former operates on the assumption of a moral positivism. It is noteworthy that most—though certainly not all—parents tend, at least in their own homes, to be "economists" and not "social scientists." The same can be said for law-enforcement officers, and for good reasons. At the intuitive level, they understand the language and logic of deterrence. It is helpful to ask whether most people would want social scientists to determine the nature and future of the economy and financial markets.

If we assume from the outset that retribution or just reprisal *does* generally deter (even if not always), an important question necessarily follows: *Should* we deter evil? And if so, in what manner and to what degree? In the logic of just-war moral reasoning, when an injustice has occurred, the *just* response is a response *in kind*. Common sense militates that we do not cut off the hands of children who steal cookies, but neither do we simply slap the wrists of people who rape, murder, and maim. Thus, we may speak of a "just reprisal," which has retribution and restoration in view. This just retribution distinguishes itself from revenge or retributivism in fundamentally important ways. Just reprisal is more than a legal concept. Rather, it is foremost a moral good rooted in natural moral law—that universal bar of justice, known through reason, to which all people and all nations are held accountable. Where natural law is ignored or eclipsed, social and legal dilemmas abound, and moral rot eventually sets in, yielding catastrophic consequences where spiritual renewal does not intervene.[2] And where moral discrimination and the concept of just retribution are called into question or denied, society will view punishment—any form of punishment—to be cruel, absurd, and irrational. Consequently, sentences for crimes resulting in incarceration will be understood to have foremost or solely a *rehabilitative rather than a penal* goal. Justice, hence, takes on primarily a *therapeutic* rather than *retributive* character.[3]

Does deterrence always work? Our argument loses nothing by conceding the obvious: no, it does not *always* work. But this is a different question than whether deterrence *usually* works. Both of us have observed firsthand that people respond to the fear of negative consequences—Tim in the context of military service, Daryl in the

---

[2]The two most likely scenarios, following moral decay in society, are a "softer" or a "harder" form of totalitarian rule. While it is true that democratic government has built-in checks and balances, and while these balances do retard the speed with which a society degenerates, these balances are foremost *procedural* and do not effect the moral foundations of a people. When a *whole people*—and *everything in that culture*—is full of putrefaction and moral rot, it is only a question of time until the system collapses and a new elite must step in to fill the power vacuum that results. This general pattern, we think, is borne out both by recent history and human nature.

[3]Hereby we do not wish to deny a rehabilitative or therapeutic element in justice. We do, however, wish to emphasize that justice is not truly justice where and when it eliminates the retributive element. Indeed, retributive justice, properly understood, is restorative and pedagogical in its character. In part 4, "Just-War Tradition and the Theologian," we devote more detailed discussion to the distinction between retribution and revenge.

context of criminal justice. And as teachers, both of us have observed the same as well, albeit in different proportions, with regard to our students. But a much more telling example can be drawn from the streets of our nation's cities. To illustrate: in the early 1990s, law-enforcement authorities in Washington, D.C., were finding it increasingly difficult to find witnesses to corroborate evidence against murder suspects. Many of these cases, as it happened, were drug-related. Why was it so difficult to find witnesses to testify against murder suspects? Were the crimes all occurring with no one present? Hardly. The real problem was that potential witnesses were terrified to testify, because if they did, they did so under the threat of death.

Does punishment deter? We need not look merely to heated debates that rage between social scientists and economists. Simply ask any parent, or any drug dealer on the street, for that matter, and wisdom will be forthcoming.

Q. 86 What about nonlethal weapons?

Generally speaking, the just-war tradition supports the use of any weapon, lethal or nonlethal, that minimizes destruction or alleviates unnecessary pain and suffering. Nonlethal weapons have been defined as being "explicitly designed and primarily employed so as to incapacitate personnel or material, while minimizing fatalities, permanent injury to personnel, and undesired damage to property and the environment."[4] They span the entire spectrum of technology and emerging technologies and include such things as firearms that inflict blunt trauma but are not intended to be fatal (by using rubber and plastic bullets), tear gas or other noxious vapors such as CS (one form of tear gas) or CN, sticky and slippery foams, pepper spray, acoustic rays, projectile netting, chemical calmatives, and directed energy heat ray systems. Unlike conventional lethal weapons that destroy their targets through blast, penetration, and fragmenta-

---

[4]*Policy for Non-Lethal Weapons*, United States Department of Defense, Directive No. 3000.3, July 9, 1996, cited in Nick Lewer, ed. *The Future of Non-Lethal Weapons: Technologies, Operations, Ethics and Law* (London: Frank Cass, 2002), 1. See also Department of Defense, Joint Publication 1-02, *Department of Defense Dictionary of Military and Associated Terms*, April 12, 2001 (as amended through September 17, 2006), 376–77.

tion, nonlethal weapons do not destroy the target and usually have effects that are reversible.

In recent years, the development of nonlethal weapons has gained much attention by both domestic law-enforcement agencies and the military, who have increasingly deployed them with success. However, there have also been instances in which, for numerous reasons, the use of nonlethal weapons has been disastrous.[5] For this reason, David A. Koplow points out that "the very name 'non-lethal' is at least partially misleading: any application of force by police or military units inherently carries the potential of death."[6]

The first concerted effort at using nonlethal weapons by the U.S. military was in Somalia in 1995, where they were successfully employed. This experiment led Lieutenant General Anthony C. Zinni, USMC, the commander who decided to use them, to conclude, "I think the whole nature of warfare is changing."[7] Without question, new technologies have transformed the battle space in many ways, with nonlethal weapons being one significant example.

Nonlethal weapons fit well within the just-war perspective in that their use is based on right intention. The goal in deploying them is to control damage, which has direct links to aspects of discrimination and proportionality. However, by doctrine, nonlethal weapons are never used without the support of lethal weapons.

Post-conflict concerns (*jus post bellum*) must also be figured into the context of conflict, and nonlethal weapons may, on occasion, provide an opportunity for ensuring future stability and peace. In this way, the use of nonlethal weapons is an effect of following the principle of proportionality and has consequences across all levels of warfare—tactical, operational, and strategic. When possible, it avoids cataclysmic damage or destruction of critical infrastructure.[8]

There is an extensive and strong body of international law governing armed conflict that includes prohibitions and restrictions on specific weapons, but as with many aspects of the law, existing standards are inadequate for contemporary technologies and circumstances.[9] There

---

[5]For an excellent overview of nonlethal weapons and their recent use, see David A. Koplow, *Non-Lethal Weapons: The Law and Policy of Revolutionary Technologies for the Military and Law Enforcement* (Cambridge: Cambridge University Press, 2006).
[6]Ibid., 3.
[7]Cited in ibid., 29.
[8]Ibid., 29–30.
[9]See, e.g., W. Michael Reisman and Chris T. Antoniou, eds. *The Laws of War: A Comprehensive Collection of Primary Documents on International Laws Governing Armed Conflict* (New York: Vintage

is surely some irony in the fact that under the 1993 Chemical Weapons Convention, some nonlethal weapons were declared prohibited from military use yet permitted in domestic law enforcement. The desirability of using such weapons is understandable in instances of close-quarter combat where civilians, hostages, human shields, or noncombatants who, forced to take up weapons, may be part of the mix. In such instances, the use of nonlethal chemical weapons to sort out combatants from noncombatants would be desirable. The counterargument is that any aspect of chemical warfare is to be regarded as anathema. The reasoning here is that the use of chemical weapons to incapacitate the enemy could be the beginning of the slide toward the use of more lethal weapons. Historical precedent for this slippery slope is seen in World War I and the Iran-Iraq War. In these two conflicts we witness the two major uses of chemical weapons in the twentieth century; both started using tear gas and escalated to deadly chemicals.[10]

The development and use of nonlethal weapons provides an enormous opportunity to limit the destructiveness of war. However, nonlethal weapons may also expand rather than limit the just causes for engaging in war, even though the lethality and destruction would be less than in other warfare.[11] While no one argues that nonlethal weapons are appropriate (or available) for all, or even most, circumstances in warfare, their development and use should be vigorously pursued for eminently moral reasons.[12]

Q. 87 Are mercenaries permitted within the framework of just-war thought?

The use of mercenaries is contrary to international law and violates standards of the ethical and regulated pursuit of justice and peace in conflict. Mercenaries (and child sol-

Books, 1994). See also, Koplow, *Non-Lethal Weapons*, 35–53, for evaluation of specific laws and treaties pertaining to nonlethal weapons; and David P. Fidler, "'Non-Lethal' Weapons and International Law: Three Perspectives on the Future," in Lewer, ed. *The Future of Non-Lethal Weapons*, 27–37.
[10]Brad Knickerbocker, "The Fuzzy Ethics of Nonlethal Weapons," *The Christian Science Monitor*, February 14, 2003, accessed at http://www.csmonitor.com/2003/0214/p02s01-usmi.htm August 23, 2006.
[11]See the argument by Fidler in "'Non-Lethal' Weapons and International Law," 34–45.
[12]See Koplow's ten recommendations for future U.S. policy in "Non-Lethal Weapons," 142–65, for an overview of viable policy options.

diers) are not to be considered part of the contemporary just-war construct.[13]

A mercenary, according to international understanding, is a person who participates in an armed conflict in which he is not a national or a party to the conflict, and does so out of a desire for material compensation in excess of payment to combatants of similar ranks within the armed forces that are party to the conflict. The Protocol Additional to the Geneva Conventions of August 12, 1949, and relating to the Protection of Victims of International Armed Conflicts (Protocol 1), June 8, 1977, provides the most widely accepted international definition of a mercenary, though not endorsed by some countries, including the United States. It reads in part:

Art 47. Mercenaries

1. A mercenary shall not have the right to be a combatant or a prisoner of war.

2. A mercenary is any person who:

(a) is specially recruited locally or abroad in order to fight in an armed conflict;

(b) does, in fact, take a direct part in the hostilities;

(c) is motivated to take part in the hostilities essentially by the desire for private gain and, in fact, is promised, by or on behalf of a Party to the conflict, material compensation substantially in excess of that promised or paid to combatants of similar ranks and functions in the armed forces of that Party;

(d) is neither a national of a Party to the conflict nor a resident of territory controlled by a Party to the conflict;

(e) is not a member of the armed forces of a Party to the conflict; and

(f) has not been sent by a State which is not a Party to the conflict on official duty as a member of its armed forces.[14]

For a combatant to be described as a mercenary under this definition, according to the Geneva Convention, all the criteria (a–f) must be met.

---

[13]On the rise of child soldiers in recent years, see, P. W. Singer, *Children at War* (Berkeley: University of California Press, 2006).

[14]Protocol Additional to the Geneva Conventions of August 12, 1949, and relating to the Protection of Victims of International Armed Conflicts (Protocol 1 Article 47.c), June 8, 1977; hereafter APGC77 Art. 47.

Because of the assumption that a mercenary is essentially motivated by money, the term *mercenary* frequently carries negative con-
notations, though it can be a compliment in some contexts. There is a
blur in the distinction between a mercenary and a "foreign volunteer,"
when the primary motive of a soldier in a foreign army is uncertain.
For example, under the laws of war, members of the French Foreign
Legion and Indian Gurkhas are not mercenaries. Although they may
meet many of the requirements of Article 47 of the 1949 Additional
Protocol 1, they are exempt under clauses 47(a), (c), (d), (e), and (f).

If, after a regular trial, a captured soldier is found to be a mercenary, he can expect treatment as a common criminal and may face
execution. A mercenary may not receive the status of a prisoner of war
and cannot expect to be repatriated at the war's end.

In 1989, the United Nations passed resolution 44/34, the International Convention against the Recruitment, Use, Financing and Training of Mercenaries. It became effective in October 2001.[15] Known
usually as the "UN Mercenary," Article 1 contains the definition of a
mercenary. Article 1.1 is similar to Article 47 of Protocol 1; however,
Article 1.2 broadens the definition to include a nonnational recruited
to overthrow a "Government or otherwise undermin[e] the consti-
tutional order of a State; or undermin[e] the territorial integrity of a
State"; a mercenary "is motivated to take part therein essentially by
the desire for significant private gain and is prompted by the promise
or payment of material compensation." Additionally, under Article
1.2 a person does not have to take a direct part in the hostilities or in
a planned *coup d'état* to be a mercenary. However, even this expanded
definition has come under criticism, and critics of the resolution argue
that the convention and APGC77 Art. 47 are designed to cover the
activities of mercenaries in post-colonial Africa and do not address
adequately the use of private military companies by sovereign states.

The significant rise and use of these military companies is problematic at many levels. The growing presence of armed and unarmed civilian contractors in war zones has created significant ethical, political,
legal, and economic debate in recent years. The legal status of civilian
contractors depends upon the nature of their work and their nation-
alities in relation to the combatants. If they have not "in fact, taken

---

[15]International Convention against the Recruitment, Use, Financing and Training of Mercenaries, A/
RES/44/34 72nd plenary meeting December 4, 1989, accessed at http://www.un.org/documents/ga/
res/44/a44r034.htm, February 18, 2008.

a direct part in the hostilities" (APGC77 Art. 47.b), these individuals are not mercenaries but civilians who have noncombat support roles and are entitled to protection under the Third Geneva Convention (GCIII 4.1.4).

The use of mercenary forces throughout European history prior to the twentieth century was very common, and just-war thinkers have addressed the topic of mercenaries since the Middle Ages.[16] What has changed over time is the nature of the mercenary as a professional soldier who is part of a larger military force acquired by warring states or princes. In American history, for example, one thinks of the thirty thousand Hessian troops employed by the British during the American Revolution. Mercenaries are those who are foreign to the conflict, are motivated primarily by financial gain, and participate directly in combat.[17]

From the viewpoint of the nation-state, there is nothing within the ethics of the just-war tradition that prohibits a small nation without adequate military resources from securing needed strength. In theory, the use of mercenaries does not present an ethical problem, even when there are numerous legal considerations. For example, David Shearer observes: "The most accepted definition of a mercenary, found in Article 47 of the 1977 Additional Protocols to the Geneva Conventions, is so riddled with loopholes that few international-law scholars believe it could withstand the rigors of the courtroom. International apathy is palpable."[18]

More recent use of mercenary forces in the twentieth century and the present is closely linked to human-rights violations and has been an ongoing concern within the United Nations. The use of mercenaries in countries such as Zimbabwe, Angola, and Sierra Leone made conflicts in those nations (and beyond their borders) intractable and eluded international ethical norms of armed conflict. Unlike professional soldiers of the past, present-day mercenaries lack the discipline,

---

[16]Frederick H. Russell, *The Just War in the Middle Ages* (Cambridge: Cambridge University Press, 1975), 241–43, 303–4. For an overview of the use of mercenaries, see P. W. Singer, *Corporate Warriors: The Rise of the Privatized Military Industry*, rev. ed. (Ithaca, NY: Cornell University Press, 2008), 19–39; also, Janice Thompson, *Mercenaries, Pirates, and Sovereigns: State Building and Extraterritorial Violence in Early Modern Europe* (Princeton, NJ: Princeton University Press, 1994).
[17]For an excellent overview on the history and use of mercenaries, see, Sarah Percy, *Mercenaries: The History of a Norm in International Relations* (New York: Oxford University Press, 2007). On recent trends and the use of mercenaries see David Shearer, "Outsourcing War," *Foreign Policy* 112 (Autumn 1998): 68–81.
[18]Ibid., 77.

ethics, and constraints of the professional soldier.[19] What is permissible is not always desirable.

The employment of private military companies (PMCs), also known as private military firms (PMFs), and contractors since the 1990s, though not considered mercenaries, has created further political, legal, and ethical debate about the viability of mercenary forces and the blurring of lines between mercenary forces and PMCs. In some respects, the services of PMCs are indistinguishable from duties of conventional infantry soldiers, although they are thought to offer greater technical proficiency. Their employment by many nations, including the United States, has been seen as one way of reducing the cost of standing military forces, and as such these companies are not viewed as falling in the same category as mercenaries.[20] PMCs between 1991 and the present have aided U.S. war efforts in numerous strategic areas, including logistics and technical training, operational support, and policing.[21]

The use of PMCs will continue to be the subject of debate. P. W. Singer notes:

> In the post–Cold War era, . . . this cross of the corporate form with military functionality has become a reality. A new global industry has emerged. It is outsourcing and privatization of a twenty-first-century variety, and it changes many of the old rules of international politics and warfare.[22]

The outsourcing of war is not new in Western history, but it creates a complex legal and ethical environment at times in what is already a difficult arena. The profit motivation of the PMC adds the dimension of business ethics to the field of military ethics and can also create an environment where just-war concerns are no longer primary. What is certain is the need to understand this revived phenomenon in contemporary warfare. As Singer notes:

[19]Michael Walzer, *Just and Unjust Wars: A Moral Argument with Historical Illustrations*, 4th ed. (New York: Basic Books, 2006), 26–29.
[20]Shearer, "Outsourcing War," 68–69.
[21]See Deborah D. Avant, "Private Military Companies and the Future of War," an April 2006 electronic publication of the Foreign Policy Research Institute, accessed at www.fpri.org/enotes/200604. military.avant.privatemilitarycompanies; site discontinued.
[22]P. W. Singer, *Corporate Warriors: The Rise of the Privatized Military Industry*, rev. ed. (Ithaca, NY: Cornell University Press, 2008), 9.

An overall global pattern is emerging, one of growing reliance by individuals, corporations, states, and international organizations on military services supplied not just by public institutions but also by the nonsovereign private market. The changes that this phenomenon portends are tectonic. The emergence of a privatized military industry may well represent the new business face of warfare.[23]

Benefits of "private" military and security services are multiple and include flexibility and quickness in response, diversity of service, specialized training and experience, and the potential for being politically less costly. Among the disadvantages are the lack of integration between private and military cultures, the cost of particular services rendered, and the lack of legal clarity (insofar as rights and responsibilities in the private and military cultures differ greatly). Because of the differences between private and military sectors as well as the motivations within each sector (and the different personal and professional ethics within each), the future of PMCs remains unclear. The use of the PMC is not prohibited by the just-war tradition, but it needs continued study with regard to that tradition.

Q. 88   How does the just-war tradition understand asymmetric warfare?

Asymmetric warfare is defined as "hostile action between forces that are vastly dissimilar in force composition, defense posture, cultural and philosophical perspectives on violence and war, and/or strategic objectives," and in which tactics and weapons employed are typically "nontraditional."[24] Often thought of as methods for "wars of the weak," tactics of weaker belligerents in asymmetric warfare in the present operational environment include (but are not limited to) terrorist tactics, use of improvised weapons, and suicide bombing. Asymmetric warfare is by no means a recent phenomenon; it has been used throughout the centuries, and many nations have had to deal with it.[25]

[23]Ibid., 18.
[24]Michael Keane, *Dictionary of Modern Strategy and Tactics* (Annapolis, MD: Naval Institute Press, 2005), 19.
[25]See Vincent J. Goulding Jr., "Back to the Future with Asymmetric Warfare," *Parameters* (Winter 2000–2001): 21–30; G. J. Bryant, "Asymmetric Warfare: The British Experience in Eighteenth-Century

What has proven to be especially vexing in our day is the combination of asymmetric warfare and idiosyncratic techniques such as the 9/11 use of airliners as missiles. In asymmetric warfare the dominant power or military force usually has the advantage in quality and quantity of military technology, forces, and strength, but it is the opponent's idiosyncratic use of civil or military technology that creates vulnerability.[26]

To the extent that asymmetric weapons and warfare violate the principles of proportionality or discrimination, they are beyond legitimacy in conflict, whether they are deployed by the weak or the strong. Where fixed moral norms are rejected, or terror is justified "in the name of God," such tactics are not out of the question. The acceptance or rejection of ethical norms and moral prohibitions is often evidenced in statements such as, "The powerful do what they can; the weak do what they must." However, such a declaration, and the thinking that underpins such a declaration, finds rejection by the moral substructure of the just-war tradition.

Q. 89   How relevant is the just-war tradition in a world of high-tech weapons?

Current technology encourages advocacy of the just-war tradition by making the *jus in bello* criteria of discrimination and proportionality more feasible. Through the use of precision-guided munitions (PGMs), joint direct attack munitions (JDAMs), and similar technologies, harm to noncombatants and unnecessary destruction are increasingly avoidable. In short, current technology lends supports for just-war moral reasoning and strengthens its viability for the future. Yet, the use of these technologies can also prompt responses by opponents that complicate moral choices. Those against whom precision weapons are used may seek new defenses, for example, using human shields as prevention against PGMs.[27] However, these moral

India," *Journal of Military History* 68, no. 2 (April 2004): 431–69; and Max Boot, *The Savage Wars of Peace: Small Wars and the Rise of American Power* (New York: Basic Books, 2002).

[26]Montgomery C. Meigs, "Unorthodox Thoughts about Asymmetric Warfare," *Parameters* (Summer 2003): 17.

[27]See, Charles J. Dunlap Jr., "Technology: Recomplicating Moral Life for the Nation's Defenders," *Parameters* (Autumn 1999): 24–53; and Norman Friedman, "Is Modern War Too Precise?" *Proceedings of the U. S. Naval Institute* 130, no. 12 (December 2004): 4, 6.

complications do not exempt new technologies from intentional ethical consideration. International humanitarian law prohibits weapons that cannot discriminate between civilian and military targets, as well as any weapons that the international community decides must not be used.[28] Thus, for example, further development and use of lasers that blind combatants has been opposed by the International Committee of the Red Cross (ICRC). What has yet to be addressed is the ethics of unmanned systems and other developing robotic systems.[29]

It would be erroneous, however, to assume that technical and tactical developments in weaponry are only a recent phenomenon. In truth, the dilemma of virtue in warfare is an ancient one. Moreover, significant changes in tactics or technology that we might take for granted today have occurred throughout the centuries, just as just-war thinking has evolved and been reapplied in fresh ways. On an ongoing basis, land, naval, and aerial warfare have all been affected by technology.

In addition, there is now the potential for space and robotic warfare. In the last decades of the twentieth century, communications, targeting, ordnance, and surveillance systems were significantly enhanced, enabling nations with those technologies advantages previously unknown. In recent years there have been tremendous advances in the use of robotic technology in land warfare, on the sea, and in the air. Unmanned aerial vehicles (UAV) such as Predator, Global Hawk, Shadow, and Raven are complemented by ground systems such as PackBot, MARCBOT, Talon, CRAM, and SWORDS. At sea there is REMUS, a system used to clear mines and explosives. Each of these systems has effectively reduced casualties and saved lives in recent conflicts. The fact of superior technical advancement does not guarantee military supremacy or ensure that particular weaponry will be used morally.[30] It simply takes ethical decision making on the battlefield to a new level. Of equal concern is the fact that international law does not keep pace with new technological developments (a problem that parallels civil law and technology issues). P. W. Singer notes:

---

[28]P. W. Singer, *Wired for War: The Robotics Revolution and Conflict in the 21st Century* (New York: Penguin, 2009), 384. Singer's volume provides a good overview of current trends in weapons technology, especially with regard to robotics. For discussions of ethics see pages 382–427.
[29]Ibid., 384–85.
[30]For an overview of the development of military technology, see Max Boot, "The Paradox of Military Technology," *The New Atlantis* 14 (Fall 2006): 13–31, and Boot's more extensive work, *War Made New: Technology, Warfare, and the Course of History, 1500 to Today* (New York: Gotham Books, 2006).

While technologic change is speeding up exponentially, legal change remains glacial. Chemical weapons were first introduced in World War I, but they weren't fully banned until eighty-two years later. Even worse, if we look back at history, the biggest developments in law only came after some catastrophe. If one-third of central Europe's population hadn't been killed in the Thirty Years' War, Hugo Grotius probably wouldn't have written *On the Laws of War and Peace*. Or, if eleven million Jews, Roma, POWs, and political prisoners weren't killed in the Holocaust, there would be no 1949 Geneva Conventions.[31]

Summarizing the increasing use of robotics and "digital warriors," Singer insightfully notes: "Man's monopoly of warfare is being broken. We are entering the era of robots at war. . . . War just won't be the same."[32]

Technology, like any instrumentality of power, has a neutral quality about it and can be used for either good or ill. Even at the earliest stages, there are always prior decisions regarding funding, design, and development before a particular technology is functional. Darrell Cole has framed the matter well: "Technology does not remove the possibility of virtue, but it does increase the possibilities for vice. . . . Every technological advance gives us one more small space for possible virtuous acts, but endless possibilities for vice."[33] In the end, the morality or immorality of any use of armed force is "not mainly a matter of the kind of force available but of who uses it, why, and how."[34]

Q. 90 How does noncombatant immunity affect conflict and war?

The idea of distinguishing between combatants and non-combatants is deeply embedded in the Western moral tradition and is also found in other traditions and cultures, such as

---

[31] Singer, *Wired for War*, 387.

[32] Ibid., 41. For a summary of recent developments, see his "Introduction: Scenes from a Robot War," 19–41.

[33] Darrell Cole, *When God Says War Is Right: The Christian's Perspective on When and How to Fight* (Colorado Springs: Waterbrook, 2002), 54. See also, A. J. Bacevich, "Morality and High Technology," *The National Interest* (Fall 1996): 37–47.

[34] James Turner Johnson, *The War to Oust Saddam Hussein: Just War and the New Face of Conflict* (Lanham, MD: Rowman & Littlefield, 2005), 21.

ancient Chinese, Hindu, Egyptian, and Hebrew cultures.[35] The protection of noncombatants in warfare is of paramount importance, and the principle of noncombatant immunity (discrimination) is central to the *jus in bello* aspect of just-war thinking. As James Turner Johnson notes: "Moral reflection has to take seriously where to draw the line between those who may be directly, intentionally targeted and those who may not. Indeed, the question of how to ensure the protection of noncombatants is one of the most important moral issues posed by contemporary armed conflict."[36] This immunity is intended not only to protect noncombatants from attack, but also to prevent noncombatants from being used either offensively or defensively as hostages or human shields.

Although the roots of noncombatant immunity in our own cultural tradition are found in the Middle Ages, we find precursors in pre-Christian cultures. The fifth-century-B.C. philosopher-warrior Sun Tzu, for example, states in *The Art of War* that when "the use of soldiers cannot be avoided, . . . the best policy is calm restraint. . . . He who delights in slaughter will not succeed in his ambition to rule."[37] In addition, rules of engagement were recognized that required just cause to begin a war, notification of pending attacks, humane treatment of prisoners and the injured, noncombatant immunity for innocents, and a commitment not to prolong war. Similarly, in *The Wisdom of Laotse*, roughly contemporary to Sun Tzu, we read: "Generally in war the best policy is to take a state intact; to ruin it is inferior to this. . . . To capture the enemy's army is better than to destroy it. . . . The worst policy is to attack cities." According to wisdom, "The slaying of multitudes should be mourned with sorrow. A victory should be celebrated with the Funeral Rite."[38]

Despite the longstanding tradition of noncombatant immunity in just-war moral reasoning, strengthening of the concept has been a much more recent development. It was only with the development of the Geneva Conventions and protocols beginning in the nineteenth

---

[35]See question 22, "Is just-war moral reasoning a uniquely religious or specifically Christian perspective on war and peace, or are there precursors?"

[36]James Turner Johnson, *Morality and Contemporary Warfare* (New Haven, CT: Yale University Press, 1999), 37–38.

[37]These moral imperatives are scattered throughout the first three chapters of *The Art of War*. We are relying on the translation, with introduction, by S. B. Griffith to Sun Tzu, *The Art of War* (Oxford: Oxford University Press, 1971).

[38]*The Wisdom of Laotse* 30–31, reproduced in *War and Peace*, Classical Selections on Great Issues, series 1, vol. 5 (Washington, DC: University Press of America, 1982), 562–63.

century and the twentieth-century rise of international humanitarian law that noncombatant immunity became a legal right, even if it often has been ignored.[39]

The principle of noncombatant immunity is a window into the heart of just-war moral reasoning and is important for many reasons. Among those identified by Colm McKeogh are the following:

- Noncombatants have committed no wrong and are innocent.
- Noncombatants are not participating in the fighting.
- Noncombatants are defenseless.
- Killing noncombatants is militarily unnecessary.
- Maintaining noncombatant immunity reduces the casualties of war.
- Sparing women, children, and others who perform essential peacetime functions permits survival.
- Killing noncombatants is contrary to the laws of war.[40]

Throughout the twentieth century the proportion of civilians and noncombatants killed in war rose dramatically. As limited warfare turned to total warfare and genocide—ethnic cleansing—and as forced flight became ends as well as means in some wars, there was often a complete breach of the principle of noncombatant immunity.[41] Such tactics, however, are completely beyond the boundaries and moral logic of just-war thinking. It is precisely for this reason that terrorism is morally reprehensible—it singles out the innocent for attack.

Noncombatant immunity should affect not only matters of tactics and targets but also technological development of new weapons. As part of the upholding of the principles of discrimination and proportionality, and of anticipating how best to serve just ends with just means, there must be ethical consideration devoted to the development of weaponry. Thus, James Turner Johnson's admonition must be taken seriously, namely, that there is "a *prima facie* obligation to develop weaponry that is inherently more discriminate and relatively

---

[39]See the helpful historical overview by Johnson, *Morality and Contemporary Warfare*, 36–37. See also Alexander B. Downes, *Targeting Civilians in War* (Ithaca, NY: Cornell University Press, 2008), for historical analysis of civilian targeting in the twentieth century.
[40]Colm McKeogh, *Innocent Civilians: The Morality of Killing in War* (New York: Palgrave, 2002), 5–13.
[41]Ibid., 140–41.

less destructive, such as by incorporating 'smart' weapons into military readiness for various kinds of contingencies, as well as by improving accuracy and lowering yields of other types of arms."[42] The rise in nonlethal weapons development is part of this perspective.[43]

Just-war thinking recognizes that in any war it is impossible not to have noncombatants die as a result of military actions. Such tragedies are inevitable but they are not *intentional*. And the fact that innocents will die in conflict does not *ipso facto* render that conflict unjust any more than a shoot-out between law-enforcement officers and bank robbers would be unjust were an innocent bystander fatally shot. Justice is based on intent, not perfection. If this were not the case, then all civilized societies would have to give up on *any* attempt at criminal justice, because those attempts will inevitably be flawed along the way. If and where belligerents intentionally intermix with a civilian population and carry on their operations amid noncombatants, they thereby assume the greater moral burden, even when from the opposite perspective the criterion of noncombatant immunity is being taken seriously.

Here we find it useful once more to illustrate from the realm of criminal justice. In the case of a potentially catastrophic violent crime, law-enforcement officers and agencies plan and calculate, wait and maneuver, consult and strategize, until they reach the point at which a particular threat appears to reach critical mass. At that point, they must decide whether or not to act and do not have the luxury to explore "further alternatives" before intercepting the *offender*. What's more, they do this in the knowledge that their attempts to spare the lives of innocent bystanders and civilians, while of paramount importance, cannot be guaranteed. Tragic though it is, the death of innocent people *in and of itself* does not render coercive force in the realm of criminal justice or international justice unjust. According to just-war moral reasoning, justice is predicated on right goals and right intention. In a fallen world, *someone* has to reckon with the responsibility of resisting evil people.

Summarizing noncombatant immunity or the "civilian ethic," Hugo Slim writes:

---

[42]Johnson, *Morality and Contemporary Warfare*, 38.
[43]See question 86, "What about nonlethal weapons?"

At its deepest point, the civilian ethic is built on a respect for all human life and the most ancient of moral injunctions that "Thou shalt not kill." Although it may not necessarily always be wrong to kill in self-defence or in certain struggles for other moral goods, it is always bad to kill. It may be necessary but is never a good in itself. As we have seen, the great majority of civilian killing is wrongful killing. It is the deliberate killing of unarmed men, women, and children and is best described as murder. . . . The main idea behind limited war and its civilian ethic is, of course, that of limited killing. This argument reasons, that even in war, one should kill as little as possible. This is because every human being's life is precious to themselves, to those who love them and, if one is religious, to God as well.[44]

Noncombatant immunity is and should be an inviolable principle of warfare. Its prominence in the ethical framework of the just-war tradition promotes justice and concerns for the innocent even in the midst of the tragedy and horror of war.

Q. 91 Aren't all wars "just" to the victor?

Speaking of the Roman way of waging war, Calgaus, a British tribal leader, declared, "They create a desolation and call it peace."[45] In the same sense, many victors declare their war efforts, war termination, and post-conflict endeavors "just," but their proclamations do not make it so. While it is true that subjectivity can never be fully removed from evaluations of one's actions, there do exist ethical standards and norms to which one can look for guidance.

According to classic just-war thinking, in order for a war to be considered just, there must first and foremost be sovereign authority, just cause, right intention, and the aim of peace.[46] Out of these primary *jus ad bellum* criteria issue several related tests—proportionality of ends (i.e., that the overall good expected from the use of force must be greater than the harm expected), last resort, and reasonable hope of success. The force employed in the war must then be in accordance with nonnegotiable *jus in bello* criteria. These require that there is

---

[44]Hugo Slim, *Killing Civilians: Method, Madness, and Morality in War* (New York: Columbia University Press, 2008), 260–61.
[45]Cited by Tacitus in *Agricola*, 30.
[46]So Thomas Aquinas *Summa theologiae* II-II Q. 40.

noncombatant protection or discrimination (i.e., no intentional targeting or harm to noncombatants) and proportionality of means (i.e., the means employed should be proportionate to the task).

Not only must the prosecution of war be just, but so too must its termination, reconciliation, and aftermath, in accordance with *post bellum* requirements.[47] Nations that wage war have a moral responsibility to do so ethically and in accordance with international law. Though no side in a conflict is morally perfect, and there has never been and will never be a war without errors, faults, failures, or shortcomings, there must never be a willing abrogation of values and ethics.

It is possible to have "peace" without justice as well as war without justice. During the Punic Wars (264–146 B.C.) the Romans and Phoenicians fought three wars. At the end of the third, the Romans laid siege to Carthage and eventually captured the city. When they did so, they massacred the citizens and soldiers, sold survivors into slavery, destroyed the city and infrastructure, and by some accounts, sowed the ground with salt so nothing could grow. It was a brutal peace, from which the phrase "Carthaginian Peace" derives.

Proclaiming a war "just" does not in fact render it so—whether before, during, or after the conflict. At the same time, neither does proclaiming a peace "just" indeed make it so, since "peace" can be either just or unjust. In the case of the latter, it can be the peace of Mafia-like rules or totalitarian oppression of dissent. In the end, some wars are justified while others are simply rationalized. That an inherently unjust war can be rationalized is not an argument against the possibility of applying just-war thinking for purposes of responsible statecraft. Upholding justice requires that we resist both the allure of "peace at any price" and the Machiavellian deception that doing evil may be a necessary means to political stability.

---

[47]Standard treatments of just-war thinking typically are limited to the two classic sets of criteria—*jus ad bellum* and *jus in bello*. We would argue that yet a third category—*jus post bellum*—of moral requirements extends naturally from these two. In recent years, given the developments in Iraq, discussions of *post bellum* obligations are beginning to emerge. We discuss *jus post bellum* in part 3, "Just-War Tradition and the Statesman."

PART 6

JUST-WAR TRADITION AND THE INDIVIDUAL

Q. 92 Why do people, including those of religious faith, disagree so strongly about war and peace?

Initially, one is tempted simply to answer "politics." This, of course, is the easy answer. And to be sure, one's own hierarchy of values as it affects economic, social, moral, cultural, and religious aspects of our lives surely expresses itself in our political sentiments and commitments. This is equally true of all people, whether or not they affirm any particular faith commitment.

From an explicitly Christian perspective, we might illustrate this diversity by means of a recent volume published under the title *Church, State and Public Justice.*[1] It contrasts five differing views of how Christian faith might enter the public arena—an arena that, as the editor notes, in the last two decades has grown rather noisy.[2] Identified for the reader are a "Catholic Perspective," a "Principled Pluralist Perspective," a "Classical Separation Perspective," a "Social Justice Perspective," and an "Anabaptist Perspective."[3] While representatives of all five positions agree that the Creator is unquestionably a God of justice, *sharp* differences exist as to (1) the role that Christians should play in society in specifically working for justice, (2) the role ascribed to government in preserving justice, and (3) responsible public policy that reflects a reasonably just society. What is the source of these sharp divisions?

The reasons are multiple, and so an easy or quick answer eludes us. Our differences over war and peace doubtless involve the *means* to uphold and defend peace, since the commodity of peace is like the air we breathe—everyone unreservedly affirms it. But our disagreements entail more. At the ideological and theological level, they are about

---

[1]Paul C. Kemeny, ed., *Church, State and Public Justice* (Downers Grove, IL: InterVarsity, 2007).
[2]Whether the public square is still "naked," to use the well-worn term coined by Richard John Neuhaus, is debatable.
[3]Whether or not one agrees with this taxonomy is beyond the scope of our discussion. At the very least, however, it does reveal the fact that among Christians (and particularly among Protestants) there is no unified political theory.

the *nature* of the interim worldly peace that is possible within human communities.[4] Thus, for example, the ideological pacifist conceives of this peace as an entity by and large achievable *apart from* political skill and statecraft. Moral theologian Oliver O'Donovan offers valuable commentary to help illustrate this point, observing that among Christians there is "a fairly profound disagreement over the limits of the operation of common grace." He says:

> A certain "statism" is implied in the pacifist position, which will not contemplate the improvisation of judgment where it is not provided for within a state structure, and to that extent cannot treat international politics wholly seriously as politics, [i.e., as] a God-given sphere of peaceful interaction. Here we begin to see why pacifism is a modern development.[5]

Undeniably, ideological and theological orientation accounts for many of our differences within the wider Christian community. So, too, does our experience. Ponder, for a moment, how the last sixty years of American experience of war have affected people's attitudes toward war, peace, and the military. From the end of World War II to the Korean War, to Vietnam, to the Cold War, to Iraq—experiences and perceptions of these wars have shaped, both consciously and subconsciously, how we view geopolitical events, regardless of whether we confess religious faith or not. For those who take their faith seriously, further factors contributing to why we disagree are still legion. For example, personal temperament and abilities doubtless play a significant role. Some of us tend to be activists, while others of us are more reflective and cerebral.

At the interpretive and hermeneutical level, some of us are "disciples" of influential religious figures and teachers; others of us have built our convictions sporadically or piecemeal, based on the accumulation of life's experiences. For some of us there exists deep confusion in our understanding of the teaching of Jesus. Was Jesus a pacifist? Does his "cleansing" of the temple constitute justified force? Was he against war? Wasn't he against retaliation? What does it mean to "turn the other cheek"? Related questions confront us. Is the Chris-

---

[4]Thus Oliver O'Donovan, *The Just War Revisited*, Current Issues in Theology (Cambridge: Cambridge University Press, 2005), 7.
[5]Ibid., 8.

tian in fact *not* to resist evil, and how is this statement to be squared with the whole weight of Scripture that requires God's people to work *against* evil? Did Jesus or John the Baptist call—or would they have called—disciples away from military service, and is this vocational mandate the meaning of Jesus' pronouncements, "Blessed are the meek" and "Blessed are the peacemakers"? Such are questions that perplex many of us. And our doubts perhaps are multiplied when we consider the standard portrait of the early church that has been popularized by historian Roland Bainton and others—a portrait that has given the impression of little or no diversity of opinion among the early Christians.[6]

A more philosophical dilemma confronts us as we wrestle with the possibility of war in an age of nuclear and mass-destructive capabilities. Can a modern war actually be "limited"? Can any modern war be just? Who decides, and when, and by what criteria? During the Cold War era, this ethical conundrum caused many believers to opt for what might be called a "nuclear pacifism." That is, although one might not *in principle* rule out the use of force in *all* situations, the sheer magnitude of destructiveness and untoward dimensions of contemporary warfare would seem to negate any *practical* possibility for war to be conducted justly. And doesn't there exist within Christian faith a basic presumption against war and coercive force?

At the ecclesial level, it is fair to say that our churches, whatever our denominational affiliation, have not always provided sound moral leadership and teaching for our congregations corporately or for believers individually on important matters of moral discourse. How will Christians be guided to reflect on issues of war and peace? And what are distinctively "Christian" reflections on war and peace? Nor have we in our churches, at least in standard teaching and preaching, made ethical formation and education a high priority. What's more, much of Christendom—particularly that rather large sector of theological conservatives in the American context—is characterized by a sacred-versus-secular split in its thinking. In some of our circles we have placed strong emphasis on evangelism, missions, church growth, and pastoral callings, while implicitly or unwittingly relegating vocational callings in the marketplace to a lesser or secondary importance. The consequences of this sort of false dichotomy are significant. At

---

[6]See the related questions in part 2, "Just-War Tradition and the Historian."

the very least, this dualism prevents thoughtful Christians from pursuing careers, for example, in law, legal theory, economics, journalism, politics and public administration, political theory, policy analysis, and even the military—careers that not only are rewarding but are also enormously strategic in terms of service to society.

Yet another factor accounting for our differences is the widespread misunderstanding—if not wholesale neglect—of what just-war moral reasoning really is. In both secular and religious contexts, the "just-war" idea suffers from multiple distortions. Among the religious, this is doubly sad because of the central place that the ethics of war and peace has had in the wider historic Christian tradition. While there are many people who simply have not had the proper resources available with which to inform themselves, others have not invested the effort to enter into a centuries-long conversation with saints and soldiers, monks and magistrates, laypersons and theologians about mainstream Christian thinking on the subject. For those who have this willingness to be guided historically and consensually, this plunge into the Christian moral tradition is nothing short of richly rewarding. Plumbing the riches of that tradition has been the aim of this volume.

Q. 93   Don't charity and resort to force or going to war stand in blatant contradiction?

A notable feature of Christian social ethics is its obligation of neighbor love. In contrast to the human tendency to define *neighbor* too narrowly (for example, limiting it to those who are *similar* to us), Jesus' teaching allows a considerable range of meaning concerning who is our neighbor. In the realm of justice, our neighbor may be any innocent third party who is suffering or oppressed or being denied basic human rights. Thus, common sense and the natural law, which call us to do good and avoid or prevent evil, undergird basic criminal justice both in the domestic and in the international context. Stated in negative terms, we attempt to protect the moral order on its borders by precepts that are *proscriptive* in nature and that constrain certain human behaviors, while, stated positively, we attempt to advance human goodness *prescriptively* in whatever ways that goodness may be expressed. In a fallen world, individual people as well as people groups and nations may not have the wherewithal to defend themselves. One expression of Christian charity, therefore, may be to defend and protect the innocent from harm's way. And in a fallen world, coercive force will always be a possibility, and on occasion a necessity.

In *Basic Christian Ethics*, ethicist Paul Ramsey develops the meaning of Christian love, as well as the specific contours of love's expression.[7] The work of charity, he rightly emphasizes, is such that it balances the needs of self and others. At the same time, it distinguishes between selfishness and rash self-sacrifice, while balancing wise self-love with mutual love between persons. We do well to consider Ramsey's line of reasoning as it applies to the defense of a third party:

> Love, which by its nature would be non-resistant where only the agent's own rights and the perhaps unjust claims of a single neighbor are involved, may change its action to resistance by the most effective possible means, judicial or military, violent or non-violent, when the needs of more than one neighbor come into view.[8]

Insofar as charity is not self-defensive by nature, it is willing to suffer insult, abuse, or self-deprivation rather than strike back at the offending party. However, this same charity, where an innocent third party is introduced to the situation, will impel human beings to develop what Ramsey calls an "ethics of protection," lest injustice be done to innocent third parties or "neighbors."[9] One might even describe this expression of love as a *preferential* ethics of protection, as Ramsey does.

Ramsey's position is not a deviation from mainstream Christian moral reflection, however, but wholly consistent with it. For Ambrose and Augustine, both of whom rejected self-defense,[10] a resort to force and war *may* regrettably be an obligation of charity. The writings of Augustine, in particular, bear out the conviction that justice and charity are not at odds. Justice is concerned with a right ordering of society for the sake of social peace, what Augustine calls the *tranquillitas*

---

[7]*Basic Christian Ethics* (New York: Scribner's, 1954), esp. chaps. 4–5.
[8]Ibid., 165.
[9]Ibid.
[10]Ambrose's views are on display in his work *On the Duties of the Clergy*. For Augustine, there is one exception, and that is a soldier who acts in self-defense and in the defense of others (*Epistle* 47, "To Publicola"). Augustine's own thinking on self-defense appears to have evolved. Earlier, he had expressed strong reservations (*On Freedom of the Will* 1.5).

ordinis. He acknowledges the existence of both a just peace—*justa pax*—and an unjust peace—*iniqua pax.* The distinction is critical. For this reason, peace *requires* the ordering of justice. Even robbers, he observes, have order and maintain a certain "peace" within their own orbit in order to plunder the innocent.[11] Peace as a good, even in its relative state this side of the *eschaton*, must be guarded since it furnishes for people the environment in which to contemplate life's mysteries. While ultimate peace that is consummated in the kingdom of God does not require restraints, penultimate peace does.[12]

Charity, as Augustine conceives of it, must motivate all that we do. It is at the center of human experience, motivating human virtue and self-sacrifice and expressing itself tangibly toward one's neighbor. It orders all human actions, even the use of coercive force and going to war for the sake of preserving justice. As a social force, this "rightly ordered love"[13] is foremost concerned with what is good—for the perpetrator of criminal acts as well as for society, which has been victimized by criminal acts. When "men are prevented, by being alarmed, from doing wrong, it may be said that a real service is done to them."[14] Not the external action per se but one's *intent* determines, in Augustinian thought, the morality of one's actions. Thus, for example, in his letter to Publicola, Augustine renders legitimate, based on the wedding of justice and charity, an exception to the prohibition of killing. It is legitimate precisely when it involves the public good—for example, in the case of the soldier or public official who carries out his public trust by establishing a justly ordered peace.[15] For this reason, Augustine can write elsewhere to Boniface, a governor of a northern African province, "Do not think that it is impossible for anyone serving in the military to please God."[16] Justice is the work of charity.

Aquinas, like Augustine before him, responds to the common objection that war is contrary to Jesus' teaching in the Sermon on the Mount not to resist evil (Matt. 5:38–39). He notes that "a man avenges the wrong done to God *and neighbor*" because of charity. And in this connection he quotes Augustine: "Those whom we have

---

[11]Augustine *The City of God* 19.11–12, 27.
[12]Ibid., 15.4; 19.112, 27; 22.24; *Epistle* 189 ("To Boniface").
[13]Augustine *The City of God* 15.22 and *Contra Faustum* 22.78.
[14]Augustine, *Epistle* 47 ("To Publicola"), trans. J. G. Cunningham, *Nicene and Post-Nicene Fathers* (*NPNF*), ed. Philip Schaff (Grand Rapids: Eerdmans, 1956), 293.
[15]Ibid.
[16]*Epistle* 189, *NPNF*, 554.

to punish with a kindly severity, it is necessary to handle in many ways against their will. For when we are stripping a man of the lawlessness of sin, it is good for him to be vanquished."[17] For Aquinas, there is just cause for war when those being attacked "deserve attack on account of some fault." That is, just cause consists in an appropriate response to prior wrongdoing.[18] It is not insignificant that in *Summa theologiae*, Aquinas's treatment of the Christian and war is situated within a wider discussion of the theological virtues[19] and narrowly within an examination of the character of *caritas*.[20]

With Augustine and Aquinas, Luther also believes that military service could be a work of charity. In *Temporal Authority: To What Extent It Should Be Obeyed* and his treatise *On War against the Turk*, he proceeds on the assumption that it is a work of Christian love to protect and defend a whole community with the sword and not let people be oppressed.[21] Luther acknowledges that slaying does not seem like it could possibly be a work of love. The "simple man," he notes, would conclude that such is not possible. In truth, however, it can be an expression of charity properly understood.

Luther offers an analogy: A good doctor in extreme circumstances may be required to amputate or destroy a hand, foot, arm, or leg that is diseased. Viewed externally, this would seem cruel and merciless. Viewed medically, the doctor wishes to cut off what is defective in order to save the body and work for the greater good. In the same way, argues Luther, the soldier fulfills his office by punishing the wicked, even when this means using lethal force. This serves the greater good of families and communities. If the sword were not employed to preserve the peace, everything in the surrounding world would be spoiled. Therefore, "war is only . . . a small misfortune that prevents a great misfortune."[22] In order to "prevent some from becoming widows and orphans as a consequence [of war or plunder]," it is "both Christian and an act of love to kill the enemy without hesitation . . . until he is conquered."[23]

---

[17] *Epistle* 138 ("To Marcellinus"), *NPNF*, 485.
[18] Thomas Aquinas *Summa theologiae* (hereafter *S.T.*) II-II Q. 40 a. 1.
[19] Ibid., Qq. 1–46. This block of teaching precedes Aquinas's teaching on the cardinal virtues (Qq. 46–170).
[20] Ibid., Qq. 23–27, 44. Notice that Qq. 34–39 are devoted to those attitudes that stand in *opposition* to charity.
[21] *Luther's Works* (hereafter *L.W.*), ed. Jaroslav Pelikan and Helmut Lehmann (Philadelphia: Fortress, 1967), 45:81–129 and 46:161–205.
[22] Ibid., 46:96.
[23] Ibid., 45:125.

In his conspicuously titled work *The Three Theological Virtues*,[24] the early-modern just-war theorist Francisco Suárez also understands and develops just-war thinking under the rubric of charity. Thereby Suárez scrutinizes the role of the state in both defensive and offensive modes: "A required mode and uniformity as to it [warfare] must be observed at its beginning, during its prosecution and after victory."[25] The moral basis for conditions that justify going to war and prosecuting war, Suárez is careful to maintain, since it is "founded upon the natural law," is "common to Christians and to unbelievers."[26]

Political ethicist Jean Elshtain rightly observes that the just-war tradition "has been called upon repeatedly in criticisms of holy wars, crusades, and wars of imperial aggrandizement."[27] Why is that? Some critics of war fail to see the profound distinction between just-war moral reasoning and other calls to arms. Whether religiously based, as in jihad or crusading, or in its secular counterpart, a militaristic *Realpolitik*, there exist no limits, no moral demarcations; violence can be justified for the purpose of imperial expansion. For just-warriors, however, "both aims and means are limited, even if one has been grievously harmed."[28]

The ethos of just-war thinking, as developed and refined in the Christian moral tradition, is aptly summarized by Oliver O'Donovan: "From the earliest attempts to understand how armed conflict might be compatible with Christian discipleship, the church has taken its bearings from the evangelical command of love."[29] Charity and the use of coercive force do not stand in contradiction, as widely assumed not merely by secular ethicists but also by their many so-called Christian counterparts. Human reason and social necessity neither sanction nor prohibit all force, only that which is morally repugnant, such as human oppression. For this reason Hugo Grotius, writing in the dust of the Thirty Years War, could maintain, "For both extremes [uncritically applying force or foreswearing all force] a remedy must be found, that

---

[24]This volume was published posthumously in 1621.
[25]*The Three Theological Virtues* 3.8.1; English translation found in James B. Scott, *The Spanish Origin of International Law: Lectures on Francisco de Vitoria (1480–1546) and Francisco Suarez (1548–1617)* (Washington, DC: Georgetown University Press, 1929), 77.
[26]Ibid., 3.8.2.
[27]*Just War against Terror: The Burden of American Power in a Violent World* (New York: Basic Books, 2003), 58.
[28]Ibid.
[29]*The Just War Revisited*, 9.

men may not believe either that nothing is [ever] allowable, or that everything [always] is."[30]

Q. 94   What about *self*-defense? Does Christian faith prohibit force in this context?

In an earlier question, we noted that both Augustine and his spiritual mentor, Ambrose, rejected self-defense, with one exception: a soldier who acts in self-defense or in the defense of others.[31] It should be noted that Aquinas, Luther, Vitoria, and Suárez disagreed.

Aquinas understands the morality of response in light of both intention and proportionality, noting that an action such as self-defense could produce a double effect, one part intended (to save a life) and the other unintended (killing the aggressor in defense).

> If a man in self-defense uses more than necessary violence, it will be unlawful: whereas if he repel force with moderation, his defense will be lawful. . . . Nor is it necessary for salvation that a man omit the act of moderate self-defense to avoid killing the other man, since one is bound to take more care of one's own life than of another's.[32]

Reprisals against criminal behavior, whether this behavior is private or state sponsored, are considered by Aquinas to be just.

In the early-modern period, both Vitoria and Suárez are writing in the context of Spain's conquest of the new world. What is noteworthy is that both affirm the right of self-defense, even when both understand that war may be declared only by the sovereign authority.[33] Following Aquinas on sovereign authority and just cause, Suárez even extends the legitimacy of self-defense to a person who has been oppressed or attacked unjustly by a king.[34] If the end is permissible, according to Suárez, then the means *necessary* to that end—that is, what is discriminate and proportionate—is justified.[35] Luther's curious response—

---

[30]*The Law of War and Peace*, trans. R. L. Loomis (Roslyn, NY: Walter J. Black, 1949), 1.1.
[31]See question 25, "What were attitudes toward military service and war among particular early fathers of the church?"
[32]*S.T.* II-II Q. 64, as cited in the Catechism of the Catholic Church, par. 2264.
[33]See *The Law of War* 1.2 and *Defense of the Faith* 6.4 respectively.
[34]*Disputationes* 3.
[35]*On War* 7.

and he is writing roughly contemporary to Vitoria—is to permit self-defense, even when he acknowledges that truly "Spirit-led" Christians may find this sort of action "rare."

> You may ask, "Why may I not use the sword for myself and for my own cause, so long as it is my intention not to seek my own advantage but to punish evil?" Answer: Such a miracle is not impossible, but very rare and hazardous. Where the [Holy] Spirit is so richly present it may well happen. . . . No one but a true Christian, filled with the Spirit, will follow this example. Where reason too tries to do likewise, it will probably contend that it is not trying to seek its own, but this will be basically untrue, for it cannot be done without grace. Therefore, first become like Samson, and then you can also do as Samson did.[36]

It is certainly true that Christ told his disciples not to fear those who might kill the body but rather fear him who has power to kill the soul (Matt. 10:28). Can we legitimately extend these words to foreign policy? Is this maxim the foundation of responsible statecraft? Consistent with the Christian moral tradition, one might argue that a Christian may be placed in situations in which defending himself might be a duty he owes to others. That is to say, sacrificing himself or failing to protect himself might actually create a greater burden or harm to others as a result.[37] Examples of this might be an ambulance driver or emergency medical technician, a military doctor or nurse, and military or governmental leaders who have been entrusted with responsibilities and lives beyond their own. Self-defense is neither negated nor given unqualified support in Scripture. Rather, it is rooted in the principle of charity, which *may or may not* resort to force, dependent upon the situation.

While biblical teaching may be said to permit abstaining from self-defense, as in the practice of Ambrose and Augustine, it cannot be said to *require* abstaining. The notion of defending oneself requires a proper understanding not only of just dealings with others but also of the self and of self-love. For this reason the Catechism of the Catholic Church, in citing Aquinas, notes: "Love toward oneself remains a fundamental principle of morality. Therefore it is legitimate to insist

---

[36]*L.W.* 45:104.
[37]Ramsey, *Basic Christian Ethics*, 176–80, develops this scenario in a plausible way.

on respect for one's own right to life. Someone who defends his life is not guilty of murder even if he is forced to deal his aggressor a lethal blow."[38] Though not explicitly, the catechism simply affirms what we know through the natural law. Thus, Samuel Pufendorf writes that both in the state of human nature and in civil society, "it is lawful for every man to defend himself."

> In Civil Society, those who are Subjects to the Civil Power . . . may then only use Violence in the Defence of themselves, when the Tim[e] and Place will not admit of an Application to the Magistrate for his Assistance in repelling such Injuries by which a Man's Life may be hazarded, or some other most valuable Good which can never be repaired . . . may be manifestly endangered.[39]

"Man is allowed to be most dear to himself," observes Pufendorf, without sinning against the "Law of Nature." He illustrates:

> Suppose a Mad-man, or a Lunatick, or one that mistakes me for some other Person who is his Enemy, should make an Attempt on my Life, I may justifiably use my Right of Self-Defence; for the Person from whom the Attempt comes, whereby my Life is hazarded, hath no Right to attack me, and I am by no means obliged to suffer Death unnecessarily; on which account it is altogether unreasonable that I should prefer his Safety to my own.[40]

According to the natural law, one may even defend oneself to the extent of using lethal force, when the aggressor is armed for the clear purpose of taking the other's life. Pufendorf is careful to distinguish between self-defense and personal revenge, since revenge of wrongs done is the task of the civil magistrate.[41] This distinction is consonant with Christian moral teaching.

As we argue in several questions in this volume, the application of coercive force—whether to defend self or to defend others—is legitimized by *intention* and *proportionality* to the situation. In this sense,

---

[38]Catechism of the Catholic Church, par. 2264.
[39]Samuel Pufendorf, *The Whole Duty of Man, According to the Law of Nature*, ed. I. Hunter and D. Saunders, trans. A. Tooke (1691; Indianapolis: Liberty Fund, 2003), 84.
[40]Ibid., 88. Pufendorf uses an analogy: while no one has the right or authority to cut off a limb or to maim out of simple pleasure, in the case of gangrene such an extreme act is justifiable *for the purpose of saving the rest of the whole body*, or at least *to preserve parts of the body that are sound*.
[41]Ibid., 87.

force has a neutral quality and can be used for just or unjust purposes. Force is per se not evil; rather, it takes on the moral character of those employing it.

Q. 95 Doesn't Gandhi demonstrate the effectiveness and necessity of pacifism?

Gandhi represents a powerful model of nonviolence extolled by religious and secular pacifists alike, and for this reason he requires our attention. Students of Indian culture and Hindu ethics, we readily grant, are better qualified than we authors to evaluate the efficacy of Gandhi's witness.

One such student, in fact, was George Orwell, who spent years as a journalist in India.[42] In the end, Orwell was left to observe, "It is difficult to see how Gandhi's methods could be applied in a country where opponents of the regime disappear in the middle of the night and are never heard from again."[43] It needs to be remembered that Orwell was writing against the backdrop of Communist tyranny in the 1940s. With millions disappearing into labor camps, the nonviolent vision seemed not to be working well in the Soviet Union. Correlatively, if we absolutize the distinction between nonviolent and violent resistance—as the nonviolent, pacifist position does—we arrive at the morally absurd position that Reinhold Niebuhr pointed out. That is, we give preference to the "nonviolent" power of a Joseph Goebbels, Hitler's extraordinary propaganda minister, over that of a military officer.[44]

But we return to Gandhi as an example, and particularly to the geopolitical context of his time. Orwell was able to praise Gandhi for his saintly status. In fact, he believed that even Gandhi's worst enemies would admit that Gandhi enriched the world simply by being alive. At the same time, Orwell rejected Gandhi's life view of *abstention*, convinced that it did not promote human welfare or compassionate relationships but rather mirrored the baseline assumption that the

---

[42]Orwell's reflections on Gandhi have been reproduced in vol. 4 of Sonia Orwell and Ian Angus, eds., *The Collected Essays, Journalism, and Letters of George Orwell*, 4 vols. (New York: Harcourt Brace Jovanovich, 1968).
[43]Ibid., 469.
[44]Reinhold Niebuhr, *Christianity and Power Politics* (New York: Scribner's, 1940), 8.

temporal world, as we know it, is something from which to be *escaped*. Such a view of ultimate reality, Orwell insisted, is inhumane.[45] But Gandhi's asceticism was the least of Orwell's concerns. The much more weighty issue was Gandhi's view that German Jews ought to commit collective suicide, thereby "arousing the world" to Hitler's violence.

Orwell is by no means the only commentator to shudder at Gandhi's moral detachment. In *Just and Unjust Wars*, Michael Walzer has argued that Gandhi's method is powerless—utterly inefficacious—against tyranny as we have known it in the last century.[46] To illustrate, consider recent estimates of the number of deaths in the twentieth century due to conventional war—about 30 million—compared with those deaths due to *political tyranny and totalitarianism*—between 100 and 200 million. (The estimate by Stephane Courtois et al. in the introduction to *The Black Book of Communism*[47] is at around 100 million.[48] The estimate of military historian Robert Conquest in his book *Reflections on a Ravaged Century*[49] is in the 170 million range.) Truly, the stench of death surrounding Marxist-Leninist ideology is extraordinary. The total estimate, in any case, dwarfs Nazism's remarkable achievement within a shorter span of years of approximately 25 million deaths, based on our current reckoning. We find ourselves powerless to grasp the significance of 100 million *or* 25 million deaths. Such figures boggle the mind. And yet we *dare not* grow numb to their reality, much of which has occurred within our lifetime. These grim realities remain before us and exist both for our benefit and for that of future generations, to teach us and to humble us. The "just warrior" such as Walzer understands this. Doubtless, Orwell understood this as well.

But if we may leave out of the discussion, for the moment, the 100–200 million people in the twentieth century who were offered up to Communist ideology, let us focus briefly on the Jewish Holocaust. Where is the efficacy of Gandhi's nonviolent pacifism as it aids European Jews and ethnic minorities? What specifically might we conclude

[45]Gandhi labeled close friendships "dangerous" since loyalty can lead a person into wrongdoing. While Orwell grants this possibility, he is inclined to believe rather that nonattachment has its roots in a desire to escape from the pain of living, since the business of loving others is genuinely hard work.
[46]Walzer's critique of Gandhi's pacifism is part of a larger commentary on nonresistance in *Just and Unjust Wars*, 4th ed. (New York: Basic Books, 2006), 332–33.
[47]Trans. J. Murphy and M. Kramer (Cambridge, MA: Harvard University Press, 1999).
[48]The authors' rough breakdown is as follows: U.S.S.R., 20 million; China, 65 million; Vietnam, 1 million; Cambodia, 2 million; North Korea, 2 million; Eastern Europe, 1 million; Latin America, 150,000; Africa, 1.7 million; Afghanistan, 1.5 million.
[49]New York: W.W. Norton, 2001.

from Gandhi's rather perverse advice to the Jews of Germany, namely, that they should *commit suicide rather than fight back against Nazi tyranny*? Is this the moral path? As Walzer poignantly remarks, in Gandhi's case, nonviolence "collapses into violence directed at oneself rather than at one's murderers."[50]

C. S. Lewis would seem to agree with Orwell and Walzer. In his view, pacifism, if it does not clothe itself in martyrdom, in the end is self-defeating.[51] But ask any Jew who was liberated by American tanks and Allied forces at the end of World War II. He or she knows that force *can* be a moral entity. In the end, we are not particularly drawn to Gandhi's vision but rather are inclined to agree with Walzer that something *must be done* proactively to resist evil. The more responsible position, it seems to us, is that of Augustine, for whom war and conquest were a sad necessity in the eyes of men of principle because of the presence of evil in the temporal world. The alternative, he believed, would be even more unfortunate if unjust men should dominate the just.[52] For this reason, Augustine insisted upon the necessity of a justly ordered peace.

Referring to events of the Second World War, Reinhold Niebuhr reminded his audience of the need "to bear witness to the truth of Christ against the secular substitutes . . . which failed to anticipate, and which may have helped to create, the tragic world in which we now live."[53] Wartime experience, as he saw it, presented us with an "opportunity to bring the truth of the Word of God to bear upon the secular roots of our present predicament."[54] Niebuhr believed that war is an expression of "divine judgment . . . visited upon men and nations"—a visitation that reveals the anthropological folly of "human progress" and human goodness, as well as the ideological folly of absolute pacifism. The issue of war, as Niebuhr saw it, forces us to reconsider our basic theological assumptions about human nature, the problem of evil, the ordering of society, and the implications of neighbor love.

What moral thinkers from Augustine to Aquinas to Reinhold Niebuhr and C. S. Lewis share in common is a type of realism about

---

[50]*Just and Unjust Wars*, 332.
[51]C. S. Lewis, "Why I Am Not a Pacifist," in *The Weight of Glory and Other Addresses*, rev. ed., ed. Walter Hooper (New York: Macmillan, 1980), 33–53.
[52]*The City of God* 4.12.
[53]*Christian Realism and Political Problems* (New York: Scribner's, 1953), 105.
[54]Ibid., 106.

human nature that counters the idealism of the world's ideologies (secular or religious), notwithstanding the nonviolent witness of Gandhi. "This, then, is why I am not a Pacifist," concluded Lewis. "If I tried to become one, I should find a very doubtful factual basis, an obscure train of reasoning, a weight of authority both human and Divine against me, and strong grounds for suspecting that my wishes had directed my decision." The "nonviolent" vision of Gandhi suggests to these mainstream moral thinkers through the ages an incongruity, since for pacifism to be a universal moral obligation it must be prescribed *for all or for none at all.*[55]

Recall Gandhi's rather distressing counsel to Jews of the Holocaust: they should *commit suicide rather than resist Nazi tyranny.* Regardless of the moral fiber that supported Gandhi's pacifist convictions, the proper moral response to the Jews—indeed to any oppressed people—is that of a wise man uttered three millennia ago:

> If you faint in the day of adversity,
>   your strength is small.
> Rescue those who are being taken away to death;
>   hold back those who are stumbling to the slaughter.
> If you say, "Behold, we did not know this,"
>   does not he who weighs the heart perceive it?
> Does not he who keeps watch over your soul know it,
>   and will he not repay man according to his work?
>   (Prov. 24:10–12 ESV)

Q. 96 Isn't pacifism a legitimate position for the religious believer who takes seriously his or her faith?

Much religious thought in our day has difficulty bridging the gap between personal conviction and public policy, between private, subjective experience and the public, social ramifications of living in the world. In truth this is a not a new challenge. To be fair, the tension between reconciling the personal and the public is a perennial issue and cannot merely be dismissed. Consider, by way of illustration, the words of Jesus, "Render to Caesar the things

---

[55]Lewis, "Why I Am Not a Pacifist," 53.

that are Caesar's, and to God the things that are God's" (Mark 12:17 ESV). They induce no less tension in any era, even when the cultural climate might vary.

It is because of this abiding tension that books such as H. Richard Niebuhr's classic *Christ and Culture*[56] are so important. They attempt, even in their imperfect way, to help us think about the relationship between faith and culture—a relationship that, at best, is tenuous. Many have followed the lead of Tertullian, whose famous rhetorical question "What does Athens have to do with Jerusalem?"—a question that has been asked by every generation of Christians—was answered in no uncertain terms. We will *not* be judged on the last day on the basis of how well we were culturally assimilated; we *will* be judged on the basis of Christ and our faith in him. Therefore, we can live in a detached sense of holiness, preserved in our Christian communities, remaining faithful to the end. Leave the business of tending the culture—a rather *messy* business indeed—to the Gentiles.

But is this the way to understand Jesus' reminder that we are "in the world but not of the world"?[57] Two generations removed, theologian John Courtney Murray reflected much on the tension between the private and the public. What bothered him in particular was the manner in which many religious Americans think about private and public morality. Approaches to morality in America, he observed, were predisposed unduly toward individualism, detachment, and subjectivism—a tendency that he believed to be especially acute among Protestants. As he saw it, this has deleterious effects on the Christian community's ability to contend for moral principle in the public arena, since public morality is not merely "the sum of private moralities."[58] Individualism's shortcomings are multiple and serious: it does not understand the special moral problems raised by human institutions; it fails to grasp the nature of politics and political values, as well as the limitations of political action; it has little sense of the differential character of morality and legality; relatedly, it is unable to develop a theory of jurisprudence; it lacks the moral resources and ability to

---

[56]New York: Harper, 1951. For current interaction with the ideas of this work, see D. A. Carson, *Christ and Culture Revisited* (Grand Rapids: Eerdmans, 2008).
[57]Cf. John 17:13–19.
[58]John Courtney Murray, *We Hold These Truths: Catholic Reflections on the American Proposition* (New York: Sheed and Ward, 1960), 277.

make moral discriminations; and, in consequence, it lacks the ability to understand and deal with public crime.[59]

There is something to be said for these concerns. They cannot simply be brushed aside as some sort of anti-Protestant rant. A recurring theme in Murray's critique is the tendency in much Christian thinking to conflate the Sermon on the Mount with public policy, that is, to confuse issues of personal discipleship with issues of statecraft. In the context of both public policy and biblical interpretation, the results are not only hermeneutically bad but ethically untenable.

Pacifism may be a dictate of the individual conscience, as it is among Christians past and present, but it must not be public policy.[60] Recall a previous question in which we observed that even Ambrose and Augustine, while they were pacifists privately and thus foreswore self-defense, nevertheless understood the distinction between private attitudes and public policy. Both, as private pacifists, could argue for the necessity of morally guided coercive force on behalf of others. When an innocent third party enters a scenario of conflict, the moral equation changes. Jesus does not say, "When a person slaps your friend on the cheek, turn to the offender his other cheek." You may be free to turn *your own* other cheek; you are *not* free to turn *that of your neighbor*. There is a difference between insult and assault. Nor does the parable of the Good Samaritan teach, by extrapolation, that the Samaritan was good because he waited until *after* the victim was mugged and robbed to assist him.[61]

In wrestling with the nature of Christian love, and the attendant duties that issue out of neighbor love, ethicist Paul Ramsey reflects at great length on seeking the other's well-being and loving others "as yourself." Of course, it is well known that self-giving has been the object of much philosophical speculation—from Plato to Nietzsche to Fromm and even to certain postmodern theorists. But Ramsey explores in a very useful and necessary way the implications of

---

[59]Ibid.

[60]Were pacifism, in fact, permitted to become public policy, then the New Testament *inter alia* would be read as a charter of political action, and we would be justified in asking questions such as, What then is the will of God for this nation's policy directives? Murray, *We Hold These Truths*, deftly handles the incongruities of this line of reasoning.

[61]No one has pressed this argument, using precisely these two scriptural illustrations, more effectively and lucidly than Paul Ramsey. See, in particular, his *Basic Christian Ethics*, esp. chaps. 3 ("The Meaning of Christian Love") and 5 ("Christian Vocation"). These two chapters inform Ramsey's work elsewhere, notably *War and Christian Conscience: How Shall Modern War Be Conducted Justly?* (Durham, NC: Duke University Press, 1961), and his massive *The Just War: Force and Political Responsibility* (New York: Scribner's, 1968).

a healthy self-love that is tethered to a love for God. At bottom, the neighbor in traumatic need must not be bypassed; rather, his highest good must be desired. This is not because he shares my Christian faith; it is because he is made in the image of God. The implications of this baseline conviction can scarcely be overstated, especially when we attempt to think about and formulate responsible public policy.

At the most practical level, it will mean what Ramsey calls a "preferential ethics of protection" for the neighbor. Let us recapitulate: Jesus, when he was alone, turned the other cheek when he was smitten and abused, he did not respond in kind, and he died without any self-defense. This was his bilateral response. So far, so good. But without distorting the New Testament text, Ramsey quite properly demonstrates aspects of a multilateral ethics of protection even in Jesus' own earthly ministry: "On occasion he showed indignation, even wrath, over injustice, using vitriolic words as weapons against the devourers of widows' houses (Luke 20:47). He was unsparing in his condemnation of the complacency of Israel's religious leaders."[62] And *unsparing* is the proper term to describe his "cleansing" of the temple. Whether the whip that Jesus used to drive the money changers was made of this or that material is irrelevant, and whether Jesus whipped people, animals, or both is also irrelevant. The whip *was* in fact used, and the Son of Man waxed *forcefully indignant*. This most assuredly does not fit the profile of the ideological pacifist, for in truth it qualifies as forceful, even violent, resistance.

However, whether Jesus forcibly resisted or not, this point is decidedly secondary. If we are seeking to identify an absolutist nonviolence mandate in the teaching of Jesus, we might also expect to find confirmation in the rest of the New Testament, especially in the teaching of John the Baptist, whose role as messianic "forerunner" was to call people to *repentance*. Alas, we are disappointed. Regarding the Baptist's teaching, the account found in Luke's Gospel is of particular interest, noting that soldiers are warned along two principal ethical lines (Luke 3:14). They are commanded not to extort money and not to accuse people falsely. These prohibitions, conjoined to yet a third— that soldiers are to be content with their wages—might strike us as rather surprising if we presume that, based on the call to discipleship and repentance, the Baptist and Jesus would summon men *away from*

---

[62]*Basic Christian Ethics*, 169.

vocational military service. In the end, neither Jesus nor John the Baptist nor the apostles called soldiers away from military service. Why? Surely, this might be viewed as a great omission, especially in the context of Christian proclamation, of which repentance is a prerequisite. In fact, when Jesus and the apostle Peter encounter soldiers, they commend them roundly for their faith.[63] This institutional participation in the military cannot merely be brushed aside as compromise with the political powers, as pacifist critics are inclined to suggest of those in the early church who served.

But the committed pacifist is likely to reply that Jesus went to the cross in a mode of passive nonresistance, as a "lamb." And so he did. In responding to this challenge, we are justified in making the distinction between the road of the Son of God as Messiah and Savior, and that of his followers. His path was instrumentally salvific; ours is not. His was a unique, once-for-all atonement for sin; ours is not. According to Ambrose, Christ would not have received defense against the wounds inflicted by his persecutors because he understood his mission, which was *to heal all through his own wounds*.[64] The path that Christ took, then, is not identical to ours, even when the writers of the New Testament call us to emulate the attitudes of Christ.

In his pastoral treatise *On the Duties of the Clergy*, Ambrose uses multiple illustrations to show the importance of the cardinal virtues and how deeply Christian they are. Not unlike ethicist Paul Ramsey closer to our time, he too advances a type of preferential ethics of protection toward his neighbor. One such illustration involves a Christian traveling with a friend. When the two encounter a robber along the way, the Christian is justified in returning blows as a legitimate means by which to defend his neighbor.

Augustine stands in fundamental agreement. Presupposing a situation in which an assassin is lying in wait, he reasons that a soldier is both commanded by the law and justified in slaying the enemy. Despite his personal renunciation of self-defense, Augustine reasons: "It is much better that one who plots against another's life should be killed rather than one who is defending his own life. A soldier who kills the enemy is acting as an agent of the law, so he can easily perform his duty without inordinate desire."[65] In the end, Augustine is able to discern

---

[63]See, e.g., Matt. 8:5–13; Luke 7:1–10; Acts 10:1–48.
[64]*On the Duties of the Clergy* 3.4.
[65]Augustine, *On Free Choice of the Will*, trans. T. Williams (Indianapolis: Hackett, 1993), 8.

the moral and social difference between private conviction (abstaining from self-defense) and public policy as an "ethics of protection."[66]

Protection of the public and of public goods, which assumes the necessity of "the sword," is not only not contrary to the teaching of the New Testament, but fully consonant with its teaching. Such, for example, is the plain meaning of Paul's teaching in Romans 13 (cf. 1 Pet. 2:13–17).[67] And what needs emphasis is that Paul's teaching on the function of political authority in Romans 13 in no way contradicts his teaching against a retaliatory spirit in Romans 12. While public protection and public defense of justice are by no means the *sole* means by which to demonstrate charity, they are most assuredly one legitimate means of doing so. Ask anyone involved in law enforcement.

Q. 97   In light of Jesus' call to "peacemaking," doesn't the New Testament require pacifism of the Christian disciple?

Certainly, standard accounts of the early church's pacifism are not without biblical justification. They proceed on the assumption that the ethics of Jesus was one of love and nonviolence. Beginning with the admonition to be peacemakers (Matt. 5:9), this view anchors itself in a reading of the Sermon of the Mount that understands Jesus' call as a call to nonretaliation and nonviolence. The resultant interpretation of Matthew 5:38–42 is that Jesus renders obsolete the *lex talionis* or "eye for eye" principle set forth in the Old Testament and that he intends the imperatives "do not resist an evil person" and "turn the other cheek" as flat and universal prohibitions of force.

Without question, the matter of retaliation challenges Christian ethics as few issues, then and now. This exhortation in Matthew 5 is placed among six case illustrations by which Jesus is reinterpreting the law. Notice what introduces this body of teaching. A common misperception about ethical living and the basis for ethics seems to persist.

---

[66] While some Christian thinkers—among them, Aquinas, Luther, and Ramsey—take Ambrose and Augustine to task for their personal views on self-defense, this concern is for us decidedly secondary.

[67] To the ideological pacifist, who chafes under the interpretation that "the sword" (the *ius gladii*) is to be understood in its more literal sense, we would simply observe that the Petrine admonitions (like their Pauline counterpart in Romans 13) are remarkably uncritical and unqualified of political authority. Moreover, first-century readers of either Romans or 1 Peter most assuredly would *not* have understood the image figuratively.

"Do not think that I have come," he warns the audience, "to abolish the Law or the Prophets; I have not come to abolish them but to fulfill them" (Matt. 5:17; see also 7:12). This declaration is framed in a clearly ethical context: the disciples' "good deeds" are to be concrete and visible to others—not hidden—and in this way glorifying to God (5:13–16). Furthermore, the righteousness of the disciples must exceed Pharisaical measures (5:20). The six case illustrations that follow, then, serve to drive home Jesus' teaching in a concrete manner. Significantly, each of the six is introduced with the rabbinic *kelal* or formulaic key, "You have heard it said. . . . But I tell you . . . ," suggesting that certain popular misunderstandings need to be exposed and rectified.

As in each of the other case illustrations, Jesus' teaching on retaliation (5:38–43) does not set aside the ethical core of the commandment; rather, Jesus shows that the violation of the commandment begins in the heart with an improper attitude and is manifest in one's practice. Contrary to much existing commentary, the *lex talionis* as a measure of just retribution is *not* being set aside by Jesus, since its intended purpose was to *limit* retribution based on proportionality. Justice demands that no more than what is proportionate to the offense be required. Moreover, private citizens could not extract retribution; rather, that was the responsibility of the judges (Deut. 19:15–21; cf. Rom. 12:17–21 and 13:1–10). By Jesus' day, rabbinic reinterpretation of "just rewards" for personal injury, which was calculated monetarily, had become illegitimate. Jesus corrects a misuse of the *lex talionis*, rather than abolishing the "law of the tooth" per se.

Just as important is the framing of the commands that follow. Not resisting evil and turning the other cheek (5:39) are contextualized among several instances of personal injury. Note the other three: the loss of an article of clothing, being conscripted to walk a second mile (in all likelihood, applying to soldiers forcing civilians to carry their gear), and lending to the person wishing to borrow. Each of these situations of daily life is personal, and all of them mirror issues of discipleship, not statecraft or policy. In terms of emphasis, then, Matthew 5–7 finds a parallel in the latter part of Romans 12, which addresses Christians' relationship to the world—specifically, handling personal injury or insult. To conflate the Sermon on the Mount and its parallel, Romans 12:17–21, with Romans 13—that is, to fail to distinguish the context and the qualification of justice properly and improperly applied—is to confuse the personal and the political. Indeed, it is to do violence to the New Testament text and to Christian social ethics.[68]

But this interpretation alone, important as it is to the teaching of our Lord as recorded in the Gospel narratives, does not suffice. Whatever we deduce from Jesus' teaching must be in accord with the teaching of his forerunner, who called men to repentance. What light does John the Baptist shed on military service, war and peace, and coercive force?

The Protestant Reformers generally held the vocation of military service to be both honorable and necessary. As evidence, Luther cites John the Baptist. When soldiers come to him with questions, the Baptist neither condemns their vocation nor calls them out of military service; rather, he exhorts them toward justice and contentment. Luther distinguishes between abuse of the office and the nature of the office itself (Luke 3).[69]

Calvin, in underscoring the nature of political authority, observes that it is the mandate of the ruler and the nature of his office "not only to restrain the misdeeds of private individuals by judicial punishments, but also to defend by war the dominions entrusted to their safekeeping, if at any time they are under enemy attack."[70] Calvin anticipates the objection. He reasons that if we object that the New Testament contains nothing permitting Christian participation in military service or war, then John the Baptist presents for us an obstacle. Why? If Christian participation in all warring is illegitimate, then the soldiers who seek out the Baptist, insists Calvin, would be directed *of necessity* to throw away their arms and leave their profession. But, to the contrary, they are admonished to do two things: act justly and be content with their wages. Military life, he concludes, is not at all prohibited.[71]

Hugo Grotius, the seventeenth-century Dutch legal theorist of deep Christian conviction, who is considered the father of international law, reasons in much the same way. The author of the magisterial work *The Law of War and Peace*—written in the wake of the Thirty Years War,

---

[68]It is significant that Ambrose, Augustine, Aquinas, Luther, and Grotius all cite popular misinterpretation in their day of the Sermon on the Mount, and Matt. 5:38–42 in particular. They all make the distinction between personal and public grievances, between matters of the heart and matters of state. All agree that the Christian must resist evil to protect others, even when the form of this resistance will vary and depend on the particular situation. And all are concerned about the common weal, which is invigorated by Christians' civic responsibility.

[69]*Whether Soldiers, Too, Can Be Saved* (L.W. 46:97); cf. *Temporal Authority* (L.W. 45:98).

[70]John Calvin, *Institutes of the Christian Religion*, ed. John T. McNeill, trans. Ford Lewis Battles (Philadelphia: Westminster Press, 1960), 4.20.11.

[71]Ibid. Luther stands in fundamental agreement with Calvin in this regard, as evidenced by his treatise *Whether Soldiers, Too, Can Be Saved.*

which decimated much of Europe—Grotius, like Calvin, ponders why the soldiers coming to John the Baptist do not renounce their military calling as inconsistent with the will of God. Grotius is struck by the fact that right motives, rather, are enjoined by the greatest Prophet who ever lived, whose message is *repentance and preparation* for the kingdom of God.[72]

With Luther, Calvin, and Grotius, we also might ponder the Lukan account describing the Baptist's encounter with soldiers (3:7–14). All of the Synoptic accounts frame John's work and message in terms of repentance. The demands of the Baptist are unflinchingly ethical: "Produce fruit in keeping with repentance!" (3:8). When some soldiers ask, "And what should we do?" John replies, "Do not extort money and don't accuse people falsely—be content with your pay" (3:14). But in addition to John the Baptist, we are justified in asking why neither Jesus nor the apostles call soldiers away from their vocation as an expression of their faith (Matt. 8:5–13; Luke 7:2–10; Acts 10:1–11:18). Surely, this omission is no mere oversight on their part.

Jesus' statements as recorded in Matthew 5:9 and 5:39 are to be understood alongside Romans 12:17–21. Jesus and Paul are proscribing *a vengeful spirit*, which is an improper application of the *lex talionis*. That is to say, we do not take justice into our own hands; rather, we are to be conciliatory by nature. Retribution, however, is not only permitted but *required* by the authorities for the common social good. Peacemaking, then, is not at odds with the work of justice. Neither is coercive force per se evil. Rather, it takes on the moral character of those applying it.

Q. 98   Aren't strife and conflict always sinful, the product of the human heart?

While this question would seem to grant the reality of human depravity, it raises the question of moral intention. Human strife is indeed inevitable, and clearly strife is a fruit of the flesh.[73] Aquinas takes up this very question in his discus-

---

[72]*The Law of War and Peace* 2.6–7.
[73]Cf. Gal. 5:20.

sion of whether war is always wrong. He grants that based on the teaching of the New Testament, it would seem that strife is always a sin if we understand strife as a form of contention, being quarrelsome, a private "warring" as it were with others that emanates from hatred and inordinate will. So, on the one hand, strife is always a sin where it manifests hatred, contradiction, contentiousness, and provocation. Fighting, of course, can mirror what Aquinas calls our "irascible contrariety," and Augustine acknowledges that war is often the manifestation of our violent lusts, cravings for power, and desire for vengeance.

But Aquinas also acknowledges that a response to provocation is not *in itself* sinful. The rightness of deeds is related to their moral intention. Self-defense and punishment are not the same as contention or strife. To be resolved to *quell strife* is not to delight in fighting. Therefore, conflict or war that is declared by a legitimate authority in response to a grievous injustice and that is motivated to secure a lasting or better peace than existed previously cannot rightly be declared sinful.[74] One can enter conflict for a noble or an ignoble purpose, armed with the proper or improper motivation.

Just-war reasoning in the Christian moral tradition proceeds on the assumption that charity—that is, love for one's neighbor—can motivate us. It can inspire what ethicist Paul Ramsey called a "preferential ethics of protection."[75] This is a discriminating love that distinguishes between guilt and innocence, justice and injustice, honor and shame. It loves others "as ourselves," in Jesus' words, which is to say, it has the neighbor's highest good in mind rather than being motivated by utilitarian self-interest or "seeking its own."[76] In Christian social ethics, the neighbor may not be bypassed (cf. Luke 10:25–37). The Samaritan was "good" precisely because of what he did in the way of sacrificial love. The point of the parable was to reveal intention. Jesus' admonition is to "go and do likewise" (v. 37). The neighbor in need, a fellow human being, is not to be bypassed. On rare occasions it *may* even be necessary to defend him by means of coercive and measured force.

---

[74]This discussion is found in Aquinas *S.T.* II-II Q. 41.
[75]*Basic Christian Ethics*, 166–84.
[76]For this reason the Christian may not invoke the sword for himself or his own cause, but he may invoke it on behalf of others for the purposes of hindering evil and helping others. This is the difference between *duellum* and *bellum*.

Q. 99   How did C. S. Lewis view war?

Lewis's views on war sprang out of deep conviction and were tempered by personal experience. As an infantry officer wounded in the First World War, Lewis experienced firsthand the death and devastation wrought by war.[77] Yet he can be understood to stand firmly within the just-war tradition, as his writings indicate. As a matter of conviction, Lewis thought that most people would become confused if they tried to sort out just-war principles and apply them to each real or potential conflict. Therefore, he encouraged citizens and soldiers, especially those of religious faith, to be keenly aware of their responsibilities vis-à-vis unlawful orders. In so doing, not only would they serve the cause of justice, but they would also provide a unified witness of moral principle to the onlooking world.

As to his own position at the time of the Second World War, Lewis declared to one friend: "I'm not a pacifist. If it's got to be it's got to be."[78] Lewis understood war to be a fact of human existence, an evidence of our fallen nature, and thus a part of human history. He believed that although the weapons of war, including nuclear weapons, might become more sophisticated, they do not change the fundamental nature of war or its participants. War, he maintained, accentuates the uncertainties of life and reminds people of the darker side of human nature, but it does not introduce any new dynamics into daily life.

In a collection of essays under the title *The Weight of Glory*,[79] Lewis asks whether to serve in a war is immoral, morally neutral, or morally obligatory. In posing this question, he realizes that it will require answering a prior question, How do we decide what is good and evil?

The typical answer is that we follow conscience. But conscience, Lewis replies, is not some autonomous faculty; rather, it can be altered by argument and persuasion and can find confirmation in our personal experience. What's more, people may be *mistaken* in the way their conscience perceives right and wrong. This leads Lewis to reason about

---

[77]For a fuller evaluation of Lewis's experiences and reflections on war, see Timothy J. Demy, "Technology, Progress, and the Human Condition in the Life and Thought of C. S. Lewis," (PhD diss., Salve Regina University, 2004), 76–84, 250–67.

[78]W. H. Lewis, ed., *Letters of C. S. Lewis* (London: Geoffrey Bles, 1966; New York: Harcourt, Brace & World, 1966), 166.

[79]C. S. Lewis, "Why I Am Not a Pacifist," in *The Weight of Glory and Other Essays*, rev. ed. (New York: HarperCollins, 2001), 64–90.

reasoning itself as a cognitive process and consider how conscience is formed. The problem, as Lewis sees it, is that very often in the process of formation, people cannot "see" what for others is self-evidently true. What, then, can we do? Nothing, says Lewis, since the supposed inability to see is most often a *refusal* to see.

Lewis does acknowledge that all people possess a moral intuition about basic good and evil. This basic intuition, what he calls the "law of nature" or the *Tao* in other of his works,[80] shows itself, for example, in the fact that all people prefer love over hatred, happiness over misery, and justice over injustice; these are "unarguable" moral facts. Having distinguished between opinion or private experience and morally intuited facts that find verification in all people based on the natural law, Lewis illustrates by way of pacifism. He finds it odd that one can claim, based on some moral sense, that "all killing of human beings is in all circumstances an absolute evil."[81] The one making this claim, Lewis believes, is "mistaking an opinion, or, more likely, a passion," for a moral intuition.[82]

How, then, Lewis wishes to know, do we decide on a question of morals? Moral judgment, he believes, depends on the meeting of facts, intuition, and reasoning, seasoned with a bit of humility. The result, to be sure, will not approximate mathematical certainty. But it will, hopefully, allow us to "reason." What, then, may we say about war that is fairly certain? For one thing, all people agree that war is horrible; this is noncontroversial. But does war do more harm than good? And how might that be measured? Lewis leaves nothing to be taken for granted. He asks whether, in fact, wars—modern wars—achieve no good, and whether they cause greater harm than good in all cases. Would Europe be better, he asks, had it submitted to Germany in 1914? On this test, he confesses, he finds the pacifist position weak, since a Germanized Europe from 1914 onward more than likely would have been evil.

At the personal level, Lewis wonders whether violence can ever be done to individuals in a manner that is lawful. If violence is always immoral, then can criminals be subjugated and punished by society? Unless violence generically can be shown universally to be wrong, then one may conclude that good people everywhere will differ, say, on the question of capital punishment. The implications for war become

---

[80]These terms are used in *Mere Christianity* and *The Abolition of Man*.
[81]Lewis, "Why I Am Not a Pacifist," 71.
[82]Ibid.

apparent. For Lewis, the belief that war is always the greater evil implies a materialist ethic. That is, it proceeds on the assumption that death and pain are the greatest of all evils. But Lewis doubts that this is true. All people die, he notes, and some in great misery. Of course, Lewis readily grants that war is awful and that it can spawn evil. But the question for him is whether war is the *greatest* evil.

Lewis also wonders why only liberal societies tolerate pacifists. Totalitarian states do not tolerate them, and yet it is precisely those states that need the pacifist influence. What does this suggest? At the very least, Lewis concludes, it does not suggest that war must or should be abolished. Those who do make calls for the abolition of war, as he sees it, tend to assume that "the great permanent miseries in human life must be curable if only we can find the right cure."[83] But more often than not, Lewis finds, the utopian "fanaticism" of "Marxists, Freudians, Eugenists, Spiritualists . . . , and all the rest" is the fruit of such thinking. And from these people, Lewis notes, "I have received no assurance that anything we can do will eradicate suffering."[84]

Finally, Lewis is perplexed that so many cultural authorities—literary, religious, and social—seem to make a strong case *against* rather than for pacifism. What's more, he takes seriously the light of religious revelation. He finds, as an Anglican, that the Thirty-Nine Articles declare it "lawful" for Christian men, in service to their society, to bear weapons and serve in wars. Moreover, the history of the church is such that its fathers collectively teach the legitimacy of the sword being used by the magistrate to protect the common weal. Why is this?

Given these consensual voices, on what then does the case for pacifism rest? This is the question that vexes Lewis. Ultimately, the entire case for pacifism, as he understands it, appears to rest on a certain statement by our Lord, "Do no resist an evil person. If someone strikes you on the right cheek, turn to him the other also" (Matt. 5:39). But does this statement not need qualification? Lewis thinks it does, believing that it can be interpreted in three ways. One is to say that it imposes a universal duty of nonresistance on all people in all circumstances. Another is that these words by Jesus are spoken as hyperbole. A third is to say that our Lord is addressing the daily trials that attend

---

[83]Ibid., 79.
[84]Ibid.

Christian discipleship, and that the disciple is being cautioned not to react out of a retaliatory, vengeful spirit toward others. In reflecting on these three options and the intended meaning of Matthew 5:38–39, Lewis asks rhetorically, "Does anyone suppose that Our Lord's hearers understood Him to mean that if a homicidal maniac, attempting to murder a third party, tried to knock me out of the way, I must stand aside and let him get his victim?"[85] Lewis thinks it impossible. "War was not what His hearers would have been thinking of," he concludes. Rather, the "frictions of daily life among villagers" were more than likely to be on the hearers' minds.[86] Not only is this for Lewis the more natural reading of Matthew, but

> it harmonises better with St. John [the] Baptist's words to the soldiers and with the fact that one of the few persons whom Our Lord praised without reservation was a Roman centurion. It also allows me to suppose that the New Testament is consistent with itself. St. Paul approves of the magistrate's use of the sword (Romans 13:4) and so does St. Peter (1 Peter 2:14).[87]

In the end, Lewis concedes, "This, then, is why I am not a Pacifist." There are simply too many impediments.

> If I tried to become one, I should find a very doubtful factual basis, an obscure train of reasoning, a weight of authority both human and Divine against me, and strong grounds for suspecting that my wishes had directed my decision. . . . It may be, after all, that Pacifism is right. But it seems to me very long odds, longer odds than I would care to take with the voice of almost all humanity against me.[88]

At a deeper level, Lewis believes that war encourages individuals to think about death and the afterlife. The temporal concerns of war direct the attention of people to the spiritual and eternal concerns of immortality. War makes death real to us, he writes in the essay "Learning in Wartime."[89] Keeping death in proper perspective, for

---

[85]Ibid., 86.
[86]Ibid., 86–87.
[87]Ibid., 88.
[88]Ibid., 88, 90.
[89]C. S. Lewis, "Learning in Wartime," in *The Weight of Glory and Other Essays* (New York: HarperCollins, 2001), 47–63.

Lewis, serves as a perpetual reminder of a marred and broken world because of sin.

Q. 100 What about Dietrich Bonhoeffer's example? How are we to reconcile his attraction to pacifism with his willingness to participate in the attempt on Hitler's life?

Trying to interpret Dietrich Bonhoeffer's experience represents a challenge to all, and this for myriad reasons. More broadly, Bonhoeffer (1906–1945) has provided inspiration for all kinds of political theology. For example, some of his admirers have been liberation theologians, utilizing him in order to justify violence. Others, in bald contrast, have advocated in his name passive resistance and absolute pacifism, and not without some justification, given Bonhoeffer's admiration of Gandhi's pacifism and his argument for self-renunciation in *The Cost of Discipleship*. But part of our challenge subsists in the fact that we find nothing definitive or conclusive in Bonhoeffer's writings of his rationale for resistance that might reconcile the tension we encounter in Bonhoeffer's life. Thus, in approaching the above question we readily acknowledge that no pat answer will suffice; one can only offer a reasoned conjecture.

And yet, as one historian observes, resistance does not occur unless persons actually intend to resist.[90] Such restating the obvious is necessary, given that people with diverse theological motives wish to co-opt Bonhoeffer for their own purposes. In attempting to understand Bonhoeffer's ultimate decision to participate in a plot to forcibly remove Hitler, we are dependent on two primary threads of understanding. One is to consider the formative influences on Bonhoeffer's political and theological thinking that inform his values, and the other is to cull the volume edited by his former student and friend Eberhard Bethge, *Letters and Papers from Prison*,[91] in which not only theological conviction, set in vignette form, but also private musings are on display. These brief, edited reflections before his death, in composite form, pro-

---

[90]So Raymond Mengus, "Dietrich Bonhoeffer and the Decision to Resist," *Journal of Modern History* 64, supp. (December 1992): S134–46.
[91]We are drawing from the enlarged edition of *Letters and Papers from Prison*, ed. Eberhard Bethge, rev. ed. (New York: Macmillan, 1971).

vide a helpful context in which to understand Bonhoeffer's actions.[92] But a bit of history behind the history will help us appreciate more fully the evolution of Bonhoeffer's thought.

Nothing in his youth suggests a predilection toward either resistance or pacifist nonresistance, although Bonhoeffer did lose an older brother in World War I and in time was increasingly inclined toward pacifism. The son of a well-respected psychiatrist, Bonhoeffer came from a family that was reasonably, though not excessively, patriotic. Having completed his *Habilitation* in Berlin in 1929, Bonhoeffer traveled to the U.S. in the fall of 1930 to study at Union Theological Seminary,[93] where he came under the influence of Reinhold Niebuhr. Niebuhr prodded Bonhoeffer toward the conviction that Christian ethics must find expression in categories that are socially useful, not merely pietistic.[94] This emphasis, as it turns out, would have enduring effects. In Bonhoeffer's thought, Niebuhr's influence stands alongside that of Swiss theologian Karl Barth, who played a critical role in the formation of "the Confessing Church" in Germany and who helped draft the Barmen Declaration in May of 1934. Both Barth and Bonhoeffer would reject the idolatrous accent on German nationalist theology, which would place both theologians at odds with much of German Protestantism. And both theologians, in our view, refrained from discussing the possibilities and conditions of justifiable armed conflict out of the fear that others would utilize those discussions to normalize the extraordinary.[95]

Two further elements must be factored into Bonhoeffer's theological outlook. One is the conjunction and reciprocity between justification and justice, on display in his work *Rechtfertigung und Recht*. A second is the matter of the "Jewish Question." That Bonhoeffer's pastor during his student days was half-Jewish and that a Jew married his sister heightened his awareness of the dilemma that shaped an understanding of the demands of justice. Bonhoeffer's dilemma,

---

[92]That *Letters and Papers from Prison* differs greatly in format from volumes such as *The Cost of Discipleship* and *Ethics* does not diminish what can mined from these brief writings.

[93]For a few months in 1939, six years after the National Socialists assumed and consolidated power, Bonhoeffer left Germany for America with a view to exposing Nazi pretensions externally. In a strange twist of fate, however, he returned to Germany to assume the significant risks that internal resistance to National Socialism would mean.

[94]Bonhoeffer writes that Protestant pietism is "a last attempt to maintain evangelical Christianity as a religion" (*Letters and Papers from Prison*, 381).

[95]In support of our position, see the fascinating essay by Oliver O'Donovan, "Karl Barth and Ramsey's 'Uses of Power,'" in Oliver O'Donovan and Joan Lockwood O'Donovan, *Bonds of Imperfection* (Grand Rapids: Eerdmans, 2003).

in time, became twofold: (1) What, therefore, should Christians' attitudes be toward Jews? (2) What does the responsible Christian do in the face of a morally illegitimate governmental regime?

In posing the question "Who stands fast?" Bonhoeffer struggles with the Christian response to the problem of evil. Several responses are for him unsatisfactory. One is what he calls the "reasonable" response. Given its naïve lack of realism about human nature (i.e., human propensity for evil), the "reasonable" person is unable to marshal the proper resources to engage moral evil and consequentially collapses into ineffectiveness. Still more pathetic to Bonhoeffer is fanaticism. The fanatic, like a bull that lacks wisdom and good discernment, rushes headlong into the red cloak, as it were, rather than the target, eventually exhausting himself in his ineffectiveness as well. Then there is the person who takes flight from public altercation and retreats into the realm of private virtue. This person will necessarily have to shut his eyes to the injustice around him, and only at the cost of self-deception can he maintain purity from the world of contamination. In contrast, there is the person of conscience who is willing to sacrifice. This person fights, even against great odds, with little or no support from others, but in the knowledge that duty, based on moral principle, holds him accountable. Authentic faith, at some point, requires responsible action, and Bonhoeffer wonders where the responsible, self-sacrificing people are in his own day.

In the same vein, Bonhoeffer ponders why among his countrymen there is a "dearth of civil courage." This is particularly perplexing for him, given the more recent history of the German people, a history that taught them the necessity of being brave, self-sacrificing, and obedient. But in learning such, many Germans did not realize the extent to which these qualities could be exploited for evil ends. Totalitarianism exposed these misplaced commitments as fundamentally flawed, preventing many Germans from engaging in responsible, morally guided action when it was needed. Bonhoeffer is left to conclude that there are situations in which true faith and moral fiber require bold action. It might be said that Bonhoeffer develops a "theology of righteous action," which leads to his active participation in the conspiracy to overthrow the *Führerstaat*.[96] In a farewell letter to Reinhold Niebuhr,

---

[96]So Dirk van Hoogstraten, "The Enemy and Righteous Action: A Hermeneutical Assessment," in John W. de Gruchy, ed., *Bonhoeffer for a New Day: Theology in a Time of Transition* (Grand Rapids: Eerdmans, 1997), 175–89; and John A. Moses, "Dietrich Bonhoeffer as Conspirator against the Hitler

written in June of 1939 following his brief visit to the U.S., Bonhoeffer writes:

> Christians in Germany will face the terrible alternative of either willing the defeat of their nation in order that Christian civilization may survive, or willing the victory of their nation and thereby destroying our civilization. I know which of these alternatives I must choose; but I cannot make that choice in security.[97]

Another small piece to the puzzle that might shed light on Bonhoeffer's "bold action" is a little-noticed reflection on the subject of "sympathy."[98] Herein he laments our "insensibility to the sufferings of others," noting that sympathy tends to grow "only in proportion to the fear of approaching disaster." But, excuse making rather than ethical courage is sadly, in his view, the rule of the day. "No one wants to meet fate head-on." Furthermore, "No one is responsible for all the injustice and suffering in the world, and no one wants to set himself up as the judge of the world." But "from a Christian point of view," he insists, "none of these excuses can obscure the fact that the most important factor, *large-heartedness*, is lacking."[99]

Though we are called to follow Christ, Bonhoeffer deems as necessary one small caveat: "We are certainly not Christ." That is to say, "we are not called on to redeem the world by our own deeds and sufferings, and we need not try to assume such an impossible burden. We are not lords, but instruments in the hand of the Lord of history; and we can share in the other people's sufferings only to a very limited degree." But "if we want to be Christians, we must have some share in Christ's large-heartedness by acting with responsibility and in freedom when the hour of danger comes. . . . Mere waiting and looking on is not Christian behavior." The Christian is "called to sympathy and action," and this calling is prompted by "the sufferings of [our] brethren."[100]

Political ethicist Jean Bethke Elshtain believes that Bonhoeffer refrained from offering any explicit justification for violent resistance because he worried that it might be used to justify situations that were

---

Regime: The Motivation of a German Protestant Revolutionary," *War & Society* 17, no. 1 (1999): 25–40.
[97] *Gesammelte Schriften*, 6 vols. (Munich: Chr. Kaiser, 1965–1974), 1:320.
[98] *Letters and Papers from Prison*, 13–14.
[99] Ibid., 13; emphasis added.
[100] Ibid., 14.

less dire than his own.[101] This explanation is certainly plausible. At the same time, there must also be traces of theological and philosophical justification in Bonhoeffer's personal decision to resort to force that might be detected along the way.[102] Already in the early 1930s, Bonhoeffer was convinced of the inevitability of another war should the Nazis come to power. In his letter to Eberhard Bethge, dated February 21, 1944, he muses: "I've often wondered . . . where we are to draw the line between necessary resistance to 'fate,' and equally necessary submission." The position he reached is that it is "impossible to define the boundary . . . on abstract principles," for both resistance and submission "must exist" and both "must be practiced." Faith, he observes, "demands this elasticity of behaviour. Only so can we stand our ground in each situation as it arises."[103] Thus, it would seem, "resistance" and "submission" for Bonhoeffer can mean different things, depending on the situation, which in the end prevents us from neatly and conclusively categorizing his "pacifism." Several writers and historians have concluded that Bonhoeffer's active resistance—that is, his "righteous action"—was galvanized by his grief over the plight of the Jews. In its "solution" to the "Jewish question," the Third Reich had finally and formally pronounced itself an illegitimate state, exalting itself as the agency of almighty God on earth and derelict of its fundamental duty in the most radical manner possible.[104]

---

[101]See her essay "Bonhoeffer and the Sovereign State," in *First Things* 65 (August–September 1996): 27–30, reproduced in Timothy J. Demy and Gary P. Stewart, eds., *Politics and Public Policy: A Christian Response* (Grand Rapids: Kregel, 2000), 115–21. Elshtain also cites the most obvious reason why Bonhoeffer did not write a justification for violence: his Nazi executioners gave him no time.

[102]This is where a uniformly "pacifist" reading of Bonhoeffer is deficient. It is mindful of Bonhoeffer's call to self-renunciation and Christ's uncontested lordship in *The Cost of Discipleship* or *Ethics*, but it is inclined to gloss over influences in Bonhoeffer's life that are not pacifist (e.g., his correspondence with Reinhold Niebuhr). One effect of this reading, for example, is to confuse the renunciation of self-defense with absolute pacifism, thereby missing a possible application of what Bonhoeffer calls large-heartedness, or empathy, *toward others*: namely, that coercive force motivated by charity in the face of evil *may* be necessary for a greater good and the protection of others. A recent volume on Bonhoeffer might well illustrate. In *What about Hitler? Wrestling with Jesus's Call to Nonviolence in an Evil World* (Grand Rapids: Brazos, 2006), Robert W. Brimlow attempts to make sense of Bonhoeffer's ultimate actions but in the end must conclude that Bonhoeffer simply got it wrong, though Brimlow acknowledges that pacifism in the face of gross evil is ineffectual. Brimlow writes, "I think he erred in how he understood the dilemma . . . Bonhoeffer was wrong in the way he understood the Hitler question" (124). Precisely what the "error" of Bonhoeffer's understanding was Brimlow does not tell us. Brimlow's answer to the question posed in the book's title, *What about Hitler?* is that we do nothing; we are not to resist evil. Rather, we repay evil with good—all manner of evil, regardless of its form—and we do not assist others who are being victimized by outrageous oppression or who are being led away to their deaths, since this would entail "violence" (151).

[103]*Letters and Papers from Prison*, 217–18.

[104]See, e.g., Ruth Zerner, "Dietrich Bonhoeffer and the Jews: Thoughts and Actions, 1933–1945," *Jewish Social Studies* 37, nos. 3–4 (1975): 235–36; Renate Wind, *Dietrich Bonhoeffer: A Spoke in the Wheel* (Grand Rapids: Eerdmans, 1992), 70; Andreas Pangritz, "Sharing the Destiny of His People," in John W. de Gruchy, ed., *Bonhoeffer for a New Day: Theology in a Time of Transition* (Grand Rapids: Eerdmans, 1997), 258–77; and Moses, "Dietrich Bonhoeffer as Conspirator," 31–39.

In the end, it would appear that Bonhoeffer stands in resistance not to state authority or coercive force per se, but to the demonic misappropriation of that authority and force, which renders it illegitimate and therefore in need of removal.[105] He stands in resistance to the state that virtually became the church in the secular realm, a state that, in Hegelian categories, was sanctified power.[106]

Q. 101   What are common misunderstandings or misuses of just-war doctrine?

A mong the most frequently occurring misrepresentations or misuse of just-war thinking (even when well-intended), three general types might be cited. One is the *misapplication* of just-war criteria. Political theorist Mark Evans cites as an example of this the frequently heard criticism by many opponents of the 2003 invasion of Iraq.[107] Critics (to the present day) have pointed to (1) the so-called "factual error" in military intelligence regarding Saddam Hussein's possession of weapons of mass destruction or (2) the "moral error" in the assumption that such weapons would have constituted just cause for regime change. A second fallacy consists of *incomplete application* of the just-war criteria.[108] Both supporters and opponents of a war—*any* war—are tempted to appeal only to particular criteria in order to justify their position. They do this on the assumption that these select criteria are sufficient to serve as justification, when in fact the criteria inform one another and are interrelated. Yet a third type of misuse is simple *misunderstanding* of the meaning of the criteria. Here, there is no shortage of anecdotal evidence from which to draw examples. In what follows, we shall illustrate the second and third categories of misuse.

---

[105]In offering a defense regarding his role in the German *Abwehr*, Bonhoeffer testifies: "If anyone wants to learn something of my conception of the duty of Christian obedience towards the authorities, he should read my exposition of Romans 13 in my book *The Cost of Discipleship*. The appeal to subjection to the will and the demands of authority for the sake of Christian conscience has probably seldom been expressed more strongly than there." *Letters and Papers from Prison*, 60.

[106]For a lucid critique of German thinking about the state that had become paradigmatic for most German elite by Bonhoeffer's day, see John A. Moses, "The Rise and Decline of Christian Militarism in Prussia-Germany from Hegel to Bonhoeffer: The End Effect of the Fallacy of Sacred Violence," *War & Society* 23, no. 1 (2005): 21–40.

[107]"Moral Theory and the Idea of a Just War," in Mark Evans, ed., *Just War Theory: A Reappraisal* (Edinburgh: Edinburgh University Press, 2005), 7.

[108]Ibid.

We choose these two illustrations as worthy of some commentary, because, in the not too distant past, they have taken the form of highly visible public statements intended to influence the American public. One is more recent and comes from a former U.S. president; the other comes in the form of a pastoral letter published by the U.S. Catholic Bishops during the height of the Cold War. We begin with the pastoral letter.

The 1983 publication of *The Challenge of Peace*[109] by the U.S. Catholic Conference represents something of a benchmark in contemporary understanding of just-war thinking and for this reason warrants our analysis. Hailed by religious leaders across the theological spectrum, the letter set forth its understanding of just-war criteria against the backdrop of Cold War tensions between the two superpowers. Under the heading of *jus ad bellum* were listed the criteria of just cause, competent authority, comparative justice, right intention, last resort, probability of success, and proportionality; under *jus in bello*, proportionality and discrimination. Apart from the lists themselves, several things are significant about the letter. One is the operating assumption spelled out by the bishops in their discussion of the criteria:

> The church's teaching on war and peace establishes a strong presumption against war which is binding on all; it then examines when this presumption must be overridden, precisely in the name of preserving the kind of peace which protects human dignity and human rights. . . . The moral theory of the "just-war" or "limited war" begins with the presumption which binds all Christians: We should do no harm; . . . how we treat our enemy is the key test of whether we love our neighbor; and the possibility of taking even one human life is a prospect we should consider in fear and trembling. How is it possible to move from these presumptions to the idea of a justifiable use of lethal force?[110]

Just-war scholars William V. O'Brien and James Turner Johnson in particular have been critical of the bishops' pastoral letter, and for good reason, given the bishops' conflation of just-war and pacifist moral reasoning. O'Brien, a fellow Catholic and at the time professor of government at Georgetown University, expresses two principal objections to *The Challenge of Peace*. On one level, he argues, it fails

---

[109]*The Challenge of Peace* (Washington, DC: United States Catholic Conference, 1983).
[110]Ibid., nos. 70 and 80.

to acknowledge the threat that totalitarianism posed to the free world during the Cold War era. For this reason O'Brien chides the bishops for their inability to identify and establish the first-order criterion of just cause in their argument, and thus, their inability to grasp what is properly foundational to just-war moral reasoning. Second, and correlatively, the bishops seem to argue that *no* just cause might justify going to war in *any* situation; after all, just-war moral theory begins with the assumption that we should do no harm.

Philosophically, this puts the bishops in a dilemma. On the one hand, they wish to acknowledge the threat of evil in the world. On the other hand, they cannot bring themselves to say that such a threat should be deterred. While they pay lip service to the just-war tradition, they alter the tradition and render it incapable of establishing justice. Their deterrence, in the end, is "disembodied."[111] O'Brien's exhortation to the church and to his own bishops is to forsake idealism and aim at moral realism.

In various writings to the present day, noted just-war historian James Turner Johnson has offered a critique of *The Challenge of Peace* that has paralleled that of O'Brien, pointing to what he believes are inherent flaws in its argument.[112] Among the more serious are the following:

- The assumption that all modern warfare is inherently unjust, given the destructive dimensions and potential of modern weaponry
- Adopting the position represented, for example, by ethicist James Childress,[113] who argues *prima facie* that it is wrong to harm, injure, or kill others, thereby setting any type of killing in opposition to the principle of benevolence[114]
- The bishops' pragmatic compromise so as to attempt to reconcile traditional just-war theory with contemporary Catholic pacifists who in principle are opposed to all war

[111]See William V. O'Brien, "The Failure of Deterrence and the Conduct of War," in Judith A. Dwyer, ed., *The Catholic Bishops and Nuclear War* (Washington, DC: Georgetown University Press, 1984), 37–63, and O'Brien, "The Challenge of War: A Christian Realist Perspective," in O'Brien and John Langan, eds., *The Nuclear Dilemma and the Just War Tradition* (Lexington: Lexington Books, 1986), 154–97.

[112]See, more recently, James Turner Johnson, "Just War, as It Was and Is," *First Things* 149 (January 2005): 14–24.

[113]Johnson notes that Childress is of a Quaker background.

[114]James F. Childress, "Just War Theories," *Theological Studies* 39 (1978): 427–45.

- Seeming digression from the church's official teaching on war and peace as set forth in the Catholic Catechism: "*Peace cannot be attained on earth without safeguarding* the goods of free persons, free communication among men, respects for the dignity of persons and peoples, and the assiduous practice of fraternity. Peace is 'the tranquility of order'[115] [*tranquillitas ordinis*]. Peace is the work of justice and the effect of charity."[116]
- Inversion of the primary and secondary or prudential just-war criteria, so as to remove the moral basis by which to adjudicate or justify the use of force[117]
- The assumption that the UN has superseded the state in terms of authority to decide when resort to armed force is necessary

More broadly, Johnson sees many of these deficiencies to have their roots in a mistaken "presumption against war," to use the language of the bishops' letter. The classical tradition, by contrast, has understood force as morally neutral and thus needing justification; hence, the *jus ad bellum* criteria of (1) just cause for intervention by (2) legitimate authority on the basis of (3) right intention. Johnson insists—properly, we think—that to recast the notion of just war with a baseline presumption against *war or coercive force* rather than against *evil or injustice* is to deviate from and not to be faithful to the tradition as it has been refined by Christian moral thinkers through the ages.[118] And indeed, just-war moral reasoning does *not* begin with the assumption that we do no harm.

A further problem with the bishops' letter, in Johnson's view, is the addition of "comparative justice"—that is, that the relative degree of rights and wrongs on both sides of a conflict be weighed and compared—a component that is not found in classical just-war thinking. The introduction of this element into just-war theory arises out of a moral calculus that has more in common with the theory of moral equivalence than with just cause and right intention. In the end it produces a relativizing effect rather than assisting us in making moral

---

[115]Here the catechism is citing Augustine.
[116]Catechism of the Catholic Church, par. 2304; emphasis added.
[117]In classical just-war moral reasoning, the prudential criteria of last resort, probability of success, and proportionality are secondary or supportive of the three core criteria.
[118]See also J. Daryl Charles, "Presumption against War or Presumption against Injustice? The Just War Tradition Reconsidered," *Journal of Church and State* 47, no. 2 (Spring 2005): 335–69.

judgments and discerning moral evil. A strength of Johnson's work is that he forces his readers—and the bishops, in this case—to engage the tradition in which just-war moral reasoning has been developed and refined. And to understand the tradition is therefore to enter into dialogue with the tradition—an inclination that is not particularly well suited to the activist age of which we are a part.

A second example of the misuse of just-war doctrine comes from former president Jimmy Carter. In an impassioned appeal to the American public that was published in the *New York Times* in early March of 2003,[119] Carter argued that "without international support," the attempted war with Iraq was a "violation" of the premises of international law. Carter's example would not be so instructive were it not for his own experience in the Oval Office and for the column's self-justification. Carter writes that having been "severely provoked by international crises, I became thoroughly familiar with the principles of a just war." To the average reader, something would seem amiss here, since there were no wars—just or unjust—during Carter's tenure in the White House. Carter, however, did preside over the Iran hostage debacle.

"For a war to be just," Carter begins, "it must meet several clearly defined criteria," and with this introduction one is poised to hear reiterated the three core qualifications that Aquinas insisted were necessary: just cause, legitimate authority, and right intention.[120] By contrast, Carter begins with a secondary qualification: "The war can be waged only as a last resort, with all nonviolent options exhausted." Carter proceeds with the claim that in the case of Iraq, "it is obvious that clear alternatives to war exist." Given the previous seventeen UN resolutions that were ignored by Iraq, the reader is not told what these "clear alternatives" were and why more than seventeen resolutions were needed to force Iraq to comply with the United Nations. Nowhere in the article is a case argued for or against just cause for military intervention. The question arises, When is "last resort" ever achieved? For the functional pacifist, it never arrives.[121] When "last resort" is not subordinated to a higher order of reasoning, namely,

---

[119]"Just War—or a Just War?" *The New York Times* (March 9, 2003).
[120]*S.T.* II-II Q. 40.
[121]Our point is not to discount legitimate disagreement over American foreign policy and policy options. It is only to observe the deficient moral reasoning and failure to enter into dialogue with the heart of the just-war tradition by a former president who, as a Nobel Peace Prize winner in 2002, should know better.

the determination of whether something is just or unjust, then it is no longer morally meaningful.

Relatedly, Carter insists that "the attackers must have legitimate authority sanctioned by the society they profess to represent." By this he means international authority, which narrowly meant (in early 2003) the votes of France, Russia, and Germany on the Security Council, all of which had an invested interest in *not* going to war with Iraq. For Carter, authority does not subsist in one's own government but rather in the United Nations. But, according to traditional just-war teaching, a body such as the UN possesses no sovereign authority, and this for several important reasons—among these: its authority is "leased" by the nations of the world; it lacks the "command-and-control" capabilities that are required for direct use of force; and it cannot be held accountable for its actions in a way that individual nations can.[122] What is absent from Carter's argument is the fact of Iraq's thumbing its nose at the previous seventeen UN resolutions and the UN's unwillingness to impose those sanctions over a period of many years.[123]

While it is tempting to view these alterations in so-called just-war thinking as merely a more recent phenomenon or to dismiss them because of Carter's remarkable ability as a *former* president to rehabilitate his image, neither response will suffice. Oliver O'Donovan believes that a recovery in the twentieth and twenty-first centuries of classical just-war moral reasoning is imperative because it has fallen "into a long disuse." We are inclined to agree. But whether or not one agrees with O'Donovan's assessment, one thing is clear: every generation will need to enter afresh into dialogue with the just-war tradition in order to be faithful to it. Writing in the 1980s at the height of the Cold War, William O'Brien was burdened by the manner in which just-war theory was misunderstood. In our time, he noted,

> it has become increasingly clear that the prescriptions of the just-war doctrine must be translated into political/military policy guidelines. If just-war doctrine is to be more than a curiosity salvaged from the history of ideas, its injunctions must be related to the practical world

---

[122]Elsewhere, Johnson has noted these deficiencies with considerable clarity in *The War to Oust Saddam Hussein: Just War and the New Face of Conflict* (Lanham, MD: Rowman & Littlefield, 2005), 59–61.

[123]Curiously, in the same column Carter acknowledges a "unanimous vote of approval in the Security Council to eliminate Iraq's weapons of mass destruction"—a vote that "can still be honored."

of statesmen and soldiers, as well as individual citizens confronting
the personal dilemmas that war brings.[124]

O'Brien's counsel strikes us as supremely relevant for our own day.

Q. 102 Aren't issues of war and peace matters of individual conscience for religious believers?

The simple answer to this question is yes. But more
needs to be said. War is one of the drastic consequences of living in a world marred and distorted by the effects of
human depravity. Religious believers are not immune to such consequences. At the same time, they are required to work for justice in
the very same imperfect world. On rare occasions, this may entail a
wartime scenario or humanitarian intervention that involves military
conflict. In our view, because of its commitment to moral restraints
on the use of force, the just-war tradition most consistently mirrors
enduring standards for war and peace.

We may illustrate this from the Judeo-Christian moral tradition,
which has played a significant role in the Western cultural understanding of war and peace. Believers throughout history have recognized
that the formulation of a doctrine of war or approach to war is a theological and biblical deduction based on the interpretation of numerous
passages in the Hebrew and Christian Scriptures (e.g., Eccles. 3:1, 8;
Matt. 5:44; 24:6–7; Acts 10:1–23; Rom. 13:1–7; 1 Tim. 2:2; and 1 Pet.
2:13–17). How those passages are interpreted determines the position
that one holds. There is no red letter version of the Bible on the doctrine
of war. Nor do we find pat answers to the question, What is the Bible's
view of war? Rather, the more appropriate question to pose is, What
view best interprets and reflects the biblical passages regarding war?

The Judeo-Christian tradition distinguishes itself by the value it
places on human and nonhuman creation, the environment, and all
that is part of the Creator's grand design. First and foremost, human
beings possess an inherent dignity and worth because they are created
in the image of God. Thus, the loss of life or taking of life in any circumstance is among the most serious and severest of life's occurrences.

---

[124]William V. O'Brien, *The Conduct of Just and Limited War* (New York: Praeger, 1981), 329.

At the foundation of Judeo-Christian thinking about war is an anthropological dualism, a belief in the dignified yet broken nature of humanity. A major (and consistent) thread throughout biblical teaching is that all of humanity and every aspect of personal and corporate life are affected by this reality. The fallen aspects of human nature affect all realms of human existence, whether social, economic, or political. These effects extend not only to interpersonal relations but international relations as well. Because war is ultimately a reflection and consequence of human nature, the fact remains that while wars are fought on the battlefields of the globe, they are waged first in human hearts.[125] It is for this reason that philosopher Arthur Holmes writes, "To call war anything less than evil would be self-deception. The Christian conscience has throughout history recognized the tragic character of war. The issue that tears the Christian's conscience is not whether war is good, but whether it is in all cases avoidable."[126] The death, destruction, horror, and personal as well as property losses of war are real issues. For a person of religious conviction to think about and wrestle with the issue of war is to struggle with the problem of evil. In order to do such reflection, there must be a broader intellectual infrastructure, a world-and-life orientation, that provides an adequate moral framework for interpreting the world, human experience, and the moral quality of human decisions.

In many of the questions posed in this volume, a recurring theme is the possibility that force can serve just purposes. That force may also be *misapplied* and serve unjust purposes is a given; human beings are moral agents. This, however, does not in itself constitute an argument against the possibility of applying force for just and moral purposes. Therefore, we contend that one cannot rightly grasp the heart of just-war reasoning without making the fundamental distinction between the commonly held presumption against *war* and the classic just-war presumption against *evil or injustice*. The difference in this starting point can scarcely be overstated. Properly understood, just-war thinking presupposes that the political community subsists in a *just and ordered peace*, the *tranquillitas ordinis* of Augustine. James Turner Johnson, more than any contemporary theorist, properly accents the difference in philosophical starting points:

---

[125]So, e.g., James 4:1–2.
[126]Arthur F. Holmes, "The Just War," in *War: Four Christian Views*, Robert G. Clouse, ed. (Downers Grove, IL: InterVarsity, 1991), 117.

In the presumption against war model, *force itself is the moral problem*, and peace is defined as the absence of the use of such force. In the just war model rightly understood, injustice and the threat of injustice are the fundamental moral problems, for in the absence of justice, the political community is not rightly ordered, and there is no real peace either in that community.[127]

Johnson underscores what is a veritable subtheme in this volume: *force in and of itself is not evil*. This postulate is consistent with our culture's religious traditions and therefore requires emphasis, given the profound differences that separate people of faith on matters of war and peace. The pacifist, if ideologically consistent, will argue that coercive force can *never* be used for just purposes. The just-war thinker, by contrast, will argue that force *can* be used for just purposes, even when it is not always required. Both positions cannot be correct. The fact that force can be misused is no argument in itself against war or coercive force. It simply underscores the bottom line of just-war theory, which is that force is both *permissible yet restrainable*, as all law-enforcement officers and agents well know. Force takes on the character of *those who apply it*, as well as the *reasons* used to justify it and the *intention* or ultimate goal with which it is employed. Consistent with our culture's religious traditions, the moral agent and the agent's intention qualify moral acts.

Q. 103   What should an individual do whose country is involved in an unjust war?

I urge, then, first of all, that requests, prayers, intercession and thanksgiving be made for everyone—for kings and all those in authority, that we may live peaceful and quiet lives in all godliness and holiness" (1 Tim. 2:1–2). With these words St. Paul admonishes believers to support those in authority over them. The goal of their prayerful and reverent service is to help preserve an environment of tranquility and quietude, in which dignity and reverence are furthered. Ultimately, such an environment requires more than simple peace, for it is possible to have peace but not justice. A dictatorial state may be at "peace" and still have extreme oppression. Therefore, we

---

[127]*The War to Oust Saddam Hussein*, 36; emphasis added.

believe that people of faith are first and foremost called to pray for a world whose peace is justly ordered.

Religious believers are required to act and participate in any realm of society and politics to the extent that they are able and have opportunity. As Augustine emphasized, we live in two kingdoms with *dual citizenships*, even while the spiritual realm has priority. If the individual decides that a war is unjust, and he or she is likely to be expected by the state to participate, then after much moral reflection based on informed understanding of national policy and the war, that individual's ethical responsibility may be in the direction of conscientious objection. This will entail a willingness to accept the legal and social consequences of that position.

In a relatively just society where political dissent is permitted, the person should do all within his or her power to inform or correct the national policy. In an unjust society where personal and collective political freedom is restricted, the individual may find it necessary to act through insurrection. Such was the circumstance of German pastor and theologian Dietrich Bonhoeffer in Hitler's Germany during World War II. After much prayer and deliberation, he believed it was necessary to try to stop Hitler through resistance and participation in the July 20, 1944, plot to kill Hitler. Bonhoeffer's position, in the end, was that it was immoral for him *not* to act. For his participation in this failed attempt, Bonhoeffer was arrested, imprisoned, and hanged.[128]

When the political claims of nation-state sovereignty collide with religious authority and personal conscience, people of faith must seriously consider the ramifications of their faith, which makes transcendent claims on their lives.[129] Augustine, whom pacifists often mistakenly portray as a quasi-crusader because of the post-Constantinian era of which he was a part, was no uncritical slave of the state. When political power coerces one to do what is wrong, then "by all means disregard the power through the fear [of God]"; the ruler might threaten "with prison, but God [threatens] with hell."[130] War, for Augustine, is not to be taken lightly and is a last resort because it is "a higher glory still to stay war itself with a word than to slay men with the sword."[131] The ethics, limits, reasons, and boundar-

---

[128]See question 100, "What about Dietrich Bonhoeffer's example?"
[129]The Judeo-Christian theological tradition typically frames these issues in terms of divine versus human sovereignty.
[130]Augustine *Sermon* 62.13.
[131]*Epistle* 229, trans. J. G. Cunningham, *Nicene and Post-Nicene Fathers* (NPNF), ed. Philip Schaff (Grand Rapids: Eerdmans, 1956), 581.

ies of political activity are circumscribed by a biblical worldview, even when Christians may disagree as to their personal responsibilities to the world in which they live.

Having argued above for the need for an informed and engaged citizenry, we turn the tables in our answer to this question of individual conscience. Political ethicist Oliver O'Donovan calls attention to one aspect of classic just-war doctrine that is very much disparaged in modern debate concerning war. It is the premise that a soldier (or potential soldier) should presume the justice of the magistrate's decisions until persuaded otherwise. Clearly, such an attitude strikes democratically oriented Westerners as undemocratic and naïve. O'Donovan's point is not to deny individual conscience—only to demonstrate that decision making with regard to armed conflict in the end cannot by nature be democratic:

> If the ordinary soldier had first to reach a clear and informed view of the right and wrong of the prince's decision—the question which of all questions he was least equipped to answer, simply from the point of view of access to the relevant information—he could never get to the point of considering his own role and responsibility.[132]

O'Donovan's point is one well-taken and needing qualified affirmation, in our view. Indeed, more often than not, citizens assume the role of amateur journalists and commentators. As O'Donovan notes, "The only form . . . in which a moral question about war can ever be put" is the question, "Are you in favor of or against United States policy?"[133]

> As soon as the first hint of future conflict passes across the airwaves, we are all on hand with our own editorials, condemning or supporting the hostilities before a shot has been fired, castigating the United States or being loyal to it, vigorously promoting that polarization of public opinion.[134]

By contrast, a "deliberating public," as O'Donovan calls it, would "move forward with its military and political representatives from situation to situation, treating each next decision as different from the last one, listening to reasons with an open mind and asking demanding questions about the explanations offered."[135]

---

[132]*The Just War Revisited*, 16.
[133]Ibid., 17.
[134]Ibid.
[135]Ibid.

Q. 104   From the standpoint of religious conviction, doesn't going to war mean that fellow Christians from different countries will kill each other?

The destructiveness of war and the human tragedies that accompany it should never be forgotten—people will die whether they profess religious faith or not. When nations confront one another in war, it is very possible and perhaps even probable that fellow believers will kill one another, given the nature of war. In instances of civil war there may even be a higher probability. This possibility illustrates the seriousness of conflict and the fact that it affects individuals, institutions, and states in many and complex ways. It also reminds us that even though an individual may perform an action that is legally and ethically justified, there is always the requirement of acting as a responsible moral agent. Every action or activity is first that of a responsible or irresponsible individual and must be initiated from personal values and beliefs; for the theist, this must be initiated in the fear of God. The actions of our hands always flow from the attitudes of our hearts. This involves an individual's intellect, will, and emotions.

When a combatant kills another combatant in war, he does so as an agent of the state. The killing of an enemy combatant is not done because the individual combatant is evil, but because force, through the combatant, is authorized by the opposing state and poses a threat to a nation and its citizens. The greater issue is not the killing of fellow religious believers—after all, believers are not a privileged class or an exempted group from the rest of humanity. Indeed, based on our shared humanity, their lives are not to be considered of greater value than those of any other faith perspective. The greater issue is the killing of any human being, regardless of faith, ethnicity, citizenship, or any other real or imposed category.

At the same time, there are definite spiritual, physical, psychological, and social dimensions in an act of killing, and there are spiritual questions and concerns regarding elation, sorrow, adrenaline, and fear in combat.[136] In part, this is why Augustine and the just-war tradition declare that there should be an attitude of remorse and reluctance on the part of the individual when entering war.

---

[136]See Dave Grossman, *On Killing: The Psychological Cost of Learning to Kill in War and Society* (Boston: Little, Brown, 1995); and Joanna Bourke, *An Intimate History of Killing: Face-to-Face Killing in Twentieth-Century Warfare* (London: Granta Books, 1999).

During World War II, writing about the topic of forgiveness, C. S. Lewis said of his experiences as an infantry officer:

> I have often thought to myself how it would have been if, when I served in the first world war, I and some young German had killed each other simultaneously and found ourselves together a moment after death. I cannot imagine that either of us would have felt any resentment or even any embarrassment. I think we might have laughed over it.[137]

Lewis's comments were made not to diminish the gravity of killing in war, but rather to underscore the power and necessity of forgiveness in the life of the believer. However, his comments are a reminder that actions taken in this life can have eternal consequences and that few things, if any, are more serious than the death of a human being who is created in the image of God. This is why, in the late Middle Ages, there was extensive debate about the role of penance in the life of the Christian warrior with many penitentiaries prescribing penance even for those who participated in a just war.[138]

The deeper question to be answered by every religious believer is whether he or she can serve in the military and, if ordered, participate in operations that will kill enemy combatants. We believe the answer to this rests in the concept of human government as a divinely sanctioned institution and that participation in every realm of government, including the military, is permissible. At the same time, we acknowledge that believers, for religious reasons, will differ as to how they answer this question. In an imperfect world, restraining evil through force to provide for corporate security may be necessary. We believe that the restraining action, whether taken by police domestically or the military externally, is a legitimate function of the state, and to the extent that an individual's conscience permits him or her to serve, that person is permitted and required to follow lawful and ethical orders, even though such orders may lead to the death of others who share the same religious convictions. Military service, ultimately, is a matter of individual conscience.

---

[137]C. S. Lewis, *Mere Christianity* (New York: Macmillan, 1943; New York: Simon & Schuster, 1996), 107.

[138]Alexander F. C. Webster and Darrell Cole, *The Virtue of War: Reclaiming the Classic Traditions East and West* (Salisbury, MA: Regina Orthodox Press, 2004), 194–202; Frederick H. Russell, *The Just War in the Middle Ages* (Cambridge: Cambridge University Press, 1975), 31–32.

Recommended Reading

The resources listed below represent only a fraction of those cited in this volume, but they commend themselves to those who want to pursue the issues we have discussed. A work's inclusion in this list does not necessarily imply the coauthors' complete agreement with its contents.

Abou El Fadl, Khaled. *The Grand Theft: Wrestling Islam from the Extremists.* San Francisco: HarperCollins, 2005.

Abrams, Elliott, ed. *Close Calls: Intervention, Terrorism, Missile Defense, and "Just War" Today.* Washington, DC: Ethics and Public Policy Center, 1998.

Anscombe, Elizabeth. "War and Murder." In *War and Morality*, edited by Richard A. Wasserstrom, 42–53. Belmont, CA: Wadsworth, 1970.

Bacevich, A. J. "Morality and High Technology." *The National Interest*, no. 45 (1996): 37–47.

Bass, Gary J. *Freedom's Battle: The Origins of Humanitarian Intervention.* New York: Alfred A. Knopf, 2008.

Belamy, Alex J. *Fighting Terror: Ethical Dilemmas.* London: Zed Books, 2008.

———. *Just Wars: From Cicero to Iraq.* Cambridge: Polity Press, 2006.

Bess, Michael. *Choices under Fire: Moral Dimensions of World War II.* New York: Alfred A. Knopf, 2006.

Biddle, Tami Davis. "Dresden 1945: Reality, History, and Memory." *The Journal of Military History* 72, no. 2 (April 2008): 413–49.

Boot, Max. *War Made New: Technology, Warfare, and the Course of History 1500 to Today.* New York: Gotham Books, 2006.

Campenhausen, Hans von. "Christians and Military Service in the Early Church." In *Tradition and Life in the Church: Essays and Lectures in*

Church History. Translated by A. V. Littledale, 160–70. Philadelphia: Fortress, 1968.

Capizzi, Joseph E. "On Behalf of the Neighbor: A Rejection of the Complementarity of Just-War Theory and Pacifism." *Studies in Christian Ethics* 14, no. 2 (2001): 87–108.

Charles, J. Daryl. *Between Pacifism and Jihad: Just War and the Christian Tradition.* Downers Grove, IL: InterVarsity, 2005.

———. "'Do Not Suppose That I Have Come . . .': The Sermon on the Mount Reconsidered." *Southwestern Journal of Theology* 46, no. 3 (Summer 2004): 47–72.

——— (with David D. Corey). *Justice in an Age of Terror: The Just-War Tradition Reconsidered.* American Ideals and Institutions. Wilmington, DE: ISI Books, forthcoming.

———. "Justice, Neighbor-Love, and the Just-War Tradition: Christian Reflections on Just Use of Force." *Cultural Encounters* (Winter 2004): 47–67.

———. "Pacifists, Patriots, or Both? Second Thoughts on Pre-Constantinian Early-Christian Attitudes toward Soldiering and War." *Logos: A Journal of Catholic Thought and Culture* (forthcoming).

———. "Presumption against War or Presumption against Injustice? The Just War Tradition Reconsidered." *Journal of Church and State* 47, no. 2 (Spring 2005): 335–69.

———. "War, Women, and Political Wisdom: Jean Bethke Elshtain on the Contours of Justice." *Journal of Religious Ethics* (June 2006): 341–69.

Christopher, Paul. *The Ethics of War and Peace.* 2nd ed. Upper Saddle River, NJ: Prentice Hall, 1999.

Claude, Inis L., Jr. "Just Wars: Doctrine and Institutions." *Political Science Quarterly* 95, no. 1 (1980): 83–96.

Clouse, Robert G., ed. *War: Four Christian Views.* Downers Grove, IL: InterVarsity, 1981.

Coady, Tony, and Michael O'Keefe, eds. *Righteous Violence: The Ethics and Politics of Military Intervention.* Melbourne: Melbourne University Press, 2005.

Cole, Darrell. *When God Says War Is Right: The Christian Perspective on When and How to Fight.* Colorado Springs: Waterbrook, 2002.

Coll, Alberto R., et al., eds. *Legal and Moral Restraints in Low-Intensity Conflicts.* International Law Studies 67. Newport, RI: Naval War College, 1995.

Cortright, David. *Peace: A History of Movements and Ideas.* Cambridge: Cambridge University Press, 2008.

Cromartie, Michael, ed. *Peace Betrayed? Essays on Pacifism and Politics.* Washington, DC: Ethics and Public Policy Center, 1990.

Demy, Timothy J., and Gary P. Stewart. *In the Name of God: Understanding the Mindset of Terrorism.* Eugene, OR: Harvest House, 2002.

Downes, Alexander B. *Targeting Civilians in War.* Ithaca, NY: Cornell University Press, 2008.

Dunlap, Charles J., Jr. "Technology: Recomplicating Moral Life for the Nation's Defenders." *Parameters* (Autumn 1999): 24–53.

Elshtain, Jean Bethke. "International Justice as Equal Regard and the Use of Force." *Ethics and International Affairs* 17, no. 2 (2003): 63–70.

———. *Just War against Terror: The Burden of American Power in a Violent World.* New York: Basic Books, 2003.

———. "Just War and Humanitarian Intervention." *Ideas* 8, no. 2 (2001): 2–21.

———. *Sovereignty: God, State, and Self.* New York: Basic Books, 2008.

———. *Women and War.* Rev. ed. Chicago: University of Chicago Press, 1995.

Elshtain, Jean Bethke, ed. *Just War Theory: Readings in Social and Political Theory.* New York: New York University Press, 1992.

Evans, Gareth. *The Responsibility to Protect: Ending Mass Atrocity Crimes Once and for All.* Washington, DC: Brookings Institution Press, 2008.

Evans, Mark, ed. *Just War Theory.* Edinburgh: Edinburgh University Press, 2005.

Feldman, Noah. *What We Owe Iraq: War and the Ethics of Nation-Building.* Princeton, NJ: Princeton University Press, 2004.

Forte, David, F., ed. *Natural Law and Contemporary Public Policy.* Washington, DC: Georgetown University Press, 1998.

Gaddis, John Lewis. *The Cold War: A New History.* New York: Penguin, 2005.

Garrett, Stephen A. *Ethics and Airpower in World War II: The British Bombing of German Cities.* New York: St. Martin's, 1993.

Guthrie, Charles, and Michael Quinlan. *Just War.* New York: Walker & Company, 2007.

Harmon, Christopher C. *"Are We Beasts?" Churchill and the Moral Question of World War II "Area Bombing."* The Newport Papers, 1. Newport, RI: U.S. Naval War College Press, 1991.

———. *Terrorism Today.* London: Frank Cass, 2002.

Harnack, Adolf von. *Militia Christi: The Christian Religion and the Military in the First Three Centuries.* Translated by D. M. Gracie. Philadelphia: Fortress, 1981.

Helgeland, John. "Christians and the Roman Army, AD 173–337." *Church History* 43, no. 2 (1974): 149–63, 200.

Helgeland, John, Robert J. Daly, and J. Patout Burns. *Christians and the Military: The Early Experience*. Philadelphia: Fortress, 1985.

Hittinger, John P. "Just War and Defense Policy." In *Contemporary Public Policy*, edited by David F. Forte, 333–60. Washington, DC: Georgetown University Press, 1998.

Hoffmann, Bruce. *Inside Terrorism*. New York: Columbia University Press, 1998.

Hoffman, Peter J., and Thomas G. Weiss. *Sword and Salve: Confronting New Wars and Humanitarian Crises*. Lanham, MD: Rowman & Littlefield, 2006.

Holmes, Arthur F., ed. *War and Christian Ethics*. Grand Rapids: Baker, 1983.

Howard, Michael, George J. Andreopoulos, and Mark R. Shylman, eds. *The Laws of War: Constraints on Warfare in the Western World*. New Haven, CT: Yale University Press, 1994.

Howard, Russell D., and James J. F. Forest, eds. *Weapons of Mass Destruction and Terrorism*. Contemporary Learning. Dubuque, IA: McGraw-Hill, 2008.

Hunter, David G. "A Decade of Research on Early Christians and Military Service." *Religious Studies Review* 18, no. 2 (1992): 87–94.

Jenkins, Philip. *God's Continent: Christianity, Islam, and Europe's Religious Crisis*. Oxford: Oxford University Press, 2007.

———. "The New Iron Curtain." *American Outlook* (Fall 2002): 24–29.

Johnson, James Turner. "The Broken Tradition." *The National Interest* (Fall 1996): 27–36.

———. *Can Modern War Be Just?* New Haven, CT: Yale University Press, 1984.

———. *The Holy War Idea in Western and Islamic Traditions*. University Park: Pennsylvania State University Press, 1977.

———. "Humanitarian Intervention, Christian Ethical Reasoning, and the Just-War Idea." In *Sovereignty at the Crossroads? Morality and International Politics in the Post–Cold War Era*, edited by Luis E. Lugo, 1237–44. Lanham, MD: Rowman & Littlefield, 1996.

———. *Ideology, Reason, and the Limitation of War*. Princeton, NJ: Princeton University Press, 1975.

———. "Just War, as It Was and Is." *First Things* 149 (January 2005): 14–24.

———. *Just War Tradition and the Restraint of War: A Moral and Historical Inquiry*. Princeton, NJ: Princeton University Press, 1981.

———. *Morality and Contemporary Warfare*. New Haven, CT: Yale University Press, 1999.

———. *The Quest for Peace: Three Moral Traditions in Western Cultural History*. Princeton, NJ: Princeton University Press, 1987.

———. *The War to Oust Saddam Hussein: Just War and the New Face of Conflict*. Lanham, MD: Rowman & Littlefield, 2005.

Juergensmeyer, Mark. *Terror in the Mind of God: The Global Rise of Religious Violence*. Rev. ed. Berkeley: University of California Press, 2003.

Kelsay, John. *Arguing the Just War in Islam*. Cambridge, MA: Harvard University Press, 2007.

———. *Islam and War: A Study in Comparative Ethics*. Louisville: Westminster John Knox, 1993.

Kelsay, John, and James Turner Johnson, eds. *Cross, Crescent, and Sword*. Contributions to the Study of Religion 27. New York: Greenwood, 1990.

———. *Just War and Jihad: Historical and Theoretical Perspectives on War and Peace in Western and Islamic Traditions*. Contributions to the Study of Religion 28. New York: Greenwood, 1991.

Kiernan, Ben. *Blood and Soil: A World History of Genocide and Extermination from Sparta to Darfur*. New Haven, CT: Yale University Press, 2007.

Krammer, Arnold. *Prisoners of War: A Reference Handbook*. Westport, CT: Praeger Security International, 2008.

Laqueur, Walter. *A History of Terrorism*. New Brunswick, NJ: Transaction, 2001.

———. *The New Terrorism: Fanaticism and the Arms of Mass Destruction*. New York: Oxford University Press, 1999.

Lewis, Bernard. *The Crisis of Islam: Holy War and Unholy Terror*. New York: Random House, 2004.

———. *Islam and the West*. New York: Oxford University Press, 1993.

———. "The Roots of Muslim Rage." *The Atlantic Monthly* 266, no. 3 (September 1990): 47–60.

———. *What Went Wrong? Western Impact and Middle Eastern Response*. New York: Oxford University Press, 2002.

Lewis, C. S. "Why I Am Not a Pacifist." In *The Weight of Glory and Other Essays*. Edited by Walter Hooper. Rev. ed., 64–90. New York: HarperCollins, 2001.

Liotta, P. H. *Dismembering the State: The Death of Yugoslavia and Why It Matters*. Lanham, MD: Lexington Books, 2000.

Mandelbaum, Michael. *The Nuclear Question: The United States and Nuclear Weapons, 1946–1976*. Cambridge: Cambridge University Press, 1979.

Marshall, Paul, ed. *Radical Islam's Rules: The Worldwide Spread of Extreme Shari'a Law*. Lanham, MD: Rowman & Littlefield, 2005.

Miller, Steven E., ed. *Strategy and Nuclear Deterrence*. Princeton, NJ: Princeton University Press, 1984.

Mueller, Karl P., et al. *Striking First: Preemptive and Preventive Attack in U.S. National Security Policy*. Santa Monica, CA: RAND Corporation, 2006.

Murray, John Courtney. *Morality and Modern Warfare*. New York: Council on Religion and International Affairs, 1959.

———. *We Hold These Truths: Catholic Reflections on the American Proposition*. New York: Sheed and Ward, 1960.

Nardin, Terry, and Melissa S. Williams, eds. *Humanitarian Intervention*. Nomos 47. New York: New York University Press, 2006.

Nasr, Seyyed Hossein. *The Heart of Islam: Enduring Values for Humanity*. San Francisco: Harper Collins, 2002.

Nasr, Seyyed Vali Reza. *Islamic Leviathan: Islam and the Making of State Power*. Oxford: Oxford University Press, 2001.

Nichols, Thomas M. *Eve of Destruction: The Coming Age of Preventive War*. Philadelphia: University of Pennsylvania Press, 2008.

Niebuhr, Reinhold. *Christianity and Power Politics*. New York: Scribner's, 1940.

———. "Must We Do Nothing?" *Christian Century* (March 30, 1932): 415–17.

Noll, Mark A. *Christians in the American Revolution*. Washington, DC: Christian University Press, 1977.

———. *The Civil War as a Theological Crisis*. Chapel Hill: The University of North Carolina Press, 2006.

O'Brien, William V. *The Conduct of Just and Limited War*. New York: Praeger, 1981.

———. "Just War Conduct in a Nuclear Context." *Theological Studies* 44 (June 1983): 191–220.

———. *Nuclear War, Deterrence and Morality*. Westminster, MD: Newman, 1967.

O'Brien, William V., and John Langan, eds. *The Nuclear Dilemma and the Just War Tradition*. Lexington: Lexington Books, 1986.

O'Donovan, Oliver. *The Just War Revisited*. Current Issues in Theology. Cambridge: Cambridge University Press, 2003.

———. *Principles in the Public Realm: The Dilemma of Christian Moral Witness.* Oxford: Clarendon, 1984.

Orend, Brian. *Human Rights: Concept and Context.* Peterborough, ON: Broadview, 2002.

———. *Michael Walzer on War and Justice.* Cardiff: University of Wales Press, 2000.

———. *The Morality of War.* Peterborough, ON: Broadview, 2006.

———. *War and International Justice: A Kantian Perspective.* Waterloo, ON: Wilfrid Laurier University Press, 2000.

Pavlischek, Keith J. "The Justice in Just War." *First Things* 144 (May 2000): 43–47.

Ramsey, Paul. *Basic Christian Ethics.* New York: Scribner's, 1954.

———. "The Ethics of Intervention." *Review of Politics* 25, no. 3 (1965): 287–310.

———. *The Just War: Force and Political Responsibility.* New York: Scribner's, 1968.

———. *The Limits of Nuclear War.* New York: Council on Religion and International Affairs, 1963.

———. *War and the Christian Conscience: How Shall Modern War Be Conducted Justly?* Durham, NC: Duke University Press, 1961.

Reed, Charles. *Just War?* New York: Church Publishing, 2004.

Regan, Richard J. *Just War: Principles and Cases.* Washington, DC: Catholic University Press of America, 1996.

Reichberg, Gregory M., Henrik Syse, and Endre Begby, eds. *The Ethics of War: Classic and Contemporary Readings.* Oxford: Blackwell, 2006.

Robinson, Paul, ed. *Just War in Comparative Perspective.* Burlington, VT: Ashgate, 2003.

Russell, Frederick H. *The Just War in the Middle Ages.* Cambridge: Cambridge University Press, 1975.

Schwartz, Stephen. *The Other Islam: Sufism and the Road to Global Harmony.* New York: Doubleday, 2008.

Shearer, David. "Outsourcing War." *Foreign Policy* 112 (Autumn 1998): 68–81.

Shue, Henry, and David Rodin, eds. *Preemption: Military Action and Moral Justification.* Oxford: Oxford University Press, 2007.

Singer, P. W. *Children at War.* Berkeley: University of California Press, 2006.

———. *Corporate Warriors: The Rise of the Privatized Military Industry.* Rev. ed. Ithaca, NY: Cornell University Press, 2008.

———. *Wired for War: The Robotics Revolution and Conflict in the 21st Century.* New York: Penguin, 2009.

Slim, Hugo. *Killing Civilians: Method, Madness, and Morality in War.* New York: Columbia University Press, 2008.

Sorabji, Richard, and David Rodin, eds. *The Ethics of War: Shared Problems in Different Traditions.* Burlington, VT: Ashgate, 2006.

Springer, Devin R., James L. Regens, and David N. Edger. *Islamic Radicalism and Global Jihad.* Washington, DC: Georgetown University Press, 2009.

Stout, Harry S. *Upon the Altar of the Nation: A Moral History of the Civil War.* New York: Viking, 2006.

Swift, Louis J. *The Early Fathers on War and Military Service.* Wilmington, DE: Michael Glazier, 1983.

Tuck, Richard. *The Rights of War and Peace: Political Thought and the International Order from Grotius to Kant.* Oxford: Oxford University Press, 1999.

Walzer, Michael. *Arguing about War.* New Haven, CT: Yale University Press, 2004.

———. *Just and Unjust Wars: A Moral Argument with Historical Illustrations.* 4th ed. New York: Basic Books, 2006.

———. "The Politics of Rescue." *Social Research* 62, no. 1 (1995): 35–40.

Webster, Alexander F. C., and Darrell Cole. *The Virtue of War: Reclaiming the Classic Christian Traditions East and West.* Salisbury, MA: Regina Orthodox Press, 2004.

Weigel, George. *Tranquillitas Ordinis: The Present Failure and Future Promise of American Catholic Thought on War and Peace.* Oxford: Oxford University Press, 1987.

Weiss, Thomas G. *Humanitarian Intervention: Ideas in Action.* Cambridge: Polity Press, 2007.

Wells, Ronald A., ed. *The Wars of America: Christian Views.* Grand Rapids: Eerdmans, 1981.

Welsh, Jennifer M., ed. *Humanitarian Intervention and International Relations.* Oxford: Oxford University Press, 2003.

Young, Frances. "The Early Church: Military, War and Peace." *Theology* 92 (1989): 491–503.

Index of Names

Aboul-Enein, Youssef H., 318n145, 320n158
Adam, 309
al-Banna, Hasan, 231
Alford, Roger P., 243
Ambrose, 62, 76, 114, 122–25, 128n124, 140, 183, 248, 252–53, 291, 294, 296, 312, 357, 362, 371, 372n66, 374n68
Anscombe, Elizabeth, 57n88
Apollinaris, 112
Arendt, Hannah, 18
Aristotle, 28, 38–40, 100, 102, 124n106, 261, 281
Arkes, Hadley, 42n44, 45
Augustine, 32, 36, 55, 62, 73, 74, 76, 93, 100n14, 113–14, 120, 122–28, 134, 139–40, 147, 148, 173, 183, 196, 253, 273, 276, 282, 287, 291, 294–96, 298, 311n125, 312, 316, 328, 357–59, 361, 362, 366, 371–72, 374n68, 376, 389n115, 393, 395, 397

Bagnoli, Carla, 195n94
Bainton, Roland, 108–9, 121, 270n46, 295, 355
Baldwin, Stanley, 221
Barclay, William, 260n27
Barth, Karl, 382
Basil, 120

Berman, Harold, 27n1
Bethge, Eberhard, 381, 385
Betz, Dieter, 259n26
Blair, Tony, 232, 234n204
Bonhoeffer, Dietrich, 327, 381–86, 395
Boniface, 126, 358
Brimlow, Robert W., 385n102
Buchanan, Allen, 217
Bullinger, Heinrich, 268

Cadoux, John, 109
Caesar, 109, 113, 115, 231, 233n200, 264, 267, 303, 323, 367–68
Caesar Augustus, 131n132
Cain, 35
Calgaus, 348
Calvin, John, 31, 58, 76, 136, 141–43, 144, 268, 326, 374–75
Campenhausen, Hans von, 122n101
Carafano, James, 239, 240, 241n225, 245–46
Carter, Jimmy, 390–91
Celsus, 116
Chesterton, G. K., 105n25
Childress, James F., 55n81, 80, 388
Christiansen, Drew, 201, 202
Christopher, Paul, 34, 201
Churchill, Winston, 220, 324–25, 326
Cicero, 41–42, 100–101, 102, 124n106, 142, 281
Claude, Inis L., Jr., 73n122

Clausewitz, Carl von, 22, 55, 93
Clement of Alexandria, 117–18
Clendenen, Avis, 284
Coady, C. A. J., 223
Cole, Darrell, 301, 344
Conquest, Robert, 46n53, 365
Constantine, 112, 120
Cornelius, 312
Courtois, Stephane, 46n53
Crawford, Neta C., 93, 213–14, 219
Cyprian, 117

David, 141, 326
Dillon, Dana, 239, 240, 241n225,
    245–46
Diocletian, 119–20
Dionysius, 118
Dipert, Randall, 217

Eliot, T. S., 27, 105n23
Elshtain, Jean Bethke, 35–36, 53n72,
    74, 91–92, 190, 210, 211, 266n36,
    328, 360, 384, 385n101
Erasmus, 143n173
Eusebius, 111, 112, 135n144
Evans, Mark, 86–87, 210, 386

Frederick (Elector of Saxony), 137n152

Gandhi, 364–67, 381
Geis, Gilbert, 28n3
Gero, Stephen, 111n54
Goebbels, Joseph, 364
Goldstone, Richard, 192–93, 293
Gratian, 147
Gray, Colin, 215–16
Grotius, Hugo, 20, 21, 32–34, 58, 76,
    89, 133–34, 149, 162–63, 167n28,
    168, 174, 178, 183–85, 194,
    196n99, 217, 238, 248, 291, 305,
    314, 323, 360–61, 374–75
Gyatso, Tenzin, 314

Harmon, Christopher C., 90–91, 212,
    230

Harnack, Adolf von, 259n26
Hashmi, Sohail, 317–18, 319n152,
    320n158, 321
Hauerwas, Stanley, 37n24
Hays, Richard, 302n115
Helgeland, John, 111–12, 121
Henry, Carl F. H., 289–91, 328
Heraclitus, 37–38
Hippolytus, 118
Hitler, Adolf, 62, 170, 207, 364–65,
    385n102, 395
Hittinger, John P., 56n82, 97n1, 160n3,
    165
Hoffman, Peter J., 236n209
Holmes, Arthur, 314, 393
Hornus, Jean-Michel, 109
Hubmaier, Balthasar, 58n91
Huntington, Samuel, 235, 236n209

Jackson, Timothy P., 302n115
Jenkins, Phillip, 210n127
Jesus, 31, 43n48, 47, 97, 109, 114n61,
    131n132, 138, 231, 251–59, 263–
    67, 270, 272–73, 275–77, 278, 280,
    283, 285–86, 292, 295, 297, 300–
    303, 312, 328, 354–55, 367–71,
    372–75, 379–80
Joab, 326
John (apostle), 272, 274, 275
John Paul II, Pope, 37n23, 48n61,
    137n152, 200n108, 265n35
Johnson, James Turner, 20–21, 66,
    79, 80–81, 89–90, 92, 102, 110,
    111n54, 112, 122n101, 147,
    148–49, 161n7, 171–72, 173n41,
    174n45, 191–92, 193, 207, 210,
    211, 212, 213–14, 217, 224n174,
    226, 227, 318n145, 321, 327, 345,
    346–47, 387–90, 391n122, 393–94
John the Baptist, 114n61, 140, 259,
    312, 355, 370–71, 374–75, 380

Kant, Immanuel, 77, 81, 217
Keohane, Robert, 217

Koplow, David A., 335
Kram, Assa von, 137

Lactantius, 119–20
Langan, John, 197n101, 242n229
Lewis, Bernard, 148n188, 232, 320
Lewis, C. S., 57n88, 68, 89, 105–6,
   253, 280n70, 298, 313, 366–67,
   377–81, 398
Little, David, 55n81
Locke, John, 150
Lu, Catherine, 194n92
Luke, 131n132, 285
Luther, Martin, 31, 32, 58, 137–40,
   142, 144, 145n178, 248, 253, 268,
   277, 296, 309, 311–12, 359, 361–
   62, 372n66, 374–75

Maimonides, 19
Mao Zedong, 237
Marcellinus, 294, 298
Marcion, 257n18, 259n26, 302
Marcus Aurelius, 44n49, 111, 112
Maritain, Jacques, 29n7
Marsden, George, 151
Martin, Troy, 284
McKeogh, Colm, 346
Meier, John P., 260n27
Meilaender, Gilbert, 44
Melanchthon, Phillip, 137n152
Melchizedek, 277
Micah, 277
Miller, William I., 252n3, 261n30
Moorhead, James H., 155
Moses, 141
Muhammad, 318, 322
Murray, John Courtney, 51n67, 54,
   55n81, 63, 66n109, 67, 265n35,
   368–69

Natsios, Andrew, 198–99
Neuhaus, Richard John, 353n2
Niebuhr, H. Richard, 288–91, 368
Niebuhr, Reinhold, 57, 61–62, 64, 267,

282n79, 288–91, 366, 382, 383,
   385n102
Noah, 279
Noll, Mark, 151, 152, 153, 155

O'Brien, William V., 63, 64–65,
   68n113, 80, 163n15, 173n41, 224,
   226–27, 387–88, 381–92
O'Donovan, Oliver, 65, 129n125, 130,
   164, 177, 210, 227–28, 229nn187–
   88, 230, 238n214, 271, 354, 360,
   391, 396
Orend, Brian, 206–7, 241–42, 324–25,
   327
Origen, 116–17, 118
Orwell, George, 364–65

Paul, 43, 97, 252, 254, 256n14,
   257n18, 262–63, 269–70, 271, 276,
   284, 297, 299, 309, 372, 375, 394
Paul VI, Pope, 64
Peter, 312, 371
Plato, 31, 38–39, 40, 47, 97, 100,
   124n106, 261, 281
Pol Pot, 192, 237
Powers, Gerard, 201, 202
Pufendorf, Samuel, 196n98, 363

Radu, Michael, 233–34
Ramsey, Paul, 51, 53n72, 63, 173n41,
   212, 217, 224n174, 226, 291, 357,
   369–70, 372n66, 376
Riley-Smith, Jonathan, 146
Robinson, Paul, 314
Rommen, Heinrich, 38, 44
Rostow, Eugene, 182
Russell, Frederick H., 128n122, 146–47

Sayers, Dorothy, 105n23
Sharon, Ariel, 219n157
Shearer, David, 339
Sigmund, Paul E., 39n29, 40
Simons, Menno, 145, 268
Singer, P. W., 340–41, 343–44
Slim, Hugo, 347–48

Suárez, Francisco, 20, 32–34, 69, 149, 174, 178, 183–85, 238, 291, 305, 314, 323, 360, 361
Swift, Louis J., 111n49

Tan, Kok-Chor, 195n94
Tertullian, 66, 110–11, 112, 114–16, 117, 118, 121, 123, 135n144, 136, 265, 270, 368
Theodosius, 124n105
Thielman, Frank, 261n27
Thomas Aquinas, 19, 27, 31, 32, 39n30, 47, 48, 49, 55, 59, 62, 66, 68, 69, 76, 125n107, 128–29, 130–31, 139–40, 161–62, 164, 178, 179, 183, 248, 253, 276, 278n61, 281, 282, 291, 295–96, 304, 312, 316, 321, 323, 358–59, 361, 362–63, 366, 372n66, 374n68, 375–76, 390
Tibi, Bassam, 318, 319n152, 321, 322n166
Timothy, 270
Tzu, Sun, 99, 106–7, 345

Urban II, Pope, 146

Vattel, Emmerich de, 217
Vitoria, Francisco de, 20, 32–34, 131–33, 149, 174, 183–85, 238, 291, 305–6, 314, 323, 361–62

Walzer, Michael, 57, 77, 102, 170, 175, 195, 196n99, 205, 207, 210, 211, 212, 213, 217, 221–24, 246–47, 324–25, 365, 366
Watson, Alan, 101
Waugh, Evelyn, 105n23
Weiss, Thomas G., 236n209
Wilberforce, William, 45
Wilken, Robert Louis, 146n182
Williams, Charles, 105n23

Yoder, John Howard, 54n74, 75, 109, 144n75, 253, 270n46, 271–74, 289–91, 295, 300–301, 302

Zacchaeus, 252, 261, 285
Zinni, Anthony C., 335
Zuhur, Sherifa, 318n145, 320n158
Zwingli, Ulrich, 58, 144, 268

Index of Scripture

Genesis
1—86, 288n86
1:26–27—97n2
1:27—278n65
2—288n86
4:1–16—35
9:1–17—278n66
9:5–6—29298
9:6—278n65, 279n67
18:25—281n74

Exodus
20:13—278n62, 278n65
21—259
21:23–25—259
21:24—259
23:6–9—281n75

Leviticus
19:9–10—291n75
19:11–14—281n76
24—260
24:17–22—260
24:20—259
34:6–7—292
34:7—292n97

Numbers
35—35n, 279
35:1–33—292n98
35:6–33—278n66

35:6–34—230n189
35:11—279
35:12—279
35:15—270
35:16–21—279
35:20–21—279
35:29–33—292n98

Deuteronomy
4:41–43—230n189,
    278n66
5:17—278n62, 278n65
19—260
19:1–13—278n66
19:1–21—230n189
19:15—260
19:15–21—373
19:17—260
19:21—259
20—98

Joshua
20:1–9—230n189,
    278n66

2 Samuel
10:12—326

Ezra
9:37—257n20

Psalms
82:3–4—104

Proverbs
10:12—104
14:31—104
16:32—104
20:3—104
24:10–12—104, 367
24:11–12—71
29:10—104

Ecclesiastes
3:1—392
3:1–5—104
3:8—104, 392
8:11—261n29

Isaiah
2:2–4—277
5:20–24—281n74
10:1–2—281n77

Joel
3:10—277

Micah
4:3—277
6:8—71n120

Matthew
4:1–11—266n37
5—256, 261
5–7—252, 373
5:3–12—259
5:9—117n80, 275, 372,
    375
5:13–16—373
5:16—256
5:17—251, 255, 255n13,
    256, 257n18, 373
5:17–19—258
5:17–20—255, 261,
    261n28, 285n85
5:18—255n13, 256
5:18–19—257
5:18–42—251
5:19—256, 258
5:20—258
5:21—278n63
5:21–22—255n12
5:21–48—256, 259, 261,
    261n28
5:27–28—255n12
5:31–32—255n12
5:38—260
5:38–39—253, 255n12,
    282, 294, 295, 358,
    380
5:38–42—259, 260n,
    372, 374n68
5:38–43—373
5:38–48—302n
5:39—140, 252, 297,
    312, 373, 375, 379
5:39–41—294
5:40—252
5:43–44—255n12
5:44—392
7:12—255, 255n13, 256,
    373
8:5–13—109n39,
    371n63, 375
8:17–48—255
10:28—280, 362

11:13—255, 255n13
12:6—258n21
15:1–9—256n17
15:2—255n10
18:4—258, 258n21
20:16—258, 258n21
20:26—258
21:12–13—258n21
22:15–22—264n32
22:21—323
22:36—255n13
22:40—255, 255n13
23:1ff.—258
23:2–12—258n21
23:3—258n22
23:4—257n19
23:8—257n19
23:11—258
23:13—268n23
23:15—258n23
23:23—255n13, 258n21,
    258n23
23:23–24—258n21
23:25—258n23
23:27—258n23
23:29—258n23
24—257, 25925
24:1–25—109n38
24:6–7—308, 392
26:52—253
26:54—253
26:56—253
26:62—258n21
26:63–65—258n21

Mark
1:12–13—266n37
7:1–13—256n17
7:3—255n10
7:5—255n10
12:13–17—264n32
12:17—323, 368

Luke
3—140, 374

3:7–14—375
3:8—375
3:14—109n39, 370, 375
4:1–13—266n37
7:1–10—109n39,
    371n63
7:2–10—375
10:25–37—376
10:35—376
19—252n4, 261, 285
20:20–26—264n32
20:25—323
20:47—370

John
1:1–51—41n48
17:13–19—368n57
18:19–24—253n7
19:1—264

Acts
1:9–11—109n38
10—312
10:1–23—392
10:1–48—371n63
10:1–11:18—375
10:1–11:48—109n39
10:2—312
17:16–34—41
17:18—42n45
17:22–31—41n47
17:30–31—41
17:31—41

Romans
1:20—97n2
2:14–15—29, 97n2, 261
2:15—35
3:11—256n14
3:31—252n5
5:1—276
6:13—114n61
6:23—114n61
7:12—256n14
11—262

12—262, 263, 269, 297,
  299, 372, 373
12:1–2—262
12:3–8—262
12:9–13—262
12:14–21—262
12:17—262
12:17–21—252, 262,
  269, 282, 294, 373,
  375
12:17–13:10—280n71
12:21—262
13—144, 144n175, 262,
  263, 267, 268, 269,
  270n46, 271, 289,
  297, 299, 372, 373,
  386n105
13:1–4—138, 311
13:1–6—263
13:1–7—164n24,
  179n58, 252, 262,
  268n41, 269, 272,
  294, 304, 392
13:1–10—373
13:3–4—141, 254,
  269n44
13:4—141, 144, 147,
  263, 269, 272n48,
  309
13:6—263
13:8–10—252n5, 256n14
13:9—278n64
13:10—284n82

1 Corinthians
2:6–10—310
9:6–7—114n61
13:13—277n59

2 Corinthians
2:14–16—114n61
6:4–7—114n61

Galatians
2:16—256n14
3:23—256n14
5:20—375n73

Ephesians
1:21—272n51
2:2—272n51
2:4–6—292
6:10–18—114n61

Philippians
2:25—114n61

Colossians
2:15—114n61
4:10—114n61

1 Thessalonians
5:8—114n61, 277n59

1 Timothy
1:18—114n61
2:1–2—179n58, 270,
  394
2:1–4—280n71
2:1–5—309
2:2—165n24, 392
2:2–4—270
2:12—304

2 Timothy
2:3–6—114n61

Titus
3:1—179n58

Philemon
1–2—114n61

Hebrews
7:2—277

James
1:25—256n14
2:8–11—252n5
2:11—278n64
4:1–2—308, 393n125

1 Peter
1:22—272n51
2—268
2:11—274
2:13–14—138, 165n24,
  280n71, 311
2:13–17—179n58,
  268n42, 269, 304,
  372, 392
2:14—380

2 Peter
1—41n48
1:5–7—41n48

Revelation
2:10—114n61
2:12—114n61
2:26–27—114n61
4:11—114n61
5:6–14—114n61
7:12—114n61
9:9–11—114n61
9:16–19—114n61
13—144n175, 270n46,
  271, 272, 289
13:1–18—114n61
16:14—114n61
17:14—114n61
19:11–16—114n61

J. Daryl Charles (MA, PhD) is Director and Senior Fellow of the Bryan Institute for Critical Thought and Practice, Bryan College. He served as 2007/2008 William E. Simon Visiting Fellow in Religion and Public Life in the James Madison Program in American Ideals and Institutions, Department of Politics, Princeton University.

Charles is author or coauthor of ten books, including (with David D. Corey) *Justice in an Age of Terror: The Just-War Tradition Reconsidered* (ISI Books, forthcoming), *Retrieving the Natural Law: A Return to Moral First Things* (Eerdmans, 2008), *Between Pacifism and Jihad: Just War and Christian Tradition* (InterVarsity, 2005), and *Virtue amidst Vice* (Sheffield Academic Press, 1997). He also coedited (with David B. Capes) *Thriving in Babylon: Essays in Honor of A. J. Conyers* (Wipf & Stock, forthcoming) and translated, from German, Claus Westermann's *The Roots of Wisdom* (Westminster/John Knox, 1994).

Charles's work focuses on a broad range of themes that concern the intersection of faith and culture, including religion in the public sphere, Protestant evangelicalism, criminal-justice ethics, bioethics, war and peace, and humanitarian intervention, and has appeared in a wide array of both scholarly and popular journals, including *First Things, Pro Ecclesia, Journal of Church and State, National Catholic Bioethics Quarterly, Journal of Religious Ethics, Books & Culture, The Weekly Standard,* and *Christian Scholar's Review.* He is a contributing editor to two journals, *Cultural Encounters* and *Touchstone,* and serves on the editorial advisory board of the journal *Pro Ecclesia.*

Timothy J. Demy (ThM, ThD; MA, PhD) is Associate Professor of Military Ethics at the U.S. Naval War College, Newport, Rhode Island. He has served as a military chaplain for more than twenty-seven years in a variety of assignments afloat and ashore with the U.S. Navy, U.S. Marine Corps, and U.S. Coast Guard, and has authored and edited more than twenty books on ethics, theology, and current issues and also contributed to numerous journals and encyclopedias. He has published and spoken nationally and internationally on religiously motivated terrorism and the role of religion in international relations.

In addition to his theological training, which he received at Dallas Theological Seminary, Demy holds advanced degrees from Salve Regina University, where he wrote on C. S. Lewis. He also earned graduate degrees in European history, international relations, and national security and strategic studies. He was the President's Honor Graduate from the U.S. Naval War College and also completed the degree Master of Studies in international relations at the University of Cambridge.

Demy is a member of numerous professional organizations, including the Evangelical Theological Society, the Center for Bioethics and Human Dignity, and the Society of Biblical Literature. He and his wife, Lyn, have been married for more than thirty years.